# The Kenneth Roberts Reader

# The Kenneth Roberts Reader

### Introduction by
### **Ben Ames Williams**

Down East Books
*Camden, Maine*

Reprinted by arrangement with
Doubleday Broadway Publishing Group,
a division of Random House, Inc.

ISBN: 0-89272-567-2

Printed and bound at Versa Press, East Peoria, Illinois

5    4    3    2    1

Down East Books
P.O. Box 679
Camden, Maine 04843
Book Orders: 800-685-7962
www.downeastbooks.com

Library of Congress Control Number: 2002101658

# Contents

# Introduction

## By BEN AMES WILLIAMS

ONCE UPON A TIME Ken Roberts and I shared a compartment on a train eastbound from Denver. The train left Denver in the evening. At the lunch hour that day we had together suffered a mildly annoying experience of which the details are unimportant; but since then, till the train's departure, we had not been alone together. As soon as the door of our compartment was closed, Ken—as Bret Harte might have put it—rose to remark that our host at luncheon had spoiled his day.

Call our host Mr. Smith. The noontime incident had not provoked in me any desire to murder this individual; but during the two hours which followed Ken's opening statement on the subject, it was impressed upon me that this was not true of Ken. He told me that Mr. Smith had spoiled his day, and he explained in some detail what he would have done to Mr. Smith if he had given free rein to his emotions. He imagined a thousand ways in which Mr. Smith during his lifetime must have spoiled the days of other men, giving full details of each case. He asserted that Mr. Smith's wife, his children, his father, his mother, and all his direct and collateral ancestors must have been confirmed day-spoilers, arguing that nothing but long-continued breeding back to the same strain could have produced such a poisonous day-spoiler as Mr. Smith. Ken spent an hour in a thorough analysis of Mr. Smith's faults; and he then proceeded to catalogue all the other days which other men had spoiled for him, and to describe how they had done so, and to try to estimate the degree of consanguinity in which they stood to Mr. Smith, basing his estimate on the relative enormity of their respective day-spoilings.

The list was a long one. I gathered—through my sympathetic tears—a general impression that for the entire span of Ken's life at least six days a week had been spoiled for him by someone; but Mr. Smith had achieved a peak hitherto approached by none!

This may seem irrelevant as an introduction to a collection of some fragments of Ken's writings; but what am I to do? To introduce Ken

Roberts, the author, to the American reading public is as unnecessary—in the familiar phrase—as to prepare an index for the dictionary. If there is any literate person in the United States who is not familiar with his work, I do not care to make that person's acquaintance. The alternative is to introduce Ken Roberts, the individual.

Did I hear someone murmur: "Individual, and how!" Perhaps! Ken and the Grand Canyon have one quality in common. Those most familiar with either of these phenomena agree that they are indescribable—and then proceed to describe them. But it may be possible to suggest Ken's impact upon the observer by citing a few of his outstanding traits—and by referring to the pages of this book for illustrative and corroborative data.

For there can be no better introduction to these, or to any other pages he has written, than some knowledge of the man himself. Once you know him, you will find him hereafter on every page.

For example—as may have been suggested by the reference to Mr. Smith and Ken's spoiled day—he is easily aroused to furious indignation;[1] and by what appears to be a law of inverse proportion, he is most violent about the little things, least violent about the big ones. He will rage for hours at an inconsiderable Mr. Smith who has spoiled his day, at rats which steal the eggs his ducks deposit around one of the ponds on his place, at sparrows which make noises near his windows when he is working, at politicians, at roadside signs—although the driveway at his home has a sentinel sign every few rods—,[2] at people who serve ketchup unlike that which his grandmother used to make, at liquor merchants so ignorant that they sell good brandy for less than the price of poor brandy, at pilots who fly low over his house, at great horned owls, at people who wish he would write another book about Benedict Arnold to tell the story of Arnold's treason, at critics who accuse him of historical inaccuracies, at Pulitzer Prize committees, at people who believe what they are told by

---

[1]See, if you doubt me, pages 10, 11, 12, 19, 55–6, 107–8, 126, 208, 212–15, 431, 455–7, 459–60 in this book.—B.A.W.

[2]Mr. Williams here implies that Mr. Roberts is somehow emulating the behavior of billboard interests—an implication without foundation in fact. I have visited Ken several times. His driveway is half a mile long, and on it are two small direction-boards reading: PRIVATE: DEAD END ROAD, NARROW AND DANGEROUS: PLEASE DON'T TRESPASS and NOT A PUBLIC ROAD. Ken says cynically that summer vacationists persistently ignore both signs. He built and maintains his own road, makes every effort to keep it unspoiled, and isn't using it to sell anybody anything, whereas the billboard interests deface public highways for personal gain. Mr. Williams' hint that there is a similarity between Ken's two direction-boards and the atrocities mentioned on pages 11, 14, 15, 17, 18 and 19, verges on the ludicrous. —NELSON DOUBLEDAY.

school histories, at readers who when one of his characters says a thing believe it is the author speaking, at all illusions and all lazy thinking.

At all these petty annoyances he flies into a towering rage; but when confronted with something which may quite justifiably raise the blood pressure, he is the mildest-mannered man that ever scuttled ship or cut a throat!

He is a hater of shams,[3] pretensions, self-deceptions, fallacies; and he particularly hates the persistent distortion of history. In what would be for him the best possible world, every history would be written with a fine impartiality and by a neutral party. He is tireless in hunting out proof that Colonials during the Revolutionary period were (a) dauntless heroes, or (b) blovalating politicians and self-seekers; the choice depending on which misconception he is at the moment engaged in setting right. He is equally tireless in proving that all British and Tories were (a) cultivated and intelligent gentlemen abused by the Colonials or (b) tyrannical rascals abusing the Colonials.

For Ken, who expects from the historian a remote impartiality, himself always has a thesis to demonstrate. His thesis is the unrecognized truth; and he will with the most laborious research write a book to prove that on a given subject everyone who believes what everyone else believes is wrong! It was characteristic of him that he began his career as a novelist by making the best possible case for Benedict Arnold.

It is doubtful whether any living man knows as much as he about the first half century of American history. A rare individual may be wiser than he in some particular field; but in an examination covering the whole picture I would back Ken against any contestant. In such matters he is a tireless and always skeptical inquirer. This being so, this persistent questioning of the accepted being so definitely his passion, it is the more remarkable that in everyday matters he is hungrily credulous.[4] Someone told me the other day that the pithy heart of a cattail stem makes a tasty salad. Cattails will forever go unmolested for all of me; but if I told Ken that, he would at the first opportunity have cattail salad for dinner. Someone once told him that skunk cabbage in the spring was edible. All his life Maine people had told him a certain common swamp plant was skunk cabbage. He believed them and sampled the plant in question and came near death as a result. In his time he has believed dietitians, dog breeders, advocates of taking exercise, advocates of not taking exercise, osteopaths,

---

[3]See, for example, pages 104, 135–38, 158–85, 186–95, 219, 230, 238, 239, 251, 259, 260, 267, 281, 286, 377, 381.—B.A.W.

[4]A few of the things he has at various times, on the mere assertion of anyone at all, so readily believed are mentioned on pages 22, 94–100, 320, 322, 324, 325, 326, 382–95, 433–5, 437, 446.—B.A.W.

quacks, critics, water dowsers, pressure-cooker salesmen, the apostles of the deep freeze, plumbers, seed catalogues, helpful friends, farm magazines. To the extent of acting on it, the man will believe—outside the field in which he is pre-eminent—literally anything. If he is told a thing is so, he tries it; if he is told it is not, he tests the truth of that statement. After an expert on such matters told him that wood ducks could not be raised from the egg in captivity, he spent some two thousand dollars to find out for himself that it could not be done![5]

But his outstanding trait—it covers not only his capacity for indignation, his intense opinions, and his tremendous capacity for believing what he is told—is his overpowering interest in everything in the world. It is true that in many respects this all-embracing interest in anything and everything has been sated. Like Owen Davis, he has found happiness in the discovery that there are a lot of things he no longer has to do. But every day brings him new interests; and each new interest must lead to action. His mind is like an unexposed film upon which everything he sees or hears makes an impression; and since impressions crowd upon him not single-spy but in battalions, he demands that pad and paper be available in every room in his house so that he can make a note of each new interest before it is crowded out of his mind by the next.

He is interested in raising ducks, in reclaiming sour land, in power lawn mowers, in painting with oils or water colors, in dogs, in scotch and gin and brandy—some of his New England ancestors must turn in their graves when they hear what he really thinks of rum; but it was he who made hot buttered rum a household word—in hay, in what others think of what he writes, in rifles, in the eradication of brown-tail moths, in woodcarving, and the application of gold leaf to enormous eagles. He is interested in things; just concrete, tangible things. I suspect, though I have never checked this,[6] that the pages of his books are heavily spiced

---

[5]Here again Mr. Williams oddly distorts facts with which I am familiar. Mr. Roberts obtained a State and Federal license permitting him to maintain, raise, and sell migratory birds on his Kennebunkport farm; and in addition to providing innumerable free lunches for marauding horned owls, foxes, mink, eagles, crows, skunks, and rats, he raised a good many hundred mallards, gray and white calls, Canada geese, China geese, and mongrel geese, some of which supplied his family and friends with food, and some of which he sold, gave away, or released for the general good of Maine wild life. His investment in incubators, hatchers, ponds, dams, breeding-boxes, wire fencing, and other material was, as Mr. Williams says, in the neighborhood of $2,000; and a clutch of wood duck eggs was once placed in the incubator—but only because the mother wood duck was killed while sitting. To deduce that Ken spent $2,000 to prove that wood ducks can't be raised in an incubator is singular reasoning.—NELSON DOUBLEDAY.

[6]I have since glanced at a random page—one page in each—in *Arundel*, in *Rabble in Arms*, in *Northwest Passage*, in *Captain Caution*, and in *The Lively Lady*; and noted these words: packs, beaver and otter skins, traders, dyed feathers, wildcat's

with nouns, the names of things; fine-sounding nouns, nouns which evoke a thousand images. Perhaps it is this which enriches his style; for his books are as toothsome as a slab of fruit cake, heavy with spice and savor.

Which reminds me that he is interested in food![7] I know no man who eats less and enjoys it more. He has tried and approved—or disapproved—of the most familiar and the rarest dishes in every country in Europe and in most states here at home. He knows the ingredients and the manner of preparation. His favorite reading is cookbooks, and each new one that comes into his hands is a challenge which the household must meet. In "The Truth About a Novel" he pleads for sympathy for Mrs. Roberts. Sympathize too, if you please, with Mr. Roberts' cook. Her life is an adventurous one.

I find that I have said little here about the book to which these remarks are presumed to be an introduction; but if I were to write as long an introduction as the book itself, my introduction would still be inadequate. The Table of Contents you might as well ignore, for you will read this book straight through—and wish for more. I am sorry Ken did not include the dinner at Dr. Campbell's in the second part of *Northwest Passage*;[8] but then there are so many passages I would be glad to see in this goodly company.

Turn the page and begin to read. You will be at once among familiar friends.

---

shoulder blade, moose-tooth pipe, bone, bearskins, canoes, pitch, pork, chickadee, supply boats, rum ration, breaker, gill, ginger, a bladder of corn meal, odor, tavern, mustached woman, a French sailor in gold earrings and a canvas petticoat, long-gun, topsail, eighteen-pound shot, weight of metal.—B.A.W.

[7]To stimulate your jaded appetite see pages 2, 3, 20–33, 37, 53, 61, 64, 71, 86–7, 92–3, 103, 238, 246, 264–6, 292, 429.—B.A.W.

[8]It is that second part of *Northwest Passage*, when Ken follows a great man from his peak down into deserved and contemptible obscurity, which lifts the novel from the category of the merely good to the company of the great. Those who did not "like"—oh, abominable word!—that second part as well as they did the first arouse in me a rage worthy even of Ken.—B.A.W.

# THE KENNETH ROBERTS READER

# This Is How It Was

THE WAY in which our family came to Arundel is a matter I set down, not to boast of my own people, since we have been simple farmers and smiths and innkeepers and soldiers and sailors, always; but so my great-grandsons may know the manner of folk from whom they sprang, and feel shame to disgrace them by taking advantage of the weak or ignorant, or by turning tail when frightened, which they will often be, as God knows I have too frequently been.

My grandfather Benjamin was a blacksmith and gunsmith in the Berwick section of the town of Kittery, his grandfather Richard having come there in 1639 from Berwick in England.

In those days the frontiers were steadily pushing eastward and northward; and to the eastward of Kittery lay the town of Wells, gradually growing in size, though populated by shiftless and poverty-stricken folk, dwelling in log huts without furniture, and constantly at odds with the Indians.

In order to obtain a blacksmith, the town of Wells, in 1670, sent a paper to my grandfather, which paper I still have in my small green seaman's chest, guaranteeing him two hundred acres of upland and ten acres of marsh if he would settle in Wells within three months, remain there for five years, and do the blacksmith work for the inhabitants for such current pay as the town could produce. This my grandfather did, albeit he spent less time at blacksmithing than in hunting with the Abenakis, by whom he was liked and trusted, as was my father to an even greater degree. It is my opinion that he was justified in spending little time in his smithy, since the only current pay the town could produce was promises that were never kept.

My father, then, was born in Wells; and when he had reached the age of seventeen, he was skilled in the arts of the blacksmith, the gunsmith, and the hunter. He had, furthermore, been blessed with nine brothers and sisters; and wishing to enjoy the pleasures of married life without falling over a child not his own whenever he turned around, he looked about and took thought for the future.

Three leagues to the eastward of Wells, along the hard white crescent-shaped beaches so plentiful in the southern portion of our province, is the Arundel River. This is a narrow river, but deeper than most of those that cut across our beaches. Therefore it has a bar farther out at sea, less easy to pass than many river bars, so that travelers view it with trepidation.

My father frequently hunted and fished near its mouth, going with friends from the Webhannet tribe of Abenakis, chiefly with young Bomazeen, the son of the wise sachem Wawa. I have heard him say he took more pleasure in the place than in any other section that had met his eye. Most men say the same thing concerning their homes; but few, to my way of thinking, have the reason for saying it that my father had.

In the spring there are quantities of salmon running upstream, easy to take with a spear because of the narrowness of the river bed. When the salmon are finished there are fat eels lying in the current riffles at low tide, so thick that in an hour one boy with a trident may fill a barrel, which is a feat I have frequently accomplished, being addicted to smoked eel with a gallon of cider before meals, or during them, or late at night when the nip of autumn is in the air, or indeed at any time whatever, now I stop to think on it.

After the eels are gone the green pollocks come up the river by the millions, fine fish to salt and dry, especially in a manner discovered by my father, which ripens their flesh to a creamy consistency, uncommonly delicious.

After the pollocks come small spike mackerel; and between seasons, when the tide rises on the bar, beautiful flat flounders lie in the sand with eyes popped out, amazed like, to betray their presence.

In the autumn come deer to paddle in the salt water, and hulking moose deer, and turkeys occasionally; also teal, black ducks, and Canada geese in long lines and wedges; while always our orchards and alder runs are filled with woodcock and that toothsome but brainless bird, the partridge, who flies hastily into a tree at the approach of a barking dog, and stays there, befuddled, until the dog's owner walks up unnoticed and knocks him down.

In the late summer, and in the spring as well, there are noisy flocks of curlews and yellow legs and plovers, wheeling above the sands in such numbers that a single palmful of small shot will kill enough for one of the juicy game pies my youngest sister Cynthia takes such pride in making and I such delight in eating.

At the mouth of the river my father found an oblong piece of farmland, set off by river and creek and beach into an easily defended section, and presenting opportunities for trade and a modest income. Since there was no white man dwelling thereabouts, probably because of the numbers of Indians who came in the summer to fish and to lie in the cool sea breezes, he took it for his own; and the Indians were content, since he traded honestly with them.

On the seaward side of our farm is a smooth white beach, half a mile in length, shaped like a hunting bow. This beach appears to face straight out to sea; but because the seacoast swings outward near this point the beach in reality faces south, toward Boston. Thus the hot winds of summer, which are southwesterly, blow in to us across the ocean, and so are cool and pleasant.

At the western end of the beach is a tumbled mass of rocks, fine for the shooting of coots or eating-ducks in spring or fall, or for capturing coarse-haired seal for moccasins, or for taking the small salt-water perches which we call cunners. These we take at any season, whenever we crave the sweetest of all chowders. I have eaten the yellow stew that Frenchmen in Quebec call boullabaze, or some such name, and brag about until their tongues go dry; and I say with due thought and seriousness that, compared with one of my sister Cynthia's cunner stews, made with ship's bread and pork scraps, a boullabaze is fit only to place in a hill of green corn to fertilize it, if indeed it would not cause the kernels to grow dwarfed and distorted.

At the eastern end of the beach and of our farm is the river mouth; and directly across the river the rocky headland of Cape Arundel pushes out to sea. Two hundred yards upstream a generous creek bears back to the westward, parallel to the beach, into a long salt marsh.

Thus our farm is protected on the south by the ocean, on the east by the river, on the north by the creek, and is open only on the west, in which direction lie the settlements; so with slight precautions one need fear no attack from any ordinary force of enemies. Even on the side toward the ocean my father found protection from French raiders; for a semicircle of reefs embrace the shore, hidden at full tide in a calm sea, but raising a smother of foam and roaring regiments of breakers when the wind blows from the east or northeast.

These ledges, covered with tangled growths of seaweed, cause the delicious odor peculiar to these parts in summer; for the prevailing winds, blowing across them, bring to shore a perfume that seems to come from the heart of the sea—an odor I know of in no other place, though there have been Frenchmen pass through here who declare the same heartening smell may be found on the coast of Brittany. This may be true, though

I would liefer hear it from an Indian than from a Frenchman if I had to depend upon it.

The truth is I love the place; and if I seem to talk overmuch of it, I only do so because I would like those who read about it to see it as I saw it, and to know the sweet smell of it, and to love it as I do.

On the highest point of this farmland my father, at the age of seventeen, with the assistance of my grandfather and Bomazeen, the son of Wawa, and a carpenter from York and Abenakis from the camp across the creek, built a sturdy garrison house of eight rooms out of logs.

From the back door he looked down on the creek and the glistening dunes that border the river mouth and the beach, and on the brown rocks of Cape Arundel, over which the sun came up to warm him at his early morning labors. From the front door he saw the sweeping crescent of beach, and the reefs with creamy breakers gamboling around and over them, and the flat salt marsh to the westward; and far away, beyond the beach and the reefs, he saw what I see today and what you, too, may see if you will come to Arundel: the blue expanse of Wells Bay with the gentle slopes of Mount Agamenticus behind it; and to the left of Agamenticus the mainland of Wells and the cliffs of York, small and blue above the water, and soothing to the eye.

It was a luxurious house by comparison with those roundabout at that time; for it had floors of boards, and bedsteads in the sleeping rooms, with mattresses resting on cords and stuffed with corn husks. In each room was a chest and a chair, and in the kitchen a table and a carved court cupboard and stout chairs. The place was a boon to weary travelers; and it was surprising how often those who passed that way were overcome with weariness at our front door.

Beside the garrison house was a smithy where my father could ply his trade when occasion rose, and sheds for horses, the whole stockaded against hostile Indians. On the riverbank was a skiff for ferrying men and horses across; and the town had given my father, in consideration for his living there, the sole right to conduct a ferry at the river's mouth.

Of my father's first wife I know little. She came from Wells and was a melancholy female, given to upbraiding my father for going alone into the wilderness during the winter months. He did this in order to trade with the Indians for beaver skins and to seek out paths and locations for Sir William Pepperell and Governor Shirley and for the Colonial Government, which knew less about the country to the north and east than a rabbit knows about fish.

Although my father never said so, I suspect he went into the wilderness to escape his first wife, and so formed the habit of roaming in the woods and living in wigwams for weeks on end—a habit from which he never recovered.

She was a sickly woman, troubled with indigestion, and bore my father no children, which was a cross to him. She was intemperate with the Abenakis, frequently attacking them with her brush broom when they came into the kitchen uninvited, as Indians always do unless at war, when they hide in bushes near the house and wait, usually in vain, for someone to stumble over them and be killed. This, too, was a source of trouble to my father. Indian wars have started with no greater provocation; and for weeks after his first wife had beaten an Indian with her brush broom he never left home without fearing that on his return he would find the house burned down.

She was finicky and would allow no servants to assist her, although my father, having accumulated a respectable amount of money through ferrying and the sale of beaver skins, would gladly have obtained one for her. This was the more annoying because the house was like to be full of travelers seeking a night's hospitality, to say nothing of the soldiers stationed there at any rumors of Indian troubles, so that his first wife was perpetually complaining and groaning about the work to be done, and there was no peace in the house.

Worst of all, she was a bad cook. Perhaps I should not set it down here, but it was a good thing for her and a good thing for my father and a good thing for the Indians and certainly a good thing for me, since without it I would never have been born, when she died of a consumption.

My father had little leisure for grieving after she had gone, even though he had been so inclined.

Settlers constantly increased, and hostile Indians from the north came more frequently to harass them; so the garrison house was too small to harbor those who sought refuge and provender. Therefore my father built a sawmill on the creek behind the house; and in this he sawed the King's pines that stood on his land; for in common with many in our province, he believed the King had no right to trees standing on a settler's land, even though they were the King's by law. Holding this law to be a foolish one, he broke it whenever he could break it unobserved, as is the custom with all of us. From these King's pines came boards forty inches in width, as free of knots as mahogany from the Sugar Islands.

With them he enlarged the garrison house, so that forty persons might live in it in comparative comfort. He covered the logs with narrow overlapping boards and erected a symmetrical ell on each side, and made a new room out of our old kitchen, a gathering-room in which to eat and drink, very comfortable. It had a fireplace so large that six people might sit within it on each side of the fire, as fine a place as ever I saw for drinking buttered rum on a cold night provided the drinker is careful, as one must always be, not so much with the rum as with buttered rum, for it is the butter, as all drinkers of this concoction know and say, that wreaks the harm. And so, when the fireside drinker must be hearty with buttered rum until the butter makes him topple, it were well he took thought to topple sidewise or backward rather than slither forward into the fire.

The walls within were sheathed with broad boards of pumpkin pine with the edges shaved thin and overlapping, so that no crack could appear, howsoever the boards might shrink; and my father obtained the services of two shipwrights, and had them make small tables with oval tops, which might be drawn before the fire and gripped between the knees by one who wished to devour a juicy black duck or a fine clam chowder.

From the town he had a license as an innkeeper and a license to dispense spirituous liquors; and all who came by the beaches stopped at the inn. In the town of Wells he secured a black woman named Malary, who had been freed from slavery along with six other slaves in the town; and Malary was held in esteem for her cooking, in especial her manner of baking beans, which manner has been nobly acquired by my sister Cynthia.

All this I know from what my father told me in my boyhood evenings; and yet how little it seems, now, that I know of him and of those times. Almost anything in the world is readily forgotten after ten years. After the passage of fifty years a happening so fades into the mists of antiquity that little is known about it except by the person who participated in it; and that little is mostly wrong. Of how my grandfather Benjamin lived and what he ate and what he wore I know next to nothing, nor do I know anything about my great-great-grandfather Richard, except that he was an ensign of Kittery in 1653, and one of three men to lay out the boundary between the towns of Kittery and Wells in 1655, because I have seen his name cut on the rock at Baker's Spring. As to how he cooked his black ducks and prevented the curse of chilblains, and whether he escaped the cruel burden of rheumatics, and what he thought about certain passages in the Bible, I must remain in darkness. Yet my great-great-grandfather, of whom I know so little, was at the height of his powers a mere one hundred years ago.

When Sir William Pepperell in 1745 sent out his call for troops to attack the French city of Louisbourg on Cape Breton, my father, being without financial cares, and having nothing of import to do at the moment, rode to the town of Berwick and enlisted in the company of Captain Moses Butler. There he met the captain's daughter Sarah.

She was tall, with brown hair and dark brown eyes and a manner of drawing in her chin when she laughed and touching her upper lip with the tip of a slender tongue, as if in delight at what had been done or said. Unlike the women of Wells and Arundel, she had schooling and had read largely in the works of Plato and Horace and Plutarch, as well as in the writings of Shakespeare and Congreve, albeit the latter, she told me, had been done secretly and after stealing the book from beneath the mattress of her mother's chamber, where it was kept hid. She could speak in French; and from her I learned a few words in that tongue, which stood me in good stead in later days.

For her education I thank God. Without it, and without her desire to see me possessed of some thoughts other than those of fish and weather and sleep, I would be crying out, along with various of my fellow-citizens of Arundel, against the useless expenditure of fifty pounds a year for the education of children in our district.

When Captain Moses Butler's company marched off to Boston, Sally Butler and her mother followed in a one-horse chaise; and before my father set foot on the ship that carried him to Louisbourg, he and my mother were betrothed.

On his return from that drunken and successful holiday, they were married; and ten years later, in the garrison house between the golden sands and white breakers of the Arundel beaches and the swirling glass-clear waters of the mill creek, there dwelt, beside myself, my father and my mother, who was the sweetest woman and the kindest, bar one, that I have known, and my sister Hepsibah and my sister Jane and my brother Ivory and my youngest sister Cynthia and my seal Eunice and my dog Ranger, who was my first dog of that name but not the last, all of them half setting dog and half spaniel, entirely black save for a white waistcoat.

Those days were happy and far less luxurious than at present, what with the stagecoach that now speeds down to Boston from Portland in two days' time, and the chinaware on our tables and our plastered walls. Yet I cannot truthfully say those times were better, though many think they were. The war is over, and the roads are easier to travel; our tools are better so that our crops are larger; and though the youths are said to be growing softer and looser from too much luxury and money, I know they will fight as bravely as ever we did, once the need of it arises; and I hope fewer of them will run away.

# Roads of Remembrance

### From FOR AUTHORS ONLY

Colonel BENEDICT ARNOLD, *leading his secret expedition against Quebec, had brought his little army up the tumbling quick water of the Kennebec; across the cruel mountain spurs of the Great Carrying Place into the winding channel of Dead River. The bitter winds of autumn cut through the men's ragged garments like knives. Snow squalls from the Canadian mountains lashed their faces. The hurricane found them strung along the river. In one night the water rose eight feet, overturning and smashing bateaux; plucking kegs of powder and bullets from the boats; washing the bulk of their little store of food down the raging stream.*

*They poled the remaining bateaux deeper into the wilderness of northern Maine, up through the waters of the Chain of Ponds, until they reached the towering wall that stood between them and Canada—the terrible mountains of the Height of Land.*

*Daniel Morgan, captain of the Virginia riflemen, came to the trail hewn by Arnold's axemen through the tangle of trees that centuries of winter storms had spread over the granite peaks. At its foot he found a messenger with instructions from Arnold. "Take one bateau across the mountains," ran the instructions, "and leave the rest behind. The men are weak from lack of food: let them carry one bateau to a company!"*

*Morgan lined up his men on the shore of the last of the Chain of Ponds. "Seven bateaux we've got," he shouted, in his great teamster's voice, "seven bateaux and we need 'em all, for supplies and medicine and the sick! We need 'em all to get to Quebec! Do we take 'em or do we leave 'em?"*

*Stumbling and slipping, laughing, cursing, coughing, the emaciated Virginians shouldered all their bateaux across the Height of Land—across five miles of desolation that caught at their feet like granite talons. When*

*they had crossed, the rags on their shoulders were stained with blood;*
*the bones of their shoulders showed through their flesh. . . .*

The Arnold Trail pushes through the forests of northern Maine, along the same route opened by Arnold's ragged companies in 1775. It twists across a shoulder of the Bigelow range, which took its name from Major Timothy Bigelow of Worcester, who climbed to its top in 1775 in the hope of seeing the spires of Quebec in the distance. From these heights it descends to the winding waters of Dead River, whose serpentine curves cling stubbornly to the shadow of Mount Bigelow. It passes through the town of Flagstaff, rising again to the beginning of the Chain of Ponds—round ponds, oval ponds, square ponds, irregular ponds, spider-shaped ponds, each one higher than the last; each one pressed deeper into the mountains that so nearly took the lives of Arnold's men a century and a half ago.

This road through the heart of the wilderness bends itself around corners with the flexibility of a snake; it traverses rocky spurs, among which lies the Chain of Ponds, with the abruptness of a roller coaster. Occasional axemen or settlers look calculatingly at the car of those who seek directions.

"Ever been over this trail before?" they ask.

"Well," they say, when they learn the trip is the first one. "you never saw nothing like it! Up and down, like going to sea in a dory! Be sure your brakes ain't slipping!"

The grades are steep. An automobilist, topping a rise, is cut off by the hood of his car from seeing either the descent beyond him or the ensuing hill. The road is edged with precipices and tumbled rocks: blue waters of ponds gleam through trees that looked down on the passage of Arnold's men. It is ancient Maine—the Maine of Abenaki huntsmen, who came from their fishing grounds on Penobscot, Kennebec, and Passamaquoddy to take beaver, sable, and otter; the far-off Maine of Father Drouillettes and Father Râle, who instructed their Indian charges in the ways of the Church, as well as in other less churchly matters; the Maine of Arnold's army, and of generations of trappers, woodsmen, and hunters.

On the trees are no signs reminding travelers of the cost of Enna Jettick shoes, or imparting the stirring information that Jonesport, home of Seth Parker, is 280 miles distant, or urging them to get a Lift with a Camel. The curves are free from the refinements which, on most of Maine's through roads, greet the eyes of beauty lovers who hasten in constantly increasing numbers to the Pine Tree State to see its widely advertised scenery—free, in short, of billboards calling attention to Burma Shave,

7-20-4 Cigars, or the Utterback-Gleason Department Store. It is a road of which any state might be proud, not only because of the difficulties surmounted in building it and its scenic grandeur, but chiefly because of its historical associations.

As yet it's a dirt road: not a finished product of cement. What it will be when finished—when the people's money has made it valuable and easily traveled—is another matter. Although Maine residents have raised their voices in condemnation of the manner in which the scenery of the state is embellished with billboards, sardine tins, old shoe boxes and lunch containers, the scenery has received as little assistance from the legislature of the state as from those who erect the billboards.

Let us examine the first fifty miles of Maine's greatest highway, between Kittery and Portland. A traveler enters Maine at the very spot where John Paul Jones's *Ranger* slid from the ways in 1777. A flawless thoroughfare of cement has replaced the winding, rutted trail of olden days.

Along this ancient road the Indians lay in wait, two centuries ago and more, for the white men who were wresting the country from the wilderness.

Down this road marched men of Maine to embark on the expedition that wrenched Louisbourg from the French; to be shot to shreds, under pigheaded Abercromby, in the abatis before Ticonderoga; to join Washington at Cambridge and Benedict Arnold on his terrible journey to Quebec. Along this road drove the old clipper captains, clip-clopping from their dignified homes in trig Maine villages, through the fairest countryside in the world, to the stately ships that showed their heels to all the vessels on the seven seas.

It was a road, not long since, of small white farms nestling in the shadow of brooding barns and sheltering elms; of old square homes built by shipbuilders and shipmasters; of lilac-scented Junes, and meadows rich in the odors of mallow and sweet-grass; of irregular stone walls; ancient taverns; solid, mellow little towns happy in the possession of architecture and tradition and family pride; of long stretches of pine woods, cool and fresh in the heat of summer; of birch-clad hill slopes, forests of oaks and sugar maples, swelling fields and flat salt marshes shimmering mistily in the warm summer sun; of life-giving breezes from the strip of deep blue sea at the far edge of all these things.

It was a beautiful road: a road for health and rest and peace of mind; a priceless possession, to be cherished and forever held in trust for the descendants of those who laid it out and made it possible. It was the essence of Maine; the gateway to the great and beautiful Maine wilderness to the north and east.

Today it is a road of big signs and little signs and medium-sized signs; of cardboard signs tacked to pine trees and wooden fences and dilapidated barns; of homemade signs tilting drunkenly in ragged fields and peering insolently from the yards and walls of furtive-looking houses; of towering signs thrusting garish, mottled faces before forests, fields, and streams, like fat, white-faced streetwalkers posing obscenely in a country lane; of little indecent litters of overnight camps, crawling at the edges of cliffs and in trampled meadows as though the countryside had erupted with some distressing disease: of windrows of luncheon boxes, beer bottles, paper bags, wrapping paper, discarded newspapers, and the miscellaneous filth of countless thoughtless tourists; of doggeries, crab-meateries, doughnut-teries, clammeries; of booths that dispense home cooking on oilcloth and inch-thick china in an aura of kerosene stoves, smothered onions, and stale grease; of roadside stands resembling the results of a *mésalliance* between an overnight camp and an early American outhouse; of forests of telephone and electric light poles entangled in a plexus of wires.

It is a road rich in the effluvia of clams in batter, frying doughnuts, sizzling lard; in tawdriness, cheapness, and bad taste, but in little else.

The National Association of Real Estate Boards has declared that "the view from the highway does not belong to the individual who owns the property along the right of way. It is a community possession." This, of course, is true; but America's lawmakers won't believe it. Maine proudly advertises its scenery, yet stands complacent and inactive while the scenery which it advertises is made hideous.

Thus the Arnold Highway through the wilderness is likely to receive as little consideration from the state that built it as from the tourists who pass over it, or from vandals who erect billboards. The billboard industry in Maine, indeed, contends that billboards are improvements on the scenery rather than affronts to nature.

Not long since a native of Maine spoke his mind concerning the state's policy of spending large sums in advertising Maine's scenery; then permitting it to be splotched with billboards.

The billboard industry made reply: "It is not true that the billboard industry is spoiling the scenery and that boards are being erected without regard to the effect they may have in ruining bits of beauty. The billboard industry requires that all billboards erected shall be so designed as to be things of beauty rather than eyesores and blots upon the landscape, and to maintain a high standard in every essential detail."

If I correctly understand this reply, it contends that a lemon pie—provided it be an artistic lemon pie—can be splashed against a Rembrandt or a Velasquez without damaging the artistic value of the painting; but to me it would seem pure vandalism.

I also feel free to add that unless billboard spokesmen were mentally deficient, they would know that nowhere in America could they find one reputable artist, one reputable architect, one reputable author, one reputable sculptor—not one man, in fact, who has to do with the arts—who would not agree that the scenery of Maine, New England, and the United States is the laughingstock of the world because of the billboards smeared across it.

But since the attitude of the state and of the billboard interests is what it is, it won't be long before Maine's newest Road of Remembrance becomes less a reminder of the ragged, starving, shoeless men from Maine, Pennsylvania, Virginia, Massachusetts, and Connecticut who forced their way through the northern forests to Quebec—less a reminder of them than of cheap automobiles, cheap shoes, cheap candy, cheap department stores, cheap cigarettes, cheap overnight camps—and of the cheap and shortsighted politicians who fail to put an end to the desecration of their native state.

This Road of Remembrance, at the Canadian border, meets the fine roads of Canada; ordinary roads which make no pretense of being Roads of Remembrance; and on them the traveler sweeps around to the shores of Lake Megantic and down the twisting valley of the Chaudière, along which Arnold's men staggered, gnawing at roasted moccasin tops and cartridge boxes, and leaving bloody footprints in the snow. No litter mars the roadside; no signboards rear themselves against the swelling fields and the forests and the riverbanks to scream the advantages of Chesterfields, Chevrolets, Burma Shave, and other products of civilization.

The Canadian liquor interests were once seized with a brilliant thought —the same brilliant thought that has struck so many earnest manufacturers in the United States: the thought that when the government, by heavy expenditures, has made a road valuable and popular, there is no reason why they should not capitalize those expensive improvements for their own private ends. Consequently the liquor interests erected signboards calling the attention of the traveling public to various distilled liquors. At this the Canadian Government, knowing that tourists prefer unsullied scenery to even the most artistic billboard advertising the most delicious intoxicant in the world, peremptorily ordered the liquor interests to remove the billboards in the greater interests of Canada. The billboards were hurriedly removed. Consequently the roads of Canada have an air of their own—a foreign air. There is a restfulness to them seldom encountered on America's Roads of Remembrance, with their overnight camps, their shoddy hot-dog stands, their glaring billboards.

Westward from Quebec one makes his way up the broad St. Lawrence, along the road followed by Burgoyne on the brave adventure intended to divide the battered and hard-pressed colonies—the adventure that ended in disaster and overwhelming defeat on the rolling cornfields of Freeman's Farm and the Heights of Saratoga.

Part way between Quebec and Montreal, in the St. Lawrence, is Lac St. Pierre; and on the far side lies the ancient town of Sorel.

A river flows into the St. Lawrence at Sorel—the river Richelieu. The Richelieu, rising in Lake Champlain, flows north to Sorel; and for centuries this river was the military highway between Canada and the American colonies: the highway for the St. Francis Indians when they set forth to destroy New England settlements; for the Marquis de Montcalm to march against the English and the colonists at Fort William Henry; for Lord Jeffrey Amherst, soldier of the King, to travel with his English and New Englanders to help James Wolfe wrest Quebec from the French; for the retreat of General Sullivan and Benedict Arnold, after the unsuccessful campaign against Canada, their army useless from starvation and smallpox.

The road from Sorel to Lake Champlain is a fine one, smooth and billboardless, bordered by neat Canadian farmhouses with roofs that curve down to overhanging eaves. It hugs the broad river, runs through the thriving city of St. John's, and passes a low, flat island in midstream—Isle aux Noix.

*The Americans were retreating from Canada before Burgoyne's army. Half dead with fatigue and fever, they dragged their bateaux, laden with guns and supplies, through the shallow quick water of the Richelieu. Ahead of them went their sick, boatload after boatload, struggling slowly up the rapid river to Isle aux Noix, crying out for relief which could not be furnished.*

*Good Dr. Meyrick went on before to Isle aux Noix. "It broke my heart," he wrote, after he had helped to disembark the sufferers, "and I wept till I had no more power to weep."*

*The army followed, the men pitching from the ranks with sickness and dying where they fell. In the days that followed, the dead were dragged in blankets to the edges of pits in this marshy island and without ceremony rolled into them in the rags in which they died. "They found not even decent sepulture, when their miseries were ended, nor any memorial of the sacrifice they made for the cause of American liberty."*

*In ten days' time the Americans moved on up the river, out of Canada and into Lake Champlain: over Lake Champlain to Crown Point—a weary journey of a hundred miles. In leaky boats they rowed for five long days and nights—a miserable and festering host. . . .*

Twenty minutes beyond Isle aux Noix the traveler enters the United States by Route No. 9, called by some the Roosevelt Highway—a Road of Remembrance.

There are billboards at once: large billboards and small billboards. It is a road of waffles. There are stretches that lead the traveler to think the road was built in memory of waffles long since dead; of waffles yet unborn; of frankfurter sausages. As soon as one enters the United States he is in the Frank and Waffle Belt. Hot waffles. Hot franks. Franks with skins and franks without skins.

It is a good road, this Roosevelt Highway. One slips along it so rapidly that one is in danger of getting his billboards mixed, especially after being in Canada, where there are no Roads of Remembrance; no billboards; nothing but the grass and the trees and the rivers, mellowed by time and marred a little, but only a little, by the hand of man.

*Reach for a Chevrolet instead of a Sweet! Try Camels for Floating Power! Chew Chryslers! Get a Lift with Burma Shave! Smoke Bromo Seltzer! You are back in the land of terrible billboards—back in Headachia!*

The Roosevelt Highway is a Road of Remembrance, built to enable the people to see this beautiful northern country: this ancient highway down which trotted the painted Indians; along which swung the French in their gay white uniforms; British in scarlet coats; Rogers' terrible Rangers in fringed buckskins and rakish Scotch caps; Americans in ragged militia jackets.

*Theodore Roosevelt's lower jaw protruded until his glistening teeth were in line with his ragged mustache. He thumped his fist upon the rostrum. "Do not," he shouted in his high-pitched voice, "do not let selfish men or greedy interests skin your country of its beauty, its riches, or its romance!"*

The ancient road from Canada winds along the shore of Lake Champlain. Far away, rising above its blue, island-dotted surface, loom the Green Mountains of Vermont, as fair a spectacle as any land affords. Billboards, near at hand, advertise hotels. Some of the hotels are a hundred miles away. Some signs are modest, built in the manner of ancient tavern signs. The majority are large and violently colored. The largest billboards advertise the worst hotels. None of them blends with the distant masses of the Green Mountains. They fail to stir the imaginations of those who would visualize the ungainly figure of Ethan Allen, leading his hard-boiled Green Mountain Boys against the British lobster-backs.

Here are signs aplenty; fine large signs. They say nothing of Indian massacres; nothing of British armies; nothing of the exploits of Rogers' Rangers. They deal with silver-fox farms; with Ausable Chasm, supposed, by the painters of the signboards, to rival the Pillars of Hercules, the Simplon Pass, the Grand Canyon of the Colorado, the Iron Gates of the Danube River, and the great falls of Albert Nyanza. Since they fail to tell us where we are, we look at the map. Ah, yes! Valcour Island . . .

*General Arnold with his fleet of gundelos and row-galleys, knocked together by New England carpenters, moved into the narrow channel separating Valcour Island from the New York shore and anchored there to delay the British fleet. Outnumbered two to one, he fought the British through a nightmare day. When darkness fell he slipped between the British ships; and at daybreak he was gone.*

*Twenty-four hours later they caught him again. He turned on them with his Congress galley, pointing the guns with his own hand; protecting the retreat of his other vessels. He fought until his galley was torn and splintered; his decks littered with dead and dying.*

*"Arnold," wrote Admiral Mahan, "ran the Congress and four gondolas ashore, pulling to windward with the cool judgment that had marked all his conduct, so that the enemy could not follow him. There he set his vessels on fire and stood by them until assured they would blow up with their flags flying. The little American navy on Champlain was wiped out; but never had any force, big or small, lived to better purpose or died more gloriously, for it had saved the Lake for that year. . . ."*

Valcour is in the Fir Balsam Pillow Belt. A multiplicity of signs announce it. The pillows are made of pure balsam. There are Lone Eagle restaurants. Lone Eagle restaurants, as might be expected from restaurants that have adopted such an illustrious name, sell only pure balsam pillows. Can it be that the countryside is flooded with impure balsam pillows?

There are signs tacked to trees: signs assuring the passers-by that Somebody's Medicine Builds Men. This, surely, is a good thought for a Road of Remembrance. Somebody's Medicine Builds Men—men, doubtless, who will neither sell nor use impure balsam pillows. Will Somebody's

Medicine build men like those tattered fighters who struggled afoot through the forests from Arnold's beached vessels to Crown Point and Ticonderoga? Evidently not.

Farther along lies the Adirondack State Park. Thanks to the activities of the New York Conservation Commission, it is a clean and de-billboarded section. More than two thousand billboards were removed from the highways in the state park by the Commission—a grievous outrage, according to the persons who contend that the Constitution of the United States protects all persons who wish to maintain eyesores on private property.

Emerging from the Adirondack State Park, the traveler approaches Lake George. Billboards, filling stations, sign-covered trees and barns reappear in regiments and battalions as the traveler nears the spot where that great French gentleman, the Marquis de Montcalm, stood chatting with his officers while his Indian allies butchered women, children, and disarmed soldiers from Fort William Henry.

They are difficult to locate, these historic spots; but one with good eyes may glimpse an occasional marker, a small bronze tablet, amid towering billboards.

The road from Lake George through Glens Falls and down the Hudson is one of the three leading billboard centers of this Land of the Free. Everything advertisable on billboards is advertised in that stretch of territory. It is a depressing land. . . . The San Francisco *Examiner*, in mid-1928, declared: "As fast as the American people invest a million to make a roadbed attractive to motorists, the signboard companies, by spending a few hundreds of dollars, make the roadsides hideous . . . and seriously depreciate that investment."

Colonel Frederick Greene, Superintendent of Public Works in the State of New York, despises Special Privilege that steals roadside beauty from the people. "As everyone knows," he writes, "a dirt road has no advertising value; but after the state has expended $50,000 or more per mile to convert a dirt road into an improved highway, traffic is immediately attracted and signs inevitably follow the traffic. Signboard companies thus reap, without return to the state, a benefit which the state has provided through the expenditure of millions of dollars."

The road along the Hudson arrives at abrupt hills: the Heights of Saratoga, around which American militia swarmed in early October of 1777 to halt Burgoyne's retreat. From the hills one looks south across the rolling plateau of Bemis's Heights. It was out of the ravines of Bemis's Heights that Benedict Arnold led American Continentals and militia against Burgoyne's light infantry and grenadiers: then hurled them against the Hessian right wing to turn the British flank and win the second battle of Saratoga: the battle that instilled confidence in the weary, wavering American colonies; the battle that whipped Burgoyne; one of the fifteen decisive battles of the world.

*Morgan's riflemen, most dreaded body of men in the Continental service, able, while running across broken ground, to load their rifles and to hit a saucer at two hundred yards, dashed from the hilltop at Bemis's Heights. Morgan himself, bellowing like a bull, was at their head.*

*They fell on the British light infantry advancing before General Fraser's right wing and opened a deadly fire. The scarlet-coated troops broke and ran in dismay. With the speed of the wind, Morgan wheeled and fell upon the British right flank with such force and impetuosity that their ranks were thrown into confusion.*

*"The finest regiment in the world," General Burgoyne called these Virginians, trained and commanded by an ex-teamster in Braddock's army—by Daniel Morgan, his back scarred with the welts of a whipping he had received in his youth from British officers. . . .*

Cowering among billboards on a rolling hilltop is an unobtrusive sign. "Colonel Morgan," it says, "held this position to prevent the retreat to the west."

On the ground where billboards pose drunkenly, Morgan's riflemen lay and prevented the escape of Burgoyne's army; hemmed in and headed off the redcoats and the blundering Hessians, so that the rolling fields and the wooded slopes of this fertile country might belong forever to all the people of America.

Billboards are thick as one continues on into Albany and descends the river through Troy, Kinderhook, and Hudson.

Hudson: there's a name that ought to bring up memories! Memories of what? Look around a bit. Wrigley's chewing gum? Campbell's soups? Ford's automobiles?

Yes, all of these; but there must be something else. Ah, yes! Hudson; Hudson! Frederick Hudson? No: that wasn't the name! Henry Hudson! That's it! Henry Hudson and the *Half Moon!*

*Henry Hudson mused idly on the romance of this limitless Western World. Resting his elbow on the taffrail of the old* Half Moon *as she wallowed slowly up the great river, he peered toward the eastward skyline.*

*"Ivory Soap," he read. "Coca-cola. Arrow shirts. Cremo cigars. Ten*

*Eyck Hotel. Nehi. June Caprice smokes Camels. Checker taxis. Philco radios. Steak and chicken dinners. Waffles. Harvard cigars. Buicks. Terraplanes. Old Golds. Green's Ale & Beer. Queen George Scotch. Seestars Brandy. Cliquot Club. Chesterfields. Halfseas Gin. Blended Rye. Ribraker Rum. Col. Bumm's Bourbon. That Good Gulf Gasolene. Soconyland."*

*Hudson shivered and rubbed his eyes. "What place is this?" he asked wonderingly.*

*High in the ratlines the wind wailed sadly. "Soconyland," it moaned. "Smokeland. Drinkland. Eatland. Guzzle-land. Speed-land. Spend-land. Noise-land. Waste-land. Tasteless-land. Get-It-However-You-Can-land. Throw-Away-Your-Birthright-land.    Not-a-Conscience-in-a-Legislature-land. . . ."*

*Hudson's elbow slipped from the taffrail; his chin descended on the water butt. Rising from the river at an acute angle, the* Half Moon *vanished behind a cloud wraith. It had ascended in search of its brother ghost, Romance.*

Discouraged at the gasolene stations, refreshment huts, and billboards that rim the New York–Albany road, the traveler strikes across the Hudson and up into the Mountain Lake Region of New Jersey. The name is redolent of romance. Mountain Lakes! It has a flavor of bosky glades; of crystal-clear tarns beneath the rocks of Lovers' Leap!

In the Mountain Lake Region the filling stations, hot-dog stands, and billboards are legion. They hide the lakes. If there is a Lovers' Leap in the vicinity, we cannot see it for giant signs announcing that Hans Breitmann's Frankfurters are endorsed by Timothy McCloskey.

Passing rapidly through the region of endorsed frankfurters, the traveler reaches a spot designated on billboards as the Eighth Scenic Wonder of the World: the Delaware Water Gap. Its outstanding scenic feature consists of billboards.

In the prudent and enterprising Pennsylvania Dutch country, hotels and businessmen of one town erect billboards in the next town. The businessmen of Bethlehem have placed billboards in near-by Nazareth. There is something vaguely familiar about these names—something that calls to mind a number of gentlemen who found themselves in serious difficulties for carrying their business into a locality where businesses had no business to be. . . .

So, in time, one comes to the long, rolling road through the most fertile country in all the world—the road across the swelling fields of Lancaster County to the little town of Gettysburg. Along it are red, white, and blue markers which bear the letter L because the highway is named in honor of Abraham Lincoln. There is a small bronze marker, too, telling those who have eyes to see that this is the Road of Remembrance.

*There was an encompassing, overwhelming, distant thudding in the air; a thudding like a thousand devils beating a thousand feather beds with a thousand sticks. Dust hung over the roadway as though the beating had continued since the beginning of time; and through the dust went a steady stream of blue-clad columns, moving perpetually to the south.*

*The sun beat down on them out of a pallid, sickly blue. Perspiration dripped from bearded cheeks to make mud splotches on wrinkled blue jackets. Guns and ammunition wagons toiled past, creaking and rattling. Officers, querulous from the blazing heat, called hoarsely to their men.*

*Along the roadside, resting in the dusty grass with heads between their knees, or dragging themselves to the rear, were the wounded—pale men, ghastly men; men with arms in slings; with bloodstained rags around legs and heads; men who limped and men who babbled.*

*"Git on up there!" bawled a capless boy who used his musket as a crutch. "They chewed hell out of us at Devil's Den! Give 'em hell, or they'll be in Philadelphy tomorrow, by God!"*

*Rolling their eyes at the white-faced boy, the blue-jacketed ranks toiled on toward Gettysburg. Ammunition wagons jolted and wailed; above them hung a smoky dust, as though the men beneath were smoldering in the fiery heat; the Union forces moved closer to the thudding of the guns.*

This is the Road of Remembrance. Tourists Accommodated. $1 Dinner: All You Can Eat for $1. Runny Mint Digestive Tablets. Cremo Cigars. Blisterine Mouth Wash. Don't Suffer from Colds: Use 666. Chew B. L. Plug. Keep Your Home Warm with Explodo Oil Burners. Take Life's Bumps on Goodrich Tires. Smoke Camels, the Nation's Sweetheart Smoke. Tourists Accommodated. Motorists Wise Simoniz. Hotel Bullethole, Gettysburg. Cannonball Lodge and Overnight Cabins: Free Digging for Bullets. Seven Miles to the Abraham Lincoln Garage and Overnight Cottages. Wear Gettysburg Overalls. Tourists Accommodated.

And *this* is the Road of Remembrance!

The road to the nation's capital, traveled at one time or another by all the great men of America, is a smear of billboards. The country between Philadelphia and New York—historic ground—is an offense to the eye, the ear, and the mind. The Boston Post Road, along which men from all the colonies trudged to press back the French and Indians, to join Washington, to fight the Mexicans, to preserve the Union, is a welter of eye-sores that daily grow larger, more brazen, more offensive. . . .

*Theodore Roosevelt shook his fist at his lethargic audience. "Do not," he implored, "let selfish men or greedy interests skin your country of its beauty, its riches, or its romance!"*

# Grandma's Kitchen

*"A Maine Kitchen" from* TRENDING INTO MAINE

It was in Grandma's home that I developed a fondness for Maine cooking, to say nothing of a few pronounced beliefs along other lines; and to the end of my days the simple foods that were the basis of most of our meals will seem to me more delicious than all the "specialties of the house" that can be produced by the world's most famous chefs.

The renowned fettuccini, be-cheesed and be-buttered with lascivious movements by the be-decorated Alfredo of Rome, has been press-agented with ecstatic cries by great authors and highly paid movie stars; but it's mushy and dreary by comparison with creamed finnan haddie prepared as my grandmother prepared it.

Frederic's pressed duck at the Tour d'Argent in Paris isn't bad, but it can't hold a candle to coot stew, properly cooked by a good Maine cook. The Bœuf à la Mode Restaurant in Paris has a world-wide reputation because of its manner of serving bœuf à la mode; and it's a pretty good dish, as is pressed duck and fettuccini; but my grandmother's corned beef hash was better—much better.

Poems have been written about bouillabaisse; but I have tried it again and again in the world's leading bouillabaisse centers, and, on the word of a dispassionate reporter, it's not to be compared with a Maine cunner, cod, or haddock chowder, made with salt pork and common-crackers.

The crisp mountain trout and sole Meunière and Marguéry over which the maîtres d'hôtel of Europe roll up their eyes so ecstatically are pleasant and nourishing fare, but they're not as good as the broiled scrod my grandmother used to make. Broiled tripe was another of her products that always set my mouth watering; so was pea soup, almost thick enough to hold a lead pencil upright; so were her fragrant and delicate fish cakes, light as a ping-pong ball, as melting in the mouth as a snowflake.

Thursday nights were big nights for the young fry in Grandmother's house, because that was the night for boiled dinner; but the biggest night of all was Saturday night. The rich scent of cooking had percolated through the house all day, and above all the other scents had risen the meaty, fruity, steamy odor of baked beans.

Ah me! Those Saturday night dinners of baked beans, brown bread, cottage cheese, Grandma's ketchup; and for a grand finale, chocolate custards! I can hear myself, a child again, begging and begging for another plate of beans—just one more plate of beans; hear the inexorable voice of authority say firmly, "You've had three plates already!" And in spite of that I can hear myself, pestlike, continuing to beg, "Just three beans! Just three more!" I usually got three additional beans, no more, no less; and always they were as delicious, as rich, as tantalizing in their toothsome mellowness as the first spoonful had been.

Others may insist on soufflés, ragouts, entremets, vol-au-vents; but I prefer baked beans cooked the way my grandmother used to cook them. Gourmets may have their crêpes suzette, their peach Melbas, their biscuit tortonis, their babas au rhum, if only I can have my grandmother's chocolate custards, sweet, smooth, cooling, and topped with half an inch of thick yellow cream.

I have heard theorists say that those of us who think back so fondly to the simple dishes we enjoyed as children are bemused by memory; that in those far-off days we had the voracious appetites, the cast-iron digestions, the lack of discrimination common to ostriches and the very young: that beans, hash, finnan haddie, and all such coarse and common fare are only delicious in retrospect.

Nothing could be farther from the truth. Hash, badly made, is disgusting; beans, poorly baked, are an offense to the palate; tripe, cooked by a mediocre cook, is revolting. But prepared by a State-of-Mainer who has the requisite touch, they are as ambrosial to me today as ever they were.

I once found myself in Palm Beach, Florida, discussing with the owner of a celebrated restaurant what should be set before a luncheon party of twelve. If, I told him, I could get the sort of hash my grandmother made in Maine, the guests would swoon with delight—but of course, I said, it was impossible.

He resented my skepticism. What, he demanded, was impossible about it? He agreed that well-made hash was indeed a dish for an epicure; and he insisted that his chef was just the one to make it.

"You're sure?" I asked. "You're sure he knows how? Everything finely chopped—moist in the center—brown and crisp on the outside?"

He was all assurance. Certainly the chef knew! I was to have no fear! My guests would talk about that hash for months! I was to leave it all to him!

There was considerable talk about that hash when the guests arrived. The thought of genuine Maine hash inflamed them; but when at last it was brought, the potatoes were cut in lumps the size of machine-gun bullets: the meat was in chunks: the whole dreadful mixture had been made dry and crumbly over a hot fire. Beyond a doubt the guests talked about that hash for the remainder of the year, but not in the way the restaurant owner had anticipated.

Years afterward, in the grill of the Barclay in New York, I was scanning the menu with two friends, preparatory to having lunch. What I'd like more than anything, I said, was the sort of hash my grandmother used to make; but that, of course, was impossible outside of Maine. My bitterness led the headwaiter to join in the conversation. His chef, he thought, could make hash that would please me—provided he knew how I liked it. I said that I had doubts: that I liked it chopped fine, extremely fine; moistened a little; cooked over a slow fire on the back of the stove until the bottom was brown and crisp; then folded over like an omelet.

"Yes," the headwaiter said, "he can do it. That's the way he makes the hash he eats himself."

Eagerly, and yet fearing the worst, I ordered hash.

"I'll have some too," one of my companions said.

"So'll I," said the other.

I advised against it. If not made correctly, I told them, it would be terrible; but they persisted. If there was a chance of getting real hash, they wanted it.

To our profound pleasure, the hash was delicious—as good as my grandmother's; and between the three of us we demolished a platterful. I must admit, however, that there was something lacking; though that something wasn't the fault of the chef. The ketchup that was produced to accompany the hash was a brilliant red, sweetish and without character. So far as I know, every ketchup on the market has a sweetish, artificial, shallow flavor that revolts the descendants of Maine's seafaring families. The chef had made hash for which no State-of-Mainer would need to apologize; but there was no ketchup comparable to my grandmother's to go with it.

Ketchup is an important adjunct to many Maine dishes, particularly in families whose manner of cooking comes down to them from seafaring ancestors. So far as I know, a sweetened ketchup in those families is regarded as an offense against God and man, against nature and good taste. This antagonism to sweetened ketchup is traceable to the days when dozens of Maine sea captains from every Maine town were constantly sailing to Cuba and the West Indies for cargoes of molasses and rum, and to Spain for salt. Captain Marryat, in *Frank Mildmay*, describes a shore excursion of ship's officers in Cuba in 1807 and complains of the lavish use of tomato sauce on all Spanish dishes. The same thing is true in Spain today, as well as in Italy, where it is customary to serve a bowl of hot tomato sauce with macaroni, spaghetti, fettuccini, ravioli, and many other dishes, so that the diner may lubricate his viands to suit himself. Under no circumstances is this tomato sauce sweetened. It is made by adding hot water to a paste obtained by boiling down tomato juice to a concentrate.

In most parts of early New England, tomatoes were called "love-apples" and were shunned as being poisonous; but that wasn't true among Maine's seafaring families. Sea captains brought tomato seeds from Spain and Cuba, their wives planted them, and the good cooks in the families experimented with variants of the ubiquitous and somewhat characterless tomato sauce of Spain and Cuba. The ketchups they evolved, in spite of the aversion to tomatoes throughout early America, were considered indispensable with hash, fish cakes, and baked beans in Maine, even in the days of love-apples.

Such was the passion for my grandmother's ketchup in my own family that we could never get enough of it. We were allowed to have it on beans, fish cakes, and hash, since those dishes were acknowledged to be incomplete without them; but when we went so far as to demand it on bread, as we often did, we were peremptorily refused and had to go down in the cellar and steal it—which we also often did. It had a savory, appetizing tang to it that seemed—and still seems—to me to be inimitable. I became almost a ketchup drunkard; for when I couldn't get it, I yearned for it. Because of that yearning, I begged the recipe from my grandmother when I went away from home; and since that day I have made many and many a batch of her ketchup with excellent results.

The recipe has never been published, and I put it down here for the benefit of those who aren't satisfied with the commercial makeshifts that masquerade under the name of ketchup:—

With a large spoon rub cooked tomatoes through a sieve into a kettle, to remove seeds and heavy pulp, until you have one gallon of liquid. One peck of ripe tomatoes, cooked and strained, makes one gallon. [This operation is greatly simplified by using one dozen cans of concentrated tomato juice.] Put the kettle on the stove and bring the tomato juice almost to a boil. Into a bowl put a pint of sharp vinegar, and in the vinegar dissolve 6 tablespoons of salt, 4 tablespoons of allspice, 2 tablespoons of mustard, 1 tablespoon of powdered cloves, 1 teaspoon of black pepper, ¼ teaspoon of red pepper. Stir the vinegar and spices into the tomato juice, set the kettle over a slow fire and let it simmer until it thickens. The mixture must be constantly stirred, or the spices settle on the bottom and burn. If made from concentrated tomato juice, an hour and a half of simmering is sufficient; but if made from canned tomatoes, the mixture should be allowed to cook slowly for three or four hours. When the kettle is removed from the fire, let the mixture stand until cold. Then stir and pour into small-necked bottles. If a half inch of olive oil is poured into each bottle, and the bottle then corked, the ketchup will keep indefinitely in a cool place. It's better if chilled before serving.

My memories of my grandmother's kitchen are fond ones. The stove was large, strategically situated near windows from which the cook could observe the goings and comings of the neighbors and divert herself while engaged in her duties. As a result, her disposition was almost free of the irritability so frequently found among cooks, and one who stood persistently beside the stove on baking days could usually obtain permission to lick the large iron spoons with which the chocolate, orange, and vanilla frostings had been applied to the cakes.

There was also an excellent chance that the cook's attention would be so caught by an occurrence in the outer world that a deft bystander could thrust a prehensile forefinger into the frosting pan and extract a delectable morsel without detection.

Opposite the stove was the pantry, with a barrel of flour and a barrel of sugar beneath the bread shelf. An excellent confection could be obtained from the sugar barrel by dropping a spoonful of water into it and carefully removing the resulting blob of moist sugar with a fork.

On the bread shelf was a fascinating hen's wing for brushing flour from the shelf into the barrel after an orgy of breadmaking; and on the cool shelf near the window, where the pans of milk stood overnight to permit the cream to rise, was a magnificent giant clamshell used to skim the cream. If one rose early in the morning, he could not only watch the delicate operation of cream removal, but might be allowed to lick the clamshell.

On the floor under the milk shelf were three gray crocks decorated with blue tracings. In one of the crocks were hermits, in another dough-nuts, and in the third sugar cookies. These crocks were dangerous to tamper with when freshly filled or almost empty; for the eagle eye of the kitchen's guardian—a muscular lady who wore a bright brown wig and answered to the name of Katie—was quick to discern the larceny, and her tongue promptly announced it in the most agonizingly penetrating voice I ever remember hearing. As a boy, at such times, I considered her totally lacking in reticence. When the hermits or doughnuts were about one-third gone, however, a reasonable number could be abstracted with almost no peril to the abstractor.

The door to the woodshed, the barn, the grape arbor, and the—well, let's call it the Rest Room—was in a third corner; and in the fourth corner was a boxlike contrivance over which, on Sunday mornings, I spent many a long hour, engrossed in polishing my grandfather's shoes. Careful as was John Singleton Copley in putting on canvas the likenesses of his sitters, I'm sure he worked no harder with his brushes than I did with mine, applying equal portions of expectoration and blacking to every crease and contour of that respected footgear; then vigorously wielding the polishing brush until my small arms ached.

Every Sunday I was rewarded for my labors with five cents—a vast sum in days when one penny purchased three licorice sticks, five all-day suckers mounted on toothpicks, or two cocoanut cakes—a delicacy which could be made to last beyond belief if wrapped in the corner of a hand-kerchief and chewed in that protective covering.

Only on every other Sunday, however, could I take an artist's delight in admiring my own craftsmanship; for my grandmother was a Congrega-tionalist and my grandfather a Baptist, and they tolerantly divided me, so to speak, between them. On one Sunday I was led by my grandmother to the Congregationalist church, to which I went willingly, knowing that at the halfway mark in the service I would be given a peppermint from the mysteriously hidden pocket of my grandmother's black silk dress; and on the following Sunday I went eagerly to the Baptist church, where I was free to crouch on the floor at my grandfather's feet during the longer reaches of the sermon, and contemplate with profound satisfac-tion the results of my labors in the kitchen.

Yes, I knew the kitchen well; and from occasionally sleeping above it, I became an expert on its intricate and absorbing sounds—not only the rhythmic thumping of the hash chopper, muffled by the mound of pota-toes and corned beef through which it was driven by Katie's tireless arms, and the occasional muted rasp when the scattered mound was reassembled for further chopping. How well I knew the delicate gritting of an iron spoon against a saucepan at the culmination of a successful frosting-making; the faint bubbling which accompanied the manufacture of doughnuts; the soft clanking that announced the removal of the lid of the mincemeat jar! Many of these sounds, of course, left me unmoved, but others brought me hurriedly down the winding back stairs—so hurriedly that I usually fell the last half-dozen steps, having learned that the compassion aroused by such a fall would unfailingly bring me a doughnut, a frosting spoon to lick, or at the worst a slice of new bread, well buttered and sprinkled with sugar.

My interest in the kitchen will help to explain why I have saved as many of my grandmother's recipes as I could—particularly the recipes for the simple Maine dishes that seem to me the best in the world.

To bake one's own beans, in these enlightened days of canned foods, is doubtless too much trouble, particularly if the cook wishes to spend her Saturday afternoons motoring, playing bridge, or attending football games —though many a Maine housewife still persists in the old-fashioned method. I can only say that there is a marked difference between canned beans and well-cooked bean-pot beans.

My grandmother's beans were prepared like this: Four cupfuls of small white beans were picked over to eliminate the worm-holed specimens and the small stones that so mysteriously intrude among all beans, then covered with water and left to soak overnight. Early the next morning, usually around five o'clock, they were put in a saucepan, covered with cold water, and heated until a white scum appeared on the water. They were then taken off the stove, the water thrown away, and the bean pot produced. In the bottom of the bean pot was placed a one-pound piece of salt pork, slashed through the rind at half-inch intervals, together with a large peeled onion; then the beans were poured into the pot on top of the pork and onion. On the beans were put a heaping teaspoon of mustard, half a cup of molasses, and a teaspoon of pepper; the bean pot was filled with boiling water, and the pot put in a slow oven. At the end of two hours a tablespoon of salt was dissolved in a cup of boiling water and added to the beans. Every hour or so thereafter the cover was removed and enough boiling water poured in to replace that which had boiled away. An hour before suppertime the cover was taken off for good and no more water added. Thus the pork, in the last hour, was crisped and browned, and the top layer of beans crusted and slightly scorched. When the beans were served, the pork was saved and the scorched beans skimmed off and thrown away. The two great tricks of bean-making seemed to be the frequent adding of small amounts of water up to the final hour of baking, so that no part of the beans had an opportunity to become dry, and the removal of the cover during the last hour. To add large amounts of water —to fill the pot to the top and let it boil down to the beans before adding more—meant that the beans would be greasy and wholly lacking in the fruity richness of properly cooked beans.

The hash trick was simpler. Into a wooden hash bowl were put three cups of cold boiled potatoes and four cups of cold corned beef from which all gristle and fat had been removed. The hash chopper was used on these until the meat and potatoes were in infinitesimal pieces. A frying pan was placed on the stove and a piece of butter the size of two eggs melted in it. A cup of boiling water was added to the butter; then the chopped potatoes and corned beef were poured in and stirred until hot.

At this point the frying pan was set back on the stove where there was no danger of burning, and the hash tamped down in the pan. At the end of a quarter hour, when a brown crust had formed on the lower side of the hash, a broad-bladed knife was inserted beneath it, and one half was deftly folded over on the other, as an omelet is folded. It was then ready to serve.

The important feature in hash-making was to make sure that the person who did the chopping shouldn't be too easily satisfied, but should lovingly labor until each piece of potato and each piece of corned beef was cut as small as possible.

Mystery has risen like a fog around Maine fish chowder. Some cooks argue that it can't be made properly without soiling eight or ten stew pans, dishes, and caldrons. A few pontifically announce that salt pork should never be used; but many contend that pork not only should be used, but should be tried out separately, the liquid fat thrown away, and only the pork scraps added to the stew. There is also a large school of thought which insists that the head and backbone must be boiled separately and the juice from them used as a basis for the chowder.

All those methods, probably, are excellent; but my grandmother believed in leaving fish heads and backbones where they belonged—in the refuse barrel at the fish market—and in soiling the fewest possible number of kitchen utensils. She had reduced the soilage to one kettle, one knife, and one spoon—which is, I believe, the absolute minimum.

Cunners, freshly taken, strike me as being the best basis for a fish chowder, but cunners are unpleasant to clean, because of the extreme slipperiness and excessive toughness of their skins and the agonizing sharpness of their back spines. If, however, two dozen medium-to-large cunners are delivered to any Maine fish market, the marketman, with professional skill, skins them and separates the usable portions from the backbones in two shakes of a lamb's tail—and the meat from two dozen cunners is about right for a small fish chowder.

Lacking cunners, my grandmother used a good-sized haddock or cod. The fish was skinned, boned, and cut into small pieces about an inch long. She sliced four large raw potatoes, boiled the slices in a quart of water, took them out and mashed them; then returned them to the water in which they boiled. She chopped three slices of salt pork and put them in a frying pan to try out. To the frying pork she added three diced onions, and when the onions had softened, she added the fish, the mashed potatoes, and the water, a pinch of white sugar, three quarters of a cup of cream, a quart of milk, salt and pepper to taste, and a teaspoon of curry powder. Just before serving she sprinkled the chowder liberally with cracker crumbs. The younger set that lived in Grandma's house always received the news that fish chowder was in the making by rubbing their stomachs and rolling up their eyes—the supreme gesture of youthful approval.

My grandmother's method of mixing and cooking fish balls was richer and juicier than that advocated by Miss Fanny Farmer in her deathless work on American cookery. She pulled half a pound of salt fish into small pieces and soaked them in cold water overnight. The next morning she changed the water and brought the fish to a boil: then mashed and chopped it until it was smooth. She boiled three good-sized potatoes for twenty-five minutes; then mashed them and stirred the fish into them. To this mixture she added five eggs, five generous teaspoons of butter and a little pepper, and beat everything vigorously together. She cooked them in deep fat, picking up generous dabs of the mixture in a potbellied spoon. The resulting fish balls, eaten with her own brand of ketchup, made ambrosia seem like pretty dull stuff.

Neither Fanny Farmer nor anyone else, so far as I know, has touched on Grandmother's chocolate custards and how she made them. Like all her other dishes, her chocolate custards were as simple and inexpensive as they were delicious. It took me many years to realize that almost everything we ate at my grandmother's was inexpensive, and that the chief reason we ate the foods we did was that she had to economize. In my childish ignorance, I thought we had hash and baked beans and finnan haddie with baked potatoes because they were the most savory dishes obtainable.

Ah, well. . . . The first step in making chocolate custards is to buy two or three dozen glass goblets—the sort shaped like large egg cups.

Three heaping tablespoons of cornstarch are dissolved in half a cup of milk. Two and one half cups of milk are heated in a double boiler. Into a saucepan are put five heaping tablespoons of sugar, two tablespoons of water, one square of cooking chocolate. This is dissolved over boiling water, then placed on the fire, boiled for two minutes, and added to the hot milk. When the mixture has the appearance of chocolate milk instead of plain milk, the half cup of milk and cornstarch is poured in. It is stirred until slightly thickened, when a half teaspoon of vanilla extract is added. It is then poured into the goblets, and the latter, when cool, are placed in the icebox. Before serving, cream is added to the surface with a gentle hand, so not to break the delicate scum.

No matter what I say, there will, I know, always be skeptics to insist that my memories play me false: that these simple old Maine dishes couldn't actually have been as good as I think they were.

Fortunately the Parker House in Boston is able to broil scrod and tripe the way my grandmother did, and the Copley Plaza in Boston is as adept at finnan haddie as she was; so when the skeptics deafen me with their shouting, I only need to drive to Boston in order to prove to my own satisfaction that they're wrong. And on Saturdays the Congress Square Hotel in Portland serves a pea soup made just as my grandmother used to make it. When I'm able, I go to Portland on Saturdays, so that I can sit high up above the city, look off across that green and rolling country to the far sharp peaks of the White Mountains, fill myself to the brim with pea soup, and think pitying thoughts of the benighted people who believe there's nothing like French cooking.

Of all the edible wild life to be found in Maine, the coot is the most difficult to handle satisfactorily; for not only is he hard to cook, but he is almost as hard to kill. The cat, popularly supposed to have nine lives, is the merest faint breath of fragility by comparison.

In late September and October coot assemble off the Maine coast in flocks of hundreds and sometimes thousands. Large as these flocks are, they've developed almost to a science the art of doing the same thing at the same moment. Thus a gunner, approaching a flock of coot, needs only to wait for the periods when all of them take it into their heads to dive together. A coot, of course, is crazy, as is shown by the expression, "As crazy as a coot"; so if a gunner moves up on a flock while it is under water, and ceases to move when the flock, with military precision, reappears on the surface, no suspicion of evil ever enters the minds of his quarry.

Eventually the hunter finds himself over a mass of submerged coot; and when they come up for air, they pop from the water in horrified amazement—a sort of ornithological eruption.

This is the moment for the hunter to lay in a month's supply of coot—provided he can make up his mind at which one of the erupting birds to aim.

Coot shooting is the most deceptive of all forms of wild-game hunting, in that a coot which seems to be dead is seldom more than momentarily dazed. In my early days, when coot were hunted from motorboats, the boat from which we gunned had an empty barrel lashed amidships. Coot that were brought down had their heads hammered briskly against the gunwale in order to discourage all further activity on their part and then were tossed into the barrel. Two or three hours later the barrel was brought ashore and its contents emptied on the lawn. Always, out of that half barrelful of seemingly defunct coot, a dozen would stagger to their feet, shake their heads as if to rid themselves of a passing headache, and waddle sturdily off in all directions.

A partridge sometimes drops dead at the impact of one small shot in a non-vital part; but fifty goose-shot frequently rattle off a coot as though his feathers and hide were Bessemer steel.

This outer toughness of the coot seems, like the hole in the doughnut, to go clear through; for when he is cooked as other water fowl are cooked, he's as inedible as an automobile tire, as redolent of fish as a glue factory. He can, however, be made edible; and my grandmother, for one, was able to stew coot so that they were as tender as black duck, and as savory.

There's an old, old recipe in Maine for stewing coot; and that recipe, I suspect, originated in the dim, dim past, probably with the Norsemen who came to Maine in their little open boats a thousand years ago. To stew coot, runs this recipe, place the bird in a kettle of water with a red building brick free of mortar and blemishes. Parboil the coot and the brick together for three hours. Pour off the water, refill the kettle, and again parboil for three hours. For the third time throw off the water, for the last time add fresh water, and let the coot and the brick simmer together overnight. In the morning throw away the coot and eat the brick.

State-of-Mainers, no matter how often they hear it, always find this recipe inordinately amusing. It used to amuse my grandmother, and I've heard her repeat that venerable recipe herself with many a quiet chuckle; yet she served coot stew whenever coot couldn't be avoided.

She had the coot skinned, never plucked; and all fat was carefully removed. The bodies were put breast down in a bowl in the ice chest after being squirted with lemon juice. Then they were put in an iron kettle with a moderate amount of water and boiled three hours, at the end of which time as many sliced potatoes were added as the situation seemed to require. Dumplings were dropped in as soon as the potatoes were done; and when the dumplings in turn were thoroughly cooked, they were temporarily removed while the remaining liquid was thickened with flour and water and salted and peppered to taste. The dumplings were then put back, and the stew was ready to serve.

There is one odd question too often asked by persons of otherwise keen intelligence. If they are told of the eating of octopus in Italy, they ask: "What does octopus taste like?" There is, of course, only one answer. An octopus tastes like an octopus; and if anybody feels an urge to ask that question about a coot, I can only say that coot stew tastes strongly of coot.

In my grandmother's house there were no alcoholic drinks, nor were there even recipes for alcoholic drinks. The State of Maine, in my grandmother's day, was perhaps a trifle odd about what was known as the Demon Rum—rum being the generic term for all alcoholic beverages. There was a deal of drinking in Maine, even when it was the one and only prohibition state in America; and in Bangor, mecca of lumbermen, a dozen saloons dispensed good cheer more or less openly in spite of the prohibition law. As for Maine sea captains, they carried cargoes of rum and would doubtless have had trouble on their hands if they hadn't issued rum rations to their crews.

I don't pretend to be psychic or vatic; but something—some little bird—tells me that my grandmother's sainted father, during his sojourn in Dartmoor Prison, took all the rum he could get and complained bitterly because there wasn't more; and that same little bird whispers to me that when my grandmother's six sea-captain brothers found themselves safely ashore in foreign ports after a hard passage, they sometimes fell so far from grace as to split a bottle of brandy with an intimate or two.

Nevertheless, my grandmother was against Rum, and so were most Maine ladies of that period. So averse to it were they that they shrank in horror from salad dressing made with claret vinegar—for even the sourest of claret came under the head of the Demon Rum.

But somehow, in our family, recipes for alcoholic beverages have been preserved. I have had occasion to mention these early Maine tipples in some of my books; and from the letters of inquiry that have reached me, peremptorily demanding the ingredients of flip or hot buttered rum, I deduce that there is almost more interest in what our forefathers drank than in what they thought.

Hot buttered rum went by no rigid measurements, and each Maine tavern and home was a law to itself. The general theory seemed to be that there was no such thing as a bad method of making hot buttered rum: that all methods were good, but that some were a little better than others.

Roughly speaking, hot buttered rum was better when made by the pitcherful or bowlful than when made by the single mugful. Also roughly speaking, the ingredients were rum, brown sugar, butter, cinnamon and boiling water; the proportions to a cupful of rum were a half gill of brown sugar, a half gill of butter, a quarter gill of powdered cinnamon, and a quart of boiling water.

A master method of making hot buttered rum, discovered by the celebrated Trader Vic of Oakland, California, is to keep on hand a few flavoring materials, and a batter made by mixing together five pounds of yellow sugar, one pound of butter, and one ounce of vanilla. This batter will keep for years in a mason jar. The proper flavoring materials are whole vanilla beans, whole cloves, and stick cinnamon.

Thus equipped, put a generous teaspoon of batter in a tumbler, drop in one vanilla bean, one small piece of stick cinnamon, and three cloves. Add an ounce-and-a-half or two-ounce jigger of rum, fill the tumbler with boiling water, stir well, and grate a little nutmeg on top.

When made in this way, the butter blends with the rum, instead of floating greasily on top to act as a clog to the system and a stopper to the rum fumes.

But don't take liberties with hot buttered rum; for although it tastes mild and harmless, it's powerful and enduring in its effects, particularly when taken in conjunction with other drinks.

In northern Maine, where winters are lingering and oppressive, early settlers made buttered rum by using hot hard cider in place of hot water; and Local Tradition—in which I put little faith—says that men have been known, at the beginning of winter, to drink too much hot buttered rum made with a base of hot hard cider, fall into a stupor, and not wake up till spring. I don't believe the story; but if I ever tried hot buttered rum made with hot hard cider, I'd handle it as I would a high explosive.

Flip was a milder and more popular beverage in Maine in the early days, though not much cheaper, since there was a period, a couple of generations before the Revolution, when rum sold for a shilling and a half a gallon.

The base of flip was beer. A two-quart pitcher was three-quarters filled with beer, to which was added a cup of rum, and sweetening matter to taste—brown sugar, molasses, or dried pumpkin. This mixture was stirred with the red-hot poker, which was kept constantly clean and hot for that purpose. Taverns which pretended to great gentility and elegance kept on hand a bowl of flip sweetener made of a pint of cream, four pounds of sugar, and four eggs, well beaten together. When a customer ordered flip, the tavern keeper poured a pint and a half of beer into a quart pewter mug, added a half cup of rum and four spoonfuls of flip sweetener, and stirred it with the red-hot poker. As in the case of hot buttered rum, hard cider was sometimes used as a base for flip. On occasions the sweetening matter was omitted from a mixture of beer and rum, in which case the drink was known as "calibogus."

Every Thursday, for years, my household has looked forward to eating pea soup for lunch. We call it split-pea soup, but we don't often use split peas. We use ordinary unsplit field peas, which we grow ourselves: not the commercial variety split by some mysterious form of processing in Wisconsin or Idaho. It is my belief that processing, by which the hard outer shell is removed from field peas to make them into split peas, does nothing whatever to improve the taste of pea soup. That, however, is merely one man's opinion.

We make our pea soup by putting three cups of field peas to soak in cold water the first thing in the morning. At ten o'clock we put the peas in a kettle with a gallon of water, two pounds of salt pork, a sliced onion, a sliced carrot, and a sliced celery stalk. When it has simmered for an hour and a half, we add a pint of strong chicken stock and a teaspoon of summer savory (sauriette) and simmer it another hour and a half. Then we rub it through a strainer and eat it with a satisfaction that never flags.

(The voluminous correspondence elicited by this chapter of *Trending Into Maine* when it was first published resulted in *Good Maine Food*, a compendium of New England recipes, by Marjorie Mosser and Kenneth Roberts, Doubleday, Doran & Co., 1940.)

## Hot Buttered Rum

*From* NORTHWEST PASSAGE

IN THE SUMMER of 1759, when Hunk Marriner and Cap Huff unexpectedly visited me in Cambridge, the College would have been something of an eye opener to those who thought of it as a nest of budding clergymen.

It was not, as the reformer Whitefield had implied a few years before, a mere seminary of Paganism; but on warm nights in the spring of the year it was likely to be a tumultuous place because of the determination of the students to show their disapproval whenever they received a bad supper in the Commons. Since this was a nightly occurrence, there was almost a regular evening hullabaloo, followed by the ringing of bells and often a sprightly throwing of brickbats against the door of a Tutor.

Edicts and warnings were issued by the Board of Overseers of the College against these frequent disorders, complaining that there were combinations among the undergraduates for the perpetration of unlawful acts; that students were guilty of being absent from their chambers at unseasonable times of night; that the loose practice of going and staying out of town without leave must cease. The students must, the Overseers insisted, make an end of profane cursing and swearing. There could be no more frequenting of alehouses; no more fetching of liquors to the chambers of undergraduates; no further entering into extravagant and enormous expenses at taverns for wine, strong beer, and distilled spirits.

Since it never seemed to occur to the Board of Overseers to see that our food was improved, the disorders naturally continued.

It even became the fashion to walk forth, on a warm evening, in search of disorders. The searchers were seldom disappointed; but when they were, they generously provided disorders of their own to keep late-comers from being disappointed too.

My rooms were on the top floor of a small house on Brattle Street; for since there were 134 students in Harvard at that time, and since only

90 could be accommodated in Massachusetts Hall, the rest of us were obliged to lodge where we could.

It was late on a June afternoon, a little before the Commons hour, that I heard my name hoarsely spoken in the street below. When I went to the open window and peered out, I saw one of my classmates pointing up at my room. Beside him Hunk Marriner and Cap Huff, all sweaty and dusty, stared upward with mouths agape.

At my shouted invitation they stumbled up the dark and narrow stairs and pushed their way into the room, seeming to fill it to overflowing, not only with their bodies and their muskets and the packages which each carried, but with a singular ripe odor compounded of rum and a musty smell unfamiliar to me.

"What's that smell?" I asked, when I had made them welcome.

"Smell?" Cap said. "Smell? I don't smell nothing, only these books here." He waved a huge hand at my desk.

"What you smell," Hunk said, "might prob'ly be either us or these skins —five sea-otter and twelve sables. Cap got 'em off to the eastward somewheres, and we're taking 'em to Boston to sell to Captain Callendar."

"Well," I said, "you're in luck! Who'd you get 'em from?"

"Oh," Cap said indifferently, "I just stumbled across 'em, and so I picked 'em up."

"Why didn't you sell 'em in Portsmouth?"

Cap's reply was impatient. "Listen: there's times I wisht I'd never bothered to pick up one of these skins. Every time anybody mentions 'em, there's as much talk about 'em as there'd be about a cartload of gold horseshoes. Prob'ly it's those skins you smell, the way Hunk says, but don't give 'em another thought, because we're going into Boston as soon as we get something to eat. Then you won't smell 'em any more."

"If you're going to eat," I said, "I'll go out and eat with you."

Hunk shook his head. "One of the reasons we stopped here was so we could leave our muskets while we go to Boston. The other reason was we didn't have any money, and we won't have any till we sell the skins. We thought maybe you'd have some."

"I haven't," I said. "This is the end of the year, and nobody has any. You'll have to go over to Commons with me for supper. Maybe you won't like the food, but it can't be helped."

"We'll like it," Cap assured me. "Anybody that's hungry likes anything, and I'm hungry enough to eat a porcupine, quills and all."

They were not, Hunk protested, suitably dressed to appear in polite society; but this wasn't true, for they had on their city clothes—homespun breeches, gray woolen stockings, and towcloth shirts—and carried brown coats tied to their belts in back. Thus a little brushing made them presentable, aside from the wrinkles in their coats and the musty flavor of stale sea-otter pelts that clung persistently to them.

Noticeable as was this faint perfume, it was wholly submerged, when we entered Commons, by a noisome fragrance that struck against us in waves as we walked down the aisle. These surges of ripeness seemed propelled against us by an undercurrent of grumbling that rose from all the tables, frequently increasing to a noisy angry clamor, only to subside again to discontented mutterings.

When we seated ourselves, it was evident that Cap and Hunk might have worn buckskin hunting clothes and coonskin caps without exciting comment; for the attention of all the students at my own table and those adjoining was riveted on the pies which were being served. They had been baked in deep dishes, about the size of a barber's bowl; and whenever one of them was placed before a newcomer, all his neighbors leaned forward to watch it opened. In every case the owner, after piercing the protective covering, used forefinger, thumb, and nose in the supreme gesture of loathing, while all adjacent colleagues groaned eloquently in unison. This, then, accounted for the resurgent clamor; and when we in turn received our own pies and opened them, we had little hope of containing our own emotion.

On the instant that I punctured the crust of mine, a hot and nauseous smell gushed upward—a smell so ripely evil that it caught at the throat and at the stomach too.

At the sight of my face, all the others at our table joined in the prevalent loud groan.

"For God's sake, what's in it?" I asked Wingate Marsh, a classmate.

"Carrion!" Marsh said. "Carrion!"

"Look here," I said to him, "these friends of mine walked all the way from Portsmouth today. Isn't there anything fit to eat?"

"Not one damned thing!" Marsh said. "There's nothing but this pie—carrion pie!" Then his eyes fixed themselves amazedly on Cap Huff, who sat beside me.

Cap had neatly folded back the crust of his pie and was eating heartily. Hunk also delved into his with no sign of repugnance.

"Hold on!" I protested. "Don't eat that! You'll be poisoned! We can't leave the table till the tutors give the word, not unless we want to be fined five shillings; but if you'll wait, I'll borrow some money and we'll go to the Tavern and get something to eat."

"What's wrong with this?" Cap asked. He scraped his bowl with his spoon; then looked amiably around the incredulously staring table. "Maybe mine was better'n what you had. Anyways, I ain't more than took the edge off my appetite, and if there's anybody wants to get rid of his pie, I'll trade him for it."

He eyed my friends innocently. "I'll trade a drink of rum for every pie. Tomorrow night I'll be coming out of Boston with some rum, and you can come around to Langdon Towne's room and collect."

With one accord the eleven other men at the table pushed their pies toward Cap. He took them all, arranging them in a semicircle in front of Hunk and himself.

"What would you figure was in these pies?" he asked, as he smiled blandly at my classmates.

Matthew Weaver of Watertown answered for all of us. "We don't know what was in yours, but ours must have been horse. Old horse, a long time dead."

Cap rolled up his eyes and swallowed hard. "No; it ain't horse: it's rabbit; but a natural good eater easy gets used to rabbits that might have lost their lives some little time back. Besides, if a rabbit's tuckered when he gets killed, he tastes kind of lively. I don't say but these was both kind of overkept and tuckered too; but on the other hand, look at all the flavor they gain by it."

Weaver stared at him incredulously. "Don't they taste *horrible* to you?"

Cap seemed to consult his inwards judicially. "No, not horrible exactly. I've had rabbit pies that you didn't have to lift the cover of, because it was already blew off. Maybe you wouldn't call it no furbelowed lady's feed, but I've seen cheeses that wasn't, either. The way to learn how to eat a pie like this is to turn your head to one side while you open it, and until it kind of dies down; but that's only for beginners. Eggs too old I don't claim I ever could master, even myself; but take a nice old kept-over rabbit and there's something mighty strong and wholesome about him. It builds up the stomach."

Samuel Wingate of Dorchester cleared his throat. "We live and learn. Just let me have my pie back, will you?"

Cap stared at him. "Your pie? I already et yours. You ain't got any! You traded it to me for a glass of rum tomorrow; and when you make a bargain, you got to keep it. Don't they learn you no morals at Harvard College?"

Sam was silent, and Cap conferred privily with Hunk, while I removed the crust from my pie and tried it. As Cap had intimated, it was not as bad as it smelled. Neither was it good.

Cap spoke benevolently to my friends. "This is how we figure it: all these pies belong to I and Hunk, but we wouldn't want to take advantage of a lot of nice young fellers—not if their education had been kind of neglected along some lines. If you fellers want to trade for what we got left, we'll trade. There's still enough of 'em so's each of you can have half a pie. You can have 'em back for a cigarro apiece, payable tomorrow night when you get your rum."

§

Word spread rapidly, seemingly, concerning my amiable and eccentric acquaintances; for when Hunk and Cap returned from Boston at dusk on the following day, there were as many as twenty undergraduates, a few of them unknown to me, lounging on the grass before the house in which I lived. As soon as Cap came in sight at the end of the street, we saw that he intended to keep his agreement. Over his shoulder was a canvas sling; and in the sling, resting above his left hip, was a five-gallon keg. Hunk was laden with a number of lesser bundles, among them a paper cylinder the size of a small cannon. Evidently their skins had sold well in Boston.

These two friends of mine, it was easy to see, had made a strong and favorable impression in a short time; for Marsh and Wingate and the others hailed them profanely, asking how much rabbit pie they'd eaten during the day, and saying they should have been at Commons for supper, as we'd had a poison-ivy soup that they'd no doubt have found appetizing.

"We've got your cigarros," Sam Wingate told Cap. "Knowing your tastes, we had 'em made specially for you out of horse hair and hoof parings."

"That's good," Cap said. "That'll be a nice change from the chopped fish skins and oakum that us country fellers have to smoke." He looked apprehensively up and down the street. "Listen! We only got five gallons in this here keg, and I been lugging it five miles, so I got a good deal of a thirst. There ain't more'n enough to give us a couple all round, so let's get out of sight somewheres and drink it pretty quick. If we don't, we'll have the whole college wanting a taste of it, and there won't be enough left for us to do more than spill on our chins."

There was some truth in what he said, for already our numbers had been augmented by other acquaintances of mine; so after Cap had dispatched Wingate and Marsh for jugs of hot water and an empty mixing bucket, we trooped upstairs to my room and disposed ourselves as best we could—most of us on the floor.

Cap placed his keg upon a table; slapped it affectionately. "This here's the medicine for food poisoning, like what you fellers prob'ly got from your insides not being built up strong and seasoned. It ain't no ordinary rum that's had all the good taken out of it by being strained and doctored and allowed to grow weak with age. This here's third-run rum, real powerful, more like food than drink. When you drink it, you can taste it. Rum's intended to take hold of you, and that's what this does. There ain't no way of concealing what it is, the way you can with old, weak-kneed rum. Why, this rum, you could put onions in it, or the powerfulest dead fish, and couldn't taste a thing different about it! It's real honest rum!" His eye fell on my wash bowl and pitcher in the corner. "Here, gimme that pitcher! First we'll try it raw; then we'll butter it, and you can see what I mean."

Worrying the bung from the keg, he decanted some of the contents into the pitcher. The room, on the instant, was permeated with an odor like that of a damp and dirty cellar in which quantities of molasses have become sour, moldy, and pungent.

Cap raised the pitcher to his lips. When he lowered it, his eyes were watery, and he gasped spasmodically, like a dying haddock.

He handed it to the man beside him. "Now you try it, but don't spill none of it on you. You're a nice-dressed little gentleman, and you don't want holes et in your clothes." He turned to Hunk. "Don't waste time unwrapping that butter and the rest of the stuff we got in Boston. This rum's more penetrating than what I figured on."

When Marsh and Wingate returned with the required utensils, they found us garrulous and in a glow from our single swallow of Cap's remedy for food poisoning.

Cap seized a bucket and went to work. In it he put two cups of maple sugar, added an inch of hot water and stirred until the sugar was dissolved. He poured in two quarts of rum, added a lump of butter the size of his fist, threw in a handful of powdered cinnamon; then filled the bucket to the brim with steaming hot water. So briskly did he stir the mixture that it splashed his shirt. And as we passed him our cups to be filled, he lectured us on the subject of hot buttered rum.

"This here," he said, "ain't the proper way to make it. I put hot water in this here, but what you ought to have is hot cider. You take three or four drinks of this, made the right way, and you don't worry about what kind of food you're eating, or about anything else, either. You can't even remember what you et five minutes after you et it.

"And it ain't a temporary drink, like most drinks. That's on account of the butter. No matter how much you drink of anything else, it'll wear off in a day or so; but you take enough hot buttered rum and it'll last you pretty near as long as a coonskin cap. Fellers up our way drink it when they're going out after catamounts, on account of catamount hunting being hard work and requiring considerable persistence. After a man's had two-three drinks of hot buttered rum, he don't shoot a catamount: all he's got to do is walk up to him and kiss him just once; then put him in his bag, all limp."

The rum in the drinks which Cap passed us had been miraculously changed. The mixture seemed mild and sweet—as harmless-tasting as a soothing syrup. Murmurs of pleasure arose from my friends as they sampled it; and the glances turned toward Cap were almost affectionate.

At their gratified murmurs, Cap scooped up a cupful for himself and drained it; then stood with eyes upraised, meditating. "Yes," he admitted, "that ain't bad! A few of those and you could play with me like a kitten." His mind seemed to slip off at a tangent. "Hunk, give Langdon Towne that stuff we got in Boston and tell him what we thought up for him."

Hunk picked up the paper cylinder which had struck me with its resemblance to a small cannon. He cleared his throat in evident embarrassment. "That rabbit pie last night——"

"Don't beat about the bush!" Cap interrupted. "You Harvard fellers can't get good food out of the folks that run this college without you make it plain how rotten it is. That's what you thought, wasn't it, Hunk?"

"Yes," Hunk said. "It seemed to us that it doesn't do much good to go around *complaining* about bad food. That's why——"

Again Cap broke in on him. "What Hunk means is that you got to *show* 'em what you think about it—show 'em hard and quick, so's they can't make any mistake about the way you feel. S'pose a feller says a lot of things to you that you don't like: you can reason with him all day without getting anywheres; but if you crack him on the jaw, he understands the way you feel about him, and he's apt to be a little more careful. Wasn't that what you had in mind, Hunk?"

"Yes," Hunk said. "We kind of figured that if we got some good stout paper——"

Cap stopped him. "Wait a minute! You ain't telling this right! You ain't used to talking, like what I am. Here, bring up those cups and let's have just the merest taste of this rum before it cools off."

We crowded around him, my friends abusing him as freely as though they had known him all their lives. They called him an old Senior Sophister; an old Butter Whelk.

They hurled questions at him, demanding to be told whether a conscience invincibly erroneous may be blameless; whether private profit ought to be the chief end of moral actions; whether the dissolution of solids in corrosive liquors is performed by attraction.

They urged him to go ahead and explain himself in English instead of using Maine dialect as heretofore.

Cap drained his own cup and whacked it on the table. With fumbling hands he set about mixing a second bucketful, and as he mixed, he discoursed. "I dunno nothing about them erroleous consciences or roguish liquors, because I ain't never had dealings with no such things; but me and Hunk have given considerable thought to this moral action I'm talking about, and if you listen, you'll get some private profit out of it."

They cheered him lustily.

"We figured it all out while we was walking into Boston. I was kind of polite about those rabbit pies last night; but we're better acquainted now, so I don't mind saying they'd 'a' made a polecat think he hadn't never smelled nothing. What you fellers want to do is make this clear to the folks that run Harvard College, and we figured how to do it, didn't we, Hunk?"

Hunk just looked at him reproachfully.

"Yes," Cap went on, "Langdon Towne knows how to draw, because me and Hunk, we've watched him and helped him. We figured if Langdon Towne drew a nice big picture of Harvard College offering a supper to a polecat, and the polecat being kind of strangled by the smell——"

The rest of Cap's speech was lost in a tumult of cheers and laughter. The next thing I knew Cap and Hunk had peeled a sheet of heavy white cartridge paper from Hunk's cannonlike cylinder and were holding it flat against the wall, while somebody else thrust a black crayon into my hand.

I stood before the cartridge paper, a little unsteady on my feet, and marked off the points of the drawing as well as I could. To represent the Harvard Overseers, I blocked out a man in Pilgrim dress, holding a dish in his extended hand; and opposite him I lightly sketched a bushy-tailed polecat clutching his nose with a paw and shrinking disgustedly from the proffered plate.

To persons slightly in liquor, matters of little humor can seem irresistibly droll; and this was the case now. As the figures developed, my audience howled and slapped themselves, rolling on the floor with uncontrollable mirth; and I, too, felt I was producing a masterpiece of comicality.

When I stepped back to look at the sketch and incidentally wipe the tears from my eyes, I found, standing close behind me, a person I had not before seen. I took him for an undergraduate, for he seemed no older than others in the room. His thin face was pale and a little pock-marked; and his eyebrows were so prominent and his eyes so small that there was a peering look to him, almost as though he stared inquisitively at life through quizzing glasses. His dress was elaborate for an undergraduate, being of rich dark brown broadcloth, with a waistcoat of orange watered silk.

"That's not bad, you know," he said to me. "Not bad at all." He fingered his lower lip. "What would you think if this gentleman"—he lightly tapped the figure of the Pilgrim—"were half concealed in the entrance of the dining hall? Then there'd be no opportunity for a misunderstanding."

He was right, of course. I went at it again, outlining the end of the Commons building, so that the Pilgrim's upper body seemed to be leaning from the open door.

While my audience whooped, the inquisitive-faced young man made another suggestion. "Try putting the dish in his other hand, and having him hold to the doorjamb with the hand nearer you. Wouldn't that give it more life?"

I did as he suggested, and was enraptured at the vitality which the sketch took on. With that I went to blacking it in, and in no time at all it seemed to me not only completed but perfect.

"Now," Cap said, "we'll all have another little drink, and then I and Hunk'll carry it out and nail it up where people can see it. Where you want it nailed? Against the President's front door?"

Disregarding the turmoil around us, the pale young man nodded and smiled at me. "That's really good. Let me take your crayon. I'll show you something—just a trick, but you might find it useful."

I gave him the crayon. Stepping close to my drawing, he made a single S-shaped line on the Pilgrim's cheek. The face as I had drawn it was merely stern and somewhat cadaverous. That one crayon stroke made it sly, narrow-minded, hypocritical, contemptuous, selfish, cruel.

I gazed from this surprisingly made-over face to the thin, inquisitive features of the stranger. "Where'd you learn to do that?"

"Oh," he said, "I've been at it since I was twelve years old. My step-father——"

He stopped suddenly. So, too, did the laughter and shouting in the room, which had rung in my ears like the roaring of breakers on a beach. In the quiet that ensued, I heard a measured knocking at the door. This was what I had feared before Cap's buttered rum had robbed me of my prudence. I knew, now, that any such gathering as this must inevitably bring down the college authorities upon us; and I saw, too late, that I had been a fool.

Seeing all the eyes in the room turned toward me, I rubbed my hand over my face in an attempt to clear my mind of rum fumes; then hoarsely called, "Come in."

The door swung open to reveal, in the light of the flickering candles, the spare, stooped form of Belcher Willard, my tutor. At sight of him those who were on the floor scrambled upright with a sound of thumping and rustling, to stand in respectful silence, as required by the college laws.

Cap and Hunk dropped the drawing which they had been holding against the wall. In the stillness I could hear it rolling itself up, as though to hide from this representative of our governing body.

Willard came in among us and walked straight to the table, on which were the keg, the pails of greasy liquid, and a score of soiled tin cups. When he raised his eyes from that odorous and offensive chaos, he looked hard at the surrounding circle of faces; then fixed his attention on me.

"Langdon Towne," he said, "you are familiar with the laws of this college. No undergraduate shall keep by him brandy, rum, or any other distilled spirituous liquors. Whosoever shall transgress against this law shall have the said liquor that is found with him taken from him, and disposed of by the President and Tutors; and he shall be further punished not exceeding five shillings."

Before I could reply, Cap Huff cleared his throat noisily. "That ain't Langdon Towne's rum. That's *my* rum. I paid five shillings for that rum —a shilling a gallon—and three shillings for the keg. I'll give it to the President if he needs it; but he can't take it and dispose of it without my say-so."

Willard looked at him from under beetling brows. "You are not a member of this Society!"

"Well, no, I ain't," Cap admitted. "I ain't a member of any society. I just stopped in to let Langdon Towne know the salmon was biting in Kittery, and if I'd known there was any feeling against rum in these parts, I wouldn't have brought this keg here."

Willard set his lips tight together. "The laws of this Society further say, that if any scholar shall entertain at his chamber or familiarly associate with any person of loose or ill character, he shall be punished by the President and Tutors not exceeding five shillings; and if he persist in so doing he shall be publicly admonished, degraded, or expelled, according to the aggravation of his offense."

Cap just stood there, scratching his head.

"Sir," I said, "Cap Huff isn't a loose or ill character—not according to my lights."

"The lights of your generation," Willard replied, "are false and audacious, and repugnant to the fundamental principles of wise and proper government."

I saw Cap stoop hastily and pick up my drawing. "I guess we'll be moving along," he said. "Hunk, you take all your stuff and I'll take the keg.

We better be getting back to Kittery." To Willard he added mildly, "I, kind of forced myself on Langdon Towne and these young fellers here. They ain't done nothing but drink a little of my rum, and there ain't no way to keep young fellers from drinking rum sometimes, no matter how many laws you make."

Willard looked disagreeable. "Your philosophical disputations have no interest for me." He stretched out a bony hand and with his forefinger tapped the drawing which Cap was attempting to stuff beneath his coat. "What is this?"

Cap put it behind his back. "That's mine."

"Indeed!" Willard said. "Indeed! Permit me to doubt it. Permit me also to remind you that the President or Tutors may require suitable assistance from any scholar for the preservation of the good order of the College; and if anyone so required shall refuse to give his assistance, it shall be looked upon as a high misdemeanor and a great contempt of the authority of the College, and be punished by degradation or expulsion."

Cap looked at him and breathed hard. "You mean if these boys don't help you to take my property away from me by attacking me, you'll up and raise all that hell with 'em?"

"Give it to him, Cap," I said.

Cap gave the roll of paper to Willard, who opened it. He slowly raised his eyes to mine. "Who did this?"

"That's mine," Cap repeated quickly. "I figured it out."

"I thought of it first," Hunk Marriner said.

The stranger who had altered the expression on the Pilgrim's face stepped close to Willard. "This is beside the point," he said mildly. "It's plain to be seen these gentlemen aren't artists, though they have other admirable qualities. I think this will settle the matter." He leaned over and scratched a few lines on the margin of the drawing. Miraculously, the lines flowed together to form a likeness of Belcher Willard; a likeness so kindly and flattering that all of Willard's grim austerity was transformed into something almost beautiful.

Willard rolled up the drawing and set his fists on his hips. He looked from the stranger to me and back again. "Most opportune! Suspiciously opportune! This Society seems to have become a resort for characters who incite our members to luxury, intemperance, or ruin. At whose invitation did you——"

"My name, sir," the young man said, "is Copley. John Singleton Copley of South Boston."

Willard laughed sourly. "I regret, sir, you are not a member of this Society, so that you could be dealt with as you deserve." He once more scanned the rest of us with a hard eye. "As for those of you who are students at Harvard College, you will report at my rooms at five tomorrow afternoon for discipline."

# The Lure of the Great North Woods

From FOR AUTHORS ONLY

ONE OF THE universally accepted truths in this skeptical world is the lure of the great north woods.

The chief foundation of the lure appears to lie in the belief that only in the great north woods may man's overwhelming desire to catch edible fresh-water fish be gratified.

For a matter of three hundred years, poets have harped on the desirability of going back to the north countree, where the towering tops of the stately pines make banners of the clouds; on the joys of faring forth along the gypsy trail, and laving the face in crystal streams at dawn among the hills; on the pleasures of resting in flowery meads while larks and throstles make glad the day.

Most of the poets who have sung of the winelike air and the wholesome fare of the glorious north countree have made lilting references to the rise of speckled beauties to the brilliant fly: to the thrilling leaps of the salmon king who boundeth up the ice-cold stream in pursuit of his evening meal of fishermen's hooks; to the outthrust jaw of the nimble bass who goeth south with an eighty-dollar reel, or words of that general import.

In other words, poets have always assumed and apparently will always assume that when one gypsies into the great north woods, one should attach sandpaper to the soles of the shoes to avoid slipping on the fish.

Poets, furthermore, seem able to reach the heart of the great north woods in one deft, sinuous leap. Whether a poet practices the art of poetry in Detroit or West 195th Street, he invariably eliminates the involved transfer from his home to the Great Outdoors, precipitating himself abruptly into soul-stirring quatrains about deftly casting a scarlet fly upon the foam-flecked pool, or how the trout leaped up at dawn to greet the rising sun.

"Come," says one of these poets—a leading advocate of gypsying away into the unspoiled northern wildernesses, "Come when the leaf comes, angle with me; come when the bee hums over the lea; come with the wild flowers—come with the wild showers—come when the singing bird calleth for thee!"

One who reads this outburst in behalf of angling and the untrammeled wilderness feels that the journey from the tumultuous and fishless marts of men to the perfumed leas where the wild bee hums is as simple as obtaining an election to the National Geographical Society.

The gay enthusiasm of the poets is admirably supported by the artists who paint the rugged north country for magazine covers and calendars. The background of these paintings is virgin forest; the immediate foreground is filled with a likeness of a gentleman picturesquely disguised in wading boots, corduroy trousers, flannel shirt, and battered felt hat, busily engaged in tearing a reluctant trout from his natural surroundings. One foot is planted on a moss-covered rock; the other rests beneath the surface of the torrent—presumably on a fish; his right hand deftly manipulates the rod; his left hand thrusts a landing net beneath the body of the trout, which stares horror-struck at its captor. The careless smile on the fisherman's face shows clearly that the whole business is attended by a minimum of fuss and exertion.

In short, those persons who have been in a position to give publicity to the great north woods have for many years been subject to what the Freudians might call a north-woods lure-complex. Just as the younger dramatists and novelists interpret everything in terms of sex, so do north-woods enthusiasts interpret everything connected with the north woods in terms of lures.

Thus has arisen the universal acceptance of the lure of the great north woods. Persons who have no idea where the great north woods begin for luring purposes are well acquainted with the fact that the lure exists. It is a great basic fact of American life, like the Constitution of the United States, the heroic spirit of '76, the consumption of baked beans in Boston, and the words of the Star-Spangled Banner—one of those basic facts concerning which little is actually known, and most of that little erroneous.

For a number of years the art of fresh-water angling in that section of Maine in which I happen to live has gradually become less and less a matter of fish-capturing and more and more a labor of worm-chaperoning. In other words, when one extracts a choice parcel of worms from the depths of the tomato bed and fares forth into the flowery meads where the bee hums over the lea with the idea of catching himself enough speckled beauties for a mess, the net result of his faring is usually to give the worms a free excursion.

If angleworms in southern Maine—and the same thing is doubtless true in many sections of America south of the great north woods—were endowed with intellect and familiar with modern advertising methods, there would be signs in worm language in centers of worm population urging worms to become fish-minded—to Get a Lift with a Fisherman.

I cannot deny that trout are still to be found in the crystal streams outside the great north woods section. They are, however, immature. They can no more make a mouthful of a medium-sized angleworm than a small boy can engulf a Virginia ham in one bite. By comparison with the speckled beauties encountered outside the great north woods, a sardine is a roistering hellion of a fish.

The reason for the immaturity of trout near inhabited areas is said by some to be due to the fact that small tin automobiles are easily obtained by the young and careless. The automobiles make it possible for them to repair in large numbers to every crystal stream and foam-flecked pool in the countryside. Arrived there, their natural lack of intellect causes them to ignore the fishing laws and retain even the smallest speckled beauty capable of digesting a worm.

For some years I annually took a little group of worms on a personally conducted tour of the local leas. On each occasion, as I wearily replaced the worms in the tomato bed at the end of the day, I resolved that on subsequent years I would forsake the haunts of men and small tin automobiles and turn to the foaming streams and the trackless forests of the north countree. Only there, I felt sure, could one go fishing and return with fish instead of with all the original worms.

Eventually the lure of the great north woods became so powerful that I broke away from the ties that bound me to civilization and went a-gypsying on the open road into the north countree with three fellow gypsies.

I had, I may add, conducted exhaustive researches into various sections of the great north woods, and had been assured by anglers of ability and experience that the country in the vicinity of a certain lake which lies in the shadow of the Height of Land on the Canadian border—Canoodlekook Lake for the purposes of this narrative—contained the very essence of north-woods lure.

It was miles from the railroad; through its primeval forests roamed the deer, the bear, the porcupine; at night, when the pale light of the moon silvered the towering tops of the giant pines, the forest glades echoed to the contralto screams of the hairy-eared lynx.

Further investigation uncovered the fact that a delightful cottage, set down on the lake shore in the midst of this wilderness, could be rented for any desired period. Not only did the persons who rented this cottage —known as Hokum Cottage for the purposes of this narrative—secure the services of its caretaker, Jake Short, enthusiastically characterized by the owner of the cottage as the best guide in the whole north country, but they also secured the use of a cook stove, icebox, bathroom complete with shower bath, and beds that would, in the owner's words, accommodate three people comfortably and four if necessary.

Since it was obvious that any person desiring to gypsy into the north country would deserve to lose his gypsying license if he wished for more than this, Hokum Cottage was engaged and urgent messages dispatched to western Pennsylvania, where two of the gypsies awaited the word to start their dash for the great north woods. Equally urgent messages were also dispatched to Jake Short, the paragon of north-woods guides, instructing him to have all in readiness.

When forces were joined in southern Maine it was apparent that among the most noticeable omissions from poems extolling the lure of the open road and the great north woods is information concerning the amount of baggage and supplies to be taken by fisherman gypsies.

Since Canoodlekook Lake lies miles from the railroad in the depths of the virgin forest, the trip had to be made by automobile; and space was consequently limited. Each gypsy, after urging the other three to restrict his personal belongings to the smallest possible compass, craved the privilege of carrying some trifle unhesitatingly condemned by the others as unnecessary.

One gypsy was refused permission to take an army revolver for defense against bears on the ground that if he met a bear, he could pretend not to see it.

Another was asked not to include rubber boots, since wet feet were to be expected on a fishing expedition. If one got into really deep water, the others argued, the boots would fill, and the owner might drown. Unmoved by these arguments, the owner of the rubber boots persisted in carrying them, thus taking up space which the other gypsies wished for themselves.

A third gypsy insisted on taking a small wire-haired fox terrier, admittedly of no assistance in the capturing of fish, because there was nobody with whom he could be left if not taken. Protests were unavailing, because the owner of the terrier was also the owner of the automobile.

A fourth gypsy wished to take an Airedale terrier on similar grounds; but since the Airedale's master didn't own the automobile, the Airedale remained at home.

The party was divided into two schools of thought concerning the amount of provisions to be taken.

One school of thought maintained that since Jake Short, caretaker of Hokum Cottage, was the best guide in the whole north country, he would without doubt await his wards with a commodious basket of brook trout, a batch of sody biscuit, a pan of flapjack batter, a hot griddle, and all the other knickknacks that play such a large part in the luring power of the great north woods.

The other school of thought held that Jake Short would be devoting his brain power to discovering new fishing grounds for his employers and would consequently have little or no time in which to bother with ordinary food.

The first school of thought advocated taking nothing of an edible nature; the second advised taking everything, from salt to canned salmon.

A compromise was finally effected, and into the interstices between the gypsies, the rubber boots, the tackle boxes, the extra overcoats and sweaters, the wire-haired terrier, and the fishing rods were packed two loaves of bread, a slab of bacon, a slab of salt pork, a can of coffee, and a can of tea.

A stop was made in the beautiful city of Portland for the purpose of adding to the already large supply of wet and dry flies possessed by the party. While a careful study of flies was being made at the counter of a sporting-goods emporium, the eye of one of the gypsies was attracted by a box of small bottles bearing the inscription, "*Fiz-faz: original fisherman's protection against mosquitoes, black flies, midges, and all other stinging insects. Rub well into face, neck, ears, hair, hands, and garments; renew when necessary. Price 35 cents.*"

Another gypsy spied a box of tubes labelled, "*Zoonga Paste: original sportsman's aid. Absolutely prevents black flies, midges, and mosquitoes from biting. Squeeze paste into palms of hands; rub well into face, neck, ears, hair, and beard. Price 35 cents.*"

Poets who have sung the glories of the great north woods, and of angling when the bee hums over the lea, have had nothing to say about pausing on the edge of flowery meads amid the piping of throstles to rub Fiz-faz or Zoonga Paste into the face, ears, and hair. According to the poets, an angler abstracts trout from the great north woods without having his attention distracted by extraneous matters; but according to the evidence on the counter of a reliable sporting-goods store, all genuine fishermen are obliged to keep themselves as well oiled as a mogul engine.

The gypsy trail led through the mountains and into rugged country. Flowery meads and leas grew fewer. The towering pines of the great north woods appeared in greater and greater numbers. There was, however, no perceptible diminution in the number of small tin automobiles.

By midafternoon the party left the railroad far behind and entered the true north woods that march back from the shores of Canoodlekook Lake. Across the lake were mountains shrouded in heavy mist. No sound broke the ominous silence of the great north country save the hoarse squawking of small tin automobiles that passed briskly along the highway. When the gypsies drew up before the door of Hokum Cottage, nestled in a rough-looking mead or lea on the lake shore, they were greeted by the finest guide in the whole north country, Jake Short himself. Jake was young and fair-haired—an upstanding, clean-cut young American, and obviously one of the finest products of the great north woods.

Releasing the wire-haired terrier and throwing the creels from the windows of the automobile, the gypsies descended and surrounded Jake.

"Anything to eat in the house?" one asked.

"Potatoes," Jake said.

"Anything else?"

"No," Jake said.

"We thought maybe you'd have some trout for us," an optimistic gypsy murmured.

"I would if I'd known you wanted some," replied Jake cheerfully.

"Well," the optimistic gypsy said, "it's early. Let's go catch some. Where can we go, Jake?"

"Well," Jake said, "to tell you the truth, I got so much work to do around here, opening these cottages and cleaning up, that I can't guide you for three-four days. I'm sorry I said I would, but that's the way it is. I didn't expect to haf to open up these cottages and get 'em cleaned, but now I got to open 'em and get 'em cleaned up, so I got to open 'em and get 'em cleaned."

"The idea is, then," the pessimistic gypsy said, "that these cottages have not only got to be opened, but cleaned as well."

"Yes," said Jake, the prince of guides. "Yes, I got to see to opening 'em and cleaning 'em."

"Well," said the gypsy who had brought rubber boots, "I suppose you've got another guide for us."

"Well, no, I haven't," Jake admitted, "but I can get you one tomorrow morning."

"Is he as good a guide as you are?" the optimistic gypsy wanted to know.

"Well, he's a good guide," Jake said unemotionally.

"Get us two guides," the pessimistic gypsy said. "Then maybe both of 'em together will be as good as one real good one."

"All right," Jake said. "Now I got to tend to opening these cottages and cleaning 'em up."

"How about helping us carry our luggage before doing your opening and cleaning?" suggested one of the more despondent gypsies.

"Sure," said the finest guide in all the great north woods. Picking up two fish baskets, one in each hand, he set off for Hokum Cottage with the easy lope of the trained woodsman, leaving the gypsies to follow with the rest of the luggage. Dropping the creels on the porch, the wonder guide continued on through the house and was about to vanish into the great northern wilderness when an agonized cry stopped him in his tracks. "We haven't anything to eat for supper," a gypsy protested, "or for breakfast either. Can you get us something?"

"Sure," said the ever reliable Jake. "What you want?"

The gypsies racked their brains. They could think of nothing but ham and eggs.

"Ham and eggs?" the prince of guides asked. "Sure! What time you want 'em?"

"By half past six tonight at the latest," the optimistic gypsy said.

"All right," Jake replied, with a look of intelligence in his keen blue eyes.

One of the gypsies showed signs of excitement. "What are these blankety-blanked little blank-blanked specks on my hands that itch so?"

"Them's midges," Jake explained. "You'll swell up nice if you let 'em bite you."

"Say," said another gypsy, who had been exploring the upper regions of Hokum Cottage, "there's a bath upstairs, just as the owner claimed; but there's no water. The shower won't work, and neither will anything else!"

All four gypsies turned expectantly to the efficient caretaker and guide, Jake Short. He nodded soothingly and, with an air of going for help, bolted hastily through the back door and vanished among the somber pines that hovered ominously over the rear of Hokum Cottage. Those melancholy trees appeared to sigh, as if in gloomy premonition of a sad event—and rightly; for Jake, the super-guide, didn't return that night, having contracted—as the gypsies learned from other sources on the following day—to guide a young lady to a dance.

Guide or no guide, and food or no food, however, the party had taken the gypsy trail for the express purpose of sampling the lure of the great north woods. Making a hasty change of costume and anointing themselves with Zoonga Paste and Fiz-faz, they collected their tackle and embarked in a rowboat. The owner of the rubber boots wore his rubber boots in the boat, although repeatedly reminded that he was in no danger of wetting his feet unless he fell overboard.

As the boat pushed off from shore, a brisk rain descended, and the gypsies were accompanied by a swarm of midges, black flies, and mosquitoes. It seems odd that in all the years during which poets have sung of the lure of the great north woods, not one of them has made even passing mention of midges and black flies. It seems so peculiar, in fact, that it gives rise to the suspicion that the poets of the great outdoors and the gypsy trail and the rugged north countree have never been north of Portsmouth, N.H., or fished for anything larger than sunfish.

The rain fell more briskly. The hardier of the black flies and midges crawled up sleeves and down neckbands in an effort to escape the inclement weather, but still the gypsies rowed back and forth across the lake, dragging artificial lures of various sizes before the indifferent gaze of the trout and salmon reputed to lurk in its cool depths. Nothing, however, developed—barring blisters on the hands of the rowers and an increase in the rainfall.

As dusk descended, the gypsies landed to discover three other fishermen also knocking off for the day. The optimistic gypsy hailed them with the frank, free camaraderie so characteristic of life in the great north woods.

"Hey," he said; "been out all day?"

One of the party turned and eyed him morosely; then replied, with all the heartiness of a big, virile, outdoors man: "Sure!"

"How many did you catch?" asked the optimistic gypsy, scraping black flies and Zoonga Paste from an eyebrow.

"How many what?" the outdoors man asked hoarsely.

"How many lakers or salmon?"

The strange fisherman looked fixedly at him; then silently climbed into an automobile and lurched away.

One of their guides, left behind with the traps, stared tolerantly at the gypsies. "They didn't ketch nawthin'," he said. "They ain't ketched nawthin' today nor yesterday nor the day before that nor the day before that."

The gypsies retired thoughtfully to the interior of Hokum Cottage. The whereabouts of the best guide in all the great north woods remained a mystery; in the so-called bathroom there was an echoing void where water should have been.

Supper consisted of boiled potatoes, bread, and bacon. This may be considered a good meal in certain parts of Ireland, provided there's enough of it; but it met with small enthusiasm in gypsy circles because of the scarcity of bacon and moistness of the potatoes, each one of which, for unknown reasons, cherished in its heart a soggy spot reminiscent of prehistoric watermelon.

It should be added, in closing the record of the first day's activities in the great north woods, that the mattresses in Hokum Cottage were evidently made on specifications customarily used in the preliminary construction of asparagus beds.

Their bottom layers seemed to be old tin cans, discarded bicycles, and broken rock. Over this, apparently, had been spread sod, corn husks, and horse-chestnut burrs.

All through the night the rain thundered on the roof of Hokum Cottage while the four gypsies sought with plaintive groans to adjust themselves to pallets that squeaked and rattled. Awed, perhaps, by these cataclysmic sounds, the noisy denizens of the great north woods for once were still.

In the morning the sodden gurgling of the rain was neutralized by the dropping of stove lids in the kitchen of Hokum Cottage, the smashing of kindling wood against table legs, the cheery crackling of flames, the rumble of masculine voices.

Investigation of these pleasant sounds showed that Jake Short, the finest guide in all the great north woods, had emerged from his trance for a sufficient time to secure the services of the two required guides, and that it was they who wrestled with the cook stove and prepared the matutinal ham and eggs, griddle cakes and coffee.

Possibly it would be better to say that it was one of them who prepared these things; for one of the new guides, Tom Mudgett by name, was of no use in the house except as a persistent narrator of romances calculated to raise the drooping spirits of discouraged fishermen.

While the other guide, Eddie Skeegins, cleverly manipulated a pan of fried potatoes, a hot griddle covered with batter, a clutch of fried eggs, and coaxed a panful of tea to that stage of development known in the great north woods as "stout," Tom draped one knee over the other, crossed his arms limply, looked worried and told his simple, manly story.

"Three of us," he said, "was up to the Beaver Dam a couple of weeks ago and caught seventy-two of the nicest trout ever you see, didn't we, Eddie? 'Nother good place is over to the Inlet. Four of us was up there three-four weeks ago and got so many we could only fish an hour and a half, wasn't we, Eddie? Dunno what those fellers want to talk about not gettin' no more fish in the lake. Gorrymighty, I been out on that lake twenty-seven time this year and ain't never come home skunked, have I, Eddie?"

Not until the eyes of the four gypsies protruded slightly from over-indulgence in griddle cakes, did they feel they were in a position to give undivided attention to the matter of Tom Mudgett's record-breaking trout catches.

"You certainly know where the fish are, Tom!" declared the optimistic gypsy. "Where'll you take us when the rain lets up?"

Mr. Mudgett looked even more worried. "Well, I dunno," he said finally. "The water'll be pretty high after this rain. I dunno where's the best place to go."

"How about the Beaver Dam where you got the seventy-two nice trout?" a gypsy asked.

"We kin go up there," Mudgett admitted. "Some people go up there and get a fine mess, and some go up there and don't get nawthin'. We might get nawthin'."

"Maybe the Inlet would be better, if you caught your baskets full in an hour and a half," suggested the optimistic gypsy.

"Yeah," Mudgett said, "only lots of times fellers go up the Inlet and never ketch a fish. Can't tell about the Inlet. We might ketch some and we might not. Ain't no way to tell. So many fellers come around here in automobiles that you can't never tell when a stream is all fished out."

"If you always have good luck on the lake, Tom," another gypsy suggested, "maybe the lake would be the best place."

"Yeah, it might," Mudgett agreed, "only you might sit out there three-four days and never git a smell of a bite."

"Then there isn't any place around here where we'd be sure of getting a few fish?" he was asked. Mudgett scratched his head dolefully and said he didn't know as there was.

The optimistic gypsy, to relieve his feelings, left Mr. Mudgett's presence and tried the shower bath to see whether it had started to work. It hadn't.

By noontime the rain had ceased and the sun was struggling to appear. After a light collation of fried potatoes, fried eggs, thick-cut bacon, tea sufficiently stout to sear an oilcloth table cover, and a mound of flapjacks and maple syrup, the four gypsies rubbed themselves well with Fiz-faz and Zoonga Paste and fared forth into the rugged northern wilderness.

Two gypsies, under the tutelage of Eddie Skeegins, entered a rowboat in company with the usual mosquitoes, black flies, and midges and rowed slowly up and down the lake for the remainder of the afternoon. Seemingly the fish were in a coma. They were indifferent to lures: apathetic toward every delicacy with which their jaded appetites were spurred.

The other gypsies, under the guidance of Tom Mudgett, bounced off into the wilderness in the automobile, left it by the roadside and plodded two miles up one side of a hill and down its far side to the Beaver Dam. Here an enterprising coterie of industrious beavers had dammed a brook until it had overflowed its banks and formed a desolate-looking bog from which emerged a forest of dying tamaracks. Access to the waters of the bog was had by means of a raft capable, if carefully handled, of holding one person. Persons not using the raft were at liberty to cast their flies among dead trees and roots in the hope of miraculously avoiding the tangled snags and somehow catching fish.

There was a plethora of trout in the waters behind Beaver Dam, for they could be felt struggling valiantly to get the bait into their mouths. After four hours of diligent fishing the two gypsies and their guide had hooked thirty-seven speckled beauties, twenty-six of which had been thrown back to mature. Eleven had been kept, though there was a strong suspicion in the gypsies' minds that when Tom Mudgett passed judgment on their length, he brought them within the law by stretching them a quarter-inch.

At sundown the gypsies and their guide, abandoning the exciting sport of measuring adolescent trout, plodded over the hill and down to the automobile. The creel containing the eleven fish was placed on the running board to be stowed away by that keen-eyed woodsman, Tom Mudgett.

Conversing cheerily, the little party started back for Hokum Cottage, secure in the knowledge that the evening menu of fried potatoes, fried eggs, fried ham, and fried tea would be augmented by eleven fried trout.

They drew up with a flourish before the cottage door and descended merrily from the automobile, happy and serene after their hours among the snags and mud of the great north woods.

Then, like a flash of lightning at a wedding, came the storm.

"Where," the pessimistic gypsy asked ominously, "is the creel with the trout?"

"It's in the automobile," said Tom Mudgett, ever ready with an answer and always wrong.

"Let's see it," the pessimistic gypsy demanded.

Tom Mudgett sprang to the automobile and looked within. The creel was not there. He lifted the driver's seat and looked beneath. It was not there. He felt in his pockets. It was not there. He looked on top of the automobile and under it. The creel was not there. In short, it wasn't anywhere. It had been forgotten.

"You had it!" Tom Mudgett said to the pessimistic gypsy, unaware of the slogan, "The customer is always right."

"I put it on the running board!" the pessimistic gypsy declared.

"You had it," Tom Mudgett repeated.

On the verge of exploding with emotion, the pessimistic gypsy rushed into the cottage and tried the shower bath. It was still dry. He leaped into the automobile and bounced back to the spot where the creel had been placed on the running board. It wasn't there. Obviously it had been picked up by somebody in a small tin automobile.

Somewhere, no doubt, the warm rays of the westering sun were illuminating the innocent features of the happy man who had stumbled on the eleven trout. Somewhere the fried food of the great north woods was being sweetened and neutralized by eleven succulent speckled beauties.

But in the hearts of those who had caught the eleven speckled beauties there was a seething whirlpool of human emotions; a mastodonic bitterness.

Things seemed brighter on the following morning. A brilliant sun shone through the kitchen window, lightly kissing Eddie Skeegins as he toyed skillfully with the fried eggs, fried ham, fried coffee, and fried flapjacks. Bright and early the four gypsies, attended by Eddie and Tom Mudgett, king of creel-forgetters, set off down the road for Derry Stream—a clear, cold mountain brook that bounded from the primeval forest, brawling among mighty boulders in all the many tongues of the great north country.

In Derry Stream the gypsies emulated the debonair gentlemen who, on calendars, stand so easily and so boldly in raging torrents. They waded the icy waters, casting their flies in spots where speckled beauties might lurk. Unfortunately, nothing worked for them as it does for the gentlemen on the magazine covers and the calendars.

There is grave doubt, too, that these debonair fishermen of the calendars would seem so debonair if they made free with the boulders and log chutes—especially the log chutes—in that section of the great north woods adjacent to Lake Canoodlekook. A log chute is a smooth slide arranged to facilitate the passage of logs over an unusually rocky section of a stream employed for logging operations. A log chute is so covered with a slick and slippery coating that one who steps on it is in imminent danger of losing not only his footing, but his dignity, his breath, the seat of his trousers, and the lower edges of his pelvic bone.

The rubber-booted gypsy attempted to strike the attitude common to fishermen on railroad posters. After wrenching his back and bouncing on five boulders in falling, he sank in eight feet of water. Several hundred gallons of water passed through him before he was rescued.

Another gypsy, stepping carelessly on the upper end of a log chute, traveled down it on that portion of his anatomy designed for such trips. When taken from the pool at the bottom, he was drained by the suspension method.

After four hours of careful fishing, Tom Mudgett had one one-pound speckled beauty, Eddie Skeegins had nine small trout, the pessimistic gypsy had four minnows which came slightly within the law, and the other gypsies had nothing at all.

On returning to Hokum Cottage the four gypsies watched Eddie Skeegins prepare to fry the ham, eggs, tea, griddle cakes, and trout. They tested the shower bath. It was still out of commission. They stared speculatively at the lumps on the surfaces of their mattresses. Then, after devouring their lunch, they silently entered their automobile and started at top speed away from the north countree and all its witchery.

Here and there, no doubt, the lure of the great north woods still exists; but in only one place may it infallibly be found. I refer, of course, to a book of poems.

## Frustration

### From NORTHWEST PASSAGE

IF THERE IS worse country—for men in a hurry—than that to the east of Memphremagog, I have yet to see it. Ordinarily, during storms in a forest, there are signs to indicate the points of the compass; and if a brook or river can be found, one needs only to go up it—or down it, as the case may be—in order to go farther on his way.

Memphremagog isn't like that. Its hills and mountains are packed together like fish balls on a platter; and wind, blowing between two hills and striking another, is twisted about so that it blows in circles. Thus rainstorms, instead of hitting trees properly and causing moss to grow on the northerly side, strike from all directions at once. As for the watercourses, there are brooks within half a mile of each other, flowing in four directions at the same time. Streams turn at right angles for no apparent reason, or make almost complete loops; and the valleys through which some of them flow are so deep and so involved that they seem to have been planned and dug by an insane god.

Our course was a snake's all the rest of that day, winding along ravines and around the shoulders of hills. The men strayed out on side excursions looking for something to shoot, so that they had to be watched and urged back into line. It seemed to me we were getting nowhere; and because of that slowness, and the howling rain-laden wind and the constant aching discomfort within me, I was irritable and apprehensive. I had the feeling someone would tread on my heels if I couldn't get forward.

The afternoon seemed no more than started before the sheets of rain and the low-lying clouds brought a dismal twilight upon us. When we came up with some of Jenkins' Rangers cutting spruce boughs, I looked at my chronometer. It was only a little past three. When I showed it to Avery, he cursed under his breath.

"What's this?" Avery asked the men. "What you stopping for?"

"Going to camp here," one of them said.

Avery spoke sharply to his own followers, who had halted. "Keep your packs on! We'll see about this!"

We pressed on to where Dunbar and Turner were helping their groups of men to settle themselves. Just beyond them the ground fell away into a ravine so broad that the far side was blurred in rain and dusk.

"Lieutenant," Avery said to Dunbar, "can't we get on a little farther? It ain't half past three yet."

Dunbar's voice was thin and tired. "It's nearly dark, Mr. Avery, no matter what the hour is. Have you seen what's ahead of us?"

He led us closer to the ravine. It was a bad one, perhaps two hundred feet deep; and while the bank on our side was steep and thinly wooded, the far side was rocky and even steeper. The distance from the level spot on which we stood to the top of the opposite bank was a good six hundred yards, and the stream at the bottom, even in the murk, was a silvery ribbon of quick water.

"If we try to cross that stream tonight," Dunbar said, "we stand to have men drowned, or lose muskets and wet what little powder we've got left. In the morning, when it's light, they'll be rested and ought to be able to cross without trouble."

Avery turned and looked behind him: raised his eyes to scan the sky: then once more stared into the ravine. Lieutenant Turner came up to us and stood staring down too. Avery eyed Turner questioningly. "What you want to camp here for? This is a hell of a place!"

"Maybe so," Turner said. "Some of these men ain't feeling too good. That's an awful easy place to break a couple legs."

"What you think?" Avery asked me.

I said I thought we ought to cross while the light held: that the water might rise much higher if the rain kept falling; I urged that we could make better time the next day if we crossed now.

Avery looked apologetically at Dunbar. "That's what I think, Lieutenant."

Dunbar nodded. "I won't try to stop you, Mr. Avery. We're each of us responsible for his party. You're subject to no one's orders but your own," and I took this to be a hint that Dunbar could get along without suggestions from Avery or me.

"Well," Avery said, "well——" He hesitated; then added: "We'll hunt on the far bank till you come up with us in the morning."

"That's not necessary," Dunbar said. "We might take a few fish from the stream for breakfast, or hunt a little on this side, so don't have us on your mind. You'll find us close behind you before night."

Avery called sharply to his men; we moved forward; and when the others saw the ravine, they pulled at their caps and fastened their powder horns and pouches more securely.

"We got to get across this tonight," Avery said. "Watch where you put your feet."

He went down the bank, slipping, saving himself by grasping at trees. I slid after him, put my foot through a tangle of dead branches, pitched headlong, and rolled against a tree with a thump that made me grunt. When Avery helped me up, I saw Dunbar's and Turner's heads thrust out over the lip, watching us. Probably, I thought, Avery and I were fools to pit our judgment against theirs; but there was nothing to do now but go on.

The men stumbled and fell repeatedly on the slippery steep slope, deep with wet leaves and soft mold. The lower we went in the ravine, the less the wind howled above us and the louder became the rushing of the stream. When we reached the bottom at last, we found a white torrent surging over boulders, and the tops of the boulders looked disgustingly slippery.

I suspected, when I felt this roaring stream pull my feet out from under me and hurl me gasping against an icy rock, that Dunbar had known best. Yet, when I reached the far bank, I was little wetter than I had been at any time during the day.

I looked back up the steep slope down which we had floundered, but I could see nobody. The top was a blur of gray treetops dimly traced against a wet obscurity.

Some of the men overturned boulders at the edge of the stream, in the vain hope of finding something living that might be eaten, and one muttered about camping here, so to fish in the morning.

"Listen," Avery said, "we'd be all day catching a mess in this stream. They won't bite in a northeaster, anyway. The place to get 'em is a pond. Maybe we'll find one tomorrow."

"You don't mean to say there's *ponds* around here!" one of the men exclaimed.

Another laughed weakly—probably because we had found ponds wherever we turned—and continued to laugh and laugh, like a girl overcome with mirth at her own brainlessness. We all laughed with him out of sympathy.

"Well," Avery said, "there ain't none of us dead yet, so we might be worse off."

We worked our way slowly up the farther declivity, holding by sodden shrubs and pulling ourselves over ledges and blown-down trees wedged precariously among them. We could just see to do it; and even so, when we worked hard to surmount bad spots, we had to rest a little until our legs stopped shaking and our muscles quivering.

When we reached the top and looked back, we saw a red glow on the bank we had left. "Look at that!" Avery cried. "That's something I ain't seen in some little time! Wouldn't Rogers give 'em hell if he saw it? Guess they must be cooking their moccasins and shirt fringes!"

He went crawling off to look for shelter and found it in a little grove of spruces pressed close against a rock. Nobody so much as mentioned a fire, probably because we would have been so long in finding dry wood. We packed ourselves into the shelter, one against the other, with our wet blankets tight around us. This is not as cold as it sounds when the weather isn't frosty, for a steam seems to lie next to the body after a time.

I had perhaps half a cup of corn left, and Avery had fifteen or twenty grains. The others had a few, so we put them all together and doled them out, one at a time, till the last kernel was gone. Everybody had eight apiece, and three had nine. I felt myself a scoundrel for being one of the three who had nine, but ate them.

The wind howled all night, and the rain slatted and hissed through the trees and on the dead leaves. Long before dawn we had slept ourselves out, and the men, in soggy misery, spoke of what sort of food would be waiting for us at Ammonoosuc. They referred longingly to John Askin, the Rangers' sutler, wishing he might be the one to bring supplies; and the Rangers' fare of which they spoke was tantalizing. They mentioned a red wine which Askin alone was able to procure: large, tender sausages; a special ham so cured that it was almost black; chocolate cakes, round red cheeses, cigars from the Sugar Islands, and a pale brown rum that could be drunk by the bottle without causing anything but a delightful exhilaration and quickening of all the senses.

When we could finally see our hands before our faces, we had been rolled in our blankets for nearly thirteen hours.

Avery crawled out from among us, wrung the water from the remnants of his Scotch cap, and made his tattered blanket into a sodden roll. "The first pond we strike," he said, "we can try the fish, but prob'ly we won't have any luck to speak of till the wind changes—nothing but little stink-pans."

A thought seemed to strike him, and he counted rapidly on his fingers. "By God!" he said. "What is this? The fifteenth?"

I said it was.

"New moon's about due," he said. "If this storm don't break pretty damned quick, we'll have weather all the way to the Ammonoosuc!" The men, busy on hands and knees with their blankets, groaned and spat.

Avery walked off toward the lip of the ravine. The sound of his footsteps in the soggy leaves ceased suddenly—so suddenly that I rose to my feet and looked after him.

He stood there, fifteen paces away, frozen, one hand before him to ward off branches, one half-raised to his cap, as a hunter freezes when he unexpectedly sees a distant deer. Thinking he *had* seen a deer, I picked up my musket and scrambled toward him. He whipped behind a tree, dropped to his knees, and looked back at me. His face, above his beard, was ghastly.

Beyond him, from the ravine, I heard an awful sound—a thin, high squeal, made by a man. I heard yells, half howl and half caterwaul, that made the skin move behind the ears, as at the shriek of a lynx.

When I reached Avery, he snapped up the lock of my musket and knocked the powder from the pan so it couldn't be fired.

The whole bottom of the ravine, at first glimpse, appeared alive with moving figures. I could distinguish men plunging downward through the trees of the opposite slope: others scurrying confusedly at the edge of the stream.

"Christ!" Avery whispered. "They'll get 'em all! Every damned one! It's an ambush!"

The confusion in the ravine became clearer to me. Upstream and downstream, in two scattered groups, were Indians crouched behind boulders: lying behind fallen tree trunks. They were painted black and vermilion. Those rushing down the bank, and stumbling jerkily at the edge of the stream, were Dunbar's, Turner's, and Jenkins' men. Rushing with them and darting among them were other black-painted Indians and a horde of small men—Frenchmen—in a brighter green than the greenish buckskins of the Rangers. There must have been two hundred Frenchmen and Indians.

If one of the stumblers broke loose from those around him and started upstream or downstream, a hidden Indian rose from behind a boulder and sank a hatchet in him.

I made out Dunbar, standing at the edge of the water, defending himself with his bayoneted musket against three Frenchmen. Seemingly the powder was wet; for not a musket was fired. An Indian came out of the foaming water behind Dunbar, split his head with a hatchet, and leaped forward on him as he fell. He knelt on Dunbar with one knee and chopped off his head.

From the struggling, confused throng came agonized cries that made me sweat and shake. I saw two Indians, upstream, holding down a Ranger, head and foot, while a third Indian dismembered him with a hatchet, although he was still alive and screaming.

"Don't let any of our men come up here!" Avery said to me. "Get 'em moving! There ain't a damned thing we can do but get out quick! If we don't——" He didn't finish: he didn't need to.

So suddenly had this horrible thing happened that our men were where I had left them, crouched over their muskets to keep off the rain while they re-primed them.

They stood up and came toward me. "Get on your packs and blankets," I said.

"Ain't we going to help 'em?" one of the men asked.

"There's two hundred to our eleven," I said. "They're out of range, and there's nothing we could do but get ourselves wiped out if a hair of us is seen. Avery says to get going."

"What about the ones that get away?" a Ranger asked.

Avery came up behind me, reached down and got his musket. He looked sick. "None of 'em got away. They killed 'em all. They're playing ball with their heads!"

I think we might have got clear away if we hadn't shot the moose; though there's no telling about such things. If we hadn't shot the moose, we might have caught up with Rogers and then Rogers would have been the one to suffer, which would have been a terrible thing for everyone. It's worse than fruitless, I find, to speculate on what might have happened under different circumstances; for too much of such speculation sometimes makes a man afraid to do anything.

It seemed best to Avery and me to bear sharply to the eastward. That direction, we knew, would bring us across the trail of Rogers' party; and by hurrying we could give him intelligence of the French and Indians and put him on his guard.

All that day the northeaster blew and the rain drove in our faces while we plodded miserably to the east. It seemed to me I had never had enough to eat, and never again could have; but in spite of our emptiness, we went on and on without a halt, clambering along watercourses, scrambling over the shoulders of hills, pulling ourselves out of ravines, dragging ourselves across bogs—and forever looking fearfully behind. We spoke no more of fishing. We would have needed bait to catch fish, and time to catch them, and a fire for cooking. It was the fire that bothered us. Its odor would have carried miles down-wind; and headed as we were, that scent would have been as good as a signpost to the French and Indians who killed Dunbar and his parties.

On the next day, the sixteenth of October, the rain stopped, but the wind held on from the northeast, howling and screaming through the treetops. That afternoon we struck tracks, bearing to the southeast. The tracks seemed to be made by between thirty and forty men; and since we knew Rogers' detachment consisted of thirty-eight in all, we were sure they were his. We made certain when, in muddy spots, we found the prints of bare feet protruding from broken moccasins. We turned along them, feeling greatly cheered and almost safe once more; and to add to our satisfaction, the northeast wind faded toward sundown. Then, when we huddled together to get what sleep we could, we saw an occasional star through the breaking clouds—a Godsend, since we dared not wrap ourselves in our blankets after seeing Dunbar's finish. We could only pull them over us, so to leave our arms and legs free.

Unfortunately the clearer weather brought a heavy frost. Our blankets froze, and to better our condition we covered ourselves a foot deep in wet leaves.

When we crawled out in the morning, we were so stiff with cold that we were like drunken men. The wind, however, had gone into the south, so we hurried cheerfully onward, hopeful of soon coming up with Rogers, of striking good hunting in warm October weather, and of an easy journey to the Ammonoosuc.

It occurred to none of us to regard the moose as an omen. We thought of her as just a cow moose, brought out of hiding by the south wind and impelled to move about in search of food. She came over a hardwood ridge in front of Avery, looking as big as a Kittery barn, and Avery let her have it in the brain for good luck; and the eleven of us jumped on her.

Moose meat has less fat than any other, so there is little nourishment to it; but it is meat, nonetheless; and not one of us had eaten meat since we ate our last fragments of bologna sausage the day before we attacked St. Francis. For eleven days we had eaten nothing but corn, and mighty little of that; so Avery had his knife into the moose's throat before she stopped kicking, and the men were on her hindquarters with knives and hatchets.

Avery stopped them. "You know better'n that! If you eat that meat fresh-killed and raw, you'll be sick! You won't be able to move!"

"I've eaten worse'n this!" one of the men said. They went right on cutting. They intended to eat: no doubt of that.

"Look," Avery said, "take off the skin first. We need it for moccasins. The rest of you open her up and take out the liver, and we'll cook it. Then we'll divide the meat and catch up with the Major and eat the rest tonight. That way it won't make anyone sick."

One of the men sat back on his heels, a chunk of bloody meat in his hand. "Cook hell! This wood here is all hard wood! It won't never burn!"

"Put that meat down, Higgins," Avery shouted. The man obeyed him reluctantly.

"Now for God's sake," Avery said, "don't eat it raw! We passed some spruce growth a ways back. I'll take Higgins and Peters, and the four of us'll go back and get a couple dead trees that'll burn. The rest of you skin her and cut her up, and by the time that's done the food'll be cooked and it'll do us some good."

They slowly went to work slitting the skin on the legs and belly.

"Come on," Avery said to me. Peters and Higgins followed us reluctantly. They were the recalcitrant ones, who had been most determined to eat. "Prime your muskets," Avery warned us. "There might be a bull moose hanging around waiting for that cow, and the waiting might have upset him."

When the four of us worked back along our trail, we found the stand of spruces that Avery had noted, two hundred yards to the rear; and wherever there are spruces, there are blow-downs of dead trees. We picked out two small ones, trimmed off the upper branches so they were easy to carry, and went to work dragging them into the clear. It was hard work freeing them. The starvation rations of the past few days seemed to have made my knees limber, but we had them almost out when Avery looked up at me. "What's that?"

I had said nothing.

"I thought you'd hurt yourself," he explained. He glanced at Peters and Higgins, struggling with their spruces: then went to them.

"Anything the matter? Didn't one of you let out a yelp?"

They stared at him in surprise.

Avery turned his head slowly toward me, a look of incredulity in his eyes. Then, leaving us, he ran out of the spruce thicket, and a little way along our tracks; crouched where the ground rose a few feet. I saw that he was peering toward where we had left our seven men and the dead moose. On the instant when he crouched, I realized sickeningly what had happened. Like Dunbar, Turner, and Jenkins, we too had been caught.

Avery sank flat on his stomach and squirmed back into the shelter of the spruces.

"Have they killed 'em?" I asked.

He shook his head. "Not with all that moose meat to be carried! They're prisoners and'll be made to carry the meat till it's eaten. Then they'll finish 'em."

He began to move off to our left, stooping. "Now we've *got* to get to Rogers."

Rogers! The thought of Rogers then was like the thought of home and safety.

§

Like four shadows we crept across our tracks, careful to leave no traces. By taking cover in depressions and behind boulders, we reached the shelter of a rocky knoll; and hidden among its ledges we watched thirty swarthy, stunted Frenchmen and a dozen painted Indians hustle our seven comrades off to the northeast. They had become beasts of burden: on their shoulders they bore gory fore- and hindquarters; bundles of moose meat; the neck and hide. Frenchmen, carrying two muskets apiece, prodded the captive Rangers with their own bayonets, amid thin bursts of distant laughter.

We were helpless. If we made a move to rescue the luckless seven, they would be instantly hatcheted and we most certainly would lose our own lives as well.

"That's where that moose came from!" Avery said bitterly. "It was moving ahead of 'em!" He looked at me despairingly. "Who'd have expected to find 'em in *front* of us?"

"You don't suppose it was their tracks we'd been following?" I asked.

"Oh, God, no!" Avery said. "That moose came on us at an angle—diagonally across our trail; and that's the way those damned French rats were moving. They must have been sent out by those that caught Dunbar. They must have known a short way to get here. If they hadn't struck us, they'd prob'ly have turned after Rogers."

"Well," I said, "they'd have caught us either way, it seems to me. I don't see how you're to blame for killing the moose. Anybody'd have killed it, under the circumstances."

The lines of trouble on Avery's young face deepened. He was hardly more than a child, and was more concerned over making a mistake than over a catastrophe to someone else.

When there was no further sight or sound of the Frenchmen and Indians, we crept back to where we had shot the moose, to see whether anything had been left. A pack of wolves couldn't have stripped the carcass more thoroughly. They had taken the nose, the tongue, the brain; even the eyes, the ears, and the intestines. Only the skull was left. "I guess they're as hungry as we are," Avery said. "I was hoping the French and Indians that were after us would starve to death; but it kind of looks as if these wouldn't be the ones."

He picked up the skull and a few scraps that lay among the blood-stained leaves. "I wish they'd left the hoofs. You can get a pretty good soup out of four hoofs and a moose head—kind of gluey; sticks to your insides."

"If we'd et it raw, the way we wanted to," Higgins said bitterly, "we'd have *something* in us, anyway."

Avery turned on him. "By God, you ain't got as much sense as a squirrel! Even a squirrel knows enough to look out for tomorrow! You'd have something in you—yes; but you'd be sick, and you'd be a prisoner, and tomorrow you wouldn't have anything in you but hatchet holes! It beats hell how full the world is of people that don't know enough to thank God they're alive!"

The outburst seemed to make him feel better. He led us down that dim trail to the southeast as though he had food in him. Speed, I knew, was urgent; for the wind had turned back into the northeast again, and the sky was covered with a dingy pall of swiftly moving clouds that foretold more rain.

We caught up with Rogers about an hour before dark. We knew we had reached him when, out of a seemingly empty forest, a bullet rattled through the branches above us, and the report of a musket whanged among the trees, echoing against far-off hills. We stood where we were, our muskets raised above our heads. I looked everywhere for the afterguard who had fired, but saw no sign of anyone until John Konkapot came out from behind a tree and made motions to someone to the rear of him. On that Sergeant Bradley and Jesse Beacham ran to him and stood waiting for us, and I own that the sight of them affected me. I had never expected to see their familiar faces again. As we came up, the three of them stared hard at the bloody moose skull under Avery's arm.

Bradley looked beyond us. "Where's the rest of your detachment, Mr. Avery?"

"Tooken," Avery said. "How far's the Major?"

Bradley turned to Konkapot. "Go on ahead and tell the Major it's Mr. Avery and Langdon Towne and two Rangers." He took the moose head from Avery and sniffed at it. "Fresh!" he exclaimed. "Where's the rest of it?"

"The French got it."

Bradley cursed feelingly and motioned Avery to go ahead. Jesse and I fell in behind them.

"Haven't you had anything to eat yet?" I asked Jesse.

"No," he said contemplatively. He plodded on silently; then thoughtfully added, "No, the weather ain't been very good for hunting." He shot a quick glance at me from under bushy white eyebrows. "How'd you get away from 'em?"

"Just luck," I said. "We got away twice—the first time when they finished Dunbar, Turner, and Jenkins."

Jesse made commiserative humming sounds. "Dunbar and Jenkins and all them men? Too bad. I'm glad you four got away. Better come and tell the Major now, I guess."

We found Rogers' detachment re-forming. At the sound of Konkapot's warning shot, the Major had thrown them out in a crescent-shaped line, and he stood in the center with Ogden and Lieutenant Grant, waiting for us. I think our misfortunes of the past few days may have had a weakening effect on me, for a wave of fondness swept over me when I stood before them—such a wave as I had only felt, as a boy, when I saw my father after a long separation.

Rogers took us in at a glance. His eyes were more staring than they had been three days before, his black hat had lost the remaining half of its cockade, and his moccasins were reinforced with strips of strouding.

Ogden, however, looked better. His face no longer resembled a greenish skull, but was merely emaciated.

"How'd they happen to get you, Mr. Avery?" Rogers asked.

"We killed a moose," Avery said. "When four of us went back to hunt firewood, the French jumped the others."

"You went *back!* Then they were in front of you!"

Avery nodded.

"How many? How far off were you when it happened? Which way'd they go?"

When Avery told him, Rogers spoke sharply to Bradley, telling him to send four sentries to the rear.

"Could we catch 'em?" he asked Avery.

Avery shook his head. "I doubt it. They'll have that moose meat to eat, and there's no telling when you'd strike the main body—the one that massacred Dunbar and Turner and all the men with 'em."

"What? What did you say?" The Major started and grunted with pain, as if he'd been kicked. "When was that? Did they kill 'em all? How do you know they did?"

"We saw it," Avery said. "It was the morning after we left you. We crossed a ravine, but Dunbar and the others stayed back on the other side. At dawn they were pushed into the ravine and ambushed. None of 'em got away."

Rogers stared at Avery. "And you were near enough to see it! How many were there?"

Avery looked sick. In a shaking voice he said: "About two hundred that we could see. There was eleven of us."

I felt called on to put in my oar. "They were out of range, Major. We couldn't have helped. If we'd been seen, they'd have got us, too."

Rogers nodded and cleared his throat. "Did they treat 'em pretty bad?"

"Yes, sir; they did. They treated 'em bad."

I heard a peculiar snuffling titter. Near us I saw Crofton crouched on the ground like a young bear. His hands were tied, he was on a rope, like a bear, and, like a bear, he swung himself from side to side and clawed at the ground.

"I told you to keep him in the rear," Rogers said angrily. "Hitch him to a tree and let him dig if he wants to!"

"Is he crazy?" I asked Jesse.

"Yes," Jesse said. "The Major found that head of his and took it away from him. Crofton's possessed to dig it up. That's all he thinks of: digging! If he ain't on a rope, so he can be pulled along, he just stays wherever he is and digs."

Rogers looked up at the sky: then down at the moose head that Bradley held. "Well," he said, "here's what we'll do. Just ahead of us there's two hills with a little valley between. It's only an hour to dark. We'll build a fire at the far end of that valley, and we'll make camp beyond the fire. That'll give us an hour to hunt for something to put with this soup bone of moose head; and if any of Avery's seven men have the luck to get away, they might hear the guns or see the fire and come in. We got to give 'em a chance. If the French should make up their minds to come this far, we'll make trouble for 'em before they ever get a look at us."

We hunted in a circle around those two hills until darkness came down on us, accompanied by more rain from the northeast. There were forty-two of us to be fed; and when we assembled around the fire we had the moose skull, six black spruce partridges, five owls, a duck-hawk, a porcupine, three red squirrels, and a crow, most of them badly damaged by musket balls. We boiled the mess in three of the kettles brought from St. Francis, dividing it as evenly as possible. It gave three cups of soup apiece. The soup wasn't rich enough to hurt an invalid, and I have no doubt it would have disgusted my Harvard classmates who caviled at a rabbit pie; but it was hot, and it went a long way toward helping us endure the rain without discouragement. We were almost contented as we sat around the fire, crunching the little bones that were left in the bottom of the kettles.

Rogers wandered restlessly among us. "Don't swallow those bones," he kept saying. "With your stomachs empty, they'll cut holes in you. Don't swallow the bones. We'll be at the Ammonoosuc before long."

Jesse Beacham, gnawing fruitlessly at a chunk of moose skull, said mildly that he'd come to think the Prodigal Son hadn't made such a bad trade when he sold his birthright for a mess of pottage. For his own part, he'd be glad to sell his birthright, or anything else, for half a mess of pottage, and would consider he was getting the best of the bargain.

There were beech trees near where we camped; so before we marched in the morning, we went to them and pawed among the sodden leaves for beechnuts—nuts so small that one must hunt an hour under the best of circumstances to find a cupful, and then from them obtain scarcely enough meat to feed a wren. In wet weather a beechnut becomes perverse and disappears entirely, leaving behind it nothing but the tantalizing burr from which it emerged.

While we thus hunted, we heard the sentries shouting, and when they came up with us, they were leading Andrew McNeal and Andrew Wansant, two of the seven who had been captured on the preceding day. Neither of the two had muskets, blankets, pouches, or powder horns.

Their Scotch caps were gone. Both were naked above the waist, and they were scratched and clawed, as if by wildcats.

We crowded around them to hear their story. The first thing Rogers wanted to know was whether the Frenchmen had seemed to be still in search of us. McNeal said no: that they were going back to the north. They were hungry, he said: worse off than we when seen at close range; and like us, they had eaten nothing for days. Their uniforms, McNeal said, were as tattered as our own; all of Wansant's and McNeal's clothes had been taken from them at once to patch garments.

The other five, McNeal said, had not yet been killed or tortured. Neither he nor Wansant had been able to understand the lingo of the French or the Indians, but from their gestures he had understood that the prisoners would be made to carry game and kettles until they returned to Canada, when they would be turned over to squaws to be tortured.

They had been given split moose bones to gnaw and had been tied back to back, in pairs. McNeal had saved a sharp-pointed sliver of moose bone. By driving the point into one of the cords that bound him, and patiently turning it round and round for two hours, he had frayed the rope and broken it. Another hour's work had freed him and Wansant; and the two of them, moving inch by inch, had crept beyond their sleeping captors.

"If it hadn't been for the noise of the rain and the wind," McNeal said, "we couldn't 'a' done it."

Wansant said simply, "I don't know yet how we done it."

"Thank God the Major lit a fire," McNeal said. "Wansant climbed a tree around midnight and thought he saw just a little glimmery spark, 'way away off. That's what kept us going."

We looked at them as at men who had been buried before our eyes, only to rise from the grave unhurt.

"Got anything to eat?" McNeal asked.

We gave them a few beechnuts. The palms of McNeal's hands were raw; and the flesh was worn from the thumb and forefinger of his right hand so that the bones and tendons showed. He tossed the nuts in his mouth and chewed them, shell and all.

On that day, which was the eighteenth of October, the country seemed to grow even worse. The streams still ran in all directions, and while we thought the rain was coming from the northeast, we couldn't be certain of it because of yesterday's unexpected double change of wind. At length even Rogers began to suspect that our compasses had gone wrong: that we might be lost. I know there are some who can find their way in the forest by the manner in which moss grows on the trees, the greater number of limbs on the south sides, and the direction of the watercourses; but if we had lacked compasses, we couldn't have done it.

Rogers shook his head at the continued downpour. "I'm going to build a camp," I heard him tell Ogden, "and get something into these men. Half of us'll fish: the rest can build fires and stand guard. We'll try to dry out the blankets, too. If this storm comes off cold, we might have a little trouble."

I called Jesse Beacham's attention to this. "A little trouble!" I said ironically. "We might have a little trouble!"

"Well," Jesse said thoughtfully, "I dunno but what he's right."

Rogers spotted a squirrel and shot him for bait, and we got our lines in the first stream we reached. If there was a trout in it longer than five inches, we couldn't find it. Five-inch trout make good enough eating, but they find difficulty in getting their mouths around hooks designed for fish considerably larger. After persistent work and endless cursing we collected a few hundred minnows, and since there is no more nourishment to a trout cooked without pork than to a handful of snow, Rogers set us to work scraping rock tripe to boil with them. Rock tripe is a greenish-gray crust that grows on boulders and ledges. When boiled it has a sickish and offensive smell, like stale paste, but supposedly it is nourishing.

We were all afternoon getting the trout and the tripe. We had become awkward and fumbling in our movements and seemed to do everything slowly. Time after time we hooked midget fish, only to have them wriggle magically from our hands and squirm between our clutching fingers to safety. Ordinarily I would have found it amusing to see a score of hairy, hollow-eyed men on hands and knees among the boulders, pawing for escaped minnows and falling clumsily on their faces; but there wasn't anything funny about it now. We needed the minnows.

When we boiled the trout and the rock tripe, the mixture was like slush from a fish pier. It wasn't for enjoyment we ate it, however, but for the strength to get us to the mouth of the Ammonoosuc. No matter how it tasted; it was food.

That was all we could talk about—food: the food we'd find at the Ammonoosuc—what sort of food it would be: whether John Askin, the Rangers' sutler, would be there with delicacies for us. Some thought he would: others were sure we would find nothing but regular army rations —salt pork, biscuit, coffee, chocolate, sugar, and rum. We didn't care what it was, so long as it was food.

Next day we came to a stream that struck a familiar chord in the breast of the Indian boy Billy; but like all Indians, he was unwilling to commit himself until he was sure. He was a good boy, as was Bub. They still carried Ogden's blanket and pack and had taken Rogers' blanket as well. They were friendly, like dogs, thin as little skeletons from lack of food, and potbellied from eating grass, buds, snails, and small snakes. They seemed to have forgotten their previous existence and to be genuinely attached to us.

The stream, a brawling, shallow one, differed from those we had encountered since we first saw Lake Memphremagog by being crystal-clear and holding steadily to one direction. It ran northwest, however; and what puzzled all of us, including Rogers, was how it could still be running to the north, toward Lake Memphremagog, when we must already be far south of the headwaters of the Connecticut, which runs almost due south.

At length Billy freely admitted to recognizing the stream. He had, he said, travelled beside it, going from the Connecticut to Memphremagog with his mother at the end of a summer of raising corn and beans in the Intervales. By following it to its source, he told the Major, we would come to a beautiful pond with an island in the middle. Only a mile from that pond, he said, was the Nulhegan River, and the Nulhegan flowed downhill into the Connecticut. Once we had come to the Nulhegan, he insisted, the Connecticut was only a short march. He put his hands on his potbelly and added apologetically, "No meat, take longer."

There are spells, as every hunter knows, when game vanishes from where it ought to be. At such times a hunter, no matter how skillful, is helpless. The forest seems stripped of birds and animals. There is no great mystery about it. Usually it results from unusual weather conditions—heavy and long-continued rains, or excessive drought—and the game has merely changed its feeding grounds, and gone to eating things no hunter expects it to eat. Partridges, for example, abandoning their usual diet of birch buds, thorn apples, and checkerberry leaves, might go into the high oaks and eat acorns, which no hunter in his right mind would think them capable of doing. That is why hunting parties of Indians so frequently starve to death in forests full of game which can't be found.

This was such a time. There were plenty of owls—little ones, with voices like the rasp of files on iron, and big ones with wild yellow eyes—but we didn't shoot them for fear of frightening something more worth having. Of all living creatures, an owl makes the worst eating, being three-fifths head and one-fifth bone, and the rest mostly voice. To make even a ghost of a meal for the forty-four of us, we would have needed eighty owls; and the entire eighty would have held no more nourishment than an equal number of trout, since they, too, are without fat.

We spread out on both sides of that brawling, clear stream, going slowly and carefully in the hope of jumping a deer; but never a deer did we see: only a damnable owl now and then, and occasionally an eagle, flapping laboriously toward some distant destination.

The sky remained overcast, and the trackless forest through which we marched was dark and somber; and that somberness was reflected in our own spirits. Only Rogers and Ogden and the Indian boys seemed cheerful; but their cheerfulness had no effect on me. I had suddenly realized that I didn't believe anything. I didn't believe we would ever find game: ever emerge from this endless forest: ever see the Connecticut: ever feel the sun's warmth or dry clothes or happiness. I didn't believe I would ever again set eyes on my home or on Elizabeth. When we rested I could only sit and brood, heavily, vacantly, sullenly resentful against all the world.

It was the same with Jesse Beacham: with Avery: with Bradley. If we were spoken to, we made no answer. When Rogers walked among us, grinning his piratical grin and telling us in his thick voice that we'd be out of the woods soon and at the Ammonoosuc before we knew it, we just sat and stared at the ground.

Billy had been right. We found the pond with the island in it, and near by the Nulhegan, running to the southeast. Dejectedly and silently we made our way down it like scarecrows half alive, watching and hoping for the deer or moose that no one ever saw.

On the 20th hope sprang up in us again, and our lowness of spirit left us, for we cut across the shoulder of a mountain and looked up a broad valley that stretched far to the north—the Connecticut Valley. Through the trees that filled the cut between the mountains we could see a broad ribbon of river, riffled and streaked with quick water. To us the Connecticut meant that the Ammonoosuc wasn't far away—the Ammonoosuc and food. We tittered weakly and made childish jokes as we stumbled toward that distant gleam.

The Cohase Intervales of the Connecticut are unlike other river intervales. The valley, at the Intervales, goes down to the river in two giant steps. It looks as though the river was once infinitely larger and deeper, held back by some vast dam, and had deposited a rich, flat river bottom at a high level. If such a dam had burst, lowering the level of the river by fifty feet, the river at that lower level would have laid down a new rich valley bottom; and that, seemingly, is what happened at the Cohase Intervales. The upper shelf of flat land is wide in some places and narrow in others: cut by incoming brooks that have made the edges of the upper shelf irregular, and occasionally left islands of earth rising from the flat surface of the lower shelf.

At the point where the Nulhegan flows into the Connecticut, the inter-vales are small and infrequent: farther to the southward they increase and flow together until they embrace the whole broad valley. Some of these intervales are clear by nature: others have been cleared in times past by northern Indians, who found the Cohase Intervales the richest and most beautiful of all the farming land within their reach.

When we came out of the forest onto the small intervale where the Nulhegan runs in, we could look down the valley for miles and see on the far side a range of mountains that put me in mind of the sharp peaks along the shores of Memphremagog. The sky was a leaden gray still, but to us it seemed blindingly brilliant; for not since we had paraded on the dance ground at St. Francis had we been clear of the forest.

While we stood looking to the southward and wondering where, among those sharp mountains, the Ammonoosuc flowed in, there was a commo-tion at the rear of the party. When I looked around, Crofton was hurrying back across the intervale toward the forest we had just left, but scrambling on his hands and knees, like an animal. He had gnawed the rope that tied him and broken it. When we shouted at him in chorus, he whirled and stared at us over the top of a bush, as a disobedient dog stares; then ambled more slowly to the edge of the forest, looked here and there, like a dog, and began to dig.

"Shall I go after him, Major?" Lieutenant Grant asked. Grant, a bluff, good-natured officer with small, squinting eyes, had been portly, even at St. Francis; but now he was cadaverous, and his once-rounded cheeks were creased and crumpled.

Rogers shook his head. "You couldn't catch him. Nobody could catch him. He's crazy. He can run forever."

Crofton, at the edge of the forest, stood up straight and peered at us. He looked like a bear standing on his hind legs. When he saw we weren't following, he dropped on all fours again, dug a little, and then, after a final apprehensive glance over his shoulder at us, he passed slowly from our sight, back into the forest.

Something about that strange departure into hell made us take furtive stock of each other in the bright light of the open intervale. What we saw wasn't reassuring. I realized for the first time that Rogers was stooped. I had noticed Ogden's stoop some days before, and knew it was due to his wound; but he had recovered from his wound now, and he still stooped. So did Lieutenant Grant. So, I realized, did Jesse, Sergeant Bradley, Whip, and most of the others. And so, it dawned on me, did I. I knew, too, why I did it. My stomach had a peculiar rubbed-together feeling—a sort of knotted tightness that could only be relieved by stooping. I wondered how long I had been doing it. I hadn't been conscious of it before. When I straightened up, I had a stomach cramp, so I stooped over again and felt better.

Next to that stoop, the thing that struck me most forcibly about my companions was their eyes. I had become accustomed to their beards and their grotesque garments—their bare feet, and the odds and ends with which their lower legs were protected from the brush—but I had been almost unconscious of their eyes until this perturbed moment. Their eyes seemed to have been pressed into their skulls with hot irons that had seared the surrounding flesh to the color of fresh liver. In those dark rings the eyes were flat and staring above noses so fleshless they resembled beaks. Between the eyebrows were deep grooves, as if from insupportable worry. Because of these eyes, and the thin beaks of noses, every man at whom I glanced—even gentle Jesse Beacham—seemed fierce and predatory. I wondered then if people I'd seen elsewhere whose look was fierce and rapacious weren't really, at heart, harassed.

§

We went as far down the Connecticut as we could that afternoon. It was bad going, because of the rain-swollen tributaries that crossed our path. Never once did we see a deer. To try for fish in the swollen streams or the muddy river would have spoiled the best part of a day, so we went on and on, thinking always of the divine food waiting for us at the Ammonoosuc.

"Not far now," Rogers said cheerfully, when somebody asked him; and we, taking him at his word, stumbled on and on.

On the 20th we found ourselves in the true Cohase Intervales. In our weariness and stooped emptiness, the labor of climbing up and down those treeless shelves—of going far from the river to skirt gullies and returning only to encounter more—was harder on us, more exhausting, than our travels through the mazes of Lake Memphremagog. It was disheartening, too, to look far ahead and see the slowness of our progress. In the forest, necessity had kept our eyes upon each succeeding step we took, and trees and thickets blocked the view; but here we could see the endlessly stretching miles, and felt ourselves snails upon them.

That was the day we lost Bradley. He came to Rogers to say his men were almost dead, and he thought he'd better hunt a little in the hills beyond the Intervales. He looked singularly defiant, but I thought nothing of it. In the condition we were in, a man's face was apt to assume all sorts of unexpected expressions without his intending it.

"Better stay with me, Sergeant," Rogers said. "We've been together a long time now. I believe you'd do well to keep on the way you are. This doesn't look like good hunting grounds to me."

"I guess we'll hunt here just the same, Major," Bradley said.

He moved off to one side with his detachment; and we expected they'd catch up with us by nightfall, or at the worst by next day; but they didn't. At night we reached the fording place, marked, as Rogers had told us weeks before, by a saddle-shaped mountain. The weather had come off cold, and the dark peaks into which we must venture on the morrow had the look of threatening blue waves. To my aching eyes they seemed to surge and roll: the sharp line of their ridges to undulate.

We built a heap of stones in the morning, so Bradley and his men might know where we had crossed: then we floundered through the quick shoal water and clambered up the sandy bank on the far side. From here, looking back, we saw, on the bank we'd left, a scant line of men making their way toward the cairn we'd set up for their guidance.

"Here comes Bradley," Rogers said. "We'll wait for him."

It was difficult to realize, watching their devious, fumbling progress, that we had moved equally slowly and gropingly across that same inter-vale.

"There's only eight of 'em," Grant remarked.

"Yes," Ogden said, "and Bradley's not one of 'em."

Since Bradley had ten men under him, that meant three were missing.

They made bad going of it crossing the river. Those who slipped and fell took a long time to regain their feet: then stood, stooped over, to cough up water. Occasionally they fell again.

They crawled up our bank weakly, like half-drowned dogs.

"Where's Bradley?" Rogers asked.

"Major," said Kelly, a redheaded Irishman from Suncook, "he went home."

"Home!" Rogers cried. "What you talking about?"

"Major, he said the Cohase Intervales was just two days from his home in Concord, and the quickest way to get back was head straight for Concord. He said all of us could have supper at his father's house day after tomorrow if we went that way."

"Concord!" Rogers said. "Where in God's name does he think Concord is?"

"Major, the sergeant said the Cohase Intervales are north west a half north from his father's house in Concord; so he took a sight—south east a half south."

Rogers' mouth twisted. "How'd it happen you didn't go with him?" he asked in a husky voice.

"We didn't like the looks of the mountains," Kelly said. "We told him we'd go our own way. We'd rather follow the Major."

Rogers stared off to the northeastward, and we stared with him. Through a gap in the hills we could see, low on the horizon, a dim silvery bulk of snow-covered mountains, like a far-off cloud.

"Who *did* go with him?" Rogers asked.

"Pomp Whipple and Lew Pote."

Rogers looked at the far, far, faint snow on the mountains. "Well," he said, "let's get moving again toward the Ammonòosuc."

Kelly spoke timidly. "Where does the Major think Bradley and them two will be landing up?"

"In the middle of the White Hills," Rogers said. "I noticed that Bradley was wearing a leather hair ribbon and some Indian jewelry. Maybe next summer somebody'll find a strip of leather and a few beads, and be Christian enough to bury what he finds with 'em. Let's get on."

Now we followed, as Rogers had promised, a blazed trail: the first we'd seen since the day the path beside the St. Francis vanished in a bog.

It took us high up over the shoulder of the mountain—a crest from which we looked back at a world devoid of life, and forward to a wilderness equally empty. Behind us the Connecticut, like a toy stream, wound back between its intervales; and on all those small drab shelves above the river nothing moved. I wondered where, in the expanse of forest and mountains beyond the river, Farrington and Campbell and Curgill still stumbled with their men—or where they might be lying, unable to move. To my vague surprise, I hardly remembered those officers. It was with difficulty, even, that I recalled their names.

Ahead of us was a rugged, wooded valley, almost inviting by comparison with those along which we had so recently struggled, and we could look straight down it, as along a gun sight, into the misty distance where our food was waiting.

"There it is," Rogers said. "There's the Ammonoosuc!" He hitched doggedly at the belt of his torn and soggy buckskins, as a man does when at last he's conquered a difficult task.

Konkapot and Captain Jacobs went ahead to the stream, hoping to surprise a deer; for they had stood the scarcity of food better than the rest of us. They could still move lightly, whereas the rest of us went blundering and staggering, kicking up noises wherever we walked.

The Ammonoosuc at last—and we were almost there. The whole valley, it seemed to me, must be a land flowing with milk and honey: a place in which we would be free at last from misery and painful endeavor. When we heard the reverberation of a musket shot, we went slipping and sliding eagerly down the rough trail, as to a banquet. In my mind was a picture of a two-hundred-pound buck—a fat, ten-point animal that might dress out to give each of the thirty-eight of us two full pounds of clear meat, a happy prelude to the great store of food awaiting us not far beyond.

What Captain Jacobs had shot was a fish eagle—a wretched bird, smelling of carrion. We made it into soup, cooking all of it, even the feet, head, and intestines. After it had been boiled half an hour, each of us had a cupful of broth, and then Rogers divided the meat. I can see him now, straddling a flat rock, with the fishy-smelling body before him, marking the carcass into thirty-eight sections. He would hold a portion behind him, in a big hand that shook: Ogden would call a name; and the man he called would go up and take the portion. An eagle is not unlike many humans of great repute: dressed up in his feathers and wings, he looks important; but divested of those trappings, he is sadly wanting in impressiveness and substance, being mostly beak, wing-bone, and leg muscle. The little portion that each of us received was a mere phantom of unsatisfactory food: a bad breath, so to speak; but it was tough, and lasted longer than five times the amount of something more savory; so our imaginations, no doubt, were strengthened by it, even though our stomachs weren't.

The valley, when we got into it, wasn't flowing with milk and honey. It was barren and miserable. We forded the rocky bed of the river, returning toward the Connecticut again. The trail, washed out by rains and long disused, dragged at our feet. The best we could do, even downhill, was twelve miles. When men tripped and fell they got to their knees like babies and pulled themselves up by clinging to saplings or low branches.

That was the 21st of October, and all that day and all the 22d we saw no more eagles nor even a chipmunk; yet, eating nothing at all, we made fifteen miles on the 22d. And when we tripped and fell, we fell forward, not minding what happened to our faces so that we fell toward the fabulous meals we'd eat at the mouth of the Ammonoosuc. Spurred on by Rogers and by the food that awaited us, we made fifteen miles through a forest stripped of wild life.

Rogers shambled back and forth along that tottering, wavering, hastening line. His voice was hoarse and rasping. "Keep your feet, Kelly!" he shouted. "Pull that man up, you, next to him, there! You, there, Wansant! Get up and move along! We're almost there! We'll be there tomorrow, sure! McNeal! Wake up, McNeal! We're almost there!"

We were forced to make camp that afternoon while it was still light; for the men were so troubled with hunger cramps that their sense of balance seemed to have gone awry. All through the day, whenever the trail had come close to the Ammonoosuc, I had found myself leaning away from the bank to avoid pitching over the edge. My hands were numb; and when I stretched myself upon the ground, the earth seemed made of prickly mist, on which I floated undulatingly. I had the impulse to ask Jesse Beacham whether he felt the same. Out of the corner of my eyes I could see him lying like a dead man, his tangled white beard pointed straight upward, but I couldn't ask him. I couldn't get the words from my brain to my tongue.

I heard Rogers' voice far away; far, far away. I had heard voices like that during a boyhood illness, coming to me from behind a screen at my bedside, faintly, as if they spoke from outside the house.

He was talking about smoke. I heard the word again and again. It woke me.

I rose and crawled forward to where Rogers talked with Ogden, Grant, and Avery.

"I tell you it's smoke!" Rogers insisted. "Open your mouth when you breathe, and breathe easy. Isn't that smoke?"

I sniffed and sniffed, and then I caught it—a faint, elusive fragrance of wood smoke.

"By James!" Ogden whispered. "I *can* smell it, Major. Sure as you're born, it *is* smoke!"

I felt rather than heard Grant laughing convulsively, breathlessly, gasping and gasping for the strength to unleash another convulsion.

Rogers' voice was exultant. "There's only one place that smoke could come from! We're there! We're all right! The food's here! We'll have it by noon tomorrow. I knew we'd make it, by God, and we have!"

§

We crawled and stumbled down the last three miles of the trail that next morning—the 23d of October—beneath cold gray skies and against a raw wind that smelled of snow; but we cared nothing for cold or snow when we heard, faint and far ahead of us, a sharp report, followed by two others in quick succession.

There was no mistaking them. They were musket shots, and we had come back again to civilization—back to a land where there were friends and food: warmth and decent homes.

Rogers raised his arms triumphantly. Holding his musket like a pistol, he fired an answering shot.

Even Jesse Beacham seemed excited. "Here we come!" he said; and he, too, sent a bullet straight upward.

"Put on the kettle!" Avery croaked. His musket spat fire at a solitary crow, high above us. It swerved and increased its speed.

Up and down the line men called jubilantly in quavering voices, their guns banging in a happy fusillade. McNeal, whose musket had been taken from him by the French, begged the loan of Avery's so to celebrate our safe arrival. He was badly off, and entitled to celebrate. Having no upper garments, he wore Avery's blanket during the day, just as Wansant wore mine. Already the damp blankets had rubbed sores on their shoulders and backs, for the skin was tight over their bones, and therefore tender.

Hungry men can smell smoke enormous distances; and the scent of it now was powerful in our nostrils. We could see, before us, the end of the Ammonoosuc Valley, blocked by the hills on the far side of a greater valley. We had come back to the Connecticut once more, and not only could we glimpse the river itself, swift and turbulent, through the naked trees, but we could see smoke lying against crowded spruces like a veil upon a bride's dark hair.

Rogers, in advance, was shouting hoarsely, thickly—shouting, I supposed, to the men who awaited us with provisions. He must have reached the juncture of the rivers. "Rogers!" I heard him shout. "Major Rogers' detachment, back from St. Francis!" It fantastically occurred to me that we might be taken for a herd of animals from the forest and shot.

Again he shouted, and now there was something in the sound of his voice that vaguely worried me—a queer uncertainty. I broke into a leaden-footed run and came out of the forest beside Ogden, Grant, Captain Jacobs, and Konkapot on a high clearing overlooking a pointed intervale, through which the Ammonoosuc ran to join the broad Connecticut. In the clearing stood a tumble-down deserted fort made of logs from which bark hung in strips. Half the logs in the palisade had rotted off, and there were holes in the roof of the log house within the palisade. In this we had no interest at all. All our eyes were upon the smoke across the river.

Rogers, fifty yards ahead of the foremost of the rest of us, slipped down the bank with a sound of rattling stones, sprawled to his knees and rose painfully to his feet. The two Indian boys slid down behind him like little brown skeletons.

On our side of the Connecticut, just below us, was the mouth of the Ammonoosuc, but there was nothing there except water and earth; the intervale was empty of any visible human life. But across the Connecticut from us we saw the foamy mouth of Wells River, entering the greater stream between high banks; and it was from the top of the southern bank of the lesser that the smoke rose and in thinning layers drifted over the Connecticut to us.

There was nothing near the fire—nothing at the water's edge: no canoe, no bateau, no food: nobody. What was a fire doing, then, burning away with no man near it, where there should have been many men and piled full sacks and boxes and great store of food. Was something wrong with our starved eyes, that they seemed to see only an abandoned fire, a nightmare ghost of a fire?

But the smell of the smoke came to us sharply on a cold and damp wind, and we knew that there are no odors in dreams, not even in nightmares. Behind me I heard men stumbling from the forest, making grunting, panting sounds.

Rogers looked quickly upstream: then down. "Rangers!" he called huskily. "Rangers!" His voice cracked. Snatching his musket from Billy, he primed and fired it.

There was desperation in the glance he threw us, and his voice was hoarse.

"They've gone and they've taken our food with 'em! They brought it and then took it away! God knows why!"

He dumped powder in his musket, rapped the butt on the ground and fired it again.

"Come back!" he shouted downstream. "Come back here!"

My knees and thighs seemed to have turned to jelly: my upper arms to pipestems. I got down the bank somehow. I think I fell head over heels down it with a dozen others, and crawled feebly from the heap like an unweaned puppy.

"Fire your guns and shout!" Rogers cried. "Look at the fire! They can't be more than a mile downriver! We got to make 'em hear us! We got to get that food back! O God! If only I had a canoe!" He went to the river's edge and waded in, up to his knees, so to see farther downstream.

We fired and fired; shouted and shouted.

"Listen!" Rogers cried at intervals. Then we'd stand with sagging legs and open mouths, listening; but never a sound did we hear save the rollicking, chuckling murmur of the flowing river.

The smoke from the fire across the Connecticut wavered and swung downstream. Cold raindrops spattered on the dry grass of the intervale with the sound of stifled tittering. Captain Jacobs and Konkapot settled back on their heels at the river's edge, their heads and hands hanging. One by one the men sank down, seeming to collapse into wasted heaps of rags and bones.

Rogers came out of the water and contemplated them. His eyes were puffy and red, like those of a weasel caught in a trap. His Rangers just lay there, looking at nothing. Some of them made groaning sounds, and some muttered; the rest were sprawled angularly, as though dead. To me they looked finished, might already have been corpses.

The rain grew more earnest: came thick, pelting and icy. Captain Ogden cast a quick look at the gray clouds that had shut down over the valley, obscuring the hills beyond Wells River; then he went close to Rogers. "You mean to say some pack of damned dirty rats brought food all the way up here and haven't waited for us?"

"They *did* wait for us," Rogers answered haggardly. "They waited clear up to almost right now. They waited for us until we heard those shots of theirs a little while ago. They waited until they heard our answering shots, and maybe that's why they left—they thought our firing was from a hostile party. I don't know. Maybe they didn't hear it: the wind was from them. Maybe they were just shooting as they started downriver."

"Downriver," Ogden repeated. "Gone downriver and left us to die here —after what we've been through?"

Abruptly Rogers' face showed an anger that I thought forced. I was watching him wanly, and it seemed to me that although a final bitter anguish had entered into him, he controlled it suddenly, seeing that if he allowed us to despair utterly we should indeed all of us, as Ogden had just said, die.

"No, damn it, no!" Rogers shouted roughly. "Don't be a fool. They're only a mile or so downriver! They heard our guns, just the way we heard theirs! They'll be back!"

"Why don't they answer, then?" Ogden cried. "That's the rule—always answer when a man's lost and you hear a musket!"

Rogers caught Ogden's arm and shook it. "I tell you that food'll be back! It'll be back!" He raised his voice. "I guarantee it! It'll be back! Now, Captain Ogden, we'll get all the men up to the fort and build a fire! Get the men on their feet and start 'em toward the fort."

Ogden just stared at him, and I knew what he meant: to have lived days and days in hell, but always with this spot where we now stood held out to us as bright Heaven if we could reach it—and then to attain it, perishing, only to find it empty: a cul-de-sac of despair and death. We too stared as Ogden did. The ghastly sarcasm of his look was upon all our faces.

Not until I saw Rogers dragging and kicking them upright did I realize that his optimistic words had been solely for their benefit: had been spoken in one last effort to save them from giving up.

"Get up!" Rogers was shouting at everybody. "Get back up the bank!

Get up to that fort and start your fires crackling! Don't you even want to be warm? Get up! Get up!" He was jerking the arms of prostrate men and pulling them upon their feet. "Get up! Get up! Shelter and warm fires! That's something, isn't it? Get up! Get up!"

Somehow, driving us, shouting at us, pulling and pushing us, he got us up the bank and into the ruined palisade. Then this grinning, bearded, tatterdemalion of a leader turned on his pack of crawling skeletons, storming at them in hoarse and breathless whispers. "By God," he panted, "I'll do my part, but you'll have to do yours! You've had as much to eat as I have, and you'll stand up on your feet like men and do what's to be done, or I'll read out your names in every town in New England! You're Rangers, and you're going to act like Rangers! I'll get food for you! I'll have food for you damned soon! I never yet promised you anything you didn't get! I promised there'd be food at this place, and there *will* be; but while I get it, you've got to make this place fit to live in. To live in, why? Because you're not fit to go any further, and when that happens, you've got to stop and live where you are, don't you? So now get to work and begin living here!"

He stopped, visibly ready to drop himself. He swept a gleaming look around the palisade and at the log house. "Clean up that house! The logs on the south side are rotten, so break 'em out! Build a fire in front of the south side. Make it a long one, and use rotten logs. Save all the sound logs. I'm going to use 'em! Get up, those of you that can work! Let's see who's still fit to be called a Ranger! The rest of you can die and be damned for all I care!"

He walked to the door of the log house and stood there, holding to the casing and looking inside.

Jesse Beacham, his face a tangle of white hair and his back so bent that it was almost a hump, followed him groaningly.

"Look at that litter!" Rogers said. "Rake it against the south wall. Then pull down the wall, pull the litter into the open and start your fire!"

He turned and stared at the rest of us out of sunken eyes. Every last man—even Andrew McNeal, from whose hands the flesh had been torn—was crawling or shambling toward the log house.

"That's better," Rogers said. "Captain Ogden, take charge of the house. Lieutenant Avery and Lieutenant Grant, put part of those men to work on the palisade. Take down the rotten logs for firewood. Save the sound logs and roll 'em over the bank, where they can't be burned. I want 'em."

He rubbed his eyes. They were so deep in his head that the rain lay in the pouches beneath them. "Here!" he said, "here! I want help. I'll take Captain Jacobs—Towne—Billy—Bub—Konkapot!" He lurched away.

Stumbling and slipping, the five of us followed him down the bank and to the edge of the intervale, where the Ammonoosuc, flowing into the Connecticut, formed a shallow backwater. He seemed to me to avoid looking downriver, or across to the intervale where the fire now had been quenched by the rain.

Rogers lowered himself heavily to his knees and pawed in the shallows at the water's edge, among dried-up plants whose dead leaves were shaped like arrowheads. With his hands he dug among them, pulling up a cluster of roots that looked like miniature sweet potatoes. He showed them to us. "You know those?" he asked Captain Jacobs.

Jacobs shook his head, as did Konkapot, Billy, and Bub.

"Well," Rogers said, "I don't recommend 'em, but you can eat 'em if you have to. They're katniss."

We repeated the word after him.

Konkapot pulled one of the roots from the cluster and raised it to his lips. Rogers took it from him.

"That's why I don't recommend 'em to hungry men," he said. "Nobody eats 'em unless he's hungry, and if he's hungry, he's apt to be in too much of a hurry. Don't eat 'em the way they are now, or they'll burn your gizzard out."

We stared at him numbly.

"Go ahead and dig 'em," Rogers said, "but don't eat 'em: not yet."

We fumbled and splashed in the shallows like draggled, hairy, feeble raccoons, until we could find no more of the roots, but Rogers, eyeing the pile we had accumulated, shook his head. "Not enough, we'll have to have more." To Captain Jacobs and Konkapot he said, "You know tawho?"

They said they didn't.

"Damn it," Rogers cried, exasperated, "your *women* do! Why don't you listen to your women once in a while!"

We carried the katniss roots to higher land, and there Rogers began to crawl through the wet, frost-bitten grass like a hound dog snuffing after a rabbit. We straggled along behind him, our heads bent before the pelting rain.

Rogers came to a halt, crouched on all fours and staring intently at a clump of withered leaves from which a dried stalk protruded. He put me in mind of a mud-stained, half-dead setter, forced by instinct to point game, even though it was the last thing he did. The leaves at which he stared had once been long and narrow.

"That's tawho," he said. "Tiger lily." He dragged out his knife. Resting on his elbows, he hacked painfully at the turf beneath the leaves and brought up a bulb the size of a crab apple. "Tawho," he repeated. "Don't eat 'em raw or they'll kill you. Bury 'em under a foot of earth with the katniss, and build a fire over 'em. Let 'em stay there all night. That draws out the poison. Then in the morning dig 'em up and eat 'em, and they'll keep you alive."

With that we began to crawl over the intervale, hunting dead tiger-lily plants, like sick cattle dejectedly foraging for a bare subsistence. My own case, as I look back on it, was no better than that of an animal. I had no memories of the past: no thoughts for the future. I wanted nothing except to stay alive.

When we returned to the fort with our load of katniss and tawho, we found the entire southern end of the log house removed and a long fire burning before the opening. Ogden, poking at the blaze, licked his lips when he saw our wretched load of roots.

"Where's Grant and Avery?" Rogers asked.

"Asleep," Ogden said. "Everyone's asleep. You'd think they were dead. Are those things good to eat?" He swallowed hard.

Rogers shook his head. "Not yet. How many sound logs did you find?"

"Twelve."

Rogers looked pleased. "Help us dig a trench for these Cohase potatoes, Captain. I guess that's all we can do today." To Captain Jacobs and Konkapot he added: "If you're too proud to go on digging, you might go back into the woods and look for game." They left us immediately, as dignified as two red skeletons could be.

While Rogers, Ogden, and I hacked out a trench with our knives, close to the fire, Billy and Bub, like two skinny squirrels, scratched away the dirt as we loosened it, and when we had buried the bulbs in the trench, we raked hot embers above them.

Rogers sat back on his haunches. "There," he said. "Those ought to keep us going till we get the raft built."

"Raft?" Ogden echoed blankly. "Raft?"

"How else can I get to Number Four, Captain?" Rogers asked. "That's where our food's gone: back to Number Four! I've got to get that food; and if it's the last thing I do, I'm going to settle with the rats that never even came where I told 'em to come—the mouth of the Ammonoosuc, not across the Connecticut where they left their damned fire! I've got to reach Number Four somehow, Captain."

"It's sixty miles, Major," Ogden protested. "You'll never make it alone!"

"I thought I'd take Billy," Rogers said mildly, "and maybe a couple of men in case I get hurt—if I can find a couple who'd risk it."

"Well," Ogden said slowly, "I guess I could make it."

"I believe I can too," I said.

I thought Rogers hadn't heard me, for he just stood there rubbing the back of one of his huge hands with the other. The dirty skin peeled off in little rolls, revealing a star-shaped red mark—an old bullet wound. Then he looked up and grinned at me wearily. "That's good. We'll make a Ranger out of you yet."

§

The rest of that day and all the next was a dim bad dream. Gray sheets of rain slanted across gray trees and gray mountains: the dirty gray river wound along a brownish-gray trough, through sodden intervales of smutty gray.

We lay in a feeble stupor through the 23d. Early on the morning of the 24th Rogers raked away the fire, unearthed the smoking brown bulbs and divided them equally among us. We had four apiece, and I could easily have eaten a bushel. Epicures, I suspect, would have scorned them; but none of the epicures I know have ever been almost dead from starvation. If they had, they would know that foods commonly regarded as repulsive by those who have always been well fed—such foods as dog, horse, snake, sea gull, wildcat, skunk, raw fish—are sweeter than ambrosia to men who are truly hungry.

All through the 24th Rogers devoted his strength to cheering up his men, and when they had swallowed their miserable portions of tawho and katniss, he did a grotesque thing: he made them shave.

"If I'm going to get food for you," he told them, "you've got to make yourselves recognizable! I can't tell you apart now; and if you keep on getting hairier while I'm away, why, when I get back here with men carrying food for you, we might take you for catamounts and shoot hell out of you instead of feeding you!"

It was a task to get some of the men to the riverbank, and an even greater task to make them soap their faces—if the soap hadn't a most horrible taste, I think we'd have eaten it long before. The disappointment of the preceding day seemed to have robbed most of them of all their remaining strength. Their razors, unused since the 13th of September, had rusted in spite of the oily rags in which they were wrapped; and their greasy beards, full of pitch, ashes, and dirt, resisted blades painfully.

When that sorry company had washed the blood from their mangled faces and used their pocket scissors on one another's matted hair, they were startling to see. The cropped heads seemed skull-like; their ravaged faces were so emaciated it seemed shameful to reveal them thus naked. And yet these barbering processes put a little new life into the men. I suppose they were reminded that, after all, they were still human beings. They were even able, when spurred on by Rogers, to hunt for lily bulbs and to unearth many times the amount we had dug the day before.

He let them go back to the log house, then; and there they lay, half-asleep and half-awake, all through the afternoon, while the downpour still thundered on the roof and Rogers made loud and hearty conversation.

"Why," he said, talking ostensibly to Ogden, Avery, and Grant, but in reality speaking to the hearing of everybody, "I'll be back here with food in ten days. You can count on it! In the meantime, you can dig lily bulbs; and even if you shouldn't shoot a deer or a moose, you'll have no trouble—no trouble worth mentioning."

He spoke to me. "Towne, you told me, back in Crown Point, that you'd made a study of the Bible. Wasn't there somebody in the Bible who went forty days without any food at all?"

It was an effort to remember. Everything I had learned in the past seemed to have retreated into the folds of my brain, like frightened sea anemones retiring into nothing; but under Rogers' insistent prodding, my memories partly revived.

"Forty days?" I said heavily. "Forty days? Yes, I think somebody in the Bible fasted forty days. Maybe it was our Lord—maybe Moses—maybe Elijah—I think maybe they all did."

"There!" Rogers cried triumphantly. "Do you hear what Towne says, all of you? Towne says even in the Bible there were men that went forty days without the slightest taste of food. Didn't have any good cooked roots—didn't have any nice hot katniss—didn't have any warm fresh tawho—no sir, not a damned thing! Not a single bite, did they, Towne?"

My brain was stirred into being a little bit more useful, and I was able to quote what Moses himself had said in Deuteronomy: that he had gone forty days and nights without eating bread or drinking water.

"Bread?" Rogers asked, and for a moment he looked blank. "Didn't have any bread? That doesn't mean that he *did* have potatoes and maybe turnips and lettuce and parsnips and . . ."

"No, no; indeed not!" I explained that when Moses said "bread," he meant edible matter of all sorts: that the word "bread" was a synonym for all food; and upon this Rogers looked relieved.

"You hear that?" he said loudly. "Moses was forty days and nights without a bite of food or a drink of water. Of course he couldn't have gone entirely without water that long, because a man can't do it, and I wouldn't ask any of you to believe that Moses went forty days without water. When Moses said he went forty days without a drink of water, he was careful to use the word 'drink.' He didn't say he didn't have a drop of water now and then—at least, according to Towne he didn't. Probably that's reasonable, because Moses was a holy man and wouldn't have said what he knew nobody could believe; so what he meant by the word 'drink' was that he never once had a real good drink of water the whole of the forty days. But when he said he didn't have any food at all, he meant just exactly what he said. It's in the Bible anyhow, so that settles it! He didn't have a single bite of food for forty days. You believe that, don't you, Ogden?"

"Me?" Ogden said. "Do I believe . . ."

"Why of course!" Rogers shouted. "Ogden believes it. Grant believes it. Avery believes it! Everybody believes it! We all know it was exactly the way Towne says Moses says it was! Well, look at the difference! Look at the water *we've* got! Never a day during the whole expedition that every last man of us couldn't have all the water he wanted. Look at the water we've got now! Good, fresh, cold rain water! What do you suppose Moses would have given for a nice mug of it, let alone buckets full? Look at sailors going crazy, hanging to spars out on the ocean after a wreck! What wouldn't they give for a millionth part of the water we got here, all around us! Look at Moses and wrecked sailors—and Elijah—without a single drink of decent water, and no food at all, let alone bushels of roasted tawho and katniss and . . ."

He was interrupted. Grant, with knobby thin hands pressed tight over his mouth, began to sputter through bony fingers, a haggard sort of tittering was heard from here and there, and then throughout the ruined fort there came the wholesome and saving sound of laughter on the air. The sound increased, grew louder and more voluminous until it finally had body and life to it.

Hell, with such laughter in it, wouldn't be altogether hell, I thought. And after all, the country through which Rogers had led us must have been worse than that through which Moses led the Children of Israel. Moses had led the Children of Israel to safety, and Rogers would do the same for us.

# An Inquiry Into Diets

### From FOR AUTHORS ONLY

ALL DIETS, according to my understanding, are wrong. I do not mean to say that all diets seem wrong to me. As a matter of fact, nearly every diet of which I have heard or read has appeared to me to be both reasonable and efficacious. What I am trying to say is that every diet, in the opinion of one or more diet experts, is either based on the erroneous ideas of a faddist, or is downright dangerous.

In my day I have seen a large number of disagreements over moot points, such as whether woman's crowning glory is or is not improved by a boyish bob, whether the Great War was or was not chiefly fought for the benefit of Rumania, whether the battle of Santiago was won by Admiral Sampson or Admiral Schley, and whether porcupines do or do not throw their quills.

By comparison with the diet question, however, all these other questions are hardly entitled to rank as moot points. The matter of diet has an infinitely higher moot content than any of them. It is as full of moot as roast pork is full of protein and calories: fuller, even, than cottage cheese is of vitamins. In my opinion it is pure moot.

My reasoning is based on the fact that experts are fairly evenly divided when delivering opinions on moot points. That is to say, if one hundred handwriting experts are summoned to court to decide whether the accused did or did not write the incriminating love letter, approximately fifty decide he did. The other fifty are equally certain he didn't. Similarly, if one hundred experts are requested to state whether beer is or is not intoxicating, one half of them will say firmly that beer is a food, like bread, and no more harmful than bread; whereas the other half will say with no less firmness that it isn't a food at all, but an alcoholic beverage, productive of crime, disease, maudlinity, and simon-pure drunkenness.

It is only on diets that the experts fail to disagree in their usual equable manner, as may be seen when one hundred diet experts are requested to pass judgment on whatever diet happens to be popular at the moment.

Ordinarily I would have no feeling whatever on the subject. Without wishing to speak highly of my own personal appearance, I may say that my weight is and has been, for some years, about right. If the life-insurance tables of weights and heights that so frequently appear in diet books are correct, a person of my height and age should weigh 172 pounds. What I actually weigh is between 165 and 172 pounds. This weight has seemed to me eminently satisfactory—not because I am infatu-ated with my appearance, but because it allows me to wear ten-year-old trousers without inconvenience.

My general health, moreover, has given me no cause for alarm. In spite of sitting at a desk, working or going through the motions of working from five to ten hours a day, Sundays and holidays included, for some seven years, I cannot at the moment recall any really troublesome ailment except a sprained thumb. By consulting my diaries, I find I had a headache on December 26, 1928; but though severe, it was not serious. I know what caused it; and it was successfully controlled by assiduous recourse to Bromo Seltzer. My physical condition, in short, has led me to feel no press-ing need for diets or diet books.

A lady of my acquaintance, however, having heard that I wrote books, and therefore suspecting me of a general knowledge of printed matter that might be of assistance to her, requested me to select for her perusal a few volumes on diet. What she wanted, she said, were books explaining how a person weighing 260 pounds can reduce to about 140 or 150 pounds in a safe and pleasing manner.

This seemed a simple request until I examined one of the large catalogs listing all books published on every conceivable subject during recent years. I then discovered that books on diet have tumbled, as the saying goes, so freely from the presses that their titles, printed in small type, fill seven pages in a volume the size of a New York telephone directory.

In order to have access to the most likely of these books, I took up the matter with an old friend, Senator George H. Moses of New Hampshire, knowing he had influence with the Congressional Library in Washington. The office staff of Senator Moses obligingly set machinery in motion; and shortly thereafter I received a dark gray mail sack which apparently held two grand pianos and a kitchen stove. When opened, however, it proved to contain merely the more authoritative publications on diet.

During the ensuing month I made a serious effort to select from the mass a few volumes that would meet the needs of my friend. I read them with scrupulous care. Whenever I rose from my desk, I stumbled over a pile of them. Whenever I wished to resume work, I had to clear diet books from desk, chair, and work table. Whenever I reached for the illuminating product of another diet expert my elbow struck a heap of eight or ten others and hurled them to the floor.

I am accustomed to dealing with masses of reference books. It is not unusual for me to spend days on end with all five fingers of my left hand marking important passages in several volumes at the same time. Consequently I was not nonplussed by the mere numbers of the diet books. What bothered me was their contents.

Hitherto, in consulting references on any given subject, I have usually been able to discard the majority as inaccurate, biased, unreliable, or untruthful, and to retain a few dependable ones as my chief sources of information. Diet books are different. Most of them are written by medical experts who have studied for years to find out exactly what happens to seven cents' worth of liver when it meets a Welch's bacillus in the upper colon of a sedentary worker aged forty-five.

Personally, I am in no position to say definitely that any great diet expert is wrong. I am only a student of diets. Obviously it takes a diet expert to catch a diet expert in a misstatement; but as I have already intimated, no diet expert hesitates to state openly that he is the first person in the world's history who has correctly answered the question of what a person ought to eat under given circumstances. The chances are that some of those who make this claim are mistaken; but there is no way, so far as I know, of finding out which are the ones.

This, it seems to me, is a serious state of affairs, and I will try to explain why. Ordinarily I would say nothing about trying to explain. I would go ahead and explain, confident of my ability to do so. Since I have been browsing among diet books, however, I am somewhat muddled, and not quite sure of anything—except that I have eaten incorrect foods all my life and must do something about it in a hurry.

No sooner had I made a beginning on the diet books than I discovered that the most recent school of diet thought believes nearly every disease in the world to be not only the result of eating improper foods, but also the result of eating proper foods in improper combinations.

I further discovered that although a person may consider himself in perfect health, and may feel comfortable and happy, he is—unless he is eating foods that the diet books say he ought to eat—as effectively poisoned as though nurtured for years on poison-ivy salads with bichloride of mercury dressing.

I also learned that nearly every disease in the world—according to the most advanced school of diet thought—can be prevented or cured by proper diet; and that the only way in which any person can save himself from a horrible illness is by ceasing to eat nearly everything to which he has hitherto been addicted and devoting the rest of his life to devouring foods he wouldn't ordinarily eat except on a bet.

It was at this point that I entirely forgot the lady who had asked me to consult diet books in her behalf and became concerned about myself.

From the first book I opened I learned, with considerable distress, that the person who permits himself to eat starches, meats, and sweets must be in a constant state of internal ferment. Not only is intestinal fermentation inevitable, but those who suffer from it are nervous, timid, afraid, irritable, and suspicious: they are quick-tempered, disagreeable, and easily offended: under the influence of intestinal ferment a splendid mind often loses its faculty of reasoning and thinking.

From the second one I discovered, with steadily growing apprehension, that if a person is so ignorant as to permit fermentable foods to pass his lips, he is doomed, because no amount of exercise, medicines, or outdoor life can counteract the harmful effects of fermented foods. They give him acidosis; and what acidosis does to him, in a quiet way, almost passes belief.

Acidosis is too large a subject for me to handle, in these few notes, except in the sketchiest manner. Not even the authors of the diet books are able to handle it satisfactorily. However, all of us are suffering from acidosis; and so far as I can tell, everybody has suffered from acidosis since the beginning of the world—unless he has been so happy as to stumble on the proper diet.

Among the unfortunates who must have been afflicted with it are Chaucer, Martin Luther, Julius Cæsar, Christopher Columbus, William Shakspere, Michael Angelo, George Washington, Napoleon Bonaparte, and all other great leaders, thinkers, fighters, and philosophers, as well as everybody who is or has ever been afraid of thunderstorms.

For many years I have been partial to large sirloin steaks, preferably those about three inches thick, which have been broiled nine minutes on each side over hot coals.

Such a sirloin steak, accompanied by a mealy baked potato, a plateful of buttered toast, and a lettuce salad thoroughly moistened with a garlic-perfumed dressing composed of two parts oil and one part claret vinegar, has always struck me as one of civilization's noblest products, especially when followed by a flaky fragment of apple pie tasting of cinnamon.

I have also viewed with favor a commodious platter of corned beef hash, or a savory mess of pea beans impregnated with pork, molasses, mustard, and onion in the proper proportion; then baked about thirty-six hours in a well-ripened bean pot.

My baked-bean record, to the best of my knowledge and belief, compares favorably with that of any New Englander. From my earliest years I have had what might almost be called an affinity for baked beans, especially when lubricated with homemade tomato catsup from which all sweetening has been religiously excluded.

When confronted with a successful baking of beans, I have frequently attacked them enthusiastically on Saturday night, gladly repeated on Sunday morning, then toyed with two or three platefuls, cold, on Sunday evening, and made a final clean-up of the bean situation at my Monday morning breakfast.

Blueberry pie, too, appeals to me strongly—especially the honest variety that makes the inside of the mouth look like a miniature stage setting of the Cave of the Winds at midnight. Blueberry pie, I have felt, is hard to beat as a climax to a tasty meal, provided the upper and under crusts are not flexible and inclined to adhere to the roof of the mouth, and if the consistency of the pie's interior is in that delicate state of transition when it is too loose to be called solid, but not sufficiently loose to be called runny.

There are, in short, a number of New England dishes that have given me pleasure for many years; and without knowing anything about it, I have taken it for granted that they were as nourishing as they were enjoyable. My ideas were probably based on the knowledge that people from my section of the country have lived on similar dishes since time immemorial, and have apparently thrived on them. That is to say, it has not been unusual for them to keep their health and strength until they were eighty-five or ninety years of age, and then meet untimely ends through being lost at sea or falling off a roof.

However, they were great bean and hash eaters, and many of them—especially the seafaring people from my section—frequently lived for weeks on end on one of the most trying dietary combinations known to dietitians: salt pork, ship's bread, and coffee tasting like a blend of boiled stockings and lobster bait.

Therefore I take it for granted, in view of what I have acquired from diet books, that they really weren't healthy at all, in spite of their long lives. Unquestionably they were victims of intestinal ferment, these seafaring New Englanders that I had always regarded as models of sturdiness. They were not, apparently, the bold mariners I had thought them, willing to crack on sail in strange waters; but must have been in a constant state of nervousness and timidity, and frequently lacking in reasoning faculties.

A casual glance into the pages of the most recently published diet books was enough to make this point clear. From one I learned my errors in regard to sirloin steak dinners, as outlined above. Beefsteak is a protein. A baked potato is a starch. The combination is dreadful. Buttered toast is largely starch, and therefore makes the terribleness more pronounced. Claret vinegar is an acid: to eat an acid with a protein is almost suicidal. As for the apple pie, it contains starch in its crust and sugar in its stuffing; and to drop those ingredients on top of steak and potatoes is little different from touching a match to a celluloid collar.

I wish to make it clear that these books are important diet books, and that I have the utmost confidence in each one at the moment I am reading it—as is the case, I believe, with all persons who read diet books. If I had not come across diet books when I did, I might never have known I had anything the matter with me—at any rate, not for thirty or forty years, when it would be too late to do anything about it.

Another book aroused me to the horrors of baked beans and tomato catsup. Baked beans are as full of starch as a dress shirt. Tomato catsup is made of acid fruit. When these are placed together in the human stomach, a fermentation takes place. Fermentation results in acidosis.

Corned beef hash is no better, unless some of the best diet books are grievously at fault. Corned beef hash is made, if made properly, by chopping corned beef and boiled potatoes together. Corned beef, unfortunately, is a protein, and potatoes are a starch. When simultaneously digested, the diet books say, the resulting fermentation is somewhat similar, in its effect on the stomach, to a lighted pinwheel.

These books aroused me as few other books have been able to do. Although I seemed reasonably healthy, I knew I couldn't be. Ever since my early youth I have been eating the wrong foods: consequently I must be badly fermented inside.

The more I thought about the matter, the more I realized that the books were right. I tired easily. Sometimes, after writing steadily for five or six hours, I would go out and play eighteen holes of golf. Within an hour or two after the golf game I would crave, let us say, a couple of lamb chops and a commodious piece of lemon meringue pie. That was a sign I was fatigued, the diet books say; for meat is nothing but a stimulant, and had I been free of fatigue, I would have craved no stimulant. Moreover, I would never have succumbed to fatigue unless suffering from acidosis. If I had been free from acidosis, I would have been content with some light viand, like a raw carrot.

One of the foremost diet books says that if a person follows the proper diet, he becomes tranquil, thoughtful, and philosophic; overwork is impossible; business worries are unknown; irritation vanishes. It was all too clear to me that I was in a bad way; for whenever my eye struck a newspaper report of the activities of the House of Representatives, I became irritated. Almost everything that was done in the House of Representatives seemed irritating; but the most frequent and explosive irritation was caused by that body's eagerness to wreck the finances of the nation; its delight in wasting more and more of the people's money; its inability to balance the budget in any sensible manner; its willingness to vote bonuses to veterans who know as little about war as the women who went without sugar in 1918, and are as little entitled to a reward; its craving to issue fiat money and generally imitate the Congress of 1786, which, through sheer ignorance and incompetence, collapsed completely and ceased to function.

When I read about such things, I not only become irritated: I become profane—so profane that my language sometimes shocks even myself.

This, of course, is another sure indication of acidosis. If I were on a proper diet, nothing could irritate me. I would remain tranquil and philosophic while reading about the House of Representatives. I would continue to be tranquil and philosophic, even though the House of Representatives should be successful in its efforts to bring the nation to insolvency and ruin.

I may as well be frank. The diet books had me, to put it crudely, scared.

If I had acidosis, I was liable to pop off at a moment's notice with any one of a score of painful and unpleasant diseases. The books insist on that, especially the newest books. If you have acidosis, they declare, bid yourself a fond farewell. Any little thing that happens to you—a sprained finger, a bruised knuckle, a hangnail, a mosquito bite—may, because of the acidosis, grow into something ruinous.

A man, perfectly healthy to all appearances, is talking and laughing with friends on Monday night. By mistake he puts the lighted end of his cigar into his mouth. He shows irritation and annoyance, which seems reasonable to those who have undergone a similar experience; but apparently he is not seriously injured. Two days later his tongue, joints, ears, and feet swell violently; and to the amazement of himself and his friends, he dies. The only ones who aren't surprised are dietitians of the acidosis school of thought; and the reason they aren't surprised is because they know that everyone who doesn't follow their diets must necessarily have acidosis, and that his organs are joyfully awaiting an excuse to cease functioning.

With all this on my mind I was, I scarcely need to say, eager to embark on any diet that would successfully free me of the curse of acidosis; but the deeper I delved in the diet books, especially those of the anti-acidosis school, the more it seemed to me that each one evinced a singular amount of irritation at the ideas of other dietitians.

As I understand it, you cannot feel irritation if you are free of acidosis. If that is correct, then the anti-acidosis experts are themselves troubled with acidosis. At all events, there was something about the situation that led me to think it might be wise to settle on a composite diet from a number of books rather than trust blindly to one book whose author might have been mistaken in his calculations.

Before deciding what to eat, however, I was obliged to consider the subject of fasting. Fasting, according to several of the most modern diet books, is a sure cure for acidosis, smallpox, acute appendicitis, pernicious anemia, rheumatism, colds in the head; for nearly every ailment, in short, that you can imagine.

Unfortunately there is a difference of opinion on the matter. I say "unfortunately" because the most earnest supporters of the fasting theory say that a thirty-day fast is easy of accomplishment: that the person participating in the fast has no desire for food after the first two or three days: that during the remainder of the fasting period there is, generally speaking, no depression; no hunger; no mental or physical fatigue; nothing but increased strength, mental clarity, and elation.

One of the diet books, written by Dr. Hay, impressed me deeply. It was being written, the author stated, during a thirty-day fast; and at the end of the thirty-day period, the author intended to subsist entirely on grapes for another thirty days.

Such a program, I scarcely need to point out, is of peculiar interest to an author; for by scattering his fasts judiciously through the course of a year, and taking proper advantage of the high food value of spinach, he ought to be able to live handsomely on an average of sixteen cents a day, or a yearly total of $58.40. If he plants his own spinach, there is no reason why he shouldn't be able to subsist for a year on as little as $27—unless I have completely misread the diet books.

In my opinion, spinach has been one of the most grossly maligned of vegetables. Until recently it was seldom placed before me without causing my acidosis to reveal itself in an outburst of irritability. I took no more pleasure in spinach-eating than I would have obtained from devouring a hooked rug. My feelings were almost violent in regard to spinach, even after I had gathered, from my first cursory survey of diet books, that it was the perfect food, fairly teeming with those great health-givers, calcium, phosphorus, iron, and vitamins.

In the early days of my diet researches, I complained to friends that I would never be able to diet successfully because of my aversion to spinach. My friends asked how I cooked my spinach. I told them that on the few occasions when it had been cooked in the mistaken belief that it was being cooked for me, it had been prepared in the conventional manner—by bringing a kettle of water to the boiling point, that is to say, and then popping the spinach into the water.

My friends exclaimed in horror at this and informed me that spinach, or any other vegetable, cooked in this manner is robbed of its most precious content: its mineral salts. That was the trouble with most people nowadays, they said: they boil their vegetables; and the mineral salts, extracted by the boiling, are thrown into the sink instead of into the stomach. Thus the people who eat the vegetables become anemic or something.

What I must do, my friends said, was to steam spinach and all other foods, so that mineral salts, vitamins, and so on would not be extracted.

Shortly thereafter I received from these kind friends a large, highly polished food steamer resembling an up-ended locomotive with the smoke stack removed. Its cover went on with nuts and bolts and was decorated with valves, dials, and other appliances. The directions for using it seemed, at first sight, a little like the instructions for manipulating a steam yacht; and when I first examined it, I doubted that it could be successfully operated without the help of two assistant engineers to watch the dials and valves, and a mechanic with a Stillson wrench to apply and remove the cover. It was complicated inside as well as out; for it contained so many wire baskets, pans, vegetable holders, and platforms that once they were abstracted they could only be replaced by an expert on picture puzzles.

To cook ten cents' worth of spinach in such an elaborate machine was baffling in the beginning because of the difficulty in getting up a full load of steam. There was a slight leakage which prevented the dial from registering the proper spinach pressure, so that after I had listened to the threatening hissing of escaping steam for an hour and forty-five minutes, it seemed best to me to remove the cooker from the fire, unscrew the nuts and bolts, throw the spinach away—mineral salts and all—and boil two eggs.

In time, however, I learned to screw down the cover over a mess of spinach so that the steam stayed where it belonged; and it was then that I discovered steamed spinach to be a truly edible vegetable. It has none of the haylike feel usually associated with boiled spinach, but has a delicate juiciness and succulence, something like the consistency of fresh asparagus. I must admit that it still tastes strongly of spinach, even when steamed; but I like it.

It might possibly be argued that since I no longer find spinach irritating, my acidosis must have left me; but I have noticed that I am undeniably irritated when I see the scenery of my native state ruined by stupidity and lack of vision, or read advertisements in which a beautiful society leader who is chiefly noted for her baked oysters claims to have stimulated her mentality by smoking Camel cigarettes. Therefore my acidosis is still with me unless the diet books are wrong about what causes irritation.

While on the subject of spinach, I feel obliged to say that a diet expert has recently issued a statement saying that spinach, in his opinion, is not only worthless as a food, but is even harmful. The information cost me nothing; and I pass it on for what it is worth.

We were, however, speaking about fasting. After reading Dr. Hay's impressive diet book, which spoke so highly of the beneficial effects of a thirty-day fast, I was in favor of cleaning up the entire acidosis situation by fasting for thirty days.

Shortly thereafter I read another authoritative book which stated casually that fasting isn't a bad thing if proper care is observed in preparing for and recovering from the fast. If precautions are not taken, the book added, the nervous system may receive a shock from which it will never recover.

This gave me, as the saying goes, pause; for I have contrived to struggle along fairly well even though I do—according to the diet books—have acidosis. It occurred to me at once that acidosis may be preferable to an incurable shock to the nervous system; so I hurriedly ran through all my diet books to see what the rest of them thought about fasting.

A large number of them seemed to have no thoughts on the subject. That is to say, they made no mention of it, which I assume they would have if they had regarded it with either favor or disfavor. One of them seemed to think that a ten-day fast might be beneficial; and another advocated fasting one day out of each month, but no more. Another declared flatly that fasting should under no circumstances be indulged in, inasmuch as it poisons the system.

Because of this divergence of opinion, I decided to do nothing definite about fasting until the diet experts are able to reach an agreement.

Having disposed of fasting to my own satisfaction, I found myself enmeshed in the subject of breakfast. Some of our leading dietitians believe that a person who wishes to be truly healthy should eat no breakfast at all; but when they have delivered themselves of this opinion, they immediately print a large number of breakfast menus. I must confess to being a trifle confused at this singular contradiction; and from time to time I wonder whether the dietitians may not be slightly confused themselves. Probably they are not. Probably their reasons for condemning breakfasts in one breath and recommending them in the next are excellent; but this is only conjecture on my part.

What to eat for breakfast is obviously one of the many baffling problems with which dietitians wrestle. According to some dietitians, there is nothing so nourishing and healthy as an egg. According to others, an egg is too rich for the human frame; and they stubbornly refuse to mention eggs in their diet books.

According to some, a griddle cake is one of the most pernicious foods yet evolved by civilized peoples; but on the other hand one of the most earnest advocates of thirty-day fasts and a breakfastless diet favors a breakfast made up of whole-wheat pancakes, maple syrup, butter, and black coffee.

Another thinks that the best of all possible breakfasts is a plate of vegetable soup.

Still another, who has specialized on the sort of foods to feed people so they may live to be excessively old and overpoweringly healthy, thinks a normal middle-aged person should have, for breakfast, melon, baked sweet potato, an extra-ripe banana with cream, and milk or cocoa. The same expert urges, as a preventive of obesity, a breakfast of melon, peaches, or berries, broiled fish, and a baked potato or a bran muffin.

Some say that coffee and tea are highly injurious. Some say they are only injurious if taken with sugar or cream. Some say they aren't injurious at all, no matter how taken.

Some say cereals are bad, and others say cereals are splendid. Some say you must not eat toast made from white bread; but others strongly recommend toast made from white bread.

Whole-wheat bread or toast, many insist, is the only sort of bread that should be eaten, and it can be eaten with anything at any time. Others say that whole-wheat bread or toast is a starch, and therefore must not—absolutely must *not*—be eaten at the same meal with meat, eggs, fish, or cheese, which are proteins, or with any food containing sugar, or with any acid fruit.

Nearly all dietitians hold out for a light breakfast; but one dietitian whose reputation is world-wide states clearly and emphatically that a frugal breakfast is bad.

In my first fright at the acidosis threat which was held over my head by so many diet books, I hurriedly abandoned the breakfast on which I have subsisted for many years, said breakfast being two eggs, two slices of dry toast, a cup of coffee, and a reasonable helping of any marmalade except quince or apricot. The eggs contained protein, the toast contained starch, and the marmalade contained sugar; and any such mixture, as I have before intimated, does shocking things to your insides—unless a number of dietitians of high standing are sadly in error.

I shifted first to tomato juice and whole-wheat toast. I seemed to be getting along on it all right, when somebody carelessly called my attention to the fact that whole-wheat toast was a starch, whereas tomato juice ranks as acid fruit—a dangerous combination according to doctors who ought to know what they're talking about.

I dropped this in a panic and turned to coddled eggs, bran embellished with milk and honey, and a spot of coffee—a breakfast strongly recommended by a diet expert whose books are regarded with veneration by large numbers of diet enthusiasts. There seemed to be something a little wrong with this breakfast, though I couldn't at the moment put my finger on the trouble. It gave me the unaccustomed feeling of having swallowed a polo ball; and at the risk of inflaming my acidosis, I was obliged to go back to my old original breakfast in order to be comfortable again.

For a time I thought the polo-ball feeling was due to the fact that my breakfast contained an improper number of calories; but a study of the calory theory convinced me that it must have been caused by something else.

The calory theory of diet is, I assume, familiar to all. Roughly speaking, the theory contends that every edible thing contains so many calories or heat units—three figs, 100 calories; one potato, 100 calories; one banana, 75 calories; one half cup beans, 100 calories; seven half walnuts, 100 calories; one egg, 75 calories; one cup skimmed milk, 90 calories; medium serving of meat, 300 calories, and so on.

The normal moderately strenuous person requires about 2,400 calories a day, whereas a coal heaver should have between 4,000 and 5,000 calories, and a heavy sitter only about 1,800 calories. If, therefore, the moderately strenuous person wishes to gain weight, he adds a few hundred calories to his diet. If he wishes to lose weight, he cuts his daily ration to about 1,200 calories.

That is the theory; but some of the modern diet books say the calory theory is all wrong: wrong and dangerous.

They say the calory theory encourages people to eat starches and proteins at the same time—which causes acidosis.

They say it permits the eating of starches, sugar, and acid fruits together—which also causes acidosis.

They point out it is little short of madness to think a coal heaver needs over 4,000 calories a day. They say if this were so, and the coal heaver were fed milk, his daily requirements would be ten quarts, which is enough to make even a rubber-skinned man explode with a loud majority report. They also say if foods are not properly combined, a man can starve to death on 4,000 calories a day and gain weight on 1,200 calories a day; and they may, of course, be right—though I haven't found them so.

I would like to have it borne in mind that I am merely quoting from the books. I have nothing whatever against the calory theory. So far as I know, it is exactly as good a theory as the acidosis theory. I am always happy to hear from readers; but I trust, in this particular case, that those who believe in the calory theory will not write long, indignant letters to show me where I am wrong. The persons to whom they should write their letters are the acidosis theorists. In fact, I may as well state here and now that if I receive vituperative letters from acidosis theorists, I shall forward them to a calory expert without comment; and if a calory theorist undertakes to drag me over the coals in a letter, I shall merely pass the letter to an acidosis expert.

I think I would probably be glad to answer all letters in person if the business of dieting were not so involved. It is so involved that persons who go into it in a serious way have little time for anything else. The most recent diet books, in extolling the advantages of an anti-acidosis diet, say that brain workers find their brains much clearer and their inventiveness greatly improved if they give up all their old habits of eating and consume only such foods as are properly combined and prepared—consume starchy foods only with starchy foods and vegetables; proteins only with other proteins and vegetables.

Authors, they say, would do infinitely more work, and better work, if they would follow this system. I have no doubt that this is true; but in my own case, I am obliged to spend so much time hunting through diet books to find out what I ought to eat, and when to eat it, and what to eat with it, and in tinkering with my vegetable steamer, and in worrying about my acidosis, that I have almost been obliged to stop writing entirely.

Possibly William Shakspere, if he could have been persuaded to cut out all liquors and restrict his foods largely to steamed vegetables and salads, might have written better plays; and then, again, he might have spent so much time steaming his spinach and thinking about his health, to say nothing of arguing with cooks who didn't care to have Shakspere or anybody else tell them how to cook vegetables, that he would have had no time at all in which to write anything.

One might think that such a small and apparently harmless thing as a drink of water would present no problem to experienced dietitians; but one who thought in that manner would be displaying lamentable ignorance.

A few diet experts think the time to drink water is when the prospective drinker thinks he would like a drink of water: when, in short, he feels thirsty. Other dietitians say this is all wrong: one should never drink when he feels thirsty, but only one half hour before meals. Others say nobody can be healthy unless he drinks at least six quarts of water a day; but this belief is derided by equally prominent dietitians, who declare firmly that large amounts of water put an intolerable burden on the heart and other organs and result in serious diseases and death. The ideal state of affairs, they say, is to drink as little water as possible. Some say no water should be drunk during meals, while others are equally positive in saying there is no better time for water-drinking.

At first blush, as the saying goes, the student of diets thinks there is one form of sustenance that has the unqualified approval of all dietitians: to wit, salads. Each and every one of them says "Eat lots of salad"—though none of them is able to dispose of salads in so few words. In that respect the diet books are somewhat similar to those that tell people how to play golf. A book on golf usually needs three chapters to tell a would-be golfer how to place his left hand on the club; and the diet books usually devote three chapters to telling their disciples to eat lots of salad. When, however, one dietitian says "salad," he means his own brand of salad: not salads advocated by other dietitians.

One of my favorite diet authors, for example, says "salads, with plenty of fine first-press olive oil and a little malt vinegar, should form a part of the midday or evening meal."

From other diet authors one learns that vinegar is all right on a salad, whereas olive oil is all wrong. "There is less danger," declares one diet authority, "from the teaspoon of alcohol in a stein of beer than from the teaspoon of oil in salad dressing."

The most modern diet books are inclined to take the opposite viewpoint. Vinegar, they think, is one of the great curses of modern life, whereas olive oil is essential to health. Vinegar on salads or on anything else, they say, must be shunned as though it contained cholera bacilli. Lemon juice must be used in place of vinegar, they declare: the man who refuses it is beyond all human help.

Others say salads should never be eaten if they contain either oil or vinegar, but should be garnished with a dressing of lemon juice and salt. Still others say salt is bad on a salad—very bad. It causes hardening of the arteries and destroys the delicate flavor of lettuce.

There are also those who protest vigorously against lemon juice, which is an acid fruit; for if a salad garnished with lemon juice enters the stomach in company with a piece of toast or a fragment of meat, eggs, fish, or cheese—with a starch or a protein, that is to say—fermentation ensues at once, and the salad eater is about as badly off as though he had inadvertently consumed a toadstool.

Before I browsed among the diet books, I was addicted to salads. Day after day, for years, I had briskly rubbed the bottom of a bowl with garlic, poured into it two large spoonfuls of olive oil, one of claret vinegar, and a teaspoon of salt, stirred it well and then tousled lettuce in it. It had never occurred to me there could be anything harmful in this. No salad dressing will blend properly without salt, to my way of thinking; and as for claret vinegar, I knew from reading Roman history that the Roman soldiers of Julius Cæsar's day marched and fought on a daily ration of red wine vinegar. Now, however, I fear such ingredients. For all I know, Rome may have fallen because the Roman soldier drank vinegar each day. I am full of fears: fuller of them than of salads.

Potatoes are either beneficial or ruinous for one who wishes to live healthfully. Some say one thing and some another.

Rice is either splendid as a food or dreadful. Several books state clearly that nations given to a rice diet have enormous endurance, and that people who live on rice can fight and toil tirelessly, whereas meat eaters fade like wilted flowers over the same tasks.

These statements baffle me. Years ago, when I was in Siberia, two American regiments, the 27th and 31st Infantry, enervated by a tour of duty in the tropical Philippines, set out on a five-hundred-mile march with two Japanese regiments fresh from the rigorous climate of the Hokkaido, the northern island of Japan. The Japanese ate rice; the Americans ate meat. The Americans outmarched the Japanese, and had to wait around, every little while, for the Japanese to catch up. Still, the dietitians, being doctors, ought to know what they are talking about when they arbitrarily announce that rice eaters have more endurance than meat eaters.

Don't eat nuts, some say. Others say nuts must be eaten.

Stick to vegetables, say others, and you'll be free of all ills. On the other hand there are many experts who issue heartfelt warnings against the indiscriminate use of vegetables. A distinguished German dietitian darkly reminds his readers that Cameroon Negroes subsist entirely on vegetables but seldom live to be more than forty years old. Others say that if you renounce meat in favor of vegetables, you will be pure as the driven snow, and will probably live a hundred years unless unexpectedly struck on the head with a club.

A great international diet specialist says firmly that a vegetable diet is unhealthful, dangerous, and irrational. In Germany, he says, he has observed patrons of vegetarian restaurants eating green vegetable soup; then carrots or spinach with potatoes, followed by apple sauce and a helping of nuts and fruits. In his opinion, all of them looked pretty sick; and he considers the diet a breeder of anemia and tuberculosis.

In the year 1604 there was dissatisfaction over the many widely different versions of the Holy Bible. Until then the best of men had, from time to time, tampered with the text to make it fit their own ideas, which were frequently peculiar; and the result had been, to put it mildly, chaotic.

King James I, consequently, called a convocation of forty-six of the leading churchmen, scholars, and educators of England and set them to work preparing an Authorized Version of the Bible. Their work, completed in 1611, was the magnificent version that has since been used by the English-speaking world.

I may, of course, be wrong; but from the enormous number of diet books now in existence, and the apparent eagerness with which each new diet is welcomed, it seems to me that diet and health have become nearly as important as religion to large numbers of people, and far more important than religion to even greater numbers. And if the noisiest of the diet doctors are correct, the welfare of America and future generations depends entirely on following the proper diet.

This being so, I cannot help but think that the Medical Profession is in urgent need of a King James who can persuade the diet doctors to unite on an Authorized Diet for the good of the country.

---

In the light of discoveries made since this chapter was written, I regard two books by Ida Jean Kain, ℞ for Slimming and Get in Shape, as the soundest, sanest, and most effective diet and weight-reducing books ever written. Both were published, 1941 and 1944, by David McKay Co., Philadelphia.

# The Glories of War

*From* RABBLE IN ARMS

. . . W<small>ITH THE MENDING</small> of my shoulder, my lethargy passed, and with its passing came a mounting rage at the troops that deserted us. Our numbers were little more than half those of Burgoyne's army. If this continued, nothing—not all the sturdy optimism of Schuyler; not all of Arnold's daring—could save us from certain and overwhelming defeat.

My brain was a mass of confused thoughts about Nathaniel—selfish thoughts, no doubt. Never, if the British won, I knew, could I bear to face my neighbors in Arundel if I owed my home, perhaps my very life, to a brother's attachment to the mistress of a British general. Nor could Nathaniel live again among the people from whom he had sprung. He might think he could, but he couldn't.

Such thoughts as these were weighing hard on me on an August morning at Stillwater when Doc had taken me to a brook above the Hudson to sop cold water on my still stiff and swollen shoulder. Twelve miles, we were, from the Mohawk, and only twenty from Albany. We had heard rumors—sad rumors—that weakness and timidity were rife among the people on the Mohawk because of the advance of St. Leger's army— that army which, in the dim past, had shouted to us that they'd see us soon at Albany. Yet, in spite of these rumors, or perhaps because of them, a company of militiamen came slouching out of camp, homeward bound— homeward bound, although the British and the Indians were converging on us from two directions.

In the frame of mind I was in, the sight of them was more than I could bear. Shirtless as I was, I got up from beside the brook and went to stand near this straggling company. Doc, protesting at my movements, continued to dab at my shoulder with a cold wet cloth.

If there were officers among the men, there was nothing to distinguish them. They were a slovenly lot, their hair unclubbed and hanging lankly around their ears: their hats tilted on the backs of their heads; their breeches torn and unbuckled; their weskits open over ragged dirty shirts; their coats off and tied over their rumps or around their muskets. The sight of my wound caught their attention, and they looked at me, which was unusual for militia, who, as a rule, loutishly ignore everything near them, barring stealable objects or girls of an age to invite bucolic pleasantries.

"God bless my soul," I said to them, "you're leaving, aren't you?"

One of them leaped in the air, kicked his heels together, and crowed like a rooster. A few laughed. The others stared doltishly.

"Where you boys from?" I asked.

"We're Quoick's milishy from Vanderheiden."

"Listen," I said. "What do you want to leave now for?"

An angry shouting arose from those farthest removed. "Come on! Come on! To hell with him! Git along!"

"Our time's up," one of the nearer men explained. "Our time was up at six o'clock this morning. We could 'a' left two hours ago."

There was a jostling among them. I heard contemptuous snorts. The whole company stirred; the men began to drift away.

"Wait," I said, "let me ask you something. What was it that led you men to enlist in the militia in the first place?"

"For God's sake," one of them cried, "push him out of the road and come ahead!"

Doc Means ceased his labors on my shoulder. "I don't believe that feller knows what's going on, Cap'n Peter," he said in his mild and quavering voice. "I wonder if he ever heard how Jennie McCrae got killed?"

The militiamen stopped in their tracks.

"Look here," I said to them. "I do believe you need to be reminded about Jennie McCrae. I can tell you she was killed, because I was up a tree near where it happened. I'd climbed it to get information so you men from Vanderheiden wouldn't get your skulls split open. I saw her killed. The man that killed her was red, the color of a red fox. He wasn't any bigger than any of you. He and his friends got into an argument over her, so he shot her in the breast. He put the muzzle against her and blew the breast right out of her. Another shot her in the back. In the back! Understand? He shot her in the back when she was lying on the ground. She hadn't done anything to any of 'em. One of the men put his foot on her and pulled off her hair. Understand? He tore it off her! Tore it off!"

I found myself shaking. My hands were trembling. My throat seemed half choked; so that I could scarcely get my breath. I had never thought of myself as a speaker, yet now I found words coming to my mouth without conscious effort—words that faintly eased the indignation that filled me—words that I spoke with all my heart, even though I hardly knew myself what I said.

"Listen to me," I said. "You owe me that much. It was over a year ago that I went in the army to keep the British away from you and your people. So far, by God, we've done it! We starved and sweated and sickened: almost drowned and damned near died a hundred times, in Canada; we built the fleet and we fought it till our ears were split and our eyes jarred loose by the guns; we held back the lousy British at Fort Ann; we chopped and chopped to hold 'em back, till the blood ran from our fingers! For over a year we've fought 'em; and you're safe and your homes are standing; and this morning your mothers put bread in the oven, and your sisters are tying ribbons in their hair and sleeping sound at night—because of what we did: because of what we've endured: because we went into this war to stop the British! To stop the British! What did *you* go into it for?"

Doc seemed to have been waiting for the question. "They went in for twenty dollars," he said promptly.

"Yes, by God!" I said to the militiamen. "I believe he's right! I believe you went in for nothing but to get your twenty-dollar bounty! I'd never have believed it if I hadn't seen you sneaking off home like a pack of yellow dogs, just when the British are getting ready to shoot your mothers in the back and rip off your sisters' scalps the way they did Jennie McCrae's. She was a nice girl! She hadn't done anything to anybody, any more than your sisters have. Twenty dollars you went in for, by God, and you can't see beyond it! Twenty-dollar men! Twenty-dollar men from Vanderheiden, New York! You'll let the British hack us to pieces and steal a nation away from us because you can't tell the difference between twenty dollars and justice—between twenty dollars and freedom—between twenty dollars and liberty! Between twenty dollars and your own country! Yes, you've got twenty dollars, so you're willing to take a chance on having your sisters scalped the way Jennie McCrae was scalped!"

One of the militiamen took a step toward me, gray-faced. "You're a liar!" he said hoarsely.

Doc Means shook his head sadly. "Pore feller!" he said. "He wants to fight, but he ain't going to be able to. His time expired at six o'clock this morning!"

"I'm a liar, am I?" I asked the gray-faced man. "How am I a liar? Two weeks ago we had sixteen hundred militia. Where are they, now that we need 'em? Gone home! Where are you going? You're going home! You're leaving us when we're lost if we don't have men! Do you know what'll happen to us if you do what not even a rat would do? Even a rat'll fight for his home! If you and all these other militia regiments run away, the British'll catch us between two fires—between St. Leger and Burgoyne—and wipe us out—starve us out—club us to death—rip off our scalps! But don't forget this: when they've got rid of us, then, by God, they'll tend to you! They'll hunt you down in the fields and woods! You'll be like woodchucks, chattering under walls! Go home, and you're doomed! Go home, and you're wrecked! Go home, and you've thrown away a nation because you can't see beyond twenty dollars!"

"Stop talking," Doc said. "You're bleeding again."

I pushed him away and shook my fist at the faces before me. The face of the gray man had, strangely, become a flaming scarlet. I saw, with a faint surprise, that all these militiamen were crimson-faced and breathing heavily, as though they had run far. "And let me tell you this," I added—somewhat thickly, I fear, since my shoulder had begun to throb and ache once more. "Nothing—nobody, could penetrate one inch into this country if you men would turn out and stay turned out! If our exertions equaled our abilities, this war'd end in one month's time! You're going home; but if you'd stay here where you belonged, we'd make a human net and a human noose for the men that killed Jennie McCrae. There'd never be a redcoat get down the Hudson or back to Canada! They'd die right here! Never a foot of our land would any Britisher ever get unless he threw in his lot with ours. There's no foreign force in the whole damned world strong enough to subdue America unless the corruption and the timidity of her own people first force her to her ruin."

I glared at the militiamen and they stared back at me. Doc caught me by the arm. "You'll stop your talking," he said shrilly, "or the future of America won't be of no interest to you. None whatever!"

He dragged me toward the brook, and as he did, I heard one of the militiamen say, "Come on! Come on out of here!" I looked back at them. A dozen, perhaps, had set off down the road, toward Albany, but the bulk of the company still stood there.

One of them moved slowly in the direction from which they had come so short a time before. Another followed him, and another. The others milled and muttered. Then, one by one, they all shuffled off after the first two—back toward Stillwater.

We watched them go. A tightness went out of my muscles. Doc cleared his throat and laughed and cleared his throat again. As if to apologize for this unprecedented throat-clearing he said faintly, "Kind of irritates my membranes, hearing all them arguments!"

. . . Doc had no sooner resumed work on my shoulder than there was a rustling in the brush below the rim of the high bank on which we stood. A man clambered up and stood staring at us. It was young Varick, one of General Schuyler's aides. He seemed almost excited. "By George," he said, "they went back! They went back to camp!"

He eyed me curiously; then added, "The general wants to speak to you. He's down here. You better come right down."

I got up heavily. "So he heard me, did he? I wouldn't have used profanity if I'd known he was down there. Is he mad?"

Varick laughed and turned away.

"I'll put on my shirt," I said.

"Come the way you are," Varick told me.

Doc picked up my shirt and coat and we followed Varick down the steep bank. At its foot was a knot of officers. I recognized Schuyler's tall figure. On the ground near him sat Arnold, drawing lines and figures on a piece of cartridge paper. Looking over Arnold's shoulder was a man in a foreign uniform, a light blue one. He was about Arnold's height; and, like Arnold, he had a round, swarthy, merry face. I knew him to be Kosciusko, an engineer officer from Poland: a great hand to lay out fortifications and trenches.

As I came up, Schuyler puckered his lips a little, and his long nose seemed to move inquiringly. When Doc, standing close behind me, again dabbed at my wound with his wet cloth, Schuyler snorted and growled. Ill at ease, I looked at Arnold, who opened his mouth at me in a wide and soundless laugh.

"So it was you, was it?" Schuyler asked. "Where did you learn such talk as that?"

"On shipboard," I said. "If seamen behave the way these militiamen do, it's a sea captain's duty to tell 'em a few things, and take a capstan bar to 'em if they don't like it." Somewhat weakly I added, "Besides, I wasn't feeling good this morning on account of my shoulder."

"Young man," Schuyler said sternly, "don't tell me a sea captain's duty! I was a sea captain when you weren't knee-high to a duck. What I asked you was where you picked up those sentiments—those sentiments about our exertions equaling our abilities, and all the rest of it."

"Sir," I said, "I didn't pick 'em up anywhere. I just spoke in anger."

"In anger, eh?" Schuyler said. "Well, now that your anger's passed, can you remember what it was you said?"

"I recall being a little sharp with 'em," I admitted, "but I don't recollect the words I used."

"I do," Doc Means said suddenly. He pressed his wet cloth against my back and held it there. "I recollect everything he said, General, and if I hadn't been afraid of inflaming this shoulder of his, I might have told him a few more things to say."

Schuyler stared arrogantly at Doc; then came around behind me. Arnold and Kosciusko joined him.

"He's got treat vairy prooty," Kosciusko said. "Thass vairy jonteel: vairy nice wound."

"Yes," Doc agreed, "that's a handsome hole."

"How is he?" Schuyler asked Doc. "Is he fit to travel?"

"Well," Doc said, "if he don't overdo it and don't go near no doctors, and don't excite himself over militia, he ought to be all right."

I was irritated by their attitude. They might have been examining a shoat. "There isn't a thing the matter with me," I said. "I can do anything that doesn't require me to use that arm."

I heard Arnold's harsh voice say, "In some cases, General, rest can be more irritating than action, and I believe this is one of 'em."

The three of them moved around in front of me again. "I'm taking you at your word," Schuyler said. "I want you to start south the first thing tomorrow morning. I want you to tell the story of Jennie McCrae to the people that don't seem to understand this war. Varick, where's that map?"

He took the map his aide gave him. "Connecticut's promised us men," he said to me. "They promised 'em three weeks ago. Where are they? Where are the Rhode Island regiments? God knows! We've had our share of Massachusetts men, but they go home! They go home!" He ran his finger down the map. "Go there and there and there! Cross over into Massachusetts and work down into Connecticut—Peekskill, Hartford, New Haven, Providence, Taunton—make a circle that ends at Bennington. Understand? When you reach Bennington, you can stop talking and come back here.

"You ought to take a month to it. A month's not too long. No: a month's not long enough. You'll have to take five weeks. You'll have a horse. You can take your friend, here, and he can have a horse too. Stop at every settlement. Stop at every village. Call the people together. Tell 'em the story of Jennie McCrae. Tell 'em that if we don't get men, the same thing'll happen to their womenfolks that happened to Jennie McCrae. Tell 'em what you told that militia company."

He put his hands behind his back and seemed to brace himself more firmly. "You've probably heard the stories they're telling about me.

They've gone all over the country. You'll have to take those stories into account. You'll have to keep my name out of it. When you ask for men, tell 'em they'll be led by General Arnold. Is that clear?" His voice was as calm and unruffled as though he discussed the possibility of rain. He was a great man—a great patriot, unselfish and generous.

I said everything was clear.

"Travel fast," Schuyler said. "We've got to have men. We've got four thousand: they've got double that. Theirs are old soldiers: ours aren't. Travel fast and get men. If we can have men, they can't get past us. I'll send other men by other routes to do the same thing you'll be doing. If we don't get men—if we don't get men——"

Arnold put in a cheerful word. "Let 'em draw their own conclusions as to what'll happen if we don't get men!"

"Ha, ha!" Kosciusko said. "I theenk that is vairy well! Vairy well hindeed! The pipple who are tol' about thees dead lady will be vairy motch hannoy! I, too, am 'orribly hannoy about thees dead lady. You weel see: they weel come hout, vairy motch hangry."

"It's high time they got angry!" Arnold said. "High time!"

Schuyler turned to Varick. "You'll have to find a uniform for Captain Merrill somewhere. God knows where you'll find such a thing, my boy, but I want it found. We'll have to make him look like a soldier somehow. We can't send him on such an errand looking like a scarecrow."

"Let me attend to it, General," Arnold said. "You've got enough on your mind. I think I can find horses and a uniform for Captain Merrill, and I'd like a word with him before he goes."

When Schuyler nodded, Arnold said to me carelessly, "Be at my quarters at eight o'clock tonight, and wait there till I come."

Doc and I climbed back to the high land above the river, leaving Schuyler, Arnold, and Kosciusko studying the lines on the square of cartridge paper.

As we went, Doc shook his head. "Now what would any feller want to be a general for?" he asked in puzzled tones. "It looks to me like it ain't much different from being tied to a runaway horse, except that you don't get so much exercise out of it."

Doc's thoughts were of no account to me. I could think of nothing except that on top of all that had happened to me, I was now to be sent ignominiously off for five long weeks on duties that any preacher or any wordy lawyer could perform—off to places where I could be of no more help to Nathaniel, if he needed me, than a mouse would be—where Ellen Phipps, now only twenty miles away within the British lines, would be as distant as the stars.

. . . It was ten o'clock that night before Arnold came back to the log house in which he had his headquarters, and where Doc and I waited on a bench outside. We thought he had forgotten about us, for he popped into the cabin without giving us so much as a glance, and we heard him telling his aide to do this and do that. The aide came hurrying out; and a little later Arnold's Negro servant appeared in the doorway and called us in. We found the general with his coat off, writing at his little field desk. "Here's your orders," he said, without looking up. "Your uniform's over there in the corner. It's a plain blue one. If it's too small, you can have it made larger in the first town you come to. My servant's got your horses. They're in the barn with mine. Sleep there tonight and be on your way by sun-up tomorrow."

He pushed his field desk from him and hooked his feet around the legs of his camp stool. In the light of the two candles before him, his swarthy face looked lumpy and angry.

"Look here," he said, "when Schuyler ordered you out to spread the story of Jennie McCrae this morning, you had your brother on your mind, didn't you?"

"Yes," I admitted, "I did."

"I thought so. Well, we've all got something on our minds in addition to this war. Even a militiaman spends a lot of time worrying for fear his family'll starve to death if he doesn't go home. It's hard for him to remember that they'll starve to death just as quick—maybe quicker—if the British beat us. Most people don't look very far ahead."

"Not more'n two inches," Doc said gently.

I said nothing.

Arnold eyed me morosely. "If you're tempted to start thinking about your own troubles," he went on, "you might give a moment's thought to Schuyler. He's sacrificed everything to hold this army together. He's got it in a position where, if we can get more men, we can turn on Burgoyne and hold him back. He's been rewarded by being called a coward and a traitor. Tonight his officers, even, turned on him."

"Turned on him?" I asked, unable to believe my ears. "How could they turn on him?"

"I'll tell you how," Arnold said. "We had word today that St. Leger's army has Fort Stanwix surrounded. If that fort falls, the whole Mohawk Valley falls. The whole Mohawk Valley'll turn Tory to save itself from being butchered. If the Mohawk Valley turns Tory, all of New York'll turn Tory; and if that happens, we're whipped. So there's no way out of it: we've got to drive St. Leger back from Fort Stanwix. You see that, I trust."

"Certainly I see it."

"Our brigadier generals don't see it," Arnold said. "Tonight Schuyler asked for a brigadier general to lead a relief column against St. Leger. Not one offered himself. Not one! They sat there like bumps on a log."

"Didn't they have anything to say?"

"Yes," Arnold said slowly, "they did. One of 'em, back in a dark corner, said, 'He means to weaken the army.' Schuyler heard him. Schuyler heard him say it. After all that Schuyler's done, he heard himself called a traitor by his own officers."

"What did he do?"

"Nothing. He can't let his personal affairs interfere with what's got to be done."

"And what about Fort Stanwix?" I asked.

"Oh," Arnold said, "I was sent up here to make myself useful, so I volunteered to march to its relief. I'll take a brigade and start tomorrow." His glance was satirical. "We all have our troubles, you see. I just had word from Congress that they'd voted on whether to restore me to my proper rank or not. They voted not to do it. Yes, they voted not to do it. And in spite of all Schuyler's done for their safety, they voted to call him down to Philadelphia to face a court-martial. He'll be relieved of his command to sit in a hot room in Philadelphia trying to prove he *isn't* a traitor—trying to satisfy a lot of politicians that he *hasn't* played the coward."

I found myself sweating with rage. "Who'll take his place?"

Arnold seemed not to hear. "I mention these things to you," he said, "because you've got your work cut out for you, and because injustices seem to improve your vocabulary. If you're going to get men for us in New England, you've got to forget your personal troubles. You've got to be in a rage over the injustice and the pettiness that's choking this country to death!" He jumped up suddenly and thrust his swarthy face close to mine. "You've got to forget everything but our needs! Coax 'em! Shout at 'em! Fight 'em! Hammer 'em! Curse 'em! Get men, and more men, and more men! By God, they've got to come out! They've got to fight! They've got to stand a few of the things we've stood! They can't stay back there, rotting in their feather beds, chewing and spitting and stuffing themselves with food while we're chased and shot at like a lot of rats! God damn it, they can't! They can't!"

He sat down as suddenly as he had risen. My throat was dry and I was shaking all over.

"Can you do that?" Arnold asked quietly. "Can you forget your brother and do that?"

"Yes," I said. The word almost choked me.

Arnold nodded. "Then there's nothing more to be said, except this: I haven't recommended you for promotion because if you're promoted you'll have to spend most of your time sitting in corners and writing letters asking for things that don't exist and explaining something you didn't do to people who won't believe you, no matter what you write. I want you to stay a captain, like Nason, until we have less need for good scouts. Understand?"

When I said I did, he glowered at me. "You've been a good officer, and don't think I'm not appreciative. Sometime I may be able to show you that I am."

With that, abruptly, he seemed to become impatient and irascible. Complaining bitterly of the letters he must write, he rose and almost pushed us from his cabin, as though he had never wanted to see us in the beginning and hoped never to see us again.

§

God knows how our horses had escaped from the commissaries who supplied us with horse meat in place of beef; for they were certainly on the verge of death from old age. Nonetheless, they carried us, which was something, even though our legs were sore from kicking them with spurless heels.

We plodded south to Albany and through the neat towns along the Hudson: then crossed the river to the road that carried us across the lower corner of Massachusetts and over the rolling hills of Connecticut. After we had been two days at Hartford, talking and haranguing continually, as we did everywhere, we went off to the eastward into northern Connecticut and Rhode Island, then swung up into Massachusetts and made a wide curve to the northward through Attleboro, Framingham, Fitchburg, and Northfield—a curve that seemed even more endless than our trip to the westward with the Indians.

I found it difficult, at first, to bring myself to speak earnestly to little groups of people. I felt like a pretentious, play-acting fool, mouthing the story of Jennie McCrae a dozen times a day. I grew hoarse, begging these silent farmers to come to their country's aid. Every phrase that fell from my lips, I felt, was stale and flat: as unconvincing as an advertisement of a sale of calicoes.

Doc shook his head. "You better get mad," he said. "You're thinking about yourself and how you look in that nice blue uniform of yours, and you ain't making no effort to get your dander up! You can't get 'em mad if you ain't mad yourself. Get aggravated at something!"

It occurred to me, then, to fix my attention on the most doltish of the men who listened: to lash myself into a fury over his ignorance and unconcern: to have him in mind when I threatened the lot of them with mutilation and death unless they came out against Burgoyne. The first time I did it, a man was waiting for us when we unhitched our horses. It was the dolt, and he had a musket over his shoulder.

When we set off, he followed us. Doc frowned at him. "Where you going?"

"Agin Burgine," the man said.

"We're going east," Doc said. "Burgoyne's over there." He pointed to the westward. The dolt hung his mouth open so a robin might have nested in it. We rode away, and when we looked back, the man was plodding off in the opposite direction.

Those to whom I talked had little to say, after the manner of New Englanders, and it was hard to tell what effect my appeals had on them. The men, at times, seemed uncomfortable, staring at each other from the corners of their eyes. The older women listened to me with lips pressed tight together and their shoulders drawn up. I couldn't be sure whether they disapproved of me, or of Burgoyne and his Indians, or of the whole war. Occasionally, when I told how the Indian had put his foot on Jennie's shoulder and torn off her scalp, a child would set up a frightened squalling, and there would be a deal of throat-clearing and foot-shuffling from the grown-ups. But on the whole, we seemed to be accomplishing nothing.

Others, we learned, had been sent by Schuyler into various sections of New England to tell the story of Jennie McCrae. I hoped they were making more impression on their audiences than was I. We were wasting our time, I said to myself over and over: wasting time that might have been spent in doing something—though God knew what—for Nathaniel.

But Schuyler had said to take five weeks, and so we took five weeks to it. We rode and talked and rode and talked. News reached us—news that made crowds turn out when they heard we were coming.

The news of Bennington was the first we heard. Burgoyne, still at Fort Edward, had sent a thousand Germans and a few Indians to the eastward, to capture horses and provisions that our people had collected at Bennington. John Stark with militia from New Hampshire and Vermont had surrounded both the slow-moving Germans and the Indians with them and had either killed or captured every mother's son of them.

The second piece of news had to do with Arnold. He had set out to relieve Fort Stanwix accompanied by a brigade of Massachusetts troops. By a trick he had led St. Leger's troops and Indians to think his force was enormous; and because of this, St. Leger and all his men had turned and raced precipitately back to Canada. Thus Arnold had not only relieved Fort Stanwix, but had robbed Burgoyne of one of the weapons with which he had planned to stab us in the heart.

The third piece of news was that Congress had removed General Schuyler from the command of the Northern Army and replaced him by General Gates. From the jubilation with which this news was received in New England, Schuyler might have been a Nero and Gates a Cæsar; but my recollection of Gates, fussing among his disordered papers at Ticonderoga like a hen scratching for grubs in a barnyard, set me to ruminating apprehensively on the monstrous ignorance of mankind.

And then, as the heat of August gave way to the clear days and the frosty nights of September, the countryside seemed to take on new life. We became conscious of men on the roads—not the usual farmers walking to town: not idlers killing time; but men off on serious business: men moving perpetually to the westward: men with muskets on their shoulders, trudging along toward some far destination. They had water flasks in the pockets of their weskits: blankets over their shoulders: little sacks of corn meal tied to their belts. When we shouted at them to know where they were going, they invariably answered, "Agin Burgine." They said it stolidly, as if going against Burgoyne was something that had to be done.

They traveled in groups, or singly, or in twos and threes. We saw them meeting and talking, and continuing onward together. Once, watching six countrymen shamble past a farmhouse, their muskets held carelessly, as if they were off on a rabbit hunt, we saw a boy burst from the farmhouse carrying a musket twice as long as himself—a boy with enough freckles to cover a topsail. An old green overcoat was tied around his waist by the arms. A woman stood in the farmhouse door and watched him go.

He ran along behind the six shamblers, worrying a tin whistle from his pocket. His musket troubled him, but he clutched it under his arm; and on his whistle he tootled a jig tune that pierced the ears like a knife. Yet it had a swing to it. One of the six men took the boy's musket. The tune grew even shriller, almost like a squirrel screaming in melodious agony. The six men got themselves into a sort of line, shouldered their muskets, and went trudging to the westward a little faster, laughing shamed bucolic guffaws at their sudden military air.

Whenever we found ourselves on a straight road, in daylight hours, we were sure to see a man or two, or a handful of men, always going west.

As we went farther west ourselves, these handfuls became larger. The travelers flowed together and made groups that imperceptibly swelled in size, as a trickle of water down a mountainside grows somehow into a brook.

When we rode at night, eager to be back with our friends again, we saw fires in the fields, with men asleep around them. In villages we began to encounter companies drilling. The groups along the roads, even, halted occasionally to drill. The sound of drums, too, struck against our ears with increasing frequency—solitary drums at first: then two or three drums together at the head of a company: then drums and fifes.

We began to have the feeling that the whole country was on the move, drifting to the westward, toward the Hudson, "agin Burgine."

When we reached Bennington, Schuyler had said, our work would be done and we could come back; so it was an unutterable relief, on the thirty-fifth day of our travels, when we rode into that hilly little town.

It was not, however, a relief that lasted long; for we were conscious at once of women talking in farmyards, standing on doorsteps, hanging from their windows, talking and talking, and staring toward the westward.

When we stopped to ask the reason for all this talking and staring, they claimed to have heard there had been a battle, though they were unable to say where they had heard the news, or how. Seemingly the rumor had sprung up in the night, like a toadstool. Vague as the rumor was, it led us to urge our weary horses onward with what speed we could.

"It's what I've been afraid of!" I said to Doc. "I've been afraid there'd be a battle, and that Nathaniel might be taken prisoner while I was away. For God's sake, try to get some speed out of that nag of yours."

"Listen," Doc said, "this nag has carried me nigh onto four hundred miles and ain't showed no speed yet. Neither has yours, so what's the use of talking like that? If there's been a battle, it's all over! Half the trouble in this world comes from trying to figure how to change things that can't be changed, on account of having happened."

Fret and fume as I would, I could make Doc go no faster, and it was not until the twenty-second day of September that we came back again to the Hudson and saw once more the rolling fields above Stillwater, and to the north the misty Heights of Saratoga. We crossed the river on a clumsy scow into an atmosphere as altered, since we had left Stillwater in August, as the leaves of the trees had been altered by September frosts.

In place of the surly, ragged, unshaven men we had seen a month before, straggling furtively away in little groups and companies, we now saw, moving blithely along the river road, as if bound for a fair, a thin unending stream of men afoot, messengers a-horseback, officers in blue uniforms, farmers driving herds of cows, army teamsters bawling flatly in the ears of lethargic oxen. Here and there the stream split to flow around ammunition carts and supply wagons.

"Look at that!" Doc said, when we came up from the ferry and walked our horses into Stillwater. "Look at that! They got shoes, all of 'em! Every last one of 'em's got on shoes with soles!"

It was true. Not a man was barefoot. Their breeches were homespun, but without rents or holes. Their hair was combed and tied. They had a healthy and well-fed appearance; and what was most astonishing, there was nothing of weariness or discouragement about them.

Their faces were tanned and cleanly shaven: they were alert, as men in a city are alert, moving about their businesses. They were friendly, too, as if they owned something in common. It was the same sort of friendliness I had often seen among American seamen in a foreign port.

We had an even greater surprise when we reached Bemis's Tavern on the river road. The river road here was blocked by entrenchments extending from the cliff to the river, and we were obliged to turn up the slope to our left and make our way to the heights above Bemis's Tavern. It was on that high land that Doc had washed the wound in my shoulder (a hurt now entirely healed) on the day when Schuyler had heard me speaking harshly to the militia.

All those heights, since we had left them, had become a sort of great fort. They were rimmed with earthworks in which were bastions and redoubts, with cannon in the embrasures. Enclosed by the earthworks was a city of tents and board shelters grouped around a parade ground; and on the parade ground was a regiment of Continentals, white belts crossed on their chests, drilling as smartly as any soldier could desire, while militia companies, profiting by the example of the smarter Continentals, went through evolutions of their own.

These fortifications, I knew, must be the ones that Arnold and Kosciusko had been laying out the day before I left; and I saw at a glance that they were good ones, for they overlooked the lowland and blocked the heights, so that an enemy, striving to move south on either the upper or the lower road, would have the devil's own time doing it.

Seeing a young officer hard at work directing incoming militiamen where to go, I drew rein beside him and asked whether General Arnold was around. The young officer stared at me in high good humor. "*Is* he!" he exclaimed delightedly. "Is he *around!*" Words seemed to fail him.

He was a lieutenant, and I gave him a cold look, at which he hastily told me to go straight up the road I was on: then to take the road to the north.

"You'll see his hut on the left," he said, "just after you get beyond the fortifications."

We passed through a series of clearings in the forest that covered most of that high land, and located Arnold's headquarters in a log cabin near a larger house—a cabin little larger than a dog kennel. I gave my horse to

Doc to hold and explained myself to a sentry. The voice that answered my knock, to my surprise, was Varick's. I went in to find him copying letters in a book.

"Good!" he said, when he looked up and saw me. "Good! I'm glad you're back! Your friends have been pestering the life out of me to know when to expect you."

I was stabbed by a score of sudden fears—fears for Nathaniel; for Ellen. "I'll join them," I said, "as soon as I get a receipt for these horses. I want to get rid of 'em before they drop dead on my hands. We heard there'd been a battle. I hope none of my friends were hurt."

Varick looked at me curiously. "Is that all you've heard? That there's been a battle?"

I nodded.

"You've got a lot to learn." Then he added, "Since General Schuyler was called down, Livingston and I have the honor to be helping General Arnold. Livingston's his aide, and I do what I can." Varick spoke feelingly. "General Arnold has been a true friend to General Schuyler, and it's a privilege to be associated with him."

This was high praise; for like Schuyler, Varick was a man of distinction and breeding, as was Livingston, who later became a judge in the Supreme Court of the United States.

When Varick had written the receipt, he pushed back his stool and looked me over appraisingly. "General Arnold's gone out to take a look at the British lines," he said. "He'll want to see you tonight. How did you find things to the eastward? Can we count on more men?"

"They're pouring out," I told him. "They're moving up by the thousands. Who won the battle?"

Varick went to the door and looked out at Doc and the horses. When he came back he said, "Nobody won it, but the British *would* have won it if it hadn't been for General Arnold. Make no mistake about that! As it is, we're just where we were before the battle, except that the place where we fought stinks with dead bodies. It was the devil of a fight! Don't think it wasn't! And if it hadn't been for General Arnold, the British army'd be in Albany right this minute."

His voice sounded bitter—not at all as it should have sounded after such a feat.

"I'm certainly glad to hear it," I said. "Congress can't refuse to give General Arnold his proper rank after he's done a thing like that."

"I wouldn't be too sure of that," Varick said. "They won't have to do anything about it if they don't know he was in the battle."

"I don't believe I know what you mean."

Varick snorted. "I'm not surprised you don't. I'll tell you what happened. Last Friday morning, the 19th, your friend Nason and his scouts came running in to say the British had started for us. General Gates wanted to sit here and wait: sit behind the entrenchments while the British brought up their artillery without hindrance. Why, they'd have blown us to bits!

"General Arnold went to Gates and begged him and begged him to send men to attack the British before they could get their cannon out of the woods. Arnold said we could beat 'em in the woods, but not if we waited for them to take their time and attack us where they pleased. He said we didn't have enough men to fight the British way: we'd got to fight our own way. He kept at Gates for two hours before Gates gave in. Even then Gates wouldn't let Arnold have as many men as he needed: as many men as he asked for."

Varick's voice rose. "If Gates had given him the men he asked for, we'd have run the British off the top of Freeman's Farm right then and there! We'd have pitchforked 'em into the Hudson River, lock, stock, and barrel. That would have been the end of Mr. Burgoyne, Esquire!"

I felt myself growing hot under the collar. "Why didn't Gates do it? Why didn't he?"

"Why?" Varick asked slowly. "Why, because he's an old gray rat. A timid, scuttling, old gray rat!" He eyed me defiantly. Finding I made no objections to his choice of words, he leaned forward eagerly. "Look! Arnold took what he could get—Morgan's and Dearborn's riflemen and Learned's brigade and some New York troops: he took 'em through the woods and met the British at Freeman's Farm, a mile from here. He hit the British so hard you could hear it all the way to Albany! Nobody else could have done what he did! He pulled those men of ours along behind him as if he'd been a hurricane! He pulled 'em and drove 'em and lashed 'em and dragged 'em. He slammed 'em against the British till the British had the blind staggers. No troops in the world ever fought better than our men fought for Arnold! Why, the British brought up all their reinforcements, trying to get through. Arnold fought 'em for five hours—fought 'em till dark—without getting one damned bit of help from that old gray rat Gates, and he held the British right where they started from! He damned near had 'em on the run! I tell you there was never a hotter fight than that one!"

"But look here," I said. "What was it you meant by saying they wouldn't have to give Arnold his proper rank if they didn't know he was in the battle!"

"I'll tell you what I meant," Varick said in a low voice. "Arnold can't get his proper rank unless Congress gives it to him. What Congress learns about the battle, they learn from the report sent to 'em by Gates—by Gates and his aide Wilkinson." He cursed in a way that surprised me; for Varick was a gentleman.

Then he said, "Gates's report to Congress didn't mention Arnold. Without Arnold we couldn't have won, but Gates gave him no credit. According to Gates, there wasn't any Arnold in the battle. According to Gates and Wilkinson, Arnold wasn't on the field! Congress will never know, officially, that Arnold won the battle of Freeman's Farm!"

"That's not possible!" I said. "Men don't do things like that."

"Don't they?" Varick asked. "You don't know Gates and Wilkinson! They're politicians! How do you suppose Gates got himself put in command of this army? He got himself put in command of this army by making Congress believe the troops wouldn't fight under anyone but himself!

"He persuaded Congress to take out Schuyler—damn his dirty little gray soul to hell! How do you suppose he's going to hold his command if it's Arnold that wins battles: if it's Arnold the troops want to fight under: if it's Arnold that stops the British: if it's Arnold that saves this country from ruin! Gates can't allow it! He won't have it! He won't let Arnold's name be mentioned in dispatches! He won't admit Arnold's alive, even! It's got to be Gates that wins battles! Gates that thinks of what to do! Gates, the damned gray rat!"

"Wait a minute," I said. "Where was Gates during the battle?"

"In his headquarters," Varick said. "He was in his headquarters!"

"He was in his headquarters?" I repeated heavily.

My mind seemed to halt at that picture of Gates, stooped and near-sighted and sly-eyed, squatting in a dark room while Arnold led and lashed and dragged his ragged, hungry troops, smashing the advance of those glittering, scarlet columns.

Varick and I stared at each other like two blockheads. I tried to think of something to say and couldn't. For the thousandth time within the year, I could only have confused thoughts—a baffled wonderment as to why I should remain in such an army when it contained men like Gates and Wilkinson, Easton and Brown, Hazen and Bedel—men who would sacrifice the welfare of their own country—the comfort and the lives of their fellows—to their own warped ambitions. It angered me to think that I must live in mental torture over Nathaniel's fate, when Nathaniel's motives were more worthy than those that filled the incomprehensible minds of folk accepted as our leaders.

I felt a bitter resentment that my fellow countrymen should so persistently bow down to mediocrity: that small men should pursue their devious ways unhindered, and great men be discredited and reviled. I thought, vaguely, that if only I could emerge alive from what lay before us: if only I could find some way to save Nathaniel—to keep his name clean—if only I could do that, wars and armies and Congresses, for all of me, could go to hell, where they belonged.

Yet, as these things struggled in my mind, I suddenly seemed to catch the faint scent of oak chips and marsh mud: to hear the screaming of mackerel gulls in swift flight above our shipyards in Arundel: to see our workmen, on an autumn evening, stumbling up the slope to drink from the pail beside our well and then go safely off to their suppers. Strangely, too, there flashed into my mind the freckled boy who had run from the farmhouse to join that shambling stream that flowed and flowed "agin Burgine": the face of the woman who had come to the farmhouse door and watched him go. . . .

I felt a faint, unpleasant stirring of something I can only call responsibility, and dimly sensed that no matter what others might be, I was, through no act or wish of my own, a part of the land and the people: an unalterable part of the land and the people. I had an obscure realization that the land and the people were stronger in me than love or hate or fear or aversion to discomfort—that such poor fools as I were doomed to endure war perpetually, just as clouds are perpetually created to shed fertility on a little square of earth, and then perish.

"He was in his quarters!" I murmured again. I couldn't comprehend it. "Why did he stay there? Why didn't he——"

"God knows!" Varick said. "Why did he act like a blackguard when he took command of this army? When Gates arrived here, General Schuyler, in spite of the mistreatment he'd received, offered him help and hospitality; and do you know what Gates did? He wouldn't even do Schuyler the courtesy to invite him to a council of war. Why? Why? There's no way of telling! There's no way of accounting for the acts of a man like that!"

He threw up his hands in a gesture of disgust, made a rasping sound in his throat, as if to clear it of Gates's very name; then said hopelessly: "It's no use talking about it. Arnold's a true friend to Schuyler, and a great leader. Gates is neither, but he's in command and he can wreck all of us if he sees fit. Talk won't change things!"

I thought best to take this as a hint. "Sir," I said, "do you know where my friends are camped?"

He laughed. "I do indeed! They're camped on the slope of the next ravine, where they can be convenient to the British pickets."

I wondered why he laughed.

We left our horses tied to the fence behind Arnold's headquarters and followed the road to the north. The rolling country on both sides of the road was forested with hardwood groves and stands of pine; and as Doc Means said, there were no more signs of British in the neighborhood than of buffaloes. For that matter, once we were out of sight of Arnold's head-quarters and a single near-by farmhouse, there were no signs of anything. There were no tents, no sentries, no pickets, no passing on the road. We could not see the Hudson, even; and our own camp with its surrounding fortifications was entirely concealed behind us.

It was when the road dipped into a sharp ravine that we heard something strange. At first it seemed to be the hoarse growling of an animal, followed by the yapping of other smaller animals. "By Grapes!" Doc said. "If I was in any civilized section, I'd say that was some kind of a den of bears; but being off here in the woods this way, I shouldn't wonder if Cap Huff had something to do with it, though that growling certainly don't sound like none of my acquaintances."

We pushed down the ravine. The growling became a human voice struggling with passages from the song "Yankee Doodle." The accompanying yapping proved to be other humans, demonstrating, from time to time, the proper rendition of that same song. Then we heard Cap Huff bawling at the top of his lungs.

"No!" he was saying. "No! How in God's name you ever expect to get to be an American if you keep saying 'Shdug'! It's 'Stuck'! Ess, tee, yew, uck, Stuck! 'Stuck a feather in his cap and called it macaroni!' Come on, now! Get it right this time, or you don't hold Grettle tonight!"

We came into a cleared space on the side of the ravine. A lean-to, made of fir branches, faced the north, and on the low bunks within it sat or lay Tom Bickford, Joseph Phipps, and two Indians who seemed to be almost disguised because of the garish red-and-white caps they wore—the only means by which our Indians could be distinguished from those who fought with the British. One was Natanis, and the other Lewis Vincent, that friend of Verrieul's who had helped us escape from the Sacs and Foxes.

Before them stood Cap Huff, as red-faced and sweaty as ever, in close communion with an odd-looking youth who had yellow hair, broad hips, and a habit of standing with such rigidity that he tilted backward. Thus his stomach was thrust forward and he appeared to be fat, which he was not. He had on the fragments of a pair of once-white breeches, a green coat from which the sleeves and tails had been removed, and the remnants of a pair of dragoon's boots.

When Cap saw us he seized the strange-looking youth by the front of his sleeveless green coat and shook him violently. "Hey!" he bawled in deafening tones. "Nix more sing. Veer drink! Brink drink!" He stared earnestly and anxiously into the young man's eyes. The young man nodded solemnly, and with a groan of relief Cap joined the others in greeting us.

"Gosh," Cap cried, "we thought you was going to miss all the fun, Cap'n Peter! You too, old Catamount!" He slapped Doc affectionately, then contorted his face horribly, jerking both his thumb and his head toward the strange youth, who was fumbling beneath the spruce-tips of one of the bed places.

"What you think of *him*, hey?" he whispered hoarsely. "He's one of them Hessians you've heard about. Name of Konrad! We ain't making no effort to memorize his last name—not till he learns some English so's we can speak his name in a translated form."

"Where'd you get him?" I asked.

"Got him in the battle," Cap said. "I thought I captured him, but he claims he deserted to us on account of liking my looks. He says he's going to be an American from now on, just like me, and I guess we ain't going to be able to do nothing to stop him!"

He sighed and muttered something about Konrad being a greater responsibility than a sick hound.

"What was the battle like?" I asked him.

"About the same as any battle," Cap said indifferently. "Of course, fighting in the woods don't present the opportunities that city fighting does, but I picked up this Konrad, and four Hessian canteens full of English rum, and a gold gorget. I might 'a' done worse. The truth is, I took this Konrad to carry those canteens. That's what he's doing now: digging up one of the canteens. He tends to our needs, when we got any. He'd be kind of a funny feller if he wasn't so much of a nuisance to talk to. You have to holler at him so loud it gives you a headache."

Cap might have been a boy with a new puppy, so wrapped up was he in Konrad. "Think up something for him to do," he urged me proudly. "He's the helpfullest thing ever you see! Cooks, sews, sings hymns, mends stockings, knits, cleans muskets, makes shoes, and waits on table. I dunno what they want to put fellers like that in an army for! You can get soldiers anywhere, but it's a terrible hard thing to get a waiter that won't spill pork drippings down your neck and bring you hoss meat when you order beef. Now you take those thirty-five hundred Hessians with Burgoyne—there's thirty-five hundred waiters just ruined for no reason at all."

"Where's Nason?" I asked.

"Out with Arnold," Cap said. "Him and Arnold, they go out together all the time, just keeping their ears to the ground. That Arnold, he knows what the English figure on doing before they do themselves. He keeps his ear so close to the ground a mole could lick it."

Konrad hurried to us with a huge wooden canteen and a drinking cup made from a gourd. He gave Cap the cup; filled it with eager care: then stood beaming upon him with idolatrous admiration. Cap exhaled gustily and, with a gracious gesture, indicated to Konrad that he should serve all of us.

"By God," Cap said, as Konrad brought the cup to me, "I dunno what people want to do so much hollering against these Hessians for! I'd ruther have one belong to me than a ox or a steer, any day. I'll bet if people in this country ever get to understanding these Hessians's ways, and how smart and attached they are if you let 'em, everybody'd want one or two of 'em. In the first place, they learn quicker'n a tame crow does, and you can call 'em anything you want to—you can even take and call 'em names you wouldn't like to call a crow, because of course they don't understand you. It's a mighty nice relief, sometimes, to call a man a whole lot of horrible names without having to fight about it. Yes, sir, these here Hessians are useful!"

"When'll Nason be back?" I asked him.

"I dunno," he said carelessly. "Prob'ly he won't be back till it's about time for us to go gunning for pickets." He looked up at the heavy sky. "This'll be a nice night for picket-shooting—good'n dark, and not too wet. We ought to get us a picket apiece, a night like this."

I found his reference to pickets puzzling. "How can you——"

Cap laid his hand on my arm. "Listen, I want to tell you what I told all the rest of our people. When we have another battle, keep your eyes open for a she-Hessian. Maybe you'll come across one when we go picket-shooting. If you do, don't let her get hurt: bring her back, so's I can go into the business of breeding 'em when the campaign's over."

I tried to speak, but he crowded closer to me, breathing heavily. "You ought to hear the stuff he's learned. He's *smart!* He speaks pieces for us regular. Soon's we get 'Yankee Doodle' taught to him, he'll be as good an American, pretty near, as anyone there is. I dunno but what he's better than a lot of these New York folks, right now. Konrad, he thinks the whole of America's a pretty good place; but a lot of these New Yorkers, they think there ain't no place in America worth a damn, outside of New York."

He turned sharply to Konrad and shouted, "Sprick English!"

Konrad clapped his hands to his side, standing so straight that he leaned backward. In a high, monotonous, unaccented voice he said loudly, "Cheneral Gates iss der greadest cheneral in der vurld." Then he looked at Cap with eager attention. Cap hooked his thumbs in his belt, surveyed Konrad proudly, and strolled away carelessly. Suddenly he turned and raised a forefinger in a signal. Konrad protruded his tongue and forced air noisily around it, making a disgusting sound at which Tom Bickford, Joseph Phipps, and Lewis Vincent burst into immoderate laughter.

Cap glowed with pride. "Didn't take over fourteen or fifteen hours to learn him that. Konrad's smart!"

"Look here," I said, "can't you think about anything but Konrad?"

Cap eyed me morosely. "What else would I think about?"

"What else? Why, anything else that's of interest to me! How did Lewis Vincent get here? How is it you can go gunning for British pickets without having your scalps snatched off? Have you heard any news of— any news of my brother?"

Tom Bickford answered for him. "That was the first thing we asked Lewis Vincent, Cap'n Peter, when he got away and joined us. He couldn't get away till after the Western Indians went home. That's how it happens we're able to be so free with their pickets."

He spoke more earnestly. "It's lots of fun, Cap'n Peter: honest. There aren't any Indians to bother us, hardly. They went home a week after Jennie McCrea was killed. They felt Burgoyne was being too strict with 'em."

"Listen!" Cap said savagely. "For three years I ain't heard about nothing but war! I've had war for breakfast, war for dinner, war for supper—and damned little else! I've had war morning, noon, and night, and some of the nights have been a week long. I've had a bellyful of war, out in these damned dark woods, playing tag with wolves and dead men, and not knowing when some red-coated poop-head'll pop around in back of me and blow off the top of my skull. For God's sake, shut up about the war! Lemme talk to Konrad and forget about it for five minutes, will you?"

Doc scanned him closely. "You're sick."

"I *ain't* sick!" Cap shouted. "I'm tired of this lousy war! I'm tired of folks that tell you to do things they ain't got the gizzard to do themselves! I'm tired of this clay-faced louse Gates and this little antimire Wilkinson, prowling around here and getting the credit for what me and George Washington and Schuyler and Arnold done! For God's sake, ain't it enough to have to fight in a lousy war like this without having to talk about it?"

Cap glared at us, breathing heavily; and for a time we said nothing at all. It was Tom Bickford who broke the silence. "We been a little nervous, Cap'n Peter," he explained, "on account of the rumors we been hearing about General Arnold. We hear General Gates wants to drive him out of here. We don't believe we'd feel very comfortable if we had to fight the British under anyone but General Arnold."

"Nonsense!" I said. "We stopped at his headquarters on the way down, and if there'd been any danger of Arnold leaving, Varick would have said so. You ought to see the way the militia's piling in! There's thousands of 'em on the road, all headed this way!"

"Yes, we heard so," Tom said. "That's one thing that's got us worried. If the militia ever starts to run, and Arnold isn't here to stop 'em, they'll get in a panic and run forever. They'll carry everything with 'em—scouts and Continentals and everybody."

"Everybody but Konrad," Cap said bitterly. "That thick-headed Hessian, he'd sit right here waiting for me to come and lead him away by the hand!"

Hard on Cap's words I heard the roar of a heavy gun, straight out in front of us. "What's that?" Doc asked.

"That's their sunset gun," Cap said. "They ain't a mile from us, hardly. If they're that close, how do you s'pose I'll have time to get back here and look out for Konrad in case anything happens?"

It was still light when Nason came down the path carrying a slab of beef which Cap seized with a deal of muttering and complaining. "Raw!" he said contemptuously. "Fresh and raw! That kind of meat's not only tasteless: it's weakening! You'd think you was eating jellyfish! Why don't you get salt pork, Stevie? There ain't nothing so tasty or nourishing as salt pork." He gave the meat to Konrad, who took it to the fire before the lean-to.

Nason seemed glad to see us, though like most of our Arundel people, he was not one to make a display of emotion. I could tell he was glad because he came up close and looked at us. "I saw Varick and heard you'd got back," he said. "Did you get to Arundel on your travels?"

When I said I hadn't, he nodded soberly and said, "I hope we'll be back there before very long."

"You *hope* we will!" Cap shouted. "What the hell's *that* mean! Has anything happened?"

"Well," Nason said, "nothing to worry over."

"My God!" Cap bawled. "Something *has* happened! Something's happened to Arnold! I knew damned well something was going to happen when I saw that little stink-wit Wilkinson in camp! What was it happened to Arnold? I suppose Gates promoted eighteen or twenty corporals over his head!"

"No," Nason said. "Gates just took Morgan's regiment of riflemen away from Arnold's division, without any explanation."

"Oh, is that so?" Cap asked heavily. "He took Morgan's regiment away from him, did he? Why didn't he take an arm and a leg and a couple of his eyes, too?"

Nason turned to me. "Maybe you didn't know that Washington sent Morgan and his riflemen up to Schuyler before Congress threw Schuyler out of the army. It's the greatest regiment in the world. Every man in it can shoot the head off a hummingbird at thirty paces."

"I never see 'em shoot hummingbirds," Cap remarked sourly, "but I saw 'em working on British officers up at Freeman's Farm. It's God's wonder the British got any officers left! Every time one of 'em came out in the open, where Morgan's men could get a look at him, there'd be about seven bullets hit him. You could hear 'em hit, like a squash pie hitting a barn door."

Nason nodded. "That's right. Arnold used that regiment the way you'd use a whip. He snapped it at 'em, first thing, and it made the British jump and scatter. When he'd rubbed 'em raw with it, he threw his other brigades straight at 'em and busted 'em wide open."

"Why did Gates take it away from him," I asked, "and when did it happen?"

"It just happened," Nason said. "We just heard about it, an hour ago. Wilkinson issued general orders saying Colonel Morgan's corps was to take instructions only from headquarters. As to why it was done, your guess is as good as mine. I'd say it was to aggravate Arnold—make him so mad he'd have to quit."

"Now, listen, Stevie," Cap said, exasperated, "he *can't* quit! The British may sail into us again tomorrow, or next day! He *can't* quit!"

Nason looked at him coldly. "What would *you* do," he asked, "if I'd told you to give orders to Natanis and Joe Phipps, and you did, and then I went to 'em and said, 'Don't pay any attention to what that big moose tells you! He doesn't know what he's talking about!' What would you say to that?"

Cap snorted. "What would I say? I dunno as I'd say much, but I'd get me a tent peg and bust it over that thick head of yours!"

"Well," Nason said, "generals don't bust tent pegs on each other, especially if one of 'em's the commanding general. If Gates insults Arnold, after what he's done for this army, there's only one thing left for Arnold to do."

"Now wait a minute, Stevie," Cap said. "If Arnold goes away, who'll lead us? Gates can't lead us. When there's a battle he has to stay in his quarters to make the beds and empty the pots. Who else is there besides Gates?"

"Lincoln," Nason said. "General Lincoln just came over from New Hampshire."

Cap's voice was incredulous. "Lincoln! I saw him once. He's the fat one, ain't he?"

Nason nodded.

Cap snorted. "How the hell would Lincoln lead us? He's so fat he can't hardly straddle a horse! If he led us, he'd have to be pushed in a wheelbarrow! How would you feel if you was being encouraged to climb that hill at Freeman's Farm by a fat general in a wheelbarrow?"

Nason said nothing.

"Stevie," Cap said, "Arnold ain't going to leave us, is he?"

"Yes. He's asked Gates for a pass for himself and his aides, so he can go down and join Washington, where he'll be allowed to make himself useful."

Cap made an ineffectual hissing sound. We sat there, staring at the darkness of the forest across the ravine. I saw from the attitude of these men that in all that Northern Army there was only one leader in whom they had confidence. Without him, I wondered, what would become of all of us?

Konrad lifted the kettle from the fire—a stew of boiled meat and potatoes. We took it from him and ate in silence.

When we were finished, Cap studied his knuckles. "If we ain't responsible to nobody but Arnold," he said to Nason, "and if Arnold's going to leave the army, why don't we take it easy tonight? Why don't we stay right here and get a good night's sleep?"

"We'll do the same as usual," Nason told him. "Those British pickets have to be tended to, no matter what happens to Arnold."

Cap rose and stretched himself. "Well, it's dark enough, ain't it? What you waiting for?"

"What'll I do?" I asked Nason. "I told Varick I'd see Arnold tonight."

"Keep away from him," Nason said. "You're under my orders, and you'll kill pickets with the rest of us."

Tom, Cap, Joseph Phipps, and the others stirred about, gathering up their muskets, powder horns, hatchets, and shot pouches. Konrad, standing stiffly by the small fire before the lean-to, seemed to me to be shivering in the dank night mist that rose from the ravine.

Doc stepped close to him. "Why," he said feebly, "he's crying. He's crying his eyes out!"

Cap came and looked in Konrad's face. "Yes," he admitted, "he certainly is! I wisht I could break him of it. Every time we go out picket-shooting, he cries. Sometimes he cries mornings and afternoons too. What you s'pose is the matter with him, old Catamount?"

"Prob'ly he's homesick," Doc said mildly. "Prob'ly he gets to thinking he won't never see no one he likes, ever again."

Cap sighed gustily. "Well," he said, "I s'pose I'll have to let the damned old cry-baby have Grettle. I hate to do it, because every time we let him have Grettle near our bed-places, we all have fleas pretty bad next morning."

He went to the back of the lean-to and pulled at a chain. A raccoon, malevolent-looking in the firelight, was dragged protestingly from behind the bottom logs of the rear wall. "Here you are, Konrad," Cap said wearily. "Here's this pet flea farm of yours."

Konrad fell to his knees and gathered the raccoon in his arms. The small animal, with a look of incredible craftiness on its masked features, paddled at Konrad's chin with paws like small black hands; then pressed its pointed nose to the man's neck.

As we crossed the ravine in single file behind Nason, we could hear Konrad lavishing noisy kisses on Grettle.

"Listen to that!" Cap said wonderingly. "If I was as homesick as all that, I couldn't get along with nothing so small as a raccoon! I'd want a tame bear, or maybe a moose."

In spite of Cap's open contempt, I suspected that more than one of us had a fellow feeling for Konrad—especially if it was true, as Doc believed, that he feared he might never see anyone he loved, ever again.

# Education

### "Concerning Education" in FOR AUTHORS ONLY

A STRIKING FEATURE of higher education in America is the large number of educators who have written books, brochures, and essays to prove that the American system of education is all wrong. Americans in general, they say, and in particular the parents responsible for sending young men and young women to college, have no comprehension of what education should be.

They add that no undergraduate understands the true meaning of education or the need of having a trained mind; that the American system of education is designed to give sketchy and worthless education to the masses, and to condemn the occasional brilliant student to an equally sketchy and worthless education; that there are few, if any, trained minds engaged in the art of teaching in America; that the welfare of America depends on the development of trained minds; and that something ought to be done about it immediately.

Educators are clear in their explanations of what it is that constitutes an untrained mind. An untrained mind is one that contains a small amount or a large amount of superficial and unrelated information, all of which, to its possessor, seems of equal value.

A mind loaded with little scraps of information on Egyptian history, archery, zoology, cheese-making, oriental art, psychology of hotel management, child guidance, the poets of the Renaissance, advertising technique, scoutcraft, and similar intellectual detritus is not trained, but is what might be called a human New England attic—a repository of useless and forgotten things.

It is more difficult to obtain from an educator a definition of a trained mind. A composite definition, obtained from English and American educators of the highest standing and of unquestioned ability, is somewhat as follows:

> A trained mind is one that has learned through extensive reading of books dealing with several related subjects, as well as through the guidance of competent teachers, to understand why the subjects are related; to criticize intelligently the statements and opinions encountered in its reading; to distinguish between that which is false and worthless and that which is genuine and worthy; to think, in short, for itself, and to go on thinking for itself through life; to speak and write clearly and logically on any subject concerning which it has formed an opinion; and to have a sincere appreciation of and respect for intellectual pursuits.

It is the contention of these educators that the man or woman with a trained mind will lead a happier, fuller, and more valuable life, no matter what his occupation or position, than he can possibly lead if his mind is untrained.

It is also their unalterable belief that any man with a trained mind can go farther in every field of activity apart from law, medicine, engineering, or any of the sciences than can the man who has specialized in that particular field without having the advantage of a trained mind.

If an educator who holds such beliefs is asked to be specific, he is usually glad to oblige. He might, for example, be specific about two young men who intend to enter what is known, in university circles, as the profession of journalism.

One of them, to prepare himself for his life work, attends a university and devotes himself for three years to a course corresponding to the Oxford University course of Modern Greats. Modern Greats consists of the study of Philosophy, Politics, and Economics. In Philosophy, the young man learns the history of Philosophy from Descartes, obtains a first-hand knowledge of the chief philosophical writers, and familiarizes himself with Moral and Political Philosophy. In Politics he studies British Political and Constitutional History since 1760, digs into Political Institutions, and specializes on some particular period either of Political History or of Social and Economic History. In Economics he must read and master authoritative books on Economic Theory and Economic Organization. In addition to these subjects, he must choose two further subjects for special study—subjects from a list which offers a wide choice in Philosophy, Politics, and Economics; and on top of it all he must, before he graduates, show ability to translate two modern languages.

By writing weekly essays on the books he is reading—essays which must express his own ideas and opinions—he becomes at least reasonably proficient at handling the English language; and by taking, at the end of, his years of study, a series of examinations covering everything he has studied, he demonstrates his ability to use his brain. He has learned nothing whatever about journalism, but he has what educators regard as a trained mind.

The other young man attends an American university where he specializes in journalism. He attends lectures on the American newspaper; on the nature of news; on the methods of gathering and writing news; on the technique of editing, copyreading, rewriting, headline writing, the handling of telegraph copy and syndicated material; on press agents and press-agenting; on the editing of small-town newspapers; on feature writing, editorial writing, critical writing and reviewing; on the laws having to do with the press and its freedom; on newspaper policy and management; on writing for magazines; on the writing of advertisements; and on the best method of throwing an indignant subscriber out of the office.

At the end of two years or so of study, he receives a bachelor's degree in Journalism, or a certificate in Journalism, and is declared fit to go out and get a job as a reporter, or do anything at all that any newspaper editor or owner is willing to let him do.

It may or may not be worthy of note that in neither of the great English universities can an undergraduate find instruction in any such subject as journalism. English magazines, however, are full of advertisements of schools of journalism which are confident of their ability to teach anyone everything there is to know about journalism in six months for the equivalent of twenty-five dollars—and to teach it by mail to boot.

At all events, the two young men enter newspaper work. The educators maintain that the result is almost inevitable. No matter what the two young men are set to doing, they say, the momentary advantage may go to the one who studied the theories of journalism; but the permanent advantage will rest with the possessor of the trained mind. The latter masters the technical details of his new calling in a day or two: then, by reason of having a trained intelligence, applies those details more effectively than the man with the untrained mind can possibly apply them.

The sole function of a college or a university, these educators insist, is the training of minds: not the technique of trades or businesses. Properly trained minds, they say, can master any trade or business in a few months, or a few weeks, if not a few days—or even in a few minutes.

The following excerpt from the London *Morning Post* of December 28, 1933, would be seized upon by educators in support of their claims. The true meat of the excerpt lies in its last paragraph.

Salisbury, Wednesday. Disguised in a flowing cassock, a medieval craftsman is repiecing the priceless stained glass of the Cathedral with no tools but a blow-lamp and an Afghan dagger.

The Reverend Stanley Baker, a Vicar-Choral of Salisbury Cathedral, is probably the only Doctor of Divinity who has ever become a Cathedral glazier. To save the hard-pressed Cathedral from expense, he is himself putting together its long-lost thirteenth-century windows from hundreds of fragments.

For the last seven years Dr. Baker has been searching for the ancient glass of the Cathedral, which was knocked out and dumped somewhere in Salisbury during the last century. He struck a find under the old Town Ditch, and another in the vaults of the Cathedral, and others elsewhere, in sufficient quantity to build up at least a few complete lancets of "grisaille" or patterned, figureless glass of the kind once so abundant in Salisbury Cathedral.

But his own funds were exhausted, and he shrank from asking the Cathedral Chapter, at such a time of depression, to bear the expense of fitting the fragments together again. He determined to do the work himself.

"I had five minutes' talk with a glazier," he told me in his workshop. "After that," he added with a twinkle, "an average intelligence and the priceless asset of a classical education came to my rescue."

American colleges and universities, the educators insist, are too prone to give courses in, let us say, glazing, the elements of canoe-building, ribbon-matching and advanced millinery, single and double tap-dancing, or the theory and practice of diaper-making. They are apt to forget that a man who learns to be a glazier may not be able to do anything else, whereas a man with a well-trained mind can learn the principles of glazing in five minutes. Then, if he finds glazing not to his liking, he can turn to journalism or to cooking or to politics or even to the writing of novels.

It is unfortunate, say the educators—unfortunate for everybody—that American parents and American taxpayers cannot have a different attitude toward education. They do not send their sons to colleges so that their minds may be trained, but because they believe that four years of attendance at any college, no matter how sketchy and worthless the instruction dispensed there, will enable their sons and daughters to get better jobs and earn more than they could earn if they had not gone to college for four years.

By holding this belief, conscientious educators declare, parents display a complete lack of understanding of the proper functions of a college or university. Colleges and universities that cater to this belief, they add, rob the nation of the services of minds that might otherwise be properly trained. Instead of graduating men equipped to become statesmen, bankers, journalists, teachers, authors, and businessmen of the highest class, they turn out second-raters and third-raters: men without mental resources; men in whom public spirit, public duty, and social purposes are not guiding motives; men who look with approving eyes on luxury, self-indulgence, and greed; men who condone sharp and unethical practices; men whose conversation deals not with things of the mind, but solely with golf, business affairs, food, drink, sport, contract bridge, and a few other equally stimulating subjects.

The common sense and sound judgment of the American people ought, of course, to make it possible for them to decide whether or not these contentions are true. While they are engaged in deciding, we will shift the scene to Oxford University for a glimpse of young Englishmen engaged in having their minds trained for the greater glory of the British Empire.

# An American Looks at Oxford

### From FOR AUTHORS ONLY

MANY THINGS, in England, are not what they seem when examined from a distance. The best English newspapers, seen at long range, appear to the casual observer to be organs for conveying news to the reading public in the regulation manner. If closely scrutinized, however, their front pages are found to be entirely devoid of news. The news is concealed in the bowels of the paper, beneath headlines seemingly designed to imply that nothing is happening anywhere.

What one gets, on the front pages of the most respectable English dailies, is a cloud of diminutive advertisements: lost dogs; stolen brooches; fishing rights on the river Usk; small service flat with water laid on; freehold property in Herts; alcoholic excess and its treatment; or young gentlewoman contemplating journey by motor-bike to South Africa and desirous of renting side-car privileges to congenial traveling companion for fifty guineas inclusive.

Similarly, it is thought by persons unfamiliar with England that Englishmen universally keep to the left-hand side of the road—as indeed they do, in theory. In practice, on the contrary, they keep to the right almost as much as to the left. As a result, many of the best brains in England are perpetually trying to understand why English automobiles and bicycles must so frequently be removed from hedgerows and pried apart with crowbars.

There is also the little matter of pronunciation. The person who thinks that the good old English name of Levenson-Gower is pronounced Levenson-Gower is grievously mistaken. It is pronounced Lewson-Gaw.

An Englishman who enunciated the word Pytchley as one might expect would be socially ostracized. Its first syllable should be Pie.

Belvoir is not Belvoir, but Beaver. Beaulieu is Bewley. The word Hants does not, as might be expected, refer to ghosts or spooks, but is the English abbreviation of Hampshire. To anybody but an Englishman, it doesn't make sense, any more than the word Mumps would make sense as an abbreviation of Massachusetts, or Nerts as an abbreviation of New York.

A preparatory school, instead of fitting a boy for a university, prepares him to stay away from home for the remainder of his life. An English preparatory school relieves the British parent of the necessity of bothering with his offspring from the seventh to the fourteenth year.

And finally, central heat occasionally encountered in a few of the stately homes and caravanserais of England is not heat at all unless augmented by open fires.

Oxford University is generally believed by undergraduates of American universities to be a cloistered educational machine which, by a mystic combination of medieval architecture and teaching, is able to stuff any young man into one end of the mill and turn him out at the other in three years' time a highly cultured British gentleman—a finished product with no rough edges, no flaws, no mental blanks: education's finest flower.

Unless I have been greatly misinformed, a considerable number of American educators not only hold the same belief, but have somehow picked up the idea that if an American university wishes to follow in Oxford's footsteps, it can best do so by erecting residential halls with Gothic exteriors and University Club interiors, and arranging to have every undergraduate pumped full of information, enthusiasm, and inspiration once a week by a master mind known as a Tutor.

These beliefs are somewhat at variance with the facts.

Oxford University, like Cambridge University, is located in one of the flattest, lowest, and dampest sections of England; and for that reason, possibly, the students are not encouraged to remain in residence for protracted periods. Eight consecutive weeks of college life is as much as any Oxford undergraduate is thought capable of enduring.

An undergraduate arrives in Oxford in October and stays there during eight chilly and depressing weeks. Then he goes away—"goes down," in the Oxford idiom—for a month and a half, during which time he travels on the Continent or otherwise diverts himself in order to recuperate from his first eight weeks of discomfort.

On returning to Oxford he stays another eight weeks, from the middle of January to the middle of March—an extremely cold and unhealthy season. Then he goes down for the spring vacation—or "vac," in the patois, to rhyme with "lack"—and remains down for six weeks, in order to give spring an opportunity to gain a foothold in England and make life bearable once more.

Then he comes back for the delightful spring or Trinity term, acknowledged by every Oxford enthusiast to be the cream of all Oxford terms. During Trinity term the hedgerows are filled with throstles; the lush countryside echoes to the dull thuds of the college crews as they indulge in their innocent pastime of bumping each other on the historic Thames—locally pronounced Isis; Oxford's medieval rooms are no longer refrigerator-like, so that undergraduates can get up in the morning without well-nigh freezing to death.

In spite of the acknowledged beauty, richness, and glamour of Oxford in the spring, the undergraduate still feels that eight weeks of it is all he can stand; so down he goes for the third time, at the end of eight weeks, for his long vac.

Apparently it is felt by the university authorities that these three stretches of eight weeks constitute a severe mental and physical strain; for the long vac lasts four months—enough of a recuperative period to enable anybody to recover from almost anything.

Americans are somewhat baffled by this twenty-four-week year that obtains at Oxford, as well as by the fact that Oxford students are able to graduate after three years' work. Persons accustomed to the four-year college course of American universities feel that Oxford students must toil constantly and at terrific pressure in order to be transformed, in the mere space of seventy-two weeks, from gawky schoolboys into such finished products as statesmen, authors, historians, and cultured British gentlemen. In another place I shall attempt to clear up this little matter of the amount of work done at Oxford.

Most puzzling, to an American, of all the features of Oxford University, is the fact that the closer one approaches it, the more vague and scattered it becomes. The university fades into a sort of unfathomable fog; and here and there, in the fog, appear colleges enclosed in high walls faintly reminiscent of the walls of the Elmira Penitentiary or the old State Prison in Charlestown, Massachusetts.

These colleges seem to have no heads; no governing bodies; no administrative centers. At the gate of each college is a small room in which lurks a porter resembling a blend of a bank cashier and the proprietor of a small livery stable of the 1895 period.

The porter of an Oxford college is popularly supposed to possess an enormous fund of practical knowledge; but to an American he occasionally appears lamentably ignorant. One says to him—shouting loudly, so to be heard above the thunderous roarings and hootings of the traffic that is rapidly shaking the gargoyles from Oxford's medieval towers—"Is this Oxford?"

"No, sir," the porter says. "This is Christ Church."

"Christ Church College?" you ask.

The porter looks annoyed. "Ow, no, sir!" he says. "Just Christ Church!"

"But it's a college, isn't it?" you ask.

"Ow, yes, sir!" the porter admits. "But it's not called so. I mean to say, it's Christ Church. Yes, sir! Ah—were you wishing to see anyone in Christ Church—*in statu pupillari*, sir?"

"No," you say, "I'm looking for the university. Can you tell me where the president's office is?"

"President, sir?" the porter says. "What president?"

"Why," you say, "the president of Oxford University."

The porter looks baffled. "There's no president of the university, sir. There's a chancellor, but he wouldn't be in Oxford, sir. He has almost nothing to do with us, sir."

"But," you say, "he must have an office and a secretarial staff. He can't attend to the affairs of the university without an office and a few secretaries, can he? Where's his office?"

"I really couldn't say, sir," the porter says. "I never heard of such a thing."

You are conscious of a vague irritation. "All right," you say, "all right. If there's no president to see, I'll see the dean. There's a dean's office, isn't there? Where's the dean's office?"

"What dean, sir?" the porter asks.

"The dean of Oxford University, of course," you say.

The porter shakes his head. "I never heard of such a thing, sir. Some of the colleges have deans, sir; but not the university, sir. What would the university do with a dean, sir, if I might ask?"

Your irritation gives way to profound exasperation. "Look here," you say. "Isn't there *anybody* connected with this university that a person can talk to? Where's the Athletic Association? I'll talk to the graduate manager."

"Athletic Association, sir?" the porter asks. "Athletic Association? Graduate Manager? Really, sir, I think there's some mistake. Was it Oxford you were thinking of, sir, or some other place?"

You give it up and stumble helplessly away, dodging the innumerable bicyclists that sweep perpetually in shoals and coveys through the streets of Oxford. Oxford University, you realize, is a strange state of affairs— one of those misnamed British institutions, like the most desirable schools in England, which are called public schools, in spite of being private schools of an almost painfully exclusive and expensive nature.

Let us, at this point, set our imaginations to work on a hypothetical American university whose external features might bear a faint resemblance to Oxford.

The first requisite would be a noisy community of some 50,000 souls—the town of Deerhampton, say—located in a dank, flat section of New England. The ideal place for it would be Cape Cod, where the town would be constantly exposed, during the winter months, to damp and bitter blasts from every direction, just as is Oxford.

The town should be cut by streets and alleyways so narrow that any pedestrian who ventures into them is in constant danger of having an automobile fender or bicycle lamp driven into his back.

Into this imaginary town of Deerhampton a group of American colleges should be inserted—a group consisting, let us say, of such men's colleges as Amherst, Bates, Bowdoin, Colby, Dartmouth, Hamilton, Haverford, Hobart, Middlebury, Swarthmore, and Williams, each one reduced in size to two or three hundred men. There should also be three or four women's colleges such as Goucher, Wellesley, Wells, and Vassar, similarly reduced in size. These colleges, in spite of being transported to Deerhampton, would retain their own traditions and customs, their own rivalries and dislikes, their own social and athletic peculiarities; their own instructors, libraries, dining halls, private barrooms; even their own presidents.

Each college would be housed in its own set of buildings, which—for greater ease in the supervision and control of inmates—would be fortress-like structures in the form of a hollow square, or of a double hollow square. Any attempt on the part of an undergraduate to enter or leave one of these fortress-like structures after the hour of midnight would be regarded as a heinous offense, almost on a par with homicide, and would result in immediate expulsion.

This group of colleges, because of being concentrated in Deerhampton, would be known as the University of Deerhampton—and that, roughly speaking, is the situation existing in Oxford.

Oxford University is made up of twenty-six colleges, of which twenty-two are men's and four are women's. Each one has its own customs and peculiarities.

Brasenose College, known to Oxford undergraduates as B. N. C., is, in theory, inclined to encourage and coddle such athletes as choose to find shelter within her walls.

Magdalen College, pronounced Maudlin, has the reputation of being the resort of the wealthiest and most aristocratic, not to say snootiest, undergraduates. It was at Magdalen that the Prince of Wales devoted several eight-week terms to the pursuit of Oxford culture; and even today there are Magdalen undergraduates who haven't recovered from this fact.

Christ Church is supposed to house the more politically inclined students.

True intellectuals and young gentlemen of what are known, in Oxford, as esthetic tendencies are thought to be found in larger numbers in Balliol College than in any other.

Peculiarities of this sort give rise to frequent pointed comment from members of other colleges. In addition to Balliol's reputation for intellectuality, she is also said to be favored by students who come to Oxford from among the dark-skinned peoples of His Majesty's Indian possessions. One of the oddities of an educated Englishman, in spite of the reputedly high quality of the culture he receives, is that he seems unable to distinguish between shades of skin, just as he seems unable to realize that there is any difference in the American language spoken by a Harvard professor, a Vermont farmer, and a Chicago gangster. Consequently the many brown people in Balliol are referred to as "black men"—especially by members of Trinity College, whose high, spike-crowned walls adjoin those of Balliol.

When the Trinity undergraduates indulge too freely in the Oxford pastime known as a "binge" or "blind"—a "blind" being a drunken brawl of a more violent nature than can even be imagined by the undergraduates of an American college—they assemble beneath the walls of Balliol and shout hoarsely, "Bring out your black men!"

It is said that a Trinity man went to Balliol to hunt for a friend, but seemed to encounter only dark faces. When, therefore, he finally met a white man, he raised his hat politely and, in imitation of Henry M. Stanley in darkest Africa, murmured, "Dr. Livingstone, I presume."

*Trader Horn*, in the days of that book's popularity, was shown at one of the Oxford "flicks"—"flick" being the name applied by Oxford undergraduates to a moving-picture house. During the course of the film, a canoe full of black men appeared on the screen, paddling energetically downriver, whereupon voices rose from the audience, crying ironically, "Well rowed, Balliol!"

It is difficult to tell, at Oxford, whether an undergraduate prefers to be known for his university or for his college. To describe him as an "Oxford man" is never considered adequate. He is Oxford and Oriel, or Oxford and New College, or Oxford and Corpus Christi. A daily paper, reporting the activity of any group of Oxford undergraduates, would be guilty of gross negligence if it failed to specify the college of which each undergraduate is a member.

If the activity is one of great importance, such as a football game between Oxford and Cambridge, or a boat race between Oxford and Cambridge, every newspaper in the British Empire is almost morally obligated to mention not only each player's college but his school as well. Seemingly an Englishman can contentedly remain in ignorance of the height and weight of a university football player; but no truehearted Briton will tolerate any concealment of the name of the player's preparatory school.

An English newspaper that, either deliberately or through carelessness, omitted this information, would probably be prosecuted under the Defense of the Realm Act. Certainly indignation would run high, and letters would be written to the London *Times* in which bitter references would be made to the evil days on which England has fallen and the degeneracy of modern times. Thus an Oxford Rugby football team is described as being composed of H. G. Owen-Smith (Diocesan College, South Africa, and Magdalen), A. L. Warr (Bromsgrove and Brasenose), P. Cranmer (St. Edward's, Oxford, and Christ Church). H. D. B. Lorraine (captain) (Glenalmond and Christ Church), and so on.

These peculiar circumstances are mentioned in order to show that an Oxford college is something more than it appears to the untrained eye, in spite of the prevalent American feeling that a passable imitation of an Oxford college can be obtained by building Gothic residential halls in almost any college town.

Those who persist in that belief are apt to find something wrong with it. If there weren't something wrong with it, I am under the impression that other English universities would have dallied with the scheme. Other English universities, however, have let it severely alone. Only at Oxford and Cambridge are the undergraduates divided into self-governing colleges. London University, Durham University, Manchester University, Birmingham University, and all other English institutions of higher education are operated on an entirely different basis—a basis similar to that of an American university.

In many ways, an Oxford college bears a striking resemblance to an American college fraternity that has grown unusually large and in the growing has acquired a permanent governing board of wise and tolerant men who guide the mental activities of the younger members of the society.

It may be that many will take exception to this likening of an Oxford college to an American fraternity, on the ground that members of an Oxford college, instead of occasionally addressing each other as "Brother White" or "Brother Black," may for months, if not for years, daily pass each other on the street without speaking. This, to hear Oxford men tell it, is an old Oxford custom due more to shyness or timidity than to any inherent desire to be rude or offensive.

A Rhodes scholar spoke to me of this quaint Oxford habit and shook his head in a puzzled way as he did so. "You get pretty sick of Oxford when you first come here," he said. "Most of the time it's cold—so cold that you never seem warm; and nobody speaks to you. You wonder whether you're queer: afflicted, maybe, with some sort of curse that makes Englishmen ashamed to associate with you. You may go to a party and sit beside another undergraduate and have a few cups of mulled claret with him. He may have a few cups too many and fall under the table, and you may pull him out and drag him home. These Oxford boys don't know how to drink, any of 'em. Well, ordinarily you'd think that after such an experience, the two of you would be on speaking terms, wouldn't you?"

I said I would indeed think so.

The Rhodes scholar shook his head. "No," he said. "You're wrong. If you meet him on the street the next day and try to catch his eye, he'll look down his nose, or he'll be awfully busy looking the other way; or if he sees you soon enough, he'll cross the street or maybe go up an alley."

"Why will he?" I asked.

"Oh," the Rhodes scholar said, "he'll be afraid that if he looks at you, or says something, you may not recognize him. He's afraid to risk having his feelings hurt."

"What's the reason for that?" I asked.

"Well, I'll tell you," he said. "A lot of Oxford and Cambridge undergraduates went to big public schools before they came to the university, and English public-school men have a splendid opinion of themselves. They don't think much of people who didn't go to a public school. They can't go around talking to everyone, for fear of speaking to someone who's socially inferior. A public-school man would be frightfully annoyed if the head of his college should suggest that he share rooms with a non-public-school man. That's why an Oxford undergraduate is cautious about speaking. Either he's afraid you're a public-school man—or that you're not."

"Isn't there anything to be done about it?" I asked.

"Yes," the Rhodes scholar said. "If you look straight at him and speak to him sort of firmly, he'll be taken by surprise. He'll look up, and you'll see his face move a little—twist into a sort of worried smile. It won't be much of a smile, but it's an admission that you're alive. After you've done that two or three times, it's safe to write him a note and ask him to tea, especially if you're an American. Americans are regarded as peculiar fish, but not bad eggs at times; so if he knows you're an American, he'll come, probably; and after that he knows you. He'll never act very happy about it, though—not in public. They don't go around saying, 'Hello!' to each other—not to any noticeable extent. As for saying, 'Hello, Eddie!' or 'Hello, Mortimer'—well, that just isn't done at all!"

"What if you aren't an American?" I asked. "What if you're a Rhodes scholar from Australia or Canada or South Africa?"

Again the Rhodes scholar shook his head. "You're out of luck. Out of luck." He muttered a few words on the subject of the relations between the English and their colonists that would have been highly distressing to the English-speaking Union. The English public-school man has little use for American Rhodes scholars, and practically none at all for Canadians, South Africans, Australians, and New Zealanders.

In spite of this oddity, and other Oxford peculiarities that I shall take up in the proper place, I must persist in holding to it that an Oxford college has more of the flavor of an American fraternity than of a residential hall. The members of an Oxford college profess to hold other Oxford colleges in more or less mild contempt, just as the members of American fraternities pretend to scorn other fraternities.

Oxford colleges, like American fraternities, brag of their distinguished graduates and hang their portraits on the walls of the college halls. Oxford colleges have their uncongenial members, and so does every American fraternity. It is the fashion, in Oxford colleges, to complain bitterly of the food served in the college halls, and the same thing is true in American fraternities. Oxford colleges do not, it is true, have mysterious secrets; but neither do American fraternities, in spite of all their pretense of secrecy and mystery. Except as regards size and dignity, they have strong points of similarity.

Consequently, alterations in the American educational system, it seems to me, might as readily have their rise in American fraternities, properly directed by persons capable of making education fashionable, as in expensive residential halls which are generously donated to American universities in the belief that they may somehow result in a system of education similar to that of Oxford University.

Roughly speaking, the features in which Oxford differs from an American college—and by an American college I mean a college proper, like

Williams College or Bowdoin College, or that section of an American university devoted to the study of the Liberal Arts—are the manner of life within an Oxford college; the forms of athletics in which its members indulge; the enormous amount of time given to activities that have nothing whatever to do with studies; the method of study followed by undergraduates; the keen respect with which a fair percentage of Oxford undergraduates regard learning, education, and the art of teaching; and the perpetual effort on the part of teachers to develop in their students sound judgment and a critical sense rather than to stuff them with facts.

This effort is not always successful. It may or may not be a jolt to the numerous critics of American educational systems to learn that a surprisingly large number of Oxford graduates—according to the English themselves—go down each year with no sounder judgment, apparently, than is possessed by a good bird dog, and with a critical sense that is, to put it mildly, somewhat spotty.

Oxford is something of a shock to an American who has heard, for years on end, that all American college men are standardized and the stereotyped result of mass production, whereas all Oxford undergraduates are individualists with widely divergent characteristics.

One's first impression of the Oxford undergraduate, on viewing him in his native haunts, is that he is wearing a uniform imposed on him by the university. In fact, this unofficial Oxford dress is so striking in its uniformity that one is at first puzzled to tell one undergraduate from another. To the newcomer, they all look alike, as do the residents of a Chinese city to an untrained eye.

The basis of this standardized Oxford garb is a Harris tweed jacket, usually a somewhat offensive shade of brown. Harris tweed is a thick and hairy form of homespun chiefly noteworthy for the fact that when made into a garment, it immediately takes on the appearance of having been worn for twelve or fifteen years and slept in for the past month.

In addition to his Harris tweed jacket, which is frequently patched on the elbows with leather, the Oxford undergraduate wears gray flannel trousers which might have been used for wiping the floor or drying dishes. It may be that the singular shapelessness and griminess of the Oxford man's gray flannels are due to the long hours he spends, during the winter, on his knees before a coal fire, attempting to coax life into it and warmth into himself. Whatever the cause, no steps, apparently, are ever taken by an Oxford undergraduate to remedy the pitiable condition of his trousers.

In the coldest weather—and Oxford's coldest weather is able to make the winter climate of Siberia seem mild and relaxing—this official Oxford garb is augmented by a violently colored wooly muffler twisted around the neck and thrust into the bosom of the Harris tweed jacket. It is also embellished, on semiformal occasions, by what is known as a gown. When an Oxford undergraduate meets his tutor, he wears a gown. When he goes out at night he must, in theory, wear a gown or be subject to a small fine in case he is apprehended by one of the two university proctors. These gowns are sleeveless jacket-length garments of sleazy black cloth, and undergraduates strive to give them a well-worn look at the earliest possible moment. They do this by using them as poker-holders and fire screens, pressing them close against the front of their fireplaces to make their cannel-coal fires burn more briskly. Consequently most gowns are ragged in the extreme and have unsightly holes burned in them.

Why Oxford undergraduates should consider it necessary to protect their necks but not their heads during their winter peregrinations is one of the most abstruse of Oxford mysteries; but such is the case. In spite of wearing a muffler that must use up the wool of a whole sheep, and a Harris tweed jacket with the texture of an old-fashioned horse blanket, the undergraduate wears no hat. He pedals himself, hatless, around the tortuous streets of Oxford on a battered bicycle which he calls a push-bike, regardless of the bitter wind that howls down from the Irish Sea and wails about his ears. He frequently tucks himself into the seat of an automobile little larger than a go-cart and careers, still hatless, into the teeth of the frigid blasts that hurtle across the frostbound Cotswold Hills.

The manner in which an Oxford undergraduate exposes his head should, possibly, be taken into consideration by the American educators who try to explain education by means of graphs, questionnaires, and algebraic formulas. They, doubtless, could derive a great lesson from the amount of abuse the brains of Oxford undergraduates are able to stand without suffering noticeable ill effects.

There is so much admiration in many parts of America for what is known as the Oxford educational system that no part of that so-called system, it seems to me, should be overlooked. One of the outstanding features of Oxford undergraduate life that is never mentioned by educators, or by any of the authors who baffle everybody, themselves included, by writing long and puzzling books on educational problems, is the excessive cold that permeates every room in every Oxford college during sixteen out of the twenty-four weeks of the university year.

Many of Oxford's beautiful buildings are not as medieval as they look, in spite of the fact that some of the colleges were founded back in the thirteenth and fourteenth and fifteenth centuries. The heating arrangements in general use, however, are almost as medieval as the buildings are supposed to be; and the normal winter temperature of most rooms is about what one might expect to find in a receiving vault in northern Russia.

If a room has any heating arrangement at all—and many undergraduates shiver miserably in rooms that have none—it is a fireplace about the size of half a Gladstone bag. In this diminutive aperture a few fragments of cannel coal are coaxed to a tarry-smelling glow that can be felt for a distance of three or four feet, provided one takes up a position immediately before the fireplace.

Influential members of the faculty are occasionally permitted to install central heat in houses belonging to one of the colleges, but never until the matter has been discussed in solemn conclave and at great length by the governing board of the college, and until it has been pointed out by the more scholarly dons that plain living is essential to high thinking. Even then it is usual for the central heating not to work.

If it is true that high thinking is dependent on plain living, it seems odd that educators who think highly of the Oxford system do not suggest the adoption of unheated rooms in American universities in order to improve American educational standards.

Strangely enough, Oxford undergraduates do not seem properly to appreciate the privilege of living and studying in unheated rooms.

The Bodleian Library at Oxford is not only one of the most justly celebrated libraries in the world, but also one of the coldest. Certainly, so far as I am concerned, it *is* the coldest, and the next coldest is that housed in the Radcliffe Camera, just across the street from the Bodleian. A brace of partridges, hung in either the Bodleian or the Radcliffe Camera during early October, would keep until April.

Those who pursue the bubble knowledge in the Bodleian in winter do so huddled in overcoats, their feet wrapped in rugs, their breaths rising in little clouds of fog, their faces pinched, and their noses a pale blue from the cold, their fingers almost too numb to clutch a pencil.

The Bodleian is suffering from several other things besides lack of heat. Although catacombs and chambers have been excavated beneath it as well as beneath the adjoining streets, in order to provide additional shelf space, the Bodleian still doesn't know what to do with all its books. It is also in a bad way from an almost complete congestion of its cataloguing system, whose shortcomings make American librarians burst into screams of agony. It consists of a set of enormous volumes in which are pasted, on long strips of paper—and occasionally in the wrong place—the titles of the new books acquired by the library.

A student who goes to the Bodleian to read may spend half a day in silent thought before receiving his books; for after he has run down the required titles in the giant catalogs, phlegmatic attendants must prowl in search of them through caverns measureless to man. It is believed by Oxford undergraduates that attendants frequently lose their way in the Bodleian labyrinths and have to be rescued by search parties. Since books cannot be removed from the Bodleian, a visit to it for reading purposes is a serious business, particularly in winter.

During my stay in Oxford I was approached by a group of undergraduates, who called my attention to the fact that the Rockefeller Foundation was presenting the Bodleian with three fifths of the amount required to build more commodious quarters for itself, and that it was also providing funds for the librarian and the architect to make a tour of inspection of American libraries. These young men wished to know how they could go about it to put in a plea with the Rockefeller Foundation.

It was their hope that the Rockefeller Foundation would persuade Oxford University to install centrally heated reading rooms in the new library building for the specific use of undergraduates.

Probably, they said, the librarian would express disgust at the idea on the ground that central heat would be bad for the books, in which case they wanted to urge the Rockefeller Foundation to take the librarian's claims *cum grano salis*. In their opinion he would be, so to speak, talking through his hat.

And anyway, they said, even though artificial heat might possibly be bad for books, the unheated rooms were even worse for undergraduates. Their thought seemed to be that it was poor economy to preserve a binding unmarred for an extra five hundred years if, in the preserving, a few hundred promising young men contracted incurable illnesses.

Having myself been numbed and shriveled by the cold of the Bodleian, I cheerfully transmit, to the Rockefeller Foundation, this unofficial but none the less heartfelt plea from the undergraduates of Oxford.

It is always pleasant to see libraries receiving assistance, though it occurs to me that England, able to purchase the Codex Sinaiticus from Russia for $500,000, is not yet reduced to such penury that her libraries should be obliged to turn to America for succor.

Since the Rockefeller Foundation is playing fairy godmother to libraries and consequently to those who read books, it seems only reasonable to interpolate a word for those who write the books on which the libraries depend.

Civilized nations are patronizing lending libraries with increasing frequency. They read more books but buy less. Although they crave reading material, they are seemingly averse to rewarding the authors who provide it. When an author's work is purchased by a lending library, it is rented to an unlimited number of readers; but from these readers the author receives nothing—a state of affairs in which there is small justice and less nourishment. Ninety-five per cent of America's authors are today unable to exist by the writing of books, unless they can first be serialized in magazines—which in most cases is out of the question. If a generous and resourceful organization like the Rockefeller Foundation would devise a method whereby authors might obtain, from lending libraries, an infinitesimal percentage of the sums received on loaned volumes, authors would be able to make a living from what they write; and the ultimate benefit to literature would be inestimable. It would, I suspect, be as beneficial to America and the world as an addition to the Bodleian, the control of malaria in Russia, or the excavation of a city in ancient Greece.

The British Society of Authors has attempted to remedy this unfortunate situation, but has found itself impotent. The Authors' League of America is at work on it; and I plead with the Rockefeller Foundation to give American authors at least as much help as it has given the Bodleian Library.

If this plea makes no appeal, I have another—a plea that the Rockefeller Foundation make, in its gift to the Bodleian, some provision for research rooms in which British authors may have access to books that will tell them how Americans talk.

At the present moment there is not, in England, any English author capable of delineating an American with any degree of accuracy, though England is littered with authors possessed to hurl barbed darts into the quivering body of at least one American.

I have made earnest efforts to discover where English writers unearth their peculiar ideas of American speech, and so far as I can tell they get them from two sources—gangster films and the "say, pardner" school of cowboy fiction.

Wherever they get them, they get them wrong; and the Bodleian Library and the Rockefeller Foundation would be accomplishing a noteworthy literary achievement if they could develop even one British author equipped with the knowledge, the mentality, and the craftsmanship to depict Americans as they are.

I mention this delicate matter in this place because it may possibly be fraught with a deep, pregnant meaning for educators, who seem to be able to get pregnant meanings out of almost anything. Education, in the two great English universities, is said by the English to give Oxford and Cambridge men a deeper culture, a greater respect for learning, than can be obtained from American universities with their mass-production evils. If this is true, I find it difficult to understand why the graduates of American universities are so free with gifts to their alma maters, and why Oxford and Cambridge men, to put it conservatively, are not.

One would think that since the Bodleian is one of the brightest jewels, if not the transcendent gem, in Oxford's glittering crown, it could obtain all necessary support from its vast numbers of cultured, brilliant, appreciative, wealthy sons. One would think so, but one would have another think coming.

When the Bodleian needs help, Oxford's cultured sons have their noses deep in a book or are otherwise engaged, and the Bodleian must accept largesse from a country that is generally believed by the English—and particularly by British authors—to care nothing for culture, and to be the great nursing home of materialism, commercialism, Uncle Shylocks, and college graduates who say, "Wa-al, I reckon that thar cathedral is real cute."

Walter de Merton was a statesman and bishop who founded Merton College, Oxford, around the year 1264. He advanced the doctrine that a college should benefit from such "happy fortune" as might fall to the lot of its graduates in subsequent life. "That doctrine," a distinguished Oxford graduate has written, "is one that sadly needs emphasizing in Oxford."

Here again, it seems to me, is an opportunity for educators to work out another set of graphs and formulas which shall seek to discover whether, in the American educational system, there aren't advantages not yet apparent to English educators, and whether there isn't something about the Oxford system slightly less perfect than the English think.

I would not care to give the impression that a visitor's enthusiasm is not stirred by Oxford. Nobody can help being favorably impressed. One who studies there will enjoy himself enormously, provided he can stand the cold, afford the high cost of living, and endure the first twenty-four weeks without succumbing to homesickness and pneumonia.

What is more, he will, if so inclined, receive a peculiar form of mental training that will, in theory, enable him to forge ahead in his chosen profession or business with startling rapidity. So, at least, I am told by Oxford dons and undergraduates.

It is impossible to obtain corroboration of this statement, since Oxford does not collect statistics or publish reports on her graduates or undergraduates. In spite of being in Oxford for a month and a half, and asking hopefully for statistics in scores of places, I was never given a statistic.

If anybody tells you anything at Oxford, you must take his word for it; whereas if you are told something at an American university, a score of books, pamphlets, and bulletins are produced to prove it. An equal number of books, pamphlets, and bulletins can usually be found to disprove whatever you hear; so an American university, with its tons of statistics, is not much better off than Oxford, with its perpetual statistic-famine.

There has been a deal of loose conversation in the United States concerning the advisability of transferring various features of the Oxford educational system to America, but usually those who do the talking overlook some of the features which have the greatest effect on Oxford and Cambridge undergraduates. For one thing, there is the matter of scouts, which at Cambridge are termed gyps.

The influence of the scout on the Oxford undergraduate is profound. An English boy, destined for a university, is shipped away from home at the mature age of eight, or seven, or sometimes even six. He is first placed in a preparatory school, where he remains until he is thirteen or fourteen. He then moves to a public school, such as Eton, Winchester, Harrow, Rugby, or Charterhouse, where he is taught such subjects as will enable him to pass his university examinations.

Long years ago a young Englishman of position was of necessity educated in his home by a private tutor. This was both inconvenient and expensive; so, in time, groups of tutors were concentrated in schools, and young Englishmen of position attended them. These schools were called public schools to differentiate them from private residences; but the name was and still is the only public thing about them. They are the very pinnacle of scholastic privacy and exclusiveness. Consequently English public-school boys emerge from school with all the ripe knowledge of life that might be gained by a chicken in an incubator, and come up to the university to have their critical senses developed and their judgment made sound and infallible in three short years of twenty-four weeks each.

What they seem to need, according to American students at Oxford who have studied English undergraduates with some care, is a nannie or nurse, together with a few brisk kicks to drive the snobbishness from them. A nurse, however, is not considered good form at an English university; so the university supplies its students with scouts to take the place of nurses.

A scout is a servant whose duty it is to watch, feed, wake, advise, lay fires for, serve tea to, check up on, and clean up after the six or eight young men in one entry of a college building. Thus every Oxford undergraduate has a scout, whether he wants one or not.

Sometimes a scout is, or thinks he is, the perfect British manservant; and sometimes, alas, he is a slovenly old thing with an insecure memory and a bad habit of wearing tennis shoes because his feet hurt. He is, however, a servant who says "sir" to the callowest of youths, and replies "Thank you" to the most outrageous orders. This, coupled with the fact that every undergraduate at Oxford is assigned a bedroom and an adjoining study to himself, soon gives the most babylike undergraduates the feeling of being masters in their own homes.

In effect, they set up housekeeping in a big, serious way as soon as they arrive in Oxford. The results are immediately noticeable. They develop an air of assurance. They balance teacups on the arms of chairs and pass plates of scones to visitors with the aplomb of old married women. They are able to ask and answer questions without blushing, stammering, or falling over a rug, even while manipulating a teapot with one hand and a dish of tarts with the other.

In spite of being, as the saying goes, still wet behind the ears, they almost at once, thanks to their activities in directing and bossing their scouts, achieve the appearance of men of the world. This appearance is too often ascribed to the tutorial system of instruction, whereas in reality the scout should receive the credit.

To one accustomed to life in an American college, Oxford University seems exasperatingly nosy. Undergraduates are not supposed to enter a pub—a public drinking place—of which there are some three hundred in the town of Oxford. If they do so, they are liable to be severely progged and fined ten shillings by the two university proctors, each of whom stalks the streets of Oxford in the cool of the evening clad in cap and gown and accompanied by two paid minions in bowler hats and sack suits —swift-footed minions, in theory, supposedly capable of overtaking any undergraduate who flees a proctor's presence. These minions are called "bulldogs" or "bullers."

The proctorial system at Oxford is a source of never-ending argument in undergraduate circles. The number of undergraduates progged and fined ten shillings a night is large. On dull nights it may run as low as thirty. On brisk nights, when the progging is good, it may reach a hundred or even two hundred. Undergraduates like to argue as to who gets the money. Some think the proctors get it all. Others think it goes to provide sherry for high officers of the university. Certainly enough prog money has been taken in, during the past half century, to build a new Bodleian Library; and equally certainly the Bodleian doesn't get it.

The operation of progging is somewhat formal. If a buller enters a pub and spots an undergraduate sucking manfully at a pint mug of the beery liquid appropriately known, in England, as "bitter," he advances and lifts his bowler hat, at the same time pronouncing the fatal words, "Are you a member of this university, sir?"

Sometimes an undergraduate runs, if the pub has a back door; but experience has taught him that evasion is fruitless. He therefore says, "Yes," whereupon the buller politely invites him to step outside and speak to the proctor.

The proctor, usually too dignified to enter the pub in person, stands in the street like a black cloud and receives the guilty undergraduate with a frosty British stare. "What is your name and college, sir?" he asks. On learning, he sends the undergraduate home with instructions to report himself at the proctor's office the next day. On the following morning, in the proctor's office, the proctor again fixes the guilty undergraduate with a supercilious gaze and asks coldly: "You were found in the bar of the Lamb and Kettle public house at eight-twenty o'clock last night?"

The undergraduate admits it.

"That will be ten shillings," the proctor says, making a note in a ledger.

This ends the incident—unless the undergraduate is progged a second time, in which case he must pay twenty shillings. A third offense costs thirty shillings. A fourth offense is usually disastrous.

Newly arrived American, Australian, and Canadian undergraduates resent the annoying activities of the bullers, and frequently argue that the entire proctorial system could be revolutionized if, on several successive nights, a buller should unexpectedly be socked on the jaw. So far, however, nobody has appeared with sufficient initiative to organize any such revolt.

Restrictions in vogue at American colleges seem mild indeed by comparison with Oxford restrictions at which no complaints are made.

Those who are permitted by the proctors to have automobiles, for example, can use them only in the afternoon and until nine o'clock at night. Undergraduates are supposed never to attend flicks or movies except in the evening. Under no circumstances can they be out of their colleges or—in case they live in accredited lodgings—out of their rooms after midnight.

The penalty for this latter crime is expulsion. One cannot escape his doom by staying out all night; for his scout must report him if his bed has not been slept in. If he lives in lodgings and transgresses against the twelve o'clock rule, his landlady is obliged to carry the news to the authorities. Sometimes she doesn't. During my stay in Oxford, an undergraduate was out of lodgings after midnight. He was an unpleasant young man and owed his landlady a great deal of money.

"If you report me," he told her, "I won't pay you what I owe." After some thought, she concluded to keep silent. Not long afterward the unpleasant young man decided to leave the university. When the landlady asked for her money, the young gentleman laughed heartily. "If you press me," he told her, "I'll tell the proctors you didn't report me, and you'll lose your license."

Fortunately for careless undergraduates, there are methods of scaling the walls of every Oxford college in spite of their height; in spite of the broken glass and barbed wire that stud the tops of some, and the bristling chevaux-de-frise of pointed steel that guard the tops of others; in spite of the iron bars that make every lower window impassable.

Some colleges are more impregnable than others. There are only two well-known ways of scaling the walls of Christ Church after midnight, whereas there are sixteen methods of surmounting the barriers of Merton.

To an American, the manner of study at Oxford proves peculiarly puzzling. At first blush one receives the impression that an Oxford degree can be obtained with a minimum of mental exertion—and certainly, in spite of the widespread belief to the contrary, there are many young men who go down from Oxford at the end of their three years with brain cavities almost completely vacant.

At second and succeeding blushes, however, one realizes that degrees can be taken in more ways than one, and that one of the methods necessitates genuine cerebral functioning—though it is not easy to discover how, when, and where the Oxford undergraduate toils.

The two forms of Oxford degrees are known as Pass Degrees and Honours Degrees. The Pass Degree, to put it bluntly, is within the reach of any undergraduate capable of reading a motion-picture title without moving his lips. A student working for a Pass Degree studies a subject somewhat sketchily, takes an examination in that subject whenever he is ready to take it, and is then permitted to forget the subject, which he usually does with celerity. The amount of work done by an Oxford undergraduate studying for a Pass Degree is similar to, though a little less tiring than, the amount done by the average American college student.

An Honours Degree, on the other hand, requires a vast amount of reading in enormous numbers of books, some of them the heaviest and dullest books ever written in the English language.

A student delving into English literature might be obliged to read, let us say, all available poems and other writings of Algernon Bickerwell, and also read extensively in books having to do with the life and times of King Elmer II, under whom Algernon Bickerwell lived and labored, as well as other volumes dealing in detail with the political and economic policies of King Elmer's chancellors, prime ministers, and privy councilors, to say nothing of browsing in a few tomes touching on the family history of King Elmer's consort, born the Princess Margarine of Bierbrau.

Nor can he, like the candidate for a Pass Degree, permit any of these things to slip from his mind. He must hold all of them in his head for a year—possibly for two years—and then be able to sit down and write a treatise about the whole business—not a treatise that merely explains what he has read, but a treatise which puts two and two together and gets six; a treatise purporting to make clear:

(A) Why the poetry of Algernon Bickerwell should display internal evidences of a marked dissatisfaction with the sociological conditions existing in Germany during the Bierbrau period;

(B) What influence the poetry of Algernon Bickerwell had upon the architectural peculiarities of the English cathedral towns;

(C) What attitude Algernon Bickerwell might have taken in his celebrated "Ode to a Titmouse" if King Elmer had married an English duchess instead of a princess of Bierbrau; and

(D) four or five other moot points designed to show whether or not the student is able to think about what he has read, and if so, how much.

The basis of all Oxford education is reading. Students do not attend classes or recitations. They read. They may, if they wish, go to lectures; but since these are not obligatory, and since most undergraduates claim to find lectures a bore, they frequently stay in their rooms and read while the lecturer discourses to empty seats.

Not only do Oxford undergraduates read such books as are obligatory, but a surprising number of them find time to do a fair amount of reading on the side. When they depart on short or long vacs, they carry a wide assortment of volumes recommended by their tutors; and these books, in theory, they read while vacationing. I say, "in theory" because most Oxford men state frankly that if they read everything they are supposed to while on vacation, they would have no time for sleep or other diversions. When they come up again to Oxford, they write little essays for their tutors—essays showing what they have read and what they think of it. Undergraduates assure me they do not have to think correctly: they merely have to think.

Reading, at Oxford, is inextricably tangled with the Oxford tutors, or, as they are laughingly called by the Oxford set, dons.

The term "don," it should be explained, is a loose popular term applied to any senior member of any one of Oxford's colleges. It has baffling features. A member of the governing body of an Oxford college is a "fellow." Most fellows are also tutors, and therefore dons. A professor, on the other hand, is not a college officer, but a university officer. The university selects a professor to lecture, to do research work: then, since the university only exists as a group of colleges, it arbitrarily wishes the professor off on one of the colleges. It says to the college: "Give this man a home; give him room and food, and admit him on equal terms to your society." Thus all professors of the university are fellows of a college, but most fellows of a college are not professors of the university.

Anybody who finds himself confused by this clear and simple statement of fact will be no worse off than most Oxford undergraduates, and may possibly begin to understand why it is that the loose popular term "don" is so widely used in Oxford, where loose popular terms are supposedly frowned upon as being frivolous and superficial.

Some dons are young and alert. Other dons are old and crusty and ride around on battered push-bikes with their academic robes billowing about them. Some, it must be reluctantly confessed, look not unlike Snyder the Talking Ape in his great bicycle act.

Every Oxford undergraduate is supposed to have two tutors: one for his morals and one for his intellect. The moral tutor and the academic tutor may be the same man; but whether they're the same or different men, the moral tutor is not overworked.

The academic tutor, however, has his hands full. He may tutor as many as thirty undergraduates. Thirty is about as many as any one tutor is considered capable of handling.

An Oxford don who has dallied with several glasses of sherry and polished off a couple of bottles of port will occasionally be candid concerning the youths who come to him for their tutorials, and will reveal the fact that tutoring the average Oxford undergraduate, owing to the seemingly porridge-like content of his brain cavity, is as exhausting as trying to climb Mount Everest.

Thus it may be seen that an Oxford don, conversing on the subject of his pupils, sounds strikingly like an American professor giving vent to frank opinions on the same topic.

Every week an Oxford undergraduate visits his tutor for a tutorial.

He goes to the tutor's study with an essay based on the books which the tutor advised him to read in the week just past. He reads the essays to the tutor, who crouches over the cannel-coal fire or stands in front of it, exposing the seat of his trousers to the gentle glow and cutting off the heat from the shivering reader.

If the tutor is a good one, the undergraduate is helped. He is helped to see his own shortcomings and is prodded, if possible, into using his mind. He and the tutor argue and discuss and wrangle. The tutor may even go so far as to give him a glass of sherry, and, generally speaking, a pleasant time is had by all.

Not all Oxford tutors, contrary to general opinion in American educational circles, are good ones. Some of them, according to Oxford undergraduates, are extremely sticky. Others are said to be foul and even rotten.

It is difficult to get an exact definition of stickiness and foulness as applied to an Oxford tutor. The general idea seems to be that he is not helpful. Undergraduates frequently fall asleep while engaged in a conference with a sticky tutor, unless I have been misinformed, and only wake in time to be told what to read during the ensuing week.

Yet it is felt at Oxford that sticky tutors are not particularly harmful, the theory being that if the student has sufficient brain power to recognize his tutor's stickiness, he probably has enough brains to educate himself in spite of the tutor; whereas, if he cannot sense that his tutor is sticky, he hasn't the mentality to learn anything, no matter who might tutor him.

That, then, is the tutorial system: an undergraduate is told what to read; and if he is reading for honors, everything he reads is somehow supposed to have a bearing on everything else he reads. When he has completed his week's reading, he writes an essay on it and reads the essay to the tutor. The tutor's main task is to goad the undergraduate into applying his wits to his studies, as well as his eyes and his memory—to make certain he won't unquestioningly accept the statements contained in books, but will critically examine them for truth and falsity.

The student is free of the tiresome drudgery of going to classes, and is relieved as much as possible from the burden of examinations. He has only two official examinations: one at the end of his first year; then no more until the end of his third or last year. Thus, so long as he does his reading, the Oxford undergraduate is, within reason, free to do as he pleases.

Even the best of tutors is forced to admit that the stimulating of Oxford undergraduates to think for themselves is a Herculean task. For a year, tutors say, and sometimes for two years, Oxford undergraduates are inclined to be inarticulate, slow, and backward. Then the brains of some of them begin to function, albeit with a deal of squeaking and rattling. They are on their way to having trained minds.

As for the undergraduates, they behave tolerantly toward their tutors' apparently insatiable demand for personal opinion. "It doesn't take you long to learn," one of them told me, "that if your tutor asks for your personal opinion, you mustn't say you haven't one. You only need to make any silly guess at an opinion. That satisfies him, because then he can set you right."

It is the fixed belief of many Americans who have studied at Oxford that America doesn't need to borrow a great deal from England in order to work out a method of training undergraduate minds that will be at least as successful as the method in use at Oxford. Their belief is based on the peculiar fact that the finest flowers of the Oxford system of education frequently appear to have the mentality, to put it mildly, of trustful children. If this statement is questioned, the cases of Dr. Busch and Captain James Brynar Owen may be cited.

Some years ago a lecture was announced in Oxford. The giver was a distinguished German savant, Dr. Busch—a man with a luxuriant beard, a deep and convincing voice, and a fund of astounding scientific information of a metaphysical nature. It was common knowledge, before his lecture, that his academic reputation in Germany was enormous. Few were familiar with his works; but since it was definitely known that everybody knew all about him, nobody was willing to admit ignorance.

Dr. Busch lectured before an imposing assemblage of Oxford dons and professors. The hall was so full of intelligence that a rock thrown at random into the audience would have struck at least five trained minds. The peculiar feature of Dr. Busch's lecture was that although it didn't make sense, it made a great and favorable impression on the Oxford dons. None of them understood what Dr. Busch was driving at, but each one failed to mention that fact, and not only applauded the doctor heartily but agreed with everyone else that it was a magnificent effort—a *tour de force*—a great privilege to hear.

On the following day it was discovered that Dr. Busch was a Balliol undergraduate who had put on false whiskers and embarked on the lecture by way of winning a bet with a fellow undergraduate. No statement made in his lecture possessed any meaning; but the trained minds that heard him had somehow failed to get to the bottom of that fact.

On another occasion the Agricultural Engineering Research Institute of Oxford University found itself in need of a director. Word went out concerning this need; and in the course of time an impressive-looking gentleman arrived among Oxford's trained minds with all sorts of testimonials as to his high ability. He also laid claim, in well-modulated tones, to a degree from Cambridge University—the Degree of Doctor of Science. The trained minds, sitting in conclave on the doctor, exercised their highly developed critical judgment and decided he was just the man for the job. It never occurred to them to write to Cambridge to verify the doctor's credentials.

So the doctor directed the Agricultural Engineering Research Institute for seven years, ending with 1931. In 1931 somebody accidentally discovered that his accounts were not quite right. Irregularities turned up with dizzying rapidity; and Oxford's trained minds were shocked to learn that the doctor, by adroit manipulation, had made the university liable for a loss of some hundreds of thousands of pounds.

He was brought to trial, when it was disclosed that he had never taken any degree at all from Cambridge, that his testimonials were bogus, and that his best ideas concerning Agricultural Engineering Research had come from being hit on the head by a shell fragment during the war.

This belated revelation left Oxford's trained minds completely speechless, so the Law took the matter into its own hands and sent the doctor away to exercise his talents in jail.

There is no doubt that educators are correct when they say the training given to undergraduate minds in Oxford University is a splendid thing; but if American students at Oxford know what they're talking about, it isn't safe for anyone to be as profoundly satisfied with the Oxford variety of trained mind as are the English. Nothing is perfect: not even an Oxford education.

## Oxford Oddities

*From* FOR AUTHORS ONLY

MOST CONVENTIONAL BELIEFS are erroneous but difficult to alter. For centuries to come, probably, it will be generally thought that all Italians are lovers of fine music; that all Americans, in 1776, were eager to fight for their country; that mongrel dogs are less subject to illness than thoroughbreds; that all fat men are jolly; and that beautiful women are mentally deficient.

It is a widely held belief, in England, that American college students are equipped with half-portion brains, and that all of those brains, because of some peculiarity of American climate, are standardized, so that they are incapable of independent thought. This belief is nurtured and encouraged by American educators, although there is no more truth to it than to the once popular New England belief that tomatoes and strychnine were equally beneficial as foods.

It is generally thought in America, on the other hand, that England is almost entirely populated by highly polished conversationalists, scintillating speakers, able historians, far-seeing statesmen, great authors, famous poets, astute editors, penetrating essayists, and gallant sportsmen, all of whom have achieved a superior and blinding polish because of the cultural advantages of Oxford and Cambridge universities. This belief is fostered—innocently, of course—by the English themselves, and especially by English educators trained at Oxford and Cambridge. The English do not intentionally deceive: they merely hold a high opinion of themselves, and have long considered everything English not only better than anything anybody else possesses, but a great deal better than it actually is.

It is true that the Englishman's admiration of his own institutions occasionally results in mild protests, as when that eminent English churchman, Dean Inge, remarked: "We English pride ourselves on our business capacity, which is very moderate; our energy in industry, in which we are rather deficient; our political wisdom, which shows itself chiefly in our distrust of logic and our conviction (by no means always right) that force is no remedy."

It doesn't necessarily take a churchman like Dean Inge to discover the flaws in this intense English enthusiasm for everything English. One who examines English newspapers with any care discovers a constant flow of editorial complaint from scattered complainers over the decay, not to say extinction, of English statesmanship, the weaknesses of the English school system, the poverty of English poetry, the collapse of English culture into the lap of Mass Production, the triviality of English literature, the abysmal stupidity of most English films, and the dreadfulness of modern English architecture.

Those who visualize England as a land of quaint villages and fine substantial hand-made things would be somewhat shocked to find Mr. A. L. Maycock, writing in *Blackwood's Magazine* on Oxford and Cambridge universities, referring despondently to the difficulty of preventing modern

English vulgarians from destroying the beauties of an English university town. "A healthy and vigorous public opinion," he says sadly, "would swiftly make this destruction impossible. At present, however, it seems doubtful whether any such public opinion exists; for a generation brought up in the modern welter of ugliness and vulgarity is insensitive to mere beauty, and knows no decent reverence for the past."

Mr. Maycock speaks of the new towns of England: "There you have ugliness unredeemed by the smallest gleam of beauty; ugliness concentrated and multiplied; ugliness absolute and of the nadir. Two outstanding examples are the railway towns of Swindon and Crewe." He speaks of the various styles of building exemplified in the unparalleled activities of this age—Pimlico Palladian, Gas-Pipe Gothic, the Clark's College Style, Lobster Gothic. He even suggests explosives for purposes of demolition of some of the English college architecture that American educators seem willing to copy in the hope of conferring some of the blessings of the Oxford system on America.

Even those two grand old English stand-bys, reading and sportsmanship, are under suspicion. Both have been attacked: one by Mr. Cosmo Hamilton, the eminent English author; the other by Mr. W. I. Bryant, a member of the amateur All-England Football Team.

Mr. Hamilton complained that the majority of England's brighter bright people had never heard of Shakespeare, Dickens, Thackeray, Wells, Kipling, or Shaw, and that in another fifty years a vast peptonized culture would be set up in England that would make the act of reading "as barbaric as being decent and considerate toward other human beings."

Mr. Bryant pointed out that English sportsmanship was not all it was cracked up to be; for although amateur teams and their followers were regarded as the very apex of sportsmanship, the opposite was coming to be the case, and audiences of sporting Englishmen were continually urging players to injure their opponents.

I mention these interesting matters because of another conventional belief widely held in America—the belief that all the results of an English university education are better than anything that America can produce. Since most Englishmen heartily concur in this belief, one doesn't have to be a superman to know there's something wrong with it, just as there seems to be something wrong with most conventional beliefs. Neither does one have to be a trained observer to discover that there are a few unpleasant features to Oxford University—features that have no counterpart in any American university.

Why it is that these unpleasant features are never mentioned in any of the massive books on education written by all the deep educational thinkers in both America and England, I cannot say. It can't be because the educators don't know about them. Nobody can visit Oxford for more than a day, or talk to any Rhodes scholar for half an hour, without receiving an overwhelming amount of information on the various brands of viciousness that are scattered through every Oxford college. Books and brochures by Oxford undergraduates are continually mentioning the esthetic young men who rouge their cheeks and fingernails; who chatter in languid, sibilant voices; who attend pajama parties, wear single earrings, and address one another in feminine superlatives.

The captain of one of the major-sports teams in one of the best American universities commented feelingly, while pursuing his studies at Oxford, on the prevalence of what he termed "pansies" among Oxford undergraduates.

"You hear about such people in American colleges," he said, "but you seldom see 'em. Over here they're on every side of you—on the teams, on the crews: all over the place."

He and scores of other Americans and Colonials—Australians, South Africans, New Zealanders—told me, with fascinated disgust, of "binges" they had attended at Oxford—binges at which, when the inhibitions of the English undergraduates had been removed by liquor, young men would be discovered on couches and in commodious easy chairs, eagerly embracing and kissing. . . . "There are fairies at the bottom of my garden," declares a popular English song. Rhodes scholars are unable to speak with authority on gardens, but they unhesitatingly insist that there are too many fairies at the bottom of every Oxford college.

I am unable to explain the estheticism of Oxford, nor are Rhodes scholars able to explain it to the satisfaction of a detached observer. Some think it has its origin in the fag system of the English public schools—the system which permits an older boy to give any sort of order to a younger boy and be implicitly obeyed. Others blame it on the fact that English boys of the so-called upper classes are sent away to school at the age of six, seven, or eight, receive practically no home training, and then come up to a hard-drink university where many of them think it smart to drink themselves into a state of semi-insanity and turn to any sort of convenient depravity. Others think it the mark of a decadent civilization. As a matter of fact, nobody is able to explain the pansyish leanings of English youth. From time to time there are outbreaks of letters and arguments in the London *Times* on the subject of what the English delicately term "the public-school evil," but the letters and arguments never arrive at any conclusion; and they probably never will.

Rhodes scholars find this estheticism a perennial source of conversation

—not only because they have encountered nothing like it in all their American university experience, but because they are vaguely apprehensive that similar faults might somehow be transferred, along with English educational methods, to America. Not one of them but would like to see his own university in America borrow a few of the advantageous features of the English system. At the same time they are free to say that they would very much dislike to see any part of the Oxford system transferred to America if with it should go any small part of the virulent perversion that permeates Oxford.

What every Rhodes scholar, as well as every American university graduate who has visited Oxford, would like to see transferred to his own American college is the desire for reading with which Oxford somehow contrives to infect a fair percentage of her undergraduates.

Unlike American university towns, Oxford has the air of being a place where studying, reading, and mental activity are forever going on. It is difficult to trace the reasons for this intellectual atmosphere. Certainly it is not due to the appearance of the undergraduates; for they seldom carry books, and most of them have a vacant and unintelligent English look, particularly when pedaling at high speed around corners and in front of automobiles on their antiquated bicycles.

Nonetheless, there is an academic flavor to the place, and the town itself is a bookish one, just as the city of Munich is a beery city. In Munich there are beer halls on main streets and on side streets and all over the place; whereas in Oxford there are not only bookshops on the principal thoroughfares, but up alleys and down lanes, as well as next door to greengrocers, wine merchants, and meat shops.

The whole town, in the winter months, seems to smell of books—of damp bindings, musty pages, smoky leather, and long-dried fish glue. Some of the bookshops are small, dealing on the side in Christmas cards, diaries, calendars and framed pictures. Others are large and devoted almost exclusively to books.

Largest of all is Blackwell's, located on that short and celebrated street known as the Broad, on which also fronts Balliol College, Trinity College, several other bookshops, a pleasing antique shop, and three tailoring establishments, as well as the Sheldonian Theatre, the Old Ashmolean Museum, and the Bodleian Library.

Blackwell's is a good bookshop—a splendid bookshop. In the product of an Oxford author's pen, Blackwell's is modestly referred to as the Greatest Bookshop in the World. As I have pointed out, this feeling of acute satisfaction over Oxford's advantages is frequently encountered among Oxford men, though the feeling is not always shared by distinguished graduates of Cambridge University and of London University.

Blackwell's may or may not be the Greatest Bookshop in the World, but it is one of the most heavily patronized. Every day, at certain hours, Blackwell's is as thronged with undergraduates as a soft-drink emporium would be in an American college town. One who wishes to hurry in, buy a book, and pay for it is obliged to worm his way through crowds of silent, brooding undergraduates who stand before the shelves, lean against the counters, or block the aisles. All of them have their noses stuck in books. They are indulging in the popular Oxford sport of browsing. They are getting an idea what this book contains and what that book contains, without going to the trouble of buying the books.

Even the clerks in Blackwell's have acquired an Oxford manner. They wear brown tweed coats and shapeless gray trousers, and can only be told from undergraduates because they aren't staring at the shelves or peering into books. Nor will a Blackwell's clerk speak to you unless you speak to him first. This is due to another old Oxford custom, which is explained by a sign on the wall:

> When you visit Blackwell's no one will ask you what you want.
> You are free to ramble where you will; to handle any book; in short, to browse at leisure.
> The assistants are at your service when you need them; but unless you look to them, they leave you undisturbed.
> You are equally welcome whether you come to buy or to browse.
> Such has been the tradition at Blackwell's for fifty years.

In many ways it is difficult to be definite about the value of an Oxford education. It is difficult because of not knowing how much a man gets out of Oxford, and how much he has in him to begin with. The poet Shelley is one of the bright jewels of whom Oxford boasts, and when the subject of "turning out" great men arises, Shelley's name usually crops up. He was an undergraduate at University College, Oxford, for eleven months in 1810. Then Oxford turned him out. In other words, he was expelled. In the 123 years that have elapsed since that day, a large number of able men have had the advantage of a more complete Oxford training than Shelley had, but there has never been another Shelley.

There is no doubt, however, that an Oxford education encourages the undergraduate to read, and to read good books, and to express himself with considerable fluency as to why a book is good and why it is bad.

It makes reading and conversation fashionable and habitual, which is more than can be said for most American universities, where an undergraduate is too often regarded as queer if he indulges in any protracted amount of reading, and as almost dangerous if he persists in talking about what he reads.

This affection for books, which is so widespread in Oxford, is frequently overdone. Many of those who browse in Blackwell's are sometimes so engrossed in what they are reading that they inadvertently drop the books in their pockets and walk out without thinking to pay for them or to mention them to the clerks. They even neglect to bring them back later; and their absent-mindedness occasionally takes the strange form of causing them to hurry, with these books, to other bookstores and there to sell them secondhand.

The yearly cost, to Blackwell's, of books thus absent-mindedly removed by undergraduate booklovers is in the neighborhood of £1,000, or approximately $5,000.

Oxford dons themselves are hard put to it to explain why it is that reading, general culture, and the trained mind are viewed with so much respect by Oxford undergraduates. Some ascribe it to the tutorial system. Others think it is inculcated in undergraduates by the high quality of the English public schools and the manner in which English boys, in their public schools, are encouraged to be articulate.

This is indignantly denied by another school of thought, which declares that the chief function of English public schools is to encourage snobbery, mass production, intellectual timidity, and class distinction, as well as several other grave faults.

A large group of theorists hold that Oxford men are readers and conversationalists because of the cultivated atmosphere of the homes from which so many Oxford and Cambridge men emerge. They would like to have you think that in countless stately homes of England, for years and years, the pater, after tea, has taken his infant offspring into the study and read to him from the classics for an hour or two each day, thus giving him an undying affection for great literature.

Unfortunately this theory fails to bear up under examination, for one encounters large numbers of English undergraduates who had little more than a bowing acquaintance with their paters before being shunted off to boarding school while still the size of two peanuts laid end to end.

Still others think that the winter chill prevalent in Oxford is at the bottom of the undergraduate's respect for reading, since it makes him willing to huddle over a cannel-coal fire with a book. This opinion has little value; for the undergraduate himself blames the coldness of the buildings for his persistent indulgence in athletics as a means of keeping warm.

Still others tell you that it is the historic, mellow atmosphere of Oxford's ancient buildings that fills her sons with the love of learning. That mellow atmosphere, they say, does something to you—something besides giving you bronchitis.

For months, they declare, you shiver with the cold and hate the place. Then, on a spring evening, you see the misty moon behind the lace of Magdalen Tower; you hear the bells of Oxford rolling like the surge of the sea across the Christ Church Meadows: you become suddenly conscious of the great men of Oxford's past, looking down on you from the glowing canvases—Gainsboroughs, Raeburns, Lelys, Knellers, Lawrences—that hang in solid ranks around the cathedral-like walls of your college hall; and something happens inside you. In you, they claim, is born a love of Oxford, a peculiar respect for education, a conception of the intrinsic value of knowledge: a desire, in short, to read your head off.

The truth of the matter seems to be that reading is the fashion at Oxford, just as is the wearing of gray trousers and Harris tweed jackets.

It has become fashionable to realize and admit the value of learning and to try openly to acquire an education.

Not so many years ago, in spite of all the tutors in all of Oxford's colleges, in spite of all the public schools and all the private readings given to small sons by all the paters in all the stately homes of England, in spite of the misty moon behind Magdalen Tower and the surging bells and whatnot, any mention of books or any semblance of bookishness was viewed with suspicion at Oxford. Sport was the topic of conversation.

There was a time, in the not so distant past, when Oxford undergraduates were willing to argue that it was a finer thing for an Oxford cricketer to make a hundred runs against Cambridge than to be Prime Minister of England: a far, far better thing to win a rowing Blue than to earn the Victoria Cross.

Those days are gone, which ought to be something of an encouragement to such easily discouraged American educators as like to cry mournful cries to the effect that the college student of America doesn't know what education is and therefore cannot be educated—who think that styles, even bad ones, never change—who are, in short, licked before they start.

Such American educators as complain that education in America is being ruined by the college man's interest in matters not in any way connected with his studies would be left in a state of fawn-eyed amazement at the amount of time and energy devoted by Oxford men to extracurricular activities.

I also imagine—or fancy, to use the phrasing of Oxford dons—I also fancy that those same educators would fly into a frenzy at the amount of undergraduate drinking at which Oxford authorities seem to connive.

Each college has what is known as its "Stores" tucked away in a corner of one of its quadrangles. If you visit an Oxford undergraduate to have a cup of tea, you are apt to find yourself involved in a long and heated argument with him and three or four of his friends—an argument during which the fatheadedness of *King Lear* as a play, the detective stories of the late Wilkie Collins, the financial insanities of American legislators and executives, the qualities of low-priced American motorcars, the advantages of double-breasted dinner coats, and the shortcomings of British rule in India are comprehensively considered and dismissed. During the argument two pots of tea, a large plate of scones, a heap of cinnamon toast, and a cake the size of a washbasin are demolished, along with two bottles of sherry. Calls for more sherry reveal the distressing fact that there is no more.

"Stores are open," the tea-drinkers tell each other consolingly, reaching for their mufflers. "We'll go over to Stores." So you go over to Stores, expecting to find an extensive emporium. Instead you find one room, and that reminiscent of an old-fashioned grocery store in a small New England town. It is dimly lighted, and the wares on the shelves half obscured in a smoky fog. On the shelves are cigars, cigarettes, tobacco, biscuits and tinned goods of various sorts, and a wealth of bottles of a rich, dark hue. Behind the counter sits a benevolent old party with an account book in his lap.

Every night, before dinner, all the Stores in Oxford colleges are crowded with undergraduates busily hoisting pewter mugs of one-pint capacity and conversing in that strangely accented speech that is said to be peculiar to Oxford, a speech characterized by words that seem half chewed and half swallowed. It takes time and concentration to realize that when they say "mertrist" they are referring to a motorist, and that the words "jew cawse" have no more sinister meaning than "due course."

You worm your way through these tweed-coated groups and face the storekeeper, who stares amiably over the tops of his spectacles.

"Fairly decent sherry here," your host says.

The storekeeper's eyebrows work nervously. "Brown or pale, sir?" he asks.

He reaches behind him for bottles containing both brown and pale and fills the glasses with the skill of an old bartender, twisting the bottles neatly to prevent the overexpenditure of even one drop. Then he makes a note in his account book: "Mr. Surbiton-Jones, 4 sherries, 2/0."

The old familiar language of the barroom, couched in Oxford patois, impinges on the ear:

"I say, what about another?"

"Oh, rah-THER!"

"Oh, I say, you must have one with me, eh?"

"Look here, Davenport, that's awf'ly good of you, but I ought to be running along!"

"What rot, Faulkner! I say, Noke, draw us six more, eh?"

"I'll have a go at the sherry, St. John: filthy stuff, that bitter!"

"Three more sherries, Noke!"

"Two bottles of sherry to take out, Noke!"

"I say, Noke, two sherries!"

"Six sherries, Noke!"

Why it is that American educators talk so glibly about the Oxford system, yet remain abnormally silent on the subject of the Stores of Oxford colleges, I cannot say. It may be, of course, that their ideal is an educational system that will borrow all the hard work from other systems but none of the fun—which would be about as far from the Oxford system as they could get.

The number of extracurricular activities into which Oxford undergraduates can and do plunge is enormous. Their plunging seems, in fact, so comprehensive and so wholehearted as to leave them no time for serious study. Oxford undergraduates, however, thanks to the industry of their scouts, have breakfast in their rooms; and usually they lunch on a piece of cold meat and a cup of tea in the same solitary state. Since there are no classes to distract their attention, they can, if they will, devote their mornings to reading, and that is what a fair percentage of them do. Thus the afternoons are left free for social activity and lighthearted play.

The primary pursuit of Oxford undergraduates, apparently, is athletics. There is no such thing as compulsory athletics at Oxford; but the climate of the place is theoretically so foul that daily exercise, and plenty of it, must be taken by those who wish to escape complete mental and physical collapse.

This is the usual argument for the prevalence of athletics at Oxford. It is hardly an impressive argument, in view of the fact that the normal population of the town of Oxford is 50,000, and that the bulk of the 50,000 seems to remain in an excellent state of health in spite of indulging in no more violent form of exercise than bicycling to and from work and standing on street corners during the early evening.

Still another argument advanced for the large amount of athletic endeavor at Oxford is that young men can be fitted for the struggle with life only if they participate in some form of sport. I am glad to present these arguments as they were presented to me; for some of the educators who are eager to transfer the Oxford system to America may wish to make use of them.

What I cannot understand—though educators can doubtless do so—is why all sports are not of equal value. Oxford, for example, doesn't give its varsity players the right to wear a big O on a sweater, but awards them a Blue—the external symbols of a Blue being a blue cap and blazer. England is full of Old Blues—persons who have played for Oxford against Cambridge, or vice versa, in a major sport. Those who play in minor sports are awarded only Half Blues, and their caps and blazers are not solidly colored, but are striped like barber poles. The theory, I assume, is that sports which rate a mere Half Blue—boxing, swimming, lacrosse, fencing, and so on— are only half as healthy as major sports like cricket and Rugby and rowing, or only half-fit a young man for the struggle with life.

At all events, there seem to be more teams to the acre in Oxford than there are potatoes to the acre in Aroostook County. Every college has three crews, rowing being the great king sport at both Oxford and Cambridge; and if any two universities in America, with all their organized cheering and preliminary advertising and expensive coaching staffs, can work up as much excitement as is aroused in the undergraduates of Oxford by the races between the crews of Oxford's different colleges—races in which they bump each other along the narrow, winding Isis—I have never heard of the universities.

I went down across Christ Church Meadows on a cold December day to the long row of decorative barges against the bank—barges used by the crews as boathouses and dressing rooms.

The wind was howling out of the east, as cold as though it came straight from an icehouse. On the little stretch of narrow river immediately in front of the barges twenty eight-oared crews were sliding up and down. Another twenty were out of sight downstream. Here and there, on the towpath, men pedaled violently on ancient bicycles, bawling plaintively through megaphones to the crews. One of the bawlers was a don—an Old Blue—who had come to the river to offer advice and criticism. Another was a varsity oarsman out of last year's boat. That's the only sort of coaching they have at Oxford and Cambridge.

Forty crews on the river, on a bitter cold day in December, shows something of an interest in rowing—even more of an interest than can be found in America's leading rowing universities.

On the same day, the Cambridge University oarsmen indulged in a little intensive rowing in their frostbitten marsh country. The London *Morning Post* reported the event in its usual exuberant way:

Cambridge, Saturday. The University Trial Eights race was rowed today at Èly. The conditions were very bleak and cold, due to a fresh east wind blowing across the Fens direct from the North Sea. This did not prevent the usual large company of rowing men making the journey from Cambridge by water; and twenty-six eights, one four, three scullers, and a tub-pair accomplished the twenty miles' journey during the morning.

Two hundred and seventeen men rowing twenty miles to see a boat race between crews of their own university is, it seems to me, an excellent example of sport for sport's sake, and is worthy of a certain amount of silent thought. How they got home, I do not know; for the *Morning Post*, in a moment of journalistic inertia, overlooked this important detail. From what I have seen of Oxford and Cambridge crews, I wouldn't have been at all surprised to hear that they rowed back.

I might add that the repeated defeat of Oxford by Cambridge at rowing gives rise to more hot air in England than all the central-heating systems to be found in that tight little island. An Oxford varsity crew has seldom beaten a Cambridge varsity crew since the year of the Big Fog or thereabouts, and a favorite pastime among Englishmen is arguing over the causes. Some think it is because modern Oxford undergraduates have degenerated: others because Oxford men are too intellectual: others because Oxford men aren't trained to row before they come to college. It was even argued seriously in weighty London journals, during the winter of 1933–34, that beer was to blame. A stronger brand of beer is, in theory, brewed in Cambridge than in Oxford: consequently, it is argued that stronger beer makes stronger oarsmen.

I suspect that if the latter belief had ever been mentioned in the hearing of the late Charles Courtney, coach for many years of monotonously victorious Cornell crews, he would have roared and bellowed himself into an apoplexy. A Cornell oarsman who was discovered applying his lips to a glass of beer was forever disgraced. At Oxford and Cambridge, however, they train on beer.

While the Oxford crews are on the river, warming the ice-cold water with the rapid beat of their oar blades, the Rugby teams, the soccer teams, the field hockey teams, and all the other teams of all twenty-two of the

Oxford colleges and of several Oxford clubs are engaged in internecine strife on a score of playing fields.

Every Oxford college has its playing field, and I will go so far as to say that the percentage of playing done on those fields is higher than that done on any other university fields in the world, with the single exception of those at Cambridge.

All Oxford teams operate on a peculiarly sensible basis. They think a team should get its practice by playing games with opponents. Practicing, they argue, isn't much fun; but playing games is fun; so they play games.

An average autumn schedule of the Isis Field Hockey Club of Oxford, for example, calls for the playing of thirty-two games with various colleges of Oxford University between October 17 and November 30—thirty-two games in forty-five days. At the same time, on adjacent fields, scores of other teams strain and strive, not only at field hockey but at Rugby, track athletics, association football, and other games.

Oxford should be a paradise for sport lovers who wish to watch an unending round of excellent games under uncrowded conditions and at no expense. It is my understanding, however, that most sport lovers love sport only when they can spend $50 for seats in a cold stadium and travel a hundred miles in great discomfort and at large expense with eighty thousand other sufferers to witness a contest which they only partly understand.

The method in vogue at Oxford for selecting the members of a varsity team is interesting and not without merit, even when compared with the American system of keeping eighty or a hundred men working all season without an opportunity to play in a game.

When the Rugby teams of all the Oxford colleges start playing in the autumn, the captains of the different teams keep careful watch on the new material that appears, fresh from public schools.

If there is an outstanding player among the freshmen who present themselves at, say, the Brasenose College football field, the Brasenose captain writes a letter to the captain of the Oxford University Rugby Football Club, informing him of his find. The young man is thereupon told to report to the captain of the varsity team. He is tried out. If he is good, he is used on the team. Otherwise he goes back and plays for Brasenose.

The result of all this playing has a peculiar effect on what is known, in some localities, as the gate. At most games, even at important ones, there are not many more spectators than players. This is due to the fact that those who, in America, would be spectators are off somewhere playing a game of something against somebody else.

Even the girls' colleges have teams. They play games—field hockey particularly—against men's teams, and give a good account of themselves. I happened by the University Parks on a freezing cold November afternoon and saw what appeared to be a riot in progress between a number of young men and an equal number of what looked like twelve-year-old schoolgirls. They seemed to be hitting each other over the head and on the shins with clubs.

On investigation, the twelve-year-old schoolgirls proved to be mature women clad in a schoolgirlish garb of long black stockings and an abbreviated black dress over a white upper garment of the type known—or so I am told—as a guimpe. They comprised the field hockey team of St. Margaret's Hall—one of Oxford's colleges for women—and they were engaged in a serious struggle with the Cow Club of Oxford University.

One of the gentlemanly members of the Cow Club politely informed me that the Cow Club was recruited from various colleges of the university, and that its avowed purposes were to destroy all pictorial representations of Highland cattle and to provide homes for cows that no longer give milk.

Another singular feature of Oxford athletics is that when a team is selected to represent the university or one of the colleges, and has taken the field for the purpose of playing a game, it stays on the field until the game is over. There are no long intermissions, nor do the players leave the field to receive the mental stimulus of a pep talk from a $10,000 coach. Halfway through the game there is a five-minute intermission, during which the two teams withdraw to opposite ends of the field and each player is permitted to pep himself up by sucking half a lemon. At the end of five minutes the lemon peels are piled neatly on a plate, removed from the field, and the game is vigorously resumed.

If a member of either team is so unfortunate as to be injured, his team gets along without him until he is able to return. If he is killed or permanently damaged, his team plays as best it can without replacing him; for substitutes are unknown. From this it may possibly be apparent to many persons that the tutorial system is not the only good feature of Oxford education.

Once, back in the thirties, Yale University created enormous excitement in athletic circles, when playing Princeton, by using, throughout the game, the same eleven players. Sports writers and radio announcers referred emotionally to Yale's eleven iron men—to those giants of football who gave their all for Dear Old Yale. They cried amazed cries concerning the terrific physical strain entailed by this superhuman feat

. . . a feat performed by every Oxford and Cambridge team in every game it plays.

A number of Oxford undergraduates questioned me, one evening, about the manner in which large American universities frequently send three or four teams of substitutes against a small college team which has no substitutes. They made no comment until I asked them what they thought of the idea, whereupon one of them contented himself with remarking that it sounded like rather a nasty bit of work.

For the benefit of such American sports enthusiasts as consider English athletics tame and namby-pamby by comparison with those of America, I might add that I had the good fortune, one cold December day, to see Oxford play Cambridge at Rugby.

There were sixty thousand people at the game, which was played on neutral grounds near London. The stands were covered, and at convenient spots beneath the stands were located those sterling British institutions known as snack bars. A large percentage of the sixty thousand patronized these snack bars before the game; yet, incredible as it may seem, there were no drunks, no fights in the stands, no beating of strangers over the head by overstimulated enthusiasts.

Apparently the sixty thousand spectators had come with no ulterior motive, as is so often the case in America, and were actually eager, not to say determined, to let nothing, not even alcohol, interfere with their enjoyment of the game. This may or may not be an indication that the English understand nothing about pleasure.

The game was played on a Wednesday, that being the day after the universities had closed for the Christmas vac. Apparently it never occurs to the English to wait for Saturday in order to play big games. They play when it's convenient, and if their dates don't quite suit the convenience of the public, nobody—not even the public—seems annoyed.

My seats were on what would correspond to the 50-yard line, and cost 7/6 apiece, or $1.87—and to the best of my knowledge and belief, no football game in the history of the world was ever worth more than $1.87. The game was scheduled for 2:15. The two teams, of fifteen men each, came on the field at 2:14, hurried to the center of the field and went to playing at 2:15.

They played two 50-minute halves without taking time out or leaving the field. When the Cambridge captain was injured, he was dragged under the grandstand to recuperate, and his team played on without him. In ten minutes' time he staggered back and went to playing again.

It was as fast and exciting a contest as I ever saw, and more exciting than 90 per cent of the big American football games I have seen. It was not, however, regarded as a good game by the football experts of the London *Times* and the London *Morning Post,* both of whom intimated that they found it tiresome.

I had always been given to understand that the Oxford and Cambridge man is at all times the perfect British gentleman, who never raises his voice and never, whatever the provocation, permits himself to become excited. My informants, however, had not been strictly accurate; for as soon as the game started, all sixty thousand of the spectators began to scream and bellow in a highly emotional manner, and some were indubitably Oxford men. In my immediate vicinity three or four hundred apparent maniacs continued for nearly two hours to shout hoarsely: "ox-FORD! oxFORD! oxFORD!" only pausing occasionally to remark in conversational tones, "Well played, Cambridge."

For those able to exist in the Oxford climate without constant daily participation in sports, there are other activities—more, even, than can be discovered in an American university that goes in heavily for extracurricular activities. The only extracurricular activity that doesn't exist in Oxford is the popular American pastime of working one's way through college by any of the devices so familiar to every American university town.

An Englishman of standing will, while a public-school boy, perform the most menial services for his seniors when acting as a fag; but he would, unless I have been misinformed, prefer to be shot rather than finance his education by serving regularly in a dining hall. At all events, there are no student laundry agencies at Oxford; no pressing clubs; no waiting on table by undergraduates.

They can, however, assist themselves through Oxford in another way. If they are short of funds, have ability, and are genuinely eager to study, they can win one of the hundreds of scholarships awarded yearly by every Oxford college—scholarships which have an average value of $300.

The cost of an Oxford education can be held down to $1,200 a year provided the undergraduate is careful, buys his sherry by the case, and is able to make one tweed jacket last him for his entire college course. It is more apt to cost $2,000 a year, even when the undergraduate is only mildly interested in having a good time.

Of other extracurricular activities, especially of societies and clubs, there is a glut or spate.

There are opera societies, dramatic societies, international and religious and political groups of every denomination; hunt clubs whose members put on pink coats and spend the better part of a day chasing a fox with forty or fifty hounds, and ordinary clubs whose chief reason for existing seems to be to provide a place where the more exclusive young men can get together in private clubrooms and drink too much sherry.

It is customary, in America, for the older generation to speak with bated breath of the amount of drinking done at some of the leading American universities, but it is my considered opinion that American undergraduates are almost blue-ribboners by comparison with Oxford's clubmen and undergraduate drinkers when they let themselves go.

It was my fortune, during a part of my stay in Oxford, to live in "digs" on St. Johns Street, where a number of wealthy undergraduates live. The nightly howling, catcalling, drunken riotings, and foul language that rose from the "digs" on that street surpassed anything I ever encountered in a long acquaintance with some of the most serious drinkers in several American universities.

Occasionally a club permits its drinking to go a trifle too far. One of Oxford's most celebrated clubs is the Bullingdon, whose members are mostly peers or excessively wealthy. During my stay in Oxford the Bullingdon staged one of its routine end-of-the-term binges. If the members had been content to wind up their festivities by celebrating in the usual manner, they would have piled chairs, couches, and bathroom fixtures in the middle of the quadrangle of one of the colleges, set fire to the pile, and danced drunkenly around the blaze. In that case everything would have been taken in good part, and the leading spirits of the university would merely have remarked that Boys will be Boys.

On this particular occasion, however, it occurred to some of the club's master minds that fireworks, set off indiscriminately in a cozy college quadrangle, would make a splendid display. Fireworks were accordingly set off, with spectacular results. A senior member of the college, who was so unfortunate as to be watching the proceedings, stopped a rocket with a part of his anatomy seldom used for rocket-stopping. He was naturally annoyed and uttered a protest, at which the members of the Bullingdon, peevish at what they considered unjustified criticism, handled him, to put it conservatively, roughly. As a result, the Bullingdon was suspended by the proctors and its clubrooms closed. For a few terms the fine old drinking traditions of Oxford were carried on without open assistance on the part of the Bullingdon; and club celebrations were restricted to the more conventional couch-and-chair-burnings.

Unlike American universities, Oxford is sterile ground for the journalistically inclined undergraduate. There is, for example, no undergraduate daily paper, probably owing to the fact that there is no need for one. Oxford undergraduates, if newspaper readers by nature, read the London papers; and though London papers have their faults, an undergraduate newspaper that tried to compete with them would, in all probability, have an appearance of futility and anemia that would keep it from working up a circulation.

Newspaper work, too, is beneath the dignity of an English gentleman. He is willing to be a journalist and sit in a quiet room writing fascinating little pieces on Etruscan art or the Mystery of Stonehenge; but he would shudder profoundly at the thought of doing leg work on a train wreck or a breach-of-promise case.

There are, however, two permanent undergraduate magazines of an airy nature, the *Isis* and the *Cherwell*, both reminiscent of the worst features of a country newspaper, London *Punch* and the society section of the Palm Beach *Post*. The *Cherwell* doesn't think highly of the *Isis*, and the *Isis* regards the *Cherwell* as scarcely worthy of consideration in a literary sense. Each, however, has an excellent opinion of itself, and—in the true Oxford manner—regards itself as the training school for the great novelists and master journalists of the immediate future.

The principal difference between the *Isis* and the *Cherwell*, to the eye of the lay observer, seems to be that the *Isis* tolerates and even condones the existence of the Oxford co-ed or undergraduette, whereas the *Cherwell* either ignores her or pierces her tender skin with the poisoned barbs of satire.

The *Isis* has a woman's page, headed "The Dovecotes," on which the leading co-ed—or undergraduette—journalists are given a free hand in the reporting of sherry parties and other mixed gatherings of interest in Oxford social circles. The undergraduettes of Oxford's four women colleges have a high reputation for intellectual achievement, but their journalists express themselves on paper in a style strikingly similar to that of co-ed journalists in American universities.

The *Isis* party [they write] was *the* party of the term. Beaumont Street was just one seething mass of humanity both inside and out, and the street was lined on both sides with numerous cars. . . . There were so many male notabilities that I shall not even try to enumerate them. . . . *What a party!*

If one based his opinion on male undergraduate humor, one might leap to the conclusion that Oxford co-eds or undergraduettes not only have a pretty thin time of it, but show up badly by comparison with Oxford's male undergraduates. Such an opinion would be incorrect.

It is true that some undergraduettes, as they career through the streets of Oxford on secondhand push-bikes which have a resale value of seven dollars, have an oddly anxious look. They wear birettas instead of the conventional mortarboard caps—a biretta being a soft four-pointed headgear reminiscent of a mortarboard that has undergone a sort of fatty degeneration. They are also apt to wear the conventional academic gown, which billows out behind as they ride, something like a balloon jib.

Their worried look is probably due to their natural desire to keep their hats on, their skirts down, and their stability from being endangered by their billowing gowns.

Considered apart from their bicycles, they are not much different from girls anywhere, except that they seem a little more solid physically than American co-eds. I have been given to understand that the English climate is responsible for the sturdiness of feminine ankles in England, though some insist it is due to the heavier balbriggans affected by English girls. At all events, English undergraduettes, to my way of thinking, run about 16 to the long ton, whereas American co-eds run about 20.

Just as in American universities where co-eds are theoretically held in contempt, there is a certain amount of contact between Oxford undergraduates and undergraduettes. At eleven o'clock in the morning, for example, they may be discovered together in large numbers at Cadena's, a coffee-and-bun shop opposite the high, fortresslike walls of Balliol College, murmuring to each other in an unacademic manner while stuffing themselves with apple tarts and coffee. Dances take place on Saturday nights within the halls of the women's colleges; and the more socially inclined of the girls are seen stepping out with surprising frequency—considering that Oxford undergraduettes are supposed to read an average of one book every seventeen minutes.

I talked with several undergraduettes concerning the low opinion in which they were theoretically held by the male undergraduate, and they hastened to inform me that the male undergraduate was not, as the saying goes, so hot. They spoke sharply, in passing, of the excessive cold in Oxford during the two winter terms, and of the difficulty of obtaining baths in many of the university rooms. They made a few tart observations on the callous indifference of university authorities to undergraduettes who were taken sick: you could die, they said, and nobody'd bother to investigate.

There was supposed to be an Oxford manner, they said, but nobody knew what it was. There was supposed to be an Oxford type of essay, but nobody knew what *that* was. Supposedly an Oxford man could be distinguished from an undergraduate of any other college in the world, they said, but that wasn't so. Put him in overalls and give him another sort of haircut and you couldn't tell him from anybody else with a hot potato in his mouth.

It was their belief that Oxford men wear the worst-looking clothes in the world; that they are the most self-satisfied men in the world; that they are the vaguest young men in the world. Vagueness, they declared emphatically, is the one great distinguishing feature of an Oxford education. Oxford teaches you to be vague. If you are given an essay to write, the subject is vague, usually—something like, "Describe the importance of William I." They raised their eyes despairingly. The importance of William I, indeed! Why not the importance of the solar system?

They referred coldly to the nightly bawling and shouting of the Oxford undergraduates who had absorbed too much sherry or too much heavy beer. They spoke contemptuously of the British reserve which, in theory, is one of the earmarks of the Oxford undergraduate. "Reserve!" they exclaimed sardonically. "Reserve!"

"Then you don't like the place?" I asked.

They stared at each other and then at me.

"Like it?" one of them said. "Like it? When I first came here I thought I'd never be warm again as long as I lived! I hated it! But when spring came, it was warm and I loved it! There's nothing like it anywhere! *I* could go down on my knees and kiss every old stone in every one of its buildings!"

It is not only the *Isis* and the *Cherwell* which are, in their own minds, training schools for the great novelists and master journalists of the future. There are other Oxford publications that suffer from a similar belief— temporary publications that materialize yearly from nowhere, like May flies, dance and flutter a little above the current of university life, and then vanish. There is no way of knowing how many novelists and journalists are trained by these little publications; but certainly there are more incipient novelists and journalists in Oxford University than in any other educational institution anywhere in the world. Every Oxford undergraduate, seemingly, is willing, not to say eager, to break into print on the slightest provocation.

It is, of course, impossible to learn how many of them are engaged in writing books, but it is safe to say that three fifths of the undergraduates have planned the novel which they propose to write as soon as they have the time and the leisure.

My own private researches lead me to think that at least twenty-five per cent of Oxford's undergraduates have the half-finished manuscript of a novel tucked away in the back of a desk drawer. Each year a number of them succeed in completing books; and what is more surprising, they even succeed in getting them published.

I read carefully, during my stay in Oxford, all the books published by undergraduates during the preceding three years; and candor compels me to state that something ought to be done about it.

Most of the novels deal with the most unpleasant features of Oxford's undergraduate life, and their underlying motif is grim realism. Occasionally one is written in lighter vein and deals with the unpleasant features in a grimly humorous manner. When it comes to genuinely grim grimness, it is my belief that Oxford undergraduate authors can be as grim as, if not grimmer than, any young authors anywhere, in spite of the widespread epidemic of grim writing that now infects the younger set.

The most widely acclaimed of those Oxford novels contained a humorous interlude which described the visit to America of the highly intellectual and cultured Oxford hero. A few selections from this humorous interlude will give a fair picture of the author's artistry and accuracy, his skill at character delineation, and his powers of observation—particularly his uncanny accuracy at depicting American speech.

Mr. Kinnel, the hero, arrives in New York by plane and hastens at once to the office of America's foremost film executive. He first meets a stenographer, who says to him, "Ow! Yew're Mr. Kinnel. Waal, I guess I'm crazy not to have known yew. Why, yew've bin the sole conversation in Noo York for the last week. My, yew've tricked England some!"

He then encounters the son of the big film executive. Although the son has taken degrees at both Harvard and Oxford, the culture of the latter university has rested lightly upon him. In spite of three years of Tutorials he says to the hero, "Meet the wife, Kinnel. Miriam, this is Mr. Kinnel, whom you've read so much about in the papers. We were pals at Arxfud." He also uses such words as "gonna," "lingo," "I reckon" and "Waal," as is, of course, customary among Americans who have had educational advantages.

The wife replies to Mr. Kinnel's compliments by "showing her brilliant teeth" and remarking, "Waal, I feel the same myself about yew. I've bin reading about yew in the papers, and I've been seeing your photograph everywhere, and everyone over here's bin talking about yew. I've never laafed so much in all my life as at the idea of li'l' England swallowin' that flyin' stuff."

This lady, evidently, is a cosmopolitan character; for only occasionally does she drop her g's; and in addition to using the plain "you" and the fancy "yew," she mixes her "bins" and her "beens" indiscriminately.

Shortly after this "there entered a white-haired man with a round pimply face. Kinnel recognized the President of the United States."

The great film executive, Mr. Salmon, wastes no formalities on the nation's chief magistrate, but says to him, "Waal, take a seat." There followed a splendid passage from this outstanding sample of Oxford literature:

The President sat down and mopped his pimply and perspiring face with a small silk "Old Glory."

Mr. Salmon at once adopted a bullying tone. "I jest vant yew to see to it that we have the *Voodrow Vilson*, the *Alexander Hamilton*, and the *Abraham Lincoln* for the last fortnight in May. Get me?"

"I'll speak to the Navy Department about it. But really, Salmon, I'm scared no end about these Japs. Such mean little beasts. Like school kids."

The President of the United States blew his nose ferociously upon "Old Glory."

"Sometimes I wish I were still jest Sheriff of Lugville," he said, with something of a sob in his throat.

The President, in addition to using the good old American phrase "no end," also uses the word "Waal."

Occasionally an Oxford author who has achieved something rather unusual in the line of grim realism is thrown in the river by his brother undergraduates, who seems to think that grimness can be overdone if it strikes too close to home.

Permanent results, however, are seldom effected by throwing an author in the river. It seems to me that an undergraduate author, writing about Oxford University, represents the university at least as effectively as any member of the Oxford Fencing Team or Boxing Team or Swimming Team, all of whose members are Half Blues. My suggestion is that the university organize an Oxford University Novelists' Association, and that Quarter Blues be awarded to such novels as are fit to print. I am under the impression that if such awards existed, and were honestly distributed, no Oxford author would have received a Quarter Blue for a long, long time.

Greatest of all Oxford training schools, according to a large portion of the Oxford undergraduate body, is the Oxford Union. The Oxford Union, a visitor to Oxford is told a thousand times, is called the "Cradle of British Statesmanship." Seemingly it is called the "Cradle of British Statesmanship" because so many Englishmen who muttered their maiden speeches in the Oxford Union subsequently rose to be cabinet ministers, governors, ambassadors, even prime ministers of England.

The walls of the Oxford Union are crowded with photographs of the great men who were, in their day, presidents of this cradle of British statesmanship. Even though Oxford men are fond of saying that the older generation made a mess of things, they still stick to it that the Union has been the cradle of British statesmanship for over a hundred years.

"Who was it," you ask, "that made the mess?"

"The soldiers," they say. "The rulers; the men who governed; the old men."

"The politicians?" you ask.

"Yes, the politicians—the statesmen. They made a mess of things. There'll be none of that in the Liberal parties of the future."

"But," you say, "your statesmen were cradled here! The Oxford Union is the cradle of British statesmanship. That means, doesn't it, that statesmanship needs a new cradle?"

Apparently it means nothing of the sort, for those to whom such a question is propounded merely stare at you vaguely and murmur, "I beg your pardon?" So I pass on the information for what it is worth: the Oxford Union is the cradle of British statesmanship.

Probably half of the male undergraduates at Oxford are members of the Union. Female undergraduates are not allowed to join. If the women want a union, the men say, let 'em build their own.

The Union has two functions. Primarily it is a library where books can be easily found and borrowed, or, if desired, read in peace; and attached to the libraries are lounging rooms where undergraduates may refresh themselves and stimulate their thoughts with tea and cakes. The function for which it is best known, however, is that of a debating society, constructed and operated on the lines of the British House of Commons.

Every Thursday night, at the Oxford Union, there is a debate. The debate is held in a hall with benches on either side, like those in the House of Commons. At one end, behind a raised desk, sits the president of the Union, who is elected to serve one term only—a term being eight weeks. The presidency of the Union is one of the most eagerly sought honors in Oxford, and has twice been held by Americans—by W. J. Bland, Kenyon College, O., and Lincoln College, Oxford, 1910: killed in action, 1918; and by R. M. Corson, University of Michigan and Oriel College, Oxford, 1918. Beneath the president sit the secretary, the treasurer, and the other officers of this university parliamentary body, all in evening clothes. Around the hall, high up, runs a narrow balcony—crowded, Thursday nights, with an attentive audience of visitors and townsfolk.

The subjects debated at the Oxford Union have a certain similarity to Oxford athletics. Oxford undergraduates play games primarily for their own amusement, and not for the edification of audiences. Similarly, subjects selected for debate at the Union, instead of being weighty matters designed to catch the attention of the world's economic experts, are subjects that seem to the officers of the Union best calculated to please undergraduate debaters and to bring from them the largest amount of opinion of one sort or another. It should also be understood that the manner of debate most in favor at the Union is apt to prove slightly befuddling to an American undergraduate debater, who enters a debate with the avowed intention of debating and of producing a sufficient array of facts and figures to win. The Union debater, contrary to the orthodox debating code, prefers to inconvenience his opponents by a series of flippant remarks and to fog the issue with epigrams, puns, and verbal acrobatics of an entertaining sort. He seems to have a double aim: to enjoy himself and to provoke a laugh.

It was my privilege to hear a powerful and protracted debate in the Oxford Union. The motion was "That Borstal and Eton are a couple of fine old schools." Eton, I scarcely need to say, is one of England's most celebrated public schools. Borstal is what is known in America as a reform school. A similar debate, in American undergraduate circles, would be, "Resolved, that Sing Sing and Yale are a couple of splendid Alma Maters."

Some thirty speakers rose to the defense of either Borstal or Eton; but none, so far as I recall, bothered to produce a fact. Such a method of debating is slightly annoying to orthodox debaters, who are left with no arguments to rebut. At least half the speakers used only the sketchiest of notes, but I have heard worse and duller speeches on the floor of the United States Senate. The other half were struggling with the nightmare of maiden efforts, and it was hard to tell, as they spoke, whether they, the audience, or the officers of the Union were suffering most keenly.

The motion for debate a short time before the Borstal-Eton argument was "That this House deplores the discovery of America." The motion was lost by 57 votes, 109 voting for and 166 against. Another was "That this House refuses to swim the Channel, fly the Atlantic, climb Mount Everest, or squat on a pole." 298 voted for the motion, 159 against it, so that it was won by 139 votes.

The singular selection of subjects for Union debates frequently gives rise to misunderstandings, as was the case in February 1933, when the Union debated the motion "That this House will under no circumstances fight for King and Country." The motion was passed by 275 votes to 153 votes, whereupon an outcry arose in the land, and humorless editorial writers on England's most powerful dailies took pen in hand for the purpose of asking tremulously, "Whither England?"

Enraged Britons wrote to *The Times* from Hyderabad, Mysore, the

Straits Settlements, Johannesburg, Hongkong, Gibraltar, and Chiswick-super-Drain. Young Mr. Randolph Churchill made a special trip from London to tell the members of the Oxford Union that they mustn't behave so dreadfully, and was almost lynched for his pains. Because of his protests, however, the motion was reconsidered. It was passed again, this time by a vote of 750 to 138.

I have heard Rhodes scholars argue that any American university that borrowed the Oxford Union idea and installed an imitation Senate or House of Representatives would be well started toward making conversation, reading, and interest in national affairs fashionable among its undergraduates. They argue, too, that most American universities, with their futile fraternity systems and their useless, non-functioning senior societies, are equipped with a ready-made method of popularizing such a body and electing representatives to it.

Some Rhodes scholars even go so far as to argue that the Oxford Union idea would be almost as valuable an educational adjunct to most American universities as the Oxford tutorial system would be. From it, they say, the American undergraduate would become familiar with parliamentary procedure; he would learn how to think on his feet; he would acquire an easy manner before an audience. He would be forced to familiarize himself, through his own efforts, with national and international affairs; and in self-defence he would be forced to discuss them. In the opinion of Rhodes scholars, too, American and English educators are too busy thinking deep and confused thoughts about education to pay attention to anything so frivolous as the Oxford Union.

American educators who go to England to view with admiration the English educational system are told, by English colleagues, that the fundamental education of the British gentleman is not planted in him at Oxford or Cambridge University, or pumped into him by the tutorial system, but begins to flower much earlier—first in the culture that so richly permeates the homes of the English upper classes, and then in that peculiarly English institution, the public school.

Some of the claims made for cultured British homes are doubtless true; but England's public-school system is, to a large degree, what is sometimes known as a racket. I mention this fact reluctantly, and only because some American educators believe everything they are told in England.

English public schools must be explained in detail to Americans; for the circumstances that keep them in existence in England are unknown in America. They were originally founded for boys who could not afford private tutors; but they have come to be schools where the sons of middle-class parents can go—provided the parents have the money—without meeting too many social inferiors.

The specter of social inferiority cannot be ignored by middle-class English families; for social inferiority, in England, is a life sentence to mediocrity and oblivion. If a child goes to a school where he talks with children from the so-called lower classes, he will inevitably pick up their accents; for it seems to be an educational principle that bad speech drives out good, just as it is an economic principle that bad currency drives out good currency. The effect of this knowledge, in England, is far-reaching. Children of any moderately good family are not allowed to go out and play with casual acquaintances. Their companions must be supervised and hand-picked. Sometimes they must be sought by advertising, as shown by this clipping from the Agony column of the London *Times*:

> Lady would like to hear of child aged six to SHARE MORNING LESSONS and walk with son. Object, companionship.—Write Mrs. ——, — Ennismore Gardens, S.W. 7.

Let us suppose that the Plantagenet family of Bumsted-on-Stilton, Hants, wishes to send its young son, Plantagenet Minor, aged eight, to school. He cannot be sent to the Bumsted free school because he would learn to say gripes for grapes, lidy rather than lady, ight instead of eight, and to do all sorts of peculiar things with the English language.

Any one of these gaucheries would not only freeze a cultured English parent into a solid block of lemon ice, but would forever ruin Plantagenet Minor's social career.

Consequently Plantagenet Minor must be sent to a small private preparatory school in Bumsted. This school may be housed in an old residence and may have no more than twenty pupils; but at it Plantagenet Minor will be taught by an Oxford or a Cambridge graduate, so that his pronunciation will remain unsullied; and he will be enabled to cultivate his feelings of class superiority by wearing a small flannel jacket emblazoned on the breast pocket with the coat of arms of the old school—three golden griffons couchant, perhaps, on a portcullis rampant, or something equally appropriate.

When Plantagenet Minor finishes with his preparatory school, he finds nothing in Bumsted to compare with an American high school. If the Plantagenets wish him to have further education, they must send him away to a public school. If Bumsted were a city, it would have a free school corresponding to an American high school, and the teaching in that free school would be exactly as good as the teaching in some of the best public schools; but the conversation of the pupils would be tainted with the accents of the lower orders—of the social outcasts.

So Plantagenet Minor, whether he lives in Bumsted-on-Stilton or in a great city, goes away to a public school, where his speech will still be uncontaminated.

In order to send him to a public school, his parents frequently make extraordinary sacrifices; for the cost of education in even a small English public school may be greater than the cost of a university education in America. Twelve hundred dollars a year is not an unusual price to pay for sending an English boy to a public school.

Until the middle of the last century, life in the great English public schools was incredibly horrible. For over a century they were centers of cruelty, snobbery, and viciousness such as no nation has ever seen before or since. Then, under the influence of a few great educators, they began to improve; and at the present time they are, by comparison with the old days, educational heavens—especially the large and famous ones like Eton, Harrow, Rugby, and Charterhouse. The smaller ones, I repeat, are rackets.

I know of one near London that, in the middle thirties, housed forty boys in a remodeled private home. The tuition fee was higher than the tuition fee of most American universities. In addition, the school charged each boy thirty guineas a term or nearly twenty dollars a week for food that was, to put it mildly, inadequate. The charges for extras were extraordinary. Each boy was charged five dollars a term for fruit, and received one orange a week; he was charged two dollars and a half for baths, and in return bathed twice a week in water used by five other boys; he was charged five dollars a term for laundry and another five dollars for mending which was seldom done. The master had sent his own son, of schoolboy age, on a cruise to the Mediterranean.

What the pupils of this school receive in return for their parents' heavy expenditure of money is the right to wear the old school tie when they venture out in the great world, and the distinction of being known as "old public-school boys." Any American who fancies, in his coarse and uncultured way, that these two attributes are not particularly important has several fancies coming to him. I am indebted to Mr. Gerald Barry for the following excerpts from London papers which show the elevated condition of England's Old Boys—in their own minds. Where an American uses the word Alumnus, an Englishman uses the term "Old Boy":

From the *Evening Standard:*

P. C. Coggins added that he took Mr. Milne to the police station, where he was charged. In reply he said, "How can you charge me? I am a public-school boy!"

From the *Daily Telegraph:*

It would be, I suggest, a good thing if Old Boys of our great public schools made it a rule invariably to accost anyone, of whatever age, whom he sees wearing his school tie. This might prevent those who have no right to wear these ties from attempting to assume a virtue which they lack.

In the old school tie and the virtues which public-school boys arrogate to themselves in England lies the germ of the true Oxford manner, which is often discussed but seldom explained. Fundamentally the Oxford manner is nothing but the serene confidence that arises from a firm and unshakable belief in the divine right of Oxford. Oxford men are no more brilliant, no better-looking, no more cultured, and possessed of no greater inherent ability than countless undergraduates of American universities; but they think they are.

The Oxford manner, it seems to me, might reasonably be considered by educators who hope to transfer the Oxford system of education to America. Is it desirable to transfer the Oxford manner to America along with the Oxford system of education, or is it not? It is my impression that no educator will be able to make up his mind on this point without considerable mental agony.

Less than a hundred years ago there were only two universities in England, and they were in bad shape. Today there are only a few more than twenty, and only two that—in the words of the English—count socially. Seventy-five years ago the English public schools were terrible beyond words, and now their Old Boys consider themselves competent to run the world.

The outlook for education in America, by comparison with what England has faced, seems as rosy as an August sunrise. If the entire English educational system was revolutionized in comparatively few years, there is no reason why it can't be done elsewhere, if there should be occasion to do it. There is no reason, that is to say, unless the English have a monopoly on brains and common sense; and no reliable investigator has found any evidence of such a state of affairs at any time in the past hundred and fifty years.

# British Mysteries

*"For Authors Only" from* FOR AUTHORS ONLY

Mysteries, seemingly, are easily solved. English detective novels, for example, are laden with insoluble mysteries. Yet in the end they are all unraveled.

Let us take one at random. The dead body of Sir Hector Branksome-Gower, clad in immaculate evening kit, monocle still in place, is found suspended from a chimney top in Gower Towers, apparently suffocated by smoke.

Police Inspector Crabbe of Branksome-on-Wye is called in. Death, he states, was accidental: due merely to Sir Hector's natural desire, on the evening of his demise, to see that all of Gower Towers' many doors, windows, and other apertures were securely fastened against intruders.

This theory is satisfactory to the occupants of Gower Towers, barring Miss Enid Branksome-Gower, Sir Hector's beautiful daughter. To Miss Enid it proves vaguely disturbing. She is not a particularly bright girl, so cannot account for her unrest. She only knows it seems odd to her that her father should have climbed to the roof to look down the chimney when he might more easily have stood in a fireplace and looked up.

Fortunately one of the guests at Gower Towers at the time of Sir Hector's mishap is Arthur Yarrow, a rising young solicitor, who has come down from London to take an inventory of Sir Hector's pheasants. To him Miss Branksome-Gower imparts her doubts.

On investigation, Mr. Yarrow discovers a significant fact, overlooked by Inspector Crabbe. Sir Hector's monocle, it is true, was in place when the body was discovered; but Sir Hector was right-handed, whereas the monocle was found in the body's left eye. In other words, Sir Hector had not inserted the monocle. It had been done for him, and the person who did it had thrust it in the wrong eye.

To Arthur Yarrow, and to any other English gentleman, the inference is obvious. If Sir Hector had been alive, he would never, never, never have placed his own monocle or any other monocle in the wrong eye, or permitted it to be done for him. Better death than the slightest deviation from good form. Therefore, Sir Hector must have been dead when the monocle was inserted. The monocle had unquestionably been adjusted for one purpose and one alone: to divert suspicion. Instead of falling, Sir Hector was necessarily popped into the chimney by the same person responsible for the misplaced monocle. In a word, Sir Hector had been murdered.

Here is what is technically known as a mystery of the first water. I am not exactly sure of the meaning of the words "first water," so frequently applied to English mysteries; but I take them to mean "ripe" or "odorous" —as would be the case with water sufficiently venerable to be regarded as the first water anywhere.

At all events, here is a mystery of the first water. It is as murky and fragrant as the first water to emerge from an old aquarium. Let us examine its fascinating features. A murdered baronet; no motive for the murder; no clues; a police inspector who cannot read the address on an envelope without moving his lips; a heroine so thick-witted that she suspects everyone of the murder, including herself; an amateur detective whose free hours are few because of his gentlemanly willingness to clarify Miss Enid's unfailing misunderstanding of every situation that confronts her.

Anybody with a working knowledge of detectives or other fact-finding agencies will say at once that this mystery is insoluble. In real life, so far as I know, genuine mysteries are never solved by professional or amateur detectives unless the person responsible for the mystery goes out of his way to call the attention of the police to the solution.

In the case of the Monocle Murder, however, Mr. Yarrow achieves the impossible. He not only explains all the intricate details to Miss Enid in such a way as to make them clear to her almost nonexistent intelligence, but he solves the mystery.

His task is to find a culprit capable of putting a monocle in the left eye of a right-handed man. This turns out to be none other than the butler, a disguised American, who—being an American—naturally lacks that instinctive age-old knowledge, common to every Englishman, of the amenities of monocle-wearing.

Mr. Yarrow discovers that the butler is in reality a notorious counterfeiter who has been carrying on his nefarious work at the bottom of a chimney in the cellar of Gower Towers. Mr. Yarrow even learns the motive for the murder. Sir Hector, sniffing about the chimney tops at closing-up time, scents the powerful acids used by the butler-counterfeiter.

He complains about them to the butler, in the belief that something has gone wrong with the drains. So the butler kills him.

That is the way of it in British detective stories. No mystery is so dark or devious as to defy solution. The unfailing insight revealed in them fills me with admiration. I am unable to state the exact number of detective novels produced in England each year, but the output is large—larger and more effectively standardized, I have been led to believe, than those two other popular products of Great Britain: scotch whisky and Chippendale furniture. Yet no matter how many there are, there's never a one of them in which the mystery isn't solved.

In a British detective story everything is fully explained—everything, that is to say, except the abysmal stupidity of the heroine. Since no attempt is ever made to explain why these females are invariably mental deficients, I gather that no explanation is needed. Not only, apparently, does England expect every man to do his duty, but she also expects the heroine of every detective novel to be a cretin.

Only recently I encountered, in a detective story by that king of English detective-story writers, Mr. E. P. Oppenheim, a beautiful cretin named Félice. Although Félice was the heroine, and innocent, she preferred to be considered guilty of several dreadful crimes rather than tell the simple truth. It is axiomatic that an English mystery-story heroine should never clear herself of suspicion, just as it is axiomatic that English detective-story writers should never use the simple word "while"—not when they can use, in its place, the more elegant "whilst."

Quoting from Mr. Oppenheim's study in feminine stupidity:

Félice stole into her husband's room whilst he was dressing for dinner that evening. He dismissed his servant at once and made her comfortable in an easy chair whilst he brushed his hair.

The question at once arises: why should a wife steal into her husband's room? There was no reason for concealment. She could have entered beating a snare drum without offending the proprieties. But she preferred to steal in. Why? Because she was a true British heroine, devoid of all reasoning power.

The point of the matter, however, is this: England is full of detective-story writers who are no more baffled by the most intricate murder mystery than they would be by a hot cross bun. That being so, I have one or two mysteries of a minor nature that I am eager to submit to their searching analysis.

For example, I am at a loss to know where British authors obtain their ideas of Americans.

I am almost as mystified as to why every British author of any standing, for the past fifteen years, has apparently considered it a sacred duty to introduce a made-in-England American into every book he writes, whether the plot needs him or not.

Let us suppose that an Englishman turns out a novel dealing with the mental distress of a little group of English people residing in a remote section of Africa. That, incidentally, introduces another mystery. The characters in all recent English novels, barring mystery novels, are usually undergoing a tremendous amount of internal agony over something pretty unimportant. If these novels correctly represent the state of mind of the English people, England must be suffering from toxic poisoning caused by improper diet or bad liquor or both. I am unable, at the moment, to devote much space to this particular mystery; but it should, it seems to me, receive attention.

For the benefit of any Englishman who may wish to investigate the reasons for the mental distress now prevalent in English novels, I will say that I have heard complaints from Canadians, during the past few years, concerning the poisonous quality of the British liquor dispensed by the Quebec Liquor Commission. Any dietitian worth his salt, moreover, will willingly state that there is nothing so conducive to mental aberrations, hallucinations, morbidness, depression, lack of self-confidence, uncertainty, loss of memory—to anticipation of accident, tragedy, death—to fear of poverty, insanity, et cetera, as two or three drinks of poor whisky taken in conjunction with those favorite English foods, stringy mutton chops and soggy potatoes.

We were speaking, however, of a novel concerning an English group in darkest Africa. Into this little group, for no reason at all, suddenly dash an American and his son, both in derbies, stiff collars, and badly fitting suits of heavy black cloth. The father is a wealthy Detroit manufacturer, traveling for no apparent reason.

He says, "Wa-al, I reckon I guess we ain't fur from the lion-huntin'!"
The son says, "Sure, I guess I reckon we ain't!"

Then, having added nothing to the plot, or to any situation or character, these two representative Americans depart humorously from the picture in a small, noisy automobile. I take this example from the work of Mr. R. W. Garnett, a distinguished contributor to *Blackwood's Magazine*.

No matter where the modern English novel is laid—whether among the country houses of the Shropshire hunting set or on the outermost fringes of the British Empire—it contains an American whose talk is as accurately and painstakingly depicted as though the author had hired it done by a seller of jellied eels from Whitechapel.

One of the unfortunate features of calling an English author's attention to the misuse of American dialogue lies, it seems to me, in an Englishman's inability to recognize the misuse when it is brought to his attention. Not even when it is forcibly hammered into his attention is he able to get more than a vague glimmering of what he has done.

Recently I tried to argue the point with an English author; but the proceeding struck me as futile. My argument was based on the speech of the Detroit businessman mentioned above—"Wa-al, I reckon I guess we ain't fur from the lion-huntin'!"

That, I assured him, was not the way Detroiters talked. Back in 1760, I said, the rude trappers who traded glass beads with the Indians for beaver skins might have garbled the English language in that manner; but at the present time, thanks to Detroit's public schools, universities, libraries, and what not, such garbling is as extinct as Indians and beavers. I further suggested that a book so inaccurate and untruthful in reproducing the speech of a Detroiter might be equally worthless in other respects.

"But, my dear chap!" the author said. "You Americans are hypersensitive! Forgive me for mentioning it, I mean to say, but really, you know: really, you shouldn't be so quick on the trigger! I mean to say, it's not an insult to your entire nation, you know, when we make one of your American chaps speak naturally."

I hesitatingly advanced the thought that there was nothing natural about the speech of the Detroiter in question: that he wouldn't have said "Waal" or "I reckon I guess" or even "we ain't fur."

The Englishman's reply was politely skeptical. "Really! And what would he have said?"

Probably, I told him, he'd have said, "We're not far from the lion country, are we?" or possibly he might have added a touch of piquancy to his inquiry by asking, "What's the lion situation this morning?"

"Oh, but I mean to say," the Englishman protested, "this Detroit chap is from the western portion of the States. I mean to say, if he spoke as you say he'd have spoken, there'd be nothing about him to show he was from Detroit. I mean to say, one can't make an American, in a book, speak like everybody else, can one? He wouldn't be an American, if you know what I mean! And what a silly ass one would look if one wrote about an American in such a way that there was nothing American about him!"

In an attempt to clarify a situation that seemed to be growing hopelessly foggy, I asked my English friend to consider, for a moment, an American author who might wish to introduce into the pages of a book a conversation between the Earl of Herts and his son, the Hon. Vivyan Montacute, concerning an American college professor who has presented a letter of introduction from the president of the Society for Furthering Anglo-American Friendship. Suppose, I said to him, that the dialogue between the two should run something as follows:

The Earl bit savagely at the end of a moist, black cigar. "Coo!" he said bitterly. " 'Ere's a ruddy nuisance! 'Oo's goin' to look after this blighter if 'e comes bargin' abaht?"

The Hon. Vivyan smiled affectionately at his father. " 'Old your 'osses, guv'nor!" he said. "Don't get your blinkin' wind up over this Yank! 'E's nuffin to worry abaht, not 'alf!"

My English friend was pained. "But my dear old bean!" he protested. "The thing's impossible! Fancy any writer chap being such a stupid! Why, it's positively sickening! I mean to say, who ever heard of an Earl dropping his h's! And having him smoke a moist cigar! Why, the fellow knows nothing about our customs—nothing! A moist cigar, indeed! What I mean, there's no need making us out a lot of barbarians! I'll venture to say a member of our aristocracy wouldn't smoke a moist cigar if it were the last bit of tobacco in the world. I will indeed, by Jerve! A moist cigar's not fit to smoke! It must be dry, old fellow! So dry it crackles, I mean to say. Look here, old chap: you're having me on, eh? Why, no publisher would publish such drivel! And certainly no Englishman would read it!"

I agreed with him that every Englishman would probably resent, and rightly so, any such misrepresentation of the British upper classes. Probably, I suggested, an Englishman would feel differently about an American book laid partly among the honest peasants of the Cotswold Hills. A roughly clad shepherd, for example, sits by the side of a tiny peat fire in the quaint kitchen of a Cotswold cottage, discussing with his aged wife the American who has recently purchased the cottage for shipment to America.

"Blimey!" he says in his rough, shepherd's voice, "blimey, but it's cruel 'ard to be chucked out of one's digs wivout a blarsted word! Eighty-two years come Michaelmas Oi'm lived in these 'ere digs, by Jove, an now 'ere Oi be, throwed out like a bloomin' old straw 'at! Oi'm a good mind to give yon American what for, that Oi be!"

His gentle old wife, neat as a pin in her gray dress and white Cotswold cap, leans forward and pats his wrinkled hand. "Cruel 'ard, aye," she says, "but buck up, laddie! We're self-respectin' Cotswold folk, an' blimey if Oi'll stand for givin' an American aught! Sure an' ye're daft, laddie, to talk of *givin'!* They'll buy anything, yon Americans; an' he'll want your old Cotswold breeks an' your old smock for local color. So sell 'em to him, laddie boy, an' we'll buy ourseils a second-hand motorcar an' get out of this bloomin' rut we're in, eh what?"

My English friend stared at me. "Look here," he protested, "that's not the way they talk in the Cotswolds! I mean to say, you could travel through the Cotswolds for yahs and yahs without hearing anyone say 'Eh what!' Why, it's positively indecent! 'Blimey' and 'wivout a blarsted word' and 'digs'—in the Cotswolds! No, no, my dear chap: it won't wash! Absolutely not! Why, it's like dropping a bit of carrion in Westminster Abbey! An author who'd write a thing like that ought to be deported! In all sincerity, my dear fellow, he shouldn't be allowed to associate with sportsmen, I mean to say!"

When I attempted to call his attention to the fact that nearly every English author was guilty of a similar misrepresentation of American speech, he uttered an indulgent laugh.

"It's all your American sensitiveness!" he assured me. "You're so quick to take offense! Really, old chap, it's your great national fault. I mean to say, we hardly dare mention your slowness in entering the war, you're so sensitive about it! No, no, my dear fellow: there's no similarity whatever between the two cases you mention and the Americans that our chaps put in their novels. Absolutely none! All we do is attach certain well-recognized quirks of speech to our American characters, so they won't be mistaken for some other nationality. Surely, old chap, you must be able to see the difference between a kindly little word picture, such as that of the Detroit manufacturer, and a vicious attack on the entire aristocracy of England, as was implied in your quotation about the Earl of Herts."

As an afterthought he added, "Besides, old fellow, our best authors have lectured in America. I mean to say, they're familiar with the kentry; and you won't find 'em making the blunders that stay-at-homes make."

I drew my notebook from my pocket and flipped over the leaves to refresh my memory on a few British authors whose little mistakes concerning America had recently caught my eye. Mr. Charles Dickens, I noted, had made mention of visiting an establishment on either Long Island or Rhode Island—he had forgotten which.

Mr. Warwick Deeping had dealt with an American woman of culture, wealth, and social position and represented her as prefacing her remarks with such expressions as "Say, pardner!"

Mr. John Galsworthy had drawn an American scientist and college professor with the best of intentions, but had left a few rough edges here and there—edges so rough as to give American readers the impression that the scientist-professor was a cross between a British ham actor and an over-serious Arkansas congressman of the coonskin-cap era.

Being a big masculine chap from Wyoming, Mr. Galsworthy's professor says, "I just love it," and, "Isn't that just wonderful!" And, "I don't want any grass to grow."

Mr. Galsworthy, in placing the latter words in the professor's mouth, was evidently trying to reproduce the phrase "Don't let any grass grow under your feet"; and it must be admitted that he nearly succeeded.

Mr. Galsworthy's professor-scientist, speaking to an acquaintance, asks, with professional tact, "Were you married in a stovepipe hat, Captain?" and, on receiving a negative answer, observes, "I'm sorry about that. They seem to me so cunning."

He also addresses ladies as "Ma'am," and, in the customary manner of American professors, gets his Anglo-Americanisms somewhat scrambled by remarking, "I'm just wondering whether that guy will be in? I've a kind of impression they do most of their business over food. We should do well to go and look at the ducks in the Park."

Mr. J. B. Priestley and Mr. A. P. Herbert had proved that their powers of observation, as regards the speech of Americans, were not dependable. Mr. R. W. Garnett, son of the librarian of the British Museum, had seemingly exhumed his Americanisms from the Museum's dustiest recesses.

*Blackwood's Magazine*, that Gibraltar of British periodicals, had made much of a serial dealing with the possible state of affairs in India in the year 1957, by Mr. Hamish Blair.

Mr. Blair introduces an American—Mr. Simmonds, a young consular officer—in the first chapter. The American, obviously, is a consular officer of career; a young man, that is to say, who must have trained for his position: first by spending four years in a university: then by undergoing an intensive course of study in the State Department and the Foreign Service School in Washington.

Mr. Simmonds is depicted as "a long-limbed, neatly dressed youth in mufti . . . clean-shaven and good-looking in the American way."

I do not know how to differentiate between a youth who is good-looking in the American way and one who is good-looking in the British way or the Danish way or the German way. The author may have known, but he was careful not to let his readers into the secret.

Mr. Simmonds' first remark is, "We are hardly a noos agency, but if a citizen applies to us for information, why nat'rally we are very willin' to hand him any facts that have come to our knowledge."

He characterizes certain noises as being "con-tinual," states that the noises are "vurry simple," and assures his audience that "the consulate ain't goin' to take sides."

I closed my notebook and put it back in my pocket. Something told me that if I tried to argue with my British author friend over the likelihood of hearing, from the mouth of an American consul of career, the words "ain't goin'," I would nat'rally be vurry much out of luck. So far as I was concerned, the whole business was doomed to remain a dark mystery—unless England's detective-story writers should take the matter in hand and solve what, to Americans, must always be unsolvable.

It is barely possible, of course, that a solution of the mystery would serve no useful purpose. The Associated Detective Story Writers of England might conceivably get at the bottom of why it is that no English author can successfully reproduce the speech of an American; but at the same time the English authors might stubbornly refuse to profit by their discovery. From what I have seen and read of English authors, they would be almost certain to refuse to profit by it.

With that danger in mind, it occurs to me that those philanthropists—usually Americans—who are laboring so industriously to improve Anglo-American relations might reasonably devote some of their time and money to publishing a phrase book for British authors—a phrase book that would clear up, for all time, the British belief that a Boston clergyman, in the year 1945, talks as a Nevada bartender must have talked in 1855.

I am always pleased to see in the papers that a large number of Englishmen and Americans have met together at a dinner of the Pilgrim Society in London and exchanged enormous numbers of compliments. Such dinners, no doubt, promote good feeling between England and America. At the same time I am vaguely conscious of the fact that while the dinner is in progress, it is, in all likelihood, being nullified by thousands of British authors—possibly by hundreds of thousands of them, now that every English magazine has picked up the good old American magazine custom of carrying advertisements guaranteeing to teach any clerk or housemaid how to become a first-class author in twenty easy lessons.

While the diners are exchanging compliments, all these countless authors are hunched grimly over their desks, striving to introduce Americans into novels, plays, and short stories. The Americans they evolve, I scarcely need to say, will fit their surroundings as easily and realistically as a hippopotamus would fit a Vermont trout stream.

Those who attend the dinner will doubtless be filled with Anglo-American good feeling; but those who read the novels and the short stories are almost certain to feel differently. I am not prepared to say they will feel like shooting a few British authors; but they will think several things about British authors, as well as about the English in general, that wouldn't look well in print.

It is, of course, a friendly gesture for wealthy Americans to contribute large sums toward the restoration of English cathedrals and manor houses, but personally I feel that Anglo-American relations would be considerably enhanced if the cathedrals and manor houses were allowed to take care of themselves, and the same sums devoted to setting up a series of prizes to be awarded to those English authors most nearly successful in depicting Americans who can be recognized by persons familiar with the subject.

## Men in a Swamp

*From* OLIVER WISWELL

DURING our long, dusty walk that night, not a sound did we hear to indicate that we were passing through a part of the country plentifully populated with rebels and informers constantly at war with their even more numerous Loyalist neighbors—and not a sound could any ear have heard from us, for we walked softly in the dust; and Buell, with his scissors-grinder's box upon his back, kept his boasted bell in his coat pocket and had muffled the clapper in his big red handkerchief.

We saw distant lights while the night was young; heard the far-off barking of dogs as we plodded on through thick darkness heavy with the scents of July—bayberries, salt marshes, hay fields, barnyards.

In the small hours we crouched by the roadside to let an occasional cart creak past, the drivers as silent as dead men. We suspected, from what James had told us, that they were provision carts sent by loyal inhabitants of the island to help feed the fleet behind us.

Around three o'clock a sonorous croaking of frogs told us we had reached Demott's Mill Pond; and there we waited in the bushes, fighting mosquitoes, until the east grew pale and the blackbirds in the brush along the pond, coming to life with weak chirpings, clambered clumsily up and down the marsh grass as if stricken with rheumatic pains.

Buell, peering cautiously above the bushes, wasn't satisfied with what he saw. "There's no sheet hanging on this side of the mill, Oliver," he said, "but who knows what's on the other side? I'll go see, and don't you move. You wait here till you hear my bell ringing. That'll mean there's no sheets on the other side and that it's safe for you to come ahead. It'll also mean everybody in the house is awake, and that you'll have something to eat as soon as you get there."

He hoisted his scissors-grinder to his shoulder, took his bell by the clapper, and trudged off through the dawn mist toward the dim gray stone building at the head of the pond. Five minutes later, I heard the bell clanging the measured irregularities peculiar to scissors-grinders, and hurried down the road to be with him.

When I reached the gate, I found Buell standing in the mill yard, ringing his bell like a man possessed and staring raptly at the brightening eastern sky as a violinist stares into space while wielding his bow. In the open door, tying his apron and staring suspiciously at Buell, was a stout, ruddy man with a pale nose and jowls the color of fresh beef. He scratched his head and looked from Buell to me.

Buell suddenly stopped his ringing and pointed his bell abruptly at the miller. "Any scissors to grind?"

The miller shook his head. "Ain't you on the road pretty early?"

Buell's bell clanged. "What's hours got to do with scissors-grinding? I grind as well in the morning as in the afternoon. Got any scissors to grind?"

The miller still studied us.

"Any knives?" Buell asked patiently. "Any axes, scythes, saws, hatchets, hoes? Any bayonets to sharpen?"

The miller narrowed his eyes. "How'd you get here? By way of New York or across the Sound?"

"What difference does it make?" Buell asked. "I grind shears and grind 'em well. I sharpen scythes or sickles or anything you've got. Ain't you got *anything* to be sharpened?"

"I might have," the miller said reluctantly. "How much do you charge?"

Buell looked relieved. "That's all I wanted to know." He turned to me. "Frank James said if we could satisfy Demott, we could satisfy anyone, so I guess we're all right. What you got for breakfast, Mr. Demott?"

The miller yawned and stretched, at ease for the first time since he'd seen us. "There ain't much in the house," he said, "but I'll try to see no friend of Frank James leaves here hungry. You can have hot ale and sour-milk cheese and new bread, and maybe a little sausage and blueberry pie."

"That's pretty near all we need, Mr. Demott," Buell said heartily. "My digestion ain't what it ought to be, and personally I can't eat more'n half a pie for breakfast, and maybe a dozen sausages. More might give me trouble."

"When's Howe coming?" Demott wanted to know before I had a chance to say a word; and all the members of his household, as we met them, asked the selfsame thing as soon as they learned who we were.

Indeed, that was the first question on the tongues of all the Loyalists we met in those next few weeks. They had been harried, spied on, lied about, informed against, robbed and insulted; and they longed achingly for Howe and his army, so that they might be freed from the oppressions and the restrictions of Congress, mobs, and committees.

"By God," Demott said, filling our pewter mugs with steaming ale, "there's no telling what'll happen to the people on this island unless Howe gets here pretty quick! We're all of us under suspicion, and they can't put *all* of us in jail, the way they have Cadwallader Colden and Judge Jones. The jails are full, and so are the swamps and the brush. I guess they'll have to kill a lot of us if Howe doesn't come pretty quick."

He dropped so heavily into a chair that the floor shook. "How long before the general figures on getting here?"

"Nobody knows," I said. "His officers think he ought to bring his army across and start fighting before the end of July, but he doesn't often do as his officers think he should."

Demott looked stricken. "What'll become of us? We can't resist unless we're organized, and we can't organize without a central head. That means we'll be helpless till Howe gets here."

I knew he was suffering from that same miserable feeling of impotence that had oppressed us in Massachusetts when the mobs played hob with us and we had been unable to resist.

"He'll be here eventually," I said as reassuringly as I could. "After all, you're no worse off than Loyalists in New England."

Demott sighed. "I suppose not. I suppose we must be even better off, or there wouldn't be so many Loyalists pouring into Long Island from all the eastern provinces. Scores of 'em cross the Sound every night. That's one of the things that bothers us. The rebels won't take the trouble to send a regiment against a few men hiding in a swamp; but when there's two thousand of 'em in the swamp, they're worth capturing. There must be fifty Massachusetts Loyalists in that swamp over yonder"—he swung a hamlike fist toward the west window of the kitchen—"and maybe another hundred from Connecticut and Rhode Island, to say nothing of all who've been hunted out of towns around here by those damned horse thieves the rebels call militia!"

"Have you been in to see how they're getting along?" I asked.

"Not me," Demott said, "and don't you, either—not unless you have to! I guess it ain't comfortable. I don't see how they stand it." He looked reflective. "Of course, it's probably better than having a mob get hold of you."

"I'll have to go there," I said. "The general wants to know what's happening to 'em. What's the best way of getting in?"

"There's only one way," Demott said, "and if you insist, I'll show it to you tonight. You'll have to go in with the night's crop of Loyalists who come down from the Sound after dark."

"I'd rather go by myself," I said, "and this morning. I've got to talk to those men. The sooner I see 'em, the sooner I can find out what the general wants to know."

"Maybe so," Demott agreed, "but if the general really needs the information, you'd better do what I tell you. Otherwise he might not get it —and we want him to have the information even more than you do. Look, Mr. Wiswell: there hasn't been a day, during the past year, that we've felt safe. There's never a morning that we aren't afraid we'll be hiding in the swamps before night. A year's a long time, Mr. Wiswell—a mighty long time to be at the mercy of any cheap rascal that chooses to lead a gang of armed good-for-nothings against anyone he happens to dislike."

Buell helped himself liberally to sour-milk cheese. "Haven't you got enough people to make a gang of your own?"

"Certainly," the miller said. "This island is three-quarters Loyalist; but we can't do the things the rebels do. They send in militia from other colonies, or bring their mobs from New York. They have no homes here; no families; no belongings except what they have on their backs. We have! If we fight 'em, they seize our cattle, burn our barns and houses, and drive our families across the Sound. I can name hundreds of people, right in this neighborhood, who've been up to their necks in misery and ruin for over a year, just because they were known to be against rebellion. I hate to think what's going to happen if the Loyalists of this island ever do somehow contrive to band together and lay hands on the mobs and committeemen that mistreated such men as——"

He was interrupted by a shrill cry from the head of the stairs. "Daniel, Daniel! Foot soldiers coming around the bend at the lower end of the mill-pond!"

Demott groaned and struggled to his feet. "Hang out this sheet!" he shouted. To me he said urgently, "You and your friend better hide in a cornbin in the mill. You can dig down in it and breathe through a tube."

"Not me," Buell said. "I'm a peaceable scissors-grinder, and no one can prove different!"

"No cornbin for me," I said. "I'll take to the swamp."

"You can't! You don't know your way around! You'd have a bullet through you before night! Damn it, Mr. Wiswell, can't you understand the rebels are trying to capture all those men in the swamps, so they can force 'em into the rebel militia and put 'em to work making forts?"

"I understand," I said, "but I didn't come here without a plan."

Buell looked indignant. "Plan? Why didn't you tell me, Oliver?"

"It's so simple you might not have approved of it."

Buell was disgusted. "You'd ought to told me, Oliver! If we get separated——"

"We won't," I said. "Get outside and sharpen something, or you'll be in the militia yourself."

He swung his sharpening wheel to his shoulder, snatched a knife from the table and his bell from the floor, ran from the house, and immediately, in the front yard, his bell began to ring and his voice to bellow.

To Demott I said, "Give me the use of one of your blankets till the rebels have gone. I need a blanket, a strip of old linen, and a lump of suet the size of a robin's egg!"

Demott stared at me, then ran to the stairs. In his absence I unbuttoned the knee band of my breeches, pushed down a stocking, took the loggerhead from the kitchen fire and held it close to the flesh above my knee. Beneath the hot iron the flesh rose in an ugly-looking welt that would soon be a blister. When Demott brought me the blanket, linen, and suet, I folded the suet in one end of the linen, laid it on a hot brick beside the oven until it was melted; then pressed it over the blister and wrapped the linen around my leg. The soft suet, forced out by the pressure of the bandage, was a dirty, unhealthy white against the flesh.

As I went into the yard, thus bandaged, Buell rolled an appraising eye at my leg, but kept on with his bellowing and grinding.

Approaching us through a haze of dust that overhung the road was a long column of men—a slovenly column that marched irregularly and out of step, so that it had the look of a gigantic centipede whose feet hurt.

I lowered myself against the wall of the mill in a sunny spot and spread the blanket over my legs.

The column drew closer and closer, and from it rose a sound of babbling, a kind of chattering such as might come from a cage of animals. At the head of the column, on a sway-backed cart horse with shaggy fetlocks and droopy head, rode a paunchy, red-faced man. He had an upturned nose and little eyes that peered out from between fat lids, and looked surprisingly like a pig on horseback.

At a bellowed order from this porcine leader, the long line of men halted and shuffled their feet in the dusty road. There may have been five hundred of them, and they were as scurvy-looking as those citizen soldiers who had stared surlily at my father and me on the night we were driven out of Milton. For the most part they were pock-marked; their hair hung lankly from under sweat-stained hats; many were stockingless; and their coats were patched and foul. Even from where I lay I could hear them cursing purposelessly.

As the pig-eyed leader rode into the mill yard, Demott appeared in the doorway. He seemed pleased at the sight of the paunchy rider and greeted him heartily as Colonel Birdsall. "What brings you here at this time of day, Colonel?" he asked.

"You know damned well," Birdsall said. His voice had a squealing resonance something like that of a sow impatiently crying out for food. "I'm after the damned Tories hiding in this swamp; and I think you know a good way in, Demott!"

Demott was indignant. "I'm a law-abiding citizen, Colonel! You've never had trouble with me, and you never will! It'd be as much as my life is worth to do anything for a Tory. No, Colonel, I'm hiding no Tories!"

Birdsall yelped contemptuously. "Pah! You can't live on the edge of this swamp and not know what goes on in it! Do you deny there's Loyalists hiding in here?" His little deep-set eyes roamed to Buell and me.

Buell, seemingly uninterested in the fat colonel, pedaled so furiously at his wheel that a stream of sparks flew from the edge of the knife blade on which he worked. The colonel leveled a stumpy forefinger at him. "You, there! You ain't a native of these parts! Where you from? What you doing here?"

Buell ceased pedaling, ran his thumb over the knife blade, and held it, point first, toward the colonel. "Me?" he asked. "Why, I ain't doing nothing! I'm just sharpening this knife."

"I can see that," Birdsall said. "What I can't see's where you're from. You don't belong here, and I want to know how you got here."

"I'm from Massachusetts," Buell said, "which ain't no place for an honest scissors-grinder."

"Why not?"

"Because there ain't anything left to sharpen in Massachusetts. They sharpened up all their axes, hatchets, and bayonets for the British five years ago. Why, Colonel, you could walk half across Massachusetts, ringing your bell all the way, and not get more'n two knives to sharpen! What's *your* trade, brother, when you ain't a soldier?"

"Who, me?" the colonel asked. "I'm a drover."

"Well," Buell said, "how'd you like it if you drove a lot of cows all through this province and never found a butcher to take 'em off your hands? You wouldn't like it, would you?"

"Beef ain't knives," Birdsall said. "People have to have beef, but they can sharpen their own knives. What you say don't explain nothing! What brought you here?"

"Why, Colonel," Buell said, "everyone in Massachusetts knows folks on Long Island are whetting their knives for each other. When I heard all you people were just waiting for a chance to cut each other's throats, I hurried right over here to get some of the trade. I figured that if people want to cut each other's throats, they ought to be helped to do a good clean job. As a drover, you've had dealings with butchers, and you know that's plain ordinary horse sense."

The colonel looked doubtful, but kicked his mare in the ribs and moved over to stand above me. "Who's this? Demott, who's this? He's *another* stranger! By God, Demott, you claim you don't know what's going on in that swamp; yet there's always a stranger or two around your house— someone who can't account for himself. Who is this man?"

I spoke up in a voice of high complaint. "Colonel, I'll tell you who I am, and what's more, I think it's your duty and the duty of every compassionate man who hates King George to do something for me. . . . Even this miller here grudges to let me lie on his ground! If you want to know where I'm from, I'm from a British ship! I was sick and they wouldn't let me stay aboard."

Birdsall made a squealing protest. "You're a damned fool if you think I'll believe that! You don't catch Ben Birdsall believing it! British surgeons may not know how to take care of their sick, but they generally pretend they do!"

He leaned from his horse and poked me with the switch he carried. "What's the matter with you, you damned ministerial tool!"

I rose on one elbow. "Only a little sore on my leg that doesn't amount to anything."

"Sore? A little sore? What kind of a little sore? You mean to say the doctors on your ship drove you off because you had a little sore? Let's look at it!"

I threw back the blanket from my leg. Above and below the bandage were scaly white excrescences, extremely unhealthy-looking.

"Hm," the colonel said. "What's the matter with it? That oughtn't to bother a doctor that's worth his salt! What did they say it was?"

I covered my leg and looked around me in what I hoped was a hunted manner. "I don't believe they knew," I said.

"Gammon!" Birdsall cried. "Either they knew or they didn't! Speak up! What did they call it?"

"Well, sir," I said, "I don't think it's true. I've never been anywhere a man could get it. I don't think it's true that I've got it!"

"By God!" Birdsall whispered. "Leprosy!" He reined back his horse. "Was that what they told you you had? Leprosy?"

I swallowed and tried to groan realistically. "No, Colonel! No! They didn't say so! They didn't come right out with the word, anyhow!"

"Demott," Birdsall shouted, "get this man away from here! Give him a bag of potatoes and see he leaves at once! Understand? Get him away from this neighborhood or I'll burn your mill!"

He urged his clumsy cart horse to a trot; and as he shouted orders to his line of scarecrow troops, he repeatedly looked back over his shoulder at me in a way that was a tribute to my blister and the sincerity of my acting.

From a distance we watched Birdsall send flanking parties of militiamen around the swamp; faintly heard his bellowing voice ordering other parties to go straight in.

"Dead or alive!" we heard him shouting. "Drive 'em out dead or alive! . . . Dead or alive!"

All through the morning and the early afternoon we heard far-off shouts and shots—single detonations; ripples of musketry fire; then long silences, during which I pictured sullen, sunken-cheeked militiamen prowling from bush to bush in that dark and watery swamp, to stalk fellow countrymen as they'd have stalked wild animals.

Toward sundown they came out again, hallooing and cursing, splashed with mud and scratched with brambles from head to foot. They had, they told Demott exultantly, killed one and taken three prisoners. The hunted Loyalists, they said, had run from them like water rats; but how many there were, or why the rest had escaped, they were unable to say.

Before that night was over we found out for ourselves.

§

We lay in the brush behind the mill until Birdsall and his men went shouting down the road; and when they had gone, the whole world—

except for the diapason of sound from innumerable frogs—seemed empty of life. But Demott had told Buell and me to stay where he'd put us in the scrub behind the mill; and so we waited, with the scent of bayberry coming to us in waves, as though this war-tormented island sighingly sought our sympathy.

Not until ten o'clock did we hear stirrings and faint tappings above the all-pervasive frog chorus, and soon thereafter we saw a lantern swing in circles near the darkened mill. That was the signal for which we waited, and when we hurried to the mill yard, we found dim figures standing there in silence.

Demott himself wasn't among them, and when one of his womenfolk came out with a lantern shrouded in a bag, I remembered with what obvious sincerity Demott had sworn to Birdsall that he had never seen a Loyalist in the swamp.

Without a word being spoken, the woman turned her back upon the mill and walked into the darkness. Buell and I followed her, and one by one so did the blurred figures that had been waiting. She led us upon a path that constantly grew softer and wetter, and when she slipped the bag from her lantern and waved it, we saw, far ahead, a yellow pin point of light.

As we drew closer, the pin point became a lantern, held by a cadaverous tall man whose breeches clung to his bony legs as if he'd been wading waist-high in a river. He stood in the stern of a sedge boat—one of the flat-bottomed square-ended craft used by Long Islanders for transporting hay crops and carrying heavy burdens through their interminable marshes; and resting against the swampy shore of the black stream were five other sedge boats, in the stern of each of which sat a hollow-cheeked man peering intently and suspiciously at us. Across their knees lay short-barreled muskets.

"How many?" the man with the lantern asked, and without waiting for an answer he added, "Did you get the medicine? Did you get the band-ages?"

Our woman guide spoke up. "I got two sheets and a pail of mutton tallow," she said. "It'll have to do."

The man groaned. "Bring rags tomorrow if you can't get sheets. We could use six sheets. Bring cinchona bark, too. The fever's bad."

The woman pushed me forward. "This here's Mr. Wiswell," she said. "Dan says you're to take special care of him, because he came over from Staten Island to find out what's happening to you."

"From Staten Island?" the man repeated blankly. Then, in the light of the lantern, he suddenly changed. His eyes glittered; his emaciated limbs seemed to strengthen and take on more substance; he stood straighter. "He came from Staten Island?" he cried. "When's Howe coming?"

"Soon," I said, "soon! Soon, I think."

At that the man groaned. " 'Soon!' That's all we've heard for the past six months! Well, get in, Mr. Wiswell, and your friend too. How many in all?"

"There's eighteen," the woman said. "All forwarded and vouched for by Mayor Mathews."

Our half-seen company entered the sedge boats with a sound of thumpings and splashings. I found myself seated in two inches of water smelling strongly of fish; and behind me sat Buell, growling at the difficulty of keeping his scissors-grinder dry. The man set his lantern on the back thwart, picked up an oar and pushed his boat away from the bank. Facing backward and never once looking ahead, he sculled us into the swamp; and behind us the other sedge boats, each with a dim lantern in its stern, followed around sharp turns and through sedgy passageways like a sluggish and dimly phosphorescent marsh monster phlegmatically traversing familiar waters.

We seemed to float on a river of drumlike rumbling—a frog chorus so vast that it had a sort of solidity. We moved, too, in a dense cloud of insects whose wings made a constant shrill whining accompaniment to the resonant song of the frogs. Those damnable bugs were like dust or smoke and filtered through every aperture, no matter how small. When I opened my eyes, they dashed against my eyeballs. When I opened my mouth, it was filled with their fluttering wings. They were in my nose, ears, hair—down my neck, up my sleeves; and I felt them crawling far down inside my clothes. They pierced me with little hot itching thrusts, with slow malignant bites, with sharp vindictive stabs. When I brushed them from one part, they attacked in a score of others, tormenting me beyond endurance.

"You'll get used to 'em," the boatman said. "You got nice rich blood, and if there's anything those critters like, it's fresh meat! When they've sucked a few quarts out of you, you'll be like the rest of us, and they won't bother you so much. Where you from, Mr. Wiswell?"

"Milton," I said, "but for the last three months I've been in Halifax with General Howe."

The boatman spoke explosively. "What's he waiting for! For God's sake, why don't he come! Does he want to find us all dead when he gets here?"

"I think he wants to be sure nothing goes wrong," I said. "He's waiting for his brother, the admiral, and the fleet from England."

"By God," the boatman said, "we wouldn't need him or his brother or the fleet if he'd only send us a few officers that knew how to fight!"

He spat violently in the water, and a bullet would have made less of an impact. He poled onward, silent for a time. Then he said, "We've got some Boston men in here with us. They say Massachusetts committees are seizing the property of everybody that left their homes, and selling it for next to nothing to those the rebels favor. They say Sam Adams figures on having all you Massachusetts folks banished for good; proscribed, too, so you can be shot in a hurry in case you take it into your head to go back. This General Howe, he'd better not waste much more time."

"Banished and proscribed?" Indiscreetly I laughed aloud; and the opening of my mouth filled it with those horrible bugs. I sputtered them out. "Aren't we banished and proscribed enough already?"

The boatman slapped his sculling oar. "Now I come to think of it, one of those Massachusetts fellers—I disremember his name—was from Milton, same as you. He asked two or three times if we'd heard of anyone named Wiswell. Yes, sir, that was the name: Wiswell! Could it 'a' been you he was asking about, Mr. Wiswell?"

Hope shot up within me, as smoldering leaves burst into flame; then died again. Would I hear something of Sally—even something from her? No, I wouldn't! After what had happened to me in the past year, I knew more than to hope. The whole world, in the words of that gay old song, was turned upside down. Nothing could come out right. I only grunted in answer to the boatman and settled myself down into the wetness in which I sat.

The Aristophanes chorus of croaking was a solid sound all about us, dimming all other senses except the afflicted one of hearing, till I croaked grotesquely myself, in protest, "Hold your tongues, you damned frogs! Can't you be quiet just an instant, for God's sake?"

At one moment the marsh before us was as black as the bottom of a well; the next moment the boatman sharply turned us against a wall of sedge, thrust hard, and we passed rustling through tall grasses and came into a pool on the far side of which blinked scores of lights, like fireflies above a meadow.

A dozen smudges smoldered among those flitting lights, and smoke from them lay in a dimly seen blanket above our heads. As the lantern in our boat cleared the wall of sedge behind us, an eager babbling arose from the shore and I had the singular and unexpected feeling that here was a haven in which I would be both safe and welcome.

Individual voices came clearer to me from among those moving lights.

"What about Howe?" "Any troops landed yet?" "When's Howe coming?"

The boatman flourished his sculling oar. "The general's sent a man to see us," he cried. "I got him here—here in this boat."

The shouting on shore faded to a whispering like that of dead leaves on an autumn night.

With a sharp twist of his sculling oar the boatman drove the nose of our little craft onto dry land, and I found myself looking up into a semicircle of gaunt faces. The light of many lanterns showed eye sockets black and bearded cheeks hollow, so that these hunted creatures had the look of dead men standing upright—yet all the eyes glittered with the hope that my coming brought.

As I stepped ashore, I heard the boatman ask, "Where's the judge?" heard someone say, "They're bringing him down."

Buell climbed from the boat, swung his scissors-grinder after him, put it down behind him and sat upon it. I heard the other boats grate against the sedge bank; heard their boatmen muttering orders; felt their occupants moving up the bank and coming to a halt behind me; but still that half circle of hollow-eyed men stood like a wall before us.

"You don't suppose, do you, Oliver," Buell asked, making a pretense of anxiety, "that these people don't want us around here? Maybe we ought to go back and tell Howe there ain't any use trying to find out what's happening to Loyalists on Long Island."

A sharp voice answered. "If you're the man General Howe sent to us, you're welcomer than ice to hell; but nobody gets into this swamp without we know who he is. Judge Hendon has to talk to each man. If you'd ever had a mob after you, you'd know why."

"Brother," Buell said, "I've had more tar on me than you could get on a barn roof."

The circle of men swayed and muttered. From far behind them we heard a commotion and shouting. The shouting proved to be one sentence, oft-repeated: "Make way for the judge! Make way for the judge!"

The half circle opened, and through the lane thus formed came two men carrying a third who sat in a chair made from birch poles. When the chair was put down, the half circle closed behind it and the two bearers stood on either side, with lanterns raised shoulder-high.

Our boatman stepped forward. "Judge," he said, "this here's a Mr. Wiswell, vouched for by Demott. He and a friend want to find out what's happening here, so they can take back word to General Howe."

The judge was a frail old man with white hair and a thin ascetic face; but I could see he was seriously an invalid, for he was obviously unable to rise from his chair, and his hands were twisted as if his fingers had been bound against his palms for a long, long time, until they were stiffened and useless. His eyes, however, were quick and young, and his voice was as gentle as his smile.

"We're honored to have you here, Mr. Wiswell," he said, "and we welcome you and your friend—I don't believe I heard your friend's name, Mr. Wiswell?"

Buell spoke up briskly. "Thomas Buell, printer, repairer of military arms; maker of fashionable ornaments for military caps and cartridge boxes; painter and gilder of escutcheons; engraver of seals, dies, punches, and copper plates; marker of silver plate with elegant ciphers and arms; cutter of blocks and ornaments for printers; maker of models for canal locks, paint-grinding mills, machines for cutting and polishing crystals and precious stones; agent for Perkins' Metallic Tractors, claimed by Doctor Elisha Perkins of Norwich, Connecticut, to be a sure cure for rheumatism, gout, black spots before the eyes, dizziness, and the itch."

The judge stared contemplatively at Buell. "Indeed! Indeed, Mr. Buell! I'm a sufferer from rheumatism myself. Am I to understand that you know of metallic substances that will cure me?"

"Not me, Judge," Buell said promptly. "Those Metallic Tractors ain't good for one damned thing—except to prove that anyone who believes in 'em is a natural-born rebel."

Obviously relieved at Buell's answer, the judge turned back to me. "Your home is in Boston, Mr. Wiswell?"

"Milton," I said. "I lived in Boston a year after we were driven from our house."

"I had great respect for a gentleman of your name, Mr. Wiswell," the judge said. "Perhaps you're related to him. I refer to Mr. Seaton Wiswell."

"My father," I said. "He—he——"

I couldn't go on. The unexpected mention of my father's name by this kind old judge, the presence of this distinguished and harmless gentleman, bent and crippled with rheumatism, in a mosquito-ridden swamp, the hollow eyes and sodden, tattered garments of all those men before me, tightened my throat so that I could neither speak nor draw a full breath.

The judge's eyes darted over the men who stood behind me, then came back to mine again. "I'll expect you later in my hut, Mr. Wiswell," he said. "We're somewhat restricted in our hospitality; but we can offer you loyalty and friendship. That's *something* in these troubled days, as you've doubtless learned by now."

When we moved aside, the refugees who had accompanied us in the sedge boats came up one by one to offer their credentials. How, the judge asked each one, had he come to Long Island? With whom had he come? Where had he landed and when? To whom had he gone, and who had told him to go there? By what road had he traveled to Hempstead? Where had he stopped on the way? Had he seen any rebel militia?

Having satisfied himself about such details, he went deeper into each man's life. Where was he born? Where had he lived before coming to Long Island? Why had he decided to leave his home? Had the rebels attempted to persuade him to join their party?

On learning where each man lived, Judge Hendon summoned from among the onlookers someone from the same town or near it, and directed him to ask questions of the newcomer.

Our boatman, standing at our shoulders, enlightened us in a hoarse whisper. "The judge tripped up three of 'em last week. Rebel spies, they were."

"What happened to them?" I asked.

The boatman looked surprised. "They're still here. You'd oughta talk to 'em about how things are. They get better food and more of it than the rest of us. Of course, we can't let 'em get away, because if we did, they'd show the rebels how to get at us, and we wouldn't last long."

The stories that the judge drew from the men who had come with us from Demott's were in all likelihood not different from scores of those I had heard in Boston; yet their simplicity made them seem new and horrible.

Thomas French had been seized by Birdsall's mob on Long Island, sent across the Sound and put in Simsbury Mines. The two companions with whom he attempted to escape had been caught under water and drowned. Edward Beekman of Norwich, Connecticut, had been tarred and feathered and the sight of one eye destroyed. Charles Holcomb of Worcester, for daring to urge his neighbors not to take up arms until all other methods of reconciliation had failed, had been chained to a cart and driven over rocky roads until something inside him burst and he was left for dead beside the road. Arthur Downs of Stonington, charged with helping Loyalists seek sanctuary on Long Island, had been towed to sea in his sloop, his sloop scuttled, and he left to drown or get to shore by long swimming. Edward Johnson of Kingston, New York, for trying to lighten the lot of Loyalists sent to the jail in that town, had been hoisted halfway up a liberty pole by the heels, left there all night, and lowered as dead in the morning.

When the last man had spoken, the silent audience moved restlessly; and its whisperings were like a prolonged hiss of anger.

Judge Hendon half raised one of his distorted hands. "Kingston Jail," he said. "Weren't several gentlemen from this part of Long Island sent to Kingston Jail?"

"I only heard about one," Johnson said. "He's the one that got me into trouble—Governor Colden. They had him in a room with five other men. The rebel militia stole his coat, so he didn't have anything but breeches and shirt, and he got the fever and had to sleep on a stone floor without coverings. They didn't give him any medicines or even enough drinking water, and I just couldn't see an old man like the governor, who'd never done anybody any harm, treated like that. I took him some clothes and medicines, and a blanket and a mattress, and on that account they burned down my store and I heard they were going to put me in Simsbury Mines; but I didn't propose to rot away in that hole in the ground, so I came here."

"In your opinion," the judge asked, "was Governor Colden treated worse than other Loyalists in Kingston Jail?"

"Oh no, sir," Johnson said. "Some were treated worse; lots worse! Some had all their clothes stolen, and wore flour sacks. There's a fever room in the jail, and when a man gets fever he's put in it with a pan of potatoes beside him. That's all he gets to eat. If he doesn't have the strength to eat, he doesn't get anything."

"Are they allowed to have exercise—permitted to walk in the town?" the judge asked.

"My goodness, no!" Johnson said. "If they were let out, half the womenfolk in town'd give 'em clothes and food. That ain't allowed! Folks that are such skunks as to want peace and the right to speak their minds shouldn't get food and clothes! No, sir; they sit right there in their little coffins of cells, gasping with heat in summer and freezing in the winter! By God, Judge, can't something be done to get our people out of Kingston Jail and all the rest of the jails to the eastward?"

His voice shook and became shrill. "They haven't done a damned thing, Judge; not one damned thing! There's an awful lot of mighty fine men in Kingston Jail, Judge! Can't something be done for 'em?"

"Possibly," the judge said cautiously. "We'll hope for the best. Meanwhile, try not to bear malice. I want all you newcomers to make yourselves useful. You'll be helped to get settled, and you'll be expected to help us in return. Sometimes one of the most valuable things you can give us is cheerfulness. If only we can have that, we'll contrive to endure what we must."

He motioned to his chair bearers, who picked him up. The silent audience separated to let him through, and we moved slowly after him in a grotesque and insubstantial pageant.

§

As the crowded half circle dispersed, I began to have an idea of the size of the company that dwelt within this swamp.

Scores of dark figures, dimly seen in the lantern light, moved before me; and as we walked beside the judge's swaying chair, I could see them carrying their lanterns to little huts built in the brush beyond the open parade across which we moved. The parade was crowded, like Boston Common on a Saturday night.

They seemed a different breed from Colonel Birdsall's militia—more alert, more determined, more resourceful.

"It wouldn't be difficult, would it, Judge," I asked, "to defeat a regiment of rebels with these men here?"

"No," Judge Hendon said, "it wouldn't! You haven't met the young men who are kind enough to act as my chair bearers. The one in front is Stephen DeLancey. His uncle's General Oliver DeLancey. The one behind is John Barbarie. John and Stephen say that Birdsall's and Duyckinck's militiamen are no better than mobs, cowards at heart. They think they can train the men in this swamp to whip ten times their number of rebels; but I can't permit it, Mr. Wiswell. There's no doubt these men have the quality and the determination to whip Birdsall and Duyckinck, but they'd never be able to protect the thousands of unarmed, unorganized Loyalists on Long Island."

"Those damned rebels splash around like a lot of pigs," Barbarie said. "They talk like pigs and smell like pigs, too. If Stephen and I'd been free this afternoon, we could have killed twenty of 'em without firing a gun—the way you'd kill pigs."

"Yes, and gained nothing by it," Judge Hendon said sharply. "Dead men help no one, not even those who kill them!" He leaned forward and spoke to Stephen DeLancey. "We'd best go by way of the hospital, Stephen."

DeLancey bore to the right, and we saw before us a long hut, roofed with leafy boughs, but without sides. On each corner post hung a lantern, and by this faint light I saw a score of figures lying on beds of leaves. They were covered with tattered blankets, bed ticking, flour bags, old coats. A few lay silent, staring up at the leafy branches overhead; others tossed and turned, sighing and groaning.

"The rebels do all they can to keep us from getting medicines," the judge said. "They aim either to kill us, or capture us and force us into the rebel militia; but it seems as though our men just won't die till Howe gets here to set us free."

A dark figure rose from his knees at the far end of the long hut and came toward us. "Judge," he said, "we've got to have more men to take care of these people. They're being eaten alive by mosquitoes, and their fevers can't be kept down. Bonner just died; and I'll lose a dozen more if I can't have another ten men to trickle water on 'em and keep off the mosquitoes."

"Bonner," the judge said thoughtfully. "He got here just yesterday, didn't he? Wasn't he the one who was going to be married next week?"

The doctor looked doubtful. "Maybe so. He had five buckshot in the small of his back, and another lodged in his skull." He gave us a quick glance; then said to the judge: "When's Howe coming?"

The judge seemed not to hear him. "This is Doctor Rounds of Islip, Mr. Wiswell. The rebels drove away eighteen horses belonging to the doctor, and obliged his wife and his daughters to take refuge in New Jersey. It's hard on the doctor, Mr. Wiswell; but it's our good fortune. Probably half of us would be dead if we didn't have him to look after us."

He touched young DeLancey. "Take me out to the parade, Stephen. We'll get those ten men for the doctor." To the doctor he added, "Come to my hut when you've made your men comfortable for the night. I'll have Mr. Wiswell with me, and we'll be even more eager to hear what he has to say than he'll be to talk to us."

As we moved out to the open space, the judge repeated name after name to DeLancey, who snapped them out in a voice that must, I thought, be audible on Staten Island.

That done, the judge took us to his own hut, which, like the hospital and all the other shelters, was nothing but a roof of branches supported by four tree trunks. To my surprise, the hut already had an occupant, and it had a ready-made audience too; for on every side of it sat and stood scores of Loyalists, their eyeballs white in the lantern light; and their hands, perpetually brushing at mosquitoes, made a pale flickering, as of a half moonlight upon restless water.

Barbarie and DeLancey put down the chair beside the occupant of the hut, who was lying on a thick mat of sedge. In the light of the lanterns his thin face had a waxy pallor, but his black eyes sparkled and his lips were curved in a smile that was both patient and sardonic. The judge leaned down and looked at him, seemed reassured by what he saw; then said to me, "This is the Reverend Edmund Lane, Mr. Wiswell. One of these days he'll be a bishop, but we almost lost him this afternoon, because he thought the rebels wouldn't shoot their own countrymen. We took four buckshot out of his shoulder."

Lane moved his hand in a small gesture that took in all the men outside the hut. "They've come here for news, Judge. You'd better arrange to give it to them, or they'll stand around all night, waiting."

The judge turned to me. "Mr. Wiswell, have you any information for us in regard to General Howe's plans, and when we may expect him to move to our relief?"

"No," I said, and I spoke loudly, so that I might be heard at a considerable distance. "I'm sorry. I'm not a carrier of information, but a seeker for it. I don't know the general's plans, or how long he may be delayed before attacking. My instructions are only to find out your numbers and the conditions under which you live, and report on 'em to the general."

I heard voices muttering in disappointment, and then, after a moment or two, the word "Declaration." It was repeated from here and there, "Declaration, Declaration," until it became a general insistent outcry —"Declaration! Declaration!"

The judge looked at me apologetically. "We've all heard Congress issued a Declaration of Independence a short time ago, but nobody can tell us what was in it. Can you, by any chance, tell us what it's about?"

"Well, sir," I said, "I can give you a general idea. I can't recite it for you; but two sentences stick in my mind and I can say 'em for you word for word. Every Loyalist, almost, knows its first sentence—'When in the course of human events it becomes necessary for one people to dissolve the political bands which have connected them with another, and to assume, among the powers of the earth, the separate and equal station to which the laws of nature and of nature's God entitle them, a decent respect to the opinions of mankind requires that they should declare the causes which impel them to the separation.' "

Somewhere among the close-packed circle of listeners a man laughed abruptly, and the laughter spread as a ripple progresses upon the surface of a pool.

Judge Hendon raised his hand and the laughter died away. "Do you know who wrote the paper?" he asked.

"Thomas Jefferson, I'm told, sir."

The judge nodded. "I see: I see. You said 'one people,' did you not? 'When it becomes necessary for one people.' " He made an exasperated movement. "Four fifths of the people on this island are loyal. Two thirds of the people in New York and Pennsylvania are loyal. More than half the people in all of North America are loyal. It looks to me as though Mr. Jefferson hasn't a high respect for the opinions of mankind—not if he wants mankind to think that I, and all the others who have fled to the security of this swamp, and another million of our fellow countrymen, are not people."

"You'll be equally interested in the other sentence," I said. "It reads, 'We hold these truths to be self-evident, that all men are created equal, that they are endowed by their Creator with certain unalienable rights, that among these are life, liberty, and the pursuit of happiness.' "

"Well, well!" Judge Hendon said. "So all men are created equal! So they're endowed with the unalienable rights of life, liberty, and the pursuit of happiness!" He shook his head. "I suppose we, in this swamp, are supposed to be in possession of our liberty and engaged in the pursuit of happiness, since Mr. Jefferson declares them to be our unalienable rights."

An angry muttering rose from the crowd of listeners.

The Reverend Mr. Lane raised a protesting hand. "No profanity, please! Model yourselves on Judge Hendon. Don't make matters worse by speaking indiscreetly or with improper heat."

"Oh my, no!" Buell said. "When the neighbors tar and feather you, don't ever call 'em anything worse than 'the said neighbors.' If you get too hot about it, you can relieve yourself with 'whereas' and 'feloniously.' Like this: 'Whereas the said neighbors did feloniously tar and feather my aforesaid hide, including my aforesaid hair, my said nose and aforesaid fingernails, therefore know all men,' and so on. Yes, sir; we got to keep our passions down!"

I went on hastily. "Those two sentences are the only ones I can quote exactly, but the document speaks of the abuses suffered by residents of North America at England's hands. It says that the King of England has refused his assent to wholesome laws and plans the establishment of absolute tyranny over these states."

"That's not so," Judge Hendon said. "No colony has ever been prevented from making any law it wished. The only thing they *haven't* been allowed to do is to issue fraudulent currency and declare it legal tender. Can you give us a better example of royal tyranny and brutality, Mr. Wiswell?"

"Well, sir," I said, "the document says the King has called together legislative bodies, at places unusual, uncomfortable, and distant from the depository of their public records, for the sole purpose of fatiguing the Patriots into a compliance with his measures!"

"Yes," the judge said meditatively, "a legislative body *was* moved in Massachusetts. It was transferred from Boston to Cambridge so the legislators might be protected against mobs. I find myself strangely lacking in sympathy for Patriots who admit they can be 'fatigued' into complying with measures of which they disapprove! I fear it's a feeble and sickly patriotism that wilts before such dreadful hardships as undertaking the long, long journey between Boston and Cambridge! I don't much care for it as an argument justifying a national rebellion against constituted authority and embarking on a civil war!"

Every man without that hut was now as silent as though carved from stone.

"Another abuse mentioned," I said, "is that the King has erected a multitude of new offices and sent swarms of officers to harass our people and eat out their subsistence."

The judge looked irritated. "Five new commissioners were appointed for this whole country, and fifteen or twenty clerks to go with them. Those are the swarms who harass Americans and eat out their subsistence! How do they compare with the packs of rebel militia that pull down our homes, maim our cattle, and make the lives of our womenfolk a perpetual nightmare!"

"Well, sir," I said, "the paper says America is opposing with manly firmness the King's invasions on the rights of the people."

"Since when," Judge Hendon asked, "has a government been able to maintain its integrity without putting down rebellion and mob rule? All these so-called measures of repression were provoked by popular outrage! Doesn't this document anywhere hint that a government must protect its officers from assault and their houses from being sacked, its loyal lieges from being tarred and feathered, and the property of merchants sailing under its flags from being thrown by lawless hands into the sea?"

"No, sir," I said.

He raised his crippled hands in a half gesture of disgust. "I've heard enough! From the beginning, twelve years ago, the rebellious agitators against England have consistently disavowed any desire for independence. For twelve long years the rebel leaders have solemnly affirmed and reiterated that they only wished to obstruct and defeat a weak ministerial policy, thereby to secure a redress of grievances. At every opportunity they vowed they abhorred the thought of independence! James Otis, Alexander Hamilton, George Washington, John Dickinson—all of them said independence would be a calamity and a crime. On this ground they secured the help of Pitt, Burke, Conway, Barré. Now they've turned traitor to those who helped them. Pitt, Burke, and all the others have been made parties to a disruption of the British Empire. The men responsible for this Declaration are political hypocrites, as those of us who disagree with them have always charged. While openly disavowing a wish for independence, some of them must have been treacherously working with that end in view all the time!"

He leaned forward in his chair. "Take word to General Howe for us,

Mr. Wiswell, that the rebels are in a position where they must be utterly destroyed if they're attacked soon. *Our* country is at stake, Mr. Wiswell. The war these rebels are forcing upon us is neither just nor necessary, because without it neither their freedom nor their happiness would be impaired or imperiled. In this colony, which is overwhelmingly loyal, rebellion was instigated and made inevitable by three lawyers—all demagogues and unscrupulous users of cunning chicanery and falsehood: the uncouth, bigoted, savage, violent, sullen William Livingston; the sycophantic hypocrite William Smith, Junior, who unhesitatingly sacrifices friendship, honor, religion, or his sacred word to pride, ambition, or avarice; and a violent and acrimonious madman, John Morin Scott; by a liquor dealer and son of a convict, John Lamb; by a slop-shop keeper, Alexander McDougall; by a sailor-fish-peddler-alehouse-keeper, Isaac Sears; by a bail jumper and a coward at Quebec under fire, Donald Campbell; by Peter Livingston, whose low cunning and avarice have earned him the name of Jew Peter.

"If these men have their way with us, the population, instead of employing themselves in peaceful occupations, will engage in costly and endless struggles for political offices and grants from the public treasury. Assemblies will be tumultuous and disorderly; the voices of worthy and modest men will seldom be heard; the bold, the ambitious, the artful will hold sway. Alcibiades will rule and Socrates will be martyred, as the Smiths proposed to martyr Doctor Myles Cooper, president of King's College, by shaving his head, slitting his nose, stripping him naked, and turning him adrift! Themistocles, Xenophon, and Aristides will be banished; great Pericles will be fined and his sons put to death when laurels should be their reward. Our futures and our lives depend on leadership, Mr. Wiswell. That's the word we want taken back to General Howe."

Judge Hendon, his twisted hands held tight against his breast, stared into the steamy darkness of the swamp with the rapt gaze of a prophet.

The Reverend Mr. Lane sighed. "Put out the lanterns," he told Barbarie and DeLancey, "and have someone cut green grass for the smudges. We need all the blood we've got if Birdsall and his men take a notion to come after us again tomorrow."

Dim, silent figures moved slowly away. A black depression weighed me down.

My thoughts and fears must have come out from me like a dark cloud, for the judge said: "Remember, Mr. Wiswell, nothing's ever as hopeless as it seems—not even death. You might tell General Howe that no matter what happens to us, we'll never lose courage."

He looked up suddenly. "Who's that?"

A voice spoke from the darkness beyond the hut. "Eben Drake of Milton, Judge. I'd like a word with Mr. Wiswell."

I didn't wait to hear what the judge said, but darted from the hut toward the dark figure standing outside. "Are you one of the Drakes from Brush Hill Road?" I asked, and in spite of myself my voice shook.

"I certainly am," he said. "I worked in Vose Leighton's store, Mr. Wiswell. I had to leave because my uncle Robie worked for Mr. John Chandler up in Worcester. Everybody that had anything to do with the Chandlers was driven out, Mr. Wiswell. The Chandlers had too much money."

"I know," I said. "Were the Leightons well when you left? How was Soame? How was Mrs. Leighton and the other boys; how was—how was —how were they all?"

"I dunno, damn 'em," Drake said. "They're in the army—the rebel army; and I hope they get their come-uppance! There ain't but one in the whole damned family I'd turn my hand over for, and she's why I wanted to see you. She thought you might come to Long Island sooner or later; so she gave me the money to get here—and this for you."

He gave me a little damp wad of paper, uncertainly said, "Well——" and drifted away in the darkness. I hurried back to the hut and, with trembling hands, rekindled one of the lanterns. The letter was discolored with grime and perspiration; the ink upon it almost illegible from innumerable wettings and dryings.

I was conscious, as I scrutinized the faded writing, that Judge Hendon, Mr. Lane, and Buell were watching me when I put the precious document on the top of Buell's scissors-grinder to steady it, and as I held the lantern close above those blurred words, Buell tried to take it from me. "You'll spill the oil out of that lamp, Oliver," he said, "and first thing you know you won't have any letter at all. Why don't you let me read it for you? I've had practice reading messy writing."

"I can read it without assistance," I said.

"Oh, private matter," Buell said, and added slowly, "I see, I see." The others also seemed to see; for they ceased to stare at me, and I had the letter to myself.

I made out the words "Dearest Oliver." My eyes cleared; my hand grew steadier; sentences that had seemed a hopeless blur became readable.

Dearest Oliver [she had written]:

Two weeks ago I had a beautiful experience. I'd just stepped out of our gate upon the road when a strange man, all the color of dust, came from some bushes across the way, where he seemed to have been lurking. At first I was a little afraid of him; because there was no one else in sight; but his manner was respectful and he touched his ragged hat. He asked me if my name wasn't Sally Leighton; and when I told him Yes, he spoke to me quickly in a low voice and said, "There's a friend of yours whose name begins with O, and he asked me to tell you that he was well and hopeful, and to say that nothing's changed or ever will be." He was gone down the road before I could utter a word in answer; but oh, Oliver, I knew you'd sent it—and thank you, thank you, thank you! Inside me I've lived in sunlight ever since I saw the dust-colored man! You mustn't write to me, remember; but, oh, perhaps there'll be another dust-colored man some day?

How often, oh, how often have I wished to write you during all these long, cold months; and how often have I longed for word from you. Now spring is here, and every scene and scent and sound reminds me of spring days we spent together.

I have never seen such vast flocks of Old Shags flying north: there have been thousands and thousands, in long lines, like those we saw the day we sailed to Hingham and caught the eels and made the stew. Father says this means we shall have a hot summer. Probably so, because there have been rings around the sun for two weeks, and never a drop of rain.

The willows along the river in Dedham smell like honey, Oliver. Do you remember the day you put the mouse on the shingle for me and floated it down over the pool where the sulky big trout lay, and how we thought he'd swallowed the shingle when he struck?

Of course you remember Pie Benjamin, the town idiot? He stood outside our house every day for eight days, making whirling motions around his ears with his forefinger, and then I remembered that either you or your father had always given him a shilling every spring so he could have his winter hair cut off. I was deeply touched that he should have come to me, and I gave him a shilling for you, Oliver.

Albion, Soame, Steven, Jeremiah, and John have gone south with their regiments. Everybody says that the British are about to leave Halifax, or have already left. It's common talk that they're going to Long Island—that all their sympathizers are going with them. That's why I'm sending this letter by Eben Drake. He knows you because he worked in Father's store for six years and saw you often. I'm hoping he'll come across you on Long Island, for if you're as eager to have a word from me as I am to hear from you, you'll be glad for it.

I wonder, dear Oliver, whether you know all the things that our brave army has learned. I am sure that if you knew the cruel things your associates have been guilty of, you would have a change of heart. The Ministry is arousing the black slaves of the south to attack us, and employing savages to make uncivilized war upon our frontiers. The Ministry has sent Hessian mercenaries to butcher us. These hirelings have been told that if they allow themselves to be captured by Americans, their bodies will be stuck full of pine splinters and then slowly burned to cinders. Was anything ever more horrible, Oliver?

Oh, my dear! I can write no more; but you will understand and hear me crying out to you—see all the words that rest unwritten in my heart. Dear, dear Oliver, I'm your

SALLY

§

I read the letter the first time as a child reads a tale, seeking the passages that delight him. She had longed for word from me! She thought often of me! She still was my Sally!

I drew a deep breath and read the letter again; and this time phrases came out from it and struck upon me with hammers: "you would have a change of heart," "cruel associates," "arousing the black slaves of the south," "see all the words that rest unwritten in my heart."

When, for the third time, I read the letter through, I seemed to be in a fog of puzzlement.

Buell touched my arm. "Don't you hear the judge speaking to you, Oliver?"

"My apologies, sir," I said. "I—I didn't hear."

"You've had troublesome news, Mr. Wiswell," the judge said. "Is there anything I can do?"

I fear I spoke brusquely. "Nothing! You can do nothing! What can you do when a person doesn't see things as you see them?"

"What can you do?" the judge asked. "You can do this, Mr. Wiswell: you can remind yourself that if the lady—and of course it *is* a lady— doesn't see things as you see them, it's because she doesn't know the truth. Yet she's obviously a true lady and a reasonable one. Otherwise she'd never have written things that first made you smile as you did, even while she wrote words that later hurt you."

I couldn't say a word.

"And of course she loves you," the judge went on, "because she's try-ing to help you. She's careful to season advice with gentleness, and that's not easily done. I suspect you're fortunate in your choice."

"I'm fortunate if I can hold her," I said, "but how can I hold her when she's forever hearing that you and I and all these men in the swamps condone cruelty and butchery? My God, Judge, do men believe whatever lie they hear about an enemy?"

"Always," the judge said. "Suppose, Mr. Wiswell, you read me part of your letter—I mean the part that hurt you. I know what it is to be sepa-rated from those held dear. It's a sort of torture that's always increased by doubts."

When I did as he suggested, Judge Hendon caressed one crippled hand with the other. "I thought it might be like that, Mr. Wiswell. Your lady has heard the old shibboleths of war—all the old accusations that were made, no doubt, by the Medes and the Persians against their enemies; by the Phoenicians; by the armies of Julius Caesar. She's mistaken, Mr. Wiswell; and all she needs, I think, is your personal assurance that your side of this struggle is supported by arguments that are far from weak; that its motives and sentiments are far from base; and that the devotion and self-sacrifice shown by those who support it are not unheroic.

"You've been hurt by the lady's suggestion that you turn to the rebel viewpoint; but I think you can make her understand that a cause which is embraced and cherished by so vast a portion of American society, regardless of obloquy and disaster, can never be turned out of court summarily and contemptuously.

"It's clear from the lady's letter that the rebels are branding us to the whole world as execrable, and insisting that there is neither patriotism nor decency outside the rebel ranks.

"Well, Mr. Wiswell, you can't very well extol your own decency and patriotism; but if your lady can hear the truth from your own lips, she'll recognize it; for every true lady is by nature a Loyalist. We are the people who have land, belongings, position, and we're standing by our guns in opposition to the people who have nothing. We're the conservative people; and what has been true of conservative people in all ages and all lands is true of us. We dissent from extreme and injudicious measures, from violence, from oppression, from revolution, from reckless statements and misrepresentation. We can't stomach liars, bullies, or demagogues, or leaders without experience, ability, or sound judgment; and in the end the lady you love will never love you less for holding to such beliefs.

"There's no denying that within our ranks are a fair portion—and in this statement I'm again conservative—of the cultivation, of the moral thoughtfulness, of the personal purity and honor that exist in the American colonies. I've seen a list, Mr. Wiswell, of those in your native Massachusetts who will probably be proscribed and forever banished for no reason except that they have been conservative men. There are hundreds of them, and not one a tyrant; not one a profligate; not one a man of small consequence. Their names are those of the oldest and noblest families whose diligence and abilities founded and built up New England. They are the most substantial and influential men in Massachusetts—men of the highest integrity. Their attitude is inspired by conscientious conviction; persisted in despite all the outrages that have been done against them, and despite all the outrages that they still must suffer.

"Conservatives aren't braggarts as a rule, Mr. Wiswell; but you can safely tell your lady or anyone else in the world that the side you have chosen has so much solid fact and valid reasoning behind it that any intelligent and noble-minded American can with reason take that side, and stick to it, and go into battle for it, and if necessary die for it: even imperil all the interests of his life in defense of it without having either his reason or his integrity impeached. You never need fear that your lady will ever believe otherwise, once she hears your case from your own lips."

The words of the old judge gave me new courage. In spite of the tumultuous croaking of the frogs, the shrill whining of the mosquitoes, the dank moisture of this miserable swamp, and the hard bed on which I rested, my sleep was more profound and freer from distracting dreams than it had been for many a long and weary night.

# The Little Home in the Country

### From FOR AUTHORS ONLY

THE place for happiness, peace, rest, health, and genuine leisure is the country. Ever since the days of Horace and his emotional outbursts on the subject of his Sabine farm, literary celebrities have referred fascinatingly to the delights of escaping the dirt and tumult of cities and occupying a small cottage in a sylvan retreat or a lush meadow miles and miles from the nearest pharmacy.

In such surroundings, according to poetry, fiction, and the drama, the air is pure and fresh; the scent of flowers and the musical twittering of birds soothe the jangled nerves; by digging occasionally in the damp and fragrant earth, one easily induces unbroken slumber and raises gargantuan vegetables.

Once upon a time, inflamed by whimsical essays telling how semidecayed farmhouses or tumble-down sheds had been transformed into miniatures of the American Wing of the Metropolitan Museum at practically no expense, I acquired an ex-stable on the coast of southern Maine and undertook the pleasant task of transforming it into one of the little homes in the country that one reads about in magazines.

I anticipated no difficulty in achieving pleasing results at small cost.

The stable was not old and had been stoutly built on a stone foundation. It upheld the best traditions of little homes in the country by standing on moderately fertile ground eminently qualified to produce luxuriant vines and shrubs; and the land around it appeared too unimportant to attract the attention of other investors who would intrude on my privacy. No subtle premonition warned me that the local golf club might build a practice tee beneath my workroom windows: no ominous portent indicated that neighbors would feel an urge to place garages in my front and rear.

That little home in the country, with its surrounding half acre of land, never changed much in its outward appearance, but it required an investment, in its transition from stable to five-room summer cottage, sufficient to build a fifteen-room house with brick walls, slate roof, pergolas, six bathrooms, silver doorknobs, and landscaping by experts. In the end I abandoned it and built a farmhouse from the ground up; for I knew that if I continued to tinker on the little home, it would eventually swallow up more than enough to build a model village including Colonial library and athletic field.

It is not my wish to cast aspersion on the persons who write whimsical pieces for the papers, giving readers the idea that a farmhouse can be remodeled as cheaply and as easily as one can buy a secondhand automobile.

In most of these whimsical pieces, a young wife leads her husband into the country, shows him a semicollapsed cottage, and talks him into buying it. Then the two of them, with an old hammer, a borrowed saw, and a few secondhand nails, proceed to hammer it into perfect condition.

I do not care to say this is impossible. There may be people who can do it. I do not even wish to point the finger of suspicion at the garden experts who produce vivacious essays telling how two days' work on the part of the merest novice will transform a revolting rock pile into a captivating fernery. Probably somewhere there are those who can successfully evolve ferneries from rock piles; so far be it from me to discourage them by cynical or ill-considered remarks. I do, however, desire to cry a bitter cry against the manner in which occupants of little homes in the country, and prospective occupants of such homes, are led to embark on ventures without being warned of the grief that may await them if they permit themselves, as I once did, to believe implicitly in catalogs and incomplete directions.

This matter of incomplete directions is one that I find trouble in mentioning without profanity; and it was responsible for the motto of my first home in the country, which, in the best traditions of country homes, had a name, Stall Hall. Its motto was "Nobody Ever Told Me About That."

I had no sooner acquired my little home in the country, for example, than I felt the need of a dense hedge to intercept the dust of passing automobiles and to intimate subtly to golfers that it would cause me no ungovernable grief if they kept to the road instead of ambling across the lawn.

Hedge experts were consulted; and it was the consensus of opinion that laurel-leaf willow would make the highest, densest hedge in the shortest possible time. A number of nurserymen's annuals confirmed this opinion with the words: "Salix laurifolia. Laurel-leaf Willow. Grows eight to twenty feet, with shining, lanceolate, dark green leaves. Makes a nice screen for any unsightly object."

In spite of being vaguely resentful of the phrase "any unsightly object," I purchased and inserted, at three-foot intervals along three of our boundaries, one hundred laurel-leaf willows, each one too fragile, at the time of planting, to be used as a switch for a recalcitrant puppy.

For a few years they kept within bounds. Then they encroached upon us ruthlessly, as the rank vegetation of an East Indian jungle overwhelms an abandoned outpost of civilization. They grew so high that in addition to shutting out the golfers, they also shut out the breezes, following which they shut out the sun. Nobody, I scarcely need to state, had ever warned me of such an occurrence.

As the screen of willows grew higher and thicker, the branches arched prettily above the gate, hung languidly over the front, side, and back yards, and even stretched carelessly across the lawns to rap against doors and windows. But toward the middle of summer each year the leaves on the lower branches, which had started by being shining, lanceolate, and dark green, as advertised, took to turning a dull mud color and falling off. By early September the nice screen was denuded of leaves and was not, as one might say, quite so nice.

Before and during this phenomenon—during, that is to say, the months of June, July, and August—any person standing near the willow hedge was soon annoyed by a crawly sensation on the back of his neck. Investigation revealed small, restless black bugs with a positive flair for neck-perambulation. Further investigation showed that each one of the several billion leaves on the hedge was populated by from one to ten of these small black bugs. In addition to occupying themselves in gnawing the shine, color, and lanceolation from the willow leaves, they further disported themselves by letting go all holds and dropping from their roosts on passing dogs or humans.

Nobody had ever mentioned small black bugs when recommending the laurel-leaf willow as a nice screen for unsightly objects; so a call for help was sent to the entomological department of the University of Maine. In the course of time a young man from the university arrived, examined the bugs with care, and took away in a specimen box a hand-picked selection of insects, together with a large number that had inconspicuously dropped on the back of his neck while he was engaged in his researches.

Later the entomological department officially notified me that the bugs were "snout beetles," and that they could be eradicated by spraying the willows once before the leaves had emerged and twice afterward with a disagreeable emulsion containing arsenate of lead and soap.

This information was doubtless true; and somewhere there may be snout beetles that succumb to a triple bath of arsenate of lead and soap. Apparently, however, my snout beetles were a tough and hardy breed; for arsenate of lead merely whetted their appetite for greenery.

The snout beetles continued to multiply with inconceivable rapidity; and by the first of September each year, all leaves from the hedge were scattered in windrows on the lawn. Whenever, during the summer, my wire-haired terrier returned from a tour of the estate to cast herself on a couch, a score of snout beetles disengaged themselves from her coat and crawled restlessly about, impatiently awaiting the arrival of a human occupant on whose neck and ears they could stroll.

The snout beetles fortunately restricted themselves to willows; but other growths adjacent to my little home in the country developed additional troubles.

The literature of dwarf fruit trees has always touched a tender chord in my breast; so the acquisition of the little home was almost immediately followed by the installation of dwarf apples, pears, and plums. The apple trees, in theory, would bear richly flavored apples in three years' time; while in four years they were supposed to supply the entire neighborhood with choice fruit.

The nurseryman's annual, in referring to these particular dwarf apple trees, spoke of them as being peculiarly adapted to the little home in the country and intimated that genuine apples might be expected one year after planting. It definitely promised apples in two years.

One of these dwarf apples was a fine, healthy tree; so I trained it against the wall of the little home in the most approved manner and left it there four years, during which time it bore three blossoms but no fruit. Fearing something was troubling it, I dug it up and moved it to another location. It remained in the new location four years without bearing either blossoms or apples.

Every year, however, enormous families of small green insects known as Aphis or Aphidae appeared at the tip of each branch. I have conferred with a number of persons in an attempt to find out why aphids should exist. In each case I have been told that they act as ants' cows, and that ants milk them. This explanation, to my way of thinking, explains nothing. It fails to explain, for example, why ants should have cows.

Having small sympathy for the cow-herding aspirations of ants, I repeatedly attempted to exterminate the aphids by spraying the appleless apple trees with an offensive brown spray containing nicotine. This spray, according to people who ought to know, is bad for aphids and exterminates them in the twinkling of an eye. Possibly this is so: I would not like to come out flat-footed and deny it. My own observations showed that the spray had a slightly soporific effect on the aphids, making them drowsy for an hour or so after the spraying. They slept a little, and after their doze or siesta they carried on as usual.

While the spray was harmless to aphids, it was not without strength; for it made brown splotches on the walls of my little home. In spite of this I was unable to discontinue its use; for all genuine experts on little homes in the country firmly maintain that it ruins aphids and that nothing else does the trick. I found, however, that a more effective method of dealing with them was to take the aphid-covered branch tip between the thumb and forefinger and roll it gently back and forth. This required patience and a delicate touch, and was hard on the thumb and forefinger, which soon became a brilliant green; but it was certainly hell on aphids.

While on the subject of aphids, I must mention vines. A long and careful study of literature dealing with little homes in the country convinced me that vines are an essential feature of such a home. In the beginning, therefore, I planted hop vines to fill blank spaces that were to be filled later with slower-growing vines such as grapes, trumpet vine, and bittersweet.

The hop vine, from its advance notices in nurserymen's annuals, seemed almost perfect for my purposes. It was "useful for covering bowers, or any place where the covering is not necessary for winter; can be planted to run along shrubbery: exceedingly fast grower, covering a large trellis in a short time; heat, drought, or insects do not trouble it; leaves are large and rough."

All these things are true; but the annuals neglected several important facts about the hop—facts I was obliged to learn from painful personal contact. They neglected to state, for example, that the hop is determined to go where it is neither wanted nor needed, so that it must be picked up and shoved into a trellis by main force; that its leaves and stalks are so rough that after spending an hour nursing hop vines, one has little or no skin left on his hands; that the dead vine clings to a trellis with such enthusiasm that the old growth cannot be torn down in the late fall without demolishing the trellis as well.

After years of wrestling with hop vines, I realized that although heat, drought, and insects could not trouble them, they could and did trouble me greatly. I then discovered another little thing about the hop that nobody had told me. The root of the hop is twice as malevolent as the foliage; so that while the exposed portion of the vine is unobtrusively twisting itself around trees, shrubs, and flowers and choking them to death, the roots insinuate themselves beneath roads, in and out of walls, into water pipes, through flower beds, between brick walks, and into the bottom of fence and telephone poles. Every little while the wandering hop root sends up another hop vine to choke a shrub to death, or run up a telephone pole and interfere with telephone messages, or pry shingles off a roof. If one attempts to pull up or dig up the root and overlooks a fragment of it, that fragment grows into another hop root and sends up more shoots and spreads itself all over the place.

In the beginning I planted fifty hop vines. In the end I pulled up something like sixty-eight miles of hop roots and over eleven hundred hop vines, all offshoots of the original fifty. I eradicated them fairly well from my own estate, but they sprang up all over the adjacent golf links; and I frequently came across descendants of the original vines half a mile and more from their homes.

I experimented for a time with Concord and Catawba grape vines; but for some reason that still remains a mystery to me, they bore extremely small grapes of such acidity that persons who ate them lost the enamel from their teeth. After a few years the vines died, probably from acidosis.

I also struggled with *Bignonia radicans,* or trumpet vine, supposed to climb twenty feet, cover the side of the house, and produce showy orange-scarlet flowers. Spring after spring I planted specimens of *Bignonia radicans* and examined them carefully from day to day in search of showy orange-scarlet blossoms. No blossoms ever appeared; and the vines expired each winter.

Unfortunate as were my experiences with most vines, there was one—*Celastrus scandens* or bittersweet—that never failed. At the beginning of my vine planting I had leaned toward the grape and the trumpet vine because they were useful and beautiful. I had viewed my bittersweet vines without enthusiasm—probably because the annuals recommended bittersweet "for covering old walls or stone heaps." Yet it was only by means of bittersweet that I was able to achieve the vine-clad effect mentioned in all poetry and fiction dealing with little homes in the country. The vine-clad effect, however, was accompanied by one or two other minor matters never mentioned in any of the poems or books, and concerning which nobody had ever told me.

The bittersweet, for example, never knew when to stop. It thrust its tendrils beneath shingles, between boards, inside blinds, and through partitions. When it had covered the walls, it covered the windows, the roof, and the inside of the porch, prying off bits of wood here and there as it progressed.

For some reason unmentioned in works of reference on little homes in the country, there is a strong affinity between the young tips of bittersweet vines and the aphid family. In the case of my vines, at any rate, the tip of each bittersweet tendril acted as a summer resort for innumerable aphids; and when these tips rested against a painted surface, the aphids left unsightly smudges on it—smudges that could only be obliterated with two coats of paint.

Such tendrils are long and springy. When pruned, they sway convulsively, slapping the pruner across the mouth with tips heavily populated with aphids. As a result, for every five minutes spent by the pruner on bittersweet vines, he spends five hours removing aphids from himself—an occupation viewed with more or less suspicion in society as at present organized.

If, disgusted with aphids, he decides to let the vines remain unpruned, his little home in the country becomes so thoroughly be-vined as to resemble Alfred Tennyson peering querulously over the top of a tangled beard.

Returning again to the subject of the dwarf fruit trees that theoretically embellished my little home in the country, I am at a loss to understand how it is that the little country home of fiction is so surrounded by successful fruit trees that the owners are in constant danger of being stunned by the frequent impact of ripe apples, pears, and plums.

In spite of receiving the best of care, my apple and pear trees persistently refused to bear fruit. One pear tree, after six years of praiseworthy effort, advanced sufficiently to bear two crops of blossoms—one in June and another in August. One summer it was thought to be producing one pear. Unfortunately this was a false alarm; for the supposed pear turned out to be a species of wen or carbuncle.

Two other pear trees were peculiarly successful in the production of unsightly red eruptions on their leaves—eruptions that usually caused the leaves to curl up and fall off.

I suspect that helpful friends were partly responsible for the persistent refusal of the trees to bear fruit. Whenever a friend appeared, I asked him why it was that the trees didn't bear fruit, and the friend usually examined them vacantly, scratched their bark with his thumbnail, dug his heel into the dirt at their roots, and then suggested pruning, or spraying with something, or fertilizing with something else. These suggestions I was usually glad to follow; but the results never varied.

Before me, as I write, lies the catalog of a fruit-tree nursery which announces, in startling type, "There's money in fruit!" I do not need to be told about this. I know it is true, because I have put some of mine there. Doubtless there are people who can get it out; but I am not one of them.

There are three other matters connected with the little home in the country concerning which, so far as I know, there has been a conspiracy of silence, and concerning which I am lamentably in the dark.

Firstly, the seed catalogs and the whimsical articles about flower beds intimate that all seeds sprout with equal ease.

Secondly, the whimsical essays telling how to plant shrubs and vines assume that when a shrub or a vine is planted, it stays where it is put.

Thirdly, the whimsical pieces about Sally and Peter—or Milady and the Duke, or Best Beloved and the Humble Servant, or whatever names the whimsical writers may choose—telling how they remodel their little home in the country, always imply that the first changes, planned and executed without the assistance of an architect, are satisfactory and remain so indefinitely.

As to the first of these three matters: Each year, on perusing the catalogs that arrive as regularly as the hop vines, I am captivated, not to say enraptured, by their suggestions for raising perennials from seed. Most of them offer collections of flower seeds which, if purchased and planted, are eventually supposed to grow into plants that will provide the garden with harmony of color and continuity of bloom, to say nothing of rare and unusual flowers of astounding size and almost suffocating fragrance.

In the collections are not only such old favorites as sweet william, lupin, foxglove, and Canterbury bells, but strange blooms—*Centaurea macrocephala*, which has large yellow flower heads; *Cimicifuga racemosa*, which has stately white flowers eight feet high; *Eryngium amethystinum*, a bearer of handsome amethyst-blue flowers; or *Geum Lady Stratheden*, which produces large, dazzling, intense yellow flowers; or *Heuchera sanguinea*, noted for its delicate spikes of coral-red bells.

Year after year I invested in costly assortments of seeds with the intention of raising my own perennials. I prepared perennial beds from the richest soil and the most potent and penetrating fertilizers. Morning and evening I patiently watered the sleeping seeds, regardless of bedraggled trousers and gluttonous mosquitoes. Each year, with unfailing regularity, sweet williams, lupins, foxgloves, and Canterbury bells burst fluently from the ground; but never was there any sign of life—barring a magnificent crop of scraggy weeds—in the drills in which the seeds of the rare and costly flowers were interred.

In my time I raised enough sweet william—a flower that leaves me as cold as Australian spinach or witch grass—to carpet the duchy of Luxemburg. Lupin flourished so vigorously in my garden that aphids came from all over the state of Maine to feed on the superlative blooms that fought for position with my foxgloves. But if it hadn't been for the clear and exciting pictures of *Heuchera sanguinea* and *Geum Lady Stratheden* that were thoughtfully placed in the seed catalogs by enterprising florists, I would have ended my days in ignorance of their appearance.

Why this should be is a mystery to me. I make no complaints, and merely state it as a fact to show there are some things connected with a little home in the country that are not satisfactorily explained in the whimsical essays.

As to the second of the three matters: I originally planted shrubs and vines around my little home in the country with no anticipation of the vexation of spirit they would cause. Nowhere, in any of the whimsical essays, was there an intimation that vines needed further attention. Within a year of the original planting, however, I discovered I had made a number of mistakes in placing the shrubs and vines. When not changing the location of my front gate, I was shifting the front or back walk; when not inserting a new flower bed, I was adding some small excrescence to the house; when not excavating a water pipe, I was removing or putting in another tree or indulging in an activity that seemed, at the time, as important as it was necessary. In each case a few shrubs or vines needed to be dug up and removed to another location, as was also the case when the shrubs became too crowded, grew up over the windows, or intruded on a view.

It became almost impossible for me to meditate pleasurably upon my shrubs or vines because of the knowledge that all of them, sooner or later, would have to be moved. If ever there came a year when I was sighing with relief because there seemed to be no immediate need to move shrubs, trees, or vines, the town in which I lived elected a new road commissioner who, for lack of something better to do, came around and made me move trees that prevented automobilists from seeing around the corner on which my home was located. Consequently it seems to me that the newspapers and magazines that publish whimsical essays about tree, shrub, and vine planting would fill a long-felt want if they would print a few serious instructions telling how to plant shrubs and trees around a little home in the country in sunken pots, so that the inevitable moving may be effected with a minimum of expense and labor.

As to the third and last—but most important—of these three matters: When I converted my ex-stable into a little home, I trusted implicitly in the whimsical essays on farmhouse repairing and the evolution of little homes in general. In these dissertations, when an old stable or farmhouse is converted, it is permanently converted. Peter and Sally, the prankish converters, are content with what they have done, even down to the antique whisky bottles used as candlesticks on the mantel. Any changes in their work, one easily sees, will only be made over their dead bodies. Consequently I fondly imagined that my initial stable-converting labors were to be my last. I even went so far as to heave a sigh of relief and observe that next year, with nothing to do, I could devote all my time to literary pursuits.

On the following year, however, it became necessary to add a brick-floored front porch, replace the walls of the dining room with a more attractive wood, and repair the kitchen. On the third year it was discovered that the roof must be reshingled, and it was consequently decided to enlarge a bedroom and add another bath at the same time. On the fourth year the carpenters returned to the scene of the crime, so to speak, to install a wrought-iron balcony injudiciously purchased from a firm of house wreckers during a hurried trip through New Orleans. Since the carpenters were at work, it seemed a desirable time to build a larger closet in the guest room, renovate the sheathing on the walls, and install antique hinges and latches on the doors.

A solemn oath was then taken that no other alterations would be countenanced.

On the fifth year a dressing room with closets was built as an adjunct to the balcony installed on the preceding year. On the sixth year the bookcases and window seats of the living room were wrenched out because they failed to harmonize with newly acquired antique furniture. On the seventh and eighth years, in order to escape constant repairs, an offensive stable across the street was purchased, torn down, and built up into a workshop. On the ninth year the kitchen of Stall Hall proved unsatisfactory and was consequently rebuilt with electrical appliances, antique hinges, and what not. Following the departure of the carpenters after the débris had been cleared away, solemn vows were taken that no carpenter should ever again set foot in the house, except socially.

On the tenth year the floor of the living room sagged, and fungoid growths emerged from joints in the floor boards and cracks in the walls. The carpenters returned, tore up the floor of the living room, and ripped off the front of the house. It then developed that when the brick porch had been added on the second year, the bricks had been laid on sea sand, and an incompetent carpenter had allowed the sand to rest against the wooden sills of the house. Out of the sand had come sheets and claws of fungus, supported by pulpy roots that extended three feet into the sand. The sheets and claws had fastened on sills, floor beams, and floor boards; then spread to the walls and rotted them so that they crumbled beneath the impact of a fist. Beams measuring eight by ten inches could be ripped to pieces with the bare hands. Consequently new floor beams, a new floor, and a new front wall, all carefully protected from the contaminating touch of sand, were installed; and at the same time it seemed a good idea to build a new cement cellar and repair the cellar walls where they had been weakened by willow roots.

Between all these distressing carpenter jobs were sandwiched ventures in painting, plumbing, electrifying, glazing, and masonry.

As a result of all this, it seems to me that whenever a newspaper or a magazine prints a whimsical piece about how somebody rebuilt a little home in the country for the price of a couple of tickets to a moderately successful Broadway success, it ought also to print an editorial note informing gullible tyros that the little-home-in-the-country game is second only to horse racing as a trap for suckers.

# Palace, Italian Style

### *"The Half-Baked Palace" from* FOR AUTHORS ONLY

I$_T$ WAS in the summer of 1927 that I was stricken with the idea of building in Italy. As I recall it, the idea germinated as the result of a sudden promiscuous mixing of several unrelated circumstances.

In the first place, I had been oppressed for some time with a desire to write a novel, but had simultaneously become acutely noise-conscious.

In the second place, a relative by marriage had unexpectedly acquired, as a summer residence, a rectangular stone farmhouse, a soiled pink in color, on the outermost shoulder of a mountainous peninsula jutting into that section of the Mediterranean romantically known as the Tyrrhenian Sea.

In the third place, while I was well aware of the fact that the term "beauty-loving Italians" is what our slang-hating English cousins like to call eyewash, I was moderately certain that all Italians, even the humblest, were well equipped to perpetuate the simple—and therefore beautiful—architecture of the Italian countryside.

In the fourth place I had recently built two small houses—one in Florida, as an investment, and one in Maine, as an accident—and in both cases I had been blessed with competent builders, who built what I wanted with a minimum of fuss and expense and a maximum of ingenuity. Therefore I was satisfied that housebuilding, whether in Maine, Florida, Czechoslovakia, Italy, or any other section, is a pleasing diversion rather than an arduous labor.

I had gathered, from several years' study of the incisive writings of prominent English, French, and Italian journalists, that American workmen are universally sunk to the same jazz-mad level to which all the rest of America has fallen: that the American workman is a dishonest, hypocritical moneygrubber, whereas the European laborer is almost an artist, reveling in the possession of a creative sense that causes him to build lovingly and enduringly—unlike the slovenly jerry-builders of America. Thus I was sure that my experiences with Italian workmen would be at least as happy as those I had enjoyed with American workmen.

The soiled pink farmhouse is situated above the town of Porto Santo Stefano, on Mont' Argentario, a rugged promontory about the size of Mount Desert Island—a promontory that misses being an island by the narrowest of margins.

It is connected with the mainland by a mile-long causeway which joins it to the town of Orbetello. Few tourists cross the causeway, since the promontory has an air of being a sort of vermiform appendix to the mainland. Consequently the town of Porto Santo Stefano has a remote and medieval flavor. There is one telephone in the town, well hidden in the bowels of the post and telegraph office, whose employees are uncertain whether Philadelphia is located in North or South America; and until recently there was only one small automobile, which had little effect on the medieval atmosphere.

On a warm spring day in 1927, I skirted the shores of this promontory, passed along the base of a Spanish castle built far back in the days when Spain owned Porto Santo Stefano and other parts of Italy, and mounted a narrow donkey path leading to the pink farmhouse. The surroundings convinced me that I had at last discovered a satisfactory spot for the complete detachment popularly supposed to be a prime necessity in the writing of novels.

Directly in front of the farmhouse, ranged in a pearly blue semicircle at the outer edge of the glassy Tyrrhenian Sea, lay the cone-shaped island of Monte Cristo, hunting preserve of the King of Italy; the whale-backed island of Giglio, with the towers of the town of Giglio clinging insectlike to its highest hump; the long expanse of Elba; and behind them all, far away against the western sky, the jagged snow-clad peaks of Corsica.

Below and to the right of the farmhouse was spread the pouch-shaped harbor of Porto Santo Stefano, large enough to hold all the navies of the world. At the lower end of the pouch lay the town of Orbetello, flat on the surface like a miniature Venice; and behind it rose a Maxfield Parrish backdrop—the barren mountains of Tuscany, crowned with small towns and Etruscan ruins. Becalmed in the harbor's mouth lay a fleet of brigs and topsail schooners, their sails snow-white against the silvery blue.

The grass was dotted with wild gladioli, wild cyclamen, and poppies; the trees were loaded with velvety half-ripe almonds; the elephantine trunks of the figs were clothing themselves ineffectively in adolescent fig leaves; and the light breeze was laden with the grapelike odor of broom blossoms.

The scenery lacked only a handsomely dressed brunette, swaying lissomely to the music of a $700 accordion, to look like the Italy of the winter-tour booklets.

The pink farmhouse, however, was not, as the saying goes, so hot. In shape, angularity, and unadorned austerity it resembled an abandoned shoe factory; and it had gone so long unattended that the pink surface of its outer walls was peeling in a spotty and leprous manner.

Its walls were three feet thick, so that its interior, even on a warm day, was reminiscent of a refrigerator car; and while it possessed what was courteously known as a bathtub, the bathtub was made of battered, grease-bearing tin which, when touched, produced sharp peals of stage thunder. It could be filled at the rate of an inch every ten minutes, but bathing in it seemed considerably worse than not bathing at all.

The windows fitted loosely in their embrasures, so that any movement of the outer air evoked shrill moanings from the edges of the panes. The kitchen equipment, moreover, was sketchy, the stove being constructed of bricks in the true Italian open-hearth manner. To heat a pot of water, a handful of charcoal was placed in a trench on the top of the stove, after which the cook fanned the charcoal with a palm-leaf fan, and continued to do so at intervals until the water boiled. Thus the operation of cooking a turkey was nearly as protracted a task as burning down the Yale Bowl.

Despite its drawbacks, however, the pink farmhouse had what seemed to be marked advantages for a person suffering from an attack of novel writing. He could not, for example, be summoned to a telephone; nor could his meditations be interrupted by motorcycle exhausts, motorboat addicts, or picnickers with a hearty contempt for the laws of trespass. Synthetic or other forms of gin were unknown. Golf links and contract bridge were as remote as a Henry James heroine.

It seemed to me, in fact, that if the pink farmhouse could only be embellished with genuine bathing facilities, and with one or two rooms devoid of the receiving-vault effect so popular in present-day Italian architecture, it would be an ideal retreat for a novelist.

When, in the following autumn, I decided to return to Italy and devote a winter exclusively to writing, I paid a hurried visit to a distinguished New York architect, Mr. Charles Ewing, and placed my hopes and fears before him. With me I had a photograph of the pink farmhouse—a photograph two inches wide and three inches long.

After studying the photograph through a magnifying glass, Mr. Ewing asked the dimensions of the farmhouse. I was unable to tell him. He then observed that the house appeared to have no chimneys. We obtained a larger magnifying glass and scrutinized the photograph with even greater care, but the chimneys persistently remained hidden—a fact that has a bearing on later developments.

Mr. Ewing at last gave it as his opinion that what I wished to do would not be difficult, since labor was cheap in Italy and masons were plentiful and skillful. He had been given to understand, he said, that one only needed to show a group of Italian masons a picture of what one wanted in order to get it; for not only were they themselves masons, but their fathers before them had been masons, and their grandfathers and great-grandfathers as well—skilled masons, all of them, with a passionate love of beauty.

Since this coincided with my beliefs, I went away in a contented frame of mind; and when I returned on the following day, Mr. Ewing and his head draftsman had evolved plans calculated to make an Italian farmer throb with pleasure.

They showed, jutting from the original boxlike pink farmhouse, a rambling, L-shaped structure, one story in height and roofed with warm red tiles.

Along the inner side of the L was a loggia with arched openings fronting on the original farmhouse; and across the front of the farmhouse stretched a wrought-iron balcony that removed the gauntness which is frequently the outstanding feature of Italian farmhouses. Not only had the house become beautiful in the drawings, but it had unexpectedly become convenient as well. It had sprouted a generous living room, with French doors opening onto a terrace overlooking the harbor and the distant mountains; a large bedroom which could only be entered from the arched loggia, and so would be removed from all the noises of the house; and a commodious bathroom.

Equipped with these drawings, we embarked for Italy. Two weeks later a conference was held in the pink farmhouse on the headland above Porto Santo Stefano—a conference at which Mr. Ewing's drawings were placed before the town's leading contractor, with a request that he submit an estimate of the cost of the proposed structure.

It seemed to us at the time that the contractor, Signor Emilio Dumbo, was singularly uninterested in the plans we hoped to follow. What he scrutinized most carefully was the wrought-iron balcony across the front of the old farmhouse.

To us it was a source of pleasure that we had been able to catch the appreciative eye of an Italian beauty lover with a balcony designed in far-off America. "She is beautiful, that one: is it not true?" we asked Signor Dumbo.

He shrugged his shoulders. "The Signori perhaps do not know," he said, "that the bars of this balcony are too close together."

We were, to be frank, mortified; and yet, when we studied the balcony again, it still seemed beautiful. Its bars, even, seemed well spaced to us.

"No," Signor Dumbo said. "If the bars are as close together as this, and a *creatura* should be left upon it, the poor little one could not safely place its head between the bars. Its head would be caught, and then what an outcry! What a *rumore!* Old persons would expire from excitement, and the *creatura*, no doubt, would choke to death. *Ma che!*"

A *creatura* is an extremely young child—a child so young that it must be transported, as the Italians say, *in collo*, or in the neck—and unless Signor Dumbo was talking through his hat, all Italian balconies are built for the sole purpose of providing apertures through which *creature* can thrust their heads.

We protested mildly that the balcony was being built to improve the appearance of the house rather than for the entertainment of *creature*.

"Then you do not need it," Signor Dumbo said. "You are far in the country here. There are no processions to watch; no passing on the street; nothing but the empty sea and the olive trees. There would be small return for the great expense of erecting this balcony. Those who stood on it would not be seen, nor would they see anybody. Therefore nobody will stand on it. One stands on a balcony to be seen, *non è vero?*"

Disregarding his baffling Italian philosophy, we concentrated on the material aspects of the matter. The balcony, we pointed out, was simple. Its design was not costly. Why, we asked him, should it be expensive?

"It is the flooring that makes it expensive," Signor Dumbo explained kindly. "A balcony must have a floor six inches in thickness, made strongly of cement built around heavy bars of iron five feet in length, and the bars must be set three feet into the face of the house and cemented in place."

"But we had planned on a wooden floor."

"Wooden floor!" Signor Dumbo exclaimed. "*Ma che!* Impossible!"

"But," we said, "in America we have seen——"

"In Italy," he interrupted, "we do not build balconies that way! A wooden floor becomes weak; and *creature* stepping upon it might fall through to the ground and become permanently damaged."

We tried again to explain our theory of beautifying the old house: how the house front, naked of decoration, seemed to stick up in the air too far and to lean over backward.

"The balcony," we said, "will make the front of the house seem lower—bring it closer to the ground. It will make the house less heavy—more graceful—more beautiful. We would like to avoid a thick, heavy floor."

Signor Dumbo laughed almost pityingly. "The balcony could not make the house seem less heavy," he said, "because the balcony would be made of iron. And this is a farmhouse. A farmhouse is not beautiful and cannot be made beautiful with an iron balcony."

Somebody, we plainly saw, was all at sea concerning the effect of balconies on house fronts; but whether it was ourselves or Signor Dumbo, we could not be certain. There was no doubt, however, that if the matter of the balcony was not removed from debate, the house itself would never be built. Consequently we instructed Signor Dumbo to give the balcony no further thought; to eliminate it from his calculations. If anything was done about it, we told him, we would do it ourselves.

"And without the balcony," we reminded him, "how much would the building cost?"

Signor Dumbo brooded over the situation for a time. "It depends," he said at length, "on whether the house will be two stories in height or not."

"Since the plans call for one story," we said, "we would like to have it one story high."

Signor Dumbo wagged his thumb and forefinger in a propellerlike motion. "*Come vuole lei,*" he agreed. "As you wish; but the walls of the house will be so thick that a second story can be erected on them at small additional expense."

It struck us almost at once that to make a change of a story in an architect's drawings might result in doing some slight damage to the symmetry of the house; and later it struck us that if the walls were going to be as thick as Signor Dumbo intimated—thick enough to support an extra story—we might cut down expenses by cutting down the thickness of the walls. We then upheld the reputation of Americans for materialism by suggesting this saving.

"Impossible!" said Signor Dumbo. "The walls must be three feet in thickness."

"But isn't this unnecessarily thick?" we asked.

"No," Signor Dumbo said, "because when the *creature* arrive, a second story must be added. It is true the plans say one story, but it is God who disposes: not the architect. Ah yes! Two stories, truly, or the home will be crowded. When in time there are even more *creature*, a third story will be necessary to provide space for such *creature* as are old enough to have *creature* of their own. Unless, therefore, the lower walls are made three feet thick, they will not support the additional stories."

Cowed a little by our outcries, he finally agreed to eliminate unborn *creature* from his arguments. He then admitted reluctantly that the walls could be comparatively fragile: could be, in fact, a mere eighteen inches thick. On this basis we told him to proceed.

After twenty-four hours of more or less careful thought, he informed us that he would undertake the construction of the house, which he complimented by calling a *palazzo*, for 27,000 lire, or approximately $1,400, provided that he was not burdened with the balcony or the bathroom fittings.

To us, who had been accustomed to paying $16 for the labor of one mason for one day in America, a price of $1,400 for a rambling stone addition that changed a farmhouse into a *palazzo* seemed strikingly like a gift. We consequently accepted the proposal, and the contract was duly signed.

At a later date we discovered that the Italian word *palazzo* is apt to be misleading. Sometimes a *palazzo* is indeed a palace; but more often it is a house occupied by a landowner in contradistinction to an adjoining house occupied by a farmer or employee. In such cases a *palazzo* may be considerably inferior to the American summer-resort residences named Camp Killkare or Kum-agen Kottage.

Two days after the signing of the contract, shortly before sunrise, the sylvan quiet of the hilltop was rent by the wild and melancholy braying of what seemed like a thousand bloodthirsty donkeys, and by what certainly sounded like an argument to the death between the entire male population of Porto Santo Stefano. From amid the tumult rose the voice of Signor Dumbo, demanding that the Signore—the Mister—from America come out into the dawn and explain how the building of the *palazzo* should be commenced.

Out of all this noise, the voice of Signor Dumbo was the only thing that was what it seemed; for instead of a thousand donkeys there were six, each one laden with building material; while the passionate human outcries proved to be merely the apathetic early morning conversation of five masons, a *calcina* mixer, two stone breakers, two masons' helpers, and three donkey drivers.

Signor Dumbo, however, continued to call at intervals for the Americans; and when they appeared he shook hands warmly and inquired solicitously how large the foundations of the new *palazzo* should be.

We brought him the plans, but he elevated his shoulders and eyebrows wearily. "Signore," he said, "those are only pictures! Any man can draw a picture! What we shall build is what we shall build: a different matter indeed from a beautiful design drawn on a piece of paper!"

This was the beginning of an amiable but exhausting war between Signor Dumbo and his masons on one side, and the builders of the *palazzo* on the other; for Signor Dumbo and the masons seemed to be willing to follow almost anything except the plans.

They would, and frequently did, follow the advice of donkey drivers, cooks, casual visitors, and each other as to what the Americans wished in the way of a house; but they avoided the plans as though they were contaminated with the most virulent of germs.

Exactly why this should have been, I cannot say; but I have learned from various sources that our experience is frequently duplicated in Italy. I might add that my researches in connection with this strange phenomenon uncovered a few mysteries that make the more involved mysteries of the late Edgar Wallace seem as simple as a recipe for preparing gruel.

I am unable to explain the singular Italian belief that any person who pretends to prominence, wealth, or social position must shun simple things or the appearance of simplicity; and the further belief that, unless he does, he loses caste. Such, however, is the mysterious state of affairs in Italy.

I am no maniac, for example, on the subject of fish as a delicacy, but I am somewhat addicted to the small mackerel known to the fishermen of Maine as spike mackerel. I have, in fact, found little or no trouble in demolishing from six to eight spike mackerel at any given time, provided they have been mildly broiled and then embellished with a sauce of lemon and melted butter.

Since Porto Santo Stefano is a fishing village, we frequently demanded fish, but were always given some form of Mediterranean fish tasting vaguely like softened flannel. One day we met a fishing boat returning from a day's cruise with the usual haul of minnows; and among them, to our surprise, we detected a number of spike mackerel. Later the same day we spoke hotly with the cook, Maria Nobile, concerning this important matter. She lifted her eyebrows, as if at the demand of a wayward child. "Certainly," she said soothingly, "there are mackerel—*acertoli*—to be had; but it is better for the Signori to have a finer fish: *spigola* or *merluzzi* or *cefalo*."

We persisted in asking for mackerel.

"Ah, signore!" said the cook patiently, "*acertoli* is not a fish for *signori* —for gentlefolk: it is a fish for the *basso popolo*—for the lower orders."

This aversion to things of the *basso popolo* extends even to literature and architecture. He who thinks, for example, that an Italian author feels free to write about any grade of Italian society would be guilty of an *Americanata*. Americans, in Italian eyes, are loony. A preposterous act or belief, therefore, is an *Americanata:* an American madness.

An Italian author would feel degraded if he wrote about the *basso popolo* in the language of the *basso popolo*. Such a proceeding would be shocking and almost despicable, like stealing a horse. He must keep as far away from the *basso popolo* as he can, and write nothing but great thoughts about important personages in even more important language.

I have conferred with a number of Italians as to what benefit, if any, this mysterious belief has on Italian letters; but their replies have given me little satisfaction, since few Italians will admit to a knowledge of more than two books, these being the *Divina Commedia* of Dante, written in the early years of the fourteenth century, and Manzoni's *I Promessi Sposi*, or *The Betrothed*, first published in 1827—and as effective a sedative today as when it was first published.

Italian architectural theories are equally mysterious. It is generally agreed, outside of Italy, that old Italian farmhouses have a simple beauty that is difficult to improve; but modern Italian architects will have nothing whatever to do with that type of beauty.

It may be that an Italian architect who dared to suggest to an Italian client that he build a residence in farmhouse style would be regarded as a traitor to the glory of a nation of beauty lovers. It is certainly true that no Italian of any standing would, if he could help himself, build a house modeled on anything as contemptible as the residences of the *basso popolo*.

Small houses built by Italians of wealth and position usually include, among exterior architectural details, twenty square yards of stained glass, three hundred feet of tin lace hanging from the eaves, and as many small, haggard-looking towers as the walls can support. As for the interior arrangements, they seem to be designed by experts in crossword puzzles. The effect of the anti-*basso popolo* theory on Italian architecture is not as mysterious as the theory itself.

Not far from the pink farmhouse is the elaborate, expensive, recently erected summer home of a wealthy couple from central Italy. In order to reach their sleeping chamber, the owner must pass through the bedroom occupied by his overseer and his wife; and to reach the bathroom they must again pass through the overseer's room, as must everyone else in the house except the overseer. An equally good arrangement would have been achieved by placing the bathroom in the middle of the front hall, so constructed that it could only be entered through the roof by means of a ladder.

I have an American friend who lives in what is known as a "historical monument," near Florence—a small house dating back to medieval days and embellished with frescoes by great artists. She obtained permission from the Italian Government to add a small wing to it; and during her absence in America she entrusted the planning and building to a celebrated Italian specialist on medieval architecture.

Like all work on historical monuments, the construction was done under government supervision. When the owner saw the finished product, she found that the medieval specialist had built a charming sixteenth-century bedroom, but placed a protuberant nickel-and-porcelain washbasin in the exact center of one of the walls, above a symmetrical array of hot- and cold-water pipes.

While I am not a member of the American Institute of Architects, I suspect that if an American architect of standing should be guilty of any such collaboration with the Middle Ages, the Institute would find some way of giving him a brisk kick where it would do the most good. I have not, however, heard of the great Italian medieval specialist receiving anything but plaudits for his handling of a medieval gem.

America has been guilty of many atrocities in small-house architecture; but the best of her small-house architecture is based on the small and simple farmhouse—American, French, Italian, and Spanish—and the world has no small-house architecture to compare with it.

Small-house architecture in southern Europe is based on medieval castles and palaces, due to the universal knowledge—except among simple-minded and materialistic Americans—that a castle or a palace is more elegant and refined than a farmhouse.

Castles and palaces, however, are not easy to reproduce on fifty-foot lots; and as a result every beauty spot on the French and Italian Riviera is richly supplied with refined and elegant villas that look like mésalliances between a horsecar and the Leaning Tower of Pisa.

When Signor Dumbo demanded the measurements of the *palazzo*, we brought him the plans. It appeared, however, that they weren't what he wanted. They were, we gathered, pictures and not plans. Building, in Italy, must be done from clear, understandable plans. He drew large, clear floor plans, therefore, on the pink wall of the farmhouse with a piece of charcoal.

That, Signor Dumbo said, as he wiped his charcoal-smutted hands on the seat of his trousers, would do the trick. He then launched the operations by nodding brusquely at the five masons who were grouped around the sketch, and hurriedly descended the hill to attend to other and more important business.

In the beginning we had the satisfaction of knowing that the masons' contempt for our plans was offset by the fact that the building was being done economically.

The five masons—Pio, Nunzio, Vincenzo, Poldo, and Beppe—were paid according to age rather than according to work done. Pio, Nunzio, and Vincenzo, being young and strong, were rewarded with 30 lire a day, or approximately $1.50.

Poldo and Beppe, unfortunately, were older. Beppe had a glass eye. Both of them were somewhat tied up with the rheumatic twinges that so often result from the climatic rigors of the so-called sunny Italian winters. Consequently they were paid 21 lire a day.

The building materials were even more economical than the labor. They consisted, in large part, of the soft, porous, limestone rocks which cover a surprising portion of Italy's surface. The masons' helpers picked up a few tons in the immediate vicinity of the *palazzo;* and when the local supply showed signs of depletion, Signor Dumbo purchased several stone walls from a neighboring farmer for eleven dollars. These provided him with enough building material to construct an art museum.

The rocks were laid up into walls with the help of a substance known to the Italians as *calcina*, the chief ingredient of which is sand, the other ingredients being a moderate amount of lime and an almost infinitesimal quantity of cement. Walls so constructed soak up water like sponges, thus giving rise to one of Italy's greatest topics of conversation in building circles—*umidita*, or dampness.

At the time of which I speak, the working hours for Italian masons and their helpers varied somewhat with the seasons. During December and January they arrived before sunrise, worked until 9 A.M.; then knocked off for one hour in order to indulge in a second breakfast and an immoderate amount of noisy conversation. At 10 A.M. they returned to work and to violent arguments which engaged them until twelve, when they again knocked off to discuss a light lunch consisting of a pint of wine, a chunk of bread, several cloves of fresh garlic, and possibly three or four inches of strikingly fragrant sausage.

After a restful nap on an exposed rock pile, they would return to the job and remain until dark, laying rocks and mortar with one hand, and with the other making threatening and contemptuous gestures at those with whom they continued to argue.

As the days grew longer, they arrived at six in the morning and departed at six in the evening; and the arguments seemed to become more violent—so violent, in fact, that occasionally everyone would drop his tools to wag bunched fingers in the faces of his confreres. Thus, although the hours increased, the amount of work accomplished remained the same. What it was they argued over with such passionate intensity, I never learned: I only know their furious dialogues never touched on anything as unimportant as the plans of the house on which they were working.

When we had risen at dawn for a week in order to indulge in profane shouting on our own account—shouting whose general tenor was that we hoped, prayed, and expected the masons to follow the plans in every detail —it seemed to us we could safely leave them for a few hours.

Consequently I wedged myself into the town's one small and rickety automobile, along with Mrs. Roberts and her sister, who was amiably permitting these alterations to her summer residence, and we churned across the mountains on a three-day trip to Florence for the purpose of buying a bathroom.

We were agreed, all of us, that once this was accomplished, the worst would be over, and I could peacefully go to work on my novel, secure from interruptions and worry.

Unfortunately none of us had ever attempted to buy a bathroom in

Italy; and for the benefit of those who have never done so, I will be frank about it and admit at once that it is something of a battle.

I had never given any thought to the fact that so many large Italian hotels are equipped with bathroom fixtures from England or Germany. Since then I have thought about it often; and the thoughts that come oftenest to me are (1) no wonder bathrooms are so infrequent in Italian residences; and (2) Heaven help the man who must buy Italian bathroom supplies for a hotel of more than five rooms.

In Florence is a factory noted for the excellence of its porcelain and tile work. In the salesrooms of this factory, we were told, we would find bathroom supplies of unrivaled beauty. We went there and encountered a polite young man with dark, romantic Italian eyes.

"Do you have bathrooms?" we asked him at once.

He smiled and said he had the very finest, largest, and most elegant bathrooms. With that he led us to a bathtub nearly as large as a cabin cruiser—a tub that would have held five tons of coal.

There, he told us, was a tub as important and as beautiful as any tub that could be found anywhere in the world.

We complimented him on the tub. He begged us not to mention it. Then we broke the news to him that we proposed to have a shower bath in our bathroom: not a tub.

"Ah!" he said, deeply interested, "a *doccia*—a douche!"

"Yes," we said, "a *doccia*. Have you a *doccia*?"

"But of course!" he cried. "There is no place in Italy, or in any other country, for that matter, where you can obtain *doccias* as beautiful as our *doccias*."

We complimented him on this, and he again begged us not to mention it. He stared at the walls, then; and after a little we suggested that he show us a *doccia* or two.

He seemed faintly surprised and waved his hand toward the walls, which were decorated with an occasional tile. "There are the tiles for the *doccia*," he said. "You may have tiles depicting animals, or tiles depicting beautiful fish, or tiles depicting ships. The tiles depicting ships are appropriate for a *doccia! Veramente!* I will indeed say so! The King himself could have no more beautiful *doccia* than a *doccia* constructed of our ship tiles."

We spoke with admiration of the ship tiles, but said that plain white tiles would answer our needs.

He said politely that nice people often used plain white tiles for a *doccia*, but that with white tiles we would need a considerable number of narrow green or red tiles with which to make intricate geometrical designs on the walls. He could, he said, provide us with geometrical designs of unusual beauty.

We were obliged to confess to a dislike of geometrical designs in a bathroom, and to a preference for plain white tiles. He reluctantly admitted that plain white tiles could be *molto simpatico*—extremely sympathetic. Consequently we were not only permitted to place an order for white tiles, but were complimented on our choice of white tiles.

"And now," we told him, when the tiles had been ordered, "we would like to see a *doccia*."

"But you have got your *doccia!*" he protested.

"No, no!" we told him, "this is the only establishment we have visited, and we have no *doccia* at all."

"But, signore!" he exclaimed, "you have only now selected it—all white tiles!"

"Ah yes," we said, "the tiles! But we have no *doccia*—no squirter to spray us with water."

"Ah, signore!" he said, "that is not the *doccia!* That is merely the pipe!"

It may be that we looked helpless; for he hastened to explain that the chief essentials of a bathroom were the bathtub and the tiles.

"Ah yes," we admitted, "but how about the squirter? How about the tank? How about the lavatory? How about the thus-and-so? We have not got our bathroom until we have them."

We had a feeling that the young man with the dark, romantic eyes thought we were cretins, or at least persons who had been dropped on a hard pavement in our early youth. Nonetheless, he was patient with us.

"Ah, signore," he said, "for the squirter and the tank and the bolts and the nails, I recommend that you go to the establishment of Signor Bianco, only one little mile from here; and for the thus-and-so and the rest of the needful things it would be best to go to the establishment of Signor Bruno, a short distance in the opposite direction."

"Is there no place in this great and beautiful city," we asked him, "where we could have procured the tiles and the squirter and the pipes and the bolts and the thus-and-so at one and the same time?"

"Truly, no, signore!" he said regretfully. "Ask yourself, signore, how it would be possible for artists like ourselves to deal in pipes or in thus-and-sos!"

"Ah yes!" we said. "Ah yes! And now, in regard to our tiles, we are in somewhat of a hurry. No doubt you can let us have these quickly?"

He was all eagerness. "But of course!"

"It is because of the masons," we explained. "They will be waiting for the tiles."

"Ah, the masons!" he said knowingly. "Yes, yes! You shall have them immediately."

"It might be a good idea," we suggested, "if we should call for them tomorrow and carry them back in our automobile."

He shook his head. "Ah no, signore! That is impossible. You see, we must notify the factory of the purchase."

"And how far is the factory?"

"It is two miles from here, signore."

"But that is nothing," we assured him. "It will be a saving to you, possibly, if we should drive there and get them tomorrow."

"No," he said, "they must be carefully selected. We must be sure that you do not receive tiles of different sizes or of different shades of whiteness."

"In that case," we suggested, "it might be well to ship them to us *grande velocita.*"

There are two methods of sending goods in Italy: *piccola velocita*, which means "little swiftness," and *grande velocita*, which means "big swiftness." In other words, slow freight and express. Necessarily, *grande velocita* is slightly more expensive.

Our bathroom expert was alert to our interests to the last. "But the expense!" he exclaimed. "*Grande velocita* is extremely costly—extremely! I can send them more economically by *piccola velocita.*"

"True," we admitted, "but unless we get the tiles quickly, the masons will have nothing to do; so would it not be better to spend 30 lire for *grande velocita* than to depend on *piccola velocita* and leave the masons without work for a matter of two months?"

He bowed and smiled, seemingly in complete accord with us, and we parted with mutual expressions of esteem. I might remark in passing that the tiles reached us five weeks later, having been sent *piccola velocita*—little swiftness; and forty per cent of them were the wrong size, though practically all of them were the same color.

The purchase of the remainder of the bathroom spoiled two more days, partly because all Italy is obliged to conserve its strength by knocking off work and taking a noonday nap during the height of the day's activities; and partly because no sale could be consummated until the sales and bookkeeping forces of two establishments had been completely informed why it was that we wished to build a bathroom without a bathtub, why it was that the *doccia* would have only a cold-water pipe, how it was possible to bathe in cold water during the winter months without getting either a *raffredore banale* or a *febbre*—a cold or a fever. It was also essential that they should discover where the house was located in which the bathroom was to be placed, the name of the contractor who was doing the work, the name and position of the Italian gentleman who owned the house, and several other details in which every employee took a polite, not to say an insatiable, interest.

Eventually all pipes, tubes, faucets, nozzles, squirters, shelves, mirrors, washers, tanks, hooks, chains, screws, racks, and thus-and-sos were assembled in one spot for our approval; and around them gathered the purchasers and the entire sales staffs of the establishments who had collaborated in the assembling.

Admiringly they pointed out handles and faucets and coils of pipe to each other, enthusiastically exclaiming, "Bella!" or "Carina!"—"Beautiful!" or "Darling!"

Each piece was placed in our hands and a short and emphatic lecture given us concerning its superiority over all other varieties of fixtures. After this the collection was carefully crated and weighed, so that no unprincipled person could abstract a nozzle or a thus-and-so without the foul deed being at once apparent to anyone who cared to place the box on the scales, following which we were highly complimented on the wisdom we had displayed in our selections.

It was late in the afternoon when we arrived again in Porto Santo Stefano. Pio, Nunzio, Vincenzo, Poldo, and Beppe, surrounded by a powerful aroma of wine and fresh garlic, were preparing to descend the hill. We inspected the progress that had been made in our absence.

The plans called for a large French door six feet in width at the end of the living room overlooking the harbor; but the masonry at that end of the room showed no traces of a doorway. Not only was the wall unbroken, and eighteen inches thick to boot, but it was shoulder high.

It must be that we showed signs of perturbation; for the five masons approached us and peered doubtfully at the spot where the doorway should have been. Beppe removed his glass eye and polished it thoughtfully.

"Does the Signore seek something?" the head mason inquired.

"Only a doorway," we said.

"A doorway?" the head mason asked. "But, signore! There will be two other doorways in the room!"

"Yes," we said, "and we believe there should be one here as well. At all events, the plans say that there should be one here."

The head mason laughed deprecatingly. "If the Signore really wishes three doorways, the matter is easily arranged; but three doorways is a great many."

Unable to express ourselves in Italian, we spoke at some length in English concerning our desire for a third door. Even before we had completed our remarks, however, the head mason seemed to grasp our meaning.

"It is nothing, signore," he said soothingly. "*Come vuole lei*—as you wish!" He lifted his foot and kicked down several square feet of freshly constructed masonry. "There, signore," said he, "is your doorway." With that the five masons lifted their hats politely and vanished into the dusk.

# Doing As Romans Do

"*When in Rome——*" *from* FOR AUTHORS ONLY

W HEN in Rome, my teachers used to tell me, do as the Romans do. I am under the impression that none of my teachers had been to Rome. A few of them, I seem to recall, were a little on the heavy side, and obliged to eschew starches, sweets, and alcoholic beverages in order to keep their figures. Yet they continued to insist that when I was in Rome I should do as the Romans do.

For a time, being young and a New Englander, I believed what they told me; but gradually I began to sense that a persistent proverb quoter may readily have a worse effect on the young than a person who denies the existence of Santa Claus—a sin for which men have been fined in France, that land of ideas and personal liberty.

I learned, for example, that no food is more succulent than those great Italian national dishes that come under the head of *pasta*, and that can be obtained, perfectly cooked, in the largest Italian hotel or the most remote mountain village—dishes such as *capellini d'angeli*, which means angels' hairs, *vermicelli, spaghetti, maccheroni, fettuccini, raviole, gnocchi*, or one of their many variants.

But I have also learned that if I should persist, when in Rome, in trying to do as the Romans do—if once or twice a day I should inhale a quarter mile or so of *fettuccini* or angels' hairs, well lubricated with butter and then rendered partly non-skid by a thorough powdering of Parmesan cheese, I would soon be afflicted with dragging-down sensations, black spots before the eyes, a sharp attack of liver trouble, and a startling enlargement of the waistline.

Within a year I would be unable to button my vest, and in three years' time I would probably explode with a loud majority report.

Because of this I have long known there was something wrong with the proverb to the effect that when in Rome, one should do as the Romans do; but I didn't know the half of it until I was hopelessly committed to enlarging the pink farmhouse overlooking the Tyrrhenian Sea.

On the day after we had returned from the exhausting Battle of the Bathroom, to find that the largest doorway indicated in the architects' plans had, in our absence, been replaced with a solid mass of masonry, we called an early morning meeting of the contractor or impresario, Signor Emilio Dumbo, and the five masons—Pio, Nunzio, Vincenzo, Poldo, and the ancient glass-eyed Beppe.

To refer to a contractor as an impresario oftentimes leads unwary folk—Americans, say—to jump to the conclusion that an impresario is more artistic and beauty-loving than a mere contractor. And indeed, some of them may be, for all I know.

The shouting and arm-waving at this conference at times became so impressive as to resemble setting-up exercises; and the upshot was the assurance from Signor Dumbo that the plans would never again be changed until we had first been consulted.

Thus the situation seemed to be thoroughly cleared up. Everybody tipped his hat to everybody else, and instructions were issued that two *fiaschi*—four quarts—of red wine were to be donated to the masons, the donkey drivers, the *calcina* mixer, the rock carriers, and the masons' helpers for their noonday lunch, by way of celebrating the *entente cordiale* and a new era of understanding.

The era of understanding lasted two days; or until the masons began to build the fireplace at the end of the living room. In the wall they left a chasm large enough to serve as an entrance to the Blue Grotto at Capri; and across the top of the chasm they installed a block of cement with a small log protruding diagonally from it. When this peculiar arrangement was questioned, the masons explained that the log was placed in the cement to form the hole for the flue. When the cement was thoroughly hard, said the head mason, the log would be withdrawn and there would be the flue, going off at the desired angle.

"Would it not be better," we asked, "to have the flue go straight up?

In the plans, the chimney is directly above the fireplace, and therefore the flue does not need to go off at an angle."

"Ah," the mason said, "the Signore has forgotten that he is planning to insert a model of a ship in the wall above the fireplace!"

We reminded him that the ship model was only six inches in thickness, and that we had therefore arranged for the wall to be two feet thick at that point, so that there would be ample space for the flue to go straight up.

"Ah yes, signore," the head mason agreed, "but it is better to bend the flue around the ship model, so that there will be no danger of having the wall fall down because of thinness. If the wall should fall down, it might fall on a *creatura*—on a child. We will bend it off to the left, and then we will bend it back to the right in a half circle, and then the wall will not be too thin in any place."

We must, we told ourselves, take the matter slowly; for we were not only in a nation of beauty lovers, but we were dealing with masons whose forebears were reputed to have been artists ever since Michael Angelo was a lance jack.

"We had understood," we said, "that an eighteen-inch wall is thick enough to permit a flue to pass straight up through it."

"That is true, signore," the mason agreed.

"Well," we said, "this wall is twenty-four inches thick, and the model is six inches deep. Therefore the wall is no different than it would be without the model. It is, in short, the same as any other wall."

"How can it be the same, signore," the mason persisted gently, "when you admit yourself that the ship model is to be placed there? If the model is there, it is there, and the wall cannot be the same as if it were not there."

This argument, we felt, was not one in which we cared to entangle ourselves too deeply; so we attempted to appeal to the mason's better nature by telling him that the finished fireplace would smoke, provided the flue wandered in a half circle.

He raised his eyebrows. "How does the Signore know it will smoke, when it is not yet finished? Of course, if the Signore wishes to avoid a half circle, he can have the flue bend off to the left until it has gone beyond the ship model, and then go straight up."

We pointed out that this solution seemed faulty because the chimney would then be located in the wrong place.

The mason shrugged his shoulders and cast a sly glance at the other masons, who had dropped their work to listen to the discussion. To them he murmured a word or two, among which could be distinguished the word "*Americanata*."

In spite of feeling abashed as well as somewhat cowed, we managed to ask weakly how they proposed to build the flue.

"Ah, signore," the head mason said, "of course the chimney must be where you wish! We will bend the flue around in a half circle."

Just before we had sailed for Italy, we had encountered Mr. George Tyler, the distinguished New York theatrical manager; and he, learning we were going to Porto Santo Stefano, had presented us with a letter to an English-speaking friend of his who lived there—Signor Eduardo Bono. When, therefore, we found the masons determined not to yield in the great Flue Crisis, we hurriedly called on Signor Bono and urged him to come to our rescue—to ascend the hill and tell the masons, in purest Tuscan, where to head in.

He willingly agreed to help; but he held out small hope for success. "With these masons," he said, "one gets nowhere oftener than somewhere."

He leaped on a donkey, clattered up the hill and, after exchanging a few compliments with the masons, took up with them the discussion of the flue. From a gentle murmur their voices rose to torrential outbursts of sound. The rosemary-covered hill slopes of Mont' Argentario echoed to passionate cries. The twittering of little birds was hushed by the storm, and the green lizards crept far back in the recesses of the vineyard walls.

Signor Bono came back to us at last, a little pale, and mopping his brow. "They say," he told us hoarsely, "that they will leave it as it is: that it will not smoke."

"What do you think? Will it smoke?"

"Of course!" he said. "Of course it will smoke; but there is nothing to be done about it. Their minds are made up that it must be curved, as they have built it."

The Flue Crisis continued for upwards of a week. Protests were daily lodged with Signor Dumbo, as well as with the masons; and while the protests were courteously received, the serpentine chimney remained unchanged.

I may as well say at once that when, two months later, the first fire was kindled in the completed fireplace, no smoke passed up the flue. All of it poured into the room, at which the masons, who had gathered around the hearth to see their theories vindicated, hurried coughing and weeping into the open air. The head mason then told us that the chimney's failure to draw was not due to the flue but to the manner in which the fireplace had been built. He could, he said, rebuild the fireplace in such a way as to remedy the trouble. He spent two days knocking out rocks and relaying them. At the second tryout, the room was filled with smoke in less than thirty seconds. When we spoke with a trace of disrespect of the Italian methods of flue construction, the mason raised his shoulders and eyebrows patiently. "Ah, signore," he said, "if I could build fireplaces that would never smoke, I would not be a mason: I would be a signore and ride in my own automobile."

The fireplace was finally made workable by knocking down the wall behind and above it, cutting a new hole through the cement block, running the flue straight up, and rebuilding the wall.

The echoes of the Flue Crisis had scarcely died away when the opening guns of the Roof War put an end to all thoughts of meditative literary production. The Roof War began when we were summoned from the house in the pale gray light of a February dawn and asked how high to make the walls of the new living room.

We sent for the plans; but before they could be brought, the head mason sought to clarify the situation. "Ah, signore," he said, "your American plans are pleasing to the eye, but in America you do not know how to build roofs. Your plans, now, show the ridgepole of your *palazzo* turning at right angles, eh?"

We admitted that this was so.

"*Ma che!*" he exclaimed then, raising his shoulders and smiling with what seemed like contempt. "*Ma che!*" *Ma che* is scarcely translatable in English. Vaguely it means, "But what an idiot you are!"

"What of it?" we asked. "Why shouldn't the ridgepole turn at right angles?"

"But, signore!" the mason protested, "after the ridgepole turns at right angles, the plans show that the roof over the bedroom is unequal. On one side of the ridgepole there is twice as much roof as on the other side." He laughed noisily and, I thought, disagreeably; and the remaining masons joined him, barring Beppe, who was removing a bit of mortar from his glass eye.

"Yes," we said, "that is correct. Roofs are often built that way. There is usually a reason for it. There is a reason for this. The ridgepole has been placed over the partition between the loggia and the bedroom. The loggia is narrow, and the bedroom is wide. Thus the portion of the roof over the bedroom is wide, and the portion over the loggia is narrow, but the whole roof is supported by the partition between them."

"Oh, signore!" the mason exclaimed, impatiently waving aside our explanation, "you cannot make two roofs fit together unless they are the same."

"Would you be good enough to repeat that?" we asked him. "To us it seems to make no sense."

"Wait a minute, signore," he said. "If we try to make the bedroom roof fit into the living-room roof, they will not join properly: they will break apart. What you must do is to make the walls of the living room higher and the walls of the bedroom lower. Then the ridgepole of the bedroom can be pushed up against the wall of the living room, and the ridgepoles of the two sections will have nothing to do with each other."

I cannot, even at this late date, reproduce the other arguments advanced by the masons in support of their theory without becoming somewhat involved and even, at times, violent. It was their contention that it was next to impossible to build a roof with a valley or gutter in it; and one of the reasons for their belief, apparently, is the dearth—particularly in Tuscany—of houses whose roofs have ridgepoles that are anything but straight.

There are millions of buildings in America whose ridgepoles somewhere form L's, in which case there is a valley from the angle of the L down to the eaves. I have traveled a fair distance through the Tuscan country-side, but I have never happened to see a roof built with a valley. The reason for this, I think, is that the regulation farmhouse throughout Tuscany, when first built, is shaped like a packing box. As the family grows and accumulates more cows and pigs, the house is enlarged by setting another packing box against the original house and knocking a door between. Thus an ancient farmhouse may consist of five or six packing boxes of varying sizes joined together, some with lean-to roofs and some with ridgepoled roofs, but each roof at a different level, and each roof fitting against a wall; seldom against another roof.

The whole effect of such houses, I scarcely need to add, is picturesque and beautiful; but comfort, convenience, and sanitation do not enter into them to any noticeable degree; while their dampness is such that if shoes or garments be left unprotected in them for more than two hours, they will be covered with a thick growth of green mold somewhat resembling sphagnum moss.

In order to convince the head mason that it was possible to build a roof with an L-shaped ridgepole, we constructed a miniature *palazzo* from string and stakes, setting the stakes in the ground and outlining the eaves, ridgepole, and valleys with string.

Obviously we had the appearance of serious mental cases as we sat on the ground playing with bits of twine; and we could feel a certain sympathy for the masons, who were obliged to retire behind walls and rocks, at frequent intervals, in order to conceal their hysterical outbursts of laughter.

When the model was finished, the masons gathered around it and studied it carefully. "Oh ho!" they said to each other. "Oh ho! So that is the way they wanted it done! Ah well! Of course, then! Certainly! It is a pity they had not told us before that this is the way they wished it!"

We reminded them weakly that it was clearly shown in the plans.

"Plans!" said the head mason. "Plans! *Ma che!*"

One more halfhearted attempt was made to change the shape of the roof, but there seemed to be no malice in the effort. When the ridgepoles were being set in place, we found Signor Dumbo, the impresario, indicating to his workmen that the ridgepole should be over the center of the bedroom, whereas the plans showed that it should be supported by the wall between the room and the loggia.

We called up to him that the pole must be six feet to the left.

He shrugged his shoulders and moved his marker two feet. "*Come vuole lei!*" he said. "As you wish! Is this the spot?"

"No, no! Push it over! Let the ridgepole be supported by the partition! Another four feet!"

He reluctantly moved it another foot to the left. "*Come vuole lei!*" he said. "Is this now the spot?"

We climbed the ladder and set the pole over the partition, after which there was a general hat tipping and exchange of compliments.

It was at this juncture that the carpenter entered the picture to demonstrate his artistic ability.

Having heard from many different sources how the American workman has been ruined by a mechanized civilization which has made him into a cross between a pneumatic drill and a corkscrew, I was happy at having the opportunity to observe a wholly unmechanized product of a beauty-loving people, as yet unruined by moneygrubbing and mass production.

I know, of course, that the population of America has been ruined by these things, because I find frequent reference to that fact in the European press. I have lately read six novels, all written by Europeans and all ranking at the top of the best-selling novels in America; and in five out of these six novels there are pointed references to the machinelike standardization of Americans.

Only in Europe, I gather from these books, is there any individuality left. European workmen, they imply, are still free from our robotlike qualities: from those American stupidities and insanities which are threatening to sweep out of the crass new world to engulf the artistic and beauty-loving peoples of Europe. Unless such things were true, the books would scarcely be bought in such large numbers by the American reading public—although this point is, of course, debatable.

Since building an Italian *palazzo*, we have heard all Americans so frequently referred to as crazy that we have a feeling it is probably so. In fact, this is as good a place as any to mention three occasions on which we were universally admitted by Italians to be crazy, and even seemed more than a little that way to ourselves.

The first occasion was when we announced that the windows of the new *palazzo* must be screened with copper screens. The Italian workmen smiled surreptitiously at each other when we told them. "What you mean," they told us, "is brass screens; but brass screening is too narrow to be used on windows. There is no such thing as copper screening. There is iron and there is brass; but copper—oh ho ho! No, no, signore."

Since they persisted in this, we traveled to Rome to obtain copper screening and visited a large hardware emporium in search of it.

"Copper!" the salesman exclaimed. "There is no such thing as screening made from copper."

"We have failed to make ourselves clear," we told him. "We are speaking of copper! The metal that doesn't rust. It is possible you think we are referring to silver screens or to gold."

"Not at all, signore," said the clerk condescendingly. "We know copper well, here in Italy; but copper screens—no! The metal is too soft to be made into screens. If you wish screens for windows, you must use galvanized iron."

Before we left the shop, the salesman had called five other salesmen and the manager to tell them of the Americans' craziness, and their amusement was almost as great as their incredulity. In order to get copper screening for the *palazzo*, we were obliged to buy it at Macy's in New York and send it back to Italy by a kindly doctor on an Italian liner.

Another occasion was when we suggested to Signor Dumbo that he could prevent water from soaking into the foundation of the *palazzo* by waterproofing the coat of cement that is spread on the lower walls of an Italian house.

"No, signore," we were told. "A sidewalk three feet in width must be built around the base of the house, so that the foundation may remain dry. This is the custom throughout Italy. There is no way in which the wall itself can be made to keep out moisture."

"We have heard differently in America," we told him. "We have heard that if a cement wall is waterproofed, the water will not penetrate."

He laughed until the tears hung on his eyelashes. "Waterproof!" he exclaimed. "How would you waterproof cement? By mixing automobile tires with it? No, no, signore! Cement cannot be waterproofed!"

A third occasion was when we carelessly remarked that a lighter and more graceful effect could be obtained in a hallway by using a fine wrought-iron balustrade than by using a clumsy wooden balustrade. Only in America, we learned, could any such insane theory have been evolved. Wood is lighter than iron, is it not? Besides, iron is for outside use: not for inside use! To use iron in the inside of a house would not be beautiful! Iron outside: wood inside! To think otherwise is indeed an *Americanata!*

We made a sketchy reference to the lacelike stonework of the Alhambra, lighter-looking, even, than the frosting on a giant wedding cake; but nobody would listen: the harm had been done. Americans are crazy; and all the talk in the world cannot alter the fact. Iron lighter than wood, indeed! *Ma che!* They are crazy, and to keep them quiet it is sometimes well to humor them; for they are all millionaires, all—all! Crazy and millionaires!

The carpenter, then, unspoiled and uncrazed by American standardization, arrived to cut and adjust the roof beams and to take measurements for the door- and window-frames, which were to be constructed in his cavernlike lair on the main street of the town. With him he brought a saw—a crude buck saw with a blade adjustable at any angle—and a hammer with a warped handle. He had no other tools.

When we first saw him, he was trimming the end of a beam destined to become a ridgepole. He was lying on his back on the ground with one knee flung over the end of the long pole; and thus awkwardly situated, he was wielding his saw and perspiring heavily. After a time he rose and rolled the pole over; then threw himself on his back again and continued his sawing, drawing the saw against his chest and thrusting it vigorously from him.

We brought him two boxes and showed him how the pole could be propped on them and so sawed in what seemed to us an easier manner by placing one knee on the pole. He smiled and nodded: then kicked the pole off the boxes, lay on his back once more, and resumed his sawing.

The plans called for a tiled roof which would project, in the manner of an Italian peasant house, only a few inches beyond the wall. The masons, however, had other ideas; and while we occupied ourselves with the carpenter, they hurriedly installed the roof supports—fragile bits of wood looking more like toothpicks than beams—in such a manner that they protruded two feet beyond the walls, as do the roof supports of a Swiss chalet. They were held in place by beds of *calcina*.

We suggested to Signor Dumbo that there was nothing like this in the plans, and he admitted it was so. "But," he added, "if the roof protrudes thus, your walls will be saved from *umidita*—from dampness—in times of rain."

From what we had seen of Italian rainstorms, however, it seemed to us that they were usually accompanied by winds that blew three ways at once—up, down, and sideways. We therefore advanced the theory that if rain were accompanied by wind, the wind would blow the rain against the walls of the *palazzo* in spite of the roof. "Is it not so?" we asked.

Signor Dumbo freely admitted this peculiar feature of Italian weather. "Yes," he said, "it is so; but this is the way we build roofs here."

"But on the peasant houses—the farmhouses," we objected. "On such houses the roofs are built with no wood showing: with flat tiles protruding over the edge of the walls."

"Pah!" he said. "Only on the houses of the *basso popolo!* This is a *palazzo*."

"If you call it a *palazzo*," we agreed, "it is probably a *palazzo*; but it is also a farmhouse. And another thing: if the pieces of wood are embedded in *calcina*, so that they are wet one day and dry the next, we fear they will shortly be afflicted with dry rot; whereas if they are concealed beneath the roof, there will be no dry rot."

He shrugged his shoulders. "Yes, but roofs cannot last forever."

"True, but it might even be that a roof laid the way you are laying it would last less than fifteen years."

He looked hurt. "But, signore!" he said, "what of it? It would only be necessary to remove the roof and make it anew!"

The carpenter stole away in the midst of this argument, and in the turmoil of the ensuing days he was forgotten. Signor Dumbo amiably yielded to our protests and at last consented to construct the roof according to the plans; but we were shortly unnerved to discover that the tiles with which he proposed to cover the roof were modern interlocking tiles, different in color and shape from the old half-round tiles on the original farmhouse. It would be no exaggeration to say that the native Italian politeness and courtesy of Signor Dumbo and the masons was put to a severe test by our mulish desire to have old-fashioned tiles used on the new roof; and it would even be short of the truth to say that our difficulties over the chimney nearly provoked a revolution.

According to the plans evolved by Mr. Ewing, the chimney—a fat white shaft—was to rise nine feet from the tiled roof. Not only is this style of chimney common to many sections of Italy; but it seemed obligatory in our case because of the height and proximity of the original farmhouse, which would have resulted—if we had permitted a low chimney—in more smoke backing out of the fireplace than in ascending the flue.

In Tuscany, however, the native population has never gone in heavily for chimneys, but has usually contented itself with two tiles tilted together over a hole in the roof. Because of this Tuscany is rich in smoky rooms—not as rich as Montenegro, where there are no chimneys at all; but rich enough.

On the day following the Tile Fracas, Signor Dumbo appeared at dawn and sent up word that he would be obliged if the Signore would thrust his head from the window.

"Good morning! Good morning!" he bellowed when the head was produced as required. "A beautiful day! *Primavera in mare*—the spring of the sea! *Vento niente*—no wind!"

He cleared his throat violently and cocked an eye at us appraisingly. "This morning we erect the chimney."

"Good!" we bawled. "Good! *Molto bene!* Much well!"

"Yes," Signor Dumbo repeated, "we build the chimney. How high shall it be, signore?"

"Three meters," we told him. "Nine feet, as on the plans."

"But, signore," he protested pathetically, "one meter would be better."

"No, three meters. The plans demand it."

"Plans!" he growled. "Plans! Always the plans! The man who drew those pictures—he is in America! What does he know of this chimney?"

"Nine feet," we said.

The word that Signor Dumbo thereupon emitted was a long word, full of S's—unquestionably a foul word. "Nine feet!" he cried bitterly. "That is not a chimney! That is a Roman monument!" With that he flung angrily off down the hill, and we saw him no more that day.

Two hours later, however, the head mason sent for us. All was in readiness, he said, to begin the chimney. Should he make it, he wished to know, one foot square?

We climbed to the roof with the plans and showed him that it must be, at the base, four and one half feet by three feet. Then, not liking the obstinate look in his expressive Italian eye, we stationed ourselves on an adjacent stone wall and watched him.

When the chimney was a foot high, he laid down his trowel and held out his hands to us imploringly. "Signore," he said, "who ever saw a chimney higher than this?"

"Go ahead," we told him. "We'll tell you when to stop."

"Signore!" he expostulated. "It will blow down. Nothing as high as that can stand the wind!"

We sat on the wall for four hours, and the chimney rose, amid impassioned protests, to a height of nine feet. Two days later it withstood a sixty-mile gale; and it is my understanding that the masons have since been heard to speak admiringly of their skill in originating and erecting this masterpiece of Italian architecture.

The agonies of the Roofing Rumpus were relieved—speaking in the somber Russian sense—by a few mild arguments with the amiable and unstandardized plumber who installed the bathroom fixtures. Having been shown the height at which to place the shower, he hurriedly did the work when our back was turned; and instead of locating the shower at the indicated height, he located the curved pipe there—which brought the shower some fifteen inches lower. Thus a full-grown bather is compelled to crouch like a hunted animal in order to receive moisture above the chest level.

It was the plumber, in collaboration with Signor Dumbo, who was overcome with mirth at our suggestion that he shelter the water pipes against freezing. This was Sunny Italy: only a crazy American would think of such an idiocy—such an *Americanata*. Our suggestions were hilariously ignored, and on the following winter the pipes froze and burst, depriving us of water for upwards of a week. At the same time, since all of Sunny Italy was in the grip of a cold wave, most of the water pipes in the town of Porto Santo Stefano also burst with tremendous enthusiasm.

Practically nothing remained to be done, with the roof and chimney finished, except to install and paint the wooden door- and window-frames, whitewash the old and new sections of the farmhouse a gleaming white, and celebrate the completed job with the customary feast to the workmen—the feast known to all Italians as the *Maccheronata*.

Because of a slight error on the part of the artistic carpenter, the largest doorframes, when they arrived, were two feet too high—an error that necessitated either a complete alteration in the plans of the living room or the rebuilding of the frames at our expense. In the opinion of the masons, the proper procedure was to knock down enough masonry to permit the gargantuan doorways to be installed, even though the proportions of the living room were ruined in doing it.

The final stage of Italian building operations consists almost entirely of the knocking down of masonry. Window openings are chiseled to larger dimensions, door openings are assaulted so they may be brought to the proper size, and holes are drilled in every wall, inside and out, for the reception of door- and blind-gudgeons and ironwork of every description.

When a house is to be painted, the masons unite in drilling commodious holes in front, back, and side walls—holes large enough to hold a family of foxes; and into each hole is inserted a beam that helps to support the necessary staging. Later these holes are imperfectly filled and plastered over; and as a result all Italian houses are pockmarked with large discolorations that would be of somewhat doubtful esthetic value, even in a standardized nation of crass materialists.

Having completed the *palazzo*, therefore, the five masons joined in what sounded like a determined attempt to knock it to pieces, following which they mounted the stagings and slopped whitewash impartially on the inner and outer walls, the new tiled floors, the windows, the woodwork, and each other.

A day or two later all who had participated in the building of the *palazzo*—masons, employers, impresario, donkey drivers, *calcina* mixers, and rock carriers—assembled in the hallway of the original farmhouse for the *Maccheronata*.

International good feeling, red wine, and spaghetti were served in equal proportions, together with smaller amounts of roast goat and other comestibles dear to the hearts of Italians. The *Americani* gave lessons in the enviable art of shrill whistling through the teeth, as well as in the singing of the great American song, "Down Where the Würzburger Flows." Instruction was given by the Italian guests in the rendition of Italy's two great patriotic airs, "*Giovinezza*" and "*La Leggenda di Piave*." Compliments were exchanged freely and continuously; and when the *calcina* mixers and the donkey drivers had tied white handkerchiefs around their arms by way of disguising themselves as women, the masons danced freely and romantically with them. By this ceremony the *palazzo* was officially declared finished.

Thus, at an almost unbelievably small outlay, the crazy Americans obtained a *palazzo* whose architecture, to the surprise of the impresario, the masons, and the *Americani* themselves, is pure Italian. It is true that the rains run in rivers beneath the doors and trickle through the windows. It is true that weather stripping must be brought from America and plugged into the cracks that have opened here and there, so that every wind that blows will not whistle melodiously through them. It is true that the *palazzo* is more difficult to heat than an early-American icehouse.

It is also possible to argue that this half-baked palace could have been built far more satisfactorily and economically if we had imported an American mason and a boss carpenter from any small New England town, paid their steamship fares over and back, and disgorged high American wages for their services; for in that case we would have been free to earn a living by writing, instead of being obliged to sacrifice a winter to persuading Italian masons to build what they should have built instead of what they wanted to build.

To an Italian, however, such an argument would be only another *Americanata*—another product of a standardized and machine-made civilization; and possibly it is.

# *Country Life in Italy*

### *From* FOR AUTHORS ONLY

THERE SEEMS TO BE a more or less settled conviction among persons of education and refinement that anyone, by removing himself far enough from his accustomed place of residence, instantly escapes into an ideal existence and is filled with strength and ability to engage successfully in pursuits that elude him in localities with which he is familiar.

This theory is certainly common with architects, college professors, widows, newspaper reporters, and college students; and to the best of my knowledge it is held by all other people, including stockbrokers, taxi drivers, and actors. It is this belief that long ago gave rise to the popular household phrase "my castle in Spain," the idea behind the expression being that an isolated retreat in sunny southern Europe offers the most romantic and stimulating refuge from the troubles and annoyances of a workaday world.

There may be a great deal in this hypothesis; but during several winters spent in the equivalent of a castle in Spain, I have often had occasion to do some intensive wondering. The burden of my wondering has to do with those who yearn frequently and audibly for an isolated retreat beside the sparkling Mediterranean.

If their yearnings should be gratified, I have repeatedly wondered, would they be content; or would they suddenly suspect that their yearners were out of kilter? I know nothing about it, of course. I merely wonder. One who lives in the equivalent of a castle in Spain has plenty of leisure for wondering; for there's little to do except work and wonder.

We had a castle in Spain, but it wasn't really in Spain nor was it a castle. Some of the more romantic British novelists have written books which tend to show that life in a crumbling Spanish or Italian castle is a pure delight. It is a good idea, however, not to trust too implicitly to British authors' powers of observation. In British novels all Americans, whether bankers, attorneys, consular officers, or Harvard undergraduates, are made to talk thus: "Say, stranger, I guess I'll be etarnally lambusted ef that thar St. Paul's Cathedral of yourn ain't approximately ez big ez our Universalist Chapel out in Cattail, Georgia!" There is no evidence that British descriptions of castles in Spain are more worthy of credence.

Castles in Spain, Italy, and southern France are stone affairs, and much of the stone is missing. They are not livable in the accepted sense of the word. To live in one of them would be more uncomfortable than living on the top floor of Bunker Hill Monument during the winter months.

There were several picturesque towers near my Italian residence, perched on hilltops overlooking the sea, and in all respects like small castles. Not even Italians, inured as they are to cold and discomfort, are able to live in them; and when the towers are used at all, they are occupied by malnourished poultry. A person contemplating a protracted stay in Italy, Spain, or southern France will require living quarters cozier and more comfortable than any castle. This usually means that he must build his own living quarters; for ideas of coziness and comfort are practically nonexistent in all countries bordering on the Mediterranean.

I had two objects in building the half-baked palace. Primarily I wished a retreat so far removed from bright lights that I would be able to complete a series of novels within my normal span of years; a place so quiet and so solitary that unless one busied himself with work from dawn to dark, so to speak, he would fly off the handle with boredom; yet a place in which servants could be persuaded to stay, so that there would be no necessity to interrupt one's labors to assist in the preparation of break-fast, lunch, and dinner and in other household duties.

Secondarily, I wished to live both comfortably and cheaply while writing the novels; for a subtle sixth sense warned me that if I could not live cheaply while engaged in that luxury, I could not live at all.

At least one half of the secondary object was attained with outstand-ing success. The housekeeping and culinary departments of the half-baked palace were placed in the capable hands of two youngish Tuscans, Concetta Dassori and Maria Nobile, whose labors were rewarded by the handsome emolument of 175 lire apiece per month, regardless of whether the lira was valued at the Old Tenor of five cents or at the Rooseveltian Tenor of nine cents.

So far as I could tell, they considered themselves fortunate to have the jobs. Maria Nobile was cook and general purchasing agent of the half-baked palace; while Concetta, being able to read and write, acted as pub-lic accountant, second maid, opener of kerosene tins, clothes cleaner and presser, shoe polisher, head laundress, and mouthpiece of the peculiar, not to say *pazzi*, or dippy, Signori from America.

They rose at six-thirty, had the fires lit at seven, and brought breakfast at seven-thirty, after which Maria, who was unable to read or write, was instructed by Concetta concerning the needs of the Signori, and went sing-ing down the mountainside to make the day's purchases.

I might remark, at this point, that there is widespread misunderstanding concerning the singing and speaking voices of most Italians.

Owing to indiscriminate reading of sentimental British authors in my youth, I long labored under the misapprehension that whereas all Ameri-cans have harsh, discordant, nasal voices, all Italians have soft, melodious voices; just as I erroneously believed all Italians to be artistic and beauty-loving in contradistinction to Americans, who are crude barbarians, devoid of refinement or good taste.

For a time, therefore, I was puzzled by Maria Nobile's singing voice, for it was both lugubrious and piercing, like the shrill wail of a rusty hinge. Eventually I realized that her voice was no different from other voices in our neighborhood—voices so harsh and so raucous, when lifted in song, as to cause the fuzz on a Harris tweed coat to rise in horror.

What Maria lacked in tonality, however, she made up in close buying power. Most Italian homes, it should be understood, are not equipped with ice chests. This is no particular hardship, since an Italian housekeeper tries to buy what she needs to get her through the day, and no more. All her purchases, furthermore, are cash purchases. The entire Italian nation is on a strictly cash basis where foodstuffs are concerned. Whether the universal distrust which exists among Italians is justified, I am unable to say.

In the matter of accumulating the exact requirements for one day's subsistence, Maria Nobile, I suspect, held the world's record.

Our need for lemons has always been great. We use them on fish, in salad dressing, in soups. So we would say to Maria Nobile, "Get lemons today—plenty of lemons!" Two hours later she would climb back up the hill, singing with all the haunting melody of a buzz saw hitting a knot; and deep down in the recesses of the blue handkerchief in which the day's provisions were transported would be one lemon.

There seemed to be a persistent fear in her mind that the house might be swept, overnight, by the plague, so that half a lemon or possibly one sardine might go to waste. She improved rapidly. In February of 1931 she purchased one half-dozen lemons at one time; but subsequently her buying activities often set the whole town talking.

Instead of purchasing one third of a calf's tongue, she reached a point where she bought the whole tongue. There was a day when, if suddenly confronted with a basketful of the Signori's favorite dish—*capitoni*, or large eels—she would climb two miles up the mountain to find out whether the Signori wished an entire *capitone*. On being ordered back to buy, all *capitoni* would have been sold. Later, if shown an eel, she accepted it at once and sometimes even said, without being prompted, that she would take another, if there was another, and keep it alive in a bucket.

On returning to the half-baked palace with her day's haul of provisions, she enumerated her purchases to Concetta Dassori, who inscribed them in a blank book known as a *Quaderno*. Each night the *Quaderno* was presented to the Signora from America, who ran over it with the stub of a lead pencil, verified the addition, and sent enough money to the kitchen to keep Maria Nobile in funds during the ensuing day.

I have before me one of her *Quadernos*, each day's expenses sloppily set down on a quarter page. The entry for March 7, translated both as to items and prices, reads, "Bread 10½ cents, butter 17½ cents, flour 7½ cents, cheese 15½ cents, milk 6½ cents, fillets of veal 36 cents, fish 22 cents, potatoes 4 cents. Total $1.19½." This was a small day.

The average Old Tenor daily expenditure made by Maria Nobile for a sufficient amount of provisions to keep the Signori from America, the small white dog, also from America, Concetta Dassori, and herself was $2.00. When there were guests in the house, as there occasionally were, she could seldom get out of her shopping without squandering at least

$2.40 to keep everyone well nourished. Sometimes an unexpected item would build up the day's total to something like $3.00.

With the advent of Rooseveltian Tenor, one half of our resources were taken from us without our consent and without due process of law—a circumstance of the deepest interest to one familiar with the heartbreaking struggles of his own countrymen, from 1775 to 1783, to free themselves of similar injustices. Everything doubled in price; and our average daily expenditure for food increased to $4.05.

One of Maria Nobile's larger days, in the beginning, read thus: "Bread 10¼ cents, flour 7½ cents, butter 18 cents, sugar 34 cents, goat's milk cheese 9, milk 10, spinach 6¼, oranges 11, prunes 20, shrimps 20, ten cans of anchovies 60, oil 30, ice 2½, salt 10, jar of preserves 12½, eels (small) 10, ¼ bottle rum for the pink dessert 27, lettuce 2, two quarts red wine 25. Total, $3.45."

Three years earlier she would have resisted our efforts to make her buy ten cans of anchovies. She would have bought one can, arguing that one can is enough for anyone to eat on any one day. Under no circumstances would she have bought a quarter bottle of rum. She would have bought one wineglassful for 4 cents and lugged it up the mountain in a two-quart bottle. If we protested, pointing out that we might need more, she would raise her eyebrows and reply quietly: "If there should be need of more, I will get more."

"Ah yes," we might say, "but suppose we need more in a hurry, eh? Suppose guests arrive!"

"*Non fa niente, signori!*" she would answer. "Don't give it a thought! I would go at once to the town, and in one hour I am back, eh?"

We always had to give it up, in the early days. "Let her alone," we would say to each other. "Don't try to argue the point. If she wants to walk forty miles a day, let her walk. Keep quiet! Shut up! There's nothing to be done about it!" We wore her down eventually; but the operation took three years.

The Italian food problem could be worse than baffling. It is my fixed belief that not even France, with her reputation for culinary excellence, is able to produce at short order as many pleasing dishes as Italy; but a stranger to Italy cannot sample Italian foods until he learns what they are; and that is the problem: to learn about them in the first place.

Why it is, I do not know; but all Italians seem to go into a coma when asked for information on culinary affairs. Each morning, early, as I have said, Concetta Dassori demanded the day's menu from the Signora so that

Maria Nobile might make the day's purchases. For almost an entire winter after we had taken up our residence in the half-baked palace, the choice of foods seemed limited to spaghetti, soup made from bouillon cubes, scrambled eggs, and three varieties of fish tasting like a water-logged sofa pillow.

Meat, we had learned, was best left alone. Once or twice we had tried steaks and chops; but there is no such thing as cold storage in an Italian town: a cow or a pig or a sheep is butchered on Friday morning, say, and by Friday evening is completely devoured. Consequently a steak, prepared in the American fashion, is hard and resilient, like the sole of an English golf brogue.

Our diet, therefore, was not only tiresome, but at times it proved downright revolting. Yet Concetta Dassori, questioned concerning other possibilities in the food line, looked helpless and said, "*Non so, signora!*"—"I do not know, lady!" So did Maria Nobile. So did everyone.

It was by the merest accident that we learned about small eels and large eels—about sole and *spigola*—about the fish *palombo*—about ravioli made from spinach mashed with goat's milk cheese—about white bean soup, black bean soup, soup made from clams no larger than a ten-cent piece—about sliced tongue stewed in tomato sauce—about thin slices of beef or veal simmered with white wine, tomatoes, meat stock, and crushed garlic —about fresh sardines—about *uova d'aringhe* or herring-eggs—about *calamaretti* or little inkwells—about the snails that emerge from stone walls after the first showers of spring—about fishcakes made from transparent, threadlike fish known as *bianchetti*.

It was just before Christmas that we learned about eels. Maria Nobile had returned from the village with a handkerchief full of undesirable foods, and had then gone with Concetta Dassori to stand at what is euphemistically known as the *fontana*: the fountain—a stone watering trough in the middle of a wind-swept field—and do the week's washing. We paused to marvel at the peculiar purple color which the cold water gave their hands, and carelessly inquired whether there was anything stirring in the village.

"No, signore," Maria Nobile said. Then she added, angrily, "Only men from Rome, crowding into the fish establishments and making it difficult for one with serious duties."

"Men from Rome?" we asked. "What are men from Rome doing here?"

"It is the Christmas season," Maria Nobile said simply. "They buy *anguille*—eels."

"Eels?" we asked. "What are they buying eels for?"

"It is Christmas," Maria Nobile repeated patiently. "It is necessary for them to have eels for Christmas."

"Necessary?" we asked. "Eels necessary? What for? For pets, or for twining around the Christmas trees?"

"*Ma che!*" Maria Nobile exclaimed. "What a fool question! They must have them for eating! Everyone everywhere eats eels on the night before Christmas! These men from Rome, they come here because in Rome there is a dearth of eels."

We brooded over that one for a time. Rome was over two hours away by fast train. The eel purchasers, therefore, had undertaken a five- or six-hour trip to gratify their pre-Christmas lust for something we had always regarded as not particularly desirable.

"Well," we said at length, "if everybody eats them, why haven't we been told about them? Are they worth eating?"

"*Madonna mia,*" said Maria Nobile, "but certainly they are worth eating!"

"In that case," we told her, "scramble into your shopping clothes again and rush down to the eel establishment. We'll have to look into this."

It was only an hour's walk to the village and return, over a path so steep and rocky that donkey riders, descending it, sit well over their donkeys' hind quarters to keep them from somersaulting heels over head. Maria Nobile and Concetta Dassori were pleased to make it a dozen times a day, if necessary. Italian servants, as I have intimated, do not take jobs unless eager to work.

I have been an eel addict from that day to this. The true eel—*anguilla* —of Italy is a small eel, about as thick as a forefinger. The regular-sized eel, such as we know in America, is a *capitone*, and he is as expensive as the finest fish.

*Anguille* are usually eaten as an appetizer, before dinner; and when prepared for cooking they are first scrubbed; then cut into four-inch sections with scissors from Maria Nobile's sewing basket. The sections are skewered together, with a bay leaf between each section, and salt heavily sprinkled over the whole. They are then broiled from twenty to twenty-five minutes, raised six inches above a charcoal fire. So cooked, the flesh of the eel is juicier and sweeter than that of sand dab, pompano, whitefish, sole, or other highly lauded sea food.

The big eel, or *capitone*, is eaten, usually, as the chief dinner dish, and is prepared by cutting into one-inch sections and stewing in a casserole with a sauce made of white wine, lemon juice, butter, tomato sauce, and chopped garlic. He, too, makes vastly better eating than fish considered more genteel in circles too refined to think, even, of eels.

We had been in residence for four winters before the delicious *palombo* was discovered. Many of the finest Italian fish—*merluzzi*, for example, and *cefalo* and *dentice*—too often taste like boiled golf stockings. One day, however, Maria Nobile served a fish that brought cries of pleasure from everyone. Without hesitation I pronounced it a true gem of the ocean. Not only did it taste like halibut, but it was free of the bones that make most Italian fish extremely hazardous. What, I demanded, was the name of this splendid specimen?

It was the *palombo*, I was informed.

Well, I said, why hadn't we been told about the *palombo* long ago? What does it look like, this *palombo*?

They described a long, slender fish, pink in color. It was a baffling description. We sent out word to Maria Nobile to get a *palombo* whenever possible.

"And," said the Signora, "when one is next secured, *porta qui!* Bring it here! The Signore wishes to view its *aspetto* or aspect."

One week later a headless fish was brought in. It was, as they had said, long and pink. It was pink because it was skinned. But the tail was intact, and the tail wasn't pink. The *palombo* was a dogfish.

After a series of accidents of somewhat similar nature, we at last wrested from our Tuscan neighbors enough recipes to provide us with a varied and appetizing menu; but, as I say, it was a long, long task. So there were times when I wondered how those who yearn for a castle in Spain would react to the diet that accompanies it. From what I have seen of traveling Americans, they are thrown into a panic at the mere thought of eating an eel, an octopus, a fine mess of snails, a nice ragout of horse, or any dish flavored with a faint fragrance of garlic. I can only say that persons who must have thick steaks, juicy chops, fried chicken, and crisp waffles on their menus will be more than likely to find a castle in Spain highly repellent at mealtimes for the first quarter century or so.

Food presented difficulties, but not so many as heat. Contrary to general opinion, the countries bordering the Mediterranean are cold during late autumn, winter, and early spring; but they don't like to admit it.

Spain is cold, and southern France is cold, and Italy is no different; but whenever a bitter wind howls from out the north, and a mantle of snow descends on every hill above three hundred meters in height, and young lettuce leaves turn black around the edges, the natives shake their heads, as if puzzled, and declare nothing like it has ever been known. This is not true. Once every fifteen years, or thereabouts, the Mediterranean countries experience a warm winter—a winter so mild that no gardens freeze;

but never in anybody's knowledge have they experienced a winter warm enough to let country folk lay aside their regulation winter undershirts—hand-knitted affairs of sufficient thickness and harshness to be used as sand-paper.

Concetta Dassori and Maria Nobile wore these delicate garments. We found them hung on thorn bushes on washdays. Ordinary laundry is dried on fig trees or clotheslines, or spread over bushes; but Italian winter under-shirts must be handled differently. If hung on fig trees they would abrade the bark; if hung on clotheslines, they would chafe the lines to shreds. So they are draped on thorn bushes, since not even a thorn can damage the winter undershirt of a true Italian.

Yet the belief persists that Spain and Italy and the French Riviera are balmy and beneficent localities. Such a belief is worse than wrong: it is dangerous. I crossed, late one December, on a steamer that touched at Palermo, Naples, and Genoa; and during the voyage I met a New Yorker and his wife who had never before been in Italy. The wife remarked that she had brought a fur coat but expected to have no use for it until she reached Paris. I asked her why she thought so; and she said she had made special inquiries, when purchasing steamer tickets, as to the temperatures she would encounter in Palermo and Naples. The weather, she had been told, would be sunny and hot, like an August day at the New England seashore. Consequently she had brought summer dresses, and her husband had a wide assortment of white flannels and linens.

After she had voided herself of this information, a heavy silence ensued; and she finally broke it by saying, "What makes you look like that? Don't you believe what he told me?"

I could only say that I had spent seven winters in Italy, and parts of three others, and that my regulation indoor dress from December to April has always been what I would wear in a furnaceless house in Maine during November and December, except that when I sit at my Italian desk I must wrap an overcoat around my legs. A year ago, I told her, we had landed in Naples to find Vesuvius white with snow.

She was polite about it and said, "Did you indeed! Was it really!"; but she doubted me. Two days later we steamed into Palermo to find that beautiful harbor rimmed by snowy mountains; and down from the moun-tains moaned a wind redolent of ice and goose flesh. Vesuvius, on the following day, looked as though one of the ancient Italian goddesses had risen early in the morning and covered it with vanilla frosting. I saw the New York lady going ashore; but I could get no idea of what she was thinking, because the collar of her mink coat concealed her eyes and nose.

The strange delusion concerning the non-existence of cold which afflicts

Mediterranean countries is nothing new. I had occasion to visit Pompeii to see the new excavations undertaken by the government. The archæological expert who accompanied me called my attention to the fact that the main living room of the more important Pompeian houses was open to the sky, and that the rooms which opened off it had originally had curtains instead of doors. "They took elaborate precautions against heat," he remarked, "but none at all against cold. For nineteen hundred years we Italians have patiently endured the cold, and I think it will be our fate to endure it patiently for another nineteen hundred years."

Because of the expense of buying fuel, Italians never use enough of it; and all Italian apartments are modeled on palace rooms, with ceilings from eleven to fourteen feet high. Since warm air rises, the heat in such rooms is concentrated where it is valueless to humans. Italians deny this; but their denials lack force; for the best-selling winter remedies in Italian pharmacies are chilblain cures.

In the few centrally heated buildings in Italy, also, there is a fixed day for turning off the heat. This day is March 15. After March 15 there is no heat again until the following November. March is a cold month. It can easily be as unpleasant in Rome, Florence, Turin, or Genoa as in Paterson, N. J., or London, England. It not only can be, but it usually is. But even though a Roman March should be as cold as a Labrador February, the heat would not be turned on in Rome apartment houses after March 15. For such Italians as admit that cold exists, cold ceases on that date. Heat for heat's sake, therefore, is not understood by even the most enlightened and fortunate Italians in large cities.

All the others, however—ninety-nine per cent of those in large cities, and all residents of small towns, and hilltops that support castles in Spain or their equivalents—seem to have an ingrained horror of unseasonable warmth.

In the town at the foot of the hill on which the half-baked palace sits there is no heat during the winter. In the kitchens of the houses there are brick stoves that hold as much as two handfuls of charcoal when going full blast; but no heat can be felt by persons five feet removed. Occasionally a charcoal brazier is lighted; but it throws out little more warmth than a lightning bug. The houses are colder than storage warehouses. They are colder than the outer air—cold with a dead and penetrating chill. Their blinds are closed against the sun. This is because the sun is warm and therefore unhealthy. If you don't believe it, ask any Italian.

The inhabitants of the town in which we lived were well aware that *Americani* are *pazzi*—cuckoo—because they sit bareheaded in the winter sun. Word was repeatedly sent to the cockeyed *Americani*, by way of

Concetta Dassori or Maria Nobile, that sickness inevitably results from sitting bareheaded in the sun. The February and March sun is the worst! In April and May the sun is bad enough, God knows; but terrible illnesses come to one who exposes himself to the February and March sun!

We became object lessons to the entire village. "Look," they said of the *Americani*, "look at them if you want to see what happens to people who sit in the sun! They are *pazzi!* That's what the sun did to them! *Pazzi* from sitting in the sun! We warned them, but they went ahead, exposing themselves in March—in March, of all times!—and now they are *pazzi!* They bought the amphora from Domenichino, and so they *must* be *pazzi!* Domenichino's uncle fished it up in his net between Giglio and Monte Cristo: nothing but a dirty old amphora covered with *frutta di mare*—sea fruit—oyster shells and stone flowers and God knows what—and with a pointed base, so that it would never stand upright! But these *Americani*, they gave Domenichino thirty lire for it, when he asked only twenty-five! Thirty lire! *Ma che!* Holy smoke! And then, to make it worse, Alibrando wished to sell them the beautiful silver cup he had won in the motorcycle race, but they would not buy at all! *Madonna mia!* Was there ever such an example of *pazzeria!* I tell you the March sun will do that to any man! *Pazzi!*"

So, while the problem of living cheaply was not difficult to overcome, the problem of living comfortably among people who distrust heat was a tough one.

The first drawback was the icebox quality of all Italian rooms. The use of wood is reduced to a minimum in Italian housebuilding. All walls are thick, and constructed of porous rocks held together with an absorbent sort of weak cement. Floors are made of brick, cement, or tile. During the winter months both walls and floors radiate a chill similar to that of an iced halibut.

The second drawback was that the window- and doorframes were made of unseasoned wood set in weak cement, so that they shrank and warped and parted company, leaving upwards of a thousand cracks and holes through which cold Italian winds screamed and moaned.

The third drawback was the matter of stoves and fuel.

In every Italian city it is possible to buy oil stoves similar in shape to the regulation cylindrical American oil stove. Unfortunately they are made in Germany, and there is always something the matter with their wicks, so that when lighted they throw off noxious fumes, give dogs eye trouble, and cause humans to come down with aphasia and sleeping sickness. Kerosene, in Italy, costs the equivalent of eighty cents a gallon, which causes oil stoves to be regarded with downright aversion.

There were plenty of wood stoves, however, made of terra cotta. These are large and imposing in appearance, and have fireboxes the size of a one-gallon can. When the weather is violent, an American feels the need of both oil stoves and wood stoves—one of each in each room, plus a fireplace in large rooms. In severe weather it is possible—provided a person has good fuel and knows his stoves—to work the temperature of a fair-sized living room up to sixty in the vicinity of an open fire if it is augmented by an oil stove and a wood stove. This can only be done after an all-day struggle. The average temperature of the living room of the half-baked palace during the winter months, after the big terra-cotta stove had been burning for two hours, was fifty degrees. Fifty degrees is not warm enough for coziness, but it's hot for any Italian room in winter.

When I say that fuel is hard to get in most places in Italy, I am grossly conservative. The fuel situation cannot be adequately expressed without the use of profanity that would be considered a trifle daring by even our most outspoken younger authors, who supposedly stop at nothing. The Italian countryside is almost entirely deforested, and burnable wood not easy to find. For two years we bought wood locally. The young man who tended the vines and fig trees on the grounds of the half-baked palace would scour the neighborhood until he found a dying almond tree, and would then purchase it on the hoof, so to speak. He would grub it up, roots and all, load it on a donkey, and drag it back to the half-baked palace. It would be sawed into lengths with a saw that hadn't been sharpened since Columbus built the *Santa Maria;* and each morning a strong man came with a helper to split the lengths into firewood.

The splitting was done as follows: a block of wood was balanced on an exposed ledge of rock by the helper. On top of this block a second block was delicately placed. A dull wedge was then produced and somehow persuaded to stand poised on the upper end of the second block. The strong man then tightened the coils of black cloth that held up his trousers, expectorated on his hands, stretched, paused for a lingering look at the beautiful harbor of Porto Santo Stefano, picked up a sledge hammer, took a full swing with it, and brought it down on the wedge with a violent exhalation. The force of the blow sent a shudder along the ledge and through the half-baked palace. The wedge, being dull, slipped from the block of wood and bounded ten yards away. The top block of wood fell off the under block, and the under block fell off the ledge. The strong man put down his hammer and looked at the harbor, while the helper hunted for the wedge, readjusted the two blocks of wood, and set the stage for a second attempt. On the third or fourth try, the wedge would take hold and the block would be triumphantly pounded to fragments.

This method of obtaining fuel, while slow, was satisfactory, provided one could keep two stoves and a fireplace burning on ten sticks of wood a day—which we couldn't; and also provided nobody in the vicinity was trying to write a novel or do anything else requiring concentration. In the latter case, the continued thudding of a sledge hammer against a dull wedge was neither inspiring nor soothing. We were therefore forced to devise other means of obtaining fuel.

After conferring with the American consul general in Naples and the American consul in Leghorn, it was learned that in the small seaside town of Castiglione della Pescaia, thirty or forty miles up the coast, there was a man who had access to a sort of forest and would be willing to ship wood to us by water.

We ordered a boatload on the fifth day of January. On the nineteenth of February the woodman sent us a communication saying that the wood was in readiness and that he was waiting for the *barca*—the vessel—that was to convey it to us. Evidently the *barca* had gone on a pleasure jaunt to the Sea of Azov by way of the Cape of Good Hope, because the wood didn't reach port until May 11.

It was, however, a magnificent load of wood, made up of old table legs, old porch columns, old pieces of fishing boats abandoned around the time of the Crimean War, old wharf piling with barnacles intact, chunks of driftwood, and wonderful old cork trees with the bark still on.

We didn't learn until the following winter that if cork wood with the bark on is burned in a stove, the greasy smoke will clog a six-inch stovepipe in six weeks.

After three years of experimenting we learned how to get a winter's supply of fuel. In February we ordered two boatloads of wood from our Castiglione della Pescaia dealer, specifying that no cork trees shall be included, but giving him a free rein in the matter of driftwood and table legs. In two boatloads there are 200 *quintale*, or twenty tons, costing $160, Old Tenor, delivered at the back door of the half-baked palace. They arrived in April or May and were stacked beside the back door to dry out in the hot sun of the long Italian summer, and during the ensuing winter they kept us as comfortable as it's possible to keep in a modified castle in Spain.

As I have said, I built the half-baked palace because it seemed to me to be located in a place where there were no diversions or disturbances: a place so remote that while I was in it, I was forced to write, and write hard, in order to preserve my sanity. As to diversions, I had accurately diagnosed the situation. It is my impression that people who speak hopefully of someday occupying a castle in Spain are not bargaining for a castle that will provide no diversions whatever. Many of them, I fear, might consider a castle in Spain a trifle boring if they were unable to see a good movie once every two or three weeks, or have a few friends in for bridge occasionally, or at least press their noses against a window and watch the automobiles go by. In that case, they should stick to hotels and not settle down in a castle—not even in a modified one.

In Porto Santo Stefano there were no diversions. I was asked by friends what I found to do in Porto Santo Stefano, and I was always honest. "I work," I told them.

"Yes," they said, "but what do you do when you don't work? Play tennis?"

"No," I explained, "there's no place to play tennis. There aren't any automobiles, and nobody in the town speaks English. No; no movies, either. There was a man who spoke English, but his house is four miles from us; and anyway, he sold it and went to live in Bordighera. There's no road to our house: only a donkey path. There's no place to spend money and nothing to spend it for; so I work."

They nodded understandingly. "How's the golf there?" they persisted. "Do you get much chance to play?"

"No," I said, "there's no place to play golf. We live on a mountain. It's all rocks and stone walls. If you hit a golf ball, it would strike a rock and bounce two miles into the sea. No, there's no golf. There's nothing but work."

They looked puzzled. "Probably the neighbors keep you from getting lonely," they said.

"There aren't any neighbors," we told them. "We live out in the country. Nobody else lives out in the country. The Italians live in the town. They don't like living in the country. Anyway, we aren't lonely. We don't want to see any neighbors—not until this damned book is finished."

"Yes," they said, "but what do you *do?*"

"That's what we're trying to tell you," we said, "we work."

They shook their heads. "My God!" they said, "how can you stand it, with nothing to do or anything!"

So I wonder, occasionally, whether those who think it would be lovely to have a castle in Spain, where they could work at the things they've always wanted to do, have even a vague idea of what they're talking about.

If they have—if they're really serious about it—it would be wrong for them to get the idea in their heads that they can find a castle in Spain, Italy, or anywhere else where there'd be no disturbances. Places with no diversions, yes! But not places with no disturbances.

For a long time I thought that the only disturbances in life were the so-called benefits of civilization: an automobile into which one could step when work grew tiresome; the perpetual squawk of automobile horns; the persistent shrilling of telephone bells; people with an uncontrollable desire to play contract bridge or talk it; the utterances of politicians in the morning paper; cocktail parties; conversation concerning scarcities from persons who have never been deprived of anything. I find, however, that if it isn't one thing, it's another.

We had no automobile horns, telephones, movies, or cocktail parties in Porto Santo Stefano; but we had the airplanes and the fishing fleet, and the sparrows, and the ladies from the village who wanted to sell jugs and mugs, and the three sheep, and the family parties that roosted outside the front gates and sang old Tuscan glees on pleasant afternoons.

There were fourteen motor-driven *paranze* in the fishing fleet—forty-footers, lateen-rigged, with five-man crews. Each *paranza* dragged a long net for half an hour; then lay to, attached the net ropes to the motor, and slowly wound it in. The winding in took another half hour and was a noisy operation: not only because of the wheezing and clanking of the motor, but because the crew of the *paranza* was engaged in what seemed to be an altercation between five brothers who had suddenly been disinherited. In reality, probably, it wasn't an altercation at all. Probably they were only touching lightly on the sardine market; but what it sounded like was the preliminary to a murder.

Sometimes the *paranze* fished all day and sometimes they fished all night, but at almost any hour one *paranza* might be found directly under the headland on which the half-baked palace is perched, its crew engaged in a heated argument. This, it seems, is a favorite spot for net hauling. From five to six o'clock at night as many as three nestled there and hauled, and the hoarse, angry voices of the haulers resounded through the half-baked palace, along with the clanking of winches and the chugging of motors, as clearly as though they were wrapped in the overcoat around my feet.

All through the morning there was usually one there; and sister vessels took up the work in the afternoon. They got in their best licks, however, from one to five in the morning, when the sea was calm. At such hours the screaming of crews and the squawking of winches sounded as though the chariot race from *Ben Hur* were in rehearsal beneath the bedroom windows.

Nothing, of course, could be done about the *paranze*, any more than anything could be done about the young men learning to fly at the Orbetello naval aviation station, at the end of the harbor. When we first arrived in Porto Santo Stefano, the Orbetello aviation station was a small affair, with two brick machine shops and a few small single-motored crates. In ten years' time it looked like a Florida real-estate development, with scores of modernistic homes for officers, machine shops resembling a New England college in its early days, and an impressive fleet of double- and triple-motored flying boats. From dawn to dark they flew, up and down and up and down the harbor, and around and around the half-baked palace, occasionally using it as a landmark across which to fly or toward which to dive. The windows buzzed and rattled as the boats howled overhead. They circled and dove at the mouth of the harbor, peppering floating targets with heavy machine guns . . . their vibration shook ink from fountain pen to manuscript . . . and we, contemplating the inevitable results of constantly increasing armaments, knew that we had come to the end of our uninterrupted Italian winters.

# The Truth About a Novel

### *From* FOR AUTHORS ONLY

THERE is no way of knowing with any certainty how large a percentage of the undergraduates of America's leading educational institutions are filled with a more or less passionate desire to earn their livings by producing novels, plays, and short stories; but from a casual survey of four large eastern universities which I once had occasion to make, I received the impression that about ninety-seven per cent of the students were desirous of breaking into literature. A few undergraduates—the more imaginative ones, possibly, or those reared in homes where authors, along with artists and persons who bet on horse races, are still regarded with a suspicious eye—had seemingly resigned themselves to accepting positions in the parental button factory or to hunting dependable jobs; but most of them, so far as I could tell, wanted to write.

My estimate of the number of would-be authors among the student class seemed excessive, so I conferred with Jesse Lynch Williams, then president of the Authors' League, whose residence in Princeton and lectures at the University of Michigan had given him unusual opportunities to observe the American college student in a state of nature. Mr. Williams considered ninety-seven per cent too high a reckoning. He felt sure that only about ninety-five, or at the outside ninety-six, per cent of American undergraduates had inclined their ears to the siren song of literature.

At all events, many young Americans nourish either a secret or an open yearning to become authors; and it has been my experience that they freely reveal their reasons for the yearning to anyone who cares to ask.

It appears to be the fixed belief of these enthusiastic young people that (1) a person needs only to write a book in order to become immediately rich and famous; (2) the work is easier and cleanlier than other forms of endeavor, and can be performed anywhere and at any time; (3) little training is needed, and no equipment except a large pad of paper, several pencils, and a place to hang the hat.

The whole business of being an author, to hear them tell it, offers the largest possible return for the smallest known outlay, and most closely approaches the ideal existence, from the viewpoint of the college student: an existence in which one gets everything for nothing, travels whenever he feels like it, plays golf every pleasant day, and has all his meals at home.

These quaint beliefs were given considerable impetus, some years ago, by the talented pen of that distinguished American author, Mrs. Edith Wharton, in her widely acclaimed novel, *Hudson River Bracketed*. The hero of that book was a callow youth in his early twenties. He becomes an author and writes a story: almost his first story, and a short story at that; but what a story! Though published in an obscure magazine operating in the red, its excellence is such that publishers and editors clamor frantically for his work, while beautiful women in high society exert themselves to win his favor. It may be true to life, of course; but such things have never happened to any authors of my acquaintance.

I know one eminent novelist who gave up newspaper reporting in order to write short stories; but he wrote eighty-six which were enthusiastically rejected before he wrote one good enough to be published. Even then he found it unnecessary to surround his home with barbed-wire entanglements in order to protect himself from ravening publishers, editors, and society ladies.

I had another friend who, after several moderately successful years of serial writing, nearly starved to death because editors suddenly became indifferent to his offerings. His sole income for one year was $246.37 and upwards of 973 rejection slips, which unfortunately cannot be eaten—a fact that may eventually lead the Carnegie Foundation, or some such charitable organization, to perform a truly great service to American letters and to struggling authors by financing a scheme to have all rejection slips printed on oatmeal cakes or bran wafers, or even on thin slices of dried beef.

Although I have never even heard of anyone, except in the pages of Mrs. Wharton's novel, who was whirled into the arms of lovely society ladies by a first short story, I have reason to believe the undergraduates of American universities think it happens every day. It is because of the many odd and interesting ideas to be found in the heads of would-be authors that I here set down an account of the work connected with the writing of a novel, the time consumed in its preparation and publication, and the earnings resulting from it. In so doing I regret the necessity of making frequent use of the personal pronoun; but it is only by using one of my own products as an example that I can be sure of presenting accurate dates and figures—which, for some reason that I will not attempt to explain, are not always procurable from authors or from publishers.

In order that would-be authors may be encouraged as much as possible, I will state at once that the novel in question is *Arundel,* and that it was by no means unsuccessful. For a time it was advertised as a best seller in New York and Boston. It was reviewed both kindly and understandingly —frequently at considerable length and with enthusiasm—by the leading newspapers in the United States. Its publishers, hopeful that its longevity might rival that of Old Parr, treated it with respectful solicitude. Consequently would-be authors cannot accuse me of presenting a peculiarly gloomy case. As a matter of fact, I consider it singularly rosy; and if there are some to whom it seems gloomy rather than rosy, then they cannot recognize rosiness when they see it, and should under no circumstances yield weakly to their craving for the sybaritic ease and the rich rewards of a literary existence.

In 1917, after several years of writing for a Boston newspaper, I surprised myself by completing a short story; and my surprise almost became apoplexy when a New York authors' agent whom I had never seen sold the story to the *Saturday Evening Post.*

Inflamed by this unexpected avalanche of good fortune, I seriously contemplated literary deeds of high emprise, among them a series of three novels dealing with the development of one family through three important periods in the history of my native state—the pioneering and revolutionary period, the shipping period, and the summer-resort period.

I even made a desultory attempt to dally with one of the books, and was dismayed to learn that I was not only painfully in the dark about what I proposed to write, but also at a loss how to write it.

Immediately after this a number of things occurred to prevent me from brooding over my own inexperience—a bit of soldiering in Siberia, for example, and several years of reporting on activities in various sections of the world for the *Saturday Evening Post*. It was not until 1925 that I made a serious effort to circumvent the ignorance that stood between me and my first novel. In that year I outlined the ground I wished to cover, and hazily concluded to start with the Louisburg Expedition in 1745, bear down heavily on some portion of the French and Indian Wars, and terminate with Benedict Arnold's march through the Maine wilderness in the autumn and winter of 1775 for the purpose of capturing Quebec.

Fired by enthusiasm, I obtained from various sources upward of thirty books on the Siege of Louisburg—diaries, records, and histories—and read them carefully. The upshot of the reading was that the Louisburg Expedition could not be made to fit my scheme.

I have no doubt that some people can write books with no equipment other than several No. 2 pencils and a large heap of white paper; but it seemed impossible for me to acquire the knack. Once I had banished the Louisburg Expedition from participation in my book, my task promised, I thought, to become simple. There was nothing left to do but lay the early portion of the story against a background of the Indian troubles which bitterly afflicted certain sections of Maine for over a century, the middle portion against the pre-Revolutionary unrest which filled New England for more than a decade, and the latter portion against the tremendous march of America's first expeditionary force up the Kennebec River, across the Height of Land, through the trackless bogs of Lake Megantic, and down the tortured bed of the river Chaudière to Quebec. Indeed, a friend of mine went so far as to remark carelessly that the story would practically write itself.

Unfortunately I could not begin the book until I had obtained definite information on the Indians of Maine: what they wore, what they ate, where they lived, how they lived, how they talked, where they hunted, how they made their weapons, what they believed, where the different tribes of the Abenaki Confederation made their homes, and how it happened that certain Indians were usually at war with the whites while others were always at peace with them. At the same time I realized I must have equally authoritative information on the white settlers who lived in southern Maine at the same period: what their houses looked like, how they subsisted, what they wore, what they ate, and so on.

Most of these bits of information, which may or may not be important or necessary, can be located, after considerable delving and cursing, in the Library of Congress, the library of the American Antiquarian Society in Worcester, Mass., the William L. Clements Library at Ann Arbor, Michigan, the Maine State Library, and the publications of the Maine Historical Society.

The chief difficulty lies in knowing what to look for. After that the only dilemma is to find a workroom large enough to assemble all reference books under the same ceiling with the No. 2 pencils, the large heap of copy paper, and the author himself. There are sometimes a few perplexities connected with persuading librarians that reference books will come to no harm if loaned to an author for an indeterminate period, but they are seldom serious.

I sincerely hope that university undergraduates who are looking forward to enjoying the easy, cleanly, meditative life of an author will not misunderstand my attitude toward the writing of books.

I would like to write them with nothing near me except a lot of No. 2 pencils and a box of pure white paper. I would be happy to escape the necessity of opening reference book after reference book, placing one on top of another on the corner of my desk until the pile towers high in air, and all for the purpose of trying to discover what method, if any, an Abenaki Indian would use to smoke out a hibernating bear from a high hollow in a tree too large to climb, or the exact position held by young Benedict Arnold with the drug-importing Lathrops in September of 1760; or whether Arnold had black hair and black eyes, as most historians claim, or brown hair and blue eyes, as was the case.

There is nothing diverting in having such a pile of books collapse, spilling the ink and hopelessly confusing the other seven reference books that are lying ready for use, with pencil stubs, old envelopes, scraps of paper, and a fountain pen or two scattered among their pages to mark passages that once seemed important to me.

Some people are inclined to speak contemptuously of novels that require the use of reference books. Such novels are occasionally damned by being called historical novels. If there is anyone able to write effectively of any period in the world's history, including the immediate present, without cluttering his desk and brain with upwards of three tons of assorted reference books smelling faintly of old glue and moldy leather, I congratulate and envy him. What is more, I doubt that it can be done. In other words, I am of the opinion that every novel which deals adequately with any period at all is a historical novel.

The preliminary steps, however, were taken at such odd moments as could be spared from regular toil, and should not be seriously regarded by would-be authors as a necessary part of the work that goes into the writing of a book.

It will be enough to touch lightly on such preliminary labors as remained. By 1926 I had become sufficiently familiar with my subject to attempt to interest a New York publishing house in the project. I broached the subject to Mr. William Briggs of Harper & Brothers. He shook his head sadly and told me frankly that there was nothing for anybody in such a book as I proposed.

Only mildly discouraged by this rebuff, I continued to collect references; and by the end of 1927 I was so far along that I approached Putnam & Co. and discussed the project with Mr. George Palmer Putnam. He was polite about it, but succeeded admirably in concealing any enthusiasm he may have felt. He would, he said, be glad to look at it when it was finished. I suggested that I might proceed with more confidence if he would advance a sufficient amount to enable me to withdraw to a secluded nook and write the book—and incidentally to assure me that I would be spared the weary task of hunting a publisher; but somehow he changed the subject in such a way that the little matter of an advance failed to receive serious consideration.

By the middle of 1928 I had rounded up all available references to Abenaki Indians, histories of most towns in southern Maine, and all known diaries, documents, letters, and biographies dealing with Benedict Arnold's expedition to Quebec and with the assault on the city by American troops in a blinding snowstorm on the last day of 1775. There were, I may say without exaggeration, a lot of these books: not quite enough to fill a freight car, but more than enough to place a severe dent in the theory that the only equipment needed in the writing of a novel is a large pad of paper, several pencils, and a place to hang the hat.

These things being assembled, there was nothing left to do but go to work—which I probably would not have done except for the insistence and encouragement of Mr. Booth Tarkington, who doubtless felt that unless I soon began to put something on paper, the year 1975 would still see me talking about what I intended to do.

A good friend, it has often occurred to me, is a highly desirable part

of every author's equipment—a friend who will listen with patient understanding to the unfolding of a plot; who will point out errors in judgment,
errors in taste, mistakes in character building, slips in grammar, weaknesses
in plot construction; who will speak reassuringly during the periods of
black depression that envelop, with more or less frequency, every writer,
causing him to declare bitterly that everything he has written is stupid,
futile, banal—is, in a word, tripe: who will, in short, somewhat lighten
the arduous labor of learning to write. Unhappily for most of us, such
friends are rare. Friends may have a world of patience and yet lack understanding; while those who possess understanding will be more than apt
to be somewhat deficient in patience.

I wish I might say that the assistance of such a friend removes all labor
from the writing of a book; but the obvious fact is that it doesn't. I learn
from my diary that the words "Arundel. Chapter I" were written on a
blank sheet of paper on September 6, 1928. I set down the date because it
is necessary, for the enlightening of would-be authors, to refer occasionally
to the amount of time consumed: not because I expect the date ever to be
made a national or even a state holiday in recognition of my labors.

Thanks to my lack of restraint in accumulating information concerning
Indians, the early settlers of Maine, Benedict Arnold, and associated matters, I was filled with an almost uncontrollable desire to tell what I knew,
and consequently felt obliged to write long chapters. They were seven
thousand, eight thousand, nine thousand words long, those early chapters,
and they took time to write: as much as six and seven days apiece. I
grumbled to Mr. Tarkington; but he patiently advised me not to worry
about their length. When I complained further that if the chapters continued to be long I would have no time for other work, he suggested that
I give up the other work. Consequently I finished the small amount of
other work that couldn't be avoided, took six completed chapters of
*Arundel* to New York and, late in December 1928, again presented myself before a publisher—in this case Mr. Russell Doubleday, of Doubleday,
Doran & Co.

"Here," I said to him, "are six chapters of a novel. I know a place in
Italy where there are no telephones, no automobiles, no golf links, no
bridge players, no friends to drop in for a week end—not even anyone
who speaks English. If you'll advance $1,000 on this book, I'll go to Italy,
crawl into a corner, and finish it in May."

Publishers are apt to be odd, as all writers eventually learn; and Mr.
Russell Doubleday showed what I considered reckless trustfulness by
handing me a check for $1,000 and a contract agreeing to publish the

book in question on a basis whereby I was to receive ten per cent of the book's retail price for the first 2,500 copies sold, fifteen per cent for the next 22,500 copies sold, and twenty per cent for all copies sold above that number. This seemed to me, and indeed was, a gratifying arrangement for a first novel; and I lost no time in packing several hundredweight of reference books into a number of ill-assorted trunks and traveling bags and embarking with Mrs. Roberts for Italy.

It seemed to me, when, on visits to Cornell, Harvard, Michigan, and the University of Illinois, I spoke with starry-eyed college students who burned to achieve fame and fortune by writing a book, that these young people were more interested in the fame and the fortune than in the methods by which such things might possibly be achieved.

None of them, I found, had ever considered the unhappy lot of an author's wife, who must too often sit alone for weeks and months on end, while her husband secretes himself in a locked chamber, only to emerge at intervals and emit mournful cries concerning his complete befuddlement and almost total lack of progress.

Yet this is a matter that requires some thought; for if an author has the misfortune to marry a lady who is not both patient and long-suffering, he is fairly certain to produce more nervous breakdowns than books.

A number of persons, when I was writing the chronicles of Arundel, politely asked where I spent my winters. When I said I spent them in Italy, they either said: "That must be wonderful!" or enviously observed: "Pretty soft!"

That is, of course, as it may be. I find, on consulting my diary, that we landed in Naples on January 8, 1929, and proceeded at once to the town of Porto Santo Stefano, arriving there on January 10. We remained there for four months. When we left, on May 2, we went direct to Naples and sailed for New York on May 4.

Each day between January 10 and May 2, with one exception, was largely spent in the romantic and stimulating occupation of sitting at a desk, facing a blank wall, and evolving out of thin air the fortunes and misfortunes of young Steven Nason from his twelfth to his twenty-seventh year. The one exception was the nineteenth day of February, when a hurried trip was made to Rome for the purpose of felicitating Mr. Samuel G. Blythe on his recovery from an attack of influenza.

The routine of all other days, including Saturdays, Sundays, holidays—both American and Italian—and festas of whatever sort, was unchanging. I here set down this routine, trusting that those who see it will bear in mind that I am seeking only to convey reliable information to would-be authors who think it must be great fun to go to Italy and write a book:

9 A.M. Retire to the workroom, wrap an overcoat around the feet to keep out the chill that rises from the tiled floors of all Italian buildings, sit down at the desk, and devote one hour to revising and rewriting the work done on the preceding two days.

10 A.M. Dip into eleven reference books to make sure of dates, weather, costumes, and sundry other matters having to do with the day's writing, and try to go on with the story until

1 P.M. Unwrap the overcoat from the feet and emerge for lunch, read the Paris *Herald* and the morning mail, curse the clownlike antics of American legislators and European statesmen, and play three games of cribbage, piquet, or backgammon with Mrs. Roberts.

2.30 P.M. Retire to the workroom, adjust the overcoat around the feet, and work for five hours.

7.30 P.M. Emerge for dinner, complain about the small amount of work accomplished during the day, and play three games of piquet, cribbage, or backgammon with Mrs. Roberts.

9.30 P.M. To bed with an armful of reference books, to brood morosely over the next day's work.

There were occasional small diversions. The persistent squawking of English sparrows weighed heavily upon me: consequently I was frequently impelled to rise from my desk and take pot shots at them from door or windows with a .22-caliber rifle.

On every other Monday morning the town barber, Dante by name, entered my workroom to favor me with a haircut, thus providing the romantic foreign flavor to be expected in Italy.

The cook, a lyric soprano who had been a pillar of strength in the local sardine factory before she was so fortunate as to land the highly desirable task of ministering to the crazy Americans, occasionally found it necessary to ask for the instructions concerning the making of American hash (*fritto Americano*) and other dainties known to be pleasing to the palates of the incomprehensible *Americani*. Ot er diversions, however, were non-existent, so that there was nothing to be done except to work, whether I felt like it or not.

Under these conditions *Arundel* made headway at the rate of about 2,200 words a day. The chapters averaged seven thousand words apiece. There were to be thirty-six chapters and a prologue; and from my diary I find Chapter 25 was finished on April 2, Chapter 26 on April 5, Chapter 27 on April 9, Chapter 28 on April 12, Chapter 29 on April 16, Chapter 30 on April 19, Chapter 31 on April 23, Chapter 32 on April 26, Chapter 33 on April 28, Chapter 34 on May 1. I beg that my readers will continue to remember that I mention these things only by way of demonstrating to would-be authors that the life of a writer of books may possibly be, as they think and say, an easy and ideal existence, but that the life of a railroad track worker or a lumberjack may often be easier, to say nothing of being less confining and more diverting.

I might also add, for the benefit of would-be authors, that their peace of mind will be considerably enhanced if they will take the precaution to marry persons capable of typing manuscripts. Mrs. Roberts typed the manuscript of *Arundel* after the longhand manuscript had been three times revised. There were 725 typewritten pages of about four hundred words each—an indication of the manner in which everyone connected with an author participates in the easy gaiety of his life.

Chapter 35 was finished on May 14, during the voyage from Naples to New York. Chapter 36 was finished in Maine on May 24; and with that, according to the beliefs of all the would-be authors with whom I had conferred in four large eastern universities, the time had come for me to reap both fame and fortune—especially fortune. I had a fat book on my hands—a book of 300,000 words, which America's leading publisher had contracted to publish; but eight and one half months had elapsed since I started to write it, and even a would-be author with no experience at all could see that I had probably, by now, frittered away the original $1,000 it had brought me.

Since the manuscript was typed, however, it could be more effectively revised than was possible while it still remained in longhand. It was therefore revised for the fourth time, a few thousand words ejected from each of the early chapters, and about one third of every page completely rewritten. The fourth revision was completed by the middle of June, at which time Mr. Tarkington arrived in Maine and suggested that I read the entire manuscript to him. When I did this, he pointed out places where the story should be pruned, and offered a number of suggestions so valuable that there were times when I felt it would be an act of simple justice to remove my own name from the title page and replace it with his. In this revision—the fifth—another fifteen thousand words were cut out, four chapters rewritten, and a moderate amount of tinkering performed throughout. The task was completed on June 27, and the manuscript was then thought to be in proper condition to meet the eye of the publisher. It was expressed to him on June 28 and eventually acknowledged with what seemed pronounced enthusiasm.

Publication being assured, it became necessary to guard against blunders by going carefully over the route followed by Arnold and his starving army up the Kennebec River, across the Height of Land and down the Chaudière, and also to make sure of the exact location of barricades, defending forces, and houses in old Quebec at the time of Arnold's attack. The Library of Congress found for me a rare manuscript map of the old city, drawn by a French engineer officer; and equipped with a copy of this I went to Quebec and obtained the assistance of Lt.-Col. G. E. Marquis, head of the Statistical Department of the Dominion Government. By pacing and measurements we found the spot where Arnold was shot, where Daniel Morgan went cursing over the first barricade of logs into a blaze of musketry fire, where the Virginians caught the Canadians on their pikeheads and pitchforked them through the windows of their guardhouse, and where Arnold's troops, having penetrated to the heart of the Lower Town, stood guard over their prisoners in the drifting snow for four hours, vainly waiting for General Montgomery, who lay at the foot of Cape Diamond, ripped to pieces by grapeshot.

As a result of these investigations, more rewriting was required—not too much, but enough to keep me from golf and mischievous idleness.·

Galley proofs—181 long strips of yellow paper about the width of the sashes once worn by high-school girls at graduating exercises—came back on September 20, slightly more than one year after I had sat myself down in the midst of a disarranged mass of reference books and hopefully written "Arundel. Chapter I" on an unblemished page. These proofs were read three times, innumerable corrections, emendations, and deletions being made at each reading; for one of the peculiar features of galley proofs is that the human eye cannot detect the most serious of the mistakes which they conceal until the third reading, or possibly until the fourth or fifth reading—and perhaps not until the twenty-fourth, if ever.

*Arundel* was finally published on January 10, 1930, one year and four months after I had begun it. It was a plethoric volume of 618 pages; and as I have said before, it received handsome treatment at the hands of critics and reviewers. I might even hazard the statement that those who read it, so far as it was possible to judge from letters of appreciation, seemed to enjoy it. Apparently it had many of the earmarks of a successful novel.

Publishers make disbursements to their carefree authors, as a rule, every six months—as soon as possible after the first of January and the first of July. Early in July 1930, therefore, I received a check for royalties on all sales made from January through June, minus the $1,000 advanced in December 1928. Twenty-two months—two months short of two years—had elapsed since I had started the book; and the check that appeared was for $1,420.95. It was, I have no hesitation in saying, extremely welcome; but it failed to measure up, somehow, to the rosy ideas of the eager, bright-eyed young people whom I had encountered in the universities—the would-be authors who had told me so trustingly that their greatest ambition was to write a book because by so doing they would become instantly rich and famous.

And the sales figures, when I finally obtained them, were not of a sort to satisfy the literary aspirant who is confident that affluence follows a best seller, just as the Constitution follows the flag. *Arundel's* 1930 record was:

| Wk. ending | Copies sold | Wk. ending | Copies sold |
|---|---|---|---|
| Jan. 15 | 3,006 | July 30 | 24 |
| 22 | 856 | Aug. 6 | 45 |
| 29 | 774 | 13 | 64 |
| Feb. 5 | 343 | 20 | 15 |
| 12 | 144 | 27 | 535 |
| 19 | 547 | Sept. 3 | 2 |
| 26 | 349 | 10 | 26 |
| Mar. 5 | 148 | 17 | 18 |
| 12 | 150 | 24 | 41 |
| 19 | 247 | Oct. 1 | 127 |
| 26 | 89 | 8 | 51 |
| Apr. 2 | 55 | 15 | 8 |
| 9 | 102 | 22 | 56 |
| 16 | 129 | 29 | 78 |
| 23 | 89 | Nov. 5 | 22 |
| 30 | 89 | 12 | 45 |
| May 7 | 31 | 19 | 56 |
| 14 | 32 | 26 | 37 |
| 21 | 34 | Dec. 3 | 37 |
| 28 | 44 | 10 | 163 |
| June 4 | 40 | 17 | 160 |
| 11 | — | 24 | 30 |
| 18 | 44 | 31 | 34 |
| 25 | 34 | Jan. 7 | 38 |
| July 2 | 228 | 14 | 29 |
| 9 | 12 | | |
| 16 | 59 | One year's | |
| 23 | 36 | total sales | 9,452 |

It was impossible for me to feel jubilant over the lamentable fact that, in a supposedly literate nation of 125,000,000 people, a "best-selling" novel of any merit whatever should be purchased by only 9,452 persons in one year. And although $2,420.95 may seem like opulence to some, it dwindles distressingly when set against the expense of accumulating a reference library, of repeatedly visiting Quebec, and of subsisting for twenty-two months, even in a land where the wage for a lyric-soprano cook is $135 a year, Old Tenor.

As for becoming famous, I wish I might encourage prospective novelists by telling how, after *Arundel* appeared, beautiful ladies sought to win my favor, and publishers almost beggared themselves to secure my next book. If authors tell the truth about themselves, and if novels and short stories tell the truth about authors, such occurrences are not unusual in literary circles. Yet somehow I have a feeling that authors, like actors, occasionally stretch a point in order to make their lot seem rosier than it is. I have heard them, for example, speak impressively of receiving hundreds of communications from admirers; but quiet investigation reveals that the author who claims to have been thus inundated has usually received eleven letters.

Not even by stretching a point, however, can I bring forward a single instance wherein ladies sought to lure me because I had written a novel. It is true that publishers made overtures; but the vagueness and caution of their approach seemed to hint at beggary for me as well as for them.

But in spite of all these minor disappointments, my own publishers so effectively convinced me that *Arundel* was a huge success that I embarked for Italy almost immediately after its publication to write *The Lively Lady*.

*Publisher's Note:* Mr. Roberts' pessimism is slightly exaggerated. Fifteen years have elapsed since *Arundel* first appeared. It has been printed in Braille for the blind by order of the Library of Congress. It was published in England—privately, Mr. Roberts cynically says; then in 1937 it was published in Germany and was a selection of the German Book Society in that year. After that the Readers' Union in London woke up and published a large English edition, and the leading publishers of Sweden, Denmark, and Italy followed suit. In America *Arundel* has quietly and steadily grown in popularity, its average yearly sales being about 5,000 copies. Its total trade sales in the United States alone at the beginning of 1945 had been 74,330, and so far another 139,000 copies have been printed in an Armed Services Edition and distributed free to United States Army and Navy personnel overseas. *Arundel* has made more friends and admirers for Mr. Roberts, both in the United States and Europe, than he realized when he wrote this chapter—or is now willing to admit.

—NELSON DOUBLEDAY

# It Takes All Kinds to Make an Army

## From ARUNDEL

WE LACKED many things in those first days before Quebec: breeches and shoes and razors and soap and shirts and blankets and hats and money and stockings and muskets and needles and thread and bayonets and pipes and tobacco. No beggars could have had less than we.

Yet we might have endured our destitution without much trouble but for two things: we lacked men to set up a proper blockade of the roads going into Quebec, and powder to make a fight in case a force should come out from the city and take us front and rear. When our powder was measured there was enough to provide each man with four rounds; and four rounds is scarce sufficient to smell up the barrel of a musket, let alone raise a dust on folk who are after your life.

Therefore the colonel, learning General Montgomery had captured Montreal and would soon march downriver to join him, made up his mind to drop back out of danger and wait for Montgomery's arrival; then return to Quebec again with enough men to blockade the roads and cut off the city's provisions, and enough powder to blow holes in everybody.

When I heard the army was to fall back, I went hunting for Cap Huff; for I had not seen him since he had been so disappointed in his personal looting of Major Caldwell's manor house.

Remembering his dislike of the French, and his desire to take home one of their queues as a souvenir, I was uneasy about him. It may be Cap was a rude and uncouth man, as some folk have ever believed and said, and seldom a beautification of the politer side of social life. Yet I found him restful because what he said never caused me to feel the need of thinking. The fact is that whatever he was, he was my friend. I need say no more to any man who has had a friend. One who has no friends could never understand my uneasiness at this time, no matter how much I might say.

I asked here and there concerning him; but no man, it seemed, had seen or heard of him for days. I sent Natanis, Hobomok, and Jacataqua to find him if they could—Natanis along the road that skirts the St. Lawrence, to the little town of Sillery; Hobomok along the main road to Montreal, running out through the town of St. Foy's; Jacataqua toward the settlements along the St. Charles River. While they hunted I sat worrying and cursing Cap for an irresponsible fool; for it had been decided that early on the following morning the army would move back through St. Foy's to Pointe-aux-Trembles, some twenty-four miles up the St. Lawrence; and God only knew what would become of Cap if he should be left alone.

Hobomok came back in the afternoon, declaring nobody in St. Foy's had seen the blundering oaf; and toward dusk Jacataqua returned from the banks of the St. Charles with similar tidings. But when Natanis came in, a little after nightfall, he had news. He had gone out along the bluff of the St. Lawrence toward Sillery, passing the tree-surrounded summer homes of wealthy Quebec folk, and had found scuffed footprints wavering toward one of them. The footprints, big as bear tracks, led to a side porch, where there was a broken window. He entered the house and found himself in a kitchen, in which were many empty brandy bottles, and a feather mattress on the floor, and on the white wall the print of an enormous hand, where its owner had leaned against the wall to raise the trap door which, in all Canadian kitchens, conceals the steps into the cellar. This print, Natanis said, must have been made by the hand of Cap Huff.

Cap had gone staggering off through the trees, bumping into them and falling down, as Natanis could see from the tracks in the snow; so Natanis trailed him. The tracks led to another summer house, where there were more empty bottles, and on the kitchen floor a bed made out of pillows.

"I think," Natanis said in conclusion, "that even still your friend cannot go far without falling down in the snow, and that if we go at once to Sillery, we shall find him before further harm is done."

We set off, the four of us, as soon as we could roll our packs. The night was dark and the snow deep; and I was glad we were groping for the roads of Canada rather than those of New England. They have a custom in Canada, because of the violent snows, of marking the roads on each side with upright pines, so that even though snow falls each day, which it often does, there are always lines of pine trees to guide the traveler on his way. It is the law, too, that after a storm each Canadian must go out with a horse and one of the squat sleighs they call carioles and drive along that portion of the road that lies before his property. Thus the roads are always clear.

Natanis showed us the first house where signs of Cap's occupancy had been discovered. The second house, he said, was half a cross beyond—half the distance between two of the crosses that the papist French plant along their roads, as thick as fence posts in Maine, each cross surmounted with all manner of implements: shears and scaling ladders and hammers and tongs and frog spears and bottles and roosters.

We came up to his second house to hear a tumult within, shouts and thumps and laughter, and then a bawling voice, familiarly hoarse, shouting the words of a song I came to know better, later:

> "*Vive la Canadienne,*
> *Vole, mon cœur, vole;*
> *Vive la Canadienne,*
> *Et ses jolis yeux doux!*
> *Et ses jolis yeux doux, doux, doux,*
> *Et ses jolis yeux doux!*"

I opened the door and walked into a dark little hall and thence into a snug warm candle-lit kitchen with strips of colored paper pasted around the windows to keep out the bitter wind and the snow powder. There were Cap and an old, old Frenchman with a queue so long he could sit on the end of it, and a younger Frenchman and his brown-faced wife. There were three brown-faced girls, two about the age of Jacataqua and the other little larger than a mosquito, and a brown-faced boy not more than five years old with a pipe between his teeth and a rope end braided into his queue to give it substance, all of them sitting before a potbellied iron stove red hot around the neck.

The boy with the pipe was perched on one of Cap's knees, and the small girl on the other. When Cap saw my face at the door he leaped to his feet, spilling his young friends on the floor.

"Ho!" Cap bawled. "It's about time you got around! Hey, Zhulie! Hey, Lizette! Friend! Friend! *Amee! Amee!*"

He bellowed in a way to deafen everybody, as was his habit when he hoped to make himself understood by persons of alien speech. His French friends stared silently and somewhat timorously at the four of us: me with my rough clothes, and Natanis and Hobomok, and Jacataqua with her hand twisted in the scruff of Anatarso's neck. We must have had a look of wildness that would have quieted a gathering of New York gaolbirds, let alone a peaceable French family.

"What in God's name have you been doing?" I asked. "I've been in a state about you, you blundering ox!"

"What are you talking about!" he exclaimed. "Can't I take a little walk without being spied on?"

"A little walk!" I cried. "How many days do you need for a little walk? Didn't you get enough walking on the Chaudière?"

"What's the matter with you!" he growled benevolently, giving Jacata-qua an affectionate slap in the ribs that set her to coughing.

"The matter is that the army moves back to Pointe-aux-Trembles at dawn tomorrow. I've been hunting you high and low so you wouldn't be left alone in this damned country and spend the rest of your days in a British prison."

Cap rubbed his red face with his vast hands.

"Tomorrow! They couldn't go tomorrow! They just got there!"

"You fool! How long do you think you've been away?"

"Two days," Cap said, scratching his head.

"Well, there's something wrong with your arithmetic, because all of us are agreed you've been gone five days."

"Like hell I have! I slept in a kitchen night before last. Last night I slept here in this kitchen with Pierre Lemoine and his wife and his mother and his son and his three daughters and a dog, and I think there was a pig as well, though maybe it was a cow."

"It's not worth arguing about," I said, "but Natanis found two kitchens where you slept, both full of empty brandy bottles. God knows how many other places you occupied!"

Cap came close to me, smelling brutally of garlic and wearing a smirk that made his round red face look like the full moon coming up out of the ocean on a hot summer night. "That accounts for it! I was put to it to understand how all that stuff could have come out of one house." He came closer and breathed on me until I near choked. "Listen, Stevie: did you ever hear of Normandy cider?"

I shook my head, strangled by his nearness.

"Why wasn't we told about it, Steven?" he demanded. "Steven, that's a great drink! They got brandy in those cellars forty years old! Fifty, some of 'em! I want to tell you, Steven: you take a gallon of that Normandy cider and add a pint of old brandy to it, and you got a drink to put hair on a pumpkin!" He shook his head, as if recalling something that gave him pain. "Listen, Steven: I can talk French!" He rolled his eyes at the ceiling, put his head on one side, and ejaculated in a high, monotonous voice: "*On Normandee noo boovong doo* see-*druh*."

"What did you mean," I asked, when I had pushed him away from me, "by saying you didn't understand how all that stuff could have come out of one house? All what stuff?"

Cap passed his hand reflectively over his moist red forehead. "Didn't I tell you about the picture? The picture of Philadelphia as Seen from Cooper's Ferry?"

I shook my head.

"Didn't I tell you about getting the cariole? Didn't I ask you whether you had any use for a fur coat or some silver knives and forks and spoons?"

"Nothing at all: you asked me nothing at all. We've just come here."

"Yes," he said thoughtfully, "I believe you're speaking the truth, since I ain't seen you for two days or five or something. Steven, I've got the most beautiful picture: Philadelphia as Seen from Cooper's Ferry."

"I could use knives and forks and spoons," I said. "Leastways, my mother could. And what was that about a fur coat?"

"Let me tell you about this picture," Cap insisted.

"What kind of fur was the coat? Was it a man's or a woman's?"

"I dunno," Cap said. "I can't hardly tell the difference between 'em. I think it was sable, though I disremember."

"Well," I said, "I want that coat."

"I got to tell you about this picture. This is the most beautiful picture in the world. Philadelphia as Seen from Cooper's Ferry. It's engraved. You can see ships on the river and people walking on shore, all as lifelike as if they was alive. I'd ruther have it than any picture I ever see! There's another one there, an oil painting, twice as big, of cows in a field; but I'd a thousand times ruther have my Philadelphia as Seen from Cooper's Ferry. You can see a cow any time, and there ain't anyone don't know what a cow looks like; but it ain't everyone that can get to Philadelphia, and looking at my picture is just like going there—better, too, in lots of ways. It don't take up near as much room as Philadelphia itself would."

He put his arm around me. My head throbbed from the fumes of his brandy-and-garlic breath. "Stevie, there ain't a man alive powerful enough to get that picture of Philadelphia as Seen from Cooper's Ferry away from me."

I got him silenced and pushed into a chair after a time. It was a quiet gathering at first, in spite of Cap's noisiness and his eagerness to have my opinion of Normandy cider strengthened with brandy. When all of us, even the brown-faced boy with the pipe, had sampled it a few times I saw that Natanis, who had been brought up in the French-Abenaki town of St. Francis, could speak this whiny French tongue with ease, and that Jacataqua could make herself understood by the two brown-faced girls. After Cap had borrowed the stubby pipe from the little boy and sucked at it and then pretended to strangle, falling to the floor with a horrible crash that shook the house and writhing there in seeming agony, there was more freedom among us.

The two brown-faced girls, Lizette and Zhulie, prepared the dinner for the next day, which they said they always did on the night before. Lizette climbed a ladder into the attic to cut a piece from the meat hanging there, and Zhulie climbed down a ladder into the cellar to get vegetables. When Cap tried to climb the ladder after Lizette, a rung broke so that he pitched down and wedged his beefy body into the hole. It seemed as though we might be obliged to cut the ladder from him, what with the bland, helpless way in which he lay where he was, refusing to move.

Nothing would do but I must master the song he had been singing; so we kept at it and kept at it, learning the verses from Lizette and Zhulie, who sat in our laps to teach us the better.

> "*Nos amants sont en guerre,*
> *Vole, mon cœur, vole;*
> *Nos amants sont en guerre:*
> *Ils combattent pour nous!*
> *Ils combattent pour nous, doux, doux;*
> *Ils combattent pour nous!*
>
> "*On passe la carafe,*
> *Vole, mon cœur, vole;*
> *On passe la carafe;*
> *Nous buvons tous un coup.*
> *Nous buvons tous un coup, doux, doux;*
> *Nous buvons tous un coup!*"

In the quiet of later days the verses would come back to me, a scrap here and a scrap there. They were about love and wine. Judging from the French songs we heard at the Taverne de Menut in St. Roque's outside of Palace Gate before we were through with Quebec, all French songs deal with these matters, nor do I know any better things for them to deal with.

My eye was taken by the dinner that Lizette and Zhulie prepared as well as they could for keeping out of the way of Cap, who would lean all over them whenever he moved, unless they dodged him, which it seemed to me they made no pointed effort to do.

They took a piece of meat, not as big as my fist, and put it in a kettle with a tight lid. With it they put a part of a cabbage and some garlic and a few potatoes and three or four turnips cut into pieces, after which they filled the kettle with water and set it on the stove. On the following day, at noon, they took it off and ate what was in it. They had put in, it seemed to me, less than enough to feed one man; but what they took out was a fine, meaty stew, enough for six or seven persons. Meanwhile it had kept heat in the kitchen, which is a good thing in winter, since the kitchen is the place where the family sleeps, and guests as well, and any living thing that happens along.

Our host, Pierre Lemoine, said little; but what he said was to the point. When we spoke of the English, with Natanis interpreting between us, he used a word that Natanis did not know. He made an effort to get at the proper meaning of this word, but could not. He said it was not only a bad word, but a worse word than any of the bad ones he had heard used by Frenchmen.

What we did to the British, Lemoine said, he did not care, provided we left no dead bodies in front of his farm during the day, to cause talk among the neighbors.

When I told this to Cap, to soften his hard feelings against the French, he nodded his head complacently, as if he had invented the French people. "That's right!" he said. "These frog-eaters ain't got any use at *all* for the British. I don't know how they'd be to fight, but they're powerful haters! They hate the English something *terrible!* They ain't bad people, either, once you get used to the awful stinks around their houses—garlic and manure and their pipes."

"Look here," I said, "I want to be sure to get that fur coat."

We finished our cider and brandy; and Cap, taking a lantern, led me through an adjoining grove of trees to one of the summer residences overlooking the St. Lawrence. It was a neat affair, a wooden house with gables; but the inside of it seemed to have been struck by a hurricane, everything overset and twisted out of place.

Cap apologized for its appearance. "I was in kind of a hurry, and I guess I wasn't standing up so very well. Seems to me I never saw a house with so many things to fall over. I moved out a lot of stuff and packed it in the cariole."

"Whose cariole?"

"Well, that old Lemoine, he told me himself I drove up to his house in it, so I guess it must be mine."

He got the fur coat from a compartment beneath the stairs. It was, as he had said, a sable coat; one that would keep Phoebe as warm as though she nestled in a feather bed.

He showed me the cellar under the kitchen, and bragged of it as though he had not only built it but filled it. The bottles were all in racks, each bottle in a hole by itself, and I had a powerful desire to taste the different liquors, some of which I had never heard tell of.

Cap brought me a bottle with "Beaune le Greve, 1761" printed on its label. He thought it must have been this, he said, on top of some brandy, that had rendered him unconscious for three days, while still leaving him able to walk about as though in full possession of his faculties. Knowing a half bottle could do us no harm, we knocked off the neck and sampled it. I found it so pleasing that I took away four bottles, though warned by Cap that brandy was more helpful in this bitter weather, and safer.

We went back to Pierre Lemoine's farm, with the Great Dipper turning slowly above us and the tremendous cold flames of the Northern Lights marching across the sky. Lizette and Zhulie came out and helped us into the warm kitchen, where we sang *"Vive la Canadienne"* until long after the hour when honest people should be asleep.

§

I thought, when I looked at the weather-beaten farmhouses of Pointe-aux-Trembles, clustered drearily around a papist chapel on the desolate bank of the broad, ice-flecked St. Lawrence, that there would be no man of our little army, ever, who would speak good of the place, or hear its name without bursting into heartfelt curses. The snow was deep, and scarce a day passed without a fresh blanket of it being laid upon us; and full five hundred of our men had no rag to their backs save the tattered remnants of the garments in which they had marched out from Cambridge in the hot September sun.

Yet, miserable as they were, they had food to put in their bellies; and they lived in the warm, snug farmhouses of the long-queued French, neater and snugger than most of those on the frontiers of Virginia and Pennsylvania and Maine. Somehow, despite the scurviness of their appearance, they were followed about by the children and seldom spurned by the farmers' sprightly daughters. So in spite of eating themselves into stupors and heating themselves to the boiling point over potbellied kitchen stoves, and then going out into three feet of snow with their threadbare coverings, and suffering from coughs and quinsies and God knows what all, they contrived to endure their misery.

In after years I heard these very folk speak of Pointe-aux-Trembles with a wagging of their heads and a smacking of their lips, as though they had found it a place of heavenly pleasure; yet I remember how full of rancor they were at the time. Thus I have learned to disbelieve the tales men tell me of the delights of their younger days.

I had thought to avoid trouble by persuading Cap Huff to give his mysterious horse and cariole to Pierre Lemoine; but Cap wouldn't hear to it.

"Steven," he said, "you ain't got the trading instinct! That horse and cariole was a gift right out of heaven; and we got to cart away a lot of stuff with us. We got to have that cariole."

"But you can't keep it! They'll take it away from you—a colonel or somebody."

"Not from me, they won't," Cap said. "Not while I got my health and my trading instinct."

We had some trouble with the packing of the cariole, because of the vast store of goods Cap had unearthed during his three days of unconsciousness. Bottles of brandy and Beaune and Spanish wine had to be protected between feather beds. On top of the beds we placed cushions, counterpanes, blankets, and other odds and ends, including a few garments for Phoebe, several dozen handsome case knives and forks, and a set of dessert knives, which I knew would be gladly received by my mother if it should be my good fortune to return to Arundel. In among these things, where we could find room, we stowed firkins of butter and lard. On top of everything we balanced ourselves, Cap carrying the rolled-up picture of Philadelphia as Seen from Cooper's Ferry, he having made as much to-do over removing it from its frame as though it had been his major general's commission from Congress, engraved on gold.

There were some of Morgan's riflemen on guard at the edge of the town when we drove up to Pointe-aux-Trembles; and their faces steamed with excitement when they saw our cariole.

"Jeeminy!" said one of them, "where you been to get feather beds!"

He was huddled into himself with the cold. I remembered I hoped to go with these men in case there was fighting at Quebec, because they were wild enough to fight their way out of any difficulty.

"Where we've been," I told him, "there's enough truck to make you rich for the rest of the winter. You ought to be there instead of here."

The rifleman looked at me for a minute, then bawled down the road to another rifleman: "Hey, Buck! Tell Old Dan to come out here, 'n' hurry!"

He felt enviously of the blankets. "Any more of these left?"

"We can take you to hundreds," Cap said. "Blankets and brandy and silver and lard and beef and French girls just a-itching to sew up the holes in your shirt."

The hulking figure of Daniel Morgan bore down on us, his eyes a pale blue in the red of his face. "What's this?" he bellowed.

"They know where there's tons of this stuff," the rifleman said.

Morgan thrust his hand between the feather beds. I knew he felt the bottles, but he drew his hand out empty and rocked himself back and forth, missing no detail of our load.

"What's that?" he snapped, rapping his finger against the rolled picture.

"Philadelphia as Seen from Cooper's Ferry," Cap said. "Prettiest picture ever I saw."

Morgan grunted. "You never saw a picture of Winchester, Virginia, then! Where'd this stuff come from?"

"Down the road a piece," I said. "There's provision wagons passing all the time on that road. Seems as if there ought to be some men down there to stop 'em from carrying food into Quebec."

"One company enough?"

"Plenty! We could show you where these places are. I was kind of figuring there might be room for us in your company in case of an attack."

"Hell, yes!" Morgan said. He took a firkin of butter and two bottles of brandy from the cariole and started away.

"Take this, too," I said, fishing out a bottle of Beaune. "You'll be surprised if you never had any." He came back for it, tucked it under his arm with a growl that might have meant anything, and hurried down the road. I gave another bottle of brandy to the rifleman who had stopped us, and we trotted briskly toward Arnold's headquarters.

"I guess it's all right, Stevie," Cap said, caressing his picture of Philadelphia as Seen from Cooper's Ferry. "Your trading instinct ain't as bad as what I thought. I'd ruther fight under Morgan than under anyone except Arnold; but ain't they the thievingest lot you ever set eyes on?"

Cap took the cariole and our belongings to hunt for Goodrich's company while I went in to see the colonel, carrying two bottles of brandy and two bottles of Beaune hidden under my coat. Ogden was acting as adjutant, and a polite young man he was, very handsome and at his ease.

"I want to see the colonel," I said.

Ogden looked at the lumps under my coat, and winked affably, a gay and frivolous officer, and a better fighter than more serious men I have known. "There's some gentlemen from Quebec with him just now, but as soon as they're out I'll put you in."

"How did they get here?"

"Carleton turned out everyone who won't bear arms against us."

"How did Carleton get to Quebec?"

"Down the river," he said angrily. "Damn him! Sailed down the day we marched here. Now we'll have hell's own time getting into the city. He's smart!"

When the Quebec gentlemen came out, solid-looking men in fur hats and coats, Ogden held the door open for me.

"Well!" Arnold said when I came in, "I was looking for you to carry word to Hanchet, at Point Levis, when we started back here. I thought you must have run into the city to pay a visit to your young woman!" He said it pleasantly enough, but his face was swarthy and nubbly. I suspicioned he was not overly pleased with me or anything else.

"I was hunting Cap Huff," I explained. "I wanted to make sure he got into no trouble with the French."

His eyes rested on the bulges around my waist, and he nodded doubtfully. "Well," he said, whipping out of his chair and spreading his coat tails before the iron stove. "Any luck?"

I took the four bottles from under my coat and stood them on his desk.

"Whoo!" he said. "Beaune le Grève! 1761! Well, it might be worse! I'd rather have this than the word I just had about a friend of yours."

"What's that?"

"Colonel McLean and his detachment of Britishers had news of our coming while they lay in Sorel. That's why they hurried into Quebec three days before we reached Point Levis. These gentlemen out of Quebec say the news was brought to McLean by a dirty, ragged, sour-faced white man traveling in a canoe with an Indian. There's no doubt it was your friend Hook."

We looked at each other gloomily.

"When is General Montgomery coming down?" I asked at length.

He shook his head, his face lumpy and bulbous. "Soon! Soon, I hope!" He glared at me. "Great grief! You'd think it was a thousand miles from Montreal, instead of a tenth of that!" I think the both of us were recalling how all of us, starving and unshod, had followed him from Lake Megantic to Point Levis in one week's time.

"Sir," I said, "you know how I feel about Mary Mallinson, she that you call Marie de Sabrevois. If Carleton's arrival puts Quebec out of our reach, I'd like to try getting in with Natanis: just the two of us."

"By God," Arnold said, picking up his chair and thumping it down on the floor so hard I thought the legs must shatter, "it *isn't* out of our reach! Not if Montgomery ever gets here, it isn't! I tell you I can take that city, Carleton or no Carleton or a dozen Carletons! All I ask is men that'll stick with me and go where I lead them, and not go whining around about danger. Danger, danger, danger! Damn it, to hear some of these namby-pambies talk, you'd think there wasn't any danger anywhere in the world except from bullets and cannon balls!" He flung himself into his chair and glared at me, moving his shoulders backward and forward inside his coat.

"Look here! It's senseless for you to think of going into the city. They'd catch you, sure as shooting. Then they'd put you in prison, and you'd be nowhere. You'd never get from the Lower Town to the Upper Town. It's like trying to climb the wall of a house without a ladder.

"Put that idea out of your head and wait till we capture it. I tell you I'm going into that city, unless all of you run away behind me! When we're in you can go where you please and do as you please. What do you say?"

I have heard a mass of tales about Colonel Arnold in these last years: how he was a horse jockey and a cheat and a braggart, and how all men hated him; but I am setting down here the things I know from following him through two campaigns. Such tales are not so, none of them. He was a brave and determined man, nor was there any soldier serving under him who would not, at his request, follow him anywhere at any time. Those who knew him had great love and respect for him, not only General Washington and General Schuyler, but all other men in his command except those who had aroused his displeasure and contempt—and God knows there were overmany to do that in those early days. Therefore I said what any other man would have said: that I would wait. Then I went away to look for Phoebe, wishing she were well out of this numbing cold and back in our kitchen at Arundel, helping my mother to hook a rug or chattering with my sisters as to what the women in Boston were wearing.

All of these towns along the St. Lawrence are eight miles apart and as like as a basketful of potatoes, some having a few more eyes than others and some having more dirt than their fellows; but all smelling the same and nearly all of them called about the same, for that matter—Saint This and Saint That and Saint T'other. They are built with a single long street; and I had no trouble finding the quarters of Goodrich's company. The entire company was crowded around the cariole in which Cap still sat, not daring to move lest his picture be snatched from him.

When he saw me he let out a bellow of relief; and I could see the men, thinking Cap aimed to keep everything for himself, were of a mind to take all from him, like the independent Sons of Liberty they were.

I said at once that we would proceed to a division, and appointed Noah Cluff bottle keeper for the company. We cleared a space in front of the farmhouse in which the men were billeted and then passed out the brandy and the Beaune, having twenty-two of the former and thirty of the latter; and while all the others were shouting over them and counting, I gave Phoebe the sable coat I had found in the summer house, a fine loose coat, such as women of wealth wear in their carioles in winter. I thought, considering her fondness for breeches and sea boots, that she would be pleased, but not overly so. Therefore I was surprised when she squealed with joy at the sight of it, and ran, still squealing, into the farmhouse.

After considerable bawling and bellowing it was decided the brandy should be mixed with Normandy cider according to the proportions advised by Cap Huff, and the Beaune drunk after the brandy had been consumed. We gave up the chair cushions and butter and lard for the men to divide as they saw fit, and carried the feather beds and the silver and the picture into the house for ourselves.

We found Phoebe in the kitchen, staring at herself in a cracked mirror. Her throat was creamy against the softness of the sable; and her cat's-eyes, twisted around her forehead like a band of wampum, glowed against her hair. There was a redness under the brown of her cheeks, almost like the redness of the Beaune. I would scarce have known her, turning her head from side to side and striving to see all of herself in the wretched fragment of mirror.

When she looked around and saw me gawking, she put her hand on her hip, stuck her nose in the air, and walked elegantly past the two of us, turning herself a little on each foot. In passing, she opened her eyes at Cap like a frightened calf, saying, "*Oh là! M'sieu!*"

Cap dropped everything and knelt on one knee, holding out his arms to her and shouting mournfully: "*On Normandee noo boovong doo seedruh!*"

"Here," I said, catching Phoebe by the arm, and noticing she was no longer the pitiful skeleton I had felt on the Chaudière, "here! Stop this nonsense! Take these things to the attic and hide them where they can't be found."

There was dissatisfaction at first, that night, over Cap's drink of cider and brandy; but opinion changed as the night wore on. Among other things, the farmer's wife danced on a table for us, jubilant and frisky, and we taught the others to sing:

"*Vive la Canadienne,
Vole, mon cœur, vole;
Vive la Canadienne,
Et ses jolis yeux doux!
Et ses jolis yeux doux, doux, doux,
Et ses jolis yeux doux!*"

Now that I think back on it, Pointe-aux-Trembles was one of the pleasantest places I have ever known.

On the last day of November we heard that General Montgomery and his troops were near at hand, together with ammunition and the clothes that had never been so needed by any body of men, I do believe, since clothes were first worn. Toward noon on the next day, the first day of

December, men went running up the road toward the point, their huge, rough, hay-stuffed moccasins flapping and padding in the snow as though they wore saddle bags on their feet. At the point we found three armed schooners, all loaded with troops, and on one of them the general.

We cheered when he came ashore; for there was no doubt he was a great leader, this tall, soldierly man, slender and of distinction, with the marks of smallpox heavy on his face. We could not cheer as heartily when we saw his aide, Aaron Burr, now a full-fledged captain, racing about on errands for his general like my dog Ranger when he suddenly comes on a spot where a fox has sat.

Nor was there a cheer in us for his troops, New Yorkers, little greater in numbers than ourselves and as worthless and unsoldierly-looking lot of youthful knaves as could be found in any gutter. We were a sad-looking assemblage, God knows, after our struggle with starvation and the flux and the wilderness, nor were we any great shakes for discipline; yet we looked to be able to handle our muskets and to endure whatever we might be set to doing, whereas these boys of Montgomery's looked like street rabble who knew how to do nothing save draw rations.

Having seen these poor wretches of his, we were not surprised, when we paraded before him that afternoon, to hear him speak highly of our soldierly appearance. Men near me opined, beneath their breaths, that he couldn't know much about soldiers, and that we might look more military if we had a few shirts among us; but just then the general announced in a ringing voice that to show what he thought of our exploit in marching to Quebec he would make each one of us a present of a suit of clothes and one dollar in hard money, and that we could draw these on the following day. Someone bawled, "Huzza for Richard Montgomery, our gallant general!" and such a cheering went up as must have made him think we considered him the greatest man in the world—which indeed we would have thought anyone who would give us garments to keep us warm and dry.

I have seen times when our army would have preferred to go naked rather than wear British uniforms; but this was not one of them. Those the general issued to us were British uniforms captured at Montreal, red coats and white woolen breeches and black woolen stockings and a fine white blanket coat to go over them, almost foppish; likewise a red cap lined with white that could be drawn down over the ears, if need be, to keep them from freezing. There was no coat big enough to fit Cap Huff. He growled and grumbled at this outrage, damning the British army for being an army of runts; but it was a circumstance for which we later had occasion to be grateful.

With the arrival of Montgomery there was tremendous activity, what with the distributing of ammunition and food and the unloading of small cannon from the sloops—cannon so small, it seemed to me, that they might be good for the killing of geese in the guzzles of Swan Island, but of no use at all for killing men inside the walls of Quebec.

With these new men we had enough to blockade the roads to the city, and so there were immediate preparations to march back again to the Plains of Abraham.

Having no wish to be once more in the bad graces of Colonel Arnold, I went with Cap Huff to the colonel's headquarters to let him know that we were going forward to Morgan's riflemen. We found a crowd of officers outside, Major Bigelow, Topham, Thayer, Church, Steele, Hubbard, Hanchet, and Goodrich, all of them neat in their white blanket coats and red caps.

Ogden came to the door, bawling for Captain Hanchet, and Hanchet hurried in, his projecting lower jaw thrust forward disagreeably, and coughing a nasty, racking cough that seemed to start somewhere around his knees.

Bigelow watched him intently and shook his head, as though there were something mislikable about Hanchet. "He was raving like a lunatic when he came up from Point Levis with his sixty men," he said. "Told everybody Arnold was giving him all the dirty jobs."

"What was the matter with Point Levis?"

"Oh," Bigelow said, "bad food and no good quarters for his men, and the likelihood of being surprised and captured by the British; and it was cold, and the river might have frozen any day."

"Yes," Captain Thayer said, as mildly as though admiring a peruke in his own hairdressing shop, "yes, and it's my understanding the wind was blowing, and might blow worse."

"Oh, much worse!" Bigelow said primly, "and it might snow; and Colonel Arnold, being angry at him, might have arranged for the sun not to shine on his side of the river!"

Thayer broke off in his laughing; for from headquarters there came a shouting in Colonel Arnold's voice. We could hear him as easily as though the windows had been open instead of sealed against the winter winds. "You're mad!" he shouted. "Mad! There isn't a man in this command that would say what you said! Danger! I'm ashamed to think one of my officers should speak of such a thing!"

Seemingly Captain Hanchet thrust in a reply here; for Arnold broke out again worse than before. "What if their enlistment *is* up on the first of January! This is December, I'll thank you to remember! They're subject to orders until midnight on December thirty-first! What do you think they are? Newborn babes? By God, Hanchet, I'll put you under arrest for this!"

There was a banging of doors from inside headquarters. The front door flew open and Arnold stood before us, his face black and lowering. "Captain Topham!" he shouted. "Captain Thayer!"

Topham and Thayer moved forward, Topham, with his rosy cheeks, looking as though he were stepping up to receive a comfit for good behavior, and Thayer so meek and mild he might have been preparing to sing a song.

"Gentlemen," said Colonel Arnold, "our cannon must be taken from the sloops and carried to Sillery by bateaux; and the same bateaux must cross to Point Levis and return with our scaling ladders. I'm informed that this is a dangerous venture, because of the floating ice in the river. Would either of you be willing to undertake it?"

Topham looked at Thayer and said, "My men are handy with bateaux!" Thayer looked at Arnold and said, "My men are ready to start at once."

Arnold smiled pleasantly. "In that case, gentlemen, I'll ask you to leave it to the fall of a coin."

The words were scarce out of his mouth when Thayer was flipping a shilling in the air.

"Heads!" Topham cried.

Thayer held out his hand, palm up, and Topham peered into it. Thayer laughed in his face, doubling up his fist and making as though to hit Topham a backhanded blow, and went in to get his orders from Arnold. Hanchet came out with a half smile on his face, though I swear I would have no part of a smile left if such a thing had happened to me; and Captain Goodrich and Captain Hubbard walked away with him down the road.

§

There was a different reception waiting for us when we returned to Quebec. Carleton, to deprive us of shelter, had burned down Major Caldwell's comfortable manor house in which we previously lodged; and the houses in the suburb of St. John, nearest to the St. John Gate, had been destroyed as well. There was more snow, and a cold so bitter that eyelids froze together if held closed overlong. On top of everything Carleton had put cannoneers from the King's frigates on the walls, so when we struggled to our posts through the snow we were kept busy dodging shells and grapeshot.

Headquarters was at Holland House in the village of St. Foy's, three miles from St. John's Gate, but many of the men were lodged in the general hospital and nunnery, a mile outside the city on the St. Charles River; for the British, out of respect for the nuns, would not shell this building. Close as the hospital was to the walls, it was too far out for Morgan and his Virginians, who had no mind to waste time in marching when there was fighting to be done; and shortly after I joined the riflemen, Morgan moved them into the very shadow of the walls, quartering them in the suburb of St. Roque.

The buildings of St. Roque comprised everything from neat small cottages and log cabins and shops and warehouses to fine stone dwellings and the most celebrated inn of all lower Quebec—the Taverne de Menut, which was a godsend to us in that awful cold. The whole suburb huddled against the base of the cliff on which the city stands; and in the space between the river and the cliff were the buildings, or what was left of them, that housed the greatest thief in all America: the palace of the chief trader of the French King. The Canadians called him the Intendant; and the stone barn where he stored the King's goods and sold them at murderous profits to the poor was called La Friponne, or The Cheat.

These were forts ready-made to our hand. Once we got into them, we could peer up at the high walls and see the sentries passing the gun ports; yet they could not shoot down at us without leaning far out over the parapet; and this, they quickly discovered, was not healthy. Neither was it possible for them to depress their cannon sufficiently to hit us, so it gave us pleasure, each day, to slip into the ruins of the palace and La Friponne and practice our marksmanship on those who showed themselves on the wall.

We heard through spies that this diversion was considered ungentlemanly by the British; but Morgan told us to go ahead and pop off all of them we could. They would call it ungentlemanly, he said, even though we set off a rocket whenever we took aim; for no American could learn to talk or act or even think in a manner satisfactory to Britishers.

Yet these damned lobster-backs on the walls, finding they could bring no cannon to bear on us, pointed mortars so to drop thirteen-inch shells on the ledges above our stations. The shells, landing on the bank with a light charge of powder behind them, would roll down against the buildings near us and explode with a crash that led us for the first time in our lives to bless the French, because they had built their walls three feet thick.

We were strewn among the wrecked rooms of La Friponne one sunny morning toward the middle of December, pecking at British sentries, and enjoying our work because the sentries stood out against the sun whereas we lay in the shadow of the cliff, when one of the gunners rolled a pill against the side of our shelter at a moment when I was lying on my stomach with my head tilted far back and my cheek and nose pressed tight against the stock of my musket.

The bomb let off with a thunderous roar and jar that almost broke my neck. At the moment of the explosion something was hurled against me so I thought the walls had fallen on me, and I fit for nothing but a shallow grave in the snow.

I made a move to roll over and found a body pinning me down. I threw it off and sat up. It was Phoebe who had fallen across me, her eyes closed and a smutch of dirt on her face, so that she gave me such a fright as I have seldom had. I hauled her up with her back against the wall and felt her all over to see whether she was hurt. She was not, because in a moment she opened her eyes and said: "Why do you come to such a terrible place as this?"

"Look here," I said, angry at the turn she had given me, "what I do is none of your business! I won't have you coming out here! It's all right for a man, but you might be hurt, so stay where you belong!"

These Britishers, stupid as they are, have the luck of the devil; for one of them succeeded in rolling another small pill against our walls. When it burst I thought Phoebe would burrow into my side.

"What have you done with your leather belt?" I asked, for I could feel it was no longer there.

"It near froze me, Steven, so I left it off."

"Yes," I said, at a loss to know why I was so put out at her, for it was pleasant to have her by me again, "yes, and not content with freezing and starving and God knows what all, you must come pushing your way into this place. What is it you want? What have you come here for?"

"I came to find you."

"Well," I said, "it wouldn't have hurt you to wait. It was in my mind to look for you tonight."

"Tonight might have been too late."

"Too late for what?"

She plucked at the matted snow on the skirt of my blanket coat. "Did you know Montgomery sent a letter to Carleton asking for the surrender of the city? That Carleton won't receive any message, or let any man come near the gates, even under a white flag?"

"Yes," I said, "I heard so. There's no secrets in this army!"

"Steven, I think I can carry a message to Carleton. Will you give me the horse and cariole that you brought to Pointe-aux-Trembles?"

The thought fair graveled me. "How can you get in with such a message, when nobody else can?"

"Why," she said, "if I wear the fur coat you gave me, and a skirt, and drive up to the gate in a lather, early in the morning, with men running and shouting behind me, they'll never think of stopping me. If I say I have important information for Carleton, they'll let me in at once."

She was right: no doubt of that; yet I had no desire to see Phoebe mixed up in any such matter. Already there were too many people on the inside of Quebec, out of my reach, but weighing perpetually on my mind —Mary Mallinson and Guerlac and Ezekiel Hook. I had no wish to have their numbers swelled by Phoebe.

"Let me hear no more of this!" I said sternly. "You might get into the city; but you'd be thrown into jail; maybe shot for a spy, even."

"Now, Steven," she said, in the same coaxing way she used when she went at me to buy the sloop, long ago, "you know the British won't shoot a woman. They won't even fire their cannon at the nunnery, though we're living in it. If they put me in gaol they'd soon let me out, for I'm no spy, and they know it; and they have too little food for themselves to feed another without need."

"Well," I said, "there's other ways of getting this letter to Carleton without having you carry it."

"What other ways?"

"Why, any God's quantity of ways. They could shoot the message over the walls with arrows in the night. They could send Mrs. Grier or Mrs. Warner with it, if you're so set on having a woman do it."

"Yes, and if they shot it over on arrows they might find it when the snow melts in the spring; or if they *did* find it Carleton wouldn't take it, any more than he will now. As for Mrs. Grier and Mrs. Warner, they have husbands; and besides, Steven, they don't have a look that would incline the sentries toward letting them pass."

"Ho!" I said, annoyed at her assurance. "Since when have people been taking you for a duchess or the governor's lady?"

"If you had eyes in your head and knew how to use them you'd know there are worse-looking women than I!"

"Belike."

She turned a little from me and did something to her hair and dress; then turned back again. "Look, Steven. *Haven't* you seen worse?" She laid hold of my arms, so that I had to look up at the triangle of creamy skin at her throat, and the pointed chin above it, and so to the rest of her: the oval cheeks, with the red blood close under them; the velvety brown of her eyes, and the thin black eyebrows that seemed traced with a quill;

the peak of hair that came down low on her forehead, so her whole face was shaped like the hearts that Arundel boys carve on the old beech tree across the creek when waiting for their sweethearts.

"Haven't you?" she said, and shook me, and smiled a little on one side of her mouth. At this, for no reason I could understand, there came into my mind all of Arundel and the things I loved—blue sea and golden sunlight: brown reefs, and the white breakers tumbling toward the hard gray sand: the sweet, warm odors of the marsh, and the fresh salt wind from over the water; the cricking of crickets on hot nights, and my mother's face, and Cynthy leaning against me to watch me eat a late supper; Ranger, with his ears cocked up and his lip curled in a grin, inviting me to take him for a hunt; the suck of the falling tide in the river, and the sweet perfume of young willow leaves in the spring.

"Haven't you?" Phoebe asked once more, while I sat and stared at her, with the rifles of the Virginians cracking on one side of us and then on the other, and the outrageous thudding of British cannon shaking the ruined wall against which we leaned.

I dropped my eyes and said, "Your nose is red." She only laughed.

"Here," I said, resolved to stop her nonsense once and for all, "such a thing as you propose is not what a woman should do: not a good woman."

"I didn't think of that," she said in a small voice. "What is a good woman, Steven?"

"You know as well as I do. A good woman doesn't go gallivanting off. She stays home and behaves herself."

"But, Steven, do you think I'm a bad woman?"

"Why, damn it," I said, not wishing to hurt her feelings, "not yet you aren't, but I don't want you to go hurroaring and hurrooing into Quebec. It wouldn't be decorum."

"You don't think ill of me for coming away with James?"

"No."

"Nor for continuing with Noah and Nathaniel and Jethro after James died?"

"No."

"Are you sure, Steven, you wouldn't think better of me if I stayed home always, instead of sailing the sloop, and lived in the kitchen, speaking ill of all my neighbors and growing to hate the faces I saw every day, like other good women in Arundel?"

"Now," I said, "all this argument is getting us nowhere! I don't propose to sit here and yawp all day. I don't think you should go, and there's an end of it. Why is it you want to do it, Phoebe?"

"Why? Why? Well, Steven, it seems to me things aren't right in the company. Goodrich and Hanchet are together all the time, talking in corners. Hubbard too. He's with them. Hanchet hates Arnold."

"That's no news!"

"I know, but he hates him worse than ever. Arnold ordered him to move into St. John with his company, and he wouldn't. Claimed it was too dangerous. Arnold said terrible things to him."

"He'd ought to shot him."

"No," Phoebe said; "he did better. He shamed him. He sent Topham and Thayer in his place, and they went. There was never anybody hated Arnold the way Hanchet does. He says he won't fight under him. Goodrich and Hubbard, they sit and listen to him, and drink brandy, and agree with everything he says."

"What else?"

"Steven, I think the men have caught it. Their enlistment is up the first of January. They want to go home. Some of them say they won't fight. Asa Hutchins says he won't. Noah and Nathaniel will, but there's a lot that won't."

She took a deep breath. "I want to be some use, instead of a burden on everyone's hands! If James could have come here and fought, then I'd have been some use. Maybe if I did something the men would be shamed into fighting. I can't sit and do nothing, Steven! I can't! I can't!"

She looked down at her hands. I saw they were clenched. The triangle of skin at her throat was as red as a maple leaf after a frost.

"Well," I said, feeling very irritated, "cover up your neck. I guess you can have the horse and cariole."

I drove out to St. Foy's with her that afternoon in the cariole, fair mazed by the figure she made. She had on a hat of sealskin, one that pulled close down onto her head. Cap Huff, she said, had got it from one of Morgan's men, paying a whole bottle of brandy for it. With it she wore the sable coat over a fine dress of gray wool begged from the nuns. On her feet were enormous winter boots, made of sealskin with the fur inside, such as Quebec ladies wear when they go in carioles.

I felt like a coachman, hunched down beside her in my dirty white blanket coat, my face all bristly with beard; and I was shamed, stealing a look at her as she sat staring down at her mittened hands, to think I had spoken of her red nose, though God knows it was red, albeit not displeasingly so.

She looked up at me as we went along, and caught me gawking at her; and though I had meant to speak to her of many things, I forgot them.

They had her to dinner at headquarters that night, while I ate pork and dumplings with the men in the kitchen. Once, when the door stood open, I heard the general speaking to her about her necklace of cat's-eyes, and caught her reply, delivered straight and pleasant, Colonel Arnold and Burr and Ogden and Bigelow and the rest of them having fallen silent to hear her.

"Indeed," she said, "I didn't know it had so great a value; but I knew I wanted it; and what we New Englanders want is apt to have a high value. If we can avoid it, we never pay full value in money for what we want, though it may be we pay in other ways. You might say this necklace cost me a piece of rope; yet in the end it amounted to more than that. I had spliced a rope to make a running noose, back in my younger days, when I was captain of a vessel in the coasting trade——"

She waited for the shout of laughter to go down; then went on: "An Indian came aboard my sloop and hankered for the rope, so I traded it to him for a snakeskin case holding three needles made from mink bones. In Portsmouth I traded these to a lady who wished them for the running of ribbons through her fripperies; and in return I took a pistol with a brass knob on the end of the butt, big enough for knocking in the heads of molasses barrels. The pistol I traded for a parrot with a sailor from the Sugar Islands; and the parrot went to the captain of a Newburyport brig in return for two stone hatchets and a magnifying glass. The hatchets near wore holes in me before I came across the mate of a brig from Ceylon who was needful of them and the glass. He traded these cat's-eyes for them; yet it may be the time and thought I put on the matter had a value, so that I did not get the necklace for nothing."

They made much of her for this speech, though it seemed to me no more worthy of remark than many I had heard her make. In more ways than one they found her diverting, as I discovered from Captain Oswald coming into the kitchen to lean against the wall and take several deep breaths.

"Holy cats!" he said, when he saw me. "I never hoped to see that!"

"See what?"

"Why," he said, "that young lady of yours was showing them the bauble on her wrist, that little leather-covered bauble, and Burr picked up her arm with both hands, pretty as you please, as if to help them see it." He wagged his head admiringly and moaned, as at a pleasant recollection.

"Where did it hit him?"

"She looked up in his face as innocent as a baby," Oswald continued. "Oh, dear! It was lovely! It just tapped his nose, by accident-like, and he's out in front, putting snow on it, to stop the bleeding."

We drove over to the Sillery Road, the one that leads into St. Louis Gate, before dawn the next morning, taking a few men with us. When it grew light we moved forward to where the straight road begins.

"Steven," she said, when I got out of the cariole, "couldn't you find an extra coat and wear a pair of them if you have to go back to lie in that awful place again."

"Don't you worry about me," I said, low in spirit to think I lacked the firmness to forbid her going. "All you have to do is finish your business and get back here where you belong."

"No messages you want taken to anybody, is there?" she asked. For the life of me I couldn't think what she was getting at. While I gawked at her she whipped up the horse and went tearing around the bend onto the straight road, the rest of us pelting after and letting off our muskets.

Heads popped into sight on the bastions that flanked the gate. We heard cheering, very faint. Still we ran on, shooting and whooping, while the cariole drew farther and farther away from us, and closer and closer to the gate. When we saw puffs of smoke along the top of the wall we came to a halt and had the pleasure of seeing the gate swing slowly open. Phoebe, plying her whip, dashed through and out of sight. We plodded slowly back, followed by the distant jeers of the city's brave defenders.

Each day, after that, I walked to headquarters to see whether word had come from Carleton in reply to the general's message, or whether Phoebe had returned; and it was such a time as comes now and again to every man—a time when everything happens except what ought to happen.

Our men had built a five-gun battery in the snow near the suburb of St. John; and the path to headquarters from our turkey-shooting post in the ruins of La Friponne led behind this battery. It was a poor thing, not only because of the small bore of the cannons, but also because the ground was hard as rock, so that the battery walls were made of snow on which water had been thrown. When, therefore, our battery began to play, the British opened on it with every cannon and mortar on the walls. There was a steady whanging and banging from the city, and shells and grapeshot racketing past at all hours, and a hellish and inconvenient bursting of bombs where they were not expected. The walk to headquarters was no pleasure at all, what with diving into the snow every few yards to escape something that could not be escaped, if so be it was bound for you.

I have heard wiseacres in New England say knowingly, when the air is sharp and biting, that it is too cold to snow; but I have seen snow aplenty fall outside the walls of Quebec when we dared not open our mouths for fear our tongues would freeze to our teeth.

Along with the increase in cannon balls we had another foot of snow, and then we had a cold snap that made the preceding cold seem like a gentle, harmless spell of weather.

With these things there came sicknesses among the men, mostly lung sicknesses that drove them out of their heads and set them to babbling of their homes and of maids they had known in other days. On top of everything came the smallpox, bowling over five men here and three men there and half a dozen in another quarter. We took turns piling them into carioles and driving them out to Sillery and putting them into empty summer houses, to die or get well.

Thus there was a deal happening; but day after day went by with no sign of Phoebe, until four days before Christmas. On that day, along about noon, which was the hour when the cannonading grew slack and the turkey shooting, as our men called their popping at British sentries, was lightest, there was a prolonged rolling of drums behind St. John's Gate—a rolling so noisy that it brought our men running to St. John from every part of the Plains of Abraham, thinking the British must be sallying on us.

From the sound, every drum in the city had been gathered in one spot. There were heads showing above the walls, all facing inward, watching what went on within.

After a deal of drumming the gates swung open and a motley throng of drummers poured out, to form a line on each side of the entranceway. When their drums were rattling and rolling with renewed violence, a small figure came marching out between those massive doors: a lonely figure, like a little boat running on a vast sea before a wall of towering thunderheads. It was Phoebe, walking very erect, even proudly, and looking neither to right nor left.

We could hear the folk on the walls jeering at her; and through it all ran the beating of the drums, rolling and thudding in time to her steps.

It is no pretty sight to see any person drummed out of a city; and I cursed the British for lousy knaves as I ran down the road to meet this small and lonely figure.

News travels fast in an army, and it must be there was knowledge of who she was and what she had done; for as she drew nearer, our men came out toward her from the houses of St. John, cheering and waving their hats. Yet we never reached her; for a cariole slid past with a scattering of snow wads from the horse's hoofs—a cariole with Burr in it. It dashed out to her, whirled around, and picked her up in less time than it takes to shell a pea. So back she came in it, riding proud and straight; and the shouting and hat waving grew violent as they came up to the houses of St. John.

I thought she would not see me; for Burr was so busy being polite to her that he might have been a puppy snuffling at a wall after a woodchuck. But as she passed me Phoebe leaned back and called, "Come to the nunnery for supper!" With that she was gone.

The general hospital for the city of Quebec, which was also a nunnery, was a long stone building overlooking the winding course of the St. Charles. It was a mile from the city walls, and on the road running past the ruins of La Friponne and through the suburb of St. Roque, where the Virginians lived. I was on my way to it before dark, decently shaved and my head cropped by a proper barber for the first time in three months, so that I felt as slick as a mackerel.

It had a dank and sour smell, that hospital and nunnery; and it was in my mind, as I prowled along the corridor, peering into room after room to find Goodrich's company, that there was smallpox in the very air, and that I would not like to have Phoebe broke out with this horrible sickness, which leaves a person scarred forever if he lays a finger to the sores that becraze him with their itching.

I found her with Jacataqua and Noah Cluff and others from the company in the big room that lets off from the kitchen. She had gone back into her gray blanket coat with its gay red sash and her blanket breeches stuffed into moccasins. She was in no amiable humor with those about her, though pleasant enough with me, bringing me a dish of meat boiled with potatoes, and a stick of French bread, log-shaped and hard; less fitted for eating purposes than for shooting from a five-inch cannon.

She took me into a corner with Jacataqua, turning her back on the rest of the company. I thought she had become haughty from dining with generals and going about with beautiful aides, though it was not long that this idea remained in my head.

"Well," she said, "I suppose you're glad to see me back."

"Yes."

"Ah," she said insolently, "if I'd known you were suffering as much as all that, I'd have come out sooner."

"If you could have come out sooner and didn't, with me walking across the plains behind that battery of sparrow guns of ours every day, so to get to headquarters to see whether you were back——"

"Hindsight's easier than foresight," Phoebe said. "It may be I'd have got out sooner if I'd hit 'em harder."

"Hit who?"

"The men who came to the cell."

"Cell!" I exclaimed.

"Of course! Did you think I had the royal apartments in the castle?"

Jacataqua burst into tears. "They sent my darling George to England in a warship to show to the King!"

"Now here!" I said. "I can't eat my supper in peace unless I have this story in order. I don't want a word out of you, Jacataqua, until Phoebe tells me the tale from the beginning."

"Steven," Phoebe said, "I could have killed that man Treeworgy!"

"Get back to the beginning quickly," I ordered.

"Well," she said, "they took me to Carleton, a quiet, pleasant gentleman. When he asked what I wanted, I took Montgomery's letter from my dress and handed it to him.

" 'What's this?' he asked, and opened it, looking first for the signature. When he saw the name he dropped the letter on the floor and set his foot on it, saying, 'I hold no communication with traitors or rebels.' Then he called an orderly and sent for someone. While he waited he never so much as turned his eyes toward me. At length the door opened and Treeworgy came in.

" 'Do you recognize this woman?' Carleton asked him.

"Treeworgy looked at me as he would at something bad, and said, 'Yes, she's a camp follower: one of the hangers-on after the men in Arnold's army.'

"If I could have reached him, Steven, I'd have crushed his skull with my little club like breaking an egg; but there were guards beside me and a table between us. Oh, Steven, I could have torn out his throat with my fingers."

"Yes, I know! That will come in good time! Get on with your tale."

"He sent Treeworgy away," she continued, "and called his orderly again, telling him to take me to the Seminary and confine me there. With that he stalked from the room without my having said a word in my own behalf." She shook her fist at me. "I was in such a rage at Treeworgy I couldn't think! Damn it, I couldn't think!"

"For God's sake," I said angrily, "do you think I haven't waked up a score of nights sweating to get at him?"

"Well," she went on, "they took me to the Seminary: pushed me into a freezing-cold room no bigger than a hogshead, with bars in the door and window. When I was able to think again I knew they had no business to put me in a cell. I screamed and wept to be taken back to Carleton. The guards laughed at me. Whenever one of them came near, I hit him with my little club and demanded an officer. I broke the hands of three of them. Two started into my cell to take away my club, but I broke the head of one. He had to be carried away. The other wouldn't come in.

"An officer came, and I told him they'd have to kill me to keep me quiet. I'd done no wrong and was determined to see Carleton again.

"He was polite, even though he laughed at me. He went away; and when he returned he led me to Carleton.

"As soon as I saw Carleton I went to talking, telling him I'd done nothing, only brought him a message from a man as honorable as he, who was fighting in a better cause—a message that any gentleman should receive as openly as it was sent; and who was he, I asked him, to sit in judgment on his fellow men when he refused, even, to hear what they had to say for themselves—and how would he like to be judged, on Judgment Day, by a Judge who would hold no communication with those he judged?

"He began to glower and blow out his mustaches, ready to tell me to be still, so I whacked his desk a fearful whack with my little club and said Treeworgy was a snake and a liar and a traitor—a disgrace to him and his army: that I was a plain sailor woman from Arundel, master of my own sloop, and married decently and in order to James Dunn of Arundel, who died of exposure in the marshes of Lake Megantic: that if he didn't let me out so I could go back to you—I mean so I could go back to my own people before Christmas—he would be what every New Englander says every English general is.

"He roared until orderlies popped their heads in at the door. When I had fallen silent he said he'd turn me loose, and glad to be rid of me, but would drum me out of the city so nobody could hear the damnable wagging of my tongue—so I might remember the contempt in which every decent Englishman holds a deluded, traitorous rebel."

"Whew!" I said, "couldn't you think of something more to say to him?"

Phoebe laughed shortly. "I thought of a deal to say to him, but I was in a hurry to get away. I didn't feel comfortable in skirts, not in this weather!"

She turned from me, her hands on her hips, to stare at a score of Goodrich's men who, having finished their supper, had drawn close to hear Phoebe. I saw Noah Cluff and Nathaniel Lord and Jethro Fish, and the butcher from York, his face red and shiny, and one Butts from Wells, with an Adam's apple that jumped up and down in his throat almost like a frog; but I saw no sign of Asa Hutchins.

"Where's Asa?" I asked.

Phoebe stamped her foot. "He deserted, that's what Asa did! Walked up to the gate last night and joined the British! Asa Hutchins from Arundel! There's a nice tale to take home! Marched through the snow and the ice with the rest of us, and starved with us, and froze, and left the blood of his bare feet on the roads, and killed Dearborn's dog, and then went and joined the British, so he could get up high in the world and shoot at us from behind stone walls!"

The men stared at her, motionless and unwinking.

"Now, Phoebe," Noah Cluff said, "Asa's young. He don't——"

"Don't tell me anything about Asa Hutchins!" she cried. "He's a deserter! He ran away! What's more, I hear there's more of you want to run away! I hear there's a lot of you came up here to fight for your country, but kind of think you'd better go home without fighting. What's the matter: don't you have a country except when it's warm? Aren't you interested in Liberty when there's snow on the ground?"

"Lot you know about it!" growled the butcher from York.

Phoebe darted to him through the men as quickly as a mackerel gull dives into a breaker for a sand eel. "Don't I!" she cried, standing a scant six inches from him. "Don't I! I know the way to fight is to fight! What was it you came up here for? To see how far you could walk?"

The butcher from York turned away. She caught him by the sleeve and turned him back again. "Go ahead! Let's have the rest of it, now you've started shouting it's a lot I know about it! Did you come up here to fight or run?"

"There ain't no woman going to talk to me like that," the butcher said, his face redder and shinier than ever.

"Why, bless me," said Phoebe, standing up to him like a bantam, "you don't mean to say you *can* fight if you don't like the way I talk, do you? Not *fight!* Not with your enlistment running out in a week! You've got to go home in a week! You couldn't run the risk of getting hurt before then, could you?"

Noah Cluff laid his hand on her shoulder. "Phoebe, they's some things you don't understand, I guess."

"Is that so! Is that so! What is it that's so clear to you mental giants, but beyond my comprehension?"

"Now, Phoebe," Noah said, patting her as one might soothe a restive horse, "you know the colonel's a hard driver, and if so be we got to serve under him——"

"Don't say it!" she cried, taking Noah by the front of the coat. "Do you suppose I don't know what you're going to say, and where you got it? All that stuff comes from Hanchet. Every last scrap of it comes from Hanchet! Hanchet, the man that's got a grievance! You remember the time the pumpkin pies were stolen at Fort Western, and how Hanchet came whining around after them? He made a personal grievance out of it!

Yes, and he did the same thing when Arnold took all the bateaux and hurried to Sartigan to get food for the rest of us. He didn't worry about how much *we* needed food, or how near *we'd* come to dying if somebody didn't hurry to get it for us! Not Hanchet! We could die and be damned for all he cared! The only thing worried him was the way Arnold seized his bateaux. He was insulted! When he was put in command on Point Levis, it was a personal grievance! When Arnold asked him to take down the cannon it was a personal grievance! Did he think about helping us, or helping the colonies? He did not! He thought about his nasty little self with his sticky-out jaw! You've got the gall to tell me I don't understand it! How many Treeworgys and Hanchets are we going to have in this army to keep us from taking Quebec?" She stamped her foot. "I understand a cry-baby when I see one, and that's what Hanchet is! He's a cry-baby! He's got Goodrich and Hubbard to crying with him; and now you've begun to cry because you see your captains crying."

" 'Tain't so," said Butts from Wells, and his Adam's apple moved convulsively. "What I say is, an enlistment's an enlistment. We enlisted till the fust of January, and what they're trying to do is get us into a fix where the fust of January won't mean nothing."

"Nothing at all!" said the red-faced butcher.

"Nothing at all, like your talk," Phoebe said. "I never heard the beat of it! According to your argument, you wouldn't eat your Thursday supper if you didn't get it till Friday morning. You know as well as I do that if you'd been asked to enlist to the first of February instead of the first of January you'd have done so. You'd have enlisted for a year! Now you're whining you can't fight because you got to go home the first of January!"

She whirled on Noah Cluff. "Are you going to fight or quit?"

"I don't rightly know, yet, Phoebe," Noah said slowly.

"What about you?" she asked Nathaniel Lord.

"Why," Nathaniel said, "I came up here to fight; so if others decide they can't, I'll go with Dearborn's company."

"How about the rest of you?"

From some of them came a grumbling murmur; from most of them, silence.

"Well," Phoebe said, "let me know when you make up your minds. As long as there's any doubt, I'm ashamed to be seen anywhere near you. I've got to look out for my reputation. Come on, Steven."

Phoebe and Jacataqua and the yellow-faced dog went back to St. Roque with me, and I got them a lodging with Mother Biard, an old brown-faced French woman who lived in a log house stuck against the cliff like a sea urchin against the side of a pool, not three minutes from the Taverne de

Menut. She sold charms, which was how I came to know about her. I have no faith in such matters, but her charms were too cheap to be passed lightly by. For one shilling she would sell a charm certain to bring its owner safe to the one he loved, or so she said. I bought one from her, since she declared she would give back the money if the charm proved ineffective. I have it still, tucked in the corner of my green seaman's chest.

# Dog Days

## "Dogs In a Big Way" from FOR AUTHORS ONLY

Dogs HAVE ALWAYS seemed to me an essential part of every well-conducted home. When I say always, I mean practically always.

Like most persons engaged in what income-tax experts jocularly term gainful endeavor, I long had visions of leading an ideal life in a rambling farmhouse of great simplicity but extreme comfort—a farmhouse containing one hundred and thirty thousand dollars' worth of conveniences, but costing about four thousand dollars.

Those visions were rosy and indefinite, except for the dogs. I had clear ideas on the dogs that would surround and inhabit the farm. I would have several utilitarian dogs: a few setters to assist me in gunning for partridges; two springer spaniels to precede me through swamps and alder thickets during the woodcock season; a dachshund to make things uncomfortable for foxes and woodchucks that have retired to their holes; and above all I wished a lot of wire-haired terriers, for no particular reason except that they pleased me, even in their obtuse and imbecilic moments. In all, I figured, I would need about forty dogs.

I clung to this idea even when, in moving about my home, I stepped on the wire-haired terrier who had the freedom of the premises at the moment. On such occasions my nerves were harrowed by a scream more blood-curdling than that of a panther. Such screams, I regret to say, more often caused irritation than sympathy, and occasionally resulted in book throwing.

I have also found my terriers capable of staging disappearing acts more baffling than those evolved by Herman the Great.

One incumbent, Serena Blandish, developed disappearing almost to a science. At one moment she reclined on the front porch, staring somnolently into space. The next moment she was gone—vanished—evaporated. All work ceased while she was hunted. I liked her, and she also had an economic value, having won blue ribbons, together with those more concrete rewards of blue-ribbon winning: canned kennel ration, bagged dog biscuit, flea powder, condition pills, and worm capsules. The countryside was scoured. The neighborhood echoed to shrill whistles. Hearts were filled with rage and despondency. Eventually she materialized from space, like an ectoplasm. At one moment the front porch was empty—deserted. The next moment she was there, staring somnolently at nothing and smelling richly of ripe fish or rotted seaweed.

Subconsciously I realized that if one lost dog can cause anguish, the losses among forty would be harrowing; while cold common sense told me that if I were in a position to step on forty dogs, I would soon be removed to a cell for observation and treatment.

Yet I continued to dream my dreams of a healthy outdoor life, surrounded by a seething mass of wire-hairs, springers, cockers, setters—almost all kinds except the little pop-eyed ones that snore.

Because of these dreams, I went into the dog-raising business—or, more properly speaking, the dog-breeding game—determined to have plenty of dogs on hand when my visionary farm should become a fact.

In the beginning it seemed a mere accident. Later it took on the aspects of a catastrophe. What happened was this:

Some years ago, with the kind assistance of American consular officers stationed in Germany, I brought home from Munich a beautiful wirehaired terrier—the dog Dick. His background was as pleasing as his appearance; for his grandfather, a French messenger dog, had been discovered in a dazed state by a German regiment out for an early morning stroll behind a heavy barrage; and the Krauts, as they were then known in American military circles, had adopted him.

Dick answered to my notion of what a good terrier should be. His facial expression was both worried and assured, and set off by fine whiskers modeled on those of Chief Justice Charles Evans Hughes. He was tough and mean where woodchucks and other vermin were concerned, but amiability itself around the house, wholeheartedly joining in dinner parties and table games by placing himself among the guests' feet and silently enduring accidental or intentional kicks.

His reputation was excellent and widespread; and it was not long before an Englishman living in a near-by town approached me with a matrimonial project for him. When the puppies should be born, I was to have the one I liked best. My frugal New England nature was pleasantly excited at the thought of obtaining, at no expenditure, an amiable descendant of a dog whose amiability was beyond question; and consequently the marriage took place.

All this occurred during that golden period when everyone was keeping cool with Coolidge; and when it was known that Dick was a proud father, a number of neighbors requested permission to pay high for the descendants of such an amiable parent. Ordinarily a dog buyer is not interested in buying anything but just plain dog; but these were boom times, when people buy unaccountable things in the line of real estate, antiques, and dogs; and on the strength of the dog Dick's amiability, his puppies brought $75 and $100 apiece. Since the Englishman seemed to be and indeed was financially embarrassed, I waived my right of selecting the pick of the litter and allowed the Englishman to sell it for his own account and risk.

In the course of time a second litter arrived. The Englishman's fortunes had not exactly improved, yet he urged me to take the best puppy for my own. I felt that a bargain was a bargain, so I thought I ought to act on his suggestion. Still, the puppy was an extra-good one—too good to take for nothing, really; so although I scarcely needed another dog at the moment, I took him home with me and arranged matters satisfactorily by making a donation to the kennel. I think I might even have kept this puppy if it had not been for the inhospitable and unnatural attitude of Dick toward his own child. He not only failed to recognize it, but in its presence his amiability vanished. When people were in sight, he affected a cold indifference; but when he thought himself free of observation, he studied it with malevolent hatred. Anybody with half an eye could see that the little newcomer had what is known as a Chinaman's chance of reaching maturity in the neighborhood of the dog Dick. Consequently I was obliged to return him to the kennels.

He was an excellent specimen of puppyhood—one of those dogs known to English terrier experts as "reg'lar little lions"; and since I had taken him, I had to do something with him. The only solution seemed to be to give him away; so I decided to send him to a friend, a former general in the American army, who had recently lost a favorite wire-haired terrier.

The puppy was duly registered in the American Kennel Club under an important-sounding title, as is the custom in the dog-breeding game— some such name as Wild Oat of Hoosegow or Royal Asafœtida Persimmon; and then, as is also the custom among dog breeders, he was given a working or everyday name. Since he was to be given to a general, he was, with striking originality, dubbed "General" in order to distinguish him from his brothers and sisters. In those days I knew little or nothing about dog breeding; and since he was learning to answer when addressed as "General," I thought it might simplify matters to register him under that name. I was at once made to realize that this is not in accordance with the best practice among the fancy. The fancy, incidentally, is the epithet applied to persons who raise dogs—particularly to those who raise dogs in England. I don't know why a dog breeder is said to belong to the fancy, and I also don't know why it isn't considered good practice by the fancy to register a dog under his everyday name.

Unfortunately for me, when the time arrived for shipping General to the general, the general's wife wrote me an almost tearful letter begging me to keep the dog. It would be her lot, she said, to attend to the upbringing of any dog that entered the home; and since she had a number of things on her mind, she was afraid that if she attempted to add dog rearing to them, she might crack. Those were not her exact words; but the underlying sentiments were even stronger.

So there I was with General on my hands, wondering what to do with him. While I was still wondering, a dog show was announced in a near-by city. Lacking anything better to do, I entered him in eight classes at this show, at two dollars per class, and had my colleague groom him for it.

The grooming of a wire-haired terrier for a show is a protracted proceeding. Six weeks before the show he is smeared with wet chalk, so that the fingers can obtain a secure grip on his wiry hair. A large part of the hair is then wrenched from him by main force—a proceeding not without peril when the hair on the tenderer portions of the stomach is attacked.

A conscientious dog plucker will spend six or eight hours on the initial grooming of a wire-haired terrier, clutching the chalk-covered and fretful dog to his bosom with one arm, and deftly wielding a stripping comb with his free hand, or pulling manfully at clumps of chalky hair. When the job is half done, the plucker has the appearance of having slept for a week in a half-filled flour barrel and of having passed his hands through a meat grinder.

Following the initial plucking, the dog is chalked and trimmed at intervals until he rounds into shape and begins to look like the pictures of wire-haired terriers in magazines. In a state of nature, the coat of a wire-haired terrier is inclined to be long and unkempt. This sometimes proves annoying to persons who buy wire-haired terriers for fifty or seventy-five dollars in the mistaken belief that their dogs will always look like the pictures of two-thousand-dollar dogs newly groomed for a show.

General rounded into shape handsomely. In private life he had developed into an arbitrary and assertive dog, strongly anti-social where cats and woodchucks were concerned. He was also insolent in his bearing, and walked proudly on his toes when taken out in public; so there was reason to think he would win enough prizes at the show to keep his mother in kennel rations, dog biscuits, and tar soap for six months.

Unfortunately he proved to be show shy. When set down in the show hall, carefully chalked and with whiskers neatly brushed, he wrenched loose from his leash, shot through the door and headed homeward with low, quavering howls. When caught, after a two-mile chase, he was chalked and combed for two hours before the road tar could be extracted from his whiskers. On being placed in the show ring, he struggled to conceal himself beneath spectators. When hauled into the open, he cowered, panting, his tail between his legs, and groveled before the judge. He was awarded two yellow ribbons and a white—two Thirds and a Fourth. When a member of the fancy wins a yellow ribbon at a dog show, he is as proud of it as of a tube of cholera bacilli. It is something to be hidden from human sight; something to be mentioned only in hushed whispers up an alley.

Notwithstanding this catastrophe, my accomplice in the venture insisted that General was a good dog—a grand dog—a reg'lar little lion. Worth keeping, he insisted, in case anything happened to the dog Dick. It was about this time that I had the thought of going into dog breeding in a big way, so to be sure of stocking my visionary farm with blue-ribbon winners, all replicas of the pictures of wire-haired terriers in the magazines. It occurred to me that if I could pick up a few lady dogs to act as wives for General, I could leave him in the kennels and let Nature take its course. My colleague approved heartily of the idea. He was to manage the kennels and let me have—if I wanted it—one dog out of each litter. The rest of the progeny were to be his.

I distinctly remember that the phrase "pick up" was always used in connection with acquiring the lady dogs. My understanding was that, if you weren't in a hurry, lady dogs of sterling parentage could be "picked up" for next to nothing. That phrase "next to nothing" was also in heavy use for a time. I do not yet know its exact meaning; but in recent years I have become wary of any commodity that is picked up for next to nothing. Roughly speaking, "next to nothing" usually proves to be twice as much as I can afford.

I had several reasons to advance to myself as to why dog raising was advisable. For one thing, I argued, it would provide work for my English confederate, who was a mill worker and had recently lost his position. For another thing, I would pay nothing for dogs in the future. If I wanted a dog, or a dozen dogs, I would merely appropriate the best ones in the kennels.

And it would be a diversion to watch the little rascals at play. Nothing like it, I told myself, for freshening up the old bean when it went stale in the middle of a novel. And who could tell, I asked myself—who could tell what great oak might someday grow from this little acorn of an idea? I knew that usually there were seven or eight puppies in a litter. Sometimes there were as many as ten. I was sure that I had heard of litters containing all of twelve, even. Still, call it seven. Suppose, just to be conservative, we had tough luck and got a mere contemptible seven. If, out of each litter, five were sold and two were kept—one a male and one a female—the kennels would grow and grow until they—well, you could never tell what would come of it!

A short time after that I heard of a lady in Washington, D.C., who had wire-haired terriers for sale. To be brief, I went there and was shown an attenuated female certain, I was assured, to make a fine matron. Just the type, she was. I picked her up for $100 and shipped her to my colleague.

She was a disappointment. It was nobody's fault: not that of the lady who sold her to me, and certainly not mine. Her chief trouble was that she was interested in everything except the charms of motherhood.

We waited an unconscionable time for her first litter. It consisted of two puppies. We waited even longer for the second. It contained three. Since my partner was obliged to subsist during this period, it was obviously impossible for me to claim any of the puppies for myself, even if I had wanted them. None, even, could be retained to build up the kennels. In fact, it became necessary for me to make a few donations to the good of the cause; for anybody could see that my colleague could hardly be expected to board two full-grown dogs for nothing, especially since they were doing next to nothing to justify their existence.

It was around this time that I became aware of a singular peculiarity of men who wished to buy dogs. They spoke freely of their experiences with liquor dealers, and of the poor quality of the stimulants for which they were obliged to pay from sixty to eighty dollars a case. Usually these gentlemen were buying dogs for their children. Good-natured ones, they asked for—"a good-natured dog that'll be a companion for my wife and kiddies." The peculiarity was that they seemed willing, if not eager, to pay sixty dollars for twelve bottles of whisky, but protested at dispensing fifty dollars for a good dog that was to be a companion to their wives and children for years to come.

My confrere felt, I think, that I had been—to put it crudely—a bit of a sucker in my first pickup. That feeling seemed to be justified, shortly after the arrival of the second small litter, when another Englishman, living in an adjoining state, reported to my partner that he was confronted with a financial stringency. He must, he wrote, part with a wire-haired terrier matron of proven worth for a mere twenty-five dollars. Obviously this was a genuine pickup, and my colleague was at once dispatched to the neighboring state in a dented automobile to do the picking.

The transaction was marred by two slips. The owner of the pickup was hospitable; and when the sale had been made, he produced a bottle of homemade ale and shared it with my partner. That was the first slip. Having consumed half the bottle, my partner took the new pickup under his arm, climbed back into his dented automobile, and rattled off toward Maine. He had rattled about seven miles when a lady charged out of a side street in a hearselike sedan and struck his dented conveyance with a sickening crash. That was the second slip. A fragment of flying glass laid open his forehead, and the steering wheel almost pushed his nose into his ear. When, therefore, a crowd assembled and hauled him out of his machine, along with a dazed wire-haired terrier, his appearance was not one to inspire confidence.

Under the best of circumstances my partner is uncommonly hard of hearing; so when an impatient policeman appeared and hurled questions at him, the replies were not satisfactory. The policeman, in short, could get nothing from him but a faint, elusive fragrance of the half bottle of ale; and in a few moments my colleague was introduced into a cell in the local jail, charged with driving while under the influence of liquor. When money had been telegraphed to straighten things out, and the dented automobile had been nursed back to health, the cost of our latest pickup had bounded up into the neighborhood of the market price on elephants.

Around this period I came across a book on wire-haired terriers; and in it were references to the manner in which a number of the most celebrated English wire-haired terriers had been picked up for next to nothing during their adolescence. I spoke to my colleague about it, and he confirmed what the book said. According to him, there were mill towns and colliery towns in England where a wire-haired terrier was as much a part of every man's personal property as his trousers. Because of that, he said, you could pick up wire-haired terriers in England—rare 'uns, too: reg'lar little lions—for a song. I asked him if he meant they could be purchased for next to nothing, and he said, "Aye! You can pick 'em up for next to nothing!"

He agreed that if we could pick up a good English dog for our kennels, it would be an excellent thing. I felt instinctively that he was right: that if we could pick up a good English dog, a new strain would be introduced into the kennels; that the very presence of an imported dog was bound to be beneficial.

Almost everyone in the dog-breeding game seems to know subconsciously that an imported dog cannot help but have a beneficial effect on American kennels. It is one of the few things a dog breeder doesn't have to be told; it appears in his head from nowhere, without warning, just as dog hairs appear on his coat sleeve.

At all events, when I next returned to my home in Maine from the half-baked palace, I returned by way of England for the express purpose of picking up a new strain for the kennel. It seemed to me that the surest way to get plenty of new strain was to pick up a young wire-haired terrier matron in a delicate condition and carry her to America for her accouchement. To show that my intentions were serious, I advertised for the matron in the London *Times*, specifying that I wished a small-sized one.

Apparently, however, something was wrong. What it was, I have no way of knowing. It hardly seems possible that in such a country of dog lovers as England there should have been no wire-haired terriers in a delicate condition; and I find it hard to believe that only one dog owner reads the London *Times*.

The fact remains that the only persons who answered the advertisement were

(a) A man in Leeds who had invented a compound for both internal and external use, guaranteed to cure mange, eczema, ringworm, inflamed eyes, colic, and sore gums, and to be an excellent preservative for shoes and harness;

(b) A young woman graduate of a nursing home for dogs, who wished to give and receive references preliminary to obtaining employment as a kennel assistant; and

(c) An ex-army officer in Bath who had in his kennels a fine young wire-haired terrier matron, exactly what I wanted, keen as mustard, price three guineas.

Bath is a five-hour train ride from London, and I had no particular desire to make a ten-hour trip unless the outlook was promising. Even though hunting a pickup, I had planned to pay considerably more than three guineas—fifteen dollars—for the new strain I proposed to inject into our tottering American kennels, and I could scarcely believe a three-guinea dog would be much of a bracer. I called the Bath gentleman on the phone, therefore, and had a chat with him—a chat couched in the British manner, so there might be no misunderstanding—and misunderstandings inevitably fall to the lot of American telephoners in England unless the recurrent form of address is used. To say, "Hello, are you the man that answered a *Times* ad yesterday?" may readily baffle all but the most cosmopolitan Englishman. It is far safer to steal up on the subject, somewhat as follows:

"I say, I say! Are you there, what? Are you there? Oh, yes, yes, yes; I say, did you, I mean, I say, did you write a note in arnser to an advertisement in the *Times*, eh?"

The gentleman in Bath understood me at once, and assured me he had just the thing—cleverest little tyke in the world—keen as mustard—a pal if ever there was one; so without more ado I caught the next express to Bath.

Dog buying in England is less of a business transaction than a social function. You cannot point at a dog and say, "I'll take that one," and leave the premises. First you must have a spot of whisky, and a little friendly chat about the war and reparations, and whether these banker johnnies know what they're about. Then you can look over the kennels; and after that your future little pal is brought out for inspection.

English kennel owners have an interesting obsession, which is that any shortcoming in a dog can be effectively concealed by assuring a possible purchaser that the dog is a pal. "You'll be getting a pal," they say, with all the tremolo stops pulled out, and with the clear implication in eye and voice that if you buy any other dog, you'll be getting a dog fiend—a sort of hyena—that will gnaw off your ears at the earliest opportunity. If I learned anything in England, it was to take a second and more careful look at any dog as soon as the word "pal" was mentioned in connection with him.

In the case of the Bath breeder, the mustard-keen little pal was a dwarfish animal whose tangled coat gave her the look of an animated mop, but not very animated. She moved reluctantly when called; and if her owner had not given her age as five years, I would have suspected her of having reached eighteen, which is about the limit for dogs. Still, if she was expecting, as they say——

"When are the puppies due?" I asked.

"I beg your pardon?" he said vacantly.

"I advertised for one that was going to have puppies," I reminded him.

"Oh, quite! Quite!" he said. "Ah, but this little thing is such a pal! Such a pal! Just a pal, she is! Keen as mustard!"

The little pal stared at him mournfully and collapsed under a table.

"You mean she's not going to have puppies?" I asked, thinking of the five-hour train ride before me.

"Ah," he said hastily, "how'd you like to take that rangy one in the kennels, eh? Make you a good price on her, by Jerve! Forty-two pounds!"

"Is she going to have puppies?" I asked hopefully.

He shook his head and sucked thoughtfully at his pipe. "Tell you what, old chap!" he said at length. "Put the thing in my hands, eh? Something's sure to turn up, what I mean! Get you a pickup for forty pounds and ship it along to you in the States."

"The fact is," I said, "this is my first visit to Bath, so I think I'll be running along to have a look at the antique shops. It must be two miles back to town, so if you wouldn't mind calling a taxi——"

"Oh, I say!" he protested. "This is Saturday! Nothing open Saturday afternoon! Whole town's shut up tight as tight! How about a spot of tea and a muffin, what?"

"Well," I said, "maybe I could catch an earlier train back to London. Long ride, you know, ha, ha, ha!"

"No train but the six-o'clock," he said. "Do you no good, going into town this hour, I mean to say. Now, see here, old chap, take that rangy one, eh? We'll say forty pounds. Dirt cheap, old fellow!"

I reached the station, minus a pal, at seven minutes before six, after having passed the wide-open doors of seven antique shops.

It began to look, then, as if I was licked. It was obvious that if I traveled to many parts of England, accepting undesired spots of whisky from kennel owners who didn't have what I wanted, my funds would soon be so depleted that I would be obliged to swim home. Even more than that, my health would be undermined. I was, in a word, despondent.

At that juncture a friend told me about a lady who had kennels in a Surrey village—one of those invariably referred to, by British real estate dealers, as Old-World Villages.

I at once made an appointment with the lady; and on arriving in the old-world village I took an old-world taxi to her home and was thoughtfully given a glass of milk and a bun before being subjected to the fatiguing experience of viewing the kennels.

I do not know the reason for the widespread belief that the English are a cold and inhospitable people; but I do know that anybody who furthers that rumor has never tried to buy a dog in England.

Almost immediately I learned from the kennel owner that she didn't have exactly what I wanted; but she had what was known to the fancy as a débutante—a lady dog, that is to say, aged eight months, who was a trifle lame from having been caught under a gate, but was being massaged daily by one of the kennel assistants—a graduate of an accredited school of dog nurses—so that she was soon expected to walk without limping. This débutante, moreover, had won a blue ribbon at a local show at the age of six months, and was regarded as a comer.

I was, as I say, despondent; and when the owner suggested that I purchase the débutante for $100 and leave her in England until she had been successfully wedded, I agreed to everything. It was not expensive, the owner assured me, to send a dog to America; and it was easy, too: as easy as—well, as easy as easy.

Probably, she said, I would have my little pal within a week or two of the day when I myself entered my own home. No trouble at all! Just go home and whitewash the kennel, and before I knew it the little pal would be there, nosing about for rats, eh?

I recall thinking that this was really a simpler and better plan than my original one, since I would not have the débutante on my hands during the ocean voyage; and because—ah well, because it was.

The débutante was bought and paid for on May 6. A few days later I sailed for home. On September 20 a cable reached me saying that the débutante—a débutante no longer, but a prospective mother—had that day been shipped from Southampton aboard the mail packet *Aquitania*.

A week or so later the little pal herself arrived in a state of almost complete collapse; and with her arrived a bulky assortment of bills calling for payment of board and lodging for one dog for several weeks, transportation of one dog and accredited dog nurse from old-world Surrey village to port of Southampton and return of nurse to old-world village, passage for one dog aboard mail packet *Aquitania*, cost of one magnificent dog house with grilled door and grilled rear window to ensure perfect ventilation, export license from His Imperial Majesty's government, fees for customs brokers, tips to stewards, transportation across the city of New York, and expressage to final destination.

I meditated, when writing the necessary checks, that while the débutante's final cost seemed enormous, it really wasn't high, since out of the litter of seven or eight puppies soon to arrive, there would be three that would go to building up the kennels; while the other four or five, being practically imported, would sell for such stiff prices that my partner would be spurred to greater endeavors.

As the weeks passed, it seemed possible that our rosiest expectations would be realized. It looked, for a time, as though the little pal might have as many as eight or nine offspring. Unfortunately she failed to produce a single progeny. All that the kennels gained, as a result of my excursion to Merrie England, was a pal; and I might add that the pal was apparently permanently unbalanced by her lonely travels. For nearly a year her timidity was such that any sudden noise sent her into a corner, from which she emerged only when encouraged with a broom. She became a mother a year later, but had cannibalistic tendencies. Her first litter contained three. Two of these she ate. Later her tastes improved a little, but not much.

As I progressed in the dog-breeding game, I slowly realized that one of its outstanding features is the difficulty of retaining in the kennels a sufficient number of dogs to provide for future growth. When large litters are needed, the litters are usually small—so small that all of them must be sold. When large litters arrive, dog buyers are stubborn about paying reasonable prices, so that the puppies are sold cheaply—so cheaply that all of them must be sold. In either case somebody is obliged to make a donation to the kennels if the kennels are to continue to exist. I scarcely need to point out who it is that must make the donation.

The very best puppies—the ones that should be saved for breeding purposes—are fairly certain to find and swallow a splintered chicken bone or a peculiarly succulent cinder and perish unexpectedly of a punctured intestine. And too often puppies must be given away. This is something that few dog breeders can escape. Maybe the out-and-out professionals can escape it, but not a part-time member of the fancy like myself. One of the singularities of the human race is that people who would shudder at the thought of soliciting a half-pound box of candy from a confectioner, or of suggesting to a grocer that he send them without charge a dozen cans of tomato soup, will freely importune a dog breeder for a dog or an author for a book. It is an understandable frailty; for to any layman it is manifestly incredible that an author should have to pay for a book he has written, or that a kennel-bred puppy represents a large part of the sole income of the kennels from which he comes. This is a painful subject; and I will content myself with remarking that whenever a puppy is given away, somebody usually has to donate its equivalent to the kennels in real money. The donor is never the Rockefeller Foundation or the Carnegie Institute.

In spite of everything, the kennels continued to exist and to provide a bare existence for my partner. Therefore, when the dog Dick went racing importantly into the dog heaven, his whiskers abristle and his black nose quivering eagerly on the scent of the ghostly rabbits, woodchucks, and foxes that must inhabit those celestial meadows, I knew exactly where to go for one of his descendants. Here at last was the justification for the time, thought, profanity, and largesse I had lavished on what is known as the dog-breeding game.

I then discovered I had no particular yearning to replace the dog Dick. He had been a good dog, and good dogs are difficult to replace. However, the house was lonely, and the rugs looked bare without a terrier lying on them and cocking his eye at me whenever I moved; so it seemed advisable to take another dog. Unfortunately, the kennels were depleted of puppies at the moment, and harbored only one of Dick's descendants—a dog a year and a half old. I knew vaguely that when a dog has lived in kennels for a year and a half he has become a kennel dog and should usually be left there. However, I wanted one of Dick's children; so I took him.

Since my partner had fed him and boarded him for eighteen months, I could scarcely expect to take him without making some sort of return; and since he was a healthy, mature dog, I knew he was worth a great deal more than a puppy. So I made a substantial donation to the kennels, and was glad to do it.

In the kennels this new acquisition had been a hearty welterweight fighter; but when removed to unfamiliar surroundings, he lost his assurance. I took him to Italy with me; and at his first sight of a donkey he was so terror-stricken that he ran nine kilometers. I thought sadly of how the dog Dick would have acted. If he had considered himself threatened by a donkey, he would have gathered up a mouthful of loose skin on the donkey's cheek and done his best to slam him over the nearest stone wall.

Still, there was nothing to be done about it; and since it is impossible to set foot out of doors in the Italian countryside without meeting from one to fifty donkeys, the new dog lived in a perpetual state of consternation. It was doubtless due to this that he quickly fell ill. Medicines were rushed from London by air mail, and other medicines were hurriedly purchased by the American consul in Florence; but in spite of everything, he died after we had owned him three months.

It was at this juncture that I began to wonder whether I wouldn't have been happier if I had never been struck by the idea of breeding dogs. Life, it seemed to me, was just one fruitless donation after another.

When I returned to America again, I found three new litters, among them several reg'lar little lions. As a matter of fact, one was a lioness, some six inches in length, with a ferocious bark similar to the noise made by the removal of five champagne corks in rapid succession.

She seemed to have brains; for when her approach to the dinner bowl was blocked by two larger brothers, she impulsively inserted her head beneath one and bit the other on the stomach. In the ensuing fracas the lioness made for the dish and helped herself until her abdomen resembled a pale pink cantaloupe.

It seemed to me this lioness would, when grown, have possibilities; so I took her home to see how she blended with the rugs. Since she blended well, I made the customary donation to the kennels and went to work teaching her to keep her nose out of candy and sandwiches.

She was given the name Serena Blandish, won two blue ribbons on the only occasion when she was placed in a prize ring, and by the time she was one year old was under the impression she had terrorized all the donkeys in Italy.

In casting up my accounts, I did a little figuring on my venture into the dog-breeding game. Unless I am greatly mistaken, Serena Blandish represented an expenditure of a trifle more than two thousand dollars, not counting dogs withdrawn from the kennels as gifts and so paid for at regular market rates. On that basis, the forty dogs I planned to have on my visionary farm would represent an outlay of $80,000; but if they should be as good as Serena Blandish, they'd be worth it.

*Publisher's Note:* Mr. Roberts came close to carrying out his early plans when he finally built his farm in Kennebunkport. Welsh terriers from his kennels turn up all over the country; and two went to sea, one as mascot for the cruiser *Augusta;* another as mascot for the destroyer *Sutherland.*

—NELSON DOUBLEDAY

## Death of a Lady

*From* THE LIVELY LADY

IT WAS thick as pea soup in the Channel: thick and choppy; and it seemed to me there was trouble in the air; for Pinky lay in my bunk, his head hanging across my legs and his beady black eyes wide open, now elevating one bushy yellow eyebrow at the stern windows, then twisting the other toward the door of the cabin, and between times growling faintly deep in his throat; so in the end he drove me to dressing and going on deck at an early hour.

I could make out nothing in the fog. Pomp, standing his trick at the wheel, his face like polished ebony from the wetness of the air, jerked his head to larboard and said he had caught a glimpse of the *Chasseur's* topgallant sail half an hour earlier. There was no breeze to speak of; only light airs from the west that left us wallowing and creaking in the oily cross-seas, with steerageway but little more; so from our reef points and top hamper there was a slatting and whacking reminiscent of a hailstorm on a barn roof. The suggestion of a barn, indeed, was one that came to me readily, because of the barnyard flavor of our waist, where there were sheep pens and crates of fowl.

One of the men brought me a cup of coffee, stout enough to hold up a nail, and I mooned idly over it, with that early-morning numbness of eye and brain which often accompanies changeable weather.

Pinky stirred himself between my ankles, where he was resting, and peered out around my leg. Feeling his stub of a tail begin to thump, I looked around myself and saw Lady Ransome had come on deck, a dark green kerchief bound around her head like a Spanish fisherwoman's, and her fur cloak wrapped tight about her. I gawked at her, my cup half raised.

"Well," I said, staring. "Well—what are you—where——"

"Is it hot?" she asked, looking at the cup.

"Yes," I said, holding it before me as if waiting for someone to throw a marlinspike at it.

"Let me have a little," she said, and took it.

"Wait; I've been drinking from it. I'll send for more."

Even while I said it, she drank what was left, watching me over the rim as she did so. I couldn't, for the life of me, think of another thing to say, and only stood looking at her until she put the cup back in my hand, which was still half open in mid-air.

"What would your aunt Cynthy say if you gave her coffee like that?" she asked. "What do they put in your coffee? Rusty iron?"

"It seems to me," I said, "it seems to me you look thinner than when I saw you in Arundel."

She seemed almost to study over her answer. "How is your mother, Captain Nason?"

"She's very well. She helped me with this sloop. No: this is a brig: she helped me with the sloop I had before this."

"When did you see her last?"

"Why, only a short time ago. Last fall. No: it was longer ago. A year ago. No: it was over a year ago: it was a year and a half ago."

Speech deserted us, and we stared at the tide streaks always to be found in the dirty gray water of the Channel, which has as many crosscurrents as one of our marsh rivers within a few minutes of flood.

Only the night before, it seemed to me, there had been scores of things I wanted to say, if I could catch her alone for a moment. Yet now that I was alone with her, and she surprising me by seeming to be in a friendly mood to boot, my brain was as muddled as a bowl of lobscouse. Nothing would rise to the surface.

"There are sticklebacks in England," she said at last. "They live in the ditches. In London I found a print of a woodcock flying with one of its babies held between its knees, as you said. Has your head hurt since that day?"

I told her it hadn't, and wondered why I had to be so dull and stupid.

"I suppose you've helped other girls cut their initials in the beech tree," she went on. "Better carvers than I. La, how crooked my letters were!" She laughed a gay little laugh, though it seemed to me she laughed overlong. "I fear you're always following after the women."

"No, I'm not," I said, hoping my voice sounded stern and truthful.

"Why," she said, "there's one under your bowsprit at this moment. Aren't you afraid she's leading you on, Captain Nason?"

"Leading—leading me on?" I stammered. "She was a ghost when we got the brig. She was pale—she looked entirely different."

"And you had her changed afterward, Captain Nason?"

"I changed her myself," I said. I intended my words to have no double meaning, but I thought she eyed me strangely.

We stared at each other. She stooped suddenly and picked up Pinky, pressing her cheek against the top of his head.

"I saw your brother," I told her awkwardly. "A pleasant young man. I saw Annie too. Did you see Annie?"

She nodded. "You said nothing to my brother about knowing me?" she said.

"No, I didn't. Did you?"

I knew she hadn't because of her sudden interest in adding to the roughness of Pinky's eyebrows. "Why was it you said nothing to him?" she asked.

"I don't know. Maybe because we're at war. No: I don't know why. Perhaps for the same reason I didn't tell my mother about your picture."

"What picture?" she asked, wide eyed.

"Why," I said, wishing I had held my tongue, "the one you—the one Annie——"

"Where is it?"

I fumbled under my coat and had to rip the button from the pocket, so clumsy were my fingers. I got out the picture at last and unwrapped the silk handkerchief from it. I glanced at it before I gave it to her. Certainly, I thought, she had grown thinner, and there was a look in her eyes that had never been in them when I first knew her, and that was not in the eyes of the miniature—a look I have seen only in the eyes of prisoners.

She gazed steadily at it, turning it between her fingers: then, before I realized what she was doing, she dropped it inside the collar of her dress.

"Here," I said, "here!" and I found myself with my hands stretched out toward her, as if to snatch it back again.

"There's been a deal of trouble over this, Captain Nason."

"But," I said, "it's—I've carried it—you can't——"

"Where did you find it?"

"It was in my coat when I sailed. It had slipped through a hole in the pocket. I've never let it out of my hands. It brings me luck!"

"Luck! Lud! It brought me more talk than was ever caused by the Great Plague! Now there'll be no more of it." She hummed a tune under her breath.

"You mean you'll tell your husband you've found it, and he'll stop talking?"

She nodded, without interrupting her humming.

"Stop a minute," I said. "Shall you tell him how I happened to have it? And where I was carrying it?"

"Of course," she said, looking abstractedly at the masthead.

"Well," I told her, "if you've been talked at till you're sick of talk, as I suspect you are, I'd give the matter more thought. I think it would be safer with me. It's brought me luck, and I'll try to see no harm comes to it."

The man at the masthead shouted, "Sail on the larboard beam!" The fog, I saw, was lighter; much lighter; but still there was no breeze to speak of.

Peer into the fog as I would, I could make out nothing.

There was confused shouting near the forecastle. 'Lisha Lord came aft to say the lookout had caught sight of a craft with two royals when the fog lightened for a moment. How far away, 'Lisha said, he was not sure. A mile; maybe less: maybe more.

"Was he sure of the two royals?" I asked him. If there were two it couldn't be the *Chasseur*. She was a brig-schooner like ourselves and carried only one.

"He says two," 'Lisha insisted.

We peered to larboard, but the fog hid what lay beyond us. We could see it drifting like smoke above the water, with little rents and alleys in it, as though it were being pushed aside, here and there, by objects invisible to us.

While we stared and stared into that blank gray wall, our mouths open and our muscles tight from our anxiety to sharpen our senses a muffled, cottony thud struck our eardrums like a ghostly finger pressed against them. We seemed to float in a thick, motionless world—a world without breath or life; and as we waited so, a burst of cavernous thuds tumbled on each other's heels irregularly, like the distant barking of two monstrous dogs.

I knew on the moment what had happened, as surely as though I had looked through the curtain of fog and seen it. The *Chasseur* had blundered into an enemy craft of some sort; and what would happen to her, with no breeze for maneuvering, God alone could tell. In no other way could the matter be explained, and our duty, as I saw it, was to find out whether it was indeed so. There were two ways, I knew, of finding out. I could send away our boats loaded with boarders; or I could run out the sweeps and move the brig herself in range. Since the *Lively Lady* moved easily, I figured she might be swept up almost as quickly as the boats could be manned and got away and rowed to an attack: also I felt that our guns would be needed, and if I depended on boats, the guns would be useless.

"Get out the sweeps, clear the waist of lumber, and pipe to quarters," I told 'Lisha Lord.

He ran down the deck. Irrelevant thoughts popped into my head, such as that 'Lisha was from Bath and as smart-looking an officer as could be found on any British man-of-war, and that we were lucky to have him to point our guns. The brig was a turmoil of running and shouting, with the shrilling of the bos'n's whistle threading through it, as is always the case in a sudden call to quarters; and over everything continued the hot, sepulchral roaring of the guns, pressing thick, moist air against our faces.

Jotham Carr ran past, to turn my cabin into a hospital, Tommy Bickford at his heels to stow my dunnage and bring me my fowling piece. The thought of the fowling piece put Sir Arthur into my head, so I caught Tommy by the arm and turned to Lady Ransome, who had been wiped from my mind by the thudding of the guns. From the waist came a disquieting baa-ing and cackling, as the men hove the livestock over the bulwarks; but there was a faint fixed smile on Lady Ransome's lips, a smile that would stay there, once she had put it on, it seemed to me, even though the whole world fell to pieces around her.

"Go with Tommy," I told her. "Get your husband and Captain Parker.

Tommy'll take you below, where there'll be no danger. Don't be afraid."

"I'm not afraid," she said.

I knew there was something I wanted to ask her, but there were too many things on my mind, such as how these other vessels might be lying, and whether 'Lisha had kept shot hot in the galley, as he had spoken of doing. She stared at me over Pinky's head, and while I was trying to remember what I wanted to say, I saw Captain Parker step on deck. Behind him was Sir Arthur, weak-looking and the color of the little sponges that grow in the rock pools of Arundel, near low-water mark; so I knew he had been made ill by our wallowing in the calm. As they appeared a burst of gunfire stopped them in their tracks.

Parker shot a quick look at the fog that hemmed us in; then peered at the men casting loose carronade slides, tricing up ports, manning the sweeps, and running like ants with shot, powder, water pails, rammers, and muskets.

"Look here," he said, stepping up to me, "what's happening here?"

"Nothing you need worry about. Go below with Lady Ransome."

Sir Arthur's face was green. "Ow!" he said. "I can't permit this."

I remembered, then, that I had wanted to speak to Lady Ransome about the miniature; but now it was too late.

"Take your husband below," I told her, "and be quick about it. Keep the dog. He'll be company. Don't let him loose. He likes the guns."

She nodded, a bright nod, and went away with Tommy, the two Englishmen following her, and Pinky peering back at me from around her arm.

Moved by the sweeps, the brig was swinging to larboard, toward the hoarse bellowing of the guns. I told myself we must see the vessels soon, since they could see each other; that it was the Ransomes' own fault, getting into this trouble; that if they hadn't wanted trouble, they should have stayed in England, where they belonged; that I hadn't lost a man so far, only poor Sip; that my mother would say that what I was doing was all right, if she were here. That's the way of it with me, I'm sorry to say: When close to trouble, I can only think small thoughts that have next to no bearing on the matter in hand.

A spout of water shot thirty feet in the air off our starboard quarter, giving me a picture of how they lay, broadside to us and two cable lengths ahead. The gun crews, silent at their stations, pointed and whispered when they saw the spout. We swept off to larboard again, so we could come up under their bows or sterns, in a position to rake. I felt movement in our topsails, the beginning of a light breeze. In the same moment the lookout shouted again, and as he shouted we saw them dimly, their top hamper showing through the dissolving fog, their hulls hidden, except for patches here and there, in layers of smoke.

We came around more, until we lay broadside to them, our bow to the westward. They were pointed northeast, a pistol shot apart. The nearer one was a ship-rigged sloop-of-war, a corvette, with British colors at her peak. Her fore-topmast was cut through at the head, its spars and gear lolloping from the cap in a tangle. The mizzenmast trailed over the counter, with the jagged stump of the mast rising from the wreckage. Through the smoke we saw her people hacking away with axes to clear the decks.

Yet there was life in her, and plenty of it. The *Chasseur*, dimly seen through the smoke, seemed a ragged wreck of the swift brig that had skimmed the waves beside us on the day before, though I well knew that a vessel, though apparently cut to pieces, could be nobly patched by a skillful crew in an hour's time. Her mainboom was shot through, her foretopgallant yard was broken in the slings, and her bowsprit dangled in splinters and festoons from her stem. Her sails were riddled and shredded from the passage of grape and round shot, so I knew the Britisher's gun crews were shooting too high. In the moment when the two craft became clear to us through the thinning fog, a man pitched over the side of the *Chasseur's* maintop, hung by a knee; then sprawled downward to the deck, turning slowly in the air and vanishing in the smoke.

"Get at them with muskets," I told Jeddy, "whenever our people can shoot without hurting the *Chasseur*. I want no gun fired till we can rake."

The breeze died again, and the guns roared thunderously, almost in our ears. A little futile spattering of musketry set in from our tops. The men were under the bulwarks, stripped to the waist; for even in cold weather there is a feeling of greater security if no coats or shirts hamper the arms or shoulders, and if belts are pulled tight at the waist to ease the shrinking in the stomach that comes with fighting.

Our eyes burned and watered with the fierceness of our peering, for there's no time to meditate when creeping into position within easy range of an enemy, waiting for the gunfire you know must come. And creep we did; for though the men drove the sweeps through the water until it whirled and sucked, we seemed to lie motionless in the oily chop, except for the lifts and lurches of the brig as the waves had their will of her. Yet we moved; for there was a sheep pen clinging against our side, with three half-dead sheep in it; draggled, wretched, staring-eyed beasts that blatted and blatted as the cold Channel chop slapped unendingly at them; and this pen moved slowly backward from our waist.

We had swept a little beyond the Britisher before she opened fire. It may be that between the men needed to work her guns and muskets against the *Chasseur* and those who chopped at her tangles of spars and cordage, she had no men to waste on us, or she may have hoped to force the *Chasseur* to strike and then engage us. Whatever the reason, we were nearly ready to turn again and sweep under her stern when she let go her starboard battery.

There was a whirring and rattling of grapeshot above us as the smoke jetted irregularly from her side, a small downrush of severed tackle, and the rasping shudder that comes from being hulled with solid shot. I moved forward to reassure the men, but they stayed where they were, those at the sweeps pushing hard; the men under the bulwarks lying tight, some with their arms over their heads to guard against splinters, and some with their faces screwed around toward the quarter-deck, grinning.

I could see the Britishers ramming home charges at the starboard ports. We would have two minutes, I knew, before the next broadside: maybe three, and maybe even four. I could make out officers on the quarter-deck as the smoke drifted away; and I wished, as I had never wished for anything in my life, for a breeze to drive us around under her stern so we could rake them off.

'Lisha Lord moved from gun to gun in the waist, tinkering with them, almost like a woman prodding at her hair, striving to get it just so. Suddenly he straightened, whirled, and jumped for the quarter-deck.

"By God," he shouted, "it's the *Gorgon*! It's the damned old *Gorgon*!"

She let off at us again, as though in protest at 'Lisha's words. We felt the push of air against us and a hellish clattering and whirring all about us, so I knew she had pointed her guns better. To this day I cannot kick a gray-winged grasshopper from the dune grass of Arundel in late summer without feeling my heart turn over in my breast; for their whirring is like that of flying wood splinters ripped from masts and yards and bulwarks by round shot. I could see splinters pass in a shimmery yellow mist, and felt a quick ache in my left shoulder, where a small splinter had driven into me, point first.

The men at a starboard sweep were sprawled on the deck, knocked there when the sweep was shattered by a round shot. Our fore-topmast swayed, then buckled with a sound of rending timber, and hung loose and draggled. A man toppled over the edge of the foretop, twisted in mid-air, and clung by his hands. I saw Moody Hailey reach down, clutch him by the back of his shirt, and heave him back into the top. One of the men crawled out from beside a carronade. Blood gushed in spurts from his neck. He reached the musket stand by the main hatch, pulled himself to his feet, then fell again and lay still, a black stream moving slowly from under him.

Jeddy hustled a new sweep to the starboard sweepers, and Rowlandson Drown bawled at his men to cut away the fore-topmast. I pulled the splinter from my shoulder, thankful when it came out easily from the bone, and told Pomp to put over the helm.

"All ships look like the *Gorgon* to you," I reminded 'Lisha. Automatically I figured that if nothing happened to us we would be in a position to rake in three minutes.

"Like hell they do!" 'Lisha said, his voice shaking as if with cold. "That's the *Gorgon!* I thought it was the *Gorgon* when I got a look at her through the fog! Now I know it! Look at her maintop netting, made in diamonds! That's mine, by God! I made it!"

It was in diamonds, as he said; and as I peered at her, wrapped in smoke and littered with her tangled top hamper, it seemed to me I could recognize, on the quarter-deck, the burly figure of Captain Bullard-Jones.

Smoke gushed from her starboard battery once more. "One—two—three!" 'Lisha counted, above the howling and rattling that followed the discharge. "Three! They can't bring the others to bear!"

"Give 'em a gun," I said. "Keep it away from the *Chasseur.*" I thanked God, as 'Lisha jumped for the long gun, that the *Gorgon* had been able to bring only three to bear; for these three had left a ragged, furry hole in our mainmast, shattered the bottom of our longboat, and stretched Rowlandson Drown on the deck; while something, though there was no way of knowing what at the moment, had happened to our steering gear. The wheel had whirled suddenly in Pomp's hands, throwing him to the deck with wrists half broken.

I saw Jeddy run to Rowlandson and pull at his arm, looking at his face; and from the way he let his arm drop and turned away I knew Rowlandson was dead.

'Lisha worked at his gun, squinting and squinting. The deck jerked as he fired, and in the same moment the sternmost gun of the *Gorgon's* starboard battery, struck fair on the muzzle by 'Lisha's shot, kicked backward and exploded.

The crew of the long gun leaped like jumping jacks, sponging and loading. "Load with one shot!" I heard 'Lisha tell them. "There's a hot one goes on top."

He ran down the deck toward the galley, slapping at the gun crews. "Steady as a rock!" he shouted. "We'll never have no such gun platform again! Right into her guts, boys!"

We crept in and crept in, closer to the *Gorgon's* stern, but slowly: as slowly, almost, as the moon comes up beyond the brown rocks of Cape Arundel. Her masts, wrapped in a tangle of sails, spars, shrouds, and running rigging, drew closer together as we brought them in line, and up through them rose white wreaths of smoke from her guns; for still she hammered at the *Chasseur*, and still the *Chasseur* hammered back, though the roars of both had a labored, weary slowness.

'Lisha ran from the galley, behind him two men with pails.

I saw a long gun emerge from one of the *Gorgon's* stern ports and slowly come to bear on us. My muscles were tight as barrel hoops, and I wanted to crouch behind the bulwark for a second—for half a second even—to do anything except stand and wait.

'Lisha Lord shouted to the gun crews of the long guns. They dumped the shot from the pails into their guns, and 'Lisha ran for the forward carronades.

The *Gorgon's* stern gun bellowed at us. It was langrage—old iron and bolts and pieces of kettles and nails—and it screamed around and over us as though the sky were filled with angry cats.

'Lisha's first shot went through the cabin windows of the *Gorgon*. His second smashed her rudder. Our men came up cheering from behind the bulwarks, all adrip from waiting. They cheered and swabbed and cheered, and last of all 'Lisha ran to the long guns loaded with hot shot.

Perspiration dropped from Jeddy's chin as he shook his fist at the *Gorgon* and screamed at her, in a shrill, cracked voice, to strike her colors.

The long guns roared out of a welter of white smoke. Aboard the *Gorgon* we heard a muffled, anguished cough, as though some great hulk of an animal had retched in deathly sickness. The smoke lifted; the cough died; then rose immediately into a roar. The wreckage of her mainmast and mizzenmast reeled; and up from her midship section sprouted a bell of planks and cordage and men and gear, a bell that blossomed into a mushroom of smoke and suddenly climbed up and up into a flame-shot column, in which moved black, broken objects, turning slowly as they mounted.

A strange silence came down upon us and on all the sea as well. It was silence, and yet not silence; for in the distance there was a rushing noise from within the column of smoke that still mounted upward from the *Gorgon*, until it seemed to hang over us like an enormous maple tree in full leaf. We heard a rasping and creaking from our damaged top hamper, and a sickening moaning from a wounded man in the foretop.

"Lower away the boats," I told Jeddy. There was a walloping splash hard by our counter, and thumps here and there on our deck, followed by a rush of falling fragments, hurtling down at us from the sides of that cone-shaped cloud.

The hull of the *Gorgon* had opened out like a melon suddenly dropped on the ground, but now her bow and stern came upright again. The opening seemed about to close; then slowly and wearily widened once more; and the bow and stern, wavering and groping as though feeling their way beneath the surface, settled deeper and deeper into the gray water of the Channel until it came to us suddenly that they were entirely gone: that there was nothing left of the *Gorgon* but a welter of planks and broken spars and splintered fragments, with heads here and there among them, and over them a vast, ever spreading umbrella of smoke. From those heads among the wreckage there rose a faint, thin piping, like the distant calling of young frogs such as we hear in Arundel on warm nights in the spring of the year.

§

The men were knotting and splicing the rigging, plugging the shot holes in our hull and nailing lead over them, and making ready to fish our wounded masts and spars as soon, almost, as the boats had been lowered away; for they knew, as well as I, that the English Channel was no place in which to waste time celebrating a victory, especially when we were helpless as a shark with his tail cut off. We would be fit to maneuver, I knew, in a half hour's time if there was nothing to worry us but our masts and spars and rigging; for no seamen in the world are so quick and handy at repairing ship as are American seamen. But in addition to our top hamper we had our rudder to consider; and when we came to look at it we found we had no rudder at all, the rudder post having been cut by a shot, and the whole machine having wrenched away. Thus we couldn't move until we made a false sternpost, or preventer sternpost, reeved a rudder of plank to it, fixed it in place, and fastened the false rudder in turn to the main chains by guys and tackles. This is the devil's own job, and we laid out the necessary gear on the quarter-deck, to save time and trouble; and into this turmoil came Sir Arthur Ransome and his wife and Captain Parker.

I think there is some good in most men, at least in those brought up among decent people, although some Englishmen seem to take pains to discourage Americans in that belief. To me Sir Arthur Ransome seemed to be such an Englishman; and I wondered where I could stow that green-faced nuisance before he offended my crew with one of his ill-considered remarks, and so got himself thrown overboard. Even as I did so he came to me, radiating offensiveness. "Look here, Nason," he said, in that whiny voice of his that set my teeth on edge.

"*Captain* Nason to you," I told him, feeling savage from anxiety as well as from the discomfort in my shoulder. "For God's sake, hold your tongue till we've put ourselves in order!"

"Ow!" he said, stiff and contemptuous, "Lady Ransome asked——"

"She's not hurt?" I snapped, conscious that the very thought made the deck seem to lurch beneath me.

"She wishes to be of assistance to your surgeon in the cabin," he said, staring at the clotted splotch on the shoulder of my shirt, so that I was reminded to put on my coat again. "I couldn't myself: very squeamish stomach on the water."

I thanked him as well as I was able. The cabin, I told him, was no place for a woman; and we could somehow make out by ourselves. I never had any doubt that Sir Arthur Ransome thought me a boor; and just then he was no doubt entirely right, though I tried to console myself by thinking he had never had to supervise the making of a preventer sternpost and rudder.

The fog was growing steadily lighter. Directly overhead was a patch of blue sky. The cat's-paws were steadying, so I knew we would soon have a breeze from the west. The boats were coming back from the wreckage of the *Gorgon;* and men were swarming in the rigging of the *Chasseur* like snails on eel grass. Her bowsprit was in place once more, though the bobstays and shrouds were not set up; a new fore-topgallant yard had been swayed onto the cap, and the main boom had been fished. I tried to make out Boyle through the glass but couldn't find him.

Jeddy came over the side while we were reeving guys through the preventer sternpost. "It was the *Gorgon,*" he said. "Those people from the *Chasseur,* they say they'll make you King of Maine when we get home."

"Well," I told him, "I'd rather have their rudder, so we'd be sure of getting home. How many did you pick up?"

"Seventeen. The *Chasseur's* boat got about thirty."

"Any officers?"

"No; only seamen and petty officers."

"Any wounded men?"

"No; they sank."

"Is Boyle all right?" I asked him.

Jeddy looked at me thoughtfully. "They got hit pretty bad, I guess; but Boyle, he only got a bullet through that gray beaver of his."

I think the thought of Rowlandson Drown lying on the deck came to both of us at the same time, because Jeddy coughed and cleared his throat and said we couldn't all be lucky; then turned away quickly to attend to the *Gorgon's* men.

A patch of sunlight showed on the water near us. Ripples lapped against our side, and it occurred to me that if my luck were what it should be, the fog would have held on and the breeze held off for another hour.

"How long, boys?" I asked the men rigging the tackles on the rudder. One said twenty minutes; another an hour. A man screamed in the cabin, so I knew Jotham Carr must be taking off an arm or a leg. It came to me that he lacked practice in such matters: that it would be better for me to help him than to stand on deck with nothing but my thoughts to keep me company. I had no more than started for the cabin when I saw the *Chasseur* wear to the north before a light westerly breeze. I thought Boyle was coming down to see what he could do for us, and I was wishful of seeing him; but it seemed strange he should wear to the north when we lay southwest of him.

I saw him crowd on his studding sails, holding steadily to his northerly course; and so rapidly did he leave us under this press of canvas that even while I gazed blankly after him, the figures on the *Chasseur's* quarter-deck faded to specks and then to pin points.

Jeddy came and stood beside me, looking after her. "Well——" he said. "Well——" And with that he launched into a string of curses that he never got out of any book, not even one of Tobias Smollett's. It was in the midst of his cursing, when he had become so involved and fanciful that the men at work on the rudder sat back on their haunches to stare up at him, that the man at the masthead shouted, "Sail!"

Jeddy stopped abruptly. The men flew at their work again. We made out the sail, far to the northward, beyond the *Chasseur*. I realized instantly that the *Chasseur* had seen it first and set off at once to intercept it; and I thought to myself that this is the way of it, often, when a friend seems to go off unfaithfully on other affairs, so that we curse him and soon thereafter lose him as a friend.

What the sail might be we couldn't tell. It looked to me like a ponderous craft. I had my suspicions, and they were such as to give me an empty feeling in my stomach and a coppery taste in my mouth; for I had no desire that our cruise should end here in the gray waters of the Channel, with us caught like a rabbit lurching and squeaking in a trap.

I could see Boyle holding straight for the sail, and knew he would do what he could; but I also knew we must make a try at helping ourselves. If she should indeed be an enemy, as I suspected, she might turn off in pursuit of Boyle if only she could see us under way. It was this, I was sure, for which Boyle was hoping.

The hole in our mainmast had been fished, and a new topmast swayed up, fidded, and stayed; so that nothing stood between us and safety except our rudder. Due east, if my reckoning was good, lay the Island of Jersey, largest of the Channel Islands. With a light westerly breeze, provided we were able to maneuver, we could turn the Ransomes adrift close to the island and be safe on the Norman coast in the little harbor of Carteret or St. Germain-sur-Ay before sundown.

I thought about it; then called Jeddy and 'Lisha Lord to the quarter-deck. The *Chasseur* was hull down, but the strange sail, which she had not yet reached, showed the tops of her bulwarks above the water. We needed no word from the man at the masthead to tell us that a ship of this size must be a seventy-four—a ship-of-the-line; and since America had no war craft larger than a forty-four-gun frigate we knew she had to be a Britisher.

"Well," I said, "we'll try steering with the sweeps, unless somebody knows a better way. If we can keep before the wind for five minutes she may run off after Boyle." They said nothing, but stood staring into the north. As we watched, the *Chasseur* hauled her wind and went off to the northwest, to windward of the seventy-four. We peered and peered, hoping to see the seventy-four go off on the same tack after her, though we knew no seventy-four ever built could sail half as fast as the *Chasseur*.

"Some of these seventy-four captains," 'Lisha said, "they ain't so bad. Either they're moss-backed old pigs, not fit for eating or killing or anything else, or they know their business."

There was a dull, distant thud, more of a throb in the air than a thud; then another; but the seventy-four came straight on. 'Lisha grunted. "Threw a couple thirty-six pounders at random! He knows his business."

"Get out the sweeps," I told them. "Run 'em through the stern ports."

We made sail and wore around. As we came before the wind the sweeps seemed almost to hold her steady. She got fresh way rapidly, held on her course for half a minute, then yawed suddenly to larboard.

"Starboard!" Jeddy bawled. The men at the sweeps pushed hard at them. The *Lively Lady* shivered a little, wallowed back toward her course, hung for a moment, then yawed again and broached to.

The seventy-four may have been three miles off; but so accurately was she pointed that if she kept on as she was, her stem would slice us neatly in two, unless we could take ourselves out of her path. The *Chasseur* had come about and shot past her to windward, and now wore across her bows once more. Boyle, we knew, was armed only with long twelves, whereas the seventy-four must carry 36-pounders or 42-pounders: consequently it was clear to us that there was nothing more for him to do. Yet he would not give up. He hove a shot at her as he passed her bows: then tacked twice in quick succession, letting off a gun each time, though he could no more hurt the lumbering hulk that surged contemptuously on her way than a woodpecker could hurt the side of a house.

Rowlandson Drown's assistant had been a gangling young man from

Quincy in Massachusetts, one James Combs. At Rowlandson's death he
had become ship's carpenter; and it was he who straightened up from the
rudder, shouting, "Get her over." With 'Lisha Lord and Jeddy climbing
around and among them like two inquisitive cats, the men put this rough
machine overboard, then lashed the upper part of the preventer post to
the brig's sternpost, and bolted the two together to keep the false sternpost from rising up or falling down. There were men under the stern,
working half submerged, with one or two entirely under water at times.

Seeing that his attempts were useless, evidently, Boyle had left the
seventy-four and was coming down on us under a cloud of sail. Behind
him the seventy-four, less than two miles distant, towered upward like an
iceberg, glistening white and no less pitiless and dangerous.

The men worked at the tackles like figures in a nightmare, slower than
anything I had ever seen; and I was so desirous of getting free of this
enormous black-stemmed vessel and the triple line of guns along its side
that I was hard put to it to get enough air into my lungs. I stood silent,
my hands clenched tight in my pockets and the nails biting into my palms.
The machine was done at last, so that Jeddy set up a shout from larboard
and 'Lisha from starboard.

With two men handling the larboard tackles and two the starboard
tackles of our makeshift rudder, the *Lively Lady* wore slowly around.
She made as though to yaw; then held steady and slipped more and more
rapidly through the water, to the south, straight away from the seventy-
four. She was a mile off by now, a tremendous big ship, making the
*Chasseur*, close astern of us, look like a pilot boat. As we picked up speed
she fired a gun. Jeddy laughed and waggled his fingers at his nose. "Growl,
you black bitch!" he said; and indeed there was a look about her of a big
black dog showing white teeth at us, in a rage at having a dinner snatched
from her jaws.

The *Chasseur* came up under our lee, her crew swarming along her
bulwarks and high on her ratlines, bawling and hurrooing at the top of
their lungs, and waving their hats and hands until the whole brig seemed
aflutter. Boyle was perched on his aftermost long gun, but his bell-topped
beaver was not on his head, so that he did not make us one of his fine
sweeping bows. Instead of that, he reached up his hands, tightly clasped
together, and shook them at us without a word. It occurred to me he
might be feeling the same tightness in his chest and throat that I felt—a
tightness that came from knowing him to be safe and grateful for our
help—and so be averse to attempting any speech.

He dragged out his gray silk handkerchief, blew his nose violently; then
smiled and nodded at me. I thought he was about to say something; but

even as I cupped my ear with my hand I saw him cast a quick glance at our fore-topmast and stand staring at it, his mouth half open. At the same moment I saw the heads of all his crew swing upward as if drawn by one string, so that every eye on the *Chasseur* was fixed on our fore-topmast.

I needed nothing more to know that we were done: not even the ripping, splintering crackle that followed immediately as our new fore-topmast gave way two thirds below its head and toppled to leeward; nor yet the second crash following close on the heels of the first when the foremast, weakened no doubt by the break during the engagement and by this additional strain, broke off close to the deck.

A hissing groan went up from the decks of the *Chasseur* as she shot ahead of us, and as we veered around, dragged by the wreckage. There was a queer, absent-minded look on the faces of our crew and of Jeddy and 'Lisha as they stared at the wreck of the foremast, almost as though they watched a cat sleeping on the deck or some similarly harmless and familiar spectacle.

Boyle, I saw, intended to speak us once more. He came into the wind, then wore around, starting to circle us. The seventy-four, still a mile astern, lumbered relentlessly on her way. I turned my eyes from her, knowing I would see enough of her before the day was done.

"Work fast," I told Jeddy. "Get out boarding axes and cut all rigging. Lower away the boats. Get the prisoners on deck and into the boats, and the wounded too."

Boyle ran under our stern, his crew as silent and watchful as though we were strangers.

"Do anything!" I heard him shout. "Anything! Prisoners? Can I take prisoners? Any belongings? Can I take anybody? Anything?"

There was the least possible chance that one boatload of people had time to pass from us to the *Chasseur*.

I turned to look at the Ransomes and Captain Parker. There was a smug look about Parker and Sir Arthur, for which I could not blame them; but Lady Ransome's face I could not see, because she was sitting on the deck, with Pinky still in her arms, and was too busy with him to notice me.

"No, indeed, thank you," Sir Arthur said, in answer to my unspoken question, and I remember how mislikable I found his pronunciation of "thank you," which was "think yaw." "No, indeed! We'll stay where we are!"

I waved to Boyle to go on. "Stand by," I called to him, "until the *Lively Lady's* gone. I don't want her taken!"

Boyle nodded vigorously; the *Chasseur* slipped away into the south;

and to me her departure seemed like that of an old, dear friend, so that my heart was like lead.

The seventy-four was close on us: no more than a half mile away. Our prisoners were on deck and our boats in the water, and Jotham Carr was seeing to bringing the wounded from the cabin. There was only one thing left to be done. Since I wished to be sure it *was* done, I warned Jeddy not to strike our colors till I returned; and with that I ran forward and down into the carpenter's quarters.

There was an old roundabout jacket belonging to Rowlandson Drown lying on the bench, where he had dropped it less than ten minutes before he was killed. I picked it up and hung it on a nail and tried not to think about it as I poured varnish over the shavings and worked with my phosphorus bottle and a match to get a light.

The drenched shavings burst into flames with a roar, and I fled back on deck pursued by a blast of heat that singed my shirt. The seventy-four, hove to at pistol-shot distance, was like a black cliff, bristling with guns. Her bulwarks, rigging and ports were aswarm with men—as many as can be found in Arundel and Cape Porpus put together.

At the sight of me, Jeddy pulled down our colors with such eagerness that I knew the seventy-four had been threatening to throw a shot at us if it was not done speedily.

I looked around, but could see nothing else that needed doing. Lady Ransome sat in the stern of the longboat, still with Pinky in her arms. Beside her sat her husband, his blanket full of belongings at his feet. I sent them away; then shouted up to the gold epaulettes shining above the gaily painted taffrail that we were on·fire and needed boats. After that, as well as I could for the·growing heaviness in my head, I took my last look at the *Lively Lady*.

They wasted no time getting us aboard, for a burning privateer is no welcome neighbor to any ship. Knowing the customs of our captors, I thought they would put us in that stinking, three-foot-high den in the bows known as the cable tier, and leave us to rot in the dark on the slime-covered coils of the cable. I have no doubt that if this seventy-four had been one of the ships used for transporting American prisoners, we would have received the same inhuman treatment suffered by thousands of captured Americans during the war; but it had fallen to our lot to be taken by the *Granicus*, Captain Wise commanding, and this Captain Wise was as pleasant and as easy to be with as any of our own great captains. Why Decatur and Perry and Lawrence and Hull and MacDonough should be quiet, companionable, polite, pleasant, thoughtful men, and the greatest of our fighters to boot, and why our incompetents should have been selfish blusterers, I do not know; but that was the truth of it. The captains I have named would not, I have heard men say, permit their crews to be whipped for offenses, and this was also true of Wise; but throughout the entire British navy of more than eight hundred ships there was hardly an officer who would not tie up any member of his crew for the smallest infraction of discipline and see his back chopped into bleeding mincemeat. I say here, in no spirit of rancor, that British naval officers, taking them by and large, were more cruel and brutal than can possibly be realized by persons who are sheltered in peaceful homes, and sleep securely on soft beds under warm blankets; so to find myself in the hands of a man like Wise was as great a surprise as to drop a hook among a school of sculpins and catch a fat beefsteak.

We were paraded before him as soon as we were aboard. He stood at the quarter-deck rail, staring down at us, a thin, tall man, possibly fifty years of age. His hair was crinkly brown, heavily shot with gray; and he had a habit of half closing his eyes before he spoke, so that he seemed about to deliver himself of an angry remark.

"I'm told," he said to us gruffly, "that the prisoners aboard your brig were well treated, and I'm a believer in turn about. I'll therefore put you to lodge on the orlop deck, and you'll be in charge of your own officers until you pass out of my control and into the hands of the Transport Office. I expect orderly conduct from you, even though I've heard that such a thing is seldom found where American seamen are concerned. Until I'm disabused you'll receive the same rations issued to the people of this man-of-war."

He turned on his heel; then swung back to us again. "I'd like to see your captain in my cabin."

When I stepped forward he nodded curtly. spoke briefly to a young officer near him, and walked off without another word. Tommy Bickford would have followed me with my duffel bag; but a red-coated marine took it from him.

I cast a final look around as I mounted to the quarter-deck of this towering vessel. Back under our lee, a smudge of black smoke pouring from her forward hatch, lay the *Lively Lady*, forlorn and untidy, her foremast dragging in the Channel chop; her mainsail lying half over the side, slack and useless, like a broken wing. A mile to the south I saw the *Chasseur* slipping toward the southeast. Even as I looked she hauled her wind and stood back toward us again, so I knew there would be no better days in store for the poor hulk we had just left. Boyle would sink her if she didn't sink herself. I tried to remember, watching her, when it was I had brought the cheese to Boyle; but I could only remember it was long, long ago.

The young officer spoke to me, sharp and haughty, ordering me to follow; and I stumbled after him with a slack and gone feeling, as though my legs and brain were stuffed with straw.

The captain's cabin in one of these British seventy-fours is a palace by itself, rising from the rear of the quarter-deck like a rich house set down at the end of a village green; and I, entering it, felt myself shabby, with something of mendicancy and disgraceful misfortune about me.

The young officer rapped at a paneled door and stood aside for me to pass in, looking as though he wished me the worst luck in the world. I entered a low-ceiled room that seemed enormous, larger than our living room in Arundel, and stood before this tall, thin, crinkly-haired captain. He had laid aside his great cocked hat and was sitting at a polished table with a hand on either knee and his lips pursed as though he intended to clap me in chains for life.

"I've been told, sir," he said, without preamble, "that you purposely set fire to a prize."

"No, sir; I did not."

"I have the word of an Englishman for it!" He eyed me coldly. "I have his word you shouted to the commanding officer of the privateer brig that annoyed me so determinedly before I came up with you. You told him to stand by until your vessel had been destroyed."

"I didn't strike my colors until after the fire had broken out," I said.

"Then you set the fire?"

"Yes, sir."

"Then in effect you set fire to British property; for you had no means of escaping and were as good as captured."

"It wasn't a prize till I struck my colors," I repeated, feeling dull and numb. "You might have blown up."

Despite my hair splitting, he gave me a courteous reply.

"So I might! So I might! I never thought of that!" He compressed his lips again and made a flirting motion with his hand. "That's no reason, however. If you destroyed a prize with no greater justification, I shall be forced to take steps. I'll be forced to make representations to the Transport Office."

There was a dull roar far astern, like the muffled rumble of a nearing thunderstorm, and I knew I would never set eyes on the *Lively Lady* again. Something seemed to go from me, so that I could hardly stand on my feet before this captain, who suddenly appeared to me more powerful than any man I had ever met. I saw he was waiting for me to speak.

"Well," I said, "there was no way out of it. I passed my word."

He frowned. "Come, come, Captain! You'd better tell me the full tale. And let me have your name, while you're about it."

"Nason; the *Lively Lady*, eighteen guns and——"

"Yes," he said, flirting his hand again, "yes, yes! Wise is my name: *Granicus*, seventy-four. Now, Captain Nason."

"Well," I said, "there it is." For the life of me I couldn't remember what he'd asked me.

Captain Wise eyed me closely. "So you passed your word, did you?"

"Yes. I couldn't get the brig till I passed my word she shouldn't fall into the hands of the British. I passed my word, and so I got her."

"Indeed! And to whom did you pass your word?"

"Robert Surcouf," I said. "Fox-faced man. Damned French pirate. Asked double what she was worth and made me give my word to boot."

"Was that Surcouf of St. Malo?"

"Yes. Surcouf. Look out for him. Had to have her, and he traded close, damn him. There's worse people than Yankees, and you can tie to it."

"And where did Surcouf get her?" he wanted to know. It seemed to me his face had come loose from its fastenings, for it appeared to slip sideways: then waver back into place.

"Get her?" I asked. "He built her! The *Revenant*. Meant *Revenge*, Jeddy said. He's a crazy little fool. She never meant *Revenge*. She's a ghost. I mean she *was* the *Ghost*. I took her out of the grave, Captain, and made her the *Lively Lady*, but now she's a ghost that's laid for good, green dress, red hair, and all."

With that, feeling somewhat upset because of the throbbing in my shoulder, I laughed at the thought of the ghost that had been laid—laughed till the tears ran down my cheeks and till I had to hang to the table. Then I found myself in a chair, drinking a glass of brandy, and heard Captain Wise at the cabin door, passing the word for the surgeon.

"Well, well," he said, "well, well, well, well! So that was the *Revenant!* Well, well, well! I should have you shot for that, my boy! Well, well, well, well! The *Revenant*."

I might have fallen asleep from the persistence with which he repeated himself and the regularity with which he nodded his head as he sat staring at me, if the surgeon had not come in, a man both pompous and obsequious, followed by a pimply-faced assistant smelling of medicines.

"Now," Wise said, "anything wrong with you? Get hurt this morning?"

"No," I said, not liking the looks of the surgeon. "Nothing. Nothing at all."

The surgeon's assistant had my coat off and whipped the shirt over my head before I could down the last of my brandy.

"Pretty!" the surgeon said, looking at my shoulder. "Sweet as a daisy.

Very finely cushioned by the deltoid muscle." He prodded me with a forefinger like a red banana. "Hm! Hard! Surprised the splinter didn't bounce off! Take out half a pint of blood and he'll be better than ever!"

He bled me, as I knew he would; for these navy surgeons bleed a man for everything under God's heaven—for headache, toothache, and footache; for burns, frostbites, loss of memory, and even loss of blood. Whenever they don't know what to do, they bleed their patients; and since they seldom know what to do they're forever bleeding someone. Yet I must admit that when he had taken a cupful of blood from my arm I felt relieved.

"How'll he do for dinner?" Captain Wise asked the surgeon, while the assistant helped me on with my shirt.

"Admirably," the surgeon said. "Ten minutes' rest and he'll be fit to eat a sheep!" He went away with his assistant, wheezing mirthfully like a porpoise clearing his nose of a vast accumulation of air and water.

"Yes," Captain Wise said, "a bite of dinner'll do you no harm. It'll occupy your mind and improve my own. I've heard monstrous strange tales about Americans, but I've had few opportunities to speak with them."

The wheezy surgeon was right; for after I had stretched myself for a time on the berth in the small gun-deck cabin in which I was stowed by the captain's orders, and had freed myself of blood and powder stains and struggled into the clean clothes Tommy Bickford had stuffed in my duffel bag, there was a stiffness in my shoulder; but the blackness that filled my brain after the blowing up of the *Lively Lady* had fallen away, as the tide falls on our Arundel beaches, though now and again a black wave came out of the receding tide and lapped at my brain once more, as I suppose must always be the case whenever a tide goes out.

Sir Arthur and Lady Ransome were in the captain's cabin when I went to it, and Captain Parker as well; and I cannot deny feeling bitter when I saw how they had become gay and lighthearted and inclined to toss scraps of gaiety to me, whether I wanted them or not.

"Ow, Captain," Sir Arthur said, as I came toward them, "we owe you an apology, I fear, for making you a trifle late for your appointment at the Island of Jersey."

I smiled as pleasantly as I could.

"Jersey!" Captain Wise exclaimed. "Weren't you getting a little deep in enemy waters?"

Sir Arthur laughed spitefully. "You'd not have thought so, Captain, if you'd heard Mr. Nason making free with our Channel, no longer ago than last night! You'd have thought the place was full of his friends! He was talking, even, of blockading Great Britain!" He stared at me. I looked from him to Lady Ransome and felt a sudden tightness in my breast to see her bend down her head as if to hide the wave of color that mounted suddenly into her face.

"I think that was Captain Boyle," I said. "It's Captain Boyle who intends to blockade you."

Captain Wise made a mildly explosive sound in his throat. "I've heard of him!" he said. "In the Indies. The whole British navy has heard of him. It wasn't Boyle—why, by God, sir, of *course* it was Boyle who squittered around me like a petrel! So that was Boyle! I nearly ran off after him when you got under way this morning. Why, I'd as soon expect to mash a flea with my best bower anchor as catch that gentleman!"

He led the way to the table and, when we were seated, looked at me sharply. "Your brig, now," he said. "How did she sail with Boyle's brig?"

"About the same," I told him. "Under favorable circumstances we did fifteen knots."

He shook his head wonderingly. "I can't account for it. Boyle's vessel was American-built, I take it."

"Yes. Baltimore-built."

"We can't build such vessels," Captain Wise said, "and if we could, we couldn't sail 'em."

Sir Arthur widened his eyes slightly. "Don't you think it possible, Captain, that Americans brag a little faster than they sail?"

Captain Wise studied Sir Arthur carefully. "No," he said at length, "no, I regret to say that doesn't explain it. We've taken a few of these fast American vessels, but had the devil's time trying to use 'em. We're afraid of their long masts, so we shorten 'em. We strengthen the hulls and find we have tubs."

"And may I ask, Captain Wise," Sir Arthur asked, "whether or not you've ever been in America? You appear to display a peculiar tolerance for its people. Ah—they shoot birds sitting!"

Captain Wise coughed. "Then I wish to God, sir, they'd be as thoughtful of us and wait till we sit!" He turned to me. "You people are different from us on sea, and I've heard you're more so on land. Yet most of you are only two or three generations out of England. How do you explain the difference, Captain Nason?"

I think I got red, and I know I spoke foolishly; for what came upon my tongue were only the stock phrases of our politician orators. "I think it's the air of liberty we breathe that makes us different. Our fathers won our freedom from British bondage; we cast off the shackles——"

Suddenly I stopped, remembering in what plight I stood myself at that lamentable moment, and seeing that the others thought it strange I should speak just then of freedom and the casting off of shackles.

Captain Wise coughed again; not even Sir Arthur looked at me, and the air seemed heavy with discomfort. It was Lady Ransome who spoke; her voice was low, and her eyes hidden by her lashes.

"Freedom," she murmured. "Yes, Americans seem to love freedom; and what will so many of them do when they're in our prisons?" She spoke the last word in so faint a voice that it was scarcely audible.

I stared at the table, unwilling to trust myself to look at her. Her husband laughed comfortably. "It's to be feared, my dear," he said, "that you've asked a question Mr. Nason will unfortunately soon be able to answer. Fortunes of war, fortunes of war!"

Lady Ransome didn't look up, and Captain Wise cleared his throat. "I was thinking about your little dog, Captain Nason. Lady Ransome tells me the dog she brought aboard is yours, but is nevertheless English. My thought was this: for a time American prisoners in English prisons were allowed to keep dogs, but there got to be too many of them, and someone gave an order they should all be killed. I'm afraid there was great lamentation: rather hard on the poor men, because seven hundred of those little comrades of theirs were destroyed on one day. Too bad, too bad!"

He assumed an air of gruffness that deceived no one. "Too bad, of course! Ah—since your little dog's already in Lady Ransome's custody and seems happy with her, it might be—you know your own business best, of course—Sir Arthur being a sportsman—ah, I thought it might be well if Sir Arthur could persuade you to—ah——"

"I'd consider it a great honor," I said, "if Lady Ransome would accept my dog: a great honor and a great relief, for to have him killed would be worse than——"

"No," Sir Arthur interrupted promptly. "The dog has points; I've noticed him, but I shouldn't want to be indebted. I don't mind purchasing the dog for my wife; but no gifts! No gifts!"

Lady Ransome looked up; her hand was at her throat, flat against it, so I could see the little indentations in the smooth skin over her knuckles. Yet the fingers seemed almost to flutter, as if she were about to make a gesture toward me; and I wondered, if her impulse carried, what that impulse would be.

"Of course," I said to Sir Arthur. "However it's done, it's a favor to me. Make the price whatever you like."

"Ow!" Sir Arthur said, "I never make an offer. *You* make the price, you know: if it's reasonable, I accept: if not, I won't, eh?"

I have no doubt, as I have said, that the man tried always to be just and fair; yet to my way of thinking he could do and say nothing gracefully.

"Would two pounds be too much?" I asked.

"Ow, not in the least," Sir Arthur said. He drew a wallet from his breast pocket, took out three bits of paper, and tossed them across the table. "I think he's worth all of three pounds, you know!"

I picked them up and put them in my pocket, unmindful of his manner in my relief at Pinky's safety.

"That's right," Captain Wise said, "that's right. You'll find use for that before you know it."

There was a knock on the door, and the captain's polite young secretary entered and bowed. "Land, sir," he said. "Wembury Point."

"Plymouth!" Sir Arthur said. "We're nearly home, eh, Nason?"

At the word "home" I turned to Lady Ransome sharply, as though she had spoken. She was staring full at me, almost haggardly; and for that moment it seemed to me, strangely, that we were actually speaking to each other, though I could not have said what the words were or even what they meant.

Suddenly she sprang up. "Plymouth?" she cried to Captain Wise. "Plymouth? But that means—Dartmoor!"

"Yes," he said, and he seemed ill at ease. "I—that is—well, really, there's nothing to be done about it: you'll go to the depot at Dartmoor, Captain Nason."


# The Prison Hulks at Chatham

### From CAPTAIN CAUTION

AT SEVEN in the morning, the ports were raised and the gratings removed from the hatches; and Marvin, shouldering his hammock and bedding, followed his fellow prisoners up the ladders to be counted. In the dusk of the day before, the French prisoners had seemed miserable, but the naked creatures who came up into the brilliant sunlight of that October day were purely horrible. To Marvin, waiting his turn, after the counting, to stack his hammock on the covered platform over the main hatch, they had the look of vicious and repulsive animals as they scuttled down the ladders again to their den on the orlop deck.

Newton came to him through the press of prisoners. "Here," he told Marvin, "come up on the forecastle. I want to show you something."

Marvin, drawing Argandeau with him, followed the small swaggering figure in the overlong greatcoat as it bustled forward and mounted nimbly to the high forecastle, from which a reek of smoke rose through a score of pipes. Four marines in threadbare scarecrow uniforms growled glumly at Newton as he stopped before them to strike an attitude that had something of the heroic about it.

"Ho!" one of the marines exclaimed. " 'Ere's the bloomin' hactor! Well, we ain't got nuffin' for yer! No tobaccer; no ole clo'es; no needles ner thread ner nails ner nuffin'!"

Clasping his hands before him, Newton raised sad eyes to the speaker's face. "Pity!" he whispered. "Have pity on a pore unfortunate woman turned into the snow with her two tender children"—he gestured dramatically toward Marvin and Argandeau—"by an unnatural and inhuman father, with never so much as a sup of rum or a measly piece of twist to hearten them against the bitter winter winds! Ah, my children! My pore, pore children! Ah, the pity of it, to see them waste before my very eyes for lack of the barest necessities of life!" He seemed to sob and droop.

One of the marines snorted. Another said angrily, "We ain't got none, I tell yer!"

"Ah, say not so!" Newton cried. He drew himself erect and thrust a hand into the bosom of his greatcoat. "None? None? In all this broad demesne, no single piece of twist? No twist in all this royal throne of kings, this sceptered isle, this earth of majesty, this seat of Mars, this other Eden, demi-paradise, this fortress built by Nature for herself against infection and the hand of war, this happy breed of men, this little world, this precious stone set in the silver sea, which serves it in the office of a wall or as a moat defensive to a house, against the envy of less happier lands,—this blessed plot, this earth, this realm, this England! No twist? Good God, no twist in England?" Passionately he struck his brow with his clenched fist, and staggered.

"Oh, 'ell!" one of the marines growled. He drew a fragment of rope tobacco from his pocket and reluctantly handed it to Newton, who examined it suspiciously, dusted it against the front of his coat, and suddenly bit off the larger part of it. He returned the remainder to the marine and, deaf to his hoarse outcries, herded Marvin and Argandeau to the starboard bulwarks.

"Now we're all right," Newton said. "Those lobsters won't bother us, for fear of losing the rest of their tobacco. Still, it's best to talk low and keep your eyes open."

The three of them stared out over the wind-swept waters of the Medway. Ahead and astern extended the long line of soiled and misshapen hulks, each one attended, as though it had spawned during the night, by a small fleet of vegetable and supply boats. Along the main channel of the river, between the hulks and the windmills and neatly hedged fields, moved brigs and ships and sloops, bound to or from the docks of Chatham.

Newton turned an uncertain eye on Argandeau. "There's some situations that require frank speaking," he said to Marvin. "Now I've got nothing against this French friend of yours; but what I've got to say is important; and if anyone should be careless enough to blab, it might be the death of us."

Marvin nodded. "What you've got to say can be said before Argandeau or not at all. He's here himself because of helping me try to stay away. If I get out, he gets out too."

"All right," Newton said hastily. "All right! That's understood. Now look here." He spat negligently at a passing supply boat. "Opposite this hulk, on shore, is a village. See it?"

"We see it," Marvin said.

"All right," Newton whispered. "That's Jillingum, that village is. Spelled 'Gillingham,' but pronounced 'Jillingum,' the way they do here. To the right of the village there's two windmills. In line with 'em, and fifty yards off shore, there's a mud bank. See it?"

Marvin nodded.

"That bank runs all the way along this reach, out of water most of the time. Sometimes only a little out. Could you swim that far at night in cold water—real cold water?"

"Easy," Marvin said.

"The mud in those banks is like glue," Newton remarked. "You go into it pretty near up to your middle. That's the trouble with getting to shore —if you swim as far as the banks, you're pretty tired, on account of having to carry things with you; so when you strike the mud, you can't get through it, sometimes. Sometimes, when the ports are opened in the morning, we see men in the mud, dead. The British leave 'em there all day—two days, sometimes—so they'll be a lesson to the rest of us." In a thoughtful voice, he added: "The crows eat 'em."

The three men stared silently at the square green fields and the slowly turning windmills, toylike against the clear sky.

"Well?" Newton asked.

"Well what?" Marvin demanded.

"Do you think you could get through the mud?"

"Why, I'd have to," Marvin said.

"Men have got through it, no?" Argandeau asked.

Newton nodded. "Three out of five got through it a month ago—Americans. Frenchmen have got through it, but mostly they were new men—privateer captains. Tom Souville got through it four times, and reached France twice, but he was captured three times and brought back."

Argandeau laughed silently. His close-cropped black head wagged gently from side to side. "Tom Souville!" he exclaimed. "When I am a young man in Calais, I have taught Tom Souville tricks in swimming. There is nothing Tom Souville can do that I cannot do."

They were silent again, staring at the distant and harmless-seeming gray thread of the mud bank.

"There's one more thing," Newton said at length. "How much can you fight?"

Marvin looked thoughtfully at his knuckles. "I don't rightly know. I never had to fight very hard. What I've had to do has come easy."

Newton felt of his upper arm and appraised him carefully.

"Well," he said slowly, "well, I'll tell you. I'll tell you just how it is. It's a hard job to escape from these hulks—a dreadful chore! 'Tisn't as if you just escaped whenever you felt like it; you've got to have money, and you've got to protect yourself from informers, and you've got to be prepared, and you've got to have the good will of the rest of the prisoners, and you've got to have the permission of the governing committee, and you've got to be relieved of your prisoner duties. Then, when all those things have been arranged, you're obliged to go to work and cut your way out. It's the hardest work in the world! If you laid out on a topgallant yard night and day for a month, trying to hand a sail that's stiff with ice, and never got it handed, it wouldn't be as hard work as getting out of these hulks, even after you've got the permission and the money."

"My money was stolen when I came aboard last night," Marvin said. "How much money does it take?"

"Wait," Newton said. "I'm coming to that. Now I'll tell you how it is: I want to get out of this place! 'Tisn't that I can't stand the bad food and the bad air and the bad clothes or the bad Frenchmen. These bad Frenchmen, they're a joke! They're so eager to take advantage of us Americans that all you got to do is to give 'em an inch of rope and they'll hang themselves. See this overcoat?"

Marvin nodded.

"That's a French coat," Newton said. "They think I'm easy because

I'm little and look worried when I gamble with 'em. The Frenchmen aren't anything as long as you watch 'em—not anything! What I can't stand is wanting to get at these English and not being able to! Listen!"

He took Marvin by the upper arms and seemed to shiver in the grip of a violent emotion. "Do you know why they take so many prisoners and starve us the way they do? It's because half of England's fattening on our hunger and nakedness and cold. The more of us they capture, the fatter England grows. Seventy-five thousand of us, French and Americans together, and the contractors take money for clothes we're supposed to get, but never do, and for food that's never fed to us! The commander of this ship, the drunken hog, fought to get the job! It pays him seven shillings a day, but he'll be a rich man in three years, hunting foxes in a red coat and talking about filthy Americans! I was secretary to a captain, I tell you, and I know what I'm talking about! I've got to get out of here! I'll blow up if I can't fight 'em!"

"I don't blame you," Marvin said thoughtfully, "but if it's as hard to escape as you say, you'd be better off, wouldn't you, to stop talking about it?"

Newton gripped the high bulwarks of the prison ship and laughed exultantly. "Stop?" he cried. "Stop? Why, no! I've just started! I've been waiting for the right men! For the right men! It's my turn to go and you're the man I want to go with. You're strong and you're big. You'll make it, and if I go with you, I'll have no trouble. This man, too"—he whirled to poke Argandeau's arched chest—"he'd get through, and the Indian you brought aboard. There's nobody else aboard this hulk I'd risk it with. I don't think the others could make it. They're weak and hungry. Most of 'em are sick. Most of 'em have been in jail too long. You're different! When I saw you come aboard, it seemed to me you must be the man I've been waiting for ever since they threw me into this"—he laughed again—"this demi-paradise; this precious stone set in the silver sea; this England!"

Marvin looked quickly over his shoulder at the four marines lounging at the forecastle rail; then stared intently at Newton.

The small man hitched up his long overcoat around him. "I'll tell you how it is," he said, and his crinkly yellow side whiskers seemed to quiver. "If you can lick a man as big as you are, and maybe a little bigger—if you've got the heart to take a pounding and give back better than you get —I can contrive for the three of us to have a chance to go." He shivered. "You're the man I've been looking for! Yes, sir, you'll make it!"

He hesitated, seeming to withdraw a little into his voluminous outer garment; then added, "Or you'll probably get killed trying."

Marvin drew a deep breath, but in spite of it, his voice trembled somewhat: "That's reasonable enough. Just show me who I've got to fight to get myself out of here."

§

Two of the long wooden benches in the lower battery had been dragged into the corner where Newton's hammock hung at night, and so arranged that they protruded from the corner in a narrow V.

At the point of the V sat Newton, flanked on each side by five committeemen. Two other committeemen sat on the deck, ten feet in advance of the point of the V; and to Marvin, who waited restlessly near them, they volunteered the information that they were thus stationed as pickets to warn away such prisoners as might be tempted to intrude on the committee's deliberations.

Nor was their office an idle one; for the deck was crowded with men, arguing, yammering, whistling, and singing; some of them cutting soup bones into miniature planks for the making of ship models; some weaving delicate boxes from fragments of straw, or carving dolls and chessmen from beef knuckles; others patrolling the deck ceaselessly, offering for sale a desirable sleeping location, the butt of a candle, or a thimbleful of grease for use in a lamp; still others trying to sell their services for the repairing of shoes or the mending of clothes. Among them moved emaciated, half-naked Frenchmen, prowling restlessly in search of unknown matters, or soliciting patronage for the gambling tables in the upper battery.

"Sheer off!" the pickets growled to all of them. "Sheer off! Committee's in session for the good of the deck! Sheer off!"

Marvin, allowed inside the picket line by Newton's orders, heard Newton address the ten committeemen.

"There's several things to come before this meeting," he told them. "First is, what's to be done about getting some kind of answer out of the American agent? There's fifty-seven Americans next door to naked, and sixty-six without coats of any kind. By December there'll be two hundred without any clothes except rags so rotten that thread won't hold 'em together. Twelve hundred new prisoner suits were supposed to be delivered last month, the French say, but they say we'll never see 'em. Osmore and the contractors keep the money, and the clothes never even get made. If we can't get help from Beasley, we'll freeze, all of us."

"How many times has he been written to?" asked a sour-visaged man whose mouth was puckered as if from the eating of persimmons.

"The committees on this hulk have written him eighteen times since August fifteenth, Captain Taylor."

The committeemen moved restlessly on their benches, and it was Captain Taylor who broke the silence again: "If the contractor would buy back our fish allowance next fish day, we might get enough to put an advertisement in *Bell's Weekly Messenger*, requesting that he pay some attention to his fellow countrymen."

"That's all right," complained a man whose head and chest were enveloped in a hood of flour sacking, "only it appears to me this taxation business is getting kind of overdone. I don't feel like these men ought to be asked to give up any more food, not even those smoked herrings. They're about starved already; so starved that if they got took sick, with the doctor paying no attention to sick men, they'd die in a minute!"

"There ain't anybody can eat the fish, Henry!" Taylor objected. "The French, they say they marked some of 'em, so they can be recognized, and they been in use for seven years—delivered at three pennies and bought back for a penny."

"Maybe so," Henry admitted, and Marvin saw that his face had an unearthly whiteness to it—the whiteness, almost, of the belly of a flatfish. "Maybe so; only the next time we get 'em, you watch me eat mine! I'm getting so I can eat anything—even a newspaper that's been wrapped round a fish!"

"Yes," Newton interrupted, "and there's another thing. Our *Statesman* subscription runs out next week, and that means twenty-eight shillings a month for the paper and sixteen shillings a month delivery charges." He laughed bitterly. "Twenty-eight shillings a month! No wonder the English don't know anything. Knowledge comes too high! Anyway, we got to sell two days' fish and one day's bread to get that renewed, provided you want it renewed."

"Want it renewed!" one of the committeemen exclaimed. "We got to have it renewed. If there ain't any news nor anything to read, there won't be anything to talk about, and we might as well be dead."

"Newton," said sour-mouthed Captain Taylor thoughtfully, "how much of that sixteen shillings goes to Osmore?"

"Probably ten," Newton said promptly. "He might get fifteen. Even so, it's no use trying to do anything about it, because the one that tried to make trouble would get the black hole for two weeks. 'Tisn't worth it! Gosh! I'd rather give up all my fish forever than get two weeks black hole!"

"I move," said Henry, from the folds of his flour sacking, "that this committee communicate with Beasley in writing for the nineteenth time, and send a letter to the President of the United States saying that the American agent for prisoners of war in England does nothing to prevent said prisoners from being treated like some sort of weasels. I also move that enough of our fish be collected and sold by the president of this lower battery to obtain the *Statesman* for another month."

"You know there's no use writing to the President of the United States," Newton objected wearily. "There's no way of getting it out except through an escaping prisoner; and if it was ever discovered on an escaping prisoner, the whole committee'd get the black hole, and all the other prisoners would have their tools and trades seized and destroyed! I'd like to hear that motion restated."

Henry jumped to his feet, pulling at the flour sacking around his throat. " 'Tain't right!" he exclaimed, his voice shaking as if with cold. "My God, you can't starve men and trample on 'em and murder 'em like this, and keep 'em gagged while you do it! You can't, I tell you! You——"

"Henry!" Captain Taylor said sharply.

Henry's voice persisted, shrill and trembling, "They treat us worse than animals, the damned rotten skunks! They can't keep me quiet! There's some way to get help—there's got to be!"

"Henry!" Captain Taylor shouted. He grasped Henry by the arm and pulled him down on the bench, shaking him roughly. "You're elected committeeman to set an example to the rest of these prisoners. See that you do it!"

Henry drew a deep and quivering breath, and the committeemen stared at their travesties of shoes, a strange and silent gathering.

"Well," Newton said at length, "we don't need it put in the form of a motion. I'll get the *Statesman* and tend to writing to Beasley again."

He cleared his throat and rose to his feet, drawing his long, ragged overcoat tight around him. "There's one more thing, and that's the question of who goes next." He eyed the committeemen significantly; and they, coming suddenly to life, fixed their eyes eagerly on him.

"We're wasting time," he went on. "Everybody wants to be next and nobody's willing to recognize the claims of anybody else. Meanwhile the food and the grease has accumulated without any work being done—no work at all! First thing you know, some of the Frenchmen, they'll get through and get stuck in the mud. Then they'll double the boat patrol, and Osmore'll have the planking sounded four times a day instead of once. This business ought to be settled, and settled now. Somebody's got to get letters out of this place, so we can get some money, and I say we ought to agree on somebody that can do it."

"I was one of the first Americans aboard this hulk!" Henry exclaimed. "You know it too! I ought to have first chance!"

"Henry," Captain Taylor said kindly, "you're wrong about this! Your spell in the black hole was pretty hard on you—harder'n you thought for, I guess. I notice you going up the ladder mornings, and you blow like a porpoise when you get on deck. You haven't been getting near enough food, and you'd never even reach the mudbank."

"I tell you I would!" Henry said. "I'd rather die trying, anyway, than not try at all!"

"Yes," Newton said, "maybe you would, but we wouldn't rather have you! Now you listen to me! I say the thing to do is to turn this over to a new man, fresh aboard."

Captain Taylor shook his head, and from the look of his mouth he might have been eating chokecherries. "No," he said, "you figure he'd be successful because he'd be strong and well fed; but you don't want to forget that these men here in this lower battery have got something almost as good as strength—they're dreadful mad! They hate the British worse than anything on earth!"

"That's what I say!" Henry exclaimed. "That's what I been trying to tell you! I'm dreadful mad, and I'd be as successful as anyone!"

Newton stared thoughtfully from Henry to Captain Taylor, who quickly lowered his eyes. "No," Newton said, "that isn't the way I figure. The way I figure is that it would be easier for everyone to agree on a new man—a man they never saw before—and I figure he'd be quicker doing the work—doing the cutting. 'Twouldn't be so hard for him to drive himself as it is for us, who've been breathing poison down here every night."

"They wouldn't agree," Captain Taylor said.

"I won't agree!" Henry stubbornly insisted.

Newton crouched down between the benches and looked up into the thin and sullen faces of the committeemen. "I had word from Osmore yesterday," he whispered. "Captain Stannage and the rest of his friends are coming aboard Saturday afternoon to get drunk again, ladies and all, damn the blowsy sluts!"

"Osmore sent you word?" Captain Taylor asked. "I suppose that means——"

"Yes!" Newton exclaimed. "It means he'll bring Little White with him. It means he aims to have a couple more of us hammered to a jelly, just to keep his friends in good spirits. Osmore told me to make the usual offer."

The committeemen growled angrily, and Captain Taylor shook his head. "I don't like it!" he said. "It's a bad business, this Little White!

I wouldn't mind if it was Frenchmen he jellied, but it goes against the grain to hear him howling his black laughter and see him smashing our people until they're no more than raw meat, and they submitting to it for the sake of a twenty-shilling note!"

Newton laughed confidently, and his crinkly yellow side whiskers seemed to bristle, so that he had the eager look of a small dog on the trail of game. "All right! But what if Little White got smashed himself when he set out to do the smashing? What do you suppose Osmore'd say, and Stannage, and those wenches of his that have been tittering at us and looking at us all summer as if we were foxes in a cage? How'd you like to watch their faces while their little pet gets some of his own medicine?"

The committeemen stared at him with eyes that suddenly glittered. Captain Taylor looked over his shoulder at the tall figure of Marvin, standing behind the two lookouts; then turned back to Newton with a sour smile. "So that's it!" he said. "Well, it's a thing we'd be powerful glad to see, all of us, and it might put heart into us, what's more; but it appears to me you're expecting too much."

"What if I'm not?" Newton demanded. "What if he can do it? Would you be willing he should be the next in line? Would you agree on him?"

"What you so anxious about him for?" Henry demanded.

Newton turned on him. "My land! Can't you see? He'd be fighting for the chance to get out, and for the money to take advantage of the chance!"

"Bring him over here," Captain Taylor said.

In response to Newton's call, Marvin stepped over one of the benches and stood between the two rows of committeemen. "Daniel Marvin, of Arundel," Newton said. "His barque was cut out of Morlaix by the *Sparrow* schooner."

The committeemen eyed him almost carelessly, as though their interest in him was slight. "Marvin?" Captain Taylor asked at length. "Marvin? Seems to me there used to be a Marvin out of Arundel in the *Talleyrand* brig, trading in Havana."

"The *Talleyrand* brig was my father's."

"H'm!" Captain Taylor said noncommittally. "Was your father cut out of Morlaix?"

"No, sir. I was aboard the *Olive Branch* barque. Captain Dorman was master—Captain Dorman, of Arundel. He was killed in the doldrums, trying to fight off a British gun brig. His daughter took command of the barque and brought her into Morlaix. She's alone there now."

The committeemen, Marvin felt, had lost all interest in him, for their glances at him were few and furtive.

"Seems to me I heard tell," Captain Taylor continued finally, "that the *Talleyrand* brig was so named because your father helped Talleyrand to buy land from General Knox."

"Yes, sir."

"What reason you got for thinking you could beat this Little White if you ain't ever seen him?" Henry demanded suddenly.

Marvin stared down at his knuckles and worked his left shoulder under his jacket. "I don't know that I could. They say he's a good fighter, and heavier than I am. Well, I've thought about him, and I believe I've figured out a way to offset his extra weight. I've figured out a new way to fight. Still, I wouldn't be interested in trying unless I knew I wasn't wasting my time."

"Wasting your time!" exclaimed another committeeman harshly. "Why, there's a standing offer of twenty pounds to the man that beats Little White! Little White's boss, Stannage, who's a friend of Osmore, made that offer. Twenty pounds to any prisoner that does it—twenty shillings to him if he tries and doesn't."

Marvin nodded. "I don't take much pleasure in fighting," he said. "I wouldn't risk it if there was nothing in it but the twenty pounds."

Newton seized Marvin's wrist and raised his arm. "Look at his reach!" he told them softly. "It's the first time we've had a man aboard with a reach like that! It's nearly as good as Little White's!"

"If you knew you weren't wasting your time," Captain Taylor reminded him, "you say you'd be interested in fighting this Little White?"

"Yes," Marvin said.

"Whether you could beat him or not?" Henry asked.

Marvin nodded. "I want to escape from this hulk," he said. "I want to get back to Morlaix. If nothing stands between me and getting there except beating this Little White, he'll have to kill me to beat me."

Newton laughed, a laugh so nervous that it was almost a titter. "There it is!" he exclaimed to the committeemen. "What more do you want than that?"

"What is it you figure we ought to agree to?" Captain Taylor asked; then puckered his mouth sourly.

"Nothing unreasonable," Marvin said. "I want to be allowed to escape, and I want the right to pick the men that work with me and go out with me—if it ever comes to that. Three others I'd want to take, no more; and all for good and sufficient reasons. I'd expect all four of us to receive the usual supplies and protection while working."

"You mean nobody else would be allowed to use your cutting, provided you're successful?" Henry demanded.

"Not for three nights—not until we've had time to get clear."

"I don't agree!" Henry declared angrily.

"Oh, here, here!" Captain Taylor said. "That's fair! If they get away, we can pass men through the bulkhead to answer to roll call, so the four won't be missed; and when the three days are up, everyone can go that has enough money and food. If one of the four should be caught, nobody else would have a chance anyway."

"Well——" said Henry weakly. He looked helplessly from one committeeman to another, his face chalk-white in the flickering light that danced across the ceiling from the reflection of the sun on the crinkled water of the Medway.

"Gorry!" exclaimed a committeeman in dogskin trousers, one of the legs being made of the skin of a red setter and the other of the skin of a coach dog. "Gorry! I say yes—whether he beats him or not!"

"No!" Captain Taylor protested sternly. "Not unless he beats him! If he's willing to try under those conditions, I say yes, and so does Henry. You do, don't you, Henry?"

"Yes," Henry said reluctantly, "I guess I do."

A glance at the other committeemen seemed to satisfy Captain Taylor, for he nodded soberly to Newton and then rose from his bench to prod inquiringly at Marvin's biceps.

"In that case," Newton said briskly, "this meeting stands adjourned and I appoint the entire committee to demand a contribution of salt from each prisoner so we can get his hands in pickle with no loss of time."

§

The barge that drew up to the landing stage of the *Crown Prince* hulk at noon on Saturday seemed to blaze with color; for the oarsmen wore uniforms of blue flannel with the arms of the Stannages on breast and back in silver, gold and red; while in the cockpit sat Stannage himself, resplendent in a hussar's uniform, all gold and scarlet. Around him clung a group of damsels in silks, furs, and feathers—damsels whose conversation seemed to Marvin, as he peered over the bulwarks at them, to consist largely of shrill laughter and shriller screams.

Between Stannage's knees crouched an enormous brown dog, thin and yellow-eyed, that panted constantly despite the chill wind that blew across the Medway, and cast longing looks over one side of the barge and then over the other. Close behind him stood a towering, smiling Negro, whose noisy laughter ran like an undercurrent beneath the high-pitched merriment of the captain's gentle companions, and whose Eastern splendor dimmed the finery of the others. On his head was perched a vast turban of yellow satin, decorated with a tall plume held in place by a glittering bauble seemingly made of pearls and diamonds; beneath his short jacket of crimson satin a broad sash of gold cloth shone dully against the velvety black of his skin; and crimson satin trousers, voluminous enough, Marvin was sure, to make a dozen potato sacks, hung to his ankles, where they were fastened by tight gold bands.

"There he is!" Newton said. "There's Little White! What you think of him, Dan?"

Marvin shook his head. "Why," he said, "he looks like a handy man to have around a pivot gun or a galley stove, provided he got a rap from a belaying pin every few minutes to remind him where he belongs."

Newton nodded. "That's something he hasn't had in some little time. These people over here, they're all excited over Molineaux, the American Negro who fought Tom Cribb. In consequence, they can't see a black man a little bigger than usual without thinking he's a fighter and making a pet of him."

Cackling hilariously, Little White, evidently at his master's bidding, leaned over and took one of the damsels beneath the arms as though she were a doll, held her for a moment over the side of the barge, so that she screamed and kicked like an excited child; then deposited her on the landing stage and spanked her briskly to start her up the gangway.

Stannage, a gaudy figure in his scarlet, fur-trimmed hussar's jacket, laughed as heartily at the playfulness of his dusky favorite as did any of the jeering prisoners that peered down at him from the bulwarks.

Marvin moved uncomfortably. "Why," he said suddenly, "this Stannage ought to have his face washed and be put to bed! He's only a child! He's never a captain—not at his age!"

"Oh, isn't he?" Newton exclaimed. "Well, he is, and he's more than a child! He's an idiot—the idiot son of rich idiots; so his family bought him a captaincy to get him out of the way. It's an old English custom! There's regiments over here officered entirely by idiots and children whose places have been bought for 'em. You can do anything with money in England; there's no place that's not for sale—church, state, army, or navy."

Mavin laughed. "I guess they're not so bad as that!" he said. "If you're trying to make me madder at them than I am, you don't need to—not by lying about 'em."

"Lying?" Newton cried. "Lying? Why—well, wait till you know 'em! Lying! It was only a couple of years ago that the Duke of York was helping Mary Anne Clarke to sell any job in England to the highest bidder! The King's son and a bawd! It's no use having merit in England, not unless you have money along with it; and if you have no money, you're no better than a criminal! They pressed me into their damned navy, and I know 'em, and I'm glad I do, because it isn't Nature for people like that to win wars from people like us. That's mighty small consolation to a man who's buried in the hulks! Mighty small, but better than nothing!"

The boyish Stannage, looking petulant, came slowly and awkwardly up the companionway, dragging his enormous and reluctant brown dog; while Little White, crowding close behind with baskets, boxes, and cloaks, rolled his eyes defiantly at the prisoners who watched him.

Argandeau, beside Marvin, sighed heavily. "It is well that I understand which is the master and which is the man," he said, "because if I did not, I might think that the smaller one was brought here by the black one for our amusement."

He watched the two gayly caparisoned figures mounting to the quarter-deck from the throng of emaciated, tattered scarecrows that packed the waist; then tapped Marvin on the arm. "In those baskets," he reminded him, "there is wine and fine food and yet more wine that they will be two hours in consuming. Two hours is no great time, so you must come now and have your dinner—two rotten carrots and a biscuit palpitating with weevils."

Marvin, climbing the ladders from the lower battery to the upper deck, mounted two hours later into a tumult so violent that the hulk seemed to shudder, as at the roaring of a storm—seemed almost to be sinking in a sea of sound.

The deck itself had become an amphitheater, and every exposed part of it, save for the quarter-deck and a square inclosure in front of the break in the poop, was massed with ragged, excited prisoners. There were prisoners clinging like ants to the two stubby signal masts; prisoners ranged in a triple tier along the high bulwarks; prisoners hanging like swarming bees against the face of the forecastle. All of them, wedged immovably in their places though they seemed to be, had freed their arms to shake a fist at the inclosure beneath the poop, so that the whole dreary hulk had the appearance of fluttering and vibrating, while from·nine hundred throats there came an angry and derisive screaming.

In the center of the inclosure, set off by ropes from the close-packed prisoners who crouched around it, strutted the towering crimson form of Little White; and from the continuous rapid movement of his grinning lips as well as from the expression of rage on the faces of the prisoners closest to him, Marvin knew he was making game of them. From time to time he turned and looked up to the baby-faced hussar captain, standing at the rail of the quarter-deck with Lieutenant Osmore, and thence to the chattering women, who now sat comfortably, wineglasses in their hands, on either side of the hulk commander and their host. There was pride and almost admiration in the smiles they gave him; and even as Marvin, preceded by Newton and followed closely by Argandeau, forced his way from the main hatch toward the ring, a woman's gayly colored silk scarf floated downward from the quarter-deck and was deftly caught by Little White—caught and flaunted proudly in the faces of the howling prisoners.

At the sight of Marvin, crawling under the ropes of the ring with the small and heavily overcoated Newton, Little White ceased his posturing and stared intently at the tall American; then, catching his eye, he thrust out his lower jaw and grimaced horribly, his mouth spreading outward so that he seemed to have the face of an ape.

Marvin stared hard at him with a horrid fascination and shivered perceptibly, whereupon the roar with which the prisoners were greeting their champion's appearance became enfeebled with misgiving and died pathetically away.

On the quarter-deck two marines thumped on the drums slung at their sides. Lieutenant Osmore placed his right hand between the first and second buttons of his coat, frowned portentously, and raised his left hand in a gesture of command. Over the hulk there fell an uneasy silence.

"You know the terms of this exhibition!" Osmore said in his shrill, domineering voice. "Captain Sir Rafe Stannage has kindly consented to permit his attendant—ah—White—ah—Little White—to display once more that art unknown to more—ah—effeminate, more cruel, and more cowardly peoples—ah—the art sprung from British hardihood and love of fair play— ah—the art of pugilism!" He inclined his head to Stannage, who was staring as though baffled at a leather strap in his left hand; and from the throng of prisoners there instantly rose a roar—short, sharp, and profoundly ironical.

"You know the terms!" Osmore repeated. "Any fighting or opprobrious remarks among the prisoners will result in two days black hole for the offenders. The rules of the exhibition will be Broughton's rules. Each round to be considered ended on the fall of one or both contestants. After each fall, each man to be brought to scratch within thirty seconds or be deemed—ah—beaten. No falling without the striking of an honest blow. Challenger to receive one pound for his brave attempt, and if successful— ah, ha-ha!—if successful, twenty guineas!" Osmore chuckled and cleared his throat importantly.

"The challenger of—ah—White—of Little White—ah—is"—he drew a

small paper from his coat and peered at it—"is one Marvin, of Arun-del."
He scanned the paper again, frowning, and repeated the word "Arun-del."

Stannage stepped to his side and looked over his shoulder. "Arun-del?
He's an Englishman?"

Osmore frowned severely down at Marvin, who stood patiently at one
side of the ring, his ear inclined to the prolonged whisperings of Newton.
"Arun-del!" Osmore exclaimed, striking the paper with his hand. "This
says Arun-del! There's no Arun-del in America!"

Marvin nodded. "A-rundle, it's pronounced."

"Never heard of the place! Where is it?" Osmore asked.

"Where?" Marvin said, looking up at him thoughtfully. "It's no great
distance from Bunker Hill and Saratoga."

A whisper arose from the men crouched at the ringside, a small dry
titter that spread through the dense masses of prisoners as ripples spread
from the dropping of a rock in a pond.

"Silence!" Osmore screamed, stamping his foot. "Silence!" He stared
balefully from one side of the crowded deck to the other, until the un-
seemly tittering had died away. "Save your damned Yankee impertinence
for another occasion or I'll clap you below hatches, all of you! You want
to see this fight, and you'll behave yourselves or not see it! I'll say this,
too: It's a lesson you need, all of you—you Frenchmen with your kicking
and knife sticking—you Spaniards and Italians with your backhanded
stilettos and daggers—you Yankees with your tomahawks and scalping
tricks! This is to do you good! You people need all the lessons you can
get in the cool courage, the restraint, the skill, and the endurance with
which the noble art of boxing has filled the breast of every truehearted
Englishman and made the British nation the mistress of the seas!"

There was a patter of applause from the young women seated at the
quarter-deck rail.

Newton cleared his throat apologetically. "I'd like to ask a question,
sir," he said. He stared up at Osmore from beside Marvin, as harmless as
a downy chicken peering from under its mother's wing.

"Be quick about it!" Osmore ordered.

"We hope you'll not permit any of your Lancashire up-and-down fighting, sir," Newton urged. "We wouldn't like to see our man killed or dis-
abled by kicking or gouging when on his back."

Osmore narrowed his eyes at Newton; then swept them quickly over
the throng of ragged men beyond. There was a small trembling among
them, and a sound like the vague shadow of stifled laughter.

Osmore's face darkened; he opened his lips as though to rebuke Newton; then seemed to cogitate. "Broughton's rules!" he snapped at length.

"You heard me say Broughton's rules! Get your man ready! Surgeon Rockett has kindly consented to fill the difficult post of referee."

He read again from his paper. "Corporals Quigg and Spratt will act for —ah—White—for Little White. For Marvin, Newton and Argandeau."

Two red-coated marines popped into the ring beside Little White, who straightway leaped into the air, crowing like a rooster and shedding jacket, trousers, waistband, and turban in a whirl of scarlet and gold. Beneath these garments he wore smallclothes of the brightest green, fastened waist and knee with yellow bands. Above them his naked torso gleamed in the pale October sunlight like polished brown wood—wood in which knots and lumps swelled unexpectedly on shoulders, arms, and back. His forehead sloped back abruptly from his broad flat nose, rising to a peak at the top of his head—a peak topped with a fuzzy semicircle of hair that had the look of a thick rope of crinkly black feathers extending over his skull and fastened to his ears on either side.

He continued to crow and leap as Newton helped Marvin to strip off his shirt, the huge brown hands flapping like wings against the green smallclothes; and even his eyes, fastened on Marvin, were black and hard as those of a giant rooster.

Marvin, resting against the ropes between Newton and Argandeau, had the look of shrinking from his black antagonist. The pearly whiteness of his chest and arms might have been thought to be the effect of fear, and the long smooth muscles hidden beneath that gleaming skin seemed, by comparison with the knobby brown bulges of Little White, almost weak and helpless. Yet it was strange but true that whereas Little White seemed to have shrunk somewhat with the removal of his gaudy plumage, Marvin seemed to have become larger.

Down from the quarter-deck came the ship's surgeon, his chin held high by his black stock, and a huge watch clutched in his hand. He crawled beneath the ropes, poked Marvin in the chest with a finger like a marlinespike, stared curiously into the yellowish eyes of Little White; then stooped over with some difficulty and, on the deck in the middle of the ring, chalked a square with three-foot sides.

"Now," he said, "if you're ready, my lads?" He popped out under the ropes. His hand rose and fell; and with that Newton hustled Marvin to one side of the chalked square, while one of the marines ran with Little White to the opposite side, so that the four men hung in a knot at the center of the ring.

The shouting of the prisoners had fallen away to a breathless hum, and through the hum rose a hoarse voice, a voice so rough and rasping as to sound less like a voice than like the scraping of a file on the strings of some vast violin. It was the voice of Little White. "Kiss mah han'," he growled. "Ah kill Americans wiff it."

Newton and the marine ran back to their sides of the ring and dodged beneath the ropes.

Little White threw himself into fighting position. His left foot and his left arm were thrust well forward; his right arm guarded his stomach and lower chest; his upper body tipped back so far that if he had raised his eyes, they would have looked straight upward into infinity. Standing so, he laughed, a deep, roaring, hyenalike laugh; for it was plain to be seen, from Marvin's posture, that Marvin was as ignorant of fighting as he was afraid of Little White. He had cramped himself sideways, his left shoulder turned in front of his body. His right foot, instead of resting squarely and flatly on the ground as a supporting platform for a blow, was poised on its toe, as, indeed, was his left foot as well. Both his knees were weakly bent, as though it was in his mind to turn at any moment and run like a coward from his powerful black opponent.

Roaring with laughter, Little White shuffled forward toward Marvin, who slipped off to one side. Roaring still, Little White shuffled after him, only to have his opponent slip off to the other side.

Nor was Little White the only one to roar. The deck of the hulk seemed almost to erupt with angry shouts of "Fight! Fight!" while Osmore, Stannage, the six women in their glowing silks and satins, and even the drummers at each side of the quarter-deck, hung far out over the rail to shout, "Fight! Fight!"

They moved around the ring, Little White shuffling forward and Marvin slipping off to left or right before him. Little White lashed out with a left-handed blow that cut a slit in Marvin's ear, and got from Marvin in return a veritable baby's tap—a breath of a hit that touched Little White's eye and was gone, like a vagrant butterfly. Again, with the evident intention of ending the fight before it had fairly begun, Little White sprang forward, his fists driving like battering rams for Marvin's mark—that triangular-shaped patch beneath his ribs and above his belt. There was the crack of a hit, but it was the impact of a black fist against a forearm; the mark itself had moved away.

The prisoners groaned and hissed. One of them, close to Newton's corner, aimed a jab at the elusive Marvin through the ropes. "Stand up to him!" he bellowed. "Get out o' there if you can't stand up to him!"

Newton rapped the bellower sharply on the forearm with the edge of his hand. "Close your face!" he said. "Can't you see it's a new way of fighting?"

The near-by prisoners howled their disgust. "Be damned to a new way of fighting!" "It's a new way of running, and a rotten one!" "Make him show what he's good for!" "Make him fight!"

Minutes passed. Blood trickled from Marvin's ear; there were red welts along his ribs from the glancing blows of Little White's knuckles; but still he slipped off to one side or to the other, and shrank away before the black man's advance.

Anger had replaced Little White's hoarse hilarity. "Stan' still!" he growled, following Marvin's erratic twistings and turnings. "Isn't one of you Americans got bottom enough to stan' up to a fighter? Light somewheres, you dirty Yankee yaller bird, so's I can knock you halfway up to Lunnon!"

To Little White's amazement, Marvin laughed. "You can't fight!" he told the black man. "You can't even throw a cross-buttock."

Little White lowered his head and charged. To the prisoners, raging at Marvin's tactics, it seemed, and was indeed the case, that Marvin, at this quick movement, stood his ground instead of slipping off to right or left. As Little White's head shot past his body, Marvin's fist came up against his opponent's throat with a sound like the impact of a dead codfish against a plank. In another instant the black man's arms were around him and the first fall had gone to Little White with a cross-buttock.

Their seconds were on them as they sprawled to the deck, hoisting them to their feet and hurrying them to the ropes for a rest of thirty seconds. Argandeau held Marvin on his knee while Newton, gabbling in his ear to make himself heard above the din of the prisoners, sponged the blood from his face and chest.

"A thirteen-minute round!" Newton told him excitedly. "A thirteen-minute round, and you're barely scratched! You're like a Baltimore schooner sailing rings round a frigate! He can't touch you! Keep it up, Dan! Your way's the best way, no matter what these fools say! Don't listen to 'em! He can't fight! He's a flipper! I told you he was a flipper! He thinks he's fighting like Molineaux, but he isn't. He's just a big black chunk of sour beef! He hits at half arm and keeps his elbows close to his body, and he'll keep doing it until he thinks he's caught you! Then he'll imitate Molineaux again and try to chop you, and you've got him! You've got him anyway! That was a beauty—a beauty! Right in the whistle! Right in the apple! He thinks he's swallowed a hen's hind foot! Oh, oh! He's fat! He's puffy! And he thinks it was an accident! He thinks he ran into it! Look at him gulp! Look at him watch you!"

Marvin glanced across at Little White, seated on the knee of a red-coated marine while another marine dabbled water on the back of his neck. There was, Marvin saw, a soft smoothness to the black skin above the green smallclothes, instead of the solid wall of corrugated muscle that should have been there; and the soft smooth surface rose and fell hurriedly. Conscious of Marvin's scrutiny, Little White blinked his small eyes, cautiously stretched his neck; then thrust out his mouth in an apelike grimace.

"Keep away from him!" Newton continued. "Keep out of his way until he's careless! Then you got him! Then you got him good! Remember what I told you!"

"Time!" the referee shouted.

Little White shuffled to the chalked square, falling into a fighting position so exaggerated that he seemed on the verge of tumbling backward. Marvin came less quickly to the scratch, and in the same cautious manner that had so enraged his fellow prisoners in the previous round—with his left shoulder thrust forward and his body bent as though he were torn with the simultaneous desire to advance and to run away.

Little White's hands revolved rapidly, and he pawed the deck with an enormous foot. "Stan' up!" he commanded hoarsely; then coughed and cleared his throat and coughed once more. "Stan' up, you ole tabby cat!"

He lurched forward to hurl murderous blows at Marvin, who shrank before him, ducking and dodging. Again and yet again Marvin's left fist flicked out, touching Little White lightly at the corner of the eye, and so faint and ineffectual were the blows that the groans and the jeering of the prisoners changed suddenly to a burst of laughter. Even Little White laughed, though he coughed when he did so, and at the corner of his eyes a smear of blood showed bright against his brown skin.

"Jes' a moment and I gits you!" he said. His voice seemed choked and strangled, and when he had spoken, he wheezed. His shuffle became swifter; and as it did, there came a hesitation into Marvin's movements—a momentary catch, as though he had faltered in deciding how to turn.

Little White bellowed hoarsely; his right hand rose high above his head, and like a flail his long black arm swept down toward Marvin's neck. Instead of slipping away, Marvin moved closer. His right fist flashed upward to land upon the brown V below the ribs. The breath went out of Little White with a hoarse hoot. He tilted suddenly forward, so that his chopping blow lost its force and landed uncontrolled against Marvin's shoulder. Marvin's left fist drove once more against the Negro's thick throat, partially straightening the black man, and once more his right fist whipped into the unprotected stomach that still quivered and jerked from the first unexpected blow. Little White clung to him with one arm—clung and fell backward, dragging Marvin with him; and the two of them plunged to the deck amid a turmoil of frenzied shouting such as might have come from ten thousand madmen, rather than from nine hundred half-fed prisoners.

Newton, dragging Marvin back to his seat on Argandeau's knee, shook like a shivered sail; and his voice trembled even more than his hands. "You got him! You got him!" He rubbed the blood from Marvin's cheek and ribs, and laughed almost hysterically. "It worked the way you said it would, and you got him!"

"Time!" bellowed Surgeon Rockett, above the howling of the prisoners.

Argandeau pushed Marvin toward the chalked square; and as Little White, coughing and blinking, stepped warily to the other side, Marvin snapped his left fist toward the black man's face. The semblance of timidity and indecision was gone from him, and he had the look of one about to taste a long-anticipated pleasure. Yet this look went from him as quickly as it had come; for as he led with his left hand, Little White half turned, threw up his head, and fell to the floor. In the same moment his second leaped at him, hustled him to his feet and dragged him back to the ropes.

Marvin, staring helplessly at Little White, felt Newton take him by the arm. "Wait!" Marvin said. He turned to the surgeon, who stood pompously outside the ring, staring at his turnip-shaped watch. "Wait! He fell without a blow! That's no fall! I didn't hit him!"

The surgeon looked up at him slowly. "You didn't what?" he asked.

"You heard me!" Marvin said. "I didn't touch him! Get him back here and make him fight!"

The surgeon laughed fatly. "You're a fine one to talk about fighting—you who did nothing but run for half an hour!"

"For God's sake!" Marvin shouted. "You——"

He stopped, staring at the pompous surgeon; then hurried to where Argandeau waited for him with outthrust knee.

Argandeau patted his shoulder, soothing him. "Remember; I have told you about these people!" he said.

The surgeon had gone to contemplating the face of his watch again. "A minute and a half he's given him!" Newton said. "Well, Dan; you do your best!"

"Time!" said the surgeon.

Marvin ran to scratch. Little White, breathing more regularly, glowered malevolently at him. Marvin grinned amiably. "You're licked, black boy! You're going to get hurt for playing tricks!"

Little White coughed and growled. Marvin slapped his outstretched left arm, a slap that tilted him forward; and as he tilted, Marvin's left fist landed wetly against his eye. Little White coughed and groaned. With hamlike hands he hammered Marvin's ribs. Marvin staggered and laughed; then rushed at Little White and drove him backward with a succession of blows to the stomach. He fell against the rope of the ring and bounced upright. When Marvin hit him in the throat and again in the stomach, he slipped to one knee and clung to the ropes.

"Foul!" he croaked hoarsely. "He bit me!"

Marvin caught him by the fringe of hair atop his head, dragged him to his feet and drove his fist against his throat. The Negro fell heavily to the deck, made vague swimming motions with his hands, and then lay still.

"Foul! Foul!" shouted Osmore and Stannage.

The pompous surgeon popped through the ropes. "Foul!" he said, brandishing his watch in Marvin's face. "The man was down!"

"No foul! No foul!" screamed the prisoners.

"No!" Marvin shouted. "Both knees and at least one hand on the floor, or the man's not down, and you know it! They're your own rules! He's down now, but he wasn't when I hit him. Don't look at me! Look at your watch, you fat swab!"

He ran to Argandeau's knee. The marine came through the ropes and dragged Little White to his corner. A hundred hands fluttered over Marvin, patting his head, his back, his thighs.

A breathless silence came upon the prisoners while they waited for the passing of the thirty seconds at whose end, according to Broughton's rules, each fighter must either toe the mark once more or acknowledge defeat. Through this silence could be clearly heard the sound of Newton's hands, slapping and kneading Marvin's arms, and of his reiterated whisper—"He'll never make it, Dan! He'll never make it! He'll never make it! He'll never make it!"

The surgeon pushed the watch in his pocket. He leaned over to look at Little White; then stared venomously at Marvin. "Time!" he said slowly. "Time!"

Marvin walked to the chalk mark in the center of the ring. He stood there alone. In the opposite corner lay Little White. Marvin, watching him, saw one black eyelid flutter. The marine pulled at the Negro's arm. He just lay there.

On the quarter-deck a woman screamed; and as if the scream had been a signal, the hulk became a bedlam of cursing, uproarious prisoners.

Newton, uttering unintelligible sounds, clambered through the ropes to throw his arms around Marvin's neck. Argandeau, tears streaming down his cheeks, embraced them both. "We win!" he blubbered. "Ah, my God! My God! I am excite! I choke! I die! We win! We win!"

Above them Stannage shook his fist at the prostrate form of Little White. "I've been sold!" he cried in his girlish voice. He leaned over the rail to point an accusing finger at Marvin. "You had no right to win! There was something wrong with it, but I don't know what! You don't deserve your twenty guineas, and I've a mind not to give them to you!" He stared about him indecisively, as if to seek support. Finding none, he fumbled in his pocket, tied some coins in a handkerchief and tossed them petulantly to Marvin; then turned suddenly to Osmore.

"Here," he said. "Where's my dog? I've been wanting to ask you all through the fight. Look at that!" He held up the empty strap and dangled it in Osmore's face.

Osmore stared at it blankly. "Your dog?" he asked. "Your dog is gone? When did you see him last?"

"After dinner," Stannage said. "One of the ladies was feeding him a sweet."

"What? You were foolish enough to let that dog run loose on this ship!" Osmore cried aghast. "I told you a week ago we had more than a dozen of these men sick from eating rats!"

Captain Stannage turned pallidly toward his six fair friends, whose sympathetically dismal exclamations pierced the air, yet went all unheard, lost under the thunder of cheering from the ragged deck below.

## It Must Be Your Tonsils

THE TONSILS, as I understand it, have innumerable ramifications and connections within the human frame—more connections, almost, than a Lee has in Virginia.

There was a day when doctors and surgeons blamed aches, pains, and swellings on such understandable weaknesses as eating, drinking, or exercising too much or too little, or on the unavoidable peculiarities of mankind or of the climate.

Old Dr. Culpepper, years and years ago, prescribed mashed henbane root, warmed and applied to the feet or the knees, as a remedy for gout. A quinsy sore throat, to his way of thinking, was best cured by swallowing a silk thread dipped in the blood of a mouse.

His advice to those who suffered from swellings was to mark the spot on a rail fence or barn door where a swine had rubbed itself: then to cut off a piece of the wood and with it rub the swollen place. This was highly efficacious, in theory, provided the sufferer utilized wood which the swine had used for similar purposes. To rub a swollen head with a piece of wood against which the swine had rubbed a swollen tail was, to Dr. Culpepper's way of thinking, waste effort.

It is safe to say that if old Dr. Culpepper were alive today his medical ideas would be more conservative. Gout, he would doubtless contend, could only be caused by infected tonsils; and he would probably frown darkly on anyone who dared suggest that henbane root, whether hot, cold, mashed, or unmashed, could act beneficially upon gout. The only way to get rid of gout, he would say, is to get rid of the tonsils.

The suggestion of using a silk thread dipped in mouse's blood as a relief for quinsy sore throat would doubtless make him equally petulant. He would insist that nothing but blemished tonsils could give rise to a quinsy sore throat; and he might even go so far as to say that the only effect to be expected from placing mouse's blood in juxtaposition with diseased tonsils would be a touch of bubonic plague.

Like many others of his fellow doctors he would, in all likelihood, blame almost everything on the tonsils: not only gout, quinsy sore throat, and swellings of various sorts, but loss of equilibrium, loss of memory, loss of appetite, roaring in the ears, rheumatism, arthritis, susceptibility to colds, sleeplessness, irritability, fatigue, neuralgia, sciatica, dark spots before the eyes, that dragging-down sensation, and other grave defects.

I do not wish to give the impression that all doctors, at the present time, blame all ills on imperfect tonsils.

There seems to be a wide difference of opinion, for example, as to what causes arthritis, and doctors are by no means united as to how it can be cured.

The extremely popular Dr. Hay says frankly that it is caused by improper diet and that anyone can rid himself of arthritis if he gives up meats, starchy foods, and alcoholic stimulants and lives almost exclusively on vegetables—except for such periods as he may wish to devote to thirty-day fasts.

The equally widely acclaimed Dr. Locke insists that arthritis is due to imperfect circulation in the extremities coupled with an improper method of standing. It can be cured, he thinks, by cleverly wrenching the joints of the feet and hands and by wedging up the inside of the shoe heels, so that the wearers have a slightly pigeon-toed appearance.

Still others attribute arthritis to needlelike crystals in the blood and joints. The crystals, they think, can be dissolved and arthritis banished by the use of powerful and offensive-tasting salts taken in conjunction with a little lemon juice.

It must be admitted, however, that the average doctor has no patience with such beliefs. They irritate him, because he knows that everybody who has arthritis also has infected tonsils. It therefore stands to reason that the infected tonsils cause the arthritis.

The average doctor seldom goes so far as to say flatly and publicly that arthritis is always blamable on infected tonsils. His reluctance to be outspoken is perhaps because many persons have infected tonsils all their lives without suffering from any ailment more severe than a cold sore. He feels free, however, to view an infected tonsil with the deepest suspicion and has no hesitation in making the most scurrilous remarks concerning its dangerous potentialities as an instigator of arthritis or any other ill.

It is not definitely known how many persons possess infected tonsils, but to unprejudiced observers they appear to be as universal in all civilized countries as is the use of handkerchiefs for nose-blowing purposes.

In spite of the prevalence of infected tonsils, nobody ever has a good word to say for them. In fact, nobody has even been heard to speak kindly of tonsils that are healthy—perhaps because there are no healthy ones. Tonsils, in short, seem as unpopular as thunderstorms and even more destructive. So far as I am able to tell, they have no value except to doctors.

During the larger part of my life, tonsils have had little or no interest for me. When I was ten years old I was subject, in common with all members of the younger set at that time, to severe colds in the head. These colds, together with painful cases of chilblains, attacked us at the beginning of the skating and punging season and usually lasted until the baseball season opened.

To those of us who were accustomed to hook rides on pungs, riding some five or six miles each evening on the runners or side boards of delivery sleighs, with wet feet, wet mittens, half-frozen ears, and all the other accompaniments of winter sports in New England in the middle nineties, a cold seemed as essential a part of winter as Christmas, comic valentines, and woollen underclothes that made the wearer itch.

Parents, however, viewed the matter in a different light, as people are apt to do when subjected to a barrage of coughs, sneezes, and snuffles for months on end. Doctors were summoned from time to time and requested to eradicate the colds; but their medicines, like those administered to cold sufferers at the present time, had no effect whatever. The doctors were even changed occasionally, and each doctor tried a different cold remedy, but to no avail.

Eventually one doctor, who may have been a trifle more advanced than the others, or may merely have been more astute, delivered the opinion that the tonsils were doubtless to blame for my protracted and seemingly incurable colds. A brief examination tended to confirm this opinion, for they were infected. That is to say, you could see them when you peered down my throat, lurking like Scylla and Charybdis on either side; and like all other tonsils, they were somewhat swollen and spongy-looking. As a result, they were taken out.

In those days the removing of a brace of tonsils was a comparatively simple matter. The technical phrase for having tonsils out was "have your tonsils out."

Things are different today. A doctor who amounts to anything doesn't take out tonsils. He performs a tonsillectomy. I am unable to state when this interesting frill was attached to tonsil removing or why. Apparently a tonsillectomy is more dignified than taking out tonsils, though why it should be I am unable to state. Dentillectomy would seem no more dignified to me than pulling a tooth, and I would feel no more important if my visits to a barber were for the purpose of having a capillectomy performed, instead of getting an ordinary haircut.

In the nineties, however, tonsillectomy hadn't been invented. Tonsil removing was just a routine job of hacking 'em out. Instead of rising at the usual hour, the patient remained in bed. The doctor arrived at 9 A.M., combed back his whiskers, removed his detachable cuffs, opened his black bag, took out about three dollars' worth of tools and appliances which he arranged on a chair seat, and then neatly placed a rubber cap over the patient's face and said, "Breathe deep."

The patient woke up an hour later in an extremely nauseated condition, surrounded by all the signs of a shockingly sanguinary encounter. As soon as the nausea had subsided and the encarnadined towels and bedclothes had been dispatched to the laundry, the tonsils were officially declared out, and the patient got up and went back to school. The carving charge, as I recall it, was in the neighborhood of ten dollars; and the expenditure was considered justified if the patient thereafter ceased to be, during the winter months, a nuisance and a plague carrier to everyone who came within sneezing range.

In my own case, the removal of my tonsils seemed to have even less effect than the removal of heavy balbriggans would have had.

It is true that I was no longer troubled with chilblains; but the chilblain, so far as I know, is one of the few human ailments that hasn't, at one time or another, been blamed on infected tonsils.

My colds, however, were as frequent and virulent as ever, and my snufflings as juicy and protracted as those of all my acquaintances. Something, no doubt, had caused my colds; but that something, obviously, was not tonsils. Twenty-five years later I learned how to control colds with moderate success by means of anti-cold injections; but during those years I would never have known that my tonsils had been tampered with. I was as unconscious of them as I had been before they were taken from me.

In the autumn of 1933 I finished a novel, *Rabble in Arms*, on which I had been toiling for two years. *Rabble in Arms* was a book of nearly nine hundred pages that had required a seemingly endless number of sixteen-hour working days; and when the final proof sheets were at last corrected, I welcomed the opportunity to turn to such comparatively light labors as investigating the activities of Adolf Hitler's young Brown Shirts and prying into the dark mysteries of Oxford University.

So far as I knew, there was nothing the matter with me; but since I had written disrespectfully of Mr. Hitler's activities as recently as 1924, it occurred to me that I had better see a doctor before departing for Germany. The Nazis, I had learned, have long memories for those who speak lightly of their policies; and I was well aware that the interiors of German jails and concentration camps, under the Hitler régime, could scarcely be classed as health resorts.

It seemed barely possible that when I re-entered Germany I might wake up some fine morning to find two or three muscular young Krauts standing by my bedside and indicating, by means of pregnant gestures with their *gummiknöckels* or steel-lined lengths of rubber hose, that all of us were taking the auto-bus for the concentration camp in about three minutes, whether I had my trousers on or not.

If this should prove to be the case, I ought, I felt, to have an accurate knowledge of my own physical condition in order to gauge my powers of endurance.

Before leaving the United States, therefore, I visited one of the leading diagnosticians on the eastern seaboard and requested him to give me what is loosely known as a good going over.

He fell to work hopefully, whacking me on the knees with a wooden hammer, listening intently to the musical functioning of my internal organs, and taking all sorts of interesting samples for close scrutiny beneath powerful microscopes.

When he had done twenty-five dollars' worth of peering, pounding, and probing, he shook his head regretfully and told me I could put on my clothes. There was nothing, he sadly admitted, the matter with me. I was in excellent shape—in better shape, he implied, than a person of my age had any right to be.

Then, as a sort of afterthought, he picked up a bundle of wooden paper cutters, told me to open my mouth, and, holding down my tongue with one of the paper cutters, intently peered within.

At once he made sounds in which distress and commiseration were equally blended. "My, my!" he said. "Ts, ts!"

He jabbed the paper cutter against the back of my throat and, regardless of my half-strangled protests, scraped it around in what was doubtless a deft manner, though to me it felt as though a hobnailed boot were being cleansed on my most delicate tissues. When he took it out and looked at it, he groaned. "Ah yes!" he said. "I thought so! My, my! Just look at that!"

I wiped the tears from my eyes and looked. I expected, from the sensation I had undergone, to see something a little larger than a first-class mutton chop; but all I saw, on the extreme tip of the paper cutter, was an infinitesimal speck of pallid moisture. Its small size was a disappointment. It seemed to me that if I scraped anything soft and moist—anything whatever—with a wooden paper cutter, I could scrape off more than the doctor had clawed from my still aching throat.

The doctor, however, seemed pleased with his haul, small as it was.

"See that?" he demanded. "My, my! You'll have to do something about that right away!"

"About what?" I asked.

"Infected tonsils!" he said. "Whole system being poisoned! Ought to come out immediately! Shouldn't delay a minute!"

I protested bitterly that my tonsils had been taken from me in my early youth. To the best of my knowledge and belief I had been devoid of tonsils since I was ten years old: yet here was a reputable doctor not only telling me that I had tonsils, but that they were dangerously infected.

He waved my protests aside. "Magnificent pair of infected tonsils," he repeated. "Focal point for all sorts of trouble! Poison draining into entire blood stream! Get right at 'em! Get rid of 'em!"

With low cunning I asked him whether the tonsils had been infected for some time.

I must, he readily admitted, have had them for years—years! For years they had been pouring poison through me, from head to heel; and it was God's wonder I wasn't a total wreck.

I reminded him that I had been working unusually hard for a long time without noticeable inconvenience, that I was able to get along on only four or five hours' sleep a night, that my brain seemed to function with reasonable clarity, that I could digest anything that was regarded as being even half edible, and that he himself had pronounced me almost disgustingly healthy—until he looked at my tonsils. If, therefore, I had been able to live comfortably with my infected tonsils for years, why couldn't I continue to do so for an indefinite period?

He refused to argue the point. I was suffering from infected tonsils, and the only thing to be done was to get rid of them. If I was unwilling to take the step before I went to England and Germany, I must—I positively must—have them attended to immediately on my return.

Satisfied with this reluctant stay of sentence, I packed my bags and departed for Oxford, England, accompanied by my tonsils.

The winter climate of Oxford is not pleasant. To judge from the large numbers of excessively old ladies and gentlemen who are daily trundled up and down its main thoroughfares in wheel chairs, and from the almost incredible age of the persons whose deaths are noted in the obituary columns of the Oxford daily newspapers, it is a healthy town in which to live.

Nonetheless, to an American who has known nothing worse than the bracing winter climate of the Maine seacoast and the exhilarating gales of southern Siberia, the Oxford climate is distinctly depressing.

The country is low, flat, and wet and frequently enveloped in dense woolly fogs resembling lemon sherbet. The conventional heating system in most Oxford residences and hotel rooms is a small fire of cannel coal which, unless constantly poked, has a dim, halfhearted appearance, not unlike that of a regular fire viewed through smoked glass.

The depressing effect of the climate is aggravated by the apparent belief on the part of Oxford landladies that the heating qualities of roast pork make up for the penetrating chill in the atmosphere and the lack of warmth in the houses. I unhesitatingly question this belief; for although the landlady of our "digs," as boardinghouses are romantically called by England's upper classes, fed us roast pork for lunch and roast pork for dinner day after day for weeks on end, we were never warm in Oxford.

At the end of a few weeks of Oxford fogs and a pork diet I became conscious of a peculiar aching in my upper arms and shoulders.

Ordinarily I would have blamed this on the pork, or on the dank chill that permeated everything in Oxford; but when the pain began to cut into my night's rest to such a degree that I decided to speak to a doctor about it, I was horrified to have the doctor call it arthritis and blame it on my tonsils.

It is true that I frankly told him an American doctor had pronounced my tonsils to be infected, instead of forcing him to do all the work himself; and I may have been a trifle injudicious in asking him whether the pain, by any chance, could be arthritis. At all events, he said at once, without a moment's hesitation, that I had arthritis, that I should see a tonsil specialist when I went to London, and that the charge for this opinion was one guinea or twenty-one shillings. Since the pain was even more pronounced when I reached London, I asked the American Embassy to provide me with the names of three tonsil specialists. This the Embassy promptly did, giving me the names of—let us say—Sir Philip Philip of Baker Street, Mr. John St. John of Wimpole Street, and Mr. Denis McDennis of Cavendish Square.

I was thus initiated into one of the oddities of British medical circles.

A general practitioner in England is known as Dr. Jones or Dr. Brown; and when you call on him for an opinion the charge is usually one guinea or twenty-one shillings.

A surgeon, however, is not known as Dr. Jones or Dr. Brown, but as Mr. Jones or Mr. Brown. He is, of course, a doctor, but he doesn't want it bruited about. If he permits the prefix "Dr." to be attached to him, somebody might suspect him of giving sugar pills to children, or doing something equally undignified.

He is much superior, socially, to an ordinary doctor, and more difficult of access. Consequently his opinions are more valuable—or so, at least, the British think. A doctor charges one guinea for saying you have throat trouble and ought to see a throat specialist; but the throat specialist charges three guineas for saying approximately the same thing.

At all events, I telephoned to that eminent tonsil specialist, Sir Philip Philip. A female attendant answered the telephone and told me coldly that Sir Philip had no free hours that day, which was Friday, or on the following Monday, nor yet on the following Tuesday, but that he could see me briefly on Wednesday, late in the afternoon.

Disheartened by this activity in tonsillar circles, I banished Sir Philip from my mind and telephoned Mr. John St. John. Mr. St. John answered the telephone himself.

Certainly, he said eagerly, he could see me today—this afternoon. Yes; if I insisted, he could even see me immediately. Yes, yes: come over at once! It meant a bit of delay in his luncheon hour, but such things were of no importance when one's health was at stake, what? By all means step in a taxi at once—Wimpole Street, eh?

I hurried over to Wimpole Street and found Mr. St. John, correctly attired in morning coat and striped trousers, awaiting me. In fact, he opened the door for me himself. Seemingly Sir Philip Philip had a corner in London's tonsils and had left little or no tonsil business for Mr. St. John.

When I briefly described my symptoms to Mr. St. John and told him what an unpleasant impression my tonsils had made on my American doctor, Mr. St. John placed me in an uncomfortable chair, pressed down my tongue with one of a bundle of wooden paper cutters, and then gasped in horror.

"Oh, by Jove!" he said. "No wonder! I mean to say, one shouldn't waste a moment! Oh, most serious! Yes, yes, yes! Oh, by all means! Just hold the head steady and I'll——"

Before I could move, he had assaulted the back of my throat with the paper cutter and had brought it out with an infinitesimal dab of gelatinous matter adhering to the front edge. He showed it to me proudly. "Took it from a pocket!" he said. "Pockets all through them, and each pocket full up! Might stay here all afternoon, taking stuff like this out of pocket after pocket! Positively frightful! My dear chap, you came here just in time!"

"Then you think this pain in my shoulders comes from my tonsils?" I asked him.

"My dear chap!" he expostulated. "Of course! You're poisoned! It might crop out anywhere! Arms, legs, body, head, feet, brain—positively anywhere! Not an instant to lose, my dear boy."

"Now wait a minute," I said. "I've got to go to Germany, and unless it's absolutely necessary I don't want to be laid up."

He was horrified. "Oh, utterly!" he insisted. "Utterly necessary! I don't wish to frighten you; but in all sincerity, my dear man, any delay might be fatal! See here, my dear chap: I'll take out a bit of the poison; and you'll see: you'll see!"

With this dark threat he produced a small suction pump with a glass nozzle. Placing the nozzle against the back of my throat, he set it in operation. The sensation was somewhat similar to reaming out the windpipe with a shotgun cleaner made of brass bristles.

When Mr. St. John at length withdrew the glass nozzle and examined it, his most pessimistic suspicions seemed confirmed. He showed me the nozzle with a triumphant air. In it was a wisp of moisture—about one quarter enough to equal the white of a hummingbird's egg.

"There you are!" he exclaimed. "Just as I told you! The entire system is at the mercy of this virulent poison! I insist upon it, my dear chap—nothing to be done but have them out! I wouldn't frighten you for worlds; but I give you my word that if my tonsils were like yours, I'd be unable to rest until I'd had them out!"

The functioning of the suction pump seemed to have weakened me and lowered my powers of resistance. Not only did my shoulders ache more violently than ever, but my back, my legs, my neck, and my head had developed aches as well. I protested feebly, however, that I had already arranged for my passage to Germany on the following Wednesday, only five days away. I could not, I told him, delay my departure beyond that date.

"Nonsense, my dear chap," said Mr. St. John. "There's nothing serious about a tonsillectomy—nothing whatever. I'll do it at your hotel or send you to a nursing home. You can walk out the next day, good as new. Have it done tomorrow, my dear chap; you'll be running about on the following day, cheerful as a cricket. Oh, absolutely! It's a new technique, my dear boy—my own; worked it out myself! There's no knife, my dear chap: no knife and no blood."

I still retained sufficient strength to question this statement. "No knife?" I asked. "How do you get 'em out?"

"I wipe them out," Mr. St. John said. "The technique's my own. I merely put a bit of gauze on my forefinger, I mean to say, and then I rub them off." He made menacing wiping motions with his forefinger.

"You mean you rub off the tonsils?" I asked.

"Absolutely," Mr. St. John said. "That's the technique. Entirely new and wonderfully successful. Give them a rub and off they come. That's why there's no blood. Now, look here, my dear chap, shall we say tomorrow morning?"

"Well," I said feebly, "how much does it cost?"

Mr. St. John was all affability. "Of course, of course," he said. "I'm glad you mentioned that. We arrange such matters to suit the individual. Last year I performed a tonsillectomy on a distinguished countryman of yours—an automobile manufacturer. He paid me three hundred guineas."

That, I told him, was nice—very nice and very generous. Unfortunately I didn't manufacture automobiles. I wrote books; and one of the peculiarities of my countrymen was that books were not essential to their happiness, whereas automobiles were.

"Oh, quite! Quite!" Mr. St. John said hurriedly. "I quite understand. Now, let me see: should we say one hundred guineas?"

"I'm afraid not," I said.

"Just a moment," Mr. St. John said. "Suppose we get at it in another way. What amount would seem reasonable to you? Be quite frank, I mean to say."

I protested that I was not familiar with the current quotations on tonsil removing.

"Come, come!" Mr. St. John said. "Name a figger! Don't be backward, my dear fellow!"

I timidly observed that twenty guineas looked as large to me, if not larger, than three hundred guineas looked to any American automobile manufacturer who had ever come to my notice.

Mr. St. John raised his eyebrows. "I could scarcely do it for that."

Enormously relieved, I looked around for my hat; but Mr. St. John stopped me. "I couldn't," he repeated, "do it for that: not for an Englishman; but an American would be different. Yes. Quite. Ah—let me see: I assume you'd have no objection to paying for an assistant to administer the anesthetic, and for a nurse, and for a few other odds and ends, eh?"

I said that I naturally expected to pay for all necessary odds and ends.

"Then we'll consider it settled," Mr. St. John said briskly. "Just name the hour and we'll have them out tomorrow, quick as a wink."

Not until later, I told him, could I let him know the exact hour; and with that I left him the conventional three guineas and tottered dejectly away to keep a luncheon engagement.

For some reason or other I was immeasurably depressed by the prospect of having my tonsils rubbed out; and I mentioned my depression to my companion at lunch. He was an Englishman with an extensive knowledge of nursing homes. The upper classes, in England, seldom go to hospitals, since hospitals cater almost wholly to the Lower Orders. They go to nursing homes, which are smaller and more exclusive than hospitals, considerably more profitable to the doctors who send patients to them, and constitute one of the many rackets from which the British seem unable to free themselves.

When my English companion heard my plans to enter a nursing home for a brief program of tonsil rubbing, he shook his head dubiously.

"Look here," he said, "did you ever see a tonsil? I mean to say, do you know how the beastly things are attached and all that sort of rot?"

I admitted that I didn't.

"Neither do I," he said, "but if they're what I think they are, a chap might rub at them all day without doing more than raise a blister on his finger. Now see here: I know nothing at all about this rubbing business—never heard of it, I mean to say. Doubtless all right and all that sort of thing; but why not stagger around to another of these tonsil chappies and see what he thinks about these confounded arms of yours, what? I mean to say, everybody thinks differently about everything nowadays, if you know what I mean. What I mean is, our banker chappies never think the same things about money and investments, and our political chappies never have the same thoughts about the League of Nations. Probably the tonsil chappies are no different. And even if they aren't, by Jerve, I wouldn't have anyone rubbing anything out of me with a bit of gauze attached to a forefinger—not until I'd seen him do a spot of rubbing on someone else, if you know what I mean."

In spite of the dull aches that filled me from head to foot, I contrived to catch his drift; and that afternoon I visited the third specialist on my list, Mr. Denis McDennis of Cavendish Square.

Having an outmoded theory that honesty is the best policy, I told him the full story—how my American diagnostician had been shocked by my tonsils several months before: how aches and pains had assailed me in Oxford: how Mr. John St. John had regarded my condition as desperate and insisted that my tonsils be immediately rubbed off bloodlessly and painlessly by means of a bit of gauze wrapped around a forefinger.

Mr. McDennis, who proved to be an Australian by birth, listened to me imperturbably. Then, after the manner of expensive doctors, he wrote down as many of the details of my past life as I was willing to divulge, after which he reached for his bundle of wooden paper cutters and proceeded to examine my throat.

To my extreme relief, he apparently had no desire to excavate any deposits either for his own amusement or for my edification, nor did he appear unduly perturbed by what he saw. In fact, he sank back lethargically in his chair after making the examination, and I was obliged to prod him into expressing an opinion.

My tonsils were, he admitted, infected, but not alarmingly so.

"Do you mean," I asked hopefully, "that I won't die if I don't have them taken out tomorrow?"

"Oh," he said, "I wouldn't advise a tonsillectomy: not tomorrow. It's quite a shock to the nervous system, I mean to say. They're deeply imbedded, you know. Oh, quite. A person of your age should make up his mind he'll have to take things easy for three or four weeks after a tonsillectomy, and won't feel his usual self for two or three months. If you're going to Germany on Wednesday with the idea of working, you shouldn't think of having a tonsillectomy."

"But," I protested, "Mr. St. John said it was nothing. He said I'd be cheerful as a cricket the day after it was done. He said——"

"Oh, quite!" Mr. McDennis murmured.

I recognized this as a British tip-off that any discussion of Mr. St. John's theories would be either unethical or unsporting, or both, and should under no circumstances be pursued as a topic of conversation. Consequently I dropped the subject; but in my coarse American way I continued to have a number of unethical and unsporting thoughts.

"What I would suggest," Mr. McDennis eventually continued, "is that if you return to America in about six months' time, you undergo a tonsillectomy. I think you will find that a tonsillectomy would increase your efficiency. You will probably feel a little better—as much as fifteen per cent better, perhaps—after the effects have worn off."

"But this arthritis," I said. "Won't it tie me in knots?"

"I fancy not," Mr. McDennis said impassively, "but I'll give you something that'll make it less noticeable. I wouldn't worry about it, if I were you. Sometimes these—ah—aches are somewhat ameliorated in more favorable climates."

He wrote out the prescription, accepted his three-guinea fee with an abstracted air, and on the following Wednesday I deserted the dank climate of England with a bottle of Mr. McDennis's ache remover in my overcoat pocket.

From that moment the aches diminished, though I am unable to state whether their diminution was due to the more bracing air and the warmer houses of Germany, or to Mr. McDennis's bitter-tasting prescription, or to the medicinal effect of German beer.

All I know is that they dwindled to a point that permitted me to swing a golf club with perfect ease, although there still remained, in my elbows, a faint discomfort that frequently resulted in a minor catastrophe when I attempted to pick up, with one hand, a typewriter or a full bean pot. The Krauts, moreover, were kind and obliging, except for their obstinate refusal to permit me to visit their concentration camps or their military training grounds at Treuenbreitzen and Jütebog; and so, in the spring of 1934, I returned to America about as well as when I went away, barring those faintly aching shoulders.

From time to time during the summer, which was a busy one, I thought guiltily of my tonsils; but the opportunity to have them out never seemed to present itself. Almost before I knew it, autumn had arrived, and with it the necessity of retiring to the half-baked palace on an Italian hilltop for the purpose of embarking on another ten-pound novel; so back to Italy I went, still accompanied by my tonsils.

It was in March of 1935, over a year after Mr. St. John, in his Wimpole Street lair, had warned me not to retain my tonsils for another day, that I awoke to the criminal folly of my procrastination.

Italian hilltops offer small opportunities for exercise, since they consist mostly of vineyards about the size of a hooked rug, set off from each other by ledges, and rock walls whose surfaces resemble enlarged nutmeg graters.

A person who is engaged in the writing of novels in such a locality, however, soon feels the need of exercise; for after sitting at a desk for upwards of ten hours a day for weeks on end, and interspersing his labors with meals in which spaghetti and other fattening foods figure largely, he begins to suspect that he may decompose unless he exerts himself physically.

In order to meet this need of exercise, I sent to the village for several yards of clothesline, made myself a number of jump ropes of different lengths, and went to work on a daily program of rope jumping.

In the beginning my movements were about as graceful as those of Eliza might have been if she had attempted to cross the ice with a piano in her arms. My endurance, too, was bad; for at the end of fifty or sixty jumps I felt as though I had run three miles and then been stepped on by a cart horse. In a week I became more adept and could jump rope freely on a tiled floor without breaking the tiles. At the same time my range increased, and I soon found myself able to make three hundred jumps at a stretch without seriously alarming the household with my wheezing.

It was on the first day of March, while I was engaged in running off a series of five hundred consecutive jumps, that the catastrophe occurred. At about the four hundredth jump I became conscious of a feeling of discomfort in my left leg. I varied my double-kick jumping with the easier double-foot hop, but the discomfort continued. Slightly alarmed by this, I slowed down to the childish hitch-and-kick jump. The discomfort left me, but something told me I had jumped enough for one day.

I hung up the rope and went back to my desk. Three hours later, when I rose to make ready for the evening spaghetti, my left knee screaked like a rusty hinge. There was an aching, burning sensation in it, so that I was obliged to walk in a crouching position, like Old Mother Hubbard hobbling to the cupboard.

I knew at once what had happened. I had put an undue strain on my knee, and the poison in my infected tonsils, seeking a weak spot in which to settle, had concentrated on the knee and given me an attack of arthritis that made my previous attack look like nothing at all.

The blame, I knew, rested entirely on myself. I had been warned by an American diagnostician: I had been doubly warned by Mr. St. John of Wimpole Street. I had disregarded their warnings; and as a result I had, figuratively speaking, got it in the neck as well as in the knee.

Too late I realized that I should have undergone a tonsillectomy during the preceding summer. If I had done so, arthritis would have passed me by.

As the weeks rolled on, my knee became worse. I tried to master it by taking long walks; but the poison from my infected tonsils, obviously, was too virulent. I limped and hobbled over the donkey paths—a distressing spectacle to behold.

Occasionally, when the pain seemed a trifle less, I bravely took the old jump rope from the hook and essayed a few jumps, only to become an almost total cripple for the remainder of the day.

Whenever I sat down in a chair or rose from one, I groaned and grumbled, and doddered painfully about in the manner of a ninety-eight-year-old State-of-Mainer dragging himself to the corner grocery to pick up the local gossip.

I became peevish and crotchety, and at frequent intervals cried loud cries to the effect that I had been a fool not to have my tonsils out a year ago; that I had learned my lesson; that I would be rid of my tonsils within one week of the day I returned to America, or know the reason why.

This time I kept my word. Five days after I landed in America I limped into the office of one of the foremost tonsil specialists in the East and submitted to another examination.

By this time my long experience with tonsils and my three-guinea conferences with London doctors had thoroughly familiarized me with the proper technical phraseology. I had, I told him, come to see him about a tonsillectomy because of arthritic tendencies. In short, I had a bum knee and a couple of bum elbows; and if these, as I suspected, were due to my tonsils, he could go right ahead and tonsillectomize me to his heart's content.

His attitude, I feel free to confess, was far from satisfactory. My tonsils, he was able to assure me, after the usual assault with the wooden paper cutters and a miniature boat hook, still were infected; and he cautiously admitted, when pressed, that I might feel better if I would submit to a tonsillectomy.

Unlike Mr. St. John of Wimpole Street, however, he refrained from making any pessimistic predictions as to what would happen to me if I persisted in dodging a tonsillectomy. As to the possible effect of a tonsillectomy on my arthritic symptoms, he refused to commit himself. That, seemingly, was my lookout.

Unlike all the other tonsil haters with whom I had come in contact, he seemed to think that he had done his duty when he proved conclusively that tonsils were infected. If the owner of the infected tonsils wished to keep them, he was at liberty to do so; if he wished to get rid of them, the doctor stood ready to perform a tonsillectomy.

In view of the passion with which my other doctors had urged me to undergo a tonsillectomy, I was naturally slightly annoyed at his lack of enthusiasm; but common sense told me that if I continued to consult doctors about my tonsils without having anything done, the financial drain would probably ruin me, even though my tonsils didn't. He was, I therefore told him, at liberty to shoot the works, and the sooner the better.

I expected him to show a faint trace of emotion when I finally agreed to take the momentous step, but he merely nodded.

What, I then asked him, should I do to prepare for the operation? Since I had been contemplating it and dodging it for nearly two years, and since it was happening to me, I naturally regarded it as something pretty important, and I saw no reason why everyone else shouldn't regard it with equal respect and awe.

The doctor, however, remained entirely unmoved. The thing to do, he said, was to go out and have dinner; then go to the hospital around nine o'clock at night and have a good sleep. At eight-thirty on the following morning, he added, he'd attend to my tonsillectomy in two shakes of a lamb's tail.

When I asked him what I should eat for dinner, he said amiably that he didn't know what I liked. Lobster, he said, made a nice dinner, as did steak or lamb chops, or even a thick slice of Penobscot salmon topped off with a commodious helping of blueberry pie.

"I suppose," I ventured, "that beer would be bad for me, just before a tonsillectomy."

"Bad?" he asked. "Bad? What's bad about it?"

I saw clearly that I might as well stop fishing for sympathy; so I went out and had a large dinner of broiled swordfish, beer, lemon pie, roquefort cheese, and coffee, following which I went to the hospital, where an impassive young thing in a white uniform handed me a half-portion night-gown that tied together at the back of the neck, and, like the present styles in women's bathing suits, covered practically nothing but two fifths of the chest.

She also handed me two pills. When I asked her what they were, she said unsympathetically that they were sleeping pills.

Two hours later she came in, woke me up, and gave me two more pills. I repeated my question and was again told they were sleeping pills.

I protested that I had already had two, but she said it was all right: that I was getting twilight sleep and still had several more pills to take, not counting the big green one around five o'clock in the morning.

Her mention of twilight sleep disturbed me. Was it possible, I asked her anxiously, that she was confusing me with someone else? I was not, I assured her, a maternity case: I was a tonsillectomy. She favored me with a false, suspicious smile and left the room as quickly as possible.

At half past seven the next morning I was handed a final pill and a pair of white cotton leggins to pull on under my half-portion nightgown, presumably for modesty's sake.

An hour later, so full of pills that I rattled when trundled along the corridor in a wheel chair, I was taken up in an elevator and pushed into the operating room, where the doctor, clad in a clean white uniform, was playing cheerfully with a trayful of knives.

Assisted by the nurses, I was shifted from one wheel chair to another, and was interested to note that when my white cotton leggins fell off during the transfer, my twilight sleep was not sufficiently powerful to keep me from feeling slightly embarrassed. When I mentioned this fact and suggested that somebody either pull up my leggins or give me another pill, the doctor said, "Just sit up straight and take it easy."

Modern tonsil removing is not at all what it was in the olden days. After I had been stabbed a few times in the back of the throat with a hypodermic needle, the doctor went to work on one side.

The primary sensation is somewhat similar to that of scraping a cluster of wax drippings from a coat sleeve with a knife blade.

The secondary sensation, when the main tonsil comes out, is vaguely reminiscent of pulling a baseball out of a pocket both tight and wet.

Having completed one side, he proceeded to tie the ends of all the newly exposed blood vessels to prevent bleeding—an operation that must be even more difficult to perform than the feat of hanging a dozen hats against a plaster wall that has no protuberances. He then did the same thing to the other side, after which he proudly showed me the extracted or ectomized tonsils.

They seemed to me to be about the size and shape of the end joint of a thumb. The time required to ectomize them had been upwards of eighteen minutes, and the whole affair had been eminently satisfactory to everyone concerned, except for the embarrassing loss of my leggins and for one other incident which was never made clear to me.

In my half-drugged state, just after the doctor had proudly displayed my still quivering tonsils to the public gaze, I thought I heard one of the attendant nurses remark, "If you aren't going to use those, I'd like to have them." What I was never able to learn was whether I had heard correctly, and whether it was my tonsils the nurse wanted, or something else, and what she planned to do with them after she got them.

I feel that I should here reveal a conspiracy that seems to be afoot to minimize the immediate aftereffects of a tonsillectomy. In my frequent conversations and conferences with high-priced specialists on the subject of tonsil removing I had been given to understand that the operation is a simple one, entirely painless: that a person whose tonsils have been snatched from him is troubled for two or three days by a slight sore throat, and that at the end of that time the entire incident passes from his mind and from his throat as well.

It is doubtless true that the operation is a simple one for those who know how to perform it properly, and it is certainly painless when properly performed, as well as practically bloodless. The person who expects to be able to forget a tonsillectomy in two or three days, however, is laboring under a grievous misapprehension, no matter how many statements he hears to the contrary.

After my nurses had wheeled me from the operating room, they rolled me back into bed, draped my dropped leggins over the back of a chair, and calmed me with an injection of morphine, as a result of which I lay lethargically during the remainder of the day and through the night.

Early the next morning a nurse came in and placed a tray upon my knees. On the tray was a breakfast that would have satisfied a boa constrictor. Its chief constituent was a beefsteak an inch and a half thick, cooked over a brisk fire, so that its edges were crisp and black. Ranged around the beefsteak were a deep dish of oatmeal, several slices of graham bread, four or five rashers of bacon, a muffin, a jar of marmalade, a pitcher of cream, a cup of strong coffee, and several soda crackers.

I sat and looked at it; then tried to swallow. I did so with great difficulty. Fortunately I had seen my tonsils after they were removed: otherwise I would have thought that something the size of a watermelon had been taken from my throat.

"Listen," I told the nurse, speaking with considerable difficulty, "I can't eat this. I couldn't eat it if I had all my tonsils. Bring me two soft-boiled eggs and make them extra soft."

"Open your mouth," the nurse said. When I opened it, she deftly tossed a powdered aspirin tablet against the back of my throat.

"Now," she said, "you eat that breakfast! The doctor ordered that breakfast. He told us just how long he wanted the steak cooked, and he said you were to eat it—all of it."

"There's a lot of gristle in that steak," I objected, "and my throat——"

"That's what he ordered," the nurse insisted. "Steak with gristle in it. You're to eat it, gristle and all."

When I again attempted to mention my throat, she stopped me. "See those soda crackers?"

I said that I did, adding that even when my health was perfect I regarded them as the lowest form of food at the breakfast hour.

"Eat 'em all," the nurse said coldly. "Don't leave so much as a crumb of those crackers! If you don't eat everything on that tray, I'll probably be fired."

I went to work on the tray. It required a few turkeylike motions of the head and neck, but I have tackled more difficult chores. The nurse watched me narrowly, and when she had seen the last soda cracker disappear she handed me a stick of gum. I thanked her and told her I never used it. "Yes, you do," she said. "You're going to use it steadily for the next ten—for the next few days. Doctor's orders."

The doctor, when he arrived, peered down my throat and seemed lost in admiration of what he saw. "Smooth as a kitty's ear," he murmured. Then he told me his theory about soda crackers and gristly steak. "The more you exercise your throat," he said, "the sooner it'll get well. Some people baby themselves after a tonsillectomy—won't eat anything but soup and milk. Their throats are sore for three weeks."

"Did you say three weeks?" I asked.

"Oh," he said carelessly, "you'll be over this in a few days."

Day after day the nurses plied me with food—fish, chops, toast, bacon, ice cream, soda crackers, cake, cheese. The second day was endurable, and so was the third.

On the fourth day the act of eating became more difficult. A mouthful of bran muffin, when it passed down the throat, seemed studded with broken bottles and rusty nails. A piece of lamb chop, pursuing its leisurely way along the esophagus, apparently had fur and claws, like an angry cat.

When I complained to my favorite nurse, she said cheerfully that the next day would be worse. She was right. Every mouthful swallowed on the fifth day was a surprise. The sensation was similar to setting off a bunch of firecrackers where the tonsils used to be. The surprising part was that no noise accompanied the act of swallowing. By rights it should have been accompanied by deafening reports, like machine-gun fire, with undertones of feline yowling and spitting.

On the fifth day I got up and went home. My first act, on rising, was to try my knee and elbows hopefully; for I thought that since the source of infection had been removed, my arthritis must have vanished. To my disappointment, both knee and elbows seemed no different than when I had entered the hospital.

The sixth day was as bad as the fifth, if not worse. Every mouthful of food set the tears to rolling down the cheeks, which made my home-coming a gay one.

The seventh day was no better.

On the eighth there was a slight improvement, accompanied during the still watches of the night by intermittent snores so violent and so noisy as to startle even the snorer.

On the ninth day I was able to swallow without wincing.

From the tenth to the fifteenth the only relic of the operation was a persistent soreness, such as might result from a prolonged siege of thunderous snoring, and a peculiar vacancy in the rear of the throat—a vacancy into which the uvula occasionally fell in the middle of a sentence, thus giving rise to a distressing choking sound.

From all this it may readily be seen that while a tonsillectomy may be, as everybody says, a simple thing, it is about as painless, in the long run, as something more complicated, like a broken leg or a Caesarean section.

As my throat returned to normalcy, I became increasingly interested in my arthritis. It was because of my arthritis that I had submitted to a tonsillectomy; and what I now wanted to know was when the poison would depart from my joints: when my old-time non-arthritic agility would return.

My knee still creaked annoyingly; but it seemed to me that since poison was no longer deluging my system, a little exercise might remove even the creak. To investigate this theory, therefore, I went to the golf links with three friends, one of whom had been a football player and graduate manager of the athletic teams of an eastern university. At the third hole my creaky knee became painful. At the sixth hole I was limping. By the tenth hole I was wincing at the finish of every shot. On the fourteenth hole I was obliged to quit.

My friend the graduate manager seemed interested. "Let's look at that knee," he said.

When I showed it to him, he poked and prodded at it. Certain of his prods were painful and others weren't.

"Who told you that was arthritis?" he asked.

"Well," I said, "the doctors seemed to think it was. They were pretty busy looking at my throat, so they didn't pay much attention to my knee, but they said anyone with a throat like mine ought to have arthritis, so that's what it is."

"Hell," the graduate manager said, "that's not arthritis! That's a pulled cartilage! I've seen thousands of 'em on the football field. You wrenched your knee and hurt the cartilage."

"Listen," I complained. "Some of the best specialists in England told me my tonsils——"

"I don't care what they told you," the graduate manager said. "Tonsils haven't any more to do with that knee than the Northern Lights have. I say it's a pulled cartilage; and I say you've got no business jumping around on it like this unless you bandage it. If you keep on this way, you'll never get over it. Then you'll go to a doctor for it, and he'll operate on you, and you'll have a stiff leg the rest of your life. Get yourself an elastic bandage and wear it whenever you exercise. If you're careful, your knee'll be well in six months. Get yourself an elastic bandage, and you can play eighteen holes of golf without being bothered at all."

"But my hands and shoulders!" I protested. "How about my hands and shoulders? Do you mean to say my hands and shoulders aren't arthritis? Are you trying to tell me they weren't caused by my tonsils?"

"I don't know anything about your hands and shoulders," he said. "All I know is that your knee is sore because of a pulled cartilage." As an afterthought he added, "Maybe your hands and shoulders are due to your teeth."

I got myself an elastic bandage for my sore knee. As the graduate manager had predicted, I was then able to play eighteen holes of golf in perfect comfort. Even the creakiness subsided, and almost at once I was able to rise from a chair without groaning and hobbling.

My hands and shoulders, however, still retained the faint arthritic discomfort that had been with me ever since those damp, dank days in England. I still hoped, once my poisonous tonsils were no longer with me, that the discomfort would disappear. I then discovered that there was a great difference of opinion as to how long it takes the system to rid itself of tonsil poison. Some said six months. Others said a year. Still others said two years. A few even went so far as to argue that if one point of infection was removed from the body, another point would set up somewhere else. Nobody seemed to know very much about it, as a matter of fact.

As time goes on I am finding more and more people who think that probably my uncomfortable hands and shoulders weren't due to my tonsils after all. They think that maybe they were caused by my unfortunate habit of leaning on my left elbow while writing—or by my teeth.

# Dissolution of a Hero

### From NORTHWEST PASSAGE

I HAD THOUGHT of the Fleet Prison as I had thought of all jails—as a stone building filled with straw-strewn cubicles from whose iron-barred doors peered wan prisoners in chains, and before which paced morose guards in uniform, jingling huge keys on iron rings; but it wasn't like that.

When I reached Ludgate Hill and walked down Farringdon Street, I found a grated window in a blank wall. Above the window were cut the words, "Pray Remember Poor Debtors Having No Allowance," and behind the grating stood a man hopefully rattling pennies in a tin cup. The cup came out of the bars appealingly toward me as I passed, and I dropped a shilling in.

A few paces beyond the window was an arched doorway—as busy a doorway as ever I saw. Messengers raced in and out; waiters with trays and hampers hurried anxiously through. Ladies whose profession was dubious made small talk with cadaverous-looking doorkeepers who stared fixedly at those who came and went.

When I stated my business to one of them, he looked helplessly baffled until I drew a shilling from my pocket. Then he became alert and loudly bellowed, "Cryer!" In response a fat man with black teeth and a nose like three ripe strawberries reluctantly and with the assistance of an eight-foot stave hoisted himself to his feet from his seat on the outer pavement and eyed me appraisingly.

"The celebrated Major Rogers," the keeper told him. "Upper side,

Number 12, but 'e'll be in Bartholomew Fair if they ain't shut off 'is credit."

The Cryer's eyes never left my weskit pocket, so I gave him a shilling too, and was led along an arched tunnel and out into the bright sunlight of a high-walled prison yard that was more like Southwark Fair than a prison.

The main building, beneath which the tunnel had brought me, was four stories high; and at each one of the scores of open windows in this huge structure was a man or woman or both, laughing, drinking, screaming, making love, holloing to people in the court below.

Above the doors and windows of the basement hung painted signs—Alderman Coffee House; Jos. Starkey, Billiards; Bartholomew Fair Wine Room; J. Cartwright, Tapster; A. Keith, Latin & French Taught; Bull & Garter Tap Room; John Figg, Barber; B. Lands, Racket Master; Bambridge, Haberdasher.

The court itself was a tumultuous throng of men, women, and children of every condition—some in rags and some dressed in the height of fashion. Crouching against the front of the prison were men huddled in foul and tattered greatcoats in spite of the warmth of the day, so that I suspected they wore next to nothing beneath. Others, stripped to shirt and smallclothes, ran furiously and with rackets drove ivory balls against the towering wall that shut the courtyard from the outer world. Still others played at skittles, missisipi, fives, cribbage, backgammon, whist, and games unknown to me. Around a tent which did duty as an alehouse, roisterers fought and sang; bedizened women strolled among the players, their shrill laughter rising penetratingly above the unending tumult of the place.

As I stood at the mouth of the tunnel, staring at the motley crew in the courtyard, I was aware of faces turned toward me. "Garnish!" I heard someone shout. "Pay or strip!" In an instant the cry was taken up on all sides, and every man in the courtyard, seemingly, stopped what he was doing to press close up to me. Those who were closest clutched at my arms and coat as if to tear off my clothes.

" 'Ere, 'ere!" the Cryer bawled, making play with his stave. "Can't you see 'e ain't no Collegian? 'E's a wisitor! Garn out of 'ere!"

The prisoners slowly dispersed, grumbling, except a few who remained to whisper urgent pleas for money, and a plump young woman in a striped skirt and a low-cut bodice, who seized the opportunity to smile kindly upon me and adjust her stocking top before my unfascinated gaze.

The Cryer lifted bushy eyebrows at me. When I shook my head, he slapped her smartly on the buttocks with his stave, ignored her outcries, and addressed me briskly. "Lucky thing for you, Master, you 'ad me along of you, or you'd be garnished proper."

"I won't forget it," I assured him. "What's the meaning of garnish? What did they mean by 'Pay or strip!'"

"Ho!" the Cryer said. "You ain't never even been in the College before, Master! Anybody wot comes in, the first thing 'e 'as to pay is Garnish, so all them old Collegians can get drunk; and if 'e ain't got no money, Master, they take 'is clo'es and sell 'em. They got to 'ave their Garnish, ain't they?"

"Do the women pay Garnish too?"

"Women!" he exclaimed. "There ain't no women in 'ere!"

Since there were at least a hundred women in sight, I could only wave my hand helplessly at them.

"Oh, them!" the Cryer said. "They didn't get put in 'ere! Nobody gets put in 'ere, only men. The women just come 'ere. Some of 'em's wives, and some of 'em's just friends of the debtors. Some of 'em's laundry ladies, and some of 'em run errands on account there's some errands that ain't delicate for a man to go on. The rest of 'em's just 'ere on business or pleasure. Glad of a chance to do pretty near anything, Master."

He became confidential. "That little gel out there in the yeller bonnet— they speak 'igh of 'er. Begins with a farden for just a mere kiss, and so on. If you 'ave a fancy to a little innocent trifling——"

"That's very kind of you," I said, "but I'm here to see Major Rogers."

"Heach man to 'is taste," the Cryer said. "I'll cry the Major in the court, an' then I'll cry 'im in Bartholomew Fair; and if 'e ain't in neither place, Master, I'll 'ave to 'ave a penn'orth o' Bob to cry 'im on the Master's Side an' the Common Side. 'Ard work, Master, cryin' out a man from among the two hundred an' forty-three debtors in this place. A penn'orth, eh, Master?"

"Yes, yes," I said. "That's agreed." His words meant next to nothing to me; but the heat of the courtyard and the stench of latrines were almost overpowering.

He stepped forward to a more commanding position in the court and in a gin-hoarsened voice bellowed, "Major Rogers."

Nobody paid the slightest attention. Not even by the turn of an eye did that idle crowd of debtors and drabs acknowledge the name that had once been the bane of the whole French army; the name that had commanded the respect of every Indian nation in North America, had put new hope into all the disconsolate traders of Canada, earned the high regard and support of the King's generals, of the King's Ministers, and of the King himself.

The Cryer turned to me, and his strawberry nose seemed to steam with annoyance. "You come along of me. Saves time, in case 'e's sleepin' in a corner an' 'as to be waked up."

I followed him into the basement of the huge building—the section evidently known to the inmates as Bartholomew Fair; and on each door the Cryer rapped with his stave and shouted, "Major Rogers!" Sometimes there was no reply; sometimes a volley of oaths and hoarse laughter answered him; sometimes he nimbly dodged a shower of dirty water or beer dregs.

" 'Ard work, Master," he assured me again. "That's the 'ell of this place —the macaronis and the beaux! A mechanic or a squire, 'e's all right; but damn these 'igh-born Mohocks that ain't never done a lick of work in their lives! They ain't got no respect for nobody! Seems like the 'arder you work, the more they 'ate you."

All the rooms in Bartholomew Fair were used as taprooms, kitchens, coffeehouses, tobacconists', barbershops, cardrooms, clubrooms, eating houses, each one as dirty as it was dark; and though we looked into every room, we found no sign of Major Rogers.

The Cryer groaned. "Mebbe it'd be best for our 'ealth's sake to 'ave a dram afore we climb to Upper Side, Master," he said hopefully. "Cruel 'ard climbin', them stairs is."

When I refused, he led me to a stairway so foul that dirt had caked on it in knobs and knots, and we stumbled up flight after flight, through an assortment of odors by comparison with which an Indian village was as fragrant as newly cut sweet grass.

In the dark gallery of the topmost floor the cries of the racket players, the shrill laughter of the women, the hoarse shouts of roisterers in the courtyard below, came to us dimly, as though choked and stifled by the stench of the place. The Cryer went confidently to a closed door, rapped upon it with his stave, and bawled, "Wisitor for Major Rogers!"

He placed his ear against the panel and nodded to me with a sly and knowing grin. " 'E's there," he whispered. From within came creakings and hurried movements; then a heavy silence.

The Cryer thumped again upon the panels, and this time a familiar voice sluggishly shouted, "Yes, yes, damn it! Nobody deaf here!"

The key turned in the lock, and the door was flung open. In the doorway stood Rogers, a little unsteady on his feet, long brown hair hanging lankly on either side of his broad face, dirty white cambric stock askew, and shirt stained with streaks and splotches.

Behind him I saw a truckle bed with a tousled gray blanket on it, a battered pine table, and two stools. Peering with feigned interest from the open window, which looked on the rear of the prison, was a young woman in a pink-and-white-striped skirt, a bright blue blouse, and shoes whose heels were so worn on the inner edges that she seemed almost to be standing on her ankle bones. She wore no stockings.

Rogers stared at the Cryer, head hanging and underlip slack. The pouches under his eyes were enormous, and glittered as if wet or newly greased. "Well, who is it?" he said thickly. "Don't wish to be disturbed when resting."

His eyes moved slowly from the Cryer's face and heavily met mine. "Oh," he said, swaying a little. "Didn't see you. Who is it? Bad light here." He caught at the doorjamb and peered hard at me.

"Why, Langdon!" he said uncertainly. "Langdon Towne!"

He shot a furtive glance at my escort; at the young woman leaning from the window; at the disheveled bed; then passed his hand clumsily over his thick lips and spoke to the Cryer. "Well, what you waiting for?"

The Cryer turned to me, showing blackened teeth. "We mentioned a dram—a penn'orth of gin, Master." His face was like that of something seen in a dreadful dream. Everything around me—Rogers, uncertain of speech and with wavering, bloodshot eyes; the wretched cell of a room and the sour stench of it; the lump of a woman, staring from the window with the same witless instinct that leads an ostrich to thrust its head beneath the sand—all of this had the quality of nightmare; and my understanding of it was as foggy as a troubled dreamer's.

I fumbled for a penny and dropped it in the Cryer's palm.

"Servant, Master," he said. "Servant, Major. Pleasure to oblige a gentleman."

He stooped and looked under the Major's arm at the woman in the window. "Glad to see you in good company for once, Sadie," he added and left us.

"Damned whelp!" the Major said. "If Fitzherbert hadn't died, I'd put an end to all this insolence! Come in, Langdon: come in! Ah—that's my nurse at the window: my nurse. Had a bad time with my leg, Langdon, my boy. Prob'ly you heard."

"Yes," I said.

"By God!" Rogers said. "I've got some scores to pay that no debtors' prison can ever take notice of! Forced the marrow right out through the bone and the flesh! Have to have a nurse look out for it—bandages and all that."

He went to the girl, who continued to stare bovinely from the window, and placed a huge hand on the small of her back, which was broad as a cow's. "You needn't wait any longer today," he said, "but if you're here tomorrow, you can look in to see how I am." He coughed in earnest of delicate health.

She withdrew herself from the window and turned a fat, expressionless, dead-white face toward the Major. "Needn't wait any longer? I come up here for them two shillings, and here I waits till I gets 'em!"

"Shillings?" Rogers repeated vacantly. "Two shillings?" He slapped his breeches pockets and seemed suddenly to recall something half-forgotten. "Damn it!" he mumbled. "That remittance was late again! Langdon, my boy, could you spare me a few shillings for a matter of a week?"

I hurriedly gave him all the silver I had. He counted it carefully, moving his thick lips—"eight, ten-and-six, eleven-and-six. Eleven-and-six, Langdon. I'll make a note of it."

He flung one of the coins to the fat girl, who picked it up with an air she tried to make disdainful and deftly concealed it somewhere about her voluminous bodice.

"Now you got your two shillings," Rogers said heavily, "suppose you get out and stay out."

"Stay out?" she asked in a strange hoarse whisper. "Don't you want me to look in tomorrow, like you said?"

"I do not!" Rogers said. "One thing I insist on's sissiplin—displin; and you, you damned fat dough-faced slut, you started getting insubordinate! Here you'll wait, you says! Well, my beauty, jus' try it! Jus' try somep'n like that on Major Robert Rogers of Rogers' Rangers! You come in here again and I'll drop you out the window, 'n' then I guess you'll think twice before you start telling a commanding officer of Rangers what you'll do an' what you won't do!"

She fled past him, and I could hear her scuffling down the gallery on her worn-out heels.

Rogers, muttering to himself, went to the bed, fumbled fruitlessly beneath the blankets, looked between the bedstead and the wall, lost his balance, and sat heavily upon the travesty of a mattress.

"Damn it," he said, passing huge fingers through his disordered hair, "these women ain't got one damned grain of reticence or anything. Show 'em a bottle of gin 'n' they ain't sassfied to drink only half it! They drink it all, unless you watch 'em; then take the bottle home to put vinegar in. You don't happen to have a drop of gin about you, do you, Langdon?"

I shook my head.

Rogers struggled to his feet. "Sit down, sit down!" he said. "Don't stand there as if you were waiting for orders! No question of rank now, my boy! Be free and easy with me—like an equal."

Then he rubbed his hand across his forehead and frowned, as if trying to remember something. "You've always—you've always——" He rubbed his brow again. "Damn it, what was it I just thought of? What is it I'm trying to say? Oh yes!" He seemed to brighten a little. "You've always looked up to me too much—that's the trouble: you've always looked up to me too much." He looked at me sternly. "Not that you oughtn't to. Of course you ought! I'm Rogers! Major Rogers! Rogers of Rogers' Rangers!"

He laughed. "But you know that, of course, because you're Langdon Towne, so what's the use of my telling you? Here, Langdon, sit yourself down on this stool while I clean up a bit; then we'll go down to Bambridge's Whistling Shop 'n' have a drop or two to old friends 'n' the Northwest Passage."

"I won't stay," I said. "I dropped in to see whether there was anything I could do——"

"Won't stay!" Rogers cried. "Never heard such nonsense! You'll stay 'n' have supper! Mos' interestin' society you'd want to meet, right here in this damned College. Good's an education—linen drapers, naval officers, prize fighters, architects, sculptors, cap'n from the Royal Hussars, poets—all of 'em up to their ears in debt, so they put 'em in prison, Langdon; the last place in the world where they'll ever have a chance to get out of debt! I tell you, Langdon, you're in good company when you're in the Fleet! No, Langdon: I ain't goin' let you go—no sir! Not till I've done the honors—'n' had a chance to think whether there's anything you can do for me, like you said. Guess I can find somep'n."

He lurched to a chest of drawers, took a tie wig and a green coat from the bottom drawer, opened a bag of flour, and with an old piece of flannel clumsily powdered the wig as well as his soiled cambric stock. He retied his hose, which were wrinkled around his ankles, tightened his knee bands, examined the shoulder of his coat, and shook his head angrily at sight of an open seam through which a corner of padding protruded. Muttering to himself, he pushed the padding out of sight with a clumsy forefinger. There was a singular stale smell to him, of perspiration and wine dregs, gin and bad tobacco.

"There," he said, clapping a laced hat on his head and taking a final look at himself in a mirror that reflected him both dimly and contortedly: "that's better!"

He ushered me out, carefully locked the door of his miserable chamber, and on his way downstairs continued his discourse, but with a tongue that seemed stiff and unmanageable.

"When I think what I been through in the last five years, Langdon, I'm s'prised every time I look in the mirror. Ain't changed at all. Have to have a little more gin than I used to, on account of my leg 'n' malaria, 'n' helps you sleep, too. Makes it hard when—ah—remittance don't come, 'n' can't get credit for gin, even if it's to be used as medicine, the way I use it. Very fortunate, you coming 'long like this, Langdon, making possible have gin again tonight. Ah—le's see, what was it, now—what was it I was jus' talking about?"

"You were saying how little you'd changed, Major."

"Yes, so I was! To tell you God's honest truth, I'd feel just about as good as I ever did if only I could get away from the damned prison an' get started on somep'n again—somep'n big. Ah, my boy, I got some real good plans, if only I could get what's owed me!"

He hurried me into the courtyard, where the throng of strollers and racket players had dwindled at the approach of the supper hour, and went limpingly down the basement stairs into the long gallery of Bartholomew Fair.

At the doorway over which hung the sign reading "College Haberdasher," he fumbled for the latch, and in his eagerness to enter almost sprawled on the floor when the door gave way. The shop was a strange one, for the owner stood behind a counter on which was nothing save two cravats, badly wrinkled, a flyspecked stock, and a half brick.

"Two Bobs," Rogers said thickly.

"You ain't got credit, Major," the man said.

Rogers' eyes rolled wildly. "Damn you, Bambridge, they're for this gentleman—my good friend Langdon Towne. One of my Rangers, Bambridge, you damned little worm—not only a Ranger but a great artist, too. So let's have a little ordinary courtesy, Bambridge! For the love of God, Langdon, give this snake three shillings!"

I gave the man a gold sovereign, and when he had bitten it and rung it on the half brick, he brought out two pint bottles of gin from under the counter. Rogers snatched one of them, wrenched out the cork, and poured half the contents down his throat. "Ah!" he sighed. "Ah! That's terrible stuff, Langdon, but it's better'n nothing. Bambridge, you damned weasel, why don't you keep something fit for gentlemen to drink?"

"Maybe for the same reason you don't never have nothing to pay me with, Major," Bambridge said.

"Impudence! Always impudence!" Rogers said sadly, then grunted and finished the remainder of his bottle in three long, lingering swallows. "Hah!" he said. "Now my young friend Langdon, come with me!"

I followed him out to the corridor, and he laid a wavering course toward the end of it, whence came a clatter of chinaware, a babel of shouting, and bursts of maudlin song. The two end rooms bore the imposing name of

Alderman's Coffee House; and the Major, bawling jovial greetings, piloted me between tables at which sat men and women who were chiefly remarkable for the dishevelment of their wigs and their garments—all of which seemed strangely askew.

In a corner of that noisy, smoky, rancid place we took possession of two stools and a greasy, rickety table. The Major planted his elbows on the table and at once went to talking rapidly, as if he feared I might have something to say that he might not care to hear. When a waiter brought us ale, boiled potatoes, and mutton swimming in a transparent gravy that tasted of hair, he chewed enormously and stared at me out of eyes watery above those glistening pouches that were the color of a russet apple.

"Le's see," he said. "Does memory play me one of its tricks—it does sometimes, my boy—or didn't I purchase two bottles of gin from Bambridge? Two, I think. Two, I swear! My dear old friend, what became of the other?"

I brought it forth. The Major said "Hah!", drew the cork, laced his ale with gin, and gulped down the contents of the mug as if he burned inside. Then upon the instant he ate voraciously again, but somehow contrived, even with his mouth packed with food, to keep on talking.

"Yes, Langdon," he said, his speech becoming thicker and thicker, "it's damn aggravating to be kept away from food 'n' drink 'n' decent lodgings jus' because you can't get what's owed to you. You know how much this damned government owes me, Langdon? Ten thousand pounds, by God! Yes, sir! A thousand pounds was all they allowed me, 'n' I'd spent ten thousand more on King's business, keeping the Indian trade for England, 'n' look at what I've got out of it! A court-martial 'n' sickness 'n' a two-shilling room on the Upper Side of the Fleet, 'n' not a penny to spend! If you value your peace of mind, Langdon, keep out of public life and don't ever try to do anything for your country!"

I could hardly bring myself to look at this miserable man—this grimy, gin-soaked giant who had been the flashing spearhead of the British attack against the French troops that had hoped to keep all of North America for the King of France—this garrulous, red-eyed, wheezy derelict whom I had known as Wobi Madaondo: the White Devil whom the Indians had feared as they feared no other English leader.

He hitched himself forward to the edge of his chair and rubbed his greasy thick lips with the back of his hand. "Now listen, Langdon; all I got to do is show 'em I'm going to get ten thousand pounds and——"

Heavyhearted as I was, I couldn't help laughing. "Ten thousand pounds! Talk sense!"

"No, listen," he insisted. " 'Tain't as hard as you think! I got some mighty fine schemes, Langdon; mighty fine. I been working on 'em—yes, 'n' I got 'em prac'lly worked out! Now you take this Northwest Passage: it's there, 'n' you know it's there, 'n' I'd 'a' got there if it hadn't been for that skunk Johnson. Why, damn him—d'you know what that rat did, right while he was having me tried for giving presents to Indians? He 'n' Claus was having a Congress 'n' giving 'em twenty bateau-loads of presents so't they'd bring their trade to Fort de Chartres! Twenty bateau-loads, by God—twice as much as I had to give 'em—'n' the Indians wouldn't pay a damned bit of attention to him!" He laughed bitterly. "God, Langdon, when I think what that old skunk did to me jus' because he wanted to hog all the credit for everything, it makes me puke!"

He groaned, drank deeply, and looked bewildered. "Well, as I was saying—jus' what was it we was discussing—had it right on the tip m' tongue——"

"You were speaking of the Northwest Passage, Major, and of——"

He slapped the table. "I cer'nly was! Johnson stopped me once, but he won't do it again. No sir! This time there won't be nobody stop me! This time I'll get there, because this time I'm going to take Englishmen with me. No sir: there ain't one damned bit o' use trying to get anything out of Englishmen if you're an American, because Englishmen know Americans ain't civilized and don't have to be treated like civilized people. Englishmen think it's an honor for Americans to be 'lowed to associate with Englishmen, 'n' honor ought to be 'nough for 'em.

"Yessir, you got to take that into account when you deal with Englishmen! Well, you know who's going with me next time? Pickersgill, by God! Yes, sir! Captain James Cook's lieutenant! Cook's been nosing around for the Northwest Passage, but he can't find it 'n' he never will; but Pickersgill's going with me, 'n' I'll find it for him, 'n' he'll collect the money for all of us. 'N' D'Arcy's going—you remember D'Arcy, don't you—Amherst's aide! Yes, sir! Pickersgill 'n' D'Arcy; 'n' this time with Pickersgill to navigate for us, 'n' Captain Cook himself to meet us when we get to the mouth of the Oregon, we're going all the way across the Pacific, 'n' come home by way of Japan and Siberia! Why, we'll be the greatest discoverers in the world! We'll bring gold 'n' ivory 'n' precious stones from Russia, 'n' all the perfumes of Araby that Lady Macbeth herself talks about, 'n' myrrh 'n' frankincense, 'n' all the spices of the gloried East—I mean the storied East. Why, hell, Langdon, those damned Tartars out there, they're just the same kind of people as Chippeways 'n' Winnebagoes. They look like 'em and act like 'em; 'n' I'll handle 'em just the same as I handled the Chippeways! I'll have an army of 'em lugging sables all the way to England for me, see if I don't!"

He laughed loudly and contemptuously. "Ten thousand pounds! Why, ten thousand pounds ain't a drop in the bocket—bucket. I'll come home with diamonds like rocs' eggs 'n' pearls that would 'a' strangled Cleopatra, 'n' enough money to buy every stick 'n' stone 'n' Lord in London. You won't never hear 'nother word about Stamp Taxes or any other kind of taxes on Americans—not by a damned sight, Langdon! Why, not even as bloody an idiot as this minny-headed Lord North would run the risk of losing a country full of diamonds 'n' pearls 'n' splices 'n' franklcense 'n' everything. Make a hell of a difference to America, 'f they let me show 'em the Northwest Passage, 'n' don't you forget it!"

He pushed himself erect in his chair and bent a stern gaze upon me. "What you lookin' so glum for, Langdon? Don't be downcast! I'll take you, too! I'll make your fortune, jus' like I used to. I'll find a place for you in this expedition, never fear! You've heard me promise, so why don't you look happier?" He stared. "You want to go, don't you?"

"No, Major."

"Why not?" he asked, frowning heavily. "Why don't you? You know it'll make you rich, don't you? Look, Carver's in London, damn pop-eyed mealy-mouthed pussycat! You know what that weasel-footed snake's been telling people? Been telling 'em I never had authority send him hunting Northwest Passage—saying he was the one invented idea of discovering Northwest Passage! Planning to write a book about his travels, they tell me, 'n' 'splain how he thought up everything all by himself, for God's sake! When he heard I was figgerin' on tryin' it again, he began to crawl around on his belly, wanting to go with me, 'n' I won't take him! Not one damned inch! Carver 'n' Atherton—they both want to go, but to hell with 'em! I'm a great feller, now they've found I've got some Englishmen going with me——"

"Have they been here to see you?" I asked.

Rogers stared at me gravely. "See me? Course not! They ain't got any money, not any more than I have. Money's the only thing that'll help me, 'n' I need more'n any of them'll ever have!"

He signaled carelessly to a waiter for more ale, and in so doing nearly fell from his stool. Righting himself, he hiccuped. "Now here's somep'n I need awful bad. You know my brother James?"

I said I hadn't that honor.

"Well," Rogers said, "he's a real good boy, James is: real good. He ain't as good a officer as me, because he's one of those fellers that stays in one place till he sends down suckers 'n' gets himself all attached to the land, kind of. He ain't good company like you 'n' me, either, but he'll work harder clearing stumps off a piece of land than I would trying to get the King's ear—damned near. He ain't got 'magination, that's James' trouble. No 'magination. Well now listen——"

He blinked, focused wavering eyes on his cracked and blackened finger-nails, and rubbed a clumsy forefinger across a star-shaped scar on the back of his hand. Into my mind flashed the picture of Ogden and me—starved, shivering, fainting, half-dead skeletons—standing in the drenching rain at the mouth of the Ammonoosuc while Rogers rubbed rolls of dirt from that same star-shaped scar and told us he was starting down the Con-necticut after food to keep us alive.

"Le's see," he said thickly. "What were we all talking about?"

"You were speaking of your brother James, Major."

"That's it," he said. "James. Somebody's got to write James—somebody he'll believe. Not me. He don't believe me. Don't believe his own brother! By God, he even thought there was something in that story Potter told about me—the one that pigeon-breasted Mohawk-marrying Roberts got him to tell—the one about me joining the French! My own brother! Me, the father of his only nephew! Didn't know I was a father, did you? Father of a li'l baby boy—li'l Arthur—born just after that damned trial, while I was in Montreal. Jus' imagine that! Innocent li'l child, 'n' 'bliged to be born under a cloud on account of Roberts 'n' the rest of those damned lying, murdering swine, Johnson 'n' Gage 'n' Claus 'n'——"

He must have been about to utter Potter's name, for he broke off, looked startled, shook his head; then said, "Poor li'l Arthur," drew a long, quivering breath, and moisture stood in his bloodshot eyes.

I tried not to think, even, of Elizabeth, the girl who, in her long-dead youth, had been horrified by uncouthness, becoming the mother of Robert Rogers' child.

The waiter set a gallon tankard of ale before us and stood looking down at Rogers.

The Major, waving him grandly to me, said, "Don't bother us, boy. There's something I wanted to tell you, Langdon."

I paid.

"Something you'd like to say to me, Major?" I asked.

"There cer'nly is, 'n' you'd never believe it, not hardly! He's here! He's in the Fleet!"

"In the Fleet!" I exclaimed. "Your brother James in the Fleet?"

"Who?" Rogers asked. "James? Hell, no, Langdon! Roberts! I'm talking about that damned screech owl of a Roberts! It's him that's in the Fleet, and not only in the Fleet, but over on the Common Side to boot. Serves him right, the dirty Mohawk-marrying screech owl! Tell you what I'll do, Langdon: I'll have him paraded for you—give you 'n idea how low a man can fall!"

He pounded heavily on the table with his pewter ale mug, and his shout for the waiter rang out above the tumult of bellowing and singing all around us almost as it had rung out at White River Falls when he told us to jump for our lives.

"Le's see," Rogers said, when the waiter answered his call. "I need a penny, 'n' I don't b'lieve I got one." He fumbled with thick fingers in his pockets. "Could you let me have a penny, Langdon?"

He took it from me, examined it closely, and held it up before the waiter. "My friend," he said, "listen to your orders! You're to go over on the Common Side 'n' find Benjamin Roberts."

"The gentleman you poured the beer over?" the waiter asked.

"The same," Rogers said. "Go get him. Tell him I got a mutual acquaintance here. Tell him he'll get some ale—not on his head, this time, but down his throat—'n' maybe some meat. He might get sixpence, even."

The waiter took the penny and went away. Rogers passed his tongue over his thick lips. "Yes, sir," he said triumphantly, "that dirty Roberts is right here in the Fleet, 'n' wha's more, he's over on the Common Side! Lives in a cell with a dozen others, 'n' don't eat unless somebody drops money at the Beggars' Grate! He'll run fifty miles for sixpence! But the bes' joke of all is who put him in the Fleet! You jus' simply wouldn't believe it if you saw it painted in one of your own pictures!" He laughed so uproariously that a disheveled fop at a near-by table rose and stared coldly at us, only to sit down quietly when he saw Rogers.

"Major," I said, "if you want to tell me something about your brother, you'll have to tell me quickly. They close the gates soon, I'm told."

He steadied himself by clutching the table edge with his huge hands. "Stay overnight—pleasure to have you share my room," he said vaguely. Then, with an effort, he fastened his eyes on mine. "You write my brother, Langdon. He's rich! Got thousans 'n' thousans of acres in New York, 'n' ain't never let go none of 'em. You tell him you saw me—health greatly impaired by confinement. Being kep' from great projects. Northwest Passage, Langdon, 'n' that ain't all, not by a damn sight! I ain't told you about the others. Listen:

"That feller Gage, he never had one damn thing to court-martial me for. He jus' tried to murder me, tha's all! He 'n' Johnson 'n' Spiesmaker, they figured anybody'd die if he got thrown onto the ballast the way I was, and took to Niagara in cold weather; but Gage was the one to blame, because he ordered the court-martial, thinking I'd be dead before I ever had to testify. Well, I'm alive, 'n' I've got a case against him, by God! I'm going to sue him!

"Ten thousand pounds? Why, hell, I'll get *fifty* thousand pounds out of that dough-faced potbelly before I'm through with him! You tell my brother that! Tell him all he's got to do is assume my obbaglations—olligations—obligations, 'n' I'll get out of here and pay him back ten times over—a hundred times! Why, it ain't possible for him to lose, Langdon!

" 'N' listen: I met the Ambassador from the Dey of Algiers before they threw me in here—feller the shape of a haystack, Langdon, 'n' mustaches like a pair of sickles, 'n' wears trousers cut like a couple balloon jibs. You know anything about Algiers?"

I shook my head, sick of his talk, sick of the Fleet, sick of everything.

"Listen," he went on, and his great red face worked, as if he prevented it by main strength from becoming slack and muscleless. "This Dey of Algiers, he needs fighters, 'n' he ain't afraid to pay for 'em. Needs good officers on his ships, 'n' good officers ashore. Got all the sholdiers he wants, but ain't got no officers that know how to show sholdiers the right way to fight. Why ain't he? Because there ain't none, only me!

"Well, this Dey of Algiers, he's got good sense. He knows about me, 'n' he knows my way of fighting is the only right way there is. His Ambassador—old sickle-whiskers—he come to see me, 'n' he says, 'You come on down to Algiers, Major,' he says, ' 'n' we'll make you a general, 'n' half of what you capture is yours,' he says. 'You'll get your general's pay,' he says, ' 'n' if you capture a ship with a cargo worth ten thousand pounds, five thousand of it's yours,' he says.

" 'Give you a house to live in,' he says, 'all blue tiles 'n' palm trees in the garden 'n' a nice view out to sea, 'n' any number of wives up to six—young ones—pick 'em out yourself—have more'n six if you want 'em,' he says, 'but the Dey won't pay for only six. Any others you'll have to buy with your own money,' he says. What you think of that! Six wives, all perfumed 'n' wearing gauze pantaloons!' "

He regarded me triumphantly, then looked concerned. "Don't tell my brother James about the six wives. Don't say nothing 'bout wives at all. Jus' tell him I can go down 'n' render valuable assistance to the Dey of Algiers, any time I get out of here, 'n' if I don't get out of here pretty damned quick, I'll most likely die of one thing or another. You know what to tell him. Jus' put in some of that Harvard College language of yours. I *got* to get out!"

Swaying on his stool, he raised his ale mug and drank sonorously; and the ale, trickling from the corners of his mouth, dripped on his soiled cambric stock. He set down the mug with a bang, pawed clumsily at the

damp spots, and made sounds of exasperation. It was a relief when someone stood at my elbow and a hesitant voice said, "I believe I've already
had the pleasure."

I looked up and saw Lieutenant Benjamin Roberts, but a pitiably different Roberts from that scarlet-coated favorite of Sir William Johnson who
had attempted to assert authority over Rogers at Oswego. His coat and
smallclothes were caked with dirt; his stockings were pulled under at the
heels to conceal holes; a soiled kerchief was tied around his neck in place
of a stock; and the hair that curled around his ears was dusty and full of
bits of straw. Everything upon him, as seemed to be the case with all the
others in that wastrels' abode, was somehow crooked—somehow im-
properly adjusted. His haggard face was thin and dirty; his lips dry; only
his eyes were the same—cat's eyes, in which, when the drooping lids were
lifted, lurked wariness, resentment, jealousy.

Rogers frowned at him, rubbed a huge hand across wavering eyes, and
laughed foolishly. "Didn't know you, Lieutenant," he said. "What you
doing in here? Somebody give you some money?"

He swayed forward, then pushed himself upright.

"The waiter told me you asked for me," Roberts said.

"Who, me?" Rogers cried. "Think I'd ask for you, you malfeaslin',
Mohawk-marryin' rattlesnake in the grass?"

"Look here, Major," I said, "you remember telling the waiter to ask
Lieutenant Roberts to join us, don't you? Sit down, Lieutenant, and have
a mug of ale. Have you had supper?"

Roberts snatched at a stool and sat close to me. "Supper?" he asked
almost whimperingly. "Supper?"

I called the waiter; ordered another plate of mutton and potatoes; another tankard of ale.

"Supper!" Rogers repeated. "Him! He ain't had a supper since Sir
William Johnson refused to honor his draft for a hundred pounds—one
hundred peeny-weeny pounds, the yeller-bellied old Mohawk! Wouldn't
spare him a hundred pounds to keep spying on me 'n' spreading his dirty
damned lies about me! Roberts, you're a dirty, chicken-breasted Mohawk-
marrier—nothing but a cheap hundred-pound debtor! Look at me! Ten-
thousand-pounder; 'n' you, you li'l pint of snow water, you ain't got
'nough resoffleness—'sourcefulness—to scratch up a hundred pounds. Jus'
a pint of snow water, half poured out!"

"I can't have this, Major," I said. "You asked Lieutenant Roberts to
come here, and the least you can do is treat him decently."

"Nothing of the sort!" Rogers said thickly. "I asked him to come over
so's you could see how far a dirty, chicken-breasted, Mohawk-marryin'

polecat would run for a quart of ale, 'n' how much he'd swallow from a offser he did his damnedest to murder. Tha's what you did, you damned tippy-toed tin sholdier! You paid Potter to swear I was going to join the French—dunno how much—not a hell of a lot—brains like yours 'n' Potter's can't think bigger'n a hundred pounds! Yes, 'n' if it hadn't been for your testimony, you damned Mohawk-marryin' skunk, the Board o' Trade would 'a' granted me sixty square miles on Lake Champlain, 'n' I'd be fixed for life 'n' wouldn't 'a' had a debt in the world!"

Roberts said never a word; and when the waiter brought the ale and put the platter of greasy mutton and gray potatoes before him, he went at them voraciously, making wet champing sounds and casting wary glances at Rogers from the corners of his eyes.

Rogers laughed drunkenly, poured himself a mug of ale with a hand so unsteady that he deluged his weskit in the pouring. He drained the mug without stopping for breath; then swayed on his seat, breathing stertorously, huge hands clutching the table, big head sagging, and focused protuberant eyes on Roberts.

"Go ahead 'n' eat, Mohawk-marrier," he said. "You think you stopped me; but you ain't! You're the one that's stopped! You 'n' Johnson 'n' Gage 'n' Claus—there ain't none of you can stop me, only for jus' a few days, as days go in this part of the world! You can't see what I see—off, off, beyond the mountains—you li'l foxes under your own li'l stone walls —I'll show you, by God—show every damned one of you blind li'l foxes— all tail 'n' no brains! Oh, God! Ain't there nobody in this whole God-damned world but li'l blind foxes! I wish—I wish——"

He paused, half rose from his stool, and his staring, bloodshot eyes swept in a dazed half circle above our heads. Then he tottered, grasped blindly at the table, sprawled to the floor with a crash, and lay motionless in ale-moistened grime.

Roberts, busy with his mutton and potatoes, didn't look up. Those at the next table disapprovingly eyed the huge body beside their stools, but made no complaint.

Roberts pushed back his plate, wiped his mouth on a shiny sleeve, filled his ale mug, and leaned toward me confidentially. "I hope, sir," he said elegantly, "that you will place no credence in the Major's words. It's true I've been shabbily treated by Sir William; but the canard about the bribe extended to Mr. Potter, sir—and on the word of an officer and a gentleman, sir, it is a canard that——"

"I know all about Potter," I interrupted.

Roberts buried his nose in his ale mug and watched me over the brim.

I rapped on the table to get the waiter's attention; and when he came and stood looking down at Rogers, his expression was one of admiration. "Strike me!" he exclaimed. "It ain't often the Major's able to get like this!"

"Will you help him to his room?" I asked.

"Pleasure, Master," he said. "Leave 'im lay till the crowd thins out; then me an' Sadie'll look out for 'im. Sadie always comes huntin' for 'im along towards midnight; an' till then, Master, 'e's as well off 'ere as a baby'd be in 'is cradle."

I felt in my pocket: then saw Roberts' eyes fixed eagerly on my hand. "Here's a shilling," I told the waiter. "Look out for him; and when Sadie comes, tell her to tell him I'll send something to the gate for him to-morrow—and that I'll write the letter he spoke of."

The waiter nodded. When I turned away, Lieutenant Roberts followed me toward the door; but when I ignored him, he left me alone and I went out from the stench and turmoil of Bartholomew Fair, across the dim and echoing courtyard of the Fleet, and beneath the arched passage into the freedom of Farringdon Street and Ludgate Hill.

Rogers, I knew, had reached the height of his career—had come to a real grandeur of soul—on that terrible day when, at the end of our retreat from St. Francis, the woodcutters had dragged our raft ashore and helped the three of us to stagger to the stockade at Number Four. I saw him as I had seen him in the flickering firelight of the fort: gaunt, barefooted, covered with bruises, hung with tattered strips of strouding. I remembered the shredded leggins hanging on his emaciated flanks; the ribs and bony chest that showed through his torn rags; the chunk of bread in his scarred, sooty, pitch-stained hands; and as if it had been yesterday I heard his thick voice saying: "Get me some beef—fat beef. I'm going back—back to my men—back to the Ammonoosuc!"

And now I had seen him so low that a man could go no lower this side of the grave. But far as he had fallen, yet something—some imperishable last glimmer of that old spirit—still survived. There was an inner force that had been warped and twisted by narrow men and a narrow woman, but that had never been wholly crushed and never could be.

More than that, I suspected that even still the man who lay in the mud of the Fleet was better than the mere sodden husk of Robert Rogers. But for Fate and Ann Potter, I suspected, there in that same grime might lie Langdon Towne. There, too, but for the grace of God, might lie any of us, our talents quenched and our best dreams beaten.

## Christmas in the Depot at Dartmoor

An ESCAPED PRISONER is a dangerous man, of course, so they put me in
Exeter jail; and I had been there three days before I got a word out of
the turnkey who brought me my hard bread, thin soup, and water—tepid
water that must have been standing in the June sun. When he did speak in
answer to my questions, I found his lingo difficult to understand.

"Noa, noa," he said. "Us bant agoin' vur tew zend ee backalong tew
Dartymoor dreckly minit: not till us cotches tha body as wuz wi' ee. Zir
Arthur hiszel, 'e yerd at tha Hall fra Dartymoor az they wuz tew or ee.
Tuther must be a urnin' tha moor. When us cotches tha body an' ast tha
tew or ee lockit up yere, than'll be time tew zend vur sojers as tew such
bad bodies can be trustit wi'."

I had a gleam of hope for Jeddy, since he was still at large, having had
the good sense to lie hid in the back room of the cottage until they had
taken me away.

"Well," I said to the turnkey, "you may not catch the other bad body;
he's not so bad, by the way, and neither am I."

" 'Ess shur that ee is!" the man said, and shook his head mournfully at
me. "A bad, bad, bad body thee'rt! Zim they do zay in Exeter town az
how they'm a purty bobbery an' stirridge at tha Hall, an' her leddyship
put oot, an' banned fra a' the gert vokes, an' gude vokes tew, an' a' on
account ov a bad, bad body fra Dartymoor. Ess fay, thee'rt a bad, bad
body, man!"

That was all I got from him; he called me a bad, bad body a thousand
times, I think; for I lay in Exeter jail two months, until mid-August,
before they took me back to Dartmoor.

Dun-colored clouds were caught against the barren face of North
Hessary as we made the final ascent from Princetown to the depot gates;
and the wisps of fog that drifted across the top of the seven crouching,

staring prison buildings seemed less like fog than like the prison smells rising perpetually from the yawning, never-shuttered windows.

In his office Captain Shortland, with his crinkly brown hair and his ruddy, jovial face, beamed at me in a manner to make me think again of the grinning, big-nosed Punches I had so often watched on the streets of Nantes, strutting on little shut-in stages and blithely whacking friends and enemies alike with great clubs.

"Hah!" he said, moving his head forward and back and lifting his shoulders at the same time, as vain men so often do to improve the set of their coats, "so you've come back to us! Good! Good! I almost like to have my boys try it, out in the great world; for they all come back—ah, most of them: hah, hah!—to more permanent quarters!"

"Do you mean the Cachot?" I asked, knowing only too well the black hole was the penalty for those caught in serious crimes and attempts to escape.

He smiled, a pleasant, regretful smile. "Yes," he said, "the Cachot." He picked up some papers from his desk. "This is a rather serious business, you know. Not the usual case! No, indeed: not the usual case! One thing on top of another!"

I waited for him to say what he had to say, thinking helplessly, as I had thought from dawn to dark during the past weeks in Exeter jail, of Emily Ransome.

"At all events," he went on, "you'll have company. Four other Americans. They tried to burn a prize; so we were forced to give them duration."

"You were forced to *what?*"

"Duration. Serious offenses, you know! Not as serious as yours, but serious enough."

"Do you mean you're putting me in the Cachot for the duration of this war?"

"That's it! I knew you'd be sensible about it."

"Wait a minute," I said. My brain was in a muddle. There was no escaping from the Cachot, I knew. It was a stone coffin. There would be no way in which I could get word from Emily; no way in which I could get word to her; and God alone knew when the war would be over.

"This Sir Arthur Ransome——" I said.

"You've got it!" Shortland smiled. "There was the burning of the *Lively Lady*, and the escape by impersonating a Frenchman—of course, you'd only get ten days in the Cachot for attempting to escape; but you see there was also breaking and entering and the destruction of property at Ransome Hall. Ransome's laid information against you for the whole affair. Nothing else to do, you know." He cleared his throat. "I'll send you in."

"Just a minute," I begged him. "Give me a hearing on this. I haven't had a trial."

"Why *should* you have a trial?" he asked. "We have Ransome's word—and Ransome's a gentleman, you see."

"Oh, my God!" I said. "There isn't a Negro in Number Four whose word wouldn't be honester! The man's working out a personal spite on me! I claim a right to be heard!"

"I've heard enough!" he said, and the geniality vanished from his face.

"No," I said. "Wait! There was no breaking or entering at Ransome Hall. And since when has it been a crime to escape from a war prison? I gave you no parole! Nobody asked me for a parole! I was captain of a privateer of eighteen guns and entitled to parole, but I asked for none. Why shouldn't I try to escape if I get the chance? Wouldn't you?"

He stuck out his jaw and blinked his eyes, and all at once the dangerous temper of the man was on his face. Captain Shortland had the record of an officer brave to rashness, a hot fighter; but his nature was brittle, and never was more than a thin cracking lacquer over the anger that seemed always smoldering underneath. "Look here," he said, "your second officer escaped with you—Tucker. Where is he?"

"How should I know where he is?"

"Well, somebody helped you get away, and when you went, Tucker went too. Now you tell us where you last saw Tucker, and who helped you, and I'll see what can be done."

"Why, then, you *can* see what can be done, can't you! My God, Captain, get me a hearing, will you? You can't put me in the Cachot like this!"

Shortland's face turned wine color. "You damned Yankees," he said, lowering his head like a bull and half whispering the words, "you think you own the whole damned earth! You keep this place in a mess with your damned screaming and complaining and bellowing for your rights, until ten of you raise more hell than a million Frenchmen. Let me tell you, you haven't *got* any rights here! And you're no judge of what I *can* do and what I *can't* do! I've got orders from the Transport Office to put you in the Cachot for duration, and that's where you go!" He raised his voice to a bellow. "Mitchell! Mitchell!"

The chief clerk popped in at the doorway.

"Oh, for God's sake!" I said. "Let me write Pellew! Let me write the American agent again—Reuben Beasley! I wrote him twice from Exeter, but he may have been away. Let me try once more!"

Shortland shouted with mirthless laughter. "Beasley! If you wait for an answer from Beasley you'll stay in the Cachot forever! He never answers letters! Not from Americans! Wouldn't you like to write the prince regent? Take him out, Mitchell!"

He left the room, slamming the door behind him. Mitchell gave me a blanket and a truss of straw and turned me over to a sentry, who led me down across the empty market place, dismal in the light of flickering lanterns. The dim, ogre-like face of Number Four glowered at us as we came to the barred gate that cut off its yard from the market. The sentry drew his bayonet along the bars with a clatter and turned to look appraisingly at me.

"We'm a-gettin' all the 'Merricans this side o' hell," he said. "Won't be none o' ee left to foight, soon, I'm a-thinkin'."

A turnkey came in answer to the racket of the bayonet against the bars, and the two of them led me to the left, along the covered walk, and finally out into the space between the circular inner wall and the high fence of iron bars. The Cachot stood snugly between the inner wall and the iron fence, looking, because of its granite sides and arched roof, unpleasantly like a tomb. As we approached, a squat figure came out from behind it and peered inquiringly at us.

"Here's another, Carley," the turnkey said. "Duration for this one, too."

The squat man came close up to me. "Duration, hey? Holy bones, you must be bad! You must 'a' spit on an admiral!"

The sentry and the turnkey laughed and left us. Carley took a key from his pocket: a huge key fastened to him by a chain. "Anyways, 'twon't be as if yez were alone, with four in for duration a'ready, and ivery wan av ye'er four thousand felly citizens fixin' to git throwed in with yez for attimptin' to brek out av the dippo. Mary help us all if thim four thousand divvles iver gits over the fince!"

A hoarse voice hailed us from the Cachot. "Mike," the voice said, "let that poor boy come to bed! He'll be gettin' his death o' cold, standin' on that damp grass!"

Carley turned the key in the lock, dragged the iron door outward, pushed me in with a sweep of his arm, and swung the door shut with a clang.

I was in a dark room, smelling powerfully of damp straw, latrines, and dirty bodies. There was a slit of dim twilight in the door, where the wicket was half open; and high up, on opposite sides, were two other slots the size of my hand—mere travesties of windows. There was no other light in the room, and the darkness was like dark wool against the eyes.

The hoarse voice spoke up. "I don't seem to recall your face, though you have a kind of familiar look."

There was a spatter of laughter which came from low down, as if from a grave.

"Jesse Smith of Stonington, Connecticut," the hoarse voice went on. "That's me! A reformed Federalist that's seen the error of his ways. Who might you be?"

"Richard Nason," I told him. "Arundel."

When Smith spoke again his voice seemed almost respectful. "Got your straw with you?"

I said I had, and immediately felt him take me by the arm.

"We got a few choice positions vacant," he told me, urging me forward. "Being last in, I took the one farthest away from the door. That's the nicest when you're last in, because it's the only one you'll get. How'd you like a nice empty space next to me, only a little further removed from the door?"

"Fine!" I told him, heartened by his folly.

He pulled the truss of straw from my shoulder, and I could hear him breaking it open. "You want to take your bearings damned careful if you have to get out of bed in the dark," he warned me, "because this is an awful easy place to get turned around in. If you get lost, you might be five or six months finding your bed again."

The other men snickered. It seemed strange to hear their laughter coming up from the floor. Being unseen and unidentified, they were unreal, like ghosts.

"Wasn't you in command of the *Lively Lady* when she sunk the *Gorgon?*" Smith asked.

"It was the *Chasseur's* fight," I told him. "We only got there at the end."

Smith rustled my straw. "There you go!" he said at length. "All smooth and soft, like corn stubble after a frost. Lay down a minute before supper and let these other jailbirds do some warbling for you."

I followed his advice, grateful to him for his flow of talk. One of the other men coughed and cleared his throat.

"Simeon Hays: Baltimoe," he said softly. "Privateer *Surprise* of Baltimoe. We-all heard about the *Gorgon*. That must 'a' been a right amusing lobster-boiling. Jim Rickor, of 'Nappolis, he's over beside the doe. Next him is 'Lisha Whitten of Newburyport, and across from Jim is John Miller. All *Surprises*. John, he used to be an Englishman, but he don't like 'em no moe, so he's an American."

"Strange he don't like 'em!" a new voice said.

Smith spoke up again. "Meet Obed Hussey," he said. "Another of them Maine Federalists."

"Jesse," the new voice protested, "that ain't right, not even in fun. I'd ruther you called me what you call the lobster-backs than be called a snivelin', English-lovin' Federalist!"

"Well," Smith said to me, "you prob'ly get the general idee."

"Supper!" a voice near the door said suddenly. The wicket slid wide open.

Smith took me by the arm and led me to the door, where each of us received a tin cup of cocoa and a quarter loaf apiece.

"Drink it where you are," Smith said. "If you try to walk round with it you might drop it, and you wouldn't get no more."

When we had given our cups to Carley and gone back to our straw again, I knew I could have eaten five loaves of bread instead of a quarter loaf, and topped off with something substantial like a sizable platter of salt fish and pork scraps and one of my aunt Cynthy's lemon pies as a sort of stopper on it.

"Can't we get more than that?" I asked.

"That's more'n we're supposed to get," Hays said. "The bread, that's fixed up for us by the prison committees. They give the money to Carley, and he buys the bread. We ain't supposed to have that much to eat. You get kind of used to it, though. Your stomach shrinks."

"Your brain don't shrink, that's the hell of it!" Jesse Smith said. "You get to thinking about baked beans and brown bread, or a nice clam chowder with sliced potatoes and onions in it and pork scraps floating around on top." I could hear him swallow hard.

"Or hash," said another voice.

"There goes 'Lisha Whitten with his hash!" Smith said bitterly. "Can't you talk about *nothin'* but hash?"

"I like hash," Whitten said. "You take a nice hash chopped up plenty fine with boiled potatoes and raw onions, and brown her——"

"Listen," Smith said harshly, "do you s'pose anybody in this Cachot don't know as much about hash as you do? We never mention food in here without you have to go to work and drag in that hash of yours. Hash, hash, hash, hash, hash! That's all you think about: just hash!"

My mind seemed like a pond that is, as our Maine people are given to saying, working. The consciousness of Emily Ransome completely filled my head, yet other thoughts seemed to rise through that consciousness as air bubbles rise from the bottom of a working pond. They rose and vanished, leaving behind the deep and unchangeable consciousness that occupied me. I could hear Jesse Smith telling about the new tunnels the

Americans were digging—tunnels large enough to let all of the five thousand American prisoners escape at one time; and simultaneously I could wonder and wonder unceasingly what in God's name had happened to Emily: where she had gone and with whom; and whether she was comfortable, with enough to eat.

"They're going down twenty feet," Jesse said, "straight down from the floors of Number Four, Number Five, and Number Six! Then they're going to level out, bring 'em together, and dig for the wall."

He told how every American in the prison had been sworn to secrecy; how an arrangement of lamps and small wooden windmills, revolved by hand, had been invented to keep the air pure in the tunnels; how the excavated dirt was concealed from Shortland and the turnkeys by being fed, handful by handful, into the streams that run through each prison yard for washing.

"They're down there now," he said, "pecking at that damned yeller gravel an' bringing it up in their pockets and shirt tails." He stopped suddenly, and I knew he had remembered some of us were in the Cachot for duration; so that no tunnel could lighten our troubles.

One of the men near the door burst into a racking, interminable fit of coughing. Another went to snoring lightly.

There was this much to be said for the Cachot, along with the many things to be said against it: it seemed to act like a drug on most of us, so that we slept easily and heavily in it, despite the roughness of its granite floor and the brutal chill that fingered at our bones both night and day.

I had my first look, the next morning, at our tomb and those who shared it with me. By the faint light that filtered through the two hand-sized slots I could see that our granite box measured six paces by six paces, and maybe fifteen feet high. The floor was made of enormous blocks: the walls of smaller ones down which there was a perpetual trickle of moisture. There was a small pile of straw for each man, and at the end opposite the door a wooden bucket for a latrine. To one side of the iron door was a shelf, and on it a bucket of drinking water. Attached to the shelf by a piece of spun yarn was a half gourd for a drinking cup. We had the clothes we lay in, and our coarse prison blanket for a wrapping and a couch. In the room there was nothing else.

The door was of iron, with an eight-inch wicket in it. Toward night Carley would open the wicket a little, so we could look out without standing on each other's shoulders. At eight in the morning Carley came in with our breakfast: a cup of hot cocoa for each of us, and a quarter loaf of bread apiece, though the bread was not supplied by the British.

Seemingly the smuggling of it to us was known and winked at. At the same time Carley would carry out and empty the bucket, renew our drinking water and look at us to see whether we were sick. At noon he brought us a bucket of soup. At night he brought us cocoa and bread again. Usually he brought it at six o'clock in summer and at four in winter, though he made the supper hour later on days when other prisoners were sent to the Cachot. He did this so the new men wouldn't have to go supperless to bed. He was a kindhearted man; and while he could do little because he had been threatened with punishment if he was caught smuggling food or liquor or newspapers to us, he did whatever he could.

Jesse explained the workings of the place to me when we had heaped our straw in piles after breakfast and covered them with our folded blankets. He was a studious-looking young man with a long mop of straight black hair that came back over his ears and hung to his coat collar behind. If it had not been for his manner of closing his eyes after saying something particularly grave, and then opening them slowly and rolling them at his hearers with an air of simulated intolerance, he would often have been suspected of being serious, which he seldom was in my hearing.

"You got to keep busy in this place," he said, "and you can't keep 'em busy unless you drive 'em. They'd rather lay and brood. On account of that, we elect a captain and a first mate every week. Me, I'm captain this week, and Obed Hussey, he's first mate. Obed ain't a bad first mate."

Obed Hussey, I saw, was tall and broad-shouldered: as fine-looking a boy as would be encountered in a month of Sundays, except for the beard on his face and the raggedness of his clothes.

Jesse addressed him ceremoniously. "Mr. Hussey, prepare the race track for the first race!"

Jesse enlightened me while Obed Hussey busied himself in spreading his blanket in the middle of the Cachot floor. "We run a series of louse races. That's one way to keep 'em busy. Every man supplies his own louse; and anybody that claims not to have one is supplied by the nearest contestant. That prevents shirking. The winner gets held up to the window to report on what's going on outside. Losers have to let the winners stand on their shoulders. It's a good idea to have your races early and late, before and after market, when there's plenty in the yard to report. Between times you got to make 'em take exercise. They don't let us out of the Cachot to exercise; don't let us out for nothing except sickness, and you got to be awful sick to be took to the hospital. If you catch jail fever, they won't let you be took to the hospital till you're mottled with it, and that's pretty late. In fact, it's too late."

"Race track prepared, Captain Smith," Obed said.

The men rose reluctantly from their piles of straw, spectral gray figures in that dim tomb, and approached the blanket, on which Obed, with a bit of lime, had drawn seven narrow alleyways.

"You got yourself a louse?" Jesse asked me.

I told him I had come in clean.

"We'll fix that," Jesse said. "Rickor, give Cap'n Nason one of your best bugs. Don't give him none of them half-growed ones, neither! Give him a good big one, so's he'll have a chance with the rest of us."

Rickor, a tired-looking, stoop-shouldered man, searched himself carefully: then handed me an active gray insect.

The men knelt in a circle around the blanket, holding their entries at one end of the alleyways.

"Are you ready?" Jesse asked.

The others growled expectantly.

"Go!" Jesse shouted.

The seven entrants were dropped on the starting line. They moved jerkily and indecisively on the rough surface of the blanket.

"I snum!" Hussey said. "I got another putterer! I ain't had a fast one in a week!" He poked at his entrant with a straw, balking him in his effort to go in the wrong direction.

"Whitten!" Jesse shouted angrily, "you're blowing on yours!"

"I ain't neither!" Whitten protested. "I got to breathe, ain't I? I wasn't doing nothin' but breathing."

"Breathe through your nose, then," Jesse said.

My entrant tacked first to starboard, then to larboard, as if in search of a safe haven; then stood still.

"What do you do when they stop?" I asked Jesse.

"Hope and pray," he replied. "They can't be touched when resting."

My insect conquered his suspicions and moved rapidly ahead.

Simeon Hays set up a shouting and snapped his fingers furiously. "Move yo' laigs, Gray Ghost!" he cried. "Come on, you li'l' gray rascal!"

His louse, a long slender one, forged across the finish line.

"That's the fifth time in three days you came in first, Sim," Jesse Smith said sourly. "Either you're tempting that insect with some kind of food, or you're holding him over on us. Lemme see you execute him right now."

Simeon obligingly cracked him between his thumbnails.

Last of all Obed Hussey glumly herded his entry across the finish line with a straw, picked him up and examined him carefully; then destroyed him.

"I declare," he said, "there's something plumb contrary about these animals of mine! If I could do it, I'd be almost tempted to clean 'em out, lock, stock, and barrel. Come on, Sim!"

Simeon Hays mounted easily to Obed's shoulders, hooked his fingers over the sill of one of the slots near the ceiling, and peered out through it. The rest of us went back to our blankets.

"It's kind of foggy up back," Simeon reported, "but you can see the hills the other side of Princetown. They's a man on a donkey on the long road, 'bout two mile away, heading north by east. Looks like a flea carryin' a littler flea. They's four Rough Alleys huntin' in the swill box back of Number One cookhouse. One of 'em's found something. Looks like a turnip! They's about two hundred men in sight. They got a Keno table pitched between Number One and Number Two. They's seven fellers playin' ketch with a ball made out of spun yarn . . ."

The rest of us lay back on our blankets in the gray gloom, striving to see into the prison yards with the eyes of Simeon Hays. It seemed to me that the world of which he spoke was a foggy, unreal world of specters and pixies. I took my miniature from my pocket and unwrapped it, holding it in the crook of my arm so I could study it unseen. The lips, I thought, moved as if to whisper to me; but in the Cachot there was no sound save the slurred Baltimore speech of Simeon Hays, telling us the few things he could see and understand of the infinitesimal happenings behind Prison Number One.

§

In the Cachot every man, I think, found his sharpest suffering from a different source. My own was the intolerable pressure of my incessant wondering: where had Emily gone, and how were things with her? What did she suffer, and what did she suffer for me? I think mine was the sharpest mental anguish there. For most of the other men, what they bore physically was enough to be busy over. Added to their special ills, we had a common bitterness in the scantiness of our food and light. Perhaps the darkness was the hardest to bear for most of us; there was never any light in that place save what filtered through the two small barred windows. Yet there were some among us who seemed most discomfortable because of the skimpiness of the rags they wore. One man would talk whimperingly an hour at a time of a fine suit of clothes he had once worn. Another bragged over and over of a beaver coat his father had given him on his fourteenth birthday; and there were others whose speech dwelt eternally on the diseases to which the Cachot, as well as the whole prison, exposed us. They would shiver and pretend to knock on wood as they spoke of jail fever, smallpox, and a violent pneumonia that set the lungs to crackling. Some found it most horrid—and indeed this was a thing oppressive to the soul—that for weeks on end we might have no more news of the world and of the movement of life upon our planet than did the very dead in the churchyard. The earth seemed to have closed over our heads and to lie heavily there.

It was not until October that we had word of how the war went, and then what we heard was horrible. Carley told us, doubtless not realizing what he added to our sorrows; for, as I have said, he was as kind as he dared be. He told us how the British had landed from their fleet in the Chesapeake and marched up to Washington, with Mr. Jefferson's militiamen running before them like frightened rabbits; and how they had put the torch to the library in Washington, to the Capitol, to the President's House, and to many public offices, as well as to the navy yard.

There was no racing on the blanket, and not even any looking out through the slit in the wall on the day after we heard that.

Perhaps it was a month after this when a New Bedford man, consigned to the Cachot for ten days, came in with news he had from a fresh draft of prisoners just brought to Dartmoor from the sea. Thus we learned how American privateers were being built in ever greater numbers and destroying more British commerce than at any time since the first two months of the war; and how British merchants were demanding the war be stopped before they were ruined. Even a hoarse and racking cheer went up from that dismal place when we thus heard of the greatest of all the privateering feats of the war: how the American privateer brig *General Armstrong* lay in Fayal harbor, neutral waters, and how she was unrightfully beset by a British sloop-of-war, a frigate, and a ship-of-the-line, and fought off four hundred men, who came in boats to take her, destroyed most of them, and then was sunk by her own captain, who reached the shore safe with all but two of his men.

Through that chill autumn we gradually hardened to the increasing cold and dampness and so kept our health. Those who came in for ten-day stretches, however, having been accustomed to the use of hammocks and to better food and to exercise, developed troubles in their lungs from sleeping on the cold granite and quickly became fit subjects for the hospital.

The chief surgeon was a man named William Dykar, who had served in America with the British in our war for independence. He was an old man, violent-tempered and opinionated, like so many officers who reach high positions in every army and navy; and he would visit no sick man in the Cachot because it was his belief that Americans could never be

trusted to speak the truth and claimed always to be sick so to escape. Therefore sick men could get no treatment in the Cachot; though if one of
them, on being released, was unable to stand, Carley would call a sentry
and take him to the hospital, where too often he died. Therefore I say,
after due thought and consideration, that this William Dykar, chief surgeon of the depot at Dartmoor from 1809 to 1814, was a deliberate and
cold-blooded murderer.

It was toward the end of October that Jesse Field, a seaman from
Townsend, Maine, was put in among us. Beyond the fact that he had
attempted to escape, and in so doing had lain full length in freezing mud
against the wall of Number Seven Prison for a matter of six hours before
being discovered, we could find out nothing from him, for he was weak
and shaken with violent chills. He lay all that day on the straw we gave
him, since he had been sent in without any; and on the following morning we saw there was a sort of brown crust on his lips and teeth. It looked
to us like typhus. When Carley came with the breakfast, therefore, I
told him to go again to Dr. Dykar and ask him for the love of God to
give an order for this man to be taken to the hospital before all of us
came down with the disease.

"I been meanin' to tell yez," Carley said. "Dykar's out! They t'run him
out!"

"Who's the new man?" I asked. "Is he a real doctor, or a murderer,
like the other?"

"Yez'll soon know!" Carley said. "His name's Magrath, and he's one of
the salt of the earth—a descendant of the Irish kings."

We went back to watching Field and to cursing our jailers for their
heartlessness. Before we knew it, almost, there was a rattling at the door,
which swung back and revealed Carley standing at the side of a tall, thin,
one-eyed man. He stood staring in at us, his mouth pursed up and pushed
to one side and his left hand feeling at his face as if he sought a beard
that wasn't there.

"How many of you in here?" he asked suddenly. His voice was deep
and pleasant, with none of the snarl in it we were accustomed to hear
from Dartmoor officials.

I came to the door and told him.

He looked me up and down. "Anything wrong with you?" he asked.

I told him there wasn't. "It's a man that came in yesterday: Jesse Field.
He looks like jail fever."

"Hm," he said. "I'll trouble you to wrap him in his blanket and bring
him out where I can see him."

Hays and I made a blanket snug around Field and brought him out. It was the first time we had been in the open air since August. The sky seemed huge and brilliant, even though heavy with gray clouds; and the air had a queer, piercing smell to it, as if drugged.

We put Field on the ground. The new doctor pulled down his eyelid and looked into his eye, then peered into his mouth.

"Call four sentries," he said to Carley. "This man goes to the hospital at once."

"Sor!" Carley said, "I'll have to be havin' an order. I'll run to the office and ask kin I have wan."

"No, you won't!" Magrath said. "You'll run to the nearest sentry! Who are you to talk about the office when I can see with half an eye you have a decent heart in you? Get along!"

He turned back to us. "Let's see this hole you live in." He walked into the Cachot, lowering his head as he passed through the door. We stayed behind, eager to have the air as long as we could.

He was pale when he came out, and there were beads of perspiration on his upper lip. "How are the vermin in there?" he asked.

"The fleas are bad," I told him, "but we keep the lice pretty well under control."

"We could do better with 'em if we had some light," Hays said.

"You have no light?" Magrath asked incredulously. "You mean you spend your lives in the dark?" The other men in the Cachot came to the door one by one, then edged, blinking, into the open, staring up at the sky and at their own raggedness.

"We're not allowed to have candles," I told him. "This is pretty brutal treatment, Doctor. If I'd ever caught one of my men treating a dog like this, I'd have knocked him into the scuppers."

Four sentries, militiamen, warmly dressed in long hooded overcoats, came up and looked wonderingly at us. I would have paid well for one of their overcoats if I had had the money, but Exeter jail had left me with only seven dollars.

"Take this man to the hospital on your muskets," Magrath said. They stood there for a second, uncertain. Magrath snapped his fingers, and they moved, then, to obey, though they were clearly reluctant.

"What are you in for?" he asked me.

"Four of these men are in on a false charge," I told him. "They're in for duration. So am I. There's more reason to what they charge me with, but I'm guilty of no crime. I'm guilty of nothing but trying to escape."

There was a commotion in the prison yard on the other side of the tall iron fence that separated the Cachot enclosure from the prisons. Prisoners shouted and ran toward the pickets. We saw Captain Shortland, followed by a militia officer, hastening toward us.

We watched him coming, stocky and strong; and the prisoners in the yard shouted in time with his footsteps, "LOB ster, LOB ster, LOB ster!" By the time he reached us he was red and angry.

"Good morning to you, Captain," Dr. Magrath said.

"Who let these men out?" Shortland demanded. "Carley! Carley! What in hell do you mean? Put these men where they belong!"

"My fault, Captain," Dr. Magrath said. "I had a report: a case of jail fever. These men, if you'll permit me to say so, Captain, should be looked after more carefully."

"*Looked* after!" Shortland said. "What in God's name do you mean? I was told to put 'em in close confinement. Should I button 'em into lace nightgowns and send 'em to bed in my guest chamber?"

"Indeed and indeed, Captain," Magrath said, "you've little leeway in carrying out your orders! Aye! What I have in mind, Captain, is that these men, after all, are prisoners of war, and I have a fixed conception of a prisoner of war. He's a man held in trust: a man for whom an accounting must be rendered when the war's over."

Shortland laughed, a sharp, mirthless bark. "Good God, Doctor," he said, "let's not have trouble at the very beginning! You know what orders are! These men are where they belong! What good is close confinement if you make it a damned lawn party, eh? These men get exactly what they deserve! Here, you, Carley! Push 'em back in the Cachot!"

Carley fussed around us like a kindly old woman, saying, "Now, byes! Now, byes!"

Magrath went on talking to Shortland in his deep, soothing voice, and we hung back against Carley's insistent pushing so we might hear as much as we could.

"Quite so, Captain," he said, "but we don't have to change close confinement to something worse, eh, Captain? Sleeping on granite, now, in this climate! There's nothing like this in all England. Did you ever try sleeping on granite, Captain?"

"No, by God!" Shortland shouted. "And until I do what these men have done I never expect to!"

"Not that, Captain!" Magrath protested: "You don't mean that! These men served their country, as I understand it. Nothing about that to deserve granite beds in winter, eh? I doubt you'd have been pleased, Captain, when you were first lieutenant of the *Melpomene*—hah, hah! There's a many of us remember that cutting-out party of yours, Captain! Suppose, instead of cutting out the *Avanturier* and winning the rank of commander, you'd fallen into the hands of the French and they'd clapped you into a black hole? Left you there with no light, and wet granite for a bed, eh?"

Shortland made a contemptuous sound in his throat. "Punishment's not punishment unless a man knows he's being punished!" he said. "Every damned one of these Americans is determined to get free! If we don't punish 'em we'll have 'em all breaking out and terrorizing the country."

"Ah," Magrath said, "I had Americans at Mill Prison before I came here. There isn't one of 'em that'll give up trying to get free because you put 'em in the Cachot when they fail. No, no! Nothing gets anywhere with 'em but kindness! The harder you are on 'em, the worse you'll find 'em. They're not Frenchmen, Captain."

"You're wasting your breath, Doctor," Shortland snapped. "I know how to handle my men!"

Magrath twisted his mouth and fingered his chin. "Yes," he said mildly. "That must be true. But let's look at the medical end of it, eh? I tell you, Captain, I don't like this African smallpox that runs about here, nor this violent pneumonia. They're like deadly poisons if not treated quickly and treated well. I must ask to be allowed to keep my eye on these men, or the guard may slip the wicket some fine morning and find all of 'em stiff as a sternpost."

They turned toward the Cachot, as if already it had become a charnel house; and when Shortland saw us still crowded in the doorway, holding it open against Carley's efforts to push us in, his face took on the look of badly cooked beef.

Before he could speak Simeon Hays shouted to Magrath: "Feed him some calomel, Doctor! His liver ain't what it ought to be!"

With that, not wishing to cause trouble for Carley, we gave ground, and the door clanged shut on us once more.

Now, whether the doctor's suggestions had some effect on Shortland, or whether the doctor himself was responsible, I don't know; but one November evening—a cold, dark twilight, when we were lying silently on our piles of straw, which had grown so shredded and moldy that they were less like straw than like dusty chaff—Carley rattled the door and pushed open the wicket.

"Here, byes!" he said. There was exultation in his voice. "I got a present for yez!"

I got up quickly, stumbling over Hays, and went to him.

"Don't nivver say I ain't give yez nothin'!" he said, handing me a piece of candle, an acid bottle, and a bundle of sulphur-tipped spunks for dipping in the bottle.

"Who are they from?" I asked.

"I dunno nawthin' about it," he said. "When yez finish with that, I'll get yez more; but pay attention to this, for the love av Mary! Whenivver yez use it, stuff the windys full of straw so the light won't show."

I doubt there are many folk, barring the blind, who know what it is to spend the greater part of their time in the thick dark. There is little I can say about it save that all of us dreaded the coming of night more than we had ever dreaded anything. Miller, the Englishman who had turned American, got the horrors one November evening. He burst out snuffling and groaning and hiccupping like a child, declaring he couldn't live another day in the place, and saying there were bells ringing in his ears, piercing his brain like knives. He carried on to such a degree that Hays and I crawled over and got our hands on him, lest he knock out his brains against the floor.

That one small point of yellow flame, almost absorbed by the dark walls of the Cachot, turned our misery into what, by comparison, seemed gaiety; for when the candle was kindled, our minds took fire from it as well, so we were able to speak, instead of lying silent and helpless. If we wished to move we could do so without stumbling over a man's legs—which was a serious business, because our legs were thin-skinned from scanty food, close confinement, and perpetual dampness. Above all we could occupy ourselves by lying around the candle as the spokes of a wheel radiate from the hub and engage in the making of hair bracelets, this being an art in which Jim Rickor had perfected himself when he should doubtless have been working at something that is known as "more useful." Because of this I have ever since been loath to say what is useful and what isn't.

Since our hair had not been cut for months—nor our beards shaved, for that matter, nor our clothes washed, nor clothes or shoes given to us to replace the rags in which we lay—we were able to pull long hairs aplenty from our own heads for the making of bracelets. These, we hoped, would serve a double purpose; for not only did they occupy our hands, but Rickor claimed they were sovereign remedies against rheumatism. Therefore we made them prodigally; and each one of us had hair bracelets on his wrists and ankles, and hair rings on his fingers, while Rickor made himself a collar, an inch and a half wide, with a neat cravat, all woven out of hair.

With the coming of December we had a fruitful subject for conversation. The month had no sooner started than Carley told us there was a rumor through the prison that American commissioners and British commissioners had met in Ghent, in Holland, to discuss peace, and were close to arriving at a decision. Thus, suddenly, we began to hope. For months we had thought of nothing in the morning except how to get through the day, and at evening how to bear one more night. But now we had rosy and heart-stirring dreams that peace might come at any moment to free us from cold and filth and aching bones, as it had come to free the Frenchmen. Every visit of Carley's was an adventure: he might, we thought, have news; and whenever he came to the wicket we held our breaths for fear we might lose a word.

Our hopes rose and fell like a fire. Jesse Smith came back to us on the ninth, swearing that if he hadn't known us in the early days of our imprisonment, he'd have taken us for haystacks because of the length of our hair and beards. He had been caught trying to scale the wall, he said; and when we asked him why he had tried to escape with peace imminent, he laughed sardonically.

"Peace!" he said. "If there's to be peace, why are the British fitting out an expedition to capture New Orleans? They don't know when they're licked! They don't know yet that we licked 'em in the Revolution! You got to lick 'em three times before it counts, and we've only licked 'em twice, so far!"

Sick at heart, we told him to hold his tongue, and set him to making a hair bracelet, loaning him our own hair for it. I can hear him now, commenting on his first bracelet.

"Hair bracelets!" he said. "My God! If the folks at home could only see me now! What if this should ever get to be known in Stonington, Connecticut! I can hear 'em, pointing at me and saying, 'There goes Jesse Smith, that was captured by the British in the war and suffered horribly, making hair bracelets! Wounded, too, he was: cut his finger on a hair!'"

But rumors of peace persisted, and so, too, did the attempts to escape, as we knew from men who were daily thrown in the Cachot.

A part of the fever to escape, it seemed to me, was due to the approach of Christmas; for Christmas is made much of in our province of Maine as well as in all New England; and as December dragged by, on snow-laden wings, our thoughts and our speech turned continually to our homes, so that we were filled with a powerful longing for them. There were times when it seemed to me I could smell, even through and above the stench of the Cachot, the odor of roasting goose, the sweet scent of spices on apple sauce, the faint mellow perfume of cider, the fragrance of mince pie. In my imagination I could see the frost figures on the windows of our large front room and catch the smell of the house: a scent of dry pine wood and cinnamon and soap and smoke, mixed with a faint trace of hay and sea air.

Christmas was a dark day, and we burned our candle all the morning so we could see to work on our hair bracelets; and Carley, instead of opening the wicket to give us our soup, unlocked the door and swung it open. Behind him we saw the doctor, tall and thin and one-eyed, wrapped in a heavy brown overcoat dusted with fine snow. From under his coat he drew a small bundle.

"Well, gentlemen," he said in his deep pleasant voice, and he wasn't being sarcastic, either, though we were the wildest and raggedest-looking men, I do believe, that ever in the history of the world had been called "gentlemen," "well, gentlemen, I wish you many, many merry Christmases—in your own country."

"We wish you the same, Doctor," said Simeon Hays. "We wish you the same, in this country or any other."

"Yes," the doctor said, clearing his throat, "yes. I appreciate that very much. Are you gentlemen quite well?"

"Why," Simeon Hays said, "considering the amount of wine we drink and the number of rich seegars we smoke, we're tollable, Doctor—tollable. Our appetite ain't too good: probably there ain't one of us could eat more than one cow, unless it was an awful small one."

"I see," the doctor said. "I wished very much to bring you something to read, gentlemen, but like most other things, that seems to be forbidden. I've brought you a small plum pudding, and Carley has a full ration for you today instead of the regular two-thirds ration. I deeply regret the plum pudding is so small, but I'm forced to say that gentlemen who've been on two-thirds rations for months are almost better off with no plum pudding at all."

He gave the bundle to Simeon Hays. Carley, overcome with emotion, rattled our bowls against his pail of soup with as much noise as though building a new wing on the Cachot.

I fished two clusters of hair bracelets from behind my pile of straw and handed one of them to the doctor. "Doctor," I told him, "we couldn't figure what to give you for a little remembrance, so we left it to each man. Oddly enough each man decided that the most useful thing would be a hair bracelet. We want you to take them as meaning we're grateful."

The doctor took the lot and examined them, smiling queerly. When he spoke, he seemed to find difficulty in expressing himself. "Why, gentlemen," he said, "this is a—this is a—I'm sure I shall never—this is a most unexpected——"

"From his childhood he's always hankered for nothing on earth so much as a hair bracelet," Simeon Hays enlightened us in a hoarse whisper.

Seeing the doctor had no desire to make a longer speech, I handed the other cluster of bracelets to Carley.

"Timothy Carley," I said, "these are for you, with thanks for past kindnesses."

"Oh, holy Mary!" Carley said, snuffling childishly. "I'm as proud of 'em as I'd be of the Garter!"

"Why, you wicked, blasphemious old man!" Simeon expostulated, very ladylike; "*whose* garter?" With that, being half starved as usual, we went for our soup.

Dr. Magrath cleared his throat. "I have one other little gift for you, gentlemen. It's only a bit of hope, so to speak; but there's worse gifts than hope. You may be quite certain that before this month is over there'll be a peace treaty signed between England and America."

We stared at him. I know that I, for one, had such a pounding in my throat that I had trouble in downing my soup; for the face of Emily Ransome came so suddenly into my mind that an enormous hand seemed to clutch at my heart and squeeze it.

Magrath smiled a lopsided smile at us, blinking his one blue eye; then the iron door clanged shut behind him.

"Well," said Simeon Hays, holding up a spoonful of soup, "here's to Christmas and freedom!"

# Experiments with a Forked Twig

THE APPARENT SUBJECT of this chapter is a small liverish-red United States Government bulletin published in 1917, 1934, and 1938 by the Government Printing Office under the auspices of the Department of the Interior. In common with most government bulletins it has a technical or meaningless title—Water Supply Paper 416; but it also has a title that seems to have genuine meaning, the latter being *The Divining Rod, A History of Water Witching, with a bibliography by Arthur J. Ellis.* Copies may be purchased from the Superintendent of Documents, Washington, D.C., for fifteen cents.

This bulletin would have considerable value if its contents were limited to the divining-rod information set down by Mr. Ellis; but unhappily somebody in the Department of the Interior had the bright idea of permitting O. E. Meinzer to write an Introductory Note to Mr. Ellis's paper on water divining. Mr. Meinzer, a geologist of high standing, has been associated with the U. S. Geological Survey since 1906, devoting his time principally to investigations of underground water. His sketch in *Who's Who in America* takes up 3 9/16 inches. He graduated from Beloit College in 1901 magna cum laude, wears a Phi Beta Kappa key, is an elder of the Presbyterian Church and a Councilor of the Boy Scouts of America, and thinks as little of water divining as he would of a barrel-ful of rattlesnakes.

Mr. Meinzer says bitterly that the whole business of water divining—which he calls "water witching"—is "thoroughly discredited" and that "it should be obvious to everyone that further tests by the United States Geological Survey" of water witching "would be a misuse of public funds." He concludes his Introductory Note with a sweeping piece of misguidance. "To all inquirers," he says, "the United States Geological Survey therefore gives the advice not to expend any money for the services of any 'water witch' . . . for locating underground water. . . ."

This brings me to the actual subject of this chapter, which is a discussion of my own experiences with water diviners—experiences that have proved to my complete satisfaction that O. E. Meinzer, in spite of his high reputation as a geologist and expert on underground water, is mistaken when he says that water dowsing is "thoroughly discredited"; that he, as a public servant, has served the public badly by advising water-hungry farmers and householders not to try to obtain a water supply by a method of which he disapproves; and that he, as a scientist, has followed highly unscientific procedure in condemning an extraordinarily useful contribution to human welfare without documenting his charges.

For the benefit of those who can't be happy unless they have access to exhaustive documentation of the success of water dowsers, I'll say at once that the best work yet produced on water dowsing is *The Divining Rod*, by Sir William Barrett, F.R.S., and Theodore Besterman, published by Methuen & Co., Ltd., 36 Essex Street W.C., London, 1926, 336 pages. This book contains innumerable well-attested cases of water diviners locating underground water supplies by the use of divining rods after geologists and professional well diggers had wasted enormous sums in fruitless attempts to find water in the same localities. Most of these cases occurred in England, Wales, or Scotland; but the authors include a few from America, and one of these American cases strikes me as being admirably designed for tossing into O. E. Meinzer's lap:

In 1901, Guy Fenley, the 14-year-old son of a highly respected citizen of Uvalde, Texas, accidentally discovered his ability to find underground water while walking with his father over the pasture of a ranch near Uvalde. This boy appeared to be able to state the approximate depth of the water as well as the direction of its flow, and to describe the strata between the water and the surface. In order to test his powers, Mr. Fenley took his son to a field at night: the boy indicated a spot where he stated water would be found at a depth of 200 feet. It is alleged that water was in fact found at 187 feet.

This being a very dry country, where the lack of water is one of the most serious difficulties to be encountered, the news of this boy's faculty soon spread. Mr. Thomas Devine took him to his ranch in the northern part of Uvalde County, where thousands of dollars had been spent in vain efforts to find water. Guy was taken to a large pasture and after two hours indicated an underground stream. This he followed for over a mile, marking a number of spots. It is stated that in each instance a fine flow of water was found. The boy was also alleged to have found water on the ranch of F. K. Moore, in Edwards County, and to have refused 500 dollars for his trouble.

Judge W. Van Sickle of the State Legislature asked the boy to come to his ranch in Brewster County, and made the following statement:

"I engaged Guy Fenley to go to Brewster County and locate two wells on the ranch owned by D. J. Combs and myself. This ranch is situated in a very dry country, known as the Glass Mountains. We had made a vain search for water on this ranch, having sunk a well to a depth of 607 feet, at a cost of $1,500, without striking water. This boy has already located two wells on the ranch, one at a depth of 250 feet and the other at a depth of 400 feet, both containing an abundant supply of pure water, and well-drilling outfits are now at work sinking other wells on the ranch, with no doubt about securing water.

"Fenley comes of a splendid family and has fine connections. He is a modest, handsome, blue-eyed boy, and to all outward appearances there is nothing about him to distinguish him from other boys of the same age. While locating the wells in Brewster County he romped and played with other boys whose acquaintance he made.

"Without citing the numerous cases and giving the names of parties for whom he has been successful in locating wells, I will say that if there is any doubting Thomas, such person can verify the truth of all my statements concerning the wonderful power of this boy by writing to anyone in Uvalde, Sanderson, or Alpine, Texas. He cannot tell the exact depth of the water below the surface, but he approximates its depth as any other person would guess at distances above the ground."

These facts were confirmed by the Hon. John N. Garner, who represents Uvalde in the State Legislature.

The Hon. John N. Garner of the foregoing paragraph was Vice President of the United States from 1932 to 1936.

If the Barrett-Besterman book, with its attested cases of successful water dowsing, isn't enough to make any reader doubt O. E. Meinzer's qualifications as a court of last appeal on the worth of the divining rod and the peculiarities of underground water, I suggest a study of the short but authoritative article which appears on page 333 of Volume 8 of the Encyclopædia Britannica (Eleventh Edition) under the heading "Divining Rod." This article concludes that:

Like the "homing instinct" of certain birds and animals, the dowser's power lies beneath the level of any conscious perception; and the function of the forked twig is to act as an index of some material or other mental disturbance within him, which otherwise he could not interpret.

It should be added that dowsers do not always use any rod. Some again use a willow rod, or withy, others a hazel-twig (the traditional material), others a beech or holly twig, or one from any other tree; others even a piece of wire or watch-spring. . . .

Modern science approaches the problem as one concerning which the facts have to be accepted, and explained by some natural, though obscure, cause.

The Encyclopædia Britannica, compiled and written by experts, does not put the stamp of approval on discredited beliefs or flim-flam games. In view of this fact, careful consideration must be given to the Britannica's statement that "modern science approaches the problem [of water dowsing] as one concerning which the facts have to be accepted."

This statement is sufficiently clear, but it can stand rephrasing for the benefit of people who condemn water dowsing without sufficient investigation.

The facts adduced by the Encyclopædia Britannica are that water dowsers, with the help of divining rods, are able accurately to locate underground veins of water that cannot be located in any other way; and these facts, in the opinion of the careful, authoritative, and hard-boiled editors of the Encyclopædia, cannot be explained by modern science, but must nevertheless be accepted.

To restate this opinion in still another way, water dowsing is a scientifically accepted fact, even though O. E. Meinzer uses a United States Government bulletin to state his personal and undocumented opinion that water dowsing is "thoroughly discredited."

Against the opinion of O. E. Meinzer, therefore, I offer the opinion of the Encyclopædia Britannica, together with my own opinion, founded on numerous successful experiments. Either the Encyclopædia Britannica and my own powers of observation are cockeyed, or O. E. Meinzer's Introductory Note to Water Supply Paper 416 is pretty unreliable stuff.

Before presenting my own experiences with divining rods and water dowsers I wish to introduce two authenticated cases of water divining.

These cases have benefited so many unfortunates that they make O. E. Meinzer's statements look sick.

A complete account of the first case can be found in *Blackwood's Magazine* for September 1932. *Blackwood's Magazine* isn't widely circulated in the United States, since it's published in Edinburgh by one of the oldest and soundest of British publishing houses; but it goes to every nook and corner of the British Empire, and, in spite of a dull-looking exterior, is rightly regarded by cultivated Englishmen as without a peer for readability and reliability.

The September 1932 *Blackwood's* contained an account of the experiences of Miss Evelyn M. Penrose while she was employed as official water dowser by the Government of British Columbia. The title of the article is "Dowsing."

In this article Miss Penrose explained that when, in 1931, the Government of British Columbia decided to employ an official water diviner, cabinet members, newspapers, and ministers furiously denounced this governmental dabbling in the black arts. Fortunately she had already convinced the British Columbia Government of her ability to locate water in apparently waterless sections; so the screams of protest were disregarded, and Miss Penrose went to work in the Okanagan Valley, the largest fruit-growing valley in British Columbia, where a seven-year drought had brought about such a ruinous shortage of water that in some parts of the valley settlers were carting water for miles from open irrigation ditches, or driving cattle a mile or two, twice a day, both winter and summer.

A water dowser's limit of endurance, she thought, was the examination of two homesteads a day for five days a week: but the need for water in the valley was so urgent that she worked seven days a week and examined as many as five and six homesteads a day for water.

It's hard, she explained, for people who do not have the water-divining gift to understand how exhausting water divining can be. The British Columbia Government understood it, she said, because during her probationary period she was accompanied on all-day dowsing expeditions by officials who were young, strong, and twice her size. They invariably returned so completely exhausted as to be incapacitated for several days thereafter.

As a result of Miss Penrose's efforts in the Okanagan Valley and the Peace River Block, there are today hundreds of individual and community wells where in early 1931 there was nothing but drought and discouragement. One young fruit grower in the center of the driest part of the valley had a magnificent orchard that was on the verge of destruction because he had no water and couldn't find any. Beneath one of the driest spots on his ranch—a spot the young man had walked over daily for years—Miss Penrose's divining rod located a water supply that yielded the young man 324,000 gallons a day.

Miss Penrose said she inherited her gift of water dowsing from her father and from a long line of Cornish forebears who were water dowsers. She had found that the water-divining gift or power usually descends from father to daughter and from mother to son. After she learned that she herself had the gift of water divining, she was distressed to find that the extreme activity of her divining rod first blistered her hands, then tore open the blisters. This forced her to abandon the conventional forked stick and use a straight metal rod balanced on the palm of her hand. At times she found the attraction of underground oil or minerals so powerful as to turn and twist her like a doll on a string, and even to pull her from her feet.

She holds that the most modern scientific explanation of water divining is that underground water, minerals, and oil give off electromagnetic waves and fields of force: that certain human beings are tuned to these waves and therefore pick them up and react to them in the same way that a radio set reacts to certain wave lengths.

In view of Miss Penrose's official record in British Columbia, how can any man be so oblivious to evidence, so stubbornly wrongheaded, as to insist that water divining is thoroughly discredited? I think I know, but I don't wish to come right out with the answer.

As a result of an article I wrote in 1943 for the *Country Gentleman* on the manner in which great horned owls had slaughtered ducks and geese on my Maine farm, I received a helpful letter from Mr. J. R. Terry of the British Columbia Department of Agriculture, Victoria, B.C. When I replied, I asked him for the latest news of Miss Penrose. He told me that Miss Penrose had returned to England and that the leading water dowser in British Columbia was Thomas G. Stewart, a long-time employee of the Canadian Department of Agriculture. Mr. Terry was kind enough to give me Mr. Stewart's address, which is 605 Foncier Bldg., 850 Hasting Street, W., Vancouver, B.C.; so I wrote Mr. Stewart for further information. A considerable correspondence ensued, and this is what I learned from it:

Mr. Stewart had dowsed for water in many parts of British Columbia for upwards of twenty-five years, during which time the wells dug as a result of his dowsing had been 96 per cent successful. He had, he said, encountered many skeptics during those years; but all of them had running water in their houses and had never known what it was to be without an adequate water supply, and belittled an honest endeavor to find a domestic supply of water. In 1937 he went to London for a meeting of the Dowsers' Association, which has four hundred members; but his enjoyment of the proceedings was marred by the discovery that the English brothers were wasting their time trying to find out what makes a divining rod move, instead of accepting the fact that it does move for certain people and devoting their efforts to finding how this peculiar gift can best be adapted to the needs of mankind.

Mr. Stewart reminded me that nobody worries, nowadays, as to why the magnetic needle points to the north, even though nobody knows the reason for it. Everyone accepts the fact and makes use of it. In certain hands, he says, the divining rod works as accurately as the magnetic needle, and he can't understand why people don't stop worrying as to the reasons and just let it work.

Since a forked branch hurts and blisters his hands, as it does the hands of everyone who does much water dowsing, Mr. Stewart makes his divining rod out of a forty-inch length of No. 9 fence wire—which is about the same as telephone wire or cement-form wire—bent in the shape of a V. With this rod he has not only located wells in all parts of British Columbia, but he has also estimated the depth of the wells with accuracy.

Here is a partial list of veins of water located by Mr. Stewart, the depths at which he estimated the veins would be found, and the depths at which the drill struck them:

Norman's Farm, Fort Langley, B.C., estimated 414; struck 405. Water overflowed.

Harry Leaf's home, Glen Valley, B.C., estimated 435; struck 440. Water overflowed.

George Campbell's home, Vanderhoof, B.C., estimated 218; struck 217. Water overflowed.

Frank Stewart's place, Heffley Creek, B.C., estimated 8; struck 8.

Burkett Jackson's place, Lower Nicola, B.C., estimated 9; struck 9.

James Sturgeon's place, Fanny Bay, Vancouver Island, estimated 3; struck 3.

Captain Logan, Cloverdale, B.C., estimated 57; struck 61.

E. Lazzos, Grand Forks, B.C., estimated 41; struck 40.

E. Thatcher's place, Halls Prairie, B.C., estimated 350; struck 358.

Christinson's place, Hixon, B.C., estimated 40; struck 30.

A. Nicolson's farm, Vanderhoof, B.C., estimated 370; struck 372.

Village of Vanderhoof, B.C., estimated 12; struck 12.

Ladysmith Fire Dept., Ladysmith, B.C., estimated 35; struck 35.

Conn's place, Halls Prairie, B.C., estimated 246; struck 240.

"and," Mr. Stewart added, when I sent him proofs of this chapter, "many dozens of others, since this list was made up, and another call today, April 1945."

Mr. Stewart believes that no water dowser is worth his salt unless he is able to estimate the depth of the water veins indicated by his divining rod. Unless this can be done, he says, the well driller may easily miss the vein by drilling beyond it, in case it is near the surface, or stop short of it in case the vein is deep.

Mr. Stewart told me three methods of determining the depth of veins. The first two, he said, were all right if the veins weren't deep.

The first he had got from T. Sorenson of Williams Lake, B.C. Sorenson stands three feet from the vein, facing it and gripping the rod by the ends, but with palms turned upward. Thus held, the rod moves downward toward the vein and remains down. It is then raised whereupon it moves downward again. He continues raising it until it ceases to move downward. Then he multiplies the number of moves by three and has the depth of the vein in feet. If, for example, it has moved downward 10⅓ times, the vein is thirty-one feet deep.

The second he got from George Swan of Denman Island. Swan stands five feet from the edge of the vein, grips his rod: then walks across the vein. As he crosses it, the rod pulls down. When five feet beyond the seam, he turns, regrips his rod and again crosses the vein, and again the rod pulls down. He continues to recross until the rod ceases to pull down: then counts 1½ feet for each time he crossed before the rod ceased to function. If it had dipped ten times, the water would be fifteen feet down.

Mr. Stewart's own method—one that has proved accurate at all depths—is as follows: he stands two feet or three feet from the vein, gripping the rod with his palms facing downward. The rod makes a complete revolution for every foot of the vein's depth. Then the rod stops and reverses itself, making the same number of revolutions in the opposite direction. Then it reverses itself once more and revolves the same number of times in the original direction. Then it stops revolving and will turn no more. In first locating the vein hold the palms facing upwards.

I gave Mr. Stewart's instructions to several Maine dowsers, but their rods refused to revolve. Thinking I might have misunderstood or misread the Stewart method, I wrote him again, asking for a more detailed description. His reply showed that I had understood him correctly, so I was forced to the conclusion that his water-dowsing faculties are more highly developed than those of most dowsers.

A brief history of authenticated cases of water divining in Maine was published in Sprague's *Journal of Maine History* for May 1915, largely based on the investigations of Calvin Chamberlain, a member of the Maine State Board of Agriculture and for fifty years a trustee of Foxcroft Academy.

The first recorded Maine water diviner was Royal Day, a deacon of the church in Monson, Maine, in 1820. In commenting on Day's unerring ability to locate underground water, Chamberlain said, "It is my belief that not a man can here be found, of ordinary intelligence and common prudence, who would venture on a well in a hard place without a resort to the water-rod. And I can further say, that not a case of disappointment or failure following its use has yet come to my knowledge."

Another celebrated Maine water diviner was William F. Gallison, a Baptist clergyman and Register of Probate. Gallison was asked to locate a spring by Colonel E. J. Mayo of Foxcroft, Maine. Gallison marked a spot on the Mayo property and said that an abundant vein of water would be found beneath that spot at a depth of between twenty-five and thirty feet. The diggers dug through earth and gravel for thirteen feet: then blasted through a solid ledge for another thirteen feet. At twenty-six feet they located a vein of water which is still there. Gallison died in 1858 with innumerable wells and springs to his credit.

An even more noted diviner was Seth Brawn of Foxcroft, Maine, who found hundreds of wells all over Piscataquis County.

In the autumn of 1880 the stream from which water was taken to supply the boilers of the spool factory in Foxcroft ran dry. Since steam was its only source of power, and the brook its only source of water, the works would have had to shut down unless water could be obtained at once. For a number of days teams hauled water from the river, half a mile distant. In their extremity the owners of the mill called upon Brawn to help them.

The lot upon which the factory was located was sparsely covered with soil; on much of it the ledges were entirely exposed, so that it wasn't a place where hit-or-miss prospecting would be practical or profitable. Brawn went over the extensive lot with his divining rod and traced three veins of water, all converging about forty yards from the boiler house. He described the situation in detail, gave the comparative size of the veins, and estimated the depth and character of the excavation that would be needed. The well was immediately dug, and his estimates proved correct in every particular.

Lower down on the same stream was an organ factory, later owned by Hughes & Son, piano manufacturers. The owners of this factory also called on Brawn for help, and he responded by locating a well so near the surface that two men, digging with pick and shovel for one hour, brought in an abundant supply of water. This was after prospecting and digging had been done in the bed of the brook without result. The spring found by Brawn furnished all the water needed by the factory. The well was only ten feet deep, and its bottom was higher than the bed of the stream and sixty feet from it.

The same year, 1880, the Piscataquis Valley Campmeeting Association built a tabernacle and cottages in Foxcroft. A fine spring of water was found upon the grounds, situated in the northwest corner, issuing from the face of the bedrock. The stables were erected in the southwest corner of the lot, next the highway, an eighth of a mile from the spring. The builders wanted a well near the stables, not only to save the labor of hauling water from the spring, but to prevent any danger of fouling the spring by taking horses there to drink.

Brawn's services were therefore enlisted. He located a vein of water near the stables, and, as was his custom, traced its course. He told the campground people that the vein which he had located for the stable well was the same vein that fed the spring in the farther corner of the grounds. When the stable well was blasted open, the campmeeting spring, an eighth of a mile away, became muddy and continued so until the work on the stable well was completed.

A farmer living on one of the rocky hills overlooking Foxcroft village desired a well. Since all parts of the farm looked equally waterless, he called on Seth Brawn and his divining rod. Brawn came, used his forked stick, and indicated a spot where the farmer would find water at a certain depth.

When work was commenced on the well, the farmer, instead of digging at the exact spot specified by Brawn, sank the shaft six feet to one side. After expending a large amount of hard labor, using quantities of powder to blast through the solid ledge, and going seven feet deeper than Brawn had told him he'd need to go, the hole showed no signs of water. The farmer, furious at his wasted labors, accused Brawn of chicanery and demanded satisfaction for his expense and trouble.

After examining the work, Brawn said, "You have not sunk your well at the spot where I told you to." The farmer replied, "I only moved over the bigness of the well, to a place more convenient for digging." Brawn directed that a hole be drilled in the wall of the shaft, about seven feet from the bottom, in the direction of the spot first indicated by him for the excavation. A small charge of powder was exploded and a copious supply of water came in; the shaft was filled and the well was a success.

Brawn continued in his work of locating wells during a long lifetime, and I have yet to hear of a report of failure. He died at Foxcroft, Maine, February 15, 1906, eighty-two years of age, retaining his faculties and power to the last.

One of the best known and most highly respected divining-rod operators in Piscataquis County was Edwin R. Haynes of Monson. During his life residence in Monson he was closely identified with the business, social, and political activities of the town. He was a charter member of Doric Lodge, F. & A. M., and its secretary for fifteen years. He was commissioned postmaster December 12, 1864, and held the office for nearly twenty-one years. He was one of the principal merchants of the place and held various town offices.

Haynes used a divining rod successfully over a long period of years. He located many veins, never failed to find water, and was accurate in estimating the depth to be excavated.

Chamberlain, in making his report, observed that it's not necessary to go to past records to authenticate the accuracy and reliability of water diviners.

Many still living within our borders [he said] possess the gift. In nearly every town in our county live many in whose hands the forked limb turns when over a water vein. Among them are men and women of the highest standing in their respective communities, and as a unit they declare that the working of the rod is emphatically not due to "unconscious movements" of the body or muscles of the operator, as so often charged by skeptics. They universally insist and know that they can do nothing whatever to prevent the rod from turning, no matter how hard they try.

We have, right here in Maine, all the necessary appliances to cure the most inveterate cases of unbelief in the water-rod, and we will gladly receive patients sent from a distance, treat them free of cost, and return them restored and in their right mind.

In our part of Maine we have a lot of water dowsers, able to locate underground veins of water by using forked twigs of the wild apple, the hazel, or the elm. In our part of Maine, too, we have a disconcerting number of people who, like O. E. Meinzer, burst into raucous and contemptuous laughter at any mention of water dowsers, and unhesitatingly class water dowsing with sea serpents, ectoplasms, and fairy godmothers.

My own experiments with wild-apple wood, hazel wands, elm branches, and other water-finding machinery have been unproductive, for none of them function for me, any more than they do for any person who hasn't a water dowser's singular sensitiveness. This sensitiveness cannot be learned or acquired by any person who doesn't have it to begin with.

I was a reporter for ten years on a Boston paper; and for twenty years after that I was a correspondent for the *Saturday Evening Post* in various parts of the United States, Europe, and the Far East. Any reputable reporter, I have found, goes out of his way to get at the truth, and makes every effort to avoid inaccuracies that might mislead his readers and damage his own reputation. With this thought in mind, I have no hesitation in saying that as a result of watching water dowsers with considerable care, I know that they possess a power as accurate and as unexplainable as that of the magnetic needle in a compass; and I have no hesitation in taking issue with O. E. Meinzer or in giving it as my considered opinion that prospective owners of country residences will save both time and money by enlisting the aid of a water dowser before embarking on any attempt to locate a water supply.

I know that dry wells can result from following the advice of the best of water dowsers; but in such cases I am certain that the water is where the dowsers' rods say it is, and that the blame for the failure to strike water is due to the difficulty of driving a straight hole through certain rock structures—a matter on which I will elaborate in another place.

My farm in Kennebunkport, Maine, Rocky Pasture, is so situated that town water is inaccessible. Consequently we were obliged to provide our own water; and to that end a well driller appeared on the premises with a drilling-rig and a trailer heavily stocked with cases of beer and canned sardines, and embarked on the task of drilling an artesian well on a level spot handy to the kitchen at an agreed price of $4.00 a foot. The spot was chosen without reason or method, so far as I could see; but since it was selected by persons familiar with housebuilding and well digging, I thought they knew what they were doing—which they emphatically didn't.

As soon as drilling started, the drill struck a ledge of rock known to well drillers as blue rock or blue marl. One of the peculiarities of blue rock is that its hardness frequently dulls or breaks the sharpest and most expensive drill point in about three seconds flat.

After two months of unflagging and thunderous effort, which would have pierced any normal rock to a depth of six hundred feet, the boring had penetrated fifty-four feet into the blue rock. The hole, moreover, was as dry as the Sahara Desert; and the well driller, having broken all his drills, announced that he would be obliged to cease and desist for a few weeks in order to repair the breakage.

It seemed to me that unless the blue rock could soon be penetrated, the well driller might be hard at work for years, leaving us waterless for the same length of time. I therefore consulted the state geologist, who obligingly came to Rocky Pasture to look into the situation. He was not encouraging, for he said frankly that the ledge of blue rock we were trying to pierce might go down three hundred feet or it might go down thirty thousand feet.

A hasty calculation satisfied me that if the blue rock should indeed prove to be thirty thousand feet thick, the well driller, who had only penetrated fifty-four feet in two months, would be approximately one hundred years getting down thirty thousand feet, and the cost of the operation would be $120,000. Since we couldn't wait one hundred years for water, and had no intention of paying anyone $120,000 for anything, we talked the well driller into accepting $216 for his dry hole, packing up his broken drills, and leaving us to clean up his empty sardine tins and beer bottles and to find another solution to our water problem.

When I conferred with old inhabitants of Kennebunkport, they pointed out that there was a marshy spot in a meadow some three hundred yards from our house, from which a trickle of water constantly oozed, even during severe droughts. There had once been a spring thereabouts, they said, and the water from it was supposedly the best obtainable anywhere around. Years ago, they said, somebody had sunk a barrel around the spring, and the barrel was always full of the best gol-rammed drinking water anybody'd want. In short, they said, the marshy spot was caused by a vein of water; and if I could find the vein, my water troubles would be over.

Unfortunately the barrel had vanished, the marshy spot was about thirty yards square, and I was at a loss to know how to locate the exact point where the spring might be expected to bubble up from the subsoil.

While I was brooding over the situation, two of my co-workers—one a contractor with whom I had gunned and fished for many years; the other a man who did farm work at Rocky Pasture for several years—came out of a near-by thicket holding freshly cut branches of wild apple about half an inch thick at the butt, about two feet long, and roughly Y-shaped.

The contractor, Raymond Grant, gripped the arms of his branch by the tips, held it upright before him, and started to cross the marshy spot. When he was almost across, the branch slowly turned downward; then jerked convulsively in his hands, like a fishing rod bending beneath the struggles of a trout. Raymond put the rod under his arm, reflectively rubbed the palms of his hands on the seat of his trousers, made a mark with his heel in the marshy sod, and said, "That's where I make it."

The other operator, Bill Brennan, took a firm grip on his own branch and approached the marshy piece from another angle. As he stepped on the wet soil, the branch dipped as though yanked earthward by an invisible cord. He walked a zigzag course, coming to a standstill at the spot Raymond had marked. The rod pointed straight down and vibrated as if afflicted with chorea. He unclenched his fingers from the rod and examined the tips of its two arms. The bark, where his fingers had gripped, was wrinkled and half peeled. The flesh of his palm and fingers had a rubbed, red look. He thrust the branch into the earth at the same spot marked by Raymond's heel.

"That's quite a vein," he said.

Raymond handed me his own rod. "Here," he said, "you try it. There's so much water down there that maybe it'll work for you."

I stepped hopefully out onto the marsh, holding the rod like an experienced water dowser; but it was like any other stick in my hands, without movement or pull. I quartered and circled the soft spot, but the rod remained as lifeless as a broom.

"I guess you don't have the knack," Raymond said, "but maybe it'll work if you hold one end while Bill holds the other."

When I did as he suggested, the rod pulled at the palms of my hands, drawn by an irresistible force.

"Try to straighten it," Raymond said. "See if you can keep it from tipping."

I couldn't do it. The downward drag, by the time we reached the marked spot, was so strong that when I resisted the attempt of that twig to pull out of my hand, it twisted and was wrenched into uselessness, after the manner of twigs too green to break. Yet the twig was too flexible for Bill, gripping the other arm of the Y, to have caused the solidity of that downward haul, even though he had tried; for it was a pull that felt as though a lively steamer trunk were dangling from its end.

"Yes," Raymond said, "that's the place, all right." He called to his workmen to bring picks and shovels, and set them to excavating a hole ten feet in diameter around the spot where the two forked twigs had done their strongest dipping. At a depth of four feet, the hole was so full of water that a gasoline pump had to be put to work. At a depth of eight feet the diggers struck gravel, and up through the gravel, exactly beneath the spot indicated by the twigs, bubbled a spring that flowed at the rate of twenty gallons a minute.

We built a stone spring house around it, with a 3,000-gallon retaining tank, installed a 500-gallon pressure tank and a Fairbanks-Morse motor, laid 800 feet of pipe from the spring to the house; and ever since we have been plentifully supplied, in spite of droughts and 40-below-zero cold snaps, with spring water that tests the same as the best mineral springs in Maine. This spring, on the test-list on page 453, is called the Home Spring.

When I asked Raymond how he had discovered that he had the gift of using a dowsing rod, he said that at one time, during his school days, there had been a sort of craze among his schoolmates for experimenting with divining rods; and on Sundays he and his friends prowled all over the countryside, attempting to develop the faculty of locating hidden springs. They experimented with willow rods, beech twigs, elm, apple wood—even with umbrella ribs. Some of the boys, he said, felt nothing at all, ever, no matter what sort of rods they used. Some felt, or thought they felt, movement in twigs, but only with certain sorts of wood. But in the hands of a favored few, the movements of the twigs were violent and uncontrollable. He seemed to think that in any rural community, a fair percentage of male school children—say 10 or 15 per cent—would prove to be susceptible to the pull of underground veins of water.

Now I had no thought at that time of posing as a champion of water diviners; but since two forked twigs in the hands of two amateur water dowsers had uncovered for me a better water supply than I could have obtained from the deepest artesian well or the most elaborate town water-supply system, I was amiably disposed toward water dowsing, and better than mildly interested in it. It didn't occur to me to take further steps in the matter, however, until the summer of 1940, when southern Maine, like many other sections of the United States, suffered a dry spell. It wasn't a super-dry spell, like the drought of the following summer; but it was dry enough to blot the water from our duckpond, in which five or six families of geese and some hundred brace of mallards, as well as several pairs of rarer ducks, made their home.

I know few things more offensive than a well-populated duckpond when its liquid content has evaporated to a rich jelly, seemingly made up of 10 per cent brown glue and 90 per cent stench. Since our duckpond had achieved this unhappy state, and would doubtless become worse before it improved, it occurred to me to call once more on Brennan and his dowsing rod.

On the following day Brennan reported that he had put a rod to work and had detected signs of underground activity about two hundred yards from our original spring. When I went with him to look over the situation, I found the indicated spot in the middle of an alder thicket on a gentle hillslope. The ground in the vicinity was as dry as a bone; yet twenty yards downhill from the marker it was black and moist.

It struck me that a spring only two hundred yards from our original spring might come from the same vein of water, and that to open that vein in more than one place might cause trouble. Brennan, however, assured me that this couldn't be the case. He had put his rod on the spring at the same time he put it on the spot under discussion, and had found that the pull exerted by the original spring was far less than the one exerted by the one he had just discovered, which he had no hesitation in characterizing as an old h'ister.

To show me what he meant, he gave me one arm of his dowsing rod to hold, holding the other himself. The behavior of the rod was almost painful, and to grip and hold it firmly was like gripping and holding a rattail file attached to the revolving spindle of a motor. Brennan started in at once to sink a hole at the indicated spot; and I had so little reason to doubt the efficacy of his dowsing rod that I set off to get two hundred feet of two-inch pipe to connect this new spring with our rapidly dwindling pond.

When I got back with the pipe, the hole was six feet deep, and water was gushing up into it so rapidly that a two-horsepower pump was just able to cope with it. As near as we could figure, it was flowing at the rate of twenty-five gallons a minute.

We built a five-foot-square box for the spring and lowered it into place. Then we hooked up the two hundred feet of two-inch pipe, bent one end to form a siphon, and lowered it into the spring. The other end opened into the duckpond. We plugged the lower end, filled the whole pipe with water: then pulled the plug. The water at once started siphoning into the duckpond from the spring, and for the rest of that dry summer we had water in the duckpond. On the test-list this spring is called the Chain of Ponds Spring.

That same summer, to rid ourselves of an unsightly alder swamp that had once been used as a neighborhood dump, we built a small pond by throwing a fifty-foot dam between two high ledges. At the beginning of the following summer the pond was a pleasing spectacle. A pair of Canada geese led seven goslings in stately circles around the shore, three pairs of wood duck and their jittery offspring gobbled innumerable mosquito larvae, and scores of toy mallards scuttled in and out of their nests in the junipers.

A few weeks later a drought had dried it almost to nothing, hundreds of fish were dying around the edges, and the ducks and goslings were in a parlous state.

As a result, Brennan again took up his dowsing rod and went on a hunt for a spring, working uphill from the duckpond so that if water were located it could be brought downhill with the minimum of exertion.

Five hundred yards uphill from that second duckpond, beyond a massive outcropping of blue stone, there was an old ice pond grown up to cattails, cranberry vines, ironwood, cat briers, and other useless scrub. It wasn't much of an ice pond, not only because of the weeds and brush, but because it usually dried up late every summer and often didn't fill again in time to produce an ice crop. It was bone dry when Bill came to me to say that his rod showed signs of water beneath its brick-hard bottom.

I didn't see how, even though there should be a spring beneath the caked mud of this old pond bottom, we could make use of it. To have done so, so far as I could see, we would have been obliged to blast a trench eight or ten feet deep through a hundred yards or more of blue stone. However, I felt I ought to know whether or not the divining rod was again telling the truth, so a hole was sunk in the tough clay of the pond bottom. Seven feet below the surface we came to a ledge, and from a hole in the ledge poured a stream of water four inches in diameter. This was at the peak of the 1941 drought, when most of the wells, ponds, and brooks in Kennebunkport had dried up and farmers were carrying water a mile and more to keep their livestock—and their families—from dying of thirst. This is known as the Ice Pond Spring. Its water has never been tested.

The dowsing rod came into play a fourth time when we set out to rid ourselves of a gypsy-moth infestation in a grove of several hundred oak trees—big trees that had been stripped of their leaves for five years running by countless millions of those destructive insects. By mid-July of each summer, every leaf had been eaten to an insubstantial skeleton, and so numerous were the caterpillars that their droppings made an endless hissing sound, like the sibilant patter of innumerable raindrops. For years I had watched this grove fade from sturdy life to premature death without being able to do anything about it, since the land didn't belong to me. Then I learned that the grove was about to be cut for firewood, so I made an extra effort and was fortunate enough to be allowed to buy it.

The state forester came to pass judgment on the grove, but wasn't optimistic about saving the trees. Most oaks died after being stripped of their leaves by gypsy moths for three successive years, he said, but he added cheerfully that I'd got to try to save them.

First, he said, I must have the grove sprayed by a high-powered sprayer. After that he would supply me with the necessary creosote and long-handled brushes, and I must apply a coat of creosote to every gypsy-moth nest on every oak in the grove. When I pointed out that there must be at least five million nests to be painted, he said cheerfully that I was probably underestimating. When I further pointed out that spraying would be impossible because there was only a marshy wood road into the grove, incapable of holding up a heavy spraying outfit, and that there was also no water with which to fill the sprayer even if the truck could be got to the grove, he said it was up to me to figure out a method of getting the truck to the grove and supplying it with water.

So, during the winter, we creosoted gypsy-moth nests by the million—little pale yellow deposits of eggs, like inch-long ovals of pallid velvet plastered on the undersides of branches on the southwest sides of tree trunks. Brennan also scoured the land near the grove with his dowsing rod held before him; and at the grove's lower edge he found a spot that set the rod to quivering and twisting. We dug there and at a depth of five feet uncovered another spring, the fourth to be located by a divining rod. We built a rough box for it, six feet square and six feet deep; and with its help, that summer, we double-sprayed the grove—which, so far as we know, hasn't harbored a gypsy moth since. This spring is not on my own farm but on an adjoining property that has been abandoned. Consequently I do not include it among the Rocky Pasture springs.

Not long after this, Raymond Lovejoy, county agent of York County, Maine, from 1919 to 1944, came down to examine into the state of our hay crop, according to his amiable yearly custom. After deciding which meadows needed lime, which ammonium nitrate, which superphosphate, which borax, and which seaweed, and after debating how much additional Reed's Canary grass to sow on the wet spots, which meadows to reseed to the magic mixture of ladino clover and orchard grass, what sections of our high land would be benefited by a sprinkling of Birdsfoot Trefoil, and settling other matters of interest only to persons providing nourishment for Holstein cows, we fell into conversation on more frivolous subjects.

"Now you take my brother," Lovejoy said. "He claims to be able to locate water by using a divining rod. Did you ever have any experience with people who claim to be able to use a divining rod?"

I told him at considerable length, and with emphasis, of the four springs that had been unerringly located by divining rods on our own farm.

"Well," Lovejoy said, "there's a lot of people around here who say there's nothing in it. There's a man in my office who can't hear the subject mentioned without getting so hot under the collar that he pretty near busts."

I urged Lovejoy to bring his skeptical friend to Kennebunkport and let him look at our springs.

He shook his head. "That wouldn't do any good. This man, he'd just claim anybody could have found those springs without using anything but ordinary common sense. He'd say everybody in the neighborhood must have known about 'em for years. He'd say only an idiot would listen to such hocus-pocus."

I took down from a shelf Volume 8 of the Encyclopædia Britannica and read him the article on Divining Rods—how the modern divining rod was originally used by prospectors for minerals in the Hartz Mountains; how scientists freely admit that the forked twig, in the hands of a dowser, is infallible as an indicator of underground water, but are unable to explain it; how Sir W. H. Preece, the English electrician, thinks a dowser's water-finding ability is due to "mechanical vibration, set up by the friction of moving water acting upon the sensitive ventral diaphragm of certain exceptionally delicately framed persons."

"How," I asked Lovejoy, "could your friend continue to insist that water dowsing, in the face of this report, is hocus-pocus?"

"You don't know how stubborn people can be," Lovejoy said.

I showed him, in *Blackwood's Magazine*, the article by Miss Penrose, and asked him what he thought his skeptical friend would have to say to these official records from British Columbia.

"I'll tell you what I think," Lovejoy said. "The York County Farm Bureau's having a fair in Dayton, Maine, in a couple of months, and I think I'll offer prizes for water dowsers. I'll make 'em perform right out in front of the grandstand. If people see it, they'll have to believe it. You can be one of the judges."

Circumstances beyond my control prevented me from being a judge at that dowsing competition, which was duly held on August 21, 1941, but I had a complete report on its interesting features. Before it was held, Lovejoy himself, at one time a profound skeptic concerning the value of divining rods and water dowsers, discovered that he, too, was affected by underground water and was able to use a divining rod successfully.

On the Dayton fairgrounds there was a judging platform, and when Lovejoy made a tour of the fairgrounds to find out whether a vein of water existed anywhere within them, he found only one vein—and that was located seven feet under the judging platform. Thus it became necessary to lay a water pipe directly over the vein, so that spectators, having seen the dowsers at work, could then see the pipe excavated and know how accurate the dowsers had been in spotting the concealed pipe.

To prevent overcrowding, no dowser under fifty years of age could enter the competition. There were five contestants. All were blindfolded: all located the water vein within three inches of the same spot. The winner, Asa Ellingwood, sixty-four, of Old Orchard, had located eight wells with no failures. Second was Joseph Vachon, fifty-four, of Emery Mills, who had located twenty-five wells with no failures. Thomas Hall of

Alfred, third, age not given, had located twelve wells with no failures. Ernest Mathews, sixty-five, West Kennebunk, winner of fourth prize, had located fifteen successful wells. C. W. Davis, seventy-four, North Berwick, winner of the fifth prize, had dowsed for water for sixty years and located so many wells he couldn't begin to remember the number.

A year after the Dayton Fair, Brennan's dowsing rod located on my own farm a fifth spring which we marked with an alder switch until such time as we might be able to dig for the spring and ditch off its overflow. Shortly afterward Lovejoy visited us again to swap a piece of venison for a brace of mallards; and when I told him about the new spring, he asked whether or not we knew how to figure the depth of a vein of water before digging for it.

When I said we didn't, he said he knew how and would give us a demonstration. Without being told where Brennan's rod had shown the new spring to be, he settled on precisely the same spot which Brennan had indicated, dropped the point of his rod on it; then took a fresh grip on the rod and rapidly stepped backward. At the start, for some unexplainable reason, the pull on the rod was gentle. Four paces from the starting point, however, the rod again dipped sharply downward.

"See that?" Lovejoy asked. "That's how it's done. You just walk backward, slow or fast, from the site of a water vein, and when the rod dips again, you've found the depth of the vein. If it dips when you're eight feet from the vein, that's its depth: eight feet. The backward dip on this spring occurred at twelve feet. When you dig this particular spring, you'll get a fair supply of water, probably, at four or five feet; but if you want the maximum flow, you'll have to dig seven or eight feet deeper."

A month later, for drainage purposes, we buried a few sticks of dynamite at the spot marked by Brennan and Lovejoy and set them off. When we examined the resulting hole, we thought the rods had at last made a mistake, for there were no signs of moisture in it. When we dug it out, we found a flat ledge of rock at the five-foot level.

The surface of that flat rock, too, was dry, except for an infinitesimal fracture that glistened a little.

On the following morning, however, the hole was full of water, and a stream trickled from it at the rate of about three gallons a minute. These two facts are important; for in them, I believe, lies the explanation of the skepticism of many professional well drillers toward the water-finding ability of water dowsers. This fifth spring is the Longmeadow Spring. Its water has not been tested.

From 1939 to 1945, fourteen springs were accurately located on my farm with dowsing rods. Seven of these springs have been given permanent boxes. The other seven, although not boxed, have been kept open so that we could know whether or not they were dependable during droughts. Of those years, three have been dry ones, and the summer of 1941 brought with it a true drought—the worst in two generations. Not one of the fourteen springs has gone dry at any time.

One of these springs, called on our test-list the Pool & Hole Spring, is in a miniature rock-sided gully ninety paces from the front door of my home and eighty paces from the spot where the well driller drilled fifty-four feet through blue rock in an attempt to strike an artesian well.

Before this spring was dug out, it was located by six local water dowsers, all working separately—Raymond Lovejoy of Sanford, Maine; his son Lieutenant Robert Lovejoy, a pilot who held a commission in both the Army and Navy air forces; William Brennan; Asa Ellingwood of Old Orchard Beach; Don Treadwell of Sanford; and Ralph Leach of Kennebunkport.

These men were asked to go independently and on different days to test that section for a vein, and all six of them settled on exactly the same spot. Treadwell and Raymond Lovejoy estimated that the main vein was eighteen feet below that spot. Since the spot was close to the house, it seemed to me that I should have the spring opened so that I could use it as an auxiliary water supply in case anything happened to our existing spring, which is eight hundred feet from the house.

We therefore started to dig a hole six feet square directly above the spot indicated by the dowsers. The digging was done at the end of a long dry spell, when there was no surface moisture near the hole. At two feet water began to well up into the hole. At three feet it was coming in so rapidly that the diggers could no longer keep on without the help of a ditch pump. Since no ditch pump was available at the time, we stopped work on the hole, which was full of water through the winter. The water remained unfrozen, as is the case with spring water. Without a pump we could only guess at the flow in the hole, our guess being three gallons a minute. Since the pull of the dowsing rods had been extremely strong at that particular spot, I argued that if we could go down eighteen feet to the vein, the flow would be much larger.

Five months later I was able to get a well digger to come in with his drilling rig. When he got his rig near the open hole, he found that he was unable to set up over it because two high-power electric lines were in his way. The question then arose as to whether or not he should drill elsewhere. Since he'd gone to considerable trouble to get his rig into a difficu't position, I told him he could drill twelve feet from the hole, on the vein.

I must here interpolate, for the benefit of those unfamiliar with the activities of water dowsers, that a water dowser's rod always takes him to one spot where the pull is stronger than at any other spot. That is the spot at which the well should always be dug. Having located that spot, however, dowsers frequently trace the vein which passes through that spot. The pull is just about as strong as the pull at the essential spot; and those dowsers who estimate depth usually estimate the depth of the vein to be the same as the depth of the specific spot. All the dowsers who used their rods to locate our Pool & Hole Spring also traced the vein; and all the dowsers, working independently, agreed exactly on the vein's course.

Having agreed that the well driller could drill on the vein since he couldn't drill in the center of the hole, I got Lovejoy, Treadwell, and Brennan to test the vein with their rods to make sure that the drill was over the vein. When all three were agreed, the driller set his rig in motion. At six feet he struck blue rock; then continued onward through blue rock another fourteen feet—a total of twenty feet. The depth of the vein had been estimated as eighteen feet.

When the six-inch bore was pumped out and light reflected into it with a mirror, the shaft was as smooth and clean as the bore of a cannon—and as dry. Not a drop of water trickled from the sides of the rock tube: yet twelve feet away was a steadily flowing spring located by the same dowsing rods that had located the vein for which the drill was searching.

The dowsers had been 100 per cent correct in locating the spring that had been dug by hand; but the drill rig, drilling a six-inch hole through hard rock, had apparently missed the vein. The driller admitted that his drill, when it struck the sloping ledge, had slipped off and entered the ledge about three inches off center. As near as I could figure it, a drill that was three inches out of plumb at a depth of six feet would be six inches out of plumb at a depth of eighteen feet. The vein fissure, being in hard blue rock of great density, might have been an extremely narrow crack, as had been the case in the Longmeadow Spring. And if this was so, then I figured that a six-inch deviation might understandably have missed it.

I have found from experience that springs often behave oddly when uncovered for the first time. Sometimes, when a hole has been dug at a spot indicated by dowsing rods, the water barely trickles into the hole. Perhaps, in four or five hours, only six inches of water will come into the excavation, the flow has obviously ceased, and the diggers freely admit that the hole is no good. Twenty-four hours later, however, the hole will be full and water flowing over the lip at the rate of two or three gallons a minute.

However, the hole drilled into the Pool & Hole Vein was completely dry; so the well driller dismantled his rig and moved a quarter of a mile to another location beside the driveway that leads into Rocky Pasture from the main highway. This spot had also strongly influenced divining rods in the hands of Lovejoy, Treadwell and Brennan. The first two had estimated that the water was twenty feet below the surface, and I was willing to gamble that three water diviners, working independently, and getting a pull at exactly the same spot, couldn't be wrong.

To my distress, this hole, when drilled and pumped out, also proved to be dry. The well driller, who had small faith in water divining, wanted to know whether or not he should go deeper. He almost never, he said, struck water under twenty-five feet, and the average depth at which he struck it, he opined, was around eighty feet. If I'd let him drill another two or three hundred dollars' worth, he hinted, I might get water and I might not. Having no faith whatever in the water-finding abilities of well drillers, I told him that I'd had enough: that I was satisfied the dowsers had been correct in indicating the spot beneath which water existed, as well as in their estimate of the water's depth, and that if it wasn't where they said it was, any further digging would merely be a waste of money.

So the well driller expressed his regrets at my hard luck and took his departure. When I broke the sad news of the two dry holes to Lovejoy, he was depressed and disheartened. He said he could neither explain nor understand it; but he was sure of one thing: the water was where he and Treadwell and Brennan had said it was, all the well drillers in the world to the contrary notwithstanding.

For the next few months I frequently and gloomily visited those two expensive dry holes. Both of them, it seemed to me, remained singularly full of water. This seemed odd, so I took a shovel with me one day and lowered the level of the surface water that stood around one of the pipe casings. When it ran off, the water level in the pipe remained constant. Stirred by a wild surmise, I sent to Montgomery Ward for two cheap pumps, set them on top of the well casings and went to pumping. Six hundred and forty strokes were needed to empty the Pool & Hole well. I waited eight minutes: then pumped it dry again in three hundred and seventy strokes. Every day or so I pump it dry and it promptly fills again. It flows about five gallons a minute, and is about as dry as the George Tavern in Glasgow, Scotland. So Lovejoy, Treadwell and Brennan had been right after all. This was the sixth spring to be pointed out by divining rods on my farm.

STATE ANALYSIS OF ROCKY PASTURE SPRINGS

| Spring at ........... | Home | Chain of ponds | Pool & Hole | Roadside | Lower Meadow | Tomato Valley |
|---|---|---|---|---|---|---|
| Serial No. | 119,472 | 119,300 | 131,017 | 131,088 | 131,089 | 131,343 |
| Date of Collection | 5/1/43 | 4/14/43 | 6/1/45 | 6/2/45 | 6/2/45 | 6/12/45 |
| Start of Analysis | 5/3/43 | 4/16/43 | 6/3/45 | 6/5/45 | 6/5/45 | 6/13/45 |
| Turbidity | 0 | 0 | 15. | 5. | 0 | 10. |
| Color | 0 | 0 | 20. | 10. | 0 | 5. |
| Sediment | sl-veg | sl-veg | ab-min | ab-min | med-veg | ab-min |
| Odor Cold. 20 C | 0 | 1V | 3-Ch Oily | 3-Ch Oily | 2-A | 4A |
| Nitrites | .001 | .001 | .001 | .003 | 0 | .001 |
| Nitrates | .01 | .015 | .01 | .01 | .02 | .01 |
| Hardness | 67. | 34. | 6. | 42. | 30. | 35. |
| Alkalinity | 7.2 | | | 7.0 | | |
| Acidity | | 6.6 | 6.3 | | 6.2 | 6.7 |
| Chloride | 12. | 9. | 12. | 10. | 7. | 6. |
| B. Coli-presumptive | 0/5 | 0.5 | 1/5 | 2/5 | 0/5 | 0/5 |
| B. Coli | 0/5 | 0.5 | 0/5 | 1/5 | 0/5 | 0/5 |
| Temperature | 50 | 46 | 46 | 48 | 46 | 48 |
| Flow per minute in gallons | 10 | 20 | 5 | 6 | 8 | 5 |

The other "dry" hole beside the road was given the same treatment and proved to be even less dry than the Pool & Hole. When emptied, it fills in five minutes, and evidently flows at the rate of six gallons a minute. On our list it is the Roadside Spring—the seventh to be found by divining rods.

The eighth was in a meadow so moist that tractors couldn't be driven across it without bogging down. I suspected that a spring was responsible, and since I wanted the meadow drained, I sent three dowsers to investigate. They found no indications of water in the wet spots; but high up above those spots, on a hillslope, they felt a strong pull. We dug there and hit the Lower Meadow Spring, which now discharges its water through a trench into a duckpond instead of spreading it ruinously over an otherwise excellent hay field.

We found the ninth spring as a result of my desire to build a storage barn in a sheltered spot, provided I could have water for it. Three dowsers agreed on two intersecting veins, one seven and one nine feet deep. The dowsers were right again, and the resulting well appears on the test-list as Tomato Valley Spring.

Other springs located on my own farm by digging at spots where divining rods showed water would be found, are No. 10, Western Point Spring; No. 11, Breakout Spring; No. 12, Between-the-Islands Spring; No. 13, Northwest Corner Spring; No. 14, Two Acre Spring; No. 15, Westgate Spring. The fourth spring we dug, as I have said, was not on my own land, so I only lay claim to fourteen springs: not to fifteen.

In no instance has a divining rod ever supplied us with faulty information.

All these water-dowsing experiments have convinced me that good dowsers are infallible at locating the proper spots to dig for water, no matter what the underground conditions may be. If, however, those underground conditions are rocky or ledgy, then the hole can't be dug by hand. A well driller must be called in, and the inability of well drillers to drill straight holes through certain sorts of rock can nullify—and too often *have* nullified—the talents of the best water dowsers in the world.

The dowsers who have helped me uncover springs and make long, involved experiments have nothing whatever to gain by misrepresenting the effect which underground water has upon their rods. They know there's nothing faked or phony about their peculiar ability, which operates equally well before skeptics and believers, at daytime or in the dark, on sunny days or in the rain, whether they're blindfolded or not, whether they wear rubber boots or leather-soled shoes, and no matter from what sort of trees their rods are cut.

They have repeatedly and cheerfully traveled fifty or sixty miles to make tests for me and have never allowed me to repay them in any way for their trouble and loss of time. Nor have they ever worried about the reputation they might lose if an ill-natured or small-minded skeptic undertook to prove they were faking—which is worthy of note, considering the number of small-minded persons in this world who spend their lives being contemptuous and skeptical about worthy things of which they're ignorant.

Their only desire is to use their ability to enable waterless households to have access to water. There wasn't one of them who hesitated to advise anyone to dig where a dowsing rod showed water, provided the well could be dug by hand; nor was there one who would advise anyone to employ a well driller to drill for that water at a cost of $6.00 a foot if the drill had to penetrate a New England ledge to reach it. The water is there if the dowsers say so; but it's where the dowsing rods say it is: not where erratic drill points happen to hit. It's not the dowsers who are unreliable: it's the drilling machines.

There seems to be a vague idea in scientific circles that the singular and undeniable affinity for, or sensitivity to, underground water on the part of water dowsers can somehow, by means of exhaustive experiments, be standardized so that water dowsing will always show successful results. This vague idea has always left me cold; for there's no way of standardizing that talent unless everything connected with its use can also be standardized.

For example, I have a crow-shooting rifle assembled for me by Major Ned Roberts, celebrated inventor of small-arms ammunition and internationally known rifle shot. It has a special stock, a special barrel, a telescope sight, and shoots a hand-made bullet from a hand-loaded R-2 case. It weighs eleven pounds, so that one should lie on his stomach to fire it to best advantage. At three hundred yards, under the watchful supervision of Major Roberts, I have fired ten bullets at a crow made of blackened cardboard and put nine of them through the crow's center. Yet that rifle, accurate as it is, cannot be aimed by an expert, locked in a vise, and fired by anyone at all with the assurance that it will score nine hits out of ten shots at three hundred yards. Three hundred yards is a long way for a bullet to travel and strike a mark three inches in diameter; and if the bullet passes through a wind current or a heat emanation while on its way, it may be deflected—not much, but just enough to make it miss the mark. Good as that rifle is, its performance just can't be standardized, no matter how often scientists may make the attempt—not unless wind and atmospheric conditions can also be standardized.

However, I suppose that scientists will continue to start their investigations of water dowsing from the wrong end for many years to come, and consequently get exactly nowhere—which is where they are now. At the present writing scientists first have to prove to themselves and others that water dowsers can locate water. They can't seem to get it through their heads that this was a proved fact when the Pyramids were rising on the banks of the Nile, during the days of the Roman emperors, and when the ancient Gauls and Britons wore cowskin pants.

I have suggested to scientists that they come to Rocky Pasture, bringing a few well diggers with them, and experiment with the veins of water that dowsers have located: that they hold one end of a dowsing rod while a dowser holds the other end: that they find out why the pull of water is stronger at one spot in a vein than at any other: that they trace veins through different types of rock, in order to find out what sort of fissures may be expected in the different types: that they measure the depths of veins, and then test the different dowsing methods of determining a vein's depth: that they try to learn why surface water, rushing through an underground pipe, has no influence whatever upon the dowsing rods of the most sensitive dowsers.

But such matters don't seem to interest scientists. They just want to find out whether water dowsers are faking when their rods jerk downward with such force as to pull the skin from the palms of their hands, and none of them are willing to take my word that the dowsers are *not* faking. The way to investigate water dowsing is to dig in the ground: not to lead blindfolded water dowsers over hidden pipes; but since I'm only an author who has ordered fifteen holes to be dug on the recommendation of water dowsers, and opened up a generous flow of water on each occasion, I obviously do not have the scientific approach. They are willing to let me experiment for them, but they insist on determining the manner in which the experiments shall be made. I have always encouraged them and been willing to play with them, in the hope that eventually they would see the light; but I think their experiments are useless. This, of course, is only one man's opinion.

Water dowsing isn't the only manifestation that completely baffles scientists. They are similarly baffled by the curve ball in baseball. They go so far as to say that there is no such thing as a curve ball in baseball: that the curve ball exists only in the beholder's eye. They have published long articles in *Life* and other magazines, illustrating their fuzzy thoughts with diagrams and photographs; and by so doing they have convinced themselves that anybody who claims to have thrown a curve ball is a prevaricator and an impostor. Every man who has played baseball, however, knows that the anti-curve-ball coterie is stupidly, overwhelmingly, and idiotically wrong. A baseball curves, in flight, exactly as a cut tennis ball swerves in its course, as a bowling ball hooks when thrown by an expert, as a billiard ball changes direction when "English" is applied to it. There isn't a third baseman living who hasn't seen a baseball curve three feet out of line in its flight across the diamond: not a catcher who doesn't shake his head in bewilderment at scientists' insistence that a thrown baseball cannot be made to curve. I find many similarities between the scientific attitude toward curved balls and water dowsing, and both attitudes, to put it mildly, are pathetic.

As I said before, the water supply for my home comes from a spring eight hundred feet distant, and the water reaches the house through a two-inch pipe buried four feet.

We had used the pipe for some years when we had trouble. An outdoor shutoff had been overlooked at the beginning of winter, and the pipe had frozen. The following spring we found the spring running low, realized that we had a break in the pipe, and didn't know where. Nobody remembered the exact course followed by the pipe, and we were confronted with the unpleasant chore of digging an 800-foot trench through hay meadows that shouldn't have been disturbed. We dug one hole over a spot where the pipe should have been, but it wasn't there.

It occurred to me that a dowsing rod ought to work as well on a pipe containing spring water as on the vein that supplied the spring; so I drove to Old Orchard and got Asa Ellingwood, who had won the Dayton dowsing contest.

Ellingwood and Brennan then took their rods and tried for the pipe. They got strong pulls all along it; and when we dug six holes at intervals on the line they indicated, we struck the pipe exactly every time.

Now the framework of this chapter was first published in the *Country Gentleman;* and after it appeared I received a number of letters which fell into three general classes: letters from persons who had the ability to use divining rods and had successfully located wells; letters from people who are gratefully using wells that were located by dowsers; and letters from water-hungry farmers who wanted to know where to go in order to get in touch with a reliable dowser who could help them escape from a waterless existence. These letters convinced me that the Department of Agriculture would be doing a great service to the country if it would instruct all county agents in every state to advertise for water dowsers, so that a list would be readily available to those who need wells.

Among the letters, too, were a few from scientists; and among the latter was a pleasant one from Professor J. B. Rhine of the Parapsychological Laboratory of Duke University. Professor Rhine and his colleagues, it developed, had been profoundly interested in water dowsing, but hadn't been able to conduct certain experiments that seemed to them to be desirable.

The experiment outlined by Professor Rhine entailed placing three dowsers at intervals along a buried pipe, each dowser to be attended by a reliable observer whose watch would be synchronized with all other watches. In a house well removed from the dowsers were to be stationed two other operatives with a pack of cards. One of the operatives was to draw a card from the pack at two-minute intervals. If the card was black, a faucet was to be opened by the second operative: if red, the faucet was to stay closed. Also at two-minute intervals the dowsers were to test the pipe with their rods to see whether or not there was any variation in the pull.

I agreed to make the experiment for Professor Rhine, and I give the results here for what they may be worth.

The dowsers were Raymond Lovejoy, Don Treadwell, and William Brennan. Lovejoy was checked by Ben Ames Williams, the author; Treadwell by Woodbury Stevens, chairman of the Kennebunkport Board of Selectmen; Brennan by Dr. James MacDonald, medical examiner of York County, Maine. The card-turning was done by Mrs. Ben Ames Williams; the faucet-turning by me.

All of the dowsers got a pull from the pipe whenever they made the tests, just as all dowsers always had when they felt for the pipe.

Brennan's reaction on every test was the same, whether water was moving in the pipe or was still. Lovejoy's rod showed weak pulls at times and stronger pulls at other times: the weak pulls corresponded to the shut-off water on 50 per cent of his tries. Treadwell's rod also showed weak and strong pulls. The strong pulls corresponded to water turn-ons on 70 per cent of his tries.

To satisfy the curiosity of Messrs. Williams, Stevens, and MacDonald, we took the dowsers to the known but undug Two Acre Spring in a near-by meadow, blindfolded them, turned them around and around; then led them in a circuitous route over the spot and the vein. The rods of all three men dipped unerringly over the spot and along the vein.

I then took them to a drainage pipe which is four feet underground and sodded over. The pipe is made of old hot-water tanks with the ends cut off. The tanks are butted together and covered at the joints with tarred paper. At the time of the experiment water was running through the pipe at the approximate rate of a hundred gallons a minute. All three dowsers walked back and forth above this pipe again and again. The water had no effect whatever on their rods.

These experiments proved one thing at least. Before Messrs. Williams, Stevens, and MacDonald took part in them, they had known little or nothing about water dowsing. If they had thought about it at all, they had thought of it as being slightly phony. After they had seen and felt dowsing rods operate, they were completely convinced that there's nothing in any way phony about water dowsing.

To keep the record clear, I add the occurrences of two days in April, 1945.

In March 1945 the *Reader's Digest* had suggested that I write an article for that magazine and had asked whether I had anything in mind. I said that I had added interesting evidence to the article on water divining originally published in the *Country Gentleman* and that a digest of it, in its revised form, might be helpful. On April 14, 1945, one of the editors replied that the editorial board had discussed the article when it first appeared, but had decided not to reprint it because of the board's skepticism about water divining—a skepticism so pronounced that the *Reader's Digest* didn't care to discuss the matter, ever again.

On the same day I received a letter from Thomas G. Stewart of Vancouver, B.C., guaranteeing the accuracy of all statements made concerning him in this chapter, and enclosing letters from Otta Giersh of Hopkins Landing, B.C., H. R. McCarthy, Princeton, B.C., and Robert E. Ferry, Wellington, B.C., all of whom—being without water—had dug for springs on spots dowsed by Mr. Stewart. All three had been rewarded by wells that supplied their houses with all the water they needed; and all three expressed their heartfelt gratitude to Mr. Stewart for the use of his dowsing rod.

On the following day Brennan reported to me the results of using his divining rod for a neighbor, Elmore Drown, whose well had dried up, leaving him waterless. Brennan went to Drown's home, cut a wild-apple rod, and tried for twenty minutes to find a water vein in likely-looking spots, but without results. He then went to an unlikely-looking spot and got such a pull, he said, as he had never felt before. It was so strong that he asked Drown for a shovel, dug two feet into gravel, and punctured a three-inch bubble that came into the hole with such force as to run out at the top.

That's evidence, and I can't understand people who steadfastly refuse to accept or even to discuss evidence. To my way of thinking, that's as bad as concealing evidence—and my unhappy experiences with historians who have consistently concealed evidence in their so-called histories have persuaded me that the concealing of evidence is a crime.

I am well aware that my unhesitating acceptance of water dowsing clearly marks me, in the minds of many of my acquaintances, as a sucker. People have been heard to laugh at my stubborn credulity until their sides were sore. Thus everybody's happy; for while they have their laughs, I have my fourteen springs.